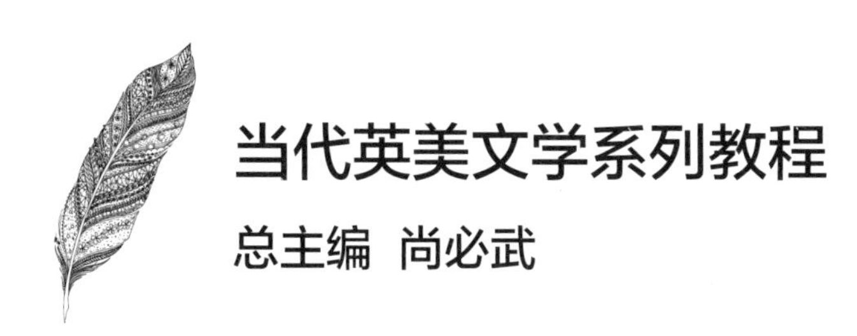

当代英美文学系列教程

总主编 尚必武

当代叙事理论教程

主　编 尚必武

副主编 汤铁丽 李亚飞 万晓蒙

内容提要

本书为“当代英美文学系列教程”之一，主要选择当代叙事发展历程中的名作（论文或著作节选）进行分析介绍，涵盖结构主义叙事学、修辞叙事学、认知叙事学、女性主义叙事学、跨媒介叙事学、非自然叙事学、非人类叙事学等叙事学主要思潮与流派。全书共分8章，每章集中于一种思潮或流派，选择2～3篇代表性作品，单篇选读篇幅在5 000～10 000词左右，每篇附有约5 000字的分析导读以及若干思考题。本书对叙事理论家及其著作的选取，不求涵盖全部，而是以权威性、代表性和重要性为首要原则，兼顾年代、流派、思潮等因素。本书主要用于英语语言文学专业研究生课程的文论教学，也适用于其他专业方向学生的选修课教学，同时也为对当代叙事学理论感兴趣的师生提供学习与阅读参考。

图书在版编目(CIP)数据

当代叙事理论教程／尚必武主编. —上海：上海交通大学出版社，2023.8

当代英美文学系列教程／尚必武总主编

ISBN 978-7-313-28611-6

Ⅰ.①当… Ⅱ.①尚… Ⅲ.①英国文学—文学研究—教材②文学研究—美国—教材 Ⅳ.①I561.06 ②I712.06

中国国家版本馆CIP数据核字(2023)第070114号

当代叙事理论教程

DANGDAI XUSHI LILUN JIAOCHENG

主　　编：尚必武

出版发行：上海交通大学出版社　　地　　址：上海市番禺路951号

邮政编码：200030　　电　　话：021-64071208

印　　制：上海文浩包装科技有限公司　　经　　销：全国新华书店

开　　本：889 mm×1194 mm　1/16　　印　　张：20.25

字　　数：508千字

版　　次：2023年8月第1版　　印　　次：2023年8月第1次印刷

书　　号：ISBN 978-7-313-28611-6

定　　价：68.00元

Preface 总序

2012年，国务院学位委员会第六届学科评议组在外国语言文学一级学科目录下设置了五大方向，即外国文学、语言学与应用语言学、翻译学、国别与区域研究、比较文学与跨文化研究。2020年起，教育部开始大力推进“新文科”建设，不仅发布了《新文科建设宣言》，还设立了“新文科研究与改革实践项目”，旨在进一步打破学科壁垒，促进学科的交叉融合，提升文科建设的内涵与质量。在这种背景下，外语研究生教育既迎来了机遇，同时又面临新的挑战，这就要求我们的研究生培养模式为适应这些变化而进行必要的改革与创新。在孙益、陈露茜、王晨看来，“研究生教育方针、教育路线的贯彻执行，研究生教育体制改革和教育思想的革新，研究生专业培养方案、培养计划的制定，研究生教学内容和教学方法的改革，最终都会反映和落实到研究生教材的建设上来。重视研究生教材建设工作，是提高高校研究生教学质量和保证教学改革成效的关键所在。”[①]从这种意义上说，教材建设是提高外语研究生教育的一个重要抓手。

就国内外语专业研究生教材而言，上海外语教育出版社推出的《高等院校英语语言文学专业研究生系列教材》占据了最主要的地位。该系列涵盖语言学、语言教学、文学理论、原著选读等多个领域，为我国的外语研究生培养做出了重要贡献。需要指出的是，同外语专业本科生教材建设相比，外语专业研究生教材建设显得明显滞后。很多高校的外语专业研究生课堂上所使用的教材基本上是原版引进教材或教师自编讲义。我们知道，“教材不仅是教师进行教学的基本工具，而且是学生获取知识、培养能力的重要手段。研究生教材是直接体现高等院校研究生教学内容和教学方法的知识载体，也是反映高等院校教学水平、科研水平及其成果的重要标志，优秀的研究生教材是提高研究生教学质量的重要保证。”[②]上海交通大学外国语学院历来重视教材建设，曾主编《研究生英语教程》《多维教程》《新视野大学英语》《21世纪大学英语》等多套本科和研究生层次的英语教材，在全国范围内产生了较大影响。

---

① 孙益、陈露茜、王晨：《高校研究生教材建设的国际经验与中国路径》，载《学位与研究生教育》2018年第2期，第72页。
② 同上。

为进一步加强和推动外语专业，尤其是英语专业英美文学方向的研究生教材建设，助力研究生培养从接受知识到创造知识的模式转变，在上海交通大学出版社的大力支持下，上海交通大学外国语学院发挥优势，携手复旦大学外文学院、上海外国语大学英语学院、北京科技大学外国语学院、东北师范大学外国语学院、中南财经政法大学外国语学院、山东师范大学外国语学院等兄弟单位，主编《当代英美文学系列教程》。本系列教材重点聚焦20世纪80年代以来的英美文学与文论，由《当代英国小说教程》《当代美国小说教程》《当代英国戏剧教程》《当代美国戏剧教程》《当代英国诗歌教程》《当代美国诗歌教程》《当代文学理论教程》《当代叙事理论教程》等8册构成。

本系列教材以问题意识为导向，围绕当代英美文学，尤其是21世纪英美文学的新类型、新材料、新视角、新话题，将文学作为一种直面问题、思考问题、应对问题、解决问题的重要途径和方式，从而发掘和彰显文学的能动性。在每册教材的导论部分，首先重点概述20世纪80年代以来的文学发展态势与特征，由此回答“当代起于何时”的问题，在此基础上简述教材内容所涉及的主要命题、思潮、样式、作家和作品，由此回答“新在哪里”的问题。本系列教材打破按照时间顺序来划分章节的惯例，转而以研究问题或文学样式来安排各章。例如，教材纳入了气候变化、新型战争、族裔流散、世界主义等问题与文学样式。在文学作品的选择标准上，教材以类型和样式的标准来分类，如气候变化文学、新型战争文学等。每个门类下均选取数篇具有典型性的作品，并对其主题特色、历史背景及其相关文学特质进行介绍，凸显对文本性敏锐的分析能力以及对相关文学研究视角及理论知识的掌握。除此之外，教材还有意识地呈现当代英美文学的新的创作手法、文学思潮和文体特征。教材的每章集中一种文学样式、类型、思潮或流派，选择2～3篇代表性作品，单篇选读篇幅在5 000～10 000词(英文)左右，每篇附有5 000字(中文)左右的分析导读以及若干思考题。教材对作家或理论家及其著作的选取，不求涵盖全部，而是以权威性、代表性和重要性为首要原则，兼顾年代、流派、思潮等因素。本系列教材适合国内高校外国文学尤其是英美文学专业的博士研究生、硕士研究生、高年级本科生、文学研究者与爱好者使用。

本系列教材在编写过程中得到了上海交通大学外国语学院、上海交通大学出版社以及国内外同行专家学者的关心、帮助与支持，特此谢忱！

尚必武

2023年3月

Foreword 前言

进入21世纪以来，叙事学研究在国内学界迅速升温，成为当下文学研究的一门显学。关于叙事学的各类研究课题、专著和论文数量呈现出爆炸式的增长。胡亚敏的《叙事学》，罗钢的《叙事学导论》，申丹、王丽亚的《西方叙事学：经典与后经典》，谭君强的《叙事学导论：从经典叙事学到后经典叙事学》等带有导论性质的专著为在国内普及和推广叙事学理论做出了重要贡献。纵观国际学界，历经半个世纪的发展，叙事学已经从经典阶段发展到后经典阶段，从单一的结构主义叙事学发展成为包含女性主义叙事学、修辞叙事学、认知叙事学、跨媒介叙事学等多个理论流派在内的叙事学。日益增长的跨学科、跨文类、跨媒介的叙事兴趣以及实用多元的叙事研究方法，催生了在高等院校讲授叙事理论的综合性资源的需求。当今国内越来越多的高校和相关专业开设了与叙事学研究相关的课程，这其中不仅包括外国语言文学专业，还包括其他人文学科，如中国语言文学、哲学、戏剧与影视学、新闻传播学等专业。了解和熟稔当代前沿理论是研究和应用叙事学的基本保证。遗憾的是，国内目前尚无系统关注当代前沿叙事理论的教材。为了进一步夯实国内叙事学的基础建设，对接国际叙事学的主要思潮与研究热点，编写一部关于当代叙事理论的教材就显得颇有必要。

内容框架

本教材主要聚焦20世纪80年代以来的叙事理论，试图弥补国内当代前沿叙事理论教材的阙如，引导学生全面认识前沿的理论和研究话题，对接国际，为培养能够与国际叙事学界的同行展开学术争鸣和对话的青年学者做好一定的知识准备。本教材主要用于外国语言文学专业研究生课程的教学，如“叙事学导论”“叙事学前沿理论”等课程，也适用于其他专业研究生的选修课或外国语言文学专业高年级本科生课程的教学，同时也可以给对叙事研究感兴趣的师生提供学习与阅读参考。本教材包括结构主义叙事学、修辞叙事学、认知叙事学、女性主义叙事学、跨媒介叙事学、身体叙事学、非自然叙事学和非人类叙事学，兼顾年代、流派、思潮等因素，力求全面、系统、深入浅出地介绍当代叙事学的主要思潮、流派和重要命题。本教材涵盖了叙事学基础理论中一些最为核心的概念以及前沿的重要术语和命题。它们作为叙事理论的重要关键词，对开展或深入叙事学研究必不可少。与此同时，本教材选取国际叙事学界的重要作品，不但将当代各个叙事学派的代表性理论文献选入其中，还纳入那些针对不同叙事学派而产生理论争鸣的文献，并提供与每一篇原文相对应的介绍性导读。这有助于学生洞悉不同叙事学理论学派的具体理论主张是如何在学界受到质疑和批评，以及如何进行修正的，进一步提升学生对叙事理论进行批判性分析的能力。

教材特色

第一，以权威性、代表性和发展性为首要原则，坚持从叙事学最具权威性和代表性的一手理论文献中选取阅读材料，并从中整理归纳出当代叙事理论发展和流变的基本线索，最大限度地呈现当代叙事理论的真实图景。这种从“原文”中学习理论的方法更能引发学生的深度思考，让学生能够从叙事理论发展史上那些具有时代意义的关键理论文献中直接学习叙事理论，更加真实地接触到叙事理论中的核心思想。

第二，以具体叙事理论文献的历时性发展流变为基本线索，使学生更好地把握当代叙事理论的发展态势和当代叙事学的基本发展脉络，在介绍性导读的指导下，对之形成更加清晰和深层次的理解；透过关于不同叙事理论派别的理论争鸣文献的细读和研究，结合相应的思考题目，有效地锻炼学生对理论的批判性思考能力。

第三，坚持从理论基础到批评实践的基本学习路径，将理论与实践相结合。本教材选取了涵盖相应文本分析内容的文献，提供文本分析的具体实例，使理论阐述具有针对性，让学生能够自然地从理论思辨过渡到文本分析，将理论运用于文本阐释中。

第四，在向学生展示主要叙事学思想的同时，也展示了叙事理论之于文本分析的启发价值。学生在掌握当代叙事学的重要术语概念的同时，能够在文献的阐释和实践中掌握运用这些术语概念的方法，并使得叙事理论的理念成为其专业学术训练的一部分。本教材旨在让学生接触当代最前沿、最权威的叙事学理论，学习叙事学研究的最新路径和批评方法，了解叙事学从“经典”到“后经典”的发展流变。本教材可以帮助学生形成前瞻性的批评视角，培养学生的理论辨析和文本批评能力，引导学生接触叙事学理论的国际前沿话题，与权威观点形成对话，进而推动国内叙事学及其他相关领域的研究者产出更多具有前沿性、创新性的成果。

编写团队

本教材主要由上海交通大学叙事学研究团队编写。具体分工如下：导论、第一章和第八章由尚必武负责，第二章和第四章由汤轶丽负责，第三章和第六章由李亚飞负责，第五章和第七章由万晓蒙负责；尚必武通读和校对了全书。

叙事学理论和批评实践的相关课程一直都是上海交通大学外国语学院研究生必修的专业课程。本教材以近年来的课程讲义为基础，并根据国际叙事学前沿话题和学生反馈不断更新内容。数位叙事学方向的硕士研究生和博士研究生在学习本课程后选择围绕非自然叙事学、身体叙事学、修辞叙事学、非人类叙事学、跨媒介叙事学等前沿话题展开研究，并在国内外权威期刊发表多篇叙事学论文，丰富和推进了我国的叙事学研究。同时，许多其他方向的研究生也在当代叙事理论相关课程的启发下，开拓了研究视角，产出诸多创新性的研究成果。同学们在课堂上所提出的问题和建议给我们带来很多启迪，也促使我们对相关问题做了更深入的思考。在这里，我们要向所有选择“叙事学”课程的同学表达最深切的谢意。同时，我们也要向出版本教材的上海交通大学出版社责任编辑张冠男女士致以由衷的谢意。她的认真细致、一丝不苟，让本书的很多舛误得以及时避免。本教材虽以讲义的形式经过数年的使用，但依然会存在不少问题，恳请读者多多批评指正，以帮助我们进一步修改完善。

尚必武

2023 年 1 月

Contents | 目录

导 论

第一节 什么是叙事?

朱光潜说:“想明白一件事物的本质,最好先研究它的起源;犹如想了解一个人的性格,最好先知道他的祖先和环境。”[①] 朱光潜以身作则,他研究诗论首先从追溯诗歌的起源开始。仿照这样的做法,我们若要研究叙事学,理应也要从研究叙事开始。尽管“叙事学有着多种多样的形式和面貌”[②],但它毕竟如茨维坦·托多洛夫(Tzvetan Todorov)所说,“是关于叙事作品的科学”[③]。杰拉德·普林斯(Gerald Prince)说得好:“既然叙事学是叙事的科学(或叙事的理论),那么叙事学范畴则依赖于叙事的定义。”[④] 在《叙事分析手册》一书中,吕克·赫尔曼(Luc Herman)和巴特·凡瓦克(Bart Vervaek)两位学者也指出:“如果叙事学是关于叙事文本的理论,那么首先要解决的就是叙事的定义。”[⑤] 换言之,要回答“什么是叙事学”,首先需要回答“什么是叙事”。只有了解和把握了“什么是叙事”,我们才能更加富有成效地研究叙事,更加有针对性地建设和发展叙事学这门学科。“什么是叙事”是叙事学研究的首要问题,所有与叙事研究有关的其他问题,诸如叙事理论的建构、叙事研究的目标、叙事研究的方法、叙事研究的重点、叙事研究的结果等,皆离不开对“什么是叙事”这个根本问题的回答。不同的叙事观会导致不同的叙事理论,产生不同的研究方法、研究目标和研究结果。

叙事定义及叙事本质的重要性已是西方叙事学界所公认的事实。令人诧异的是,叙事学的发展已经走过了将近40年的历程,但是作为其研究的对象,叙事却没有得到统一的界定。德国学者莫妮卡·弗鲁德尼克(Monika Fludernik)指出:“每种叙事理论都确立了其自身对叙事的定义。”[⑥] 这势必导致了叙事定义的多副面孔。

乔纳森·卡勒(Jonathan Culler)说:“为了使叙事成为研究的对象,我们必须把叙事从非叙事中区

---

① 朱光潜:《诗论》,合肥:安徽教育出版社,2006年,第1页。

② Andrew Gibson, “Narrative Substraction,” *Erzählen und Erzähltheorie im 20. Jahrhundert: Festschrift für Wilhelm Füger*, ed. Jorg Helbig (Heidelberg: Universitätsverlag C., 2001), p.228.

③ 张寅德编选:《叙述学研究》,北京:中国社会科学出版社,1989年,第1—2页。

④ Gerald Prince, “Surveying Narratology,” *What Is Narratology? Questions and Answers Regarding the Status of a Theory*, eds. Tom Kindt and Hans-Harald Müller (Berlin and New York: Walter de Gruyter, 2003), p.1.

⑤ Luc Herman and Bart Vervaeck, *Handbook of Narrative Analysis* (Lincoln and London: University of Nebraska Press, 2005), p.11.

⑥ Monika Fludernik, *An Introduction to Narratology* (London and New York: Routledge, 2009), p.8.

别出来。”[1] 为了实现这样的目标，叙事学家从描述叙事的现象开始，继而才对其做出界定。就描述叙事现象而言，无论是经典叙事学家还是后经典叙事学家，基本上都有一致的意见，即持有某种程度的“泛叙事”观，认为叙事无处不在。就经典叙事学家而言，罗兰·巴特(Roland Barthes)是其中的代表。他在《叙事作品结构分析导论》一文中指出：

> 世界上叙事作品之多，不计其数；种类浩繁，题材各异。对人类来说，似乎任何材料都适宜于叙事：叙事承载物可以是口头的或书面的有声语言、是固定的或活动的画面、是手势，以及所有这些材料的有机混合；叙事遍布于神话、传说、寓言、民间故事、小说、史诗、历史、悲剧、正剧、喜剧、哑剧、绘画(请想一想卡帕齐奥的《圣于絮尔》那幅画)、彩绘玻璃窗、电影、连环画、社会杂闻、会话。而且，以这些几乎无限的形式出现的叙事遍存于一切时代、一切地方、一切社会。[2]

如果说巴特是经典叙事学家中持有“普遍叙事”观的代表，那么戴维·赫尔曼(David Herman)和布莱恩·理查森(Brian Richardson)则是后经典叙事学家中持有“普遍叙事”观的代表。在《复数的后经典叙事学：叙事分析新视野》一书的“导论”中，赫尔曼写道：

> “叙事”概念涵盖了一个很大的范围，包括符号现象、行为现象以及广义的文化现象；譬如我们现在说性别叙事，也说历史叙事、民族性叙事，甚至会俗滥地说地球引力叙事。[3]

与赫尔曼相似，理查森在《叙事的近期概念及叙事理论的叙事》一文中指出：

> 现在，叙事无处不在。叙事研究继续变得更为细化，更为宏大，更为广泛，叙事研究被应用于越来越广阔的领域和学科，在从哲学、法律到表演艺术和超文本研究的领域中都变得越来越显要。[4]

在回答“什么是叙事”这个问题上，西方叙事学家采取了两种方式：对叙事现象的描述和对叙事的界定。在对叙事现象的描述上，叙事学家们几乎很少有分歧，但是在对叙事的界定上，叙事学家们则莫衷一是，观点各异。

玛丽-劳勒·瑞安(Marie-Laure Ryan)指出，探究叙事本质有两种方法：描述性方法和定义性方法。[5] 各种叙事的描述性方法之间可以“和谐共存”，这在巴特、赫尔曼、理查森等人对叙事现象的描述中即可看出。但是各种叙事的定义性方法之间则存有冲突。瑞安认为，这些冲突具体表现为六个难以解决的问题：① 叙事是否会因文化和历史时期的不同而不同？② 叙事是否预设了叙述者的语言行为？

---

① Jonathan Culler, *The Pursuit of Signs* (Ithaca: Cornell University Press, 2001), p.171.

② 罗兰·巴特：《叙事作品结构分析导论》，载张寅德编选《叙述学研究》，北京：中国社会科学出版社，1989 年，第 2 页。

③ David Herman, “Introduction,” *Narratologies: New Perspectives on Narrative Analysis*, ed. David Herman (Columbus: Ohio State University Press, 1999), p.20.

④ Brian Richardson, “Recent Concepts of Narrative and the Narratives of Narrative Theory,” *Style* 34.2 (Summer 2000), p.168.

⑤ Marie-Laure Ryan, “Narrative,” *Routledge Encyclopedia of Narrative Theory*, eds. David Herman, Manfred Jahn and Marie-Laure Ryan (London and New York: Routledge, 2005), p.345.

③ 叙事性的特征是否可以被分为不同的层次？④ 叙事性是形式还是内容？⑤ 叙事的定义是否把所有文学作品都放在同等重要的地位？⑥ 叙事是否同时要求话语/故事、能指/所指，或叙事是否可以不把文本作为自己的实现形式？在瑞安看来，第六个问题对于叙事的界定最为重要，因为它涉及了叙事的构成。[①]

在叙事学的发展史上，关于叙事的定义数不胜数。西方学者大致采取三种界定方法来定义叙事：以事件再现为主导的界定方法、以文本类型为主导的界定方法、以跨学科视角为主导的界定方法。

戴维·鲁德姆(David Rudrum)说："'再现'(有时是'呈现')被如此广泛地应用于界定叙事，以至于这种理解叙事的方式成了叙事学中少数几个常用的方法之一。"[②] 无论是在叙事学诞生之初还是在其发展到后经典阶段之后，都有很多的叙事学家从事件再现的角度出发，对叙事加以界定。把叙事看作事件再现，是西方叙事学界比较盛行的一种论点，只是在再现方式和再现手段上存有一定的差异罢了。首先，有的叙事学家直接把叙事界定为事件的再现，但没有具体明确被再现的事件之间的关系。热拉尔·热奈特(Gérard Genette)认为叙事是"一个或一序列事件的再现"。[③] 在《叙事虚构作品：当代诗学》中，施劳米什·里蒙-凯南(Shlomith Rimmon-Kenan)通过界定叙事虚构作品来审视叙事，她说叙事虚构作品是对"虚构事件的连续性叙述"。[④] 在《剑桥叙事学导论》中，H.伯特·阿波特(H. Porter Abbott)把叙事界定为"**对一个事件或一系列事件的再现**"。[⑤] 在《叙事学词典》中，普林斯把叙事界定为"一个或多个虚构或真实事件(作为产品、过程、对象和行动、结构与结构化)的再现，这些事件由一个、两个(明显的)叙述者向一个、两个或多个(明显的)受述者传达"。[⑥]

其次，虽然有的叙事学家也从事件再现的角度来界定叙事，但他们同时还强调了这些事件之间的特定次序和连接关系。例如，在《语言、叙事与反叙事》一文中，罗伯特·斯科尔斯(Robert Scholes)把叙事界定为"一序列事件的象征再现，这些事件由主题和时间连接起来"。[⑦] 在《叙事学：叙事理论导论》的第一版中，米克·巴尔(Mieke Bal)说："一个**故事**就是一个以某种方式写就的'法布拉'(fabula)。一个**法布拉**就是一系列在逻辑或时间上相关的事件。"[⑧] 在《叙事学导论》中，苏珊·奥尼嘉(Susan Onega)和加西尔·兰德(Garcia Landa)把叙事界定为"对一系列事件的再现，这些事件以某种时间或因果的方式有意义地连接在一起"。[⑨] 在《叙事：批判语言学导论》中，迈克尔·图伦(Michael Toolan)把叙事界定为

---

① Marie-Laure Ryan, "Narrative," *Routledge Encyclopedia of Narrative Theory*, eds. David Herman, Manfred Jahn and Marie-Laure Ryan (London and New York: Routledge, 2005), pp.345 - 347.

② David Rudrum, "From Narrative Representation to Narrative Use: Towards the Limits of Definition," *Narrative* 13.2 (May 2005), p.196.

③ Gérard Genette, *Figures of Literary Discourse*, trans. Marie-Rose Logan (New York: Columbia University Press, 1982), p.127.

④ Shlomith Rimmon-Kenan, *Narrative Fiction: Contemporary Poetics* (2nd edition) (London and New York: Routledge, 2002), p.2.

⑤ H. Porter Abbott, *The Cambridge Introduction to Narrative* (Second Edition) (Cambridge: Cambridge University Press, 2008), p.2.

⑥ Gerald Prince, *A Dictionary of Narratology* (Extended and Revised Version) (Lincoln and London: University of Nebraska Press, 2003), p.58.

⑦ Robert Scholes, "Language, Narrative and Anti-Narrative," *On Narrative*, ed. W. J. T. Mitchell (Chicago: University of Chicago Press, 1981), p.205.

⑧ Mieke Bal, *Narratology: An Introduction to the Theory of Narrative*, trans. Christine van Boheemen (Toronto: University of Toronto Press, 1985), p.5.

⑨ Susan Onega and José Ángel García Landa, *Narratology: An Introduction* (London: Longman, 1996), p.4.

“一系列被感知的存在一定连接关系的事件”。① 在《叙事因果》(*Narrative Causalities*, 2006)一书中,爱玛·卡法勒诺斯(Emma Kafalenos)再次把叙事界定为“一序列事件以一定次序的再现”。②

除了上述学者从事件再现的角度来界定叙事外,也有部分学者从“文本类型”(text type)的角度来界定叙事,西摩·查特曼(Seymour Chatman)、弗鲁德尼克、赫尔曼等人是其中的典型代表。文本类型是文本语言学上的一个常用术语,是对文本不同种类的称呼。根据拉斯特·费格尔(Lester Faigley)和保罗·迈耶(Paul Meyer)的论点,在文本语言学研究中,划分文本类型最简单的方式就是把文本分成“叙事”和“描述”两种模式。③ 图伊亚·弗塔嫩(Tuija Virtanen)把文本类型看作“原型的抽象”(prototypical abstractions),并初步提出了五种文本类型:叙事、描述、指导、说明、议论。④

在查特曼看来,“时间上可以控制读者接受的任何交际”都可以被看作文本,即文本是“控制时间的结构”。⑤ “文本类型”有别于“文类”(genre),文类是文本类型的一个亚类型或几个文本类型的混杂。⑥ 在《叙事术语评论》一书中,查特曼主要区分了“叙事”“议论”“描述”三种文本类型。作为文本类型的一种,叙事的特殊性在于其双重的“时间逻辑”(chrono-logic):叙事不仅包含了在时间上的外在运动(小说、电影、戏剧中再现的时长),也包含在时间上的内在运动(构成情节的序列事件的时长)。第一种运动是叙事中的“话语”,第二种运动是叙事中的“故事”。⑦ 与此相反,非叙事文本则不具有双重“时间逻辑”,它们只有时间上的外在运动,而缺乏时间上的内在运动。具体而言,描述有时被视作一种“因果链接”(causal contiguity),议论至少在信息意义上是依赖于“逻辑”(logic)的,即便不是使用严格意义上的三段论的说理逻辑,至少也是使用“省略三段论法”(enthymeme)的比较柔和的说理逻辑。

弗鲁德尼克也从文本类型的角度来界定叙事。在《走向“自然”叙事学》一书中,弗鲁德尼克提出了三种层次的文本类型:① 宏观文类层次,这一层次由交际的**功能**构成;② 文类层次,传统的文类期待在这一层次上产生作用;③ 文本表层上的话语模式。她重点区分了在宏观文类这一层次上的五种文本类型:叙事、议论、反思、对话和教导。⑧ 在《文类,文本类型还是话语类型?叙事模态性与文类划分》一文中,弗鲁德尼克又重申了这一论点,并且论述了宏观文类上的五种文本类型对于自然叙事学研究的影响。她把自然发生的话语作为叙事的一个原型,重新提出了叙事的定义问题。⑨

除查特曼、弗鲁德尼克之外,赫尔曼也从文本类型的角度对叙事做出了新的界定。不过与查特曼、弗鲁德尼克不同的是,赫尔曼以研究事件序列为目的,提出了研究文本类型的两种方法:① “横向方法”,这一方法按照层层包含的路径,把文本类型按照“文本>文本类型>文类>亚文类”的方式进行排列;② “纵向方法”,这一方法把文本类型分为“叙事”“描述”“解释”三种类型。赫尔曼认为,不同的文本

① Michael Toolan, *Narrative: A Critical Linguistic Introduction* (2nd edition) (London and New York: Routledge, 2001), p.6.
② Emma Kafalenos, *Narrative Causalities* (Columbus: The Ohio State University Press, 2006), p.2.
③ Lester Faigley and Paul Meyer, "Rhetorical Theory and Readers' Classification of Text Types," *Text* 3.4 (1983), pp.305 - 325.
④ Tuija Virtanen, "Issues of Text Typology: Narrative—A 'Basic' Type of Text?" *Text* 12.2 (1992), p.297.
⑤ Seymour Chatman, *Coming to Terms: The Rhetoric of Narrative in Fiction and Film* (Ithaca: Cornell University Press, 1990), p.79.
⑥ Ibid., p.10.
⑦ Ibid., p.9.
⑧ Monika Fludernik, *Towards a 'Natural' Narratology* (London: Routledge, 1996), pp.356 - 358.
⑨ Monika Fludernik, "Genres, Text Types, or Discourse Modes? Narrative Modalities and Generic Categorization," *Style* 34.1 (Spring 2000), pp.274 - 292.

以不同的方式来控制时间，因此文本类型理论的重要旨趣在于区分文本控制时间的不同方式。不过，赫尔曼主要从认知科学的角度出发，对“叙事”“描述”“解释”做出界定。在赫尔曼看来：

> 描述可以被看作一种认知活动，有可能成为一种话语或文本，也有可能不成为一种话语或文本。如果被文本化的话，描述可以在多种媒介中出现，也会受到多重再现规约的影响，如计算表格、人格特征列表、人种学实践等。①
>
> ……
>
> 叙事是一种认知活动，有可能是已经实现的艺术，也有可能是没有实现的艺术。这一文本类型涵盖了很多的媒介与再现规约，从手势语、电影叙事、面对面的故事讲述，到先锋试验性质的叙事文学等。②
>
> ……
>
> 解释是一种认知活动，有可能是已经实现的“物质艺术”(material artifact)，也有可能是没有实现的“物质艺术”，包含了多重再现媒介和验证过程。③

笔者以为，从文本类型角度来界定叙事方法实际上回答了“同什么比较，叙事才成为叙事”(Narrative, compared to what?)的问题。不同文本类型之间大致有三种关系：① 多种文本类型共同存在于同一文本之中，即形成混杂型文本；② 不同文本类型互不包含，相互排斥；③ 各个文本类型之间相互转化与过渡，即在一定条件下，一种文本类型可以转变为另一种文本类型。

除了从事件再现、文本类型的角度界定叙事之外，还有部分叙事学家从跨学科视角来界定叙事。回顾叙事学在后经典阶段的发展时，里蒙-凯南从建构主义的角度来阐述和界定叙事，她说：“在很多跨学科的交叉上（例如，文学与精神分析、哲学、历史学、法律研究），叙事的概念已经被扩大了。部分地受到社会科学领域中建构主义理论的影响，叙事是指感知、组织和建构意义的方式，是一种不同于逻辑和话语思维的认知模式，但绝不亚于逻辑和话语思维。”④ 詹姆斯·费伦(James Phelan)则从修辞方法的角度来界定叙事，认为叙事是“某人在某个场合为了某个目的向某人讲述某件事情的行为”。⑤ 赫尔曼从认知角度出发，把叙事看作一种“认知工具”(cognitive instrument)，在这种意义上，“叙事是一种认知结构或理解经验的方式。叙事作为文本类型，被那些以任何数量的符号媒介（书面或口头语言、漫画和绘图小说、电影、电视、以计算机为交际媒介的即时信息等）生产和导向故事的人生产和阐释出来，成为既影响故事讲述行为又受到故事讲述行为影响的交际互动手段”。⑥

叙事作为叙事学研究的对象，对其概念的界定无疑是整个学科健康发展的重要前提。一直以来，伴随叙事学不断发展的是关于叙事概念的多重界定。无论是以事件再现为主导的界定方法、以文本类型为主导的界定方法还是通过跨学科视角来界定叙事的方法，都未能在西方叙事学界达成统一。苏珊·

---

① David Herman, *Basic Elements of Narrative* (Oxford: Wiley-Blackwell, 2009), p.89.

② Ibid., p.92.

③ Ibid., p.98.

④ Rimmon-Kenan, *Narrative Fiction: Contemporary Poetics* (2nd edition), p.151.

⑤ James Phelan, *Living to Tell about It: The Rhetoric and Ethics of Character Narration* (Ithaca: Cornell University Press, 2005), p.217.

⑥ Herman, *Basic Elements of Narrative*, p.7.

奥尼嘉和加西尔·兰德指出:"叙事这一术语在潜在意义上是模糊的。"[①] 从某种意义上来说,叙事术语的模糊性或不确定性为叙事学界关于叙事定义的争论埋下了伏笔。

2000 年,《文体》(*Style*)杂志还邀请理查森作为特约主编,推出了以"叙事概念"为题的专刊。在叙事概念的讨论中,叙事的定义或"什么是叙事?"这个问题无疑是最重要的。但是想一劳永逸地界定叙事,谈何容易。实际上,西方学者还曾围绕这一话题展开了激烈的论战。在此,我们仅以戴维·鲁德姆和劳勒·瑞安之间的论战为例。

2005 年,鲁德姆在美国《叙事》杂志上发表了《从叙事再现到叙事用法:走向定义的界限》一文。在该文中,鲁德姆挑战了"叙事是对一系列或一序列事件的再现"(the representation of a series or sequence of events)这一普遍性定义。他认为关于叙事的任何定义,只要忽略了用法的重要性,就是不完整的。鲁德姆直接指出,以文本再现为基础的关于叙事的定义存有根本性的缺陷:

> 再现给"叙事是什么"提供了一个单一的概念,同时也规定了"叙事做什么"。只要叙事学一直被束缚在这个概念上,被束缚在这样的一种语言哲学观上,把"所指"(signification)的问题放在用法和实践的问题之前、之上,那么就不可能有界定叙事和对叙事的主题加以分类的满意方法。[②]

鲁德姆认为,对一系列或一序列事件的再现,并不能够给叙事提供一个完整的定义。再现或许是叙事的必要条件,但绝不是叙事的充分条件。要使得文本成为叙事,还必须要有别的东西或"额外条件"(something extra)。普林斯把这个额外条件称作"叙事性"(narrativity),即"一般叙事塑性"(general narrative configuration)动力的结果。[③] 鲁德姆认为,普林斯关于叙事性的说法并不比"事件再现"的说法高明,因为它既不能完全把叙事和非叙事区别开来,也不能给叙事提供一个清晰明确的定义。

在否定"叙事再现"和"叙事性"之后,鲁德姆走向了语言哲学关于"用法"(use)的论述。鲁德姆认为,任何再现都有很多"用法",任何关于叙事的定义,如果忽视了"用法"的重要性,都是不完整的。[④] 要区分"序列事件再现"的地位,就必须要考虑文本是如何被使用的。

在叙事定义这一论题上,鲁德姆贬抑"语义"(semantics)、褒扬"语用"(pragmatics)的立场遭到了瑞安的质疑。瑞安认为:

> 实在是因为叙事的用法太多了,因此我们不能把叙事的用法加进叙事的定义之中,我们必须依赖于文本所再现的内容。如果用法是叙事定义的基石,要不然就需要描述这些所有的用法,但这是一个不可能完成的任务,因为每天都会出现很多不同的新用法(如电子游戏、虚拟电视等),而且叙述者无法控制故事世界中受述者的行为;要不然我们就需要优先考虑某一个用法,如虚构叙事,或者用玛丽·露易·普拉特的话来说,"叙事表达文本",直接把那些诸如受到折磨的忏悔或用来解释

---

① Onega and García Landa, *Narratology: An Introduction*, p.4.

② Rudrum, "From Narrative Representation to Narrative Use: Towards the Limits of Definition," pp.202 - 203.

③ Gerald Prince, "Revisiting Narrativity," *Transcending Boundaries: Narratology in Context*, eds. Walter Grünzweig and Andreas Solbach (Tübingen: Gunter Narr, 1999), p.48.

④ Rudrum, "From Narrative Representation to Narrative Use: Towards the Limits of Definition," p.200.

理论的故事排除在外。[①]

瑞安并不完全排斥叙事的语用属性，但这并不意味着叙事的用途就可以构成叙事的定义，叙事的用法更不可能使得叙事的定义“滴水不漏”(watertight)。瑞安按照叙事的语义到语用的走向，提出了满足叙事的九个条件：

(1) 叙事必须是关于由个体存在物构成的世界的。

(2) 这个世界存在于一定的历史中，并且经历一定的变化。

(3) 这些状态的改变必须是由外在的事件所引起的，而不是由自然进化所引起的。

(4) 事件的某些参与者必须是人类或人类的代理者，这些代理者有内心的生活，而且能对世界的状态做出情感反应。

(5) 某些事件必须是由这些代理者所做出的有目的的行为，即代理者必须受到冲突的刺激，他们的行动以解决问题为目的。

(6) 事件序列必须形成一个统一的因果链条，最后走向结局。

(7) 某些事件必须是非习惯性的。

(8) 这些事件必须客观地发生在故事世界。

(9) 故事必须要有意义。[②]

根据上述九个条件，读者自己可以确定叙事的定义。也就是说，叙事不再是固定不变的“常量”，而是演变成因读者认知结构不同而有所不同的“变量”，叙事涉及读者个人的主观判断。作为“可能世界叙事学”和认知叙事学的代表人物之一，瑞安对自己在叙事概念上的“认知立场”毫不避讳。她认为，对叙事的界定存有认知因素的原因在于该定义涵盖了对于“叙事性”狭义本质的心理操作，而不是对“叙事性”的整体判断，例如再现事件发生次序的心理操作、这些事件在再现世界中引起的变化、事件对人物的意义、行动发生的动因以及行动的结果与代理者的意图的比较等。文本向读者提出了这些问题，如果读者可以解答这些问题，那么读者就可以把文本看作一个故事。[③]

瑞安还对比了小说的语用概念与叙事概念之间的差异。她认为，把文本看作小说对于读者的阅读有着至关重要的影响，但是这种辨别不能总是依赖于文本的内容或形式特征。小说属于“自上而下”的操作类型，读者必须先把文本看成小说，然后才能正确地解读它，但叙事性依赖的是“自下而上”的操作类型，读者必须让文本自己展示出其叙事地位。[④]

针对瑞安的挑战，鲁德姆在回应文章中重申了自己的立场，即如果一个文本通常被“用作叙事”(used as narrative)的话，那么它就是叙事，这与文本“被读作叙事”(read as narrative)不是一回事。具体说来，如果一个文本通常被某个“语言社区”(linguistic community)作为叙事来使用，那么该文本就是

① Ryan, “Semantics, Pragmatics, and Narrativity: A Response to David Rudrum,” *Narrative* 14.2 (May 2006), p.193.
② Ibid., p.194.
③ Ibid., pp.194－195.
④ Ibid., p.195.

叙事。虽然鲁德姆一方面接受了瑞安的质疑及其对叙事的新界定，但另一面他又否认了叙事定义的重要性，偏离了话题。他说："因为定义限制了我们对研究对象的看法，所以在界定叙事时，失去的东西会很多；又因为定义对于叙事研究没有必要，所以得到的东西会很少。"①

对鲁德姆否定叙事定义重要性的新立场，瑞安又在其个人网页中做出进一步回应。瑞安认为，虽然鲁德姆和自己有一致的观点，即叙事有太多的用法，以至于不能把这些用法整合进一个定义，但是他们却由此得出了大相径庭的结论。瑞安认为，叙事的定义应该以语义而不是语用为基础，更精确地说，应该以使用叙事的人在阅读或观看叙事时所形成的心理再现为基础。鲁德姆得出的结论是，叙事的用法太多了，以至于不能把这些用法都考虑进来，因此我们不应该努力地去界定叙事。对于鲁德姆这个论点，瑞安表示反对。她指出，鲁德姆忽视了不完美的叙事定义的"启发价值"(heuristic value)。②

无论是语义还是语用，都是叙事的重要方面。在这个论题上，鲁德姆和瑞安似乎都过于偏执，前者认为叙事的定义需要依赖叙事的"用法"，但是叙事的"用法"过多尤其导致了叙事定义的不可能性；后者认为叙事的界定必须以语义为基础，以读者对叙事的心理再现为前提。不过，同鲁德姆相比较，瑞安承认叙事定义的可能性和必要性的立场还是值得赞赏的。此外，鲁德姆和瑞安关于叙事定义的争论仅仅局限于"语义"和"语用"这两个维度，而忽略了叙事发生的重要载体——"媒介"(media)。任何形式的叙事都不可能凭空发生，必须借助发生的载体"媒介"。不同的媒介引起叙事语境的不同。在经典叙事学家看来，不同的媒介可以传递相同的叙事，但不同的媒介即便旨在讲述一个相同的故事，其自身属性也会产生不同的叙事情境，从而直接或间接地影响叙事内容的表达和传递，进而影响叙事的效果。

在《叙事学导论》一书中，弗鲁德尼克说："在21世纪的开端，叙事学非但没有走向尽头，反而非常健康和繁荣。"③ 当下，叙事学研究的兴盛和繁荣是无争的事实，不过对于"什么是叙事"这个问题的探究依然有待进一步加深。对叙事现象的观察、对叙事结构的认识以及对叙事概念的界定应该是叙事学研究的基础。只有回答了"什么是叙事"，我们才能更加明确地回答"怎么研究叙事"，才能更有新意地探讨与叙事相关的其他问题。总之，关于"什么是叙事"这个问题的讨论需要更多学者的参与。就像奥特曼(Altman)所说的那样："叙事自身被重新界定后，修正叙事分析、叙事种类以及叙事历史概念的路径也就被打开了。"④

---

① David Rudrum, "On the Very Idea of a Definition of Narrative: A Response to Marie-Laure Ryan," *Narrative* 14.2 (May 2006), p.203.

② Marie-Laure Ryan, "In Defense of Definition," in http://users.frii.com/mlryan/rudrumresponse.htm.

③ Fludernik, *An Introduction to Narratology*, p.21.

④ Rick Altman, *A Theory of Narrative* (New York: Columbia University Press, 2008), p.2.

第二节　什么是叙事学？

2002年5月，德国汉堡大学召开了一次题为“什么是叙事学”（What Is Narratology）的学术研讨会。在会议召集人汤姆·奇恩特（Tom Kindt）与汉斯-哈罗德·穆勒（Hans-Harald Müller）看来，“叙事学是什么？”“它所追求的目标是什么？”“它应该采用什么方法？”是很多国家的不同学科领域的学者都关注的问题。[①] 奇恩特与哈罗德·穆勒指出：“让‘什么是叙事学’这个问题如此紧迫的原因不是缺少可能的答案，而恰恰是答案太多了。”[②] 那么叙事学究竟是什么？我们不妨从叙事学的定义、历史源头和思想资源出发，历时地考察其本体地位。

众所周知，叙事学（英文narratology，法文narratologie）又名“叙述学”或“叙事理论”，是关于叙事的理论或科学。1969年，法国叙事学家茨维坦·托多洛夫在《〈十日谈〉语法》一书中，正式提出了“叙事学”这一概念。他在该书中写道：“这部著作属于一门尚未存在的科学，我们暂且将这门科学取名为叙述学，即关于叙事作品的科学。”[③] 在《叙事学手册》中，扬·克里斯托弗·梅斯特（Jan Christoph Meister）把叙事学界定为“一种致力于研究叙事再现的逻辑、原则和实践的人文学科”。[④] 在《叙事学词典》中，杰拉德·普林斯从以下三个方面来界定叙事学：

> （1）受结构主义启发而发展的叙事理论。叙事学研究叙事的本质形式和功能（不包括其表述媒介）并试图描述叙事能力的特征。尤其是，它检验一切叙事所共有的（在故事、叙述行为及其相互关系的层面上）和能够使一切叙事互不相同的东西并且试图解释生产和理解这些叙事的能力。
>
> （2）一种对有时序的情境与事件进行表述的语词模式的叙述研究。在这一限定意义上，叙事学忽视本身的故事层面（例如，它并不企图系统地阐述故事或情节的语法），而专注于故事与叙述文本、叙述行为与叙述文本以及故事与叙述行为之间的可能关系，具体地说，它考察语式、语态、声音等相关问题。
>
> （3）从叙事学模式和类别的角度，对特定（组合）的叙事进行的研究。[⑤]

与国外情况大致类似，傅修延在《中国叙事学》一书中写道：“叙事学又称叙述学，‘叙事’与‘叙述’是当前使用频率极高的热词，其内涵正在不断扩展与泛化，但叙事的本质应当是叙述事件，也就是通常所说的讲故事。据此而言，叙事学可以说是探寻讲故事奥秘的学问。”[⑥] 在《叙事学导论：从经典叙事学到后经典叙事学》一书中，谭君强这样界定叙事学：

---

① Tom Kindt and Hans-Harald Müller, “Preface,” *What is Narratology? Questions and Answers Regarding the Status of a Theory*, eds. Tom Kindt and Hans-Harald Müller (Berlin and New York: Walter de Gruyter, 2003), p.v.

② Ibid.

③ 张寅德编选：《叙述学研究》，第1—2页。

④ Jan Christoph Meister, “Narratology,” *Handbook of Narratology* (2nd edition), eds. Peter Hühn, Jan Christoph Meister, John Pier and Wolf Schmid (Berlin: De Gruyter, 2014), p.623.

⑤ Prince, *A Dictionary of Narratology* (Extended and Revised Version), p.66.

⑥ 傅修延：《中国叙事学》，北京：北京大学出版社，2015年，第1页。

> 叙事学，说得简单一点，就是关于叙事文本或叙事作品的理论。它在对意义构成单位进行切分的基础上，探讨叙事文本内在的构成机制，以及各部分之间的相互关系和其内在的关联，从而寻求叙事文本区别于其他类型作品的独特规律。同时，它也研究叙事、叙事性，即何种因素构成叙事，使作品具有叙事性等方面的内容。这样的研究使叙事学得以不断扩大自己的研究范围，在保持以语言媒介为核心的叙事文本作为研究基础的情况下，将研究的领域扩展到由其他媒介所构成的叙事文本中。[①]

上述叙事学定义有一个共同之处，即都认为叙事学就是寻找叙事作品所共有的规律，探寻故事讲述的奥秘或故事的语法的学问。在很多叙事理论家那里，叙事学大致等同于叙事的诗学。譬如，施劳米什·里蒙-凯南在其那本被广为接受的叙事学著作《叙事虚构作品：当代诗学》中，直接用"当代诗学"(contemporary poetics)作为该书的副标题。换言之，里蒙-凯南把该书中所讨论的叙事学看成是诗学。

什么是诗学？早期的叙事学为什么是诗学？在传统意义上，诗学一般是指关于诗歌的研究，因此被定义为"诗歌理论，尤其强调肌理与结构的原则"。[②] 在现代意义上，诗学指的是关于文学的一般理论。就如彼得·蔡尔兹(Peter Childs)和罗杰·弗勒(Roger Fowler)所指出的那样："在现代用法中，诗学不是研究诗歌或诗歌的技巧，而是文学的一般理论。"[③] 里蒙-凯南借用了以色列特拉维夫学派创始人本雅明·哈沙夫斯基(Benjamin Hrushovski)关于诗学的定义。在《诗学、批评、科学：关于文学研究领域与责任的评论》("Poetics, Criticism, Science: Remarks on the Fields and Responsibilities of the Study of Literature",1976)一文中，哈沙夫斯基写道：

> 诗学把文学作为文学的系统研究。它回答"什么是文学"的问题以及其他由此引发而来的问题，比如：什么是语言的艺术？什么是文学的形式与种类？什么是文学样式或趋势的本质？什么是某个具体诗人的"艺术"或"语言"？故事是如何被建构的？文学作品有哪些具体维度？这些维度是如何构成的？文学文本如何再现"非文学"现象？等等。[④]

在《叙事虚构作品：当代诗学》"后记"中，里蒙-凯南解释了她撰写该书的两个理论前提：第一，叙事学是诗学的一个分支；第二，叙事学的研究对象是叙事虚构作品的"类别差异"(differentia specifica)。[⑤] 换言之，叙事学重点考察叙事作品所共有的区别性特征。如果把哈沙夫斯基关于文学研究的诗学问题具体化为叙事研究的诗学问题，那么叙事诗学就是把叙事作为叙事的系统研究，具体回答什么是叙事，叙事何以是叙事，以及由此衍生而来的其他问题，如叙事形式与种类、叙事何以被建构等。

不过里蒙-凯南没有提及的是，在哈沙夫斯基那里，诗学有理论诗学(theoretical poetics)和描述诗学(descriptive poetics)之分。所谓的理论诗学涉及理论活动，根据一个问题或一系列问题的逻辑来建

---

① 谭君强：《叙事学导论：从经典叙事学到后经典叙事学》，北京：高等教育出版社，2014年，第2页。

② J. A. Cuddon, *A Dictionary of Literary Terms and Literary Theory* (Fifth Edition) (Malden: Wiley-Blackwell, 2013), p.545.

③ Peter Childs and Roger Fowler, *The Routledge Dictionary of Literary Terms* (London and New York: Routledge, 2006), p.179.

④ Benjamin Hrushovski, "Poetics, Criticism, Science: Remarks on the Fields and Responsibilities of the Study of Literature," *PTL: A Journal for Descriptive Poetics and Theory of Literature* 1 (1976), p.xv.

⑤ Rimmon-Kenan, *Narrative Fiction: Contemporary Poetics* (2nd edition), p.141.

构一套系统;描述诗学是对某类具体文学作品的文学维度做出详尽研究的学术活动。[①] 维吉尔·L.勒克(Virgil L. Lokke)评价道:"诗学呼声无论是来自本雅明·哈沙夫斯基、诺思洛普·弗莱(Northrop Frye)还是来自茨维坦·托多洛夫,都没什么区别——他们都在呼唤文学理论中的'科学性'霸权。"[②] 勒克进一步指出:"尽管新的'科学性'诗学版图包含很多领地,但没有哪一个能比'叙事学公国'(the principality of narratology)更能有效地展示新诗学的问题与抱负。"[③] 换言之,在勒克看来,叙事学是哈沙夫斯基所呼吁的科学性诗学的典型代表。从诗学类型来看,叙事学可被纳入描述诗学这一类型。在这种意义上,里蒙-凯南说:"叙事学将自身看作一套理论,或建构在逻辑上相互关联的法则的系统,这些法则构成了有规律的现象或一组现象。"[④]

受到亚里士多德《诗学》的间接影响以及结构主义语言学的直接影响,叙事学致力于揭示叙事文类的区别性特征与普遍模式,旨在建构关于叙事的诗学,这产生的后果是叙事学忽略了对文本意义的发掘与阐释,沉溺于纯理论的建构,脱离了文本生产与文本接受的历史文化语境,难以持续发展。这也是结构主义叙事学在20世纪80年代遭遇发展低谷的原因所在。在为《剑桥文学批评史》所撰写的"叙事学"条目中,普林斯写道:

> 叙事学不是阐释的女仆。相反,通过对控制叙事的主导原则的关注,叙事学没有刻画具体叙事的具体意义,而是刻画那些使得叙事产生意义的东西,叙事学是攻破文本的重要参与者。此外,叙事学还在另一场影响文学研究样式的战争中起到了重要作用。它通过考察运作于所有叙事(不仅仅是伟大的、虚构的或现存的叙事)的要素,质疑文学经典的本质,揭示出许多非经典叙事作品和经典叙事作品(从叙事上来说)都一样复杂。[⑤]

值得注意的是,普林斯特别强调:叙事学不是"阐释的女仆"(a handmaiden of interpretation)。这一观点与强调具体文本"细读"(close reading)的新批评立场截然相反。新批评的主要任务就是通过对文本的细读来发现和揭示文本的意义,将揭示文本的具体意义视作阐释的根本目的,而叙事学则背离这一诉求,致力于寻找意义得以产生的机制和要素。从这个角度来说,叙事学无视对具体文本的阐释,甚至与文本阐释截然对立。从根本上来说,早期的叙事学对阐释的排斥是因为其诗学属性。对此,我们不妨以卡勒的论述来加以说明。在《文学理论入门》一书中,卡勒这样解释诗学与阐释学之间的对立:

> 在文学研究中也有一个经常被忽视的基本区别,就是两个课题之间的区别:一个根据语言学的模式,认为意义就是需要解释的东西,并且努力证明为什么意义会成为可能。另一个与其相反,它从形式开始,力图解读这些形式,从而告诉我们这些形式究竟意味着什么。在文学研究中,这是诗学和解释学的对比。诗学以已经验证的意义或者效果为起点,研究它们是怎样取得的。(是什么使一段文

① Hrushovski, "Poetics, Criticism, Science: Remarks on the Fields and Responsibilities of the Study of Literature," p.xv.
② Virgil L. Lokke, "Narratology, Obsolescent Paradigms, and 'Scientific' Poetics; or Whatever Happened to PTL?" *Modern Fiction Studies* 33.3 (Autumn 1987), p.545.
③ Ibid.
④ Rimmon-Kenan, *Narrative Fiction: Contemporary Poetics* (2nd edition), p.141.
⑤ Gerald Prince, "Narratology," *Cambridge History of Literary Criticism: From Formalism to Poststructuralism*, ed. Raman Selden (Cambridge: Cambridge University Press, 1995), pp.129 - 130.

字在一本小说里看起来具有讽刺意味？是什么使我们对某一个人物产生同情？为什么一首诗的结尾会显得含混不清？）而解释学则不同，它以文本为基点，研究文本的意义，力图发现新的、更好的解读。①

在上文中，卡勒提到了文学研究两种相互对立的类型，即以探究具体文本的具体意义为主要目的的阐释学路径，以及从文本意义出发来探究意义产生的文本机制与形式的诗学路径。卡勒在这里所说的基于语言学模式的文学研究课题在很大程度上指的就是结构主义叙事学。

2002年，卡勒在为《结构主义诗学》撰写序言的时候，再次提到诗学与阐释学的对立。卡勒说，诗学就是"把文学装置、规约和策略理解为文学作品创造它们效果的手段。我把阐释学作为诗学的对立面，阐释实践的目标是发现或确定文本的意义。从原则上来说，这两种事业大相径庭：诗学从被验证的意义或效果出发，试图解读那些使它们成为可能的结构或装置，而阐释学则争辩意义是什么或应该是什么。英美新批评使得阐释学成为文学研究的正统方法，我认为文学研究的目标不在于发现新且合理的阐释，而在于试图理解作品怎样对读者产生效果（诸如意义的效果）"。② 可见，卡勒所拥抱和赞同的是作为诗学性质的文学研究，而这也是他在美国积极推动包括叙事学在内的结构主义文学理论的一个主要动因。为追求文学研究的科学性和客观性，结构主义者们过于聚焦叙事的"诗学"层面，把叙事看作一种形式结构，选择不介入文本阐释，视文本阐释为主观行为，忽略了具体叙事文本的内涵及其之于读者的意义，从而使得叙事学陷入发展的危机，以至于里蒙-凯南在完成《叙事虚构作品：当代诗学》一书后，不确定该书是介绍叙事学的导论还是宣告叙事学死亡的讣告。③

尽管结构主义叙事学以诗学为建构目标，不做阐释的女仆，但这并不意味着叙事学和阐释学就完全不能互补相容。波·帕特森（Bo Petterson）指出，尽管结构主义叙事学和20世纪阐释学的历史与理论基础大相径庭，前者的研究兴趣在于形式，而后者的研究兴趣在于阐释，但"很少有人注意到的是，叙事学与阐释学都对文本有兴趣"。④ 从这个角度出发，帕特森呼吁把叙事学和阐释学相结合，认为"叙事学与文学阐释学这两个方法要想获得更为牢固的基础，就必须把两者之间的链接建立起来"。⑤ 不过需要指出的是，结构主义叙事学所感兴趣的文本是广义上的叙事文本而不是具体的叙事文本。如果说叙事学因为忽略对具体文本意义的发掘与阐释而出现危机，那么其再度复兴则是源于其研究范式的及时转换，即从对叙事文类的诗学建构转入对具体叙事文本的意义阐释。

2016年夏，汉娜·梅雷托亚（Hanna Meretoja）在《故事世界》杂志上发表了题为《支持阐释》的文章。在该文中，梅雷托亚指出："我们应该在宏观层面和微观层面上理解阐释这个概念，阐释和阐释学应该在当代叙事研究领域中具有更中心的位置。"⑥ 梅雷托亚详细列举了叙事学需要"支持阐释"的三个缘由：第一，阐释是我们一直在做的东西，如果拒绝阐释，阐释就在我们背后发生。我们最好批判性地反思我们阐释世界的方式，而不是假装我们能够超越阐释实践直接进入世界。所以，与其反对阐释，倒不

① 乔纳森·卡勒：《文学理论入门》，李平译，南京：译林出版社，2008年，第64页。

② Jonathan Culler, *Structuralist Poetics: Structuralism, Linguistics and the Study of Literature* (London and New York: Routledge, 2002), pp.vii - viii.

③ Rimmon-Kenan, *Narrative Fiction: Contemporary Poetics* (2nd edition), p.135.

④ Bo Petterson, "Narratology and Hermeneutics: Forging the Missing Link," *Narratology in the Age of Cross-Disciplinary Narrative Research*, eds. Sandra Heinen and Roy Sommer (Berlin: De Gruyter, 2009), p.13.

⑤ Ibid., p.32.

⑥ Hanna Meretoja, "For Interpretation," *Storyworlds* 8.1 (2016), p.98.

如明智地用丰富而复杂的方式去介入阐释的不同维度和不同层面。第二，我们不该把阐释看作寻找隐藏的意义或内容，而要将其看作介入世界或从某种视角介入阐释对象的行为，同时需要反思此类阐释行为如何参与建构现实。第三，承认我们是阐释的动物，可以让我们反思各种不同阐释行为是如何联系的，帮助我们把文学阐释现象与更大的阐释现象关联在一起。从阐释过程来看待叙事和主体性，能够为我们概念化叙事与经验、生活与叙事、主体性和文化网络之间的关系提供一个“非还原的”(nonreductive)框架。[①] 也就是说，叙事和阐释的结合可以让我们更好地介入世界、参与建构现实。这与利斯贝特·科塔尔斯·阿尔特斯(Liesbeth Korthals Altes)所提出的叙事在融合阐释的时候需要考虑社会维度大致相同。阿尔特斯指出：“叙事学对社会维度缺乏系统的兴趣，因此失去了多样的阐释过程。”[②] 换言之，叙事学如果转向并支持阐释，就需要纳入对性别、政治、伦理、历史等社会维度的考量。关于叙事学纳入性别、政治等维度，本书将以女性主义叙事学为例加以说明；关于叙事学纳入伦理、历史等维度，本书将以修辞叙事学为例加以说明。

女性主义叙事学是叙事学由诗学转向并支持阐释的一个典型例子。20世纪80年代，这种转型非但没有即刻得到认同，反而引起了一定的争议。我们不妨以苏珊·兰瑟(Susan Lanser)所提出的女性主义叙事学及其与里莉·迪恩格特(Nilli Diengott)之间的争论为例。1986年，兰瑟在《文体》杂志发表了题为《建构女性主义叙事学》(“Toward a Feminist Narratology”)的文章，呼吁将女性主义和叙事学进行结合。兰瑟坦言，她要把叙事学和女性主义这两个看似不同的批评结合起来：前者是科学的、描述的、非意识形态的，而后者是印象式的、评价性的和政治性的。[③] 兰瑟指出，叙事学过去常常把“纯符号过程”(pure semiosis)和叙事之间的关系视作因果关系，由此导致的普遍倾向是既使文本脱离了它们的生产语境和接受语境，又使文本脱离了“政治”批评家们所说的作为文学基础的“现实世界”(real world)。[④] 为了回答具体文本中的具体阐释问题，兰瑟以《埃特金森的盒子》(*Atkinson's Casket*，1832)中一位新婚女性给其闺蜜写的一封书信为例，讨论了文本中潜藏的具有颠覆性质的女性声音。从表层文本来看，这封信夸赞了其丈夫，认为他“最为和蔼可亲”(the most amiable)，视妻子为“伴侣”(companion)，让人感觉婚姻幸福；同时，这封信也表现了女性的温顺与屈从。但如果按照书信所提示的隔行阅读方式，读者就会发现一个不同于表层文本的声音。书信批判了丈夫是“丑陋鲁莽、老不中用、嫉妒心强的怪物”(ugly, crass, old, disagreeable, and jealous monster)，视妻子为“玩偶或下贱的奴仆”(paly thing or menial slave)，表达了叙述者对婚姻的不满。针对这一特殊文本，兰瑟区分了“公开型叙述”(public narration)和“私密型叙述”(private narration)两种叙述类型。公开型叙述指的是针对文本世界之外的受述者的交流，私密型叙述指的是针对文本世界之内的受述者的交流。兰瑟指出，对于女性文本而言，公开型和私密型语境之间的区分复杂而重要。就她所讨论的这封信而言，在叙述者“我”那里，公开的文本是为男性而作的，而私密的文本是为她的闺蜜而作的。兰瑟说：“我对这个编码信件的分析表明，一种修订的诗学或许可以仔细分析和解码叙事的某些维度。”[⑤]正如兰瑟本人所说，她的研究

---

① Hanna Meretoja, “For Interpretation,” *Storyworlds* 8.1 (2016), pp.113-114.

② Liesbeth Korthals Altes, *Ethos and Narrative Interpretation: The Negotiation of Values in Fiction* (Lincoln: University of Nebraska Press, 2014), p.19.

③ Susan S. Lanser, “Toward a Feminist Narratology,” *Style* 20.3 (1986), p.341.

④ Ibid., p.344.

⑤ Ibid., p.357.

呼唤了一种叙事研究的新范式，即从脱离历史文化语境的诗学建构走向融合历史语境的文本阐释。

迪恩格特以“叙事诗学”(narrative poetics)为出发点，对兰瑟将女性主义批评和叙事学相结合的倡议提出质疑。在《叙事学与女性主义》(“Narratology and Feminism”)一文的第一条注释中，迪恩格特强调自己倾向于使用“叙事诗学”这一术语，因为这是更为准确的用来描述关于叙事的结构主义讨论的术语。[①] 实际上，我们可以把迪恩格特对女性主义叙事学的批判看成传统叙事学家对叙事诗学的固守。与里蒙-凯南类似，迪恩格特重点参照了哈沙夫斯基对诗学、批评和阐释的区分。实际上，哈沙夫斯基是在讨论阅读方式的基础上，依据文学研究者对文本的不同兴趣，将文学研究分成不同的领域。哈沙夫斯基把文学阅读划分为三个层次：第一，某个读者或听众对某个具体文学作品的反应。这种反应可以是直接的也可以是间接的，可以是粗略的也可以是精细的。我们可以说它是读者的“享受”或“美学体验”、读者对文本的理解等。这一活动从总体上来说就是个人对文学作品的欣赏或体验。这一层面没有关于文学文本的交流，大致属于读者和本人自己的交流。第二，以文字为媒介，在文学和读者之间的交流，其目的在于通过写作和讲述的形式向他人表达自己的印象、理解和评价。这一层面是一个人对多个人的交流。第三，严肃的文学研究与分析，其目的是就像科学一样，用一套知识体系和方法对文学做出客观的描述和解释。这一层面以可接受的逻辑结构、系统和方法为基础，是代表多个人的一个人对多个人展开的交流。就文学研究而言，哈沙夫斯基所重点强调的是第三种类型的阅读，并且把对文学研究的兴趣划分为三种类型，与之对应的则是三种研究领域：第一，单个文学作品(the single work of literature)，与之对应的是“阐释”；第二，作为历史存在的文学(literature in its historical existence)，与之对应的是“批评”；第三，作为文学的文学(literature as literature)，与之对应的是“诗学”。具体说来，批评研究的是文学中的现实生活；诗学是对文学作为文学的系统研究，通过一个或一组问题的逻辑来建构一个系统；阐释并不意在建构系统，而是意在发掘单个作品的意义。参照哈沙夫斯基的论述，迪恩格特绘制如下关于批评、诗学和阐释之间区别的图示：[②]

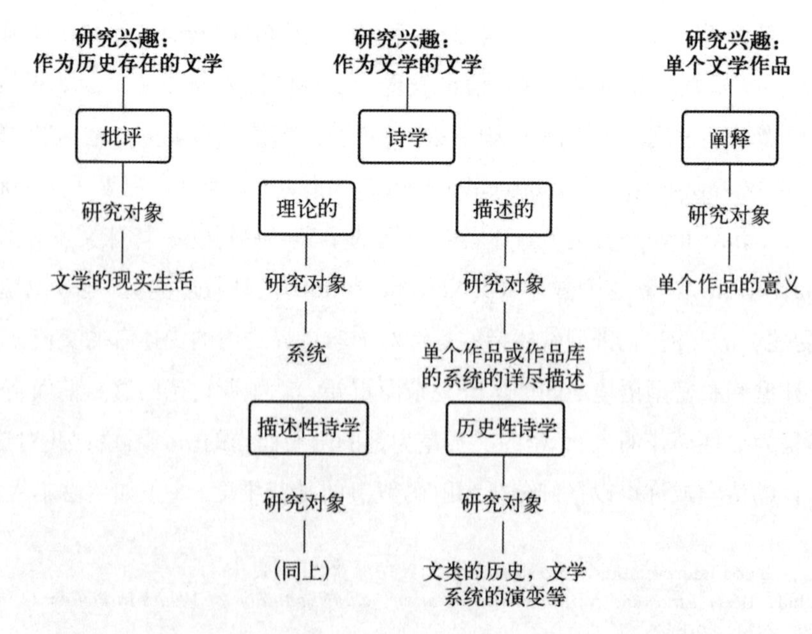

① Nilli Diengott, “Narratology and Feminism,” *Style* 22.1 (1988), p.50.

② Ibid., p.44.

在迪恩格特看来，叙事学属于理论诗学而不属于阐释。就此而言，兰瑟的问题在于混淆了叙事学的地位。[①] 迪恩格特重申："确定叙事的意义是阐释所关注的内容，而不是理论诗学所关注的内容。"[②] 至于性别是否要被纳入叙事理论的建构这一问题，迪恩格特认为，性别只对阐释有意义，但阐释既非叙事学，亦非理论诗学。

从今天的眼光来看，女性主义叙事学融合历史和语境，对叙事文本做出了具有性别意味的阐释，其地位已经牢固树立起来，它也成为当代叙事理论中一支颇有影响的流派。与女性主义叙事学对阐释的倚重一样，修辞叙事学也同样强调阐释，甚至比女性主义叙事学更加强调阐释。在《理解叙事》(*Understanding Narrative*, 1994)一书中，费伦和彼得·J.拉宾诺维茨(Peter J. Rabinowitz)倡导叙事研究的"理论实践"立场，试图把理论和阐释加以结合，让理论与实践相互启发，以这种自我反思的方式在阐释文本的同时，考察阐释的理论基础，呼吁关注阐释并给当代叙事研究注入强劲动力。他们说："有时候，船的旧结构无法很好地解决船上的具体问题，为了应对这个情况，就需要设计新船板，提出一个新设计。但过一段时间后，这个新设计又不能充分地解决船上的新问题，所以又开始了新一轮创新。"[③] 与具有诗学性质的结构主义叙事学家无视阐释的做法不同，费伦和拉宾诺维茨倡导将叙事学服务于文本阐释，同时认为叙事阐释也可以给叙事学带来变革，促使叙事学为解决新的叙事问题而不断创新，实现理论和阐释之间的互补共赢，叙事研究也由此被注入源源不断的发展动力。

叙事学对阐释的支持和拥抱使得这门学科成功走出危机与低谷，发展成为当代文学研究的一门显学，并且迅速向其他学科渗透，表现出很强的应用性。在注重阐释、向其他研究领域和学科扩张的过程中，叙事学表现出工具箱性质的实用性。2017年，澳大利亚著名叙事学家、《劳特利奇叙事理论指南》(*The Routledge Companion to Narrative Theory*, 2022)第一主编保罗·道森(Paul Dawson)在《文体》杂志第2期发表了题为《陷入叙事学的"工具箱"：叙事理论的概念与类型》("Delving into the Narratological 'Toolbox': Concepts and Categories in Narrative Theory")的文章。道森开篇指出："描述叙事理论特征最常用的一个方式是把它看成一套提供给叙事分析的'工具箱'。我认为这是一个极为糟糕的、平淡乏味的隐喻，但有趣的是该隐喻的流行让我们认识到叙事学的学科抱负。因为每当叙事学工具箱被提及的时候，它都被表述为一个方法论或元学科。"[④] 至于叙事学被视作工具箱的原因，道森从其最初较为抽象的形式主义色彩谈起：

> 众所周知，叙事学的传统就是在理论上聚焦于叙事的深层结构、叙事语法的建构以及对所有叙事特征的探寻。但是，我们知道叙事学常常被视为一种抽象的理论事业，其特征就是沉醉于分类形式、创造新词。为了改变这些印象，叙事学家们经常以可转移的实用性来推销叙事理论的输出价值。由此，"工具箱"隐喻就变得重要了。实际上，该隐喻邀请我们把叙事学的理论大厦想象为一种可使用、易上手的事业，叙事学忙于提出诸多术语和样式，以便我们在研究叙事的时候可以用到它们。[⑤]

---

① Diengott, "Narratology and Feminism," pp.43 - 44.

② Ibid., p.44.

③ James Phelan and Peter J. Rabinowitz, "Introduction: Understanding Narrative," *Understanding Narrative*, eds. James Phelan and Peter J. Rabinowitz (Columbus: The Ohio State University Press, 1994), pp.13 - 14.

④ Dawson, Paul Dawson, "Delving into the Narratological 'Toolbox': Concepts and Categories in Narrative Theory," *Style* 51.2 (2017), p.228.

⑤ Ibid., p.229.

在道森看来，叙事学原本就是抽象的理论，致力于辨析叙事的深层结构，揭示所有叙事所共享的特征，建构叙事的普遍语法，但同时为了输出的需要，又以"工具箱"的名义来宣扬其实用性，从而使得其各种术语和分类方式具有了合法性。道森在上文中指出，把抽象的叙事学比喻为实用的"工具箱"(toolbox)是"叙事学家们"(narratologists)的惯常做法。究竟是哪些叙事学家把叙事学比喻为工具箱呢？在文章中，道森提到了德国叙事学家曼弗雷德·雅恩(Manfred Jahn)。雅恩是著名的《劳特利奇叙事理论百科全书》(*Routledge Encyclopedia of Narrative Theory*，2005)的主编之一，著有影响巨大的网络版叙事学教材《叙事学 2.3：叙事理论导读》(*Narratology 2.3: A Guide to the Theory of Narrative*)。雅恩在该书第 1 章写道："本章建构一个叙事学基本概念的工具箱，并展示如何将它运用于对小说的分析。"[①] 实际上，在该书中雅恩 5 次用到了"工具箱"。譬如，在该书最开始，他写道："本教程提供一个基本的叙事学概念、方法和模型的工具箱。"[②] 在第 1 章第 19 节，他写道："除了热奈特的两种叙事基本类型(同质叙事和异质叙事)之外，我们的工具箱现在还纳入斯坦泽尔的三种叙事情境：第一人称叙述、作者式叙述(同质-显性)和人物叙述(异质-隐性，加上内聚焦)。"[③] 在第 1 章第 27 节，他又写道："在本节结束之际，我想通过另外两个例子来检验我们现在的这个工具箱。"[④] 此外，他在书中还交替使用了"分析工具"(analytical tools)以及"工具"(tools)两个概念。毫不夸张地说，雅恩对叙事学工具论持有无比坚定的立场，并将此概念贯穿叙事学研究始终。譬如，雅恩在他所撰写的网络在线版《电影的叙事学分析》(*A Guide to Narratological Film Analysis*，2021)一书中写道："本教程提供一个基本的叙事学概念、方法和模型的工具箱，并展现如何将它应用于电影分析。"[⑤]

除雅恩之外，把叙事学视为工具箱的理论家还有荷兰叙事学家米克·巴尔、德国叙事学家安斯加尔·纽宁(Ansgar Nünning)等。在《叙事学：叙事理论导论》一书中，巴尔不止一次地强调叙事学是工具。她说："这里的理论不以确定性自诩，它被看作一套工具，是一种表达和具体化我们对文本阐释反应的手段；"[⑥]"必须要清楚的是，这里讲述的整个理论都是一个读者设计，一套启发性工具；"[⑦]"叙事理论主要是一个工具箱，而不是一个关于话语类型、模式或态度的哲学。"[⑧] 在《语境主义叙事学与文化叙事学概览》("Surveying Contextualist and Cultural Narratologies")一文中，纽宁野心勃勃地提出建构文化叙事学，认为"叙事学的分析工具可以用来服务于对叙事的语境阐释"。[⑨] 纽宁坚定地认为，"所有文学家和文化史学家，如果想要研究叙事中的伦理、意识形态或政治问题，都可以从叙事学提供的工具箱中获得裨益。"[⑩] 在《叙事学手册》中，梅斯特也把叙事学看作工具。梅斯特说："叙事学是一门人文学科，

---

① Manfred Jahn, *Narratology 2.3: A Guide to the Theory of Narrative* (English Department, University of Cologne, 2021), www.uni-koeln.de/~ame02/pppn.pdf.

② Ibid.

③ Ibid.

④ Ibid.

⑤ Manfred Jahn, *A Guide to Narratological Film Analysis* (English Department, University of Cologne, 2021) www.uni-koeln.de/~ame02/pppf.pdf.

⑥ Mieke Bal, *Narratology: Introduction to the Theory of Narrative* (Fourth Edition) (Toronto: University of Toronto Press, 2017), p.viii.

⑦ Ibid., p.viii.

⑧ Ibid., p.7.

⑨ Ansgar Nünning, "Surveying Contextualist and Cultural Narratologies: Towards an Outline of Approaches, Concepts and Potentials," *Narratology in the Age of Cross-Disciplinary Narrative Research*, eds. Sandra Heinen and Roy Sommer (Berlin: De Gruyter, 2009), p.50.

⑩ Ibid., p.63.

致力于研究叙事再现的逻辑、原则和实践。在起步阶段，叙事学被结构主义方法所主导，提出了各种理论、概念和分析步骤。叙事学的概念和模式被视为启发工具，被广为使用；叙事学定理在探究和建构我们关于生产和处理不同形式、媒介、语境和交流实践的多种叙事的能力模型上扮演了一个重要角色。”①

问题在于，如果叙事学是工具箱，那么这个箱子里有多少工具？工具的数量会发生变化吗？在道森看来，叙事学好比苹果手机，工具会越来越多，工具箱也随之越来越大。他列出了叙事学工具箱不断增大的三个原因：

> 第一，我们需要改进现有的工具，尤其是当我们遇到新的叙事作品，而现有工具无法起作用的时候。
>
> 第二，我们需要创造新的工具，尤其是当我们想要扩展我们的研究对象，把很多不同媒介都包括进来的时候。
>
> 第三，我们需要把叙事学和其他批评实践结合得更为紧密，并对后者有用的时候。②

换言之，叙事学的工具箱之所以会越来越大，是因为叙事现象或需要解决的叙事问题不断涌现出来。问题是作为文学理论一个重要分支的叙事学何以成为工具箱？我们不妨回到德勒兹与福柯有关理论的对话上。1972年，在与福柯对谈时，德勒兹把理论比喻为工具箱。德勒兹说：

> 理论确确实实就像是一个工具箱。它与能指无关。它必须是有用的，而且不是对其自身有用。如果没有人用理论，从理论家(他随后就停止作为理论家)开始一直到理论，就都会失去价值或不合时宜。我们不修改理论，而是创造新的理论，我们除了创造其他理论之外，别无选择。不可思议的是，普鲁斯特这个被称为纯粹知识分子的作家，把这个问题说得清晰明了：“把我的书看成朝向外面世界的一副眼镜；如果它们不适合你，你就去另外找一副；我让你自己去寻找工具，是为了搏斗而必备的工具。”③

德勒兹以普鲁斯特把书本比喻为眼镜的例子来说明理论就如同一个工具箱。书本就如同眼镜，可以让我们看到外面的世界；当然眼镜适不适合，需要我们自己决定，选择权在我们自己手上，但前提是为了看到外面的世界，我们必须要有一副眼镜。在德勒兹看来，理论之所以有用和具有价值，是因为它是工具箱。如果一个人寻找的理论不合适，就等于在工具箱中拿错了工具，他需要去换一套合适的工具。换言之，理论之所以像一个工具箱，主要是因为它证明了其有用性，否则无论是理论家还是理论自身都失去了价值，也没有存在的必要性。在这种情况下，理论就会发生变革，甚至涌现出新理论，并继续以工具箱的性质来证明其有用性。

德勒兹关于理论是工具箱的这一观点在其他文学理论家那里得到了进一步延伸。譬如，在《理论工具箱：人文、艺术与社会科学的批评概念》(*The Theory Toolbox: Critical Concepts for the Humanities*,

① Meister, “Narratology,” p.623.

② Dawson, “Delving into the Narratological ‘Toolbox’: Concepts and Categories in Narrative Theory,” pp.229－230.

③ Michel Foucault, *Language, Counter-memory, Practice*, trans. Donald F. Bouchard and Sherry Simon (Ithaca: Cornell University Press, 1977), p.208.

Arts, and Social Sciences)一书中,杰弗里·尼伦(Jeffrey Nealon)和苏珊·瑟尔斯·吉鲁(Susan Searls Giroux)也从“有用性”角度来解释理论的工具箱性质:“如果理论是有趣或有用的,理论所做的工作不能局限于或被界定为学派和思潮。相反,我们对理论的兴趣在于把它当作一种方法,当作介入当代文化的一个较大的工具箱。”[①] 尽管20世纪被誉为文学理论的黄金世纪,从俄国形式主义、英美新批评,到法国结构主义、解构主义,再到后殖民主义、新历史主义、女性主义、性别研究、族裔研究等,各种理论流派层出不穷,但是尼伦和吉鲁反对将理论看作“流派”(school)或“思潮”(movement),而把理论视为一种“方法”(approach),视为一个可以帮助我们介入文化研究的“工具箱”。也正是在“工具箱”这个意义上,理论才“有趣”或“有用”。

近年来,叙事学积极借鉴和引入其他学科的研究方法与成果,由此涌现出诸多新的叙事学流派,譬如认知叙事学、语料库叙事学、生态叙事学等。与此同时,作为一种研究方法与参照范式,叙事学迅速向其他学科领域渗透和扩张,由此超越了其原初的文学批评领域,涌现出所谓的“应用叙事学”(applied narratology),譬如法律叙事学、音乐叙事学、舞蹈叙事学、新闻叙事学、电影叙事学、数字叙事学、建筑叙事学、游戏叙事学等。用扬·克里斯托弗·梅斯特、汤姆·奇恩特、威尔海姆·舍尔努斯(Wilhelm Schernus)等人的话来说:“现在,应用叙事学出现在所有的学科领域中,我们迟早要面对数学叙事学、无机叙事学等应用叙事学。”[②] 毫无疑问,不断涌现的应用叙事学固然得益于跨学科研究这一总体趋势与潮流,但更受惠于叙事学所提供的强有力的分析工具。在这种意义上,我们不难理解道森的观点:叙事学之所以是工具箱,是因为它也是“一个给其他学科提供工具的服务性学科”(a service discipline providing tools for other disciplines)。[③]

进入21世纪以来,叙事学非但没有死,反而在保留其核心概念与术语的同时,脱离了纯粹的形式主义色彩,充分关注语境,同时与其他相邻学科交叉发展,表现出更加强劲的发展势头。结合具体历史语境和批评气候的变化,从历时维度出发,我们不难发现叙事学的三种基本形态,即具有诗学性质的叙事学、支持阐释的叙事学以及作为工具箱的叙事学,进而给叙事学的历时考察提供另一维度。早期的叙事学,在理论源头上,可追溯至亚里士多德的《诗学》;在思想资源上,可追溯至结构主义和形式主义;在研究诉求上,致力于揭示叙事的区别性特征与普遍模式,发掘叙事意义生产的机制,发展成为具有诗学性质的学科。具有诗学性质的叙事学聚焦叙事的形式,忽略对具体文本意义的解读,脱离了文本生产的历史文化语境,不甘做阐释的奴仆,这导致其陷入发展危机。实际上,叙事学与文学阐释在对立的同时,也蕴含了互补融合的可能。随着具有意识形态色彩的政治文化批评在20世纪80年代的兴起,叙事学开始拥抱和转向阐释,将性别、政治、伦理、历史等因素纳入考量范畴,注重以语境化的方式对具体文本展开叙事分析,继而实现了从对叙事文类的诗学建构到对具体文本的叙事阐释的范式转变。叙事学在转向和支持阐释之后,不仅实现了自身的再度复兴,也实现了理论和阐释之间的互动与双赢,为叙事研究注入源源不断的发展动力。在注重阐释以及跨向其他学科领域的过程中,叙事学表现出很强的实用性,

---

① Jeffrey Nealon and Susan Searls Giroux, *The Theory Toolbox: Critical Concepts for the Humanities, Arts, and Social Sciences* (2nd ed.) (Lanham: Rowman & Littlefield Publishers, 2012), p.7.

② Jan Christoph Meister, Tom Kindt and Wilhelm Schernus, “Introduction: Narratology beyond Literary Criticism: Mediality-Disciplinarity,” *Narratology beyond Literary Criticism: Mediality, Disciplinarity*, ed. Jan Christoph Meister (Berlin: De Gruyter, 2005), p.xiv.

③ Dawson, “Delving into the Narratological ‘Toolbox’: Concepts and Categories in Narrative Theory,” p.243.

被有效地用作介入其他领域研究的“工具箱”，成为一种“有趣”或“有用”的方法。在当下和未来一段时间内，随着新的叙事现象和叙事问题的不断出现、相关方法的持续引入以及叙事学自身向其他学科的快速渗透，叙事学会表现出更为多元的特征，但诗学、阐释、工具箱稳固地构成了叙事学的三种形态。时至今日，三种形态的叙事学之间已经不再是过去“有我无你，有你无我”的相互排斥关系，而是“我中有你，你中有我”的融合并存关系。诗学形态使得叙事学持续保持理论的生产性，实现对文学、文类总体结构与规律的把握；阐释形态则使之避免了“只见森林、不见树木”的偏误倾向，能够在具体历史语境中解读具体叙事文本的意义与内涵；而工具箱形态则使之具有很强的实用性，在服务于叙事文本阐释的同时，实现了向其他学科领域的拓展，成为一门服务性学科。从某种意义上来说，三种形态的并存、融合与互补也是叙事学发展的生命力所在。

第三节　当代叙事学的思潮、发展态势与研究命题

类似于叙事学研究对象层面的划分,[①]叙事学的发展阶段也大致存在二分法与三分法的区别。就三分法而言,德国学者汤姆·奇恩特、汉斯-哈罗德·穆勒,比利时学者吕克·赫尔曼与巴特·凡瓦克,英国学者保罗·韦克(Paul Wake)等人是其中的代表。在《什么是叙事学?关于一个理论地位的问题与解答》(2003)一书的序言中,奇恩特和哈罗德·穆勒根据叙事学的发展历程,将其划分为三个阶段:第一阶段为19世纪中叶至20世纪中叶,这一时期关于叙事的研究主要由修辞与诗学范式研究、小说家的实践知识、文学批评家的个人观察三个方面构成;第二阶段为20世纪中叶至20世纪80年代,在这一时期,叙事学成为文本研究的一个独特领域,法国结构主义者的研究尤为值得称道;第三阶段是20世纪80年代后的叙事学研究,这一时期的叙事学以多元化和急速扩张为主要特征。[②] 与此划分相似,在《叙事分析手册》(2005)中,赫尔曼与凡瓦克也从叙事学生成与发展的历时角度,将其大致划分为三个阶段:结构主义叙事学、结构主义之前以及与结构主义同期的叙事学、后经典叙事学。[③] 与上述学者略有不同的是,韦克在《文学和文化理论百科全书》(2011)一书中,一方面在标题上将"叙事学"和"结构主义"并置,另一方面认为叙事学有"三个界限分明但事实上又总是融合在一起的"阶段:结构主义、经典叙事学、后经典叙事学。[④]

但是目前国际学界普遍接受的关于叙事学发展阶段的划分是戴维·赫尔曼在世纪之交所提出的二分法模式,即经典叙事学与后经典叙事学。[⑤] 据赫尔曼的解释,他采用这种划分方法是为了对比结构主义叙事学与那些结构主义者无法采用或被他们所忽视的叙事研究框架。[⑥] 德国学者安斯加尔·纽宁不仅采用经典叙事学、后经典叙事学的二分法模式,而且还就两者之间的主要区别绘制了十分详尽的图表,受到学界的普遍认可。[⑦] 后经典叙事学的两个典型特征表现在方法与媒介两个方面,即在方法上超越了经典的结构主义语言学方法,引入了一批新的研究方法,如认知方法、修辞方法、语料库方法、女性主义批评理论等;在媒介上,走出了传统的文学叙事,尤其是小说叙事的范畴,进入其他新兴的故事讲述媒介领域,如数字叙事、电影叙事等。方法与媒介层面上的超越使得后经典叙事学具有复数性质,分裂出很多分支。

---

① 叙事学研究对象层面的划分,如西摩·查特曼提出的故事与话语,热拉尔·热奈特提出的故事、叙述与话语,米克·巴尔提出的文本、故事与素材等。

② Kindt and Müller, "Preface," pp.v-vi.

③ Herman and Vervaeck, *Handbook of Narrative Analysis*.

④ Paul Wake, "Narratology and Structuralism," *The Encyclopedia of Literary and Cultural Theory*, ed. Michael Ryan (Malden: Wiley-Blackwell, 2011), p.727.

⑤ David Herman, *Narratologies: New Perspectives on Narrative Analysis* (Columbus: The Ohio State University Press, 1999).

⑥ 尚必武:《叙事学研究的新发展》,载《外国文学》2009年第5期,第98页。

⑦ Ansgar Nünning, "Toward a Cultural and Historical Narratology: A Survey of Diachronic Approaches, Concepts and Research Projects," *Anglistentag 1999 Mainz Proceedings*, eds. Bernhard Reitz and Sigrid Rieuwerts (Trier: Wissenschaftlicher Verlag, 1999), p. 358; Ansgar Nünning, "Narratology or Narratologies? Taking Stock of Recent Developments, Critique and Modest Proposals for Future Usages of the Term," *What Is Narratology? Questions and Answers Regarding the Status of a Theory*, eds. Tom Kindt and Hans-Harald Müller (Berlin and New York: Walter de Gryuter, 2003), pp.243 - 244.

无论是从研究方法还是从研究对象的范畴来看，在后经典阶段，叙事学的疆域得到前所未有的拓展，出现了诸多新的流派。譬如，在研究方法上，有认知叙事学、修辞叙事学、语料库叙事学、可能世界叙事学、女性主义叙事学、后殖民主义叙事学等。在研究对象上，在文学叙事领域，不仅有以小说为核心研究对象的小说叙事学，而且还涌现出自然叙事学（以口头叙事为研究对象）、诗歌叙事学、戏剧叙事学等，甚至出现了以研究反模仿叙事特征为主的非自然叙事学；在文学叙事研究的范畴之外，涌现出法律叙事学、音乐叙事学、绘图叙事学等。同时，随着新的文学艺术样式和交流媒介的出现，新的叙事学流派也随之出现，如以研究"绘本叙事"（graphic narrative）为主的"绘本叙事学"（graphic narratology），以及数字叙事学、博客叙事学等。而且，随着叙事学研究持续引入新方法以及新叙事形式的出现，叙事学界必将出现更多的新派别。

在当今西方叙事学界，尽管经典叙事学的价值和作用无可否认，但几乎很少有学者会承认自己在从事经典叙事学研究，他们更乐意说自己是后经典叙事学这个阵营里的一个分支或派别。抑或可以说，当代西方叙事学的发展，在很大程度上表现为后经典叙事学的发展。"后经典叙事学"这一概念最早出现在美国叙事学家戴维·赫尔曼于1997年发表的一篇题为《脚本、序列和故事：后经典叙事学的元素》（"Scripts，Sequences，and Stories：Elements of a Postclassical Narratology"）的文章中。在该文中，赫尔曼从认知科学的角度对叙事序列加以全新审视，特别是借助于认知科学的"认知草案"一说来阐释叙事序列、故事构建、叙事性等相关论题。赫尔曼认为，虽然女性主义、修辞理论、语言学、计算机科学等各种理论模式和视角均为后经典叙事学增添了活力，但他撰写该文只是为了整合一些研究叙事话语的认知因素。[①] 据此，我们不难推断，赫尔曼在该文中所讨论的后经典叙事学实质为认知叙事学。令人始料未及的是，该文发表后，后经典叙事学这一术语非但没有被学界所普遍接受，反而遭到了部分学者的质疑。例如，另一位美国叙事学家布莱恩·理查森曾就"后经典叙事学"一说，在《现代语言学会会刊》（*PMLA*）上同赫尔曼展开激烈的交锋。[②]

后经典叙事学这一概念真正为学界所熟知，是在《脚本、序列和故事：后经典叙事学的元素》一文发表的两年之后。1999年，美国俄亥俄州立大学出版社出版了由赫尔曼主编的《复数的后经典叙事学：叙事分析新视野》一书。在为该书撰写的长达三十页的"前言"中，赫尔曼对叙事学研究的现状做了全面的回顾和精辟的总结。赫尔曼认为，在借鉴了女性主义、巴赫金对话理论、解构主义、精神分析学、历史主义、修辞学、电影理论、计算机科学、语篇分析、（心理）语言学等众多方法论和视角之后，单数的叙事学（narratology）已经裂变为复数的叙事学（narratologies）。也就是说，结构主义对故事进行的理论化工作已经演化出众多的叙事分析模式。赫尔曼进一步指出，叙事诗学在过去十多年间发生了惊人的嬗变，叙事学已经从经典的结构主义阶段——相对于远离当代文学和语言学理论的蓬勃发展的索绪尔阶段——走向了后经典阶段。[③] 需要指出的是，正是这一转向使得一度消沉的叙事学逐渐走出解构思潮的阴影。

在该书出版之后，后经典叙事学这一概念逐渐为中外叙事学界所认同，成为当下叙事学研究的通用语。以色列叙事学家施劳米什·里蒙-凯南在《叙事虚构作品：当代诗学》一书第二版的"后记"中，不仅

---

① David Herman，"Scripts，Sequences，and Stories：Elements of a Postclassical Narratology，" *PMLA* 112.5（October 1997），p.1049.

② Brian Richardson and David Herman，"A Postclassical Narratology，" *PMLA* 113.2（March 1998），pp.288 - 290.

③ Herman，*Narratologies: New Perspectives on Narrative Analysis*，pp.1 - 2.

沿用了后经典叙事学这一概念，而且还对当下后经典叙事学的特征用“走向”(towards)一词加以概括，如“作为摇摆不定的走向”“作为相互修订的走向”“作为永久变化的走向”等。① 德国叙事学家安斯加尔·纽宁在《单数的叙事学还是复数的叙事学？对近期发展的评价、批判以及对未来术语使用的建议》一文中也使用了后经典叙事学这一概念。在该文中，纽宁首先进一步阐释了后经典叙事学的含义，在详细探讨经典叙事学与后经典叙事学之间关系的同时，还试图对复数的后经典叙事学加以归类。②

作为当代叙事理论的主流之一，后经典叙事学力图修正经典叙事学在诸多方面的缺失，如经典叙事学“对核心文类的武断选择；没有认识到其他文类研究的意义；将故事视作自足的产品，而不是由读者在持续修正的阅读过程中建构出来的文本；既排斥了心理力量、心理欲望，也没有考虑那些涵盖和塑造它们的文化、语用及历史语境”等，③这无疑为叙事学研究平添了许多活力与新意。在21世纪进入第二个十年的时候，西方叙事学家对这一现状做出反思。后经典叙事学的首倡者戴维·赫尔曼率先对后经典叙事学的发展阶段做出划分，提出了后经典叙事学第二阶段的设想。他认为，后经典叙事学在第一阶段的重点是引入结构主义理论之外的思想，重新评价经典模式的可能性与局限，其在第二阶段面临新的挑战，即“要加强女性主义、跨媒介、认知以及其他各种后经典方法之间更为紧密的对话”。他建议叙事理论家先并置新方法对于叙事现象的描述(叙述、视角、人物等)，接着检验这些描述的重合面，然后再探讨在那些不重合的描述面上，这些新方法在多大程度上可以互为补充，由此绘制各种后经典方法之间相互关系的图式。④

在《后经典叙事学：方法与分析》一书的“导言”中，扬·阿尔贝(Jan Alber)和莫妮卡·弗鲁德尼克再次提出了后经典叙事学的两个阶段。他们认为从赫尔曼的《复数的后经典叙事学：叙事分析新视野》一书的出版至21世纪的第十个年头，是后经典叙事学的第一阶段；后经典叙事学的第二阶段则以《后经典叙事学：方法与分析》一书的出版为起点。在这一阶段，叙事学家们需要考虑叙事学在语境上和主题上的曲折变化如何能够以成熟的方式同结构主义的核心联系起来。这并不是说要把所有的方法和模式都规定为一个整体，而是努力整合后经典叙事学研究的多重方法，发现他们之间的“重合性”(overlapping)与“冲突性”(incompatibilities)。⑤

阿尔贝和弗鲁德尼克把后经典叙事学第一阶段的主要特征归纳为“多元性”(multiplicities)、“跨学科性”(interdisciplinarities)和“跨媒介性”(transmedialities)，把后经典叙事学第二阶段的主要特征归纳为“巩固”(consolidation)与“持续多元”(continued diversification)。必须要指出的是，后经典叙事学的第二阶段是第一阶段的延续，即便是在第二阶段，后经典叙事学依旧保留了其在第一阶段的特征，即它仍然是多元的、跨学科的和跨媒介的。阿尔贝和弗鲁德尼克所言的“巩固”一方面是指巩固经典叙事学所取得的成就，另一方面是指巩固后经典叙事学在第一阶段所取得的成就；“持续多元”一方面是指研究对象持续出现的多元化，另一方面是指研究同一个叙事学问题时，综合运用多种研究方法。阿尔贝和

① Rimmon-Kenan, *Narrative Fiction: Contemporary Poetics* (2nd edition), pp.134 – 149.

② Nünning, "Narratology or Narratologies? Taking Stock of Recent Developments, Critique and Modest Proposals for Future Usages of the Term," pp.239 – 275.

③ Manfred Jahn, "Foundational Issues in Teaching Cognitive Narratology," *European Journal of English Studies* 8.1 (April 2004), p.105.

④ 尚必武：《叙事学研究的新发展》，第99页。

⑤ Jan Alber and Monika Fludernik, "Introduction," *Postclassical Narratology: Approaches and Analyses*, eds. Jan Alber and Monika Fludernika (Columbus: The Ohio State University Press, 2010), p.5.

弗鲁德尼克强调:“当代的叙事学家们的研究对象要比20年前更为多样,在研究同一个问题时,他们致力于整合很不相同的研究方法,将他们的研究建立在非常丰富的语境主义框架下。”①

赫尔曼、弗鲁德尼克、阿尔贝都强调,在后经典叙事学的第二阶段,需要审视各种后经典叙事学流派之间的关系。诚然,与学界对经典叙事学和后经典叙事学之间关系的关注相比,各种后经典叙事学流派之间的关系似乎被忽略了。就此而言,赫尔曼等人的立场是很有道理的。究竟哪些后经典叙事学派别之间的关系需要被重新探讨?在后经典叙事学的第二阶段,又有哪些热点论题值得关注?在接受访谈时,国际叙事学研究权威詹姆斯·费伦以其主编的“叙事理论与阐释”丛书和《叙事》杂志所发表的研究成果为例,罗列了当代叙事学研究的趋势,如对叙事要件的研究,把叙事形式连接到更大影响的研究,努力深化或修改具体研究方法的方法论研究,连接形式与历史的研究,用批评理论的其他分支来探讨与叙事论题之间关系的研究,关于叙事转向的研究,把叙事实践作为理论来源的研究等。②

如果说当下的后经典叙事学研究进入了第二阶段,那么在这一阶段,叙事学研究又表现出怎样的态势?又有哪些任务需要完成?对此,赫尔曼的回答是加强各种经典方法之间的更为紧密的对话,弗鲁德尼克、阿尔贝的回答是“巩固”与“持续多元”。在后经典叙事学的第二阶段,认知叙事学、修辞叙事学、女性主义叙事学、跨媒介叙事学将会继续成为强势派别。与此同时,非自然叙事学的发展势头迅猛。不过,鉴于引入方法和研究对象的多元性质,后经典叙事学的相关具体流派内部也呈现出多元的特征,认知叙事学、修辞叙事学就是如此。随着新的文学样式、叙事媒介不断涌现出来,相关的叙事学流派也应运而生,如绘本叙事学、多模态叙事学等。在研究路径上,各种后经典叙事学流派之间相互借鉴、交叉整合是后经典叙事学发展的突出特征。此外,叙事学研究的“历时”方法和“跨国界”转向日趋明显。在后经典叙事学进入第二发展阶段之后,当代西方叙事学研究主要展现出六个值得关注的动向。

第一,持续涌现的叙事学新流派。新的时代造就了文学新样式、叙事新媒介。这些文学新样式、叙事新媒介固然挑战了现有叙事理论的解释力,但同时也孕育了新的叙事学派,其典型特征表现为叙事学研究的跨媒介态势。诚如弗鲁德尼克和格雷塔·奥尔森(Greta Olson)所言:“新媒介的出现可以改变我们对故事的理解,我们也能看到新媒介如何被物质因素传递或受到物质因素的影响。”③ 就整体层面而言,叙事的跨媒介态势催发了日渐火热的“跨媒介叙事学”,代表性的研究成果有瑞安主编的《跨媒介叙事:故事讲述的语言》(*Narrative Across Media: The Languages of Storytelling*, 2004)、玛利娜·格里沙科娃(Marina Grishakova)和瑞安主编的《跨媒介性与故事讲述》(*Intermediality and Storytelling*, 2010)、瑞安和让-诺埃尔·托恩(Jan-Noël Thon)主编的《跨媒介的故事世界:建构媒介意识的叙事学》(*Storyworlds across Media: Toward a Media-Conscious Narratology*, 2014)、托恩的《跨媒介叙事学与当代媒介文化》(*Transmedial Narratology and Contemporary Media Culture*, 2016)。就某个具体的叙事媒介研究而言,首先必须要提西方学界日渐火热的绘本叙事学,其主要成果有蒂埃里·格罗恩斯坦(Thierry Groensteen)的《绘本与叙述》(*Comics and Narration*, 2011)、阿基米·黑什尔(Achim Hescher)的《阅读绘本小说:文类与叙述》(*Reading Graphic Novels: Genre and Narration*, 2016)、卡

① Jan Alber and Monika Fludernik, "Introduction," *Postclassical Narratology: Approaches and Analyses*, eds. Jan Alber and Monika Fludernika (Columbus: The Ohio State University Press, 2010), p.23.

② 尚必武:《修辞诗学及当代叙事理论》,载《当代外国文学》2010年第2期,第153—159页。

③ Monika Fludernik and Greta Olson, "Introduction," *Current Trends in Narratology*, ed. Greta Olson (Berlin: De Gruyter, 2011), p.23.

伊·米科宁(Kai Mikkonen)的《绘本艺术的叙事学》(*The Narratology of Comic Art*, 2017)等。其次是电影叙事学的研究,其主要成果有爱德华·布兰尼根(Edward Branigan)的《叙事理解与电影》(*Narrative Comprehension and Film*, 1992)、彼得·福斯塔腾(Peter Verstraten)的《电影叙事学》(*Film Narratology*, 2009)以及罗伯特·佩尔森(Roberta Pearson)与安东尼·N.史密斯(Anthony N. Smith)主编的《媒介汇聚时代的故事讲述:荧幕叙事研究》(*Storytelling in the Media Convergence Age: Exploring Screen Narratives*, 2015)。在某种程度上,由于跨媒介叙事研究突破了传统叙事研究以文字叙事作为主要考察对象的做法,也不再狭隘地将叙事看作必须涉及"叙述者"和"受述者"的特定言语行为,在后经典叙事学发展的多个不同流派之中,跨媒介叙事学呈现出颠覆性和革命性的突破意义,既涉及对经典叙事理论不同概念的重新审视和调整,也包含对不同媒介叙事潜能和表现方式的挖掘和探索,由此不但可以给叙事理论的进一步拓展和深化提供动力,还可以给媒介研究、文化研究等相关领域提供重要的理论指导和实践分析工具。此外,对原有叙事文本特征的新发现也会引发新的叙事学派,非自然叙事学就是一个明显的例子。近年来,非自然叙事学以异常迅猛的火热态势向前发展,在叙事诗学与叙事批评实践层面取得了诸多重要的研究成果,引发国际叙事学界的普遍关注。非自然叙事学以"反模仿叙事"为研究对象,以建构"非自然叙事诗学"为终极目标,迅速成长为一支与女性主义叙事学、修辞叙事学、认知叙事学等比肩齐名的后经典叙事学派。自布莱恩·理查森出版奠基式的论著《非自然的声音:现当代小说的极端化叙述》(*Unnatural Voice: Extreme Narration in Modern and Contemporary Fiction*, 2006)一书后,扬·阿尔贝、斯特凡·伊韦尔森(Stefan Iversen)、亨里克·斯克夫·尼尔森(Henrik Skov Nielsen)、玛利亚·梅凯莱(Maria Mäkelä)等叙事学家纷纷撰文立著,从多个方面探讨非自然叙事,有力地促进了非自然叙事学的建构与发展。在21世纪跨入第二个十年后,阿尔贝等人在《叙事》杂志联名发表了《非自然叙事,非自然叙事学:超越模仿模型》("Unnatural Narrative, Unnatural Narratology: Beyond Mimetic Models", 2010)一文,正式提出非自然叙事学这一概念,并从故事和话语层面对非自然叙事做出了分析。随后,西方叙事学界连续推出了《叙事虚构作品中的奇特声音》(*Strange Voices in Narrative Fiction*, 2011)、《非自然叙事,非自然叙事学》(*Unnatural Narratives, Unnatural Narratology*, 2011)、《叙事中断:文学中的无情节性、扰乱性和琐碎性》(*Narrative Interrupted: The Plotless, the Disturbing and the Trivial in Literature*, 2012)、《非自然叙事诗学》(*A Poetics of Unnatural Narratives*, 2013)、《非自然叙事:理论、历史与实践》(*Unnatural Narrative: Theory, History, and Practice*, 2015)、《非自然叙事:小说与戏剧中的不可能世界》(*Unnatural Narrative: Impossible Worlds in Fiction and Drama*, 2016)、《非自然叙事学:扩展、修正与挑战》(*Unnatural Narratology: Extensions, Revisions, and Challenges*, 2020)等多部探讨非自然叙事的论著。尽管非自然叙事学的出现及其理论主张引发了一定程度的争议,但它毕竟在研究对象层面上将人们的学术视野转向了叙事的非自然维度,即转向"反模仿"模式,以及逻辑上、物理上和人力上不可能的故事,同时又在学科理论体系层面上拓展和丰富了叙事学的基本概念与内涵。自2008年以来,几乎每届的"国际叙事学研究协会年会"都有非自然叙事学的专题论坛。作为一个热门的后经典叙事学流派,非自然叙事学值得我们持续关注。

第二,对后经典叙事学跨学科路径的重访与反思。毋庸置疑,其他学科方法的引入为叙事学的发展提供了动力和契机,叙事学实际上也是跨学科性质的产物,经典叙事学与后经典叙事学皆是如此。有论者认为,“叙事学的未来存在于其他学科的发展”。[①] 在后经典阶段,即便是对叙事学基本概念的重新审视都带有一定的跨学科性质,例如理查德·沃尔什(Richard Walsh)从认知语用学的角度对“虚构性”等概念的重新探讨。[②] 桑德拉·海嫩(Sandra Heinen)和罗伊·萨默尔(Roy Summer)在整体层面上对叙事学研究的跨学科性做了探讨。[③] 就具体后经典叙事学流派的跨学科性质而言,我们不妨以认知叙事学为例。在大量借用认知科学的理论和研究成果的基础上,叙事学家们开创了认知叙事学这一重要叙事学门类。根据《MIT 认知科学百科全书》的界定,认知科学主要包括以下领域:哲学、心理学、神经科学、人工智能、语言学与语言、认知和进化等。[④] 不同认知叙事学家以不同领域的认知科学为理论视角,从事认知叙事学研究,认知叙事学从而产生了不同的分支。例如,玛丽-劳勒·瑞安以人工智能和可然世界理论为基础进行认知叙事学研究;赫尔曼以认知语言学、心智哲学为理论基础进行认知叙事学研究;丽萨·尊希恩(Lisa Zunshine)以认知心理学为基础进行认知叙事学研究;凯·扬(Kay Young)以神经科学为基础进行认知叙事学研究等。对于认知叙事学的跨学科性质,认知叙事学家们供认不讳,且大有持续推动和发展的态势。2010 年,弗鲁德尼克分别在《文学语义学杂志》和《现代语言学会会刊》上撰文,不仅将认知语言学中的概念整合理论引入自己的自然叙事学研究,而且还对认知叙事学在 21 世纪的美好愿景做出积极乐观的展望。[⑤] 但值得注意的是,瑞安对当下认知叙事学的研究范式提出质疑,探讨了叙事学与认知科学之间存在的问题。在瑞安看来,认知叙事学研究大都采用“自上而下”(top-down)的模式,即把认知科学的相关概念直接运用于叙事分析。那么认知叙事学与认知科学之间真正的合作关系应该是怎样的呢?瑞安认为,认知叙事学与认知科学之间首先应该建构一种“循环反馈”(feedback loop)的关系,两者相互学习,以检验彼此的观点。即,认知科学的实验给叙事学以诸多新思想,而不是证实通常可以感觉到的思想,例如人脑的某个特殊区域与审美欣赏相关、发现大脑的某个部位在叙事讲述和叙事处理的过程中会被激活等。在“循环反馈”建构起来以后,我们可以通过问一些恰当的问题来研究叙事与心理之间的关联。如:什么使得叙事值得讲述?什么特征使得故事具有意义?什么再现技巧会吸引读者的注意力?故事是如何产生情感的?当某个故事是关于悲惨事件的时候,我们是否会感到快乐?什么是小说?为什么我们对根本不存在的人物的命运感兴趣?瑞安坚定地认为:“如果真的有认知叙事学这么一回事的话,它不应该是简单地借用现成的概念,将它们以自上而下的模式应用于文本,而应该是相信我们自己思维的能力,探析我们的大脑如何创造、解码和使用故事。换言之,只有当认知叙事学以自下而上的方式,从文本中得出见解的时候,它才最富有生产性。”[⑥] 瑞安实质上探讨的是叙事学的学科地位问题,即跨学科的方法固然有助于丰富叙事学研究,但在借用其他学科方法的过程中,不能忽视叙事学自身的学科地位和价值。瑞安的这一批判不仅有助于进一步深化认知叙事学,而且对其他跨学科性质的后经典叙事学派别来说也同样具有反思价值。

第三,叙事学研究的“历时转向”(diachronic turn)。众所周知,以结构主义语言学为“领先科学”的

---

① Fludernik and Olson, “Introduction,” p.22.

② Richard Walsh, *The Rhetoric of Fictionality: Narrative Theory and the Idea of Fiction* (Columbus: The Ohio State University Press, 2007); Richard Walsh, “Fictionality as Rhetoric: A Distinctive Research Paradigm,” *Style* 53.4 (2019), pp.397 - 425.

③ Sandra Heinen and Roy Sommer, *Narratology in the Age of Cross-Disciplinary Narrative Research* (Berlin: De Gruyter, 2009).

④ Robert A. Wilson and Frank C. Keil. *The MIT Encyclopedia of the Cognitive Sciences* (Boston: MIT Press, 1999).

⑤ Monika Fludernik, “Narratology in the Twenty-First Century: The Cognitive Approach to Narrative,” *PMLA* 125.4 (2010), pp.924 - 930; Monika Fludernik, “Naturalizing the Unnatural: A View from Blending Theory,” *Journal of Literary Semantics* 39.1 (2010), pp.1 - 17.

⑥ Marie-Laure Ryan, “Narratology and Cognitive Science: A Problematic Relation,” *Style* 44.4 (Winter 2010), p.489.

经典叙事学重点关注普遍的叙事特征,主要从“共时”的角度研究叙事所共享的结构。这一研究范式无疑是一把“双刃剑”:在促进叙事诗学建构的同时,也忽略了个别叙事的具体特征,尤其是叙述技巧在文学史上的演变以及读者对这些技巧的接受。就叙事文本的研究而言,结构主义叙事学重点“考察了18世纪至20世纪早期的小说文本,而把后现代主义文本,尤其是那些产生于18世纪之前的文本只当作叙事规则的例外情况来对待,且几乎完全忽略了中世纪的叙事文本。”① 为弥补“共时”范式在叙事学研究中的缺失,对“历时”范式的适时引入就显得大有必要。弗鲁德尼克是较早地倡导从“历时”角度进行叙事学研究的学者。她曾感慨,尽管叙事学研究出现了很多新的方法,“但是在理论层面上研究叙事形式和叙事功能的旨趣却比较少见”。② 在弗鲁德尼克看来,从历时的方向来研究叙事学是“一个重要的、激动人心的新研究领域”。③ 21世纪以来,“历时性”方法的重要性也逐渐显示出其独特的作用,越来越为众多叙事学家们所采用。例如,汤姆·奇恩特和汉斯-哈罗德·穆勒对半个世纪以来的西方叙事学界围绕“隐含作者”这一概念产生的争执进行了历时性梳理④;彼得·许恩(Peter Hühn)等人考察了14世纪至20世纪英国小说中的“事件性”⑤;赫尔曼等人对8世纪至21世纪英语叙事作品中的“意识再现”问题进行了研究等⑥。“历时性”范式不仅有助于审视叙事学的基本概念和叙述策略,而且对于叙事学这门学科的历史考辨是非常有益的。多萝特·伯克(Dorothee Birke)、埃娃·冯·康岑(Eva von Contzen)和凯伦·库科宁(Karin Kukkonen)指出,对叙事学的历时考察可以促使叙事学家思考如何在更大的时间轴线上定位自身及其研究路径。⑦ 虽然在《叙事理论指南》中,赫尔曼和弗鲁德尼克对叙事学的发展史做过简单的梳理,但梳理依旧不够全面、不够深入,完整的叙事学史有待书写。

第四,叙事学研究的“跨国界转向”(transnational turn)。当下,叙事学研究的跨学科、跨文类、跨媒介态势已成为学界的共识。与此相对照,叙事学研究的“跨国界转向”还没有被完全提上日程。历经半个世纪的发展,叙事学主要成为西方尤其是欧美学界的独语行为,这显然与叙事学的普适性理论构想和学科旨趣不吻合。实际上,在多元文化主义盛行的全球化时代,不同区域和不同民族的叙事学之间的合作与交流已经成为叙事学得以长足发展的必要手段。《叙事学的当代潮流》(*Current Trends in Narratology*, 2011)一书提出了后经典叙事学研究的第三种类型“比较叙事学”(comparative narratology),即“历时性地评价区域性和民族性的叙事学研究,这些视角为被视作‘主流’的英语叙事学的创新奠定了基础”。⑧ 该书的第三部分名为“历时视角的区域性和民族性研究:建构一种比较叙事学”,论述了法国的后经典叙事学研究、以色列的“特拉维夫学派”的叙事学研究等。遗憾的是,兰瑟、弗鲁德尼克、奥尔森等人没有为叙事学如何实现“跨国界转向”提出具体的策略和方案。这一缺憾在苏珊·弗里德曼(Susan Friedman)那里得到了一定程度的弥补。在《建构叙事理论的跨国界转向:文学叙事、转喻的旅行,以及弗吉尼亚·沃尔夫与泰戈尔的个案研究》一文中,弗里德曼提出了如下几个问题:能否建构一种包含很

① Fludernik, *An Introduction to Narratology*, p.110.
② Monika Fludernik, "The Diachronization of Narratology," *Narrative* 11.3 (October 2003), p.331.
③ Ibid., p.332.
④ Tom Kindt and Hans-Harald Müller, *The Implied Author: Concept and Controversy* (Berlin: de Gruyter, 2006).
⑤ Peter Hühn, *Eventfulness in British Fiction* (Berlin: de Gruyter, 2010).
⑥ David Herman, *The Emergence of Mind: Representation of Consciousness in Narrative Discourse in English* (Lincoln: University of Nebraska Press, 2011).
⑦ Dorothee Birke, Eva von Contzen, and Karin Kukkonen, "Chrononarratology: Modelling Historical Change for Narratology," *Narrative* 30.1 (January 2022), p.27.
⑧ Fludernik and Olson, "Introduction," p.4.

多跨越时空的文学叙事的跨国界叙事理论？是否应该重新概念化叙事理论的课题？这个新建立的跨国界的框架与辨别、超越或支撑文化差异的文学叙事的“普遍”规则和组成因子的叙事学课题有何相关之处？① 为了回答这些问题，弗里德曼不仅回顾了叙事的普遍性和差异性，而且提出了关于文学叙事的跨国界阅读的四种策略：修订（revision）、复原（recovery）、循环（circulation）、拼贴（collage）。她还以沃尔夫、泰戈尔兄妹的创作实践为例演示了这些阅读策略。弗里德曼呼吁：“单纯地阅读非西方的叙事是不够的，我们需要思考它们之于叙事理论的意义。”② 此外，还要“扩大我们理论化叙事的文档，即走出我们舒服的领地，同全世界范围内的叙事和叙事理论展开交流”。③ 笔者对此表示赞同，因为只有在研究对象、研究方法、研究成果上的跨国界交流，才能实现真正意义上的叙事学研究的“跨国界转向”。在这一过程中，可以借用“比较叙事学”的手段，将世界各国的叙事文本纳入研究范围，突破现有叙事学在研究方法和研究对象上的“西方中心主义”，实现建构“世界叙事学”的美好图景。

第五，对叙事学家个人学术思想的研究。顾名思义，叙事学主要以叙事为研究对象，或如费伦所指出的那样：“我们这个研究领域的主要对象是叙事或叙事理论，而不是叙事理论家本人。”④ 不过，在审视各个地区或各个机构的叙事学研究的同时，也不能忽视对于学科建设的发展起到重大推动作用的叙事学家及其个人学术思想的研究。欣喜的是，近期西方学界已经出现研究叙事学家个人学术思想的动向。譬如，“国际叙事学研究协会”会刊《叙事》杂志曾于 2006 年第 2 期刊发了一组研究韦恩·布斯（Wayne Booth）的专题论文，以表达对这位叙事理论大师的崇敬和怀念。数年后，该刊又于 2010 年第 1 期刊载了两篇研究热奈特叙事理论思想的文章，三篇研究拉尔夫·拉德尔（Rader W. Rade）叙事理论思想的文章。至于研究叙事理论家个人学术思想的意义，《叙事》杂志主编费伦的解释是：“聚焦于在深度、广度和意义上对叙事领域都起到过重大推动作用的某个叙事理论家个人的研究，可以产生有价值的学术成果。通过带领我们重新评价叙事理论家的研究，这样的文章不仅对相关核心概念做出新的解读，而且也给研究叙事理论更大的课题以及这些课题同学科发展之间的关系提供新的视角。”⑤ 有鉴于此，费伦以身作则，专门撰文讨论布斯的叙事学思想⑥，也与戴维·里克特（David Richter）合作发表了研究拉德尔学术思想的文章⑦。这个研究动向也是珍视叙事学研究遗产的表现。

第六，各种后经典叙事学流派之间的交叉整合。经典叙事学与后经典叙事学之间相互依存、相互借用，这已成为学界共识。实际上，在后经典叙事学的第二阶段，后经典叙事学流派之间表现出交叉发展的势头。《后经典叙事学：方法与分析》中的多篇论文都具有学科交叉整合的典型特征。例如，赫尔曼充分整合了认知叙事学和跨媒介叙事学两大流派；马丁·勒施尼格（Martin Löschnigg）整合了传记叙事学、认知叙事学和跨媒介叙事学的成果；阿尔贝整合了修辞叙事学、认知叙事学、跨媒介叙事学和非自然叙事学；尼尔森整合了非自然叙事学和认知叙事学等。又如，在探讨不可靠叙述这个概念时，安斯加尔·纽宁整合了修辞叙事学和认知叙

---

① Susan Stanford Friedman, “Towards a Transnational Turn in Narrative Theory: Literary Narratives, Traveling Tropes, and the Case of Virginian Woolf and the Tagores,” *Narrative* 19.1 (January 2011), p.2.

② Ibid., p.24.

③ Ibid., p.24.

④ James Phelan, “Editor's Column,” *Narrative* 18.1 (January 2010), p.2.

⑤ Phelan, “Editor's Column,” p.2.

⑥ James Phelan, “Imagining a Sequel to Wayne C. Booth's The Rhetoric of Fiction—Or a Dialogue on Dialogue,” *Comparative Critical Studies* 7.2-3 (2010), pp.243-255.

⑦ James Phelan and David Richter, “The Literary Theoretical Contribution of Ralph W. Rader,” *Narrative* 18.1 (January 2010), pp.73-90.

事学的方法。[①] 为加强后经典叙事学之间的交流和对话，当代著名后经典叙事学家费伦、赫尔曼、理查森、拉宾诺维茨、罗宾·沃霍尔（Robyn Warhol）合力推出了《叙事理论实践：四种视角的对话》（*Practicing Narrative Theory: Four Perspectives in Conversation*，2011）。可以预见的是，随着叙事学研究的逐步推进，对叙事现象解释的深入和对叙事概念辩论的深化，各种叙事学流派之间的交叉与综合也会更加深入。

上述六个态势既是后经典叙事学在第二发展阶段的特征，也是其未来发展的优势和动力所在。持续开创新的叙事学流派，可以丰富叙事学的理论范畴，应对新叙事媒介的挑战，同时也可以使叙事学与时俱进，具有时代感；加强现有的各种后经典叙事学流派之间的对话和协作，不仅有助于在理论上建构叙事诗学，而且有助于在实践上提升叙事批评的效度；反思叙事学流派自身的发展历程，则有助于辨析和去除学科发展的内在缺陷与不足，厘清学科发展脉络；引入“历时”视角有助于绘制叙事技巧流变的全景图式；挖掘和审视知名叙事学家个人的学术思想，则可以传承学术薪火；叙事学研究的“跨国界转向”，则可以突破“西方中心主义”，建构普适性的“世界叙事学”。

有鉴于当下叙事学研究盛况空前的局面，弗鲁德尼克颇感欣慰地说：“在 21 世纪之初，叙事学非但没有衰落，反而发展得很好、很繁荣。”[②] 与弗鲁德尼克的宽慰和赞许相反，《今日诗学》杂志主编梅尔·斯滕伯格（Meir Sternberg）显得有所保留，他说：“尽管叙事理论在细节问题上日渐复杂，但它依然处于幼年期，因为它的学科基础还有待建构。为确立研究目标，需要回答两个互补性的问题：① 什么是叙事？② 它与其他话语类型所共享的成分是怎样的？”[③]斯滕伯格认为：“第一个问题显然与‘叙事性’（narrativity）相关，但理论界对此关注甚少，而且也没有形成一致意见。对于与叙事相对应的相邻学科而言，第二个问题还没有被提出来。”[④] 换言之，在斯滕伯格眼里，这两个问题没有得到关注和解答，叙事学研究的目标仍然没有确立，依旧处于“幼年时期”（infancy）。

如果说弗鲁德尼克是对叙事学过去和现在做出比较，进而认可了这门学科的发展成绩，那么斯滕伯格则是对叙事学的研究现状加以反思，进而表达了对该学科未来发展的期待。无论是在经典阶段还是在后经典阶段，叙事学都取得了有目共睹的成绩，跃居为文学研究的一门显学。不可否认，当前的叙事学确实存在一定程度的不足。譬如，就叙事学的跨学科性而言，其一方面将叙事学术语单纯地引入其他学科，另一方面自然是将其他学科的理论引入叙事学，没有实现很好的双向交流。再者，叙事学陷入概念之争的僵局，叙事学界甚至出现肆意制造术语概念的现象。但这并不能否认叙事学的学科地位与活力，假如一门学科是完美无瑕、无可挑剔的，那么说明这门学科实际上已经走向了尽头，没有存在的必要了。正是因为这些不足和缺憾，叙事学才有了广阔的发展空间。如同经典叙事学的复兴以及当下叙事学这门学科的繁荣在很大程度上都归功于后经典叙事学的崛起和发展一样，叙事学的未来在很大程度上也势必依赖进入第二发展阶段的后经典叙事学。当前叙事学研究的不足需要进入第二发展阶段的后经典叙事学去面对和解决，叙事学未来发展的空间需要第二发展阶段的后经典叙事学去开创。

---

① Ansgar Nünning, “Reconceptualizing Unreliable Narration: Synthesizing Cognitive and Rhetorical Approaches,” *A Companion to Narrative Theory*, eds. James Phelan and Peter J. Rabinowitz (Oxford: Blackwell, 2005), pp.89 - 107; Ansgar Nünning, “Reconceptualizing the Theory, History and Generic Scope of Unreliable Narration: Towards a Synthesis of Cognitive and Rhetorical Approaches,” *Narrative Unreliability in the Twentieth-Century First-Person Novel*, eds. Elke D'hoker and Gunther Martens (Berlin: De Gruyter, 2008), pp.29 - 76.

② Fludernik, *An Introduction to Narratology*, p.12.

③ Meir Sternberg, “Narrativity: From Objectivist to Functional Paradigm,” *Poetics Today* 31.3 (Fall 2010), p.509.

④ Ibid., p.509.

第一章
结构主义叙事学

第一节　概　　论

盖因结构主义叙事学在20世纪六七十年代的重要影响，国内外的很多文学理论著作通常在“结构主义”范畴下讨论叙事学。加拿大文论家史迪文·邦尼卡斯尔(Stephen Bonnycastle)在《寻找权威：文学理论概论》一书中，直接将叙事学纳入结构主义范畴加以论述。在从“叙事行为”“素材与话语”“实际发生的事件与描述事件的故事”“情节发生的速度和催化材料”四个方面对叙事学加以阐释之后，邦尼卡斯尔得出结论：叙事学“是在60年代作为结构主义的一部分才变得十分重要的，而且发展迅速”。[①] 英国著名文论家拉曼·塞尔登(Raman Selden)在《当代文学理论导读》一书中，也把叙事学放置在结构主义范畴下加以讨论，并且直接使用了“结构主义叙事学”(structuralist narratology)这一名称。[②] 澳大利亚文论家理查德·哈兰德(Richard Harland)在其新著《从柏拉图到巴特的文学理论》的最后一章“法国结构主义”中，沿用了塞尔登的“结构主义叙事学”这一名称，大致论述了法国结构主义者A.J.格雷马斯(A.J.Greimas)、克洛德·布雷蒙(Claude Bremond)、茨维坦·托多洛夫、罗兰·巴特等人的叙事理论。[③]

与国外研究类似，马新国在《西方文论史》一书中沿用了西方学者的“结构主义叙事学”这一名称，将叙事学放置在结构主义理论下加以讨论，认为法国结构主义叙事学的成就集中体现在叙事理论研究领域，叙事文学成为法国结构主义者主要关注的课题材料。[④] 张首映在《西方二十世纪文论史》的第7章“结构主义”标题之下评述了叙事理论。他认为结构主义把叙事文学作品作为主要研究对象，形成结构主义叙事学，在层次、句法结构、体裁分析等方面均取得了较高的成就。[⑤]

如上所述，很多论者之所以认为叙事学隶属于结构主义，主要是因为结构主义叙事学在现代叙事理论发展史上地位显要且影响重大。1966年，法国巴黎《交际》杂志第8期出版了以“符号学研究：叙事作

---

① 史迪文·邦尼卡斯尔：《寻找权威：文学理论概论》，王晓群等译，长春：吉林大学出版社，2003年，第137页。

② Raman Selden, *A Reader's Guide to Contemporary Literary Theory* (Beijing: Foreign Language Teaching and Research Press, 2004), pp.66－87.

③ Richard Harland, *Literary Theory from Plato to Barthes: An Introduction* (Beijing: Foreign Language Teaching and Research Press, 2005), pp.219－237.

④ 马新国：《西方文论史》，北京：高等教育出版社，2003年，第431—453页。

⑤ 张首映：《西方二十世纪文论史》，北京：北京大学出版社，2005年，第169—203页。

品结构分析"为题的论文专集,其中包括巴特的《叙事作品结构分析导论》、布雷蒙的《叙事可能之逻辑》等若干叙事研究论文。特别值得一提的是,1969年,法国叙事学家托多洛夫首次提出"叙事学"这一名称。托多洛夫在《〈十日谈〉语法》一书中写道:"这部著作属于一门尚未存在的科学,我们暂且将这门科学取名为叙述学,即关于叙事作品的科学。"[①] 此后的法国结构主义叙事学发展势头尤为强劲,先后出版了大批颇有影响的叙事理论研究力作,如列维-斯特劳斯的《悲伤的热带》《野性的思维》《结构人类学》以及热奈特的《叙事话语》《新叙事话语》等。20世纪70年代,叙事学逐渐发展成为一股国际性的潮流,美国、荷兰、意大利、以色列、丹麦等国家都兴起了叙事学研究的热潮。

一、理论前奏与思想资源

可能一是因为"叙事学"这一名称由法国叙事学家(托多洛夫)提出,二是因为法国结构主义叙事学的繁荣鼎盛及其在叙事学史上的重要地位使得部分中外学者在论及经典叙事学时,言必称法国结构主义叙事学,以至于忽视了法国结构主义之前以及与之同期的其他叙事理论。在"叙事学"正式冠名之前,我们有"小说理论""小说美学""小说修辞学"的探讨,它们应该是结构主义之前的叙事理论研究。在这方面,我们自然会想到传统小说叙事理论家,如塞缪尔·理查森(Samuel Richardson)、亨利·菲尔丁(Henry Fielding)等;现代小说叙事理论家,如亨利·詹姆斯(Henry James)、E.M.福斯特(E.M. Forster)等;20世纪初的俄国形式主义者,如维克多·什可洛夫斯基(Viktor Shklovsk)、鲍里斯·艾亨鲍姆(Boris Eikhenbaum)等;英美新批评理论家,如克林斯·布鲁克斯(Cleanth Brooks)、罗伯特·潘·沃伦(Robert Penn Warren)等;德国形态学家,如奥拓玛· 席瑟尔·冯·弗莱申堡(Otmar Schissel von Fleschenberg)、贝拉德·索伊福特(Berard Seuffer)、维莱姆·迪勃琉斯(Wilhelm Dibelius)、安德烈·尧勒斯(André Jolles)、贡特尔·穆勒(Günther Müller)、艾伯拉德·拉默特(Eberhard Lämmert)等。他们都为结构主义叙事学的崛起奠定了理论基础。

在"结构主义之前及同期的叙事学"这一章中,《叙事分析手册》的作者吕克·赫尔曼和巴特·凡瓦克着力分析了有关叙事理论的六对概念:"故事与情节""讲述与展示""作者与叙述者""叙述者与读者""意识与话语""感知与话语"。在他们看来,这些都是叙事学研究的核心概念,也是引发叙事学界各种争论的主要话题。[②] 下面我们以"故事"与"情节"以及"讲述"与"展示"为例略加说明。

杰拉德·普林斯认为:"既然叙事学是叙事的科学(或叙事理论),那么它的范围就依赖于后者,即叙事的定义。"[③] 与普林斯相仿,吕克·赫尔曼和巴特·凡瓦克也认为:"如果叙事学是叙事文本的理论,那么首先要解决的就是叙事的定义问题。"[④] 但叙事的定义似乎更难把握,因为它又直接将问题转嫁给了"事件"。而与"事件"密切相关的就是叙事学史上的"故事"与"情节"之争。在结构主义叙事学盛行之前,就"故事"与"情节"的关系而言,英国小说家兼文论家E.M.福斯特的论述无疑是较为出名的一种。在福斯特看来,情节是按因果关系来安排的事件,故事是按时间关系来安排的事件。例如,"国王死了,然后王后死了"是故事,而"国王死了,王后因为悲伤死了"则是情节。但叙事究竟是什么?定义又该如

① 张寅德编选:《叙述学研究》,第1—2页。
② Herman and Vervaeck, *Handbook of Narrative Analysis*, p.11.
③ Prince, "Surveying Narratology," p.1.
④ Herman and Vervaeck, *Handbook of Narrative Analysis*, p.11.

何确定？对此，布莱恩·理查森做了总结。他认为目前关于叙事的定义大致有四种类型：时间的(temporal)、因果的(causal)、最小的(minimal)以及执行的(transactional)。第一种类型认为叙事的区别性特征是以时间顺序再现事件；第二种类型认为事件之间的因果关系最为重要；第三种类型认为任何行动或事件实际上都是叙事，因为它暗示着一种状态变化；第四种类型认为叙事不是文本的精髓或特征，而是阅读文本的一种方式。①

"讲述"与"展示"这对概念最早可追溯至柏拉图《理想国》中的diegesis与mimesis。diegesis相当于telling，即通过讲述的方式，把事件和对话通过概要的方式告诉读者，而mimesis即相当于showing，指的是通过表演的方式呈现现实。由于受到亨利·詹姆斯的"戏剧化，戏剧化!"(Dramatize, dramatize!)口号的影响，帕西·卢伯克(Percy Lubbock)曾说："只有在小说家认为故事是应该被展现的、让故事自己说自己的时候，小说的艺术才开始了。"② 依据这样的基准，卢伯克批评了那些主要采用讲述型叙述策略的小说家，如菲尔丁、萨克雷、狄更斯等。与卢伯克相左，韦恩·布斯在《小说修辞学》(*The Rhetoric of Fiction*, 1961)中表达了另外一种观点。在布斯看来，卢伯克对詹姆斯的口号阐释过了头。事实上，小说艺术并不排斥讲述策略。吕克·赫尔曼与巴特·凡瓦克由此认为：讲述与展示的结合是小说在诞生之日起就有的事，概要和场景之间的张力是任何叙事形式所共同具有的特征，也是当代小说所要探讨的中心论题之一。③

二、叙事分类与研究层面

在吕克·赫尔曼与巴特·凡瓦克看来，结构主义叙事学主要集中探讨了三个方面的问题："故事""叙事""叙述行为"。这不禁使人想起叙事学史上的"二分法"与"三分法"之争。二分法是指有的叙事学家从"故事"和"话语"两个方面来研究叙事学，认为故事是被叙述的内容，话语则是叙述故事的手段，即故事是what，而话语是how。这类叙事学家主要以法国的托多洛夫和美国的查特曼为代表。托多洛夫受到俄国形式主义者什可洛夫斯基和艾亨鲍姆关于"素材"(fabula)与"内容"(sjuzet)的影响，在1966年提出了"故事"与"话语"两个概念来区分叙事作品的素材和表达形式。而查特曼则直接将他的一本专著以《故事与话语》命名，以表明他的二分法立场。

与二分法相对，在西方叙事学界，一部分数量相当的学者提出叙事学研究的三分法。例如，热奈特在《修辞格Ⅲ》一书中提出了三分法："故事"(histoire)，即被叙述的内容；"叙述话语"(récit)，即用于叙述故事的文本；"叙述行为"(narration)，即产生话语的行为与过程。热奈特的这一划分方法得到了里蒙-凯南的赞同。里蒙-凯南的《叙事虚构作品：当代诗学》一书也采用了"故事""文本""叙述"的三分法。巴尔在《叙事学：叙事理论导论》中虽然也采用了三分法，即"文本""故事"与"素材"，但是其在单个章节标题下的研究内容与热奈特、里蒙-凯南不尽相同。

赫尔曼与凡瓦克倾向于叙事学的三分法研究。他们将自己的三分法术语同热奈特、里蒙-凯南、巴尔的术语进行比较，得出如下的对比图式：

① Brain Richardson, "Recent Concepts of Narrative and the Narratives of Narrative Theory," p.169.
② Percy Lubbock, *The Craft of Fiction* (New York: Viking Press, 1963), p.62.
③ Herman and Vervaeck, *Handbook of Narrative Analysis*, p.16.

吕克・赫尔曼与巴特・凡瓦克	热奈特	里蒙-凯南	巴尔
故事(story)	故事(histoire)	故事(story)	素材(fabula)
叙事(narrative)	叙述话语(récit)	文本(text)	故事(story)
叙述行为(narration)	叙述行为(narration)	叙述(narration)	文本(text)

叙事学的三分法对比[①]

在赫尔曼和凡瓦克看来,故事同任何的深层结构一样,都是读者从具体文本中获得的抽象结构。因此,在故事这一条目下,他们又深入探讨了三个方面的问题,即“事件”(events)、“行动素”(actants)和“背景”(setting)。

三、主要特征与诗学本质

在《叙事作品结构分析导论》一文中,罗兰・巴特开门见山,指出了叙事的普遍性:

> 世界上叙事作品之多,不计其数;种类浩繁,题材各异。对人类来说,似乎任何材料都适宜于叙事:叙事承载物可以是口头的或书面的有声语言、是固定的或活动的画面、是手势,以及所有这些材料的有机混合;叙事遍布于神话、传说、寓言、民间故事、小说、史诗、历史、悲剧、正剧、喜剧、哑剧、绘画(请想一想卡帕齐奥的《圣于絮尔》那幅画)、彩绘玻璃窗、电影、连环画、社会杂闻、会话。而且,以这些几乎无限的形式出现的叙事遍存于一切时代、一切地方、一切社会。[②]

正是因为叙事的“无处不在”,所以我们必须正视叙事、研究叙事。由此,叙事也便有了被确立为研究对象的合法理据。那么,接下来的问题便是如何研究叙事。在巴特和其他经典叙事学家看来,索绪尔的结构主义语言学似乎是一个可资参照的范式。巴特曾这样陈述借鉴结构主义语言学方法的缘由:“结构主义不正是通过成功地描写‘语言’——言语来自语言,我们又能借语言再生言语——来驾驭无限的言语的吗?面对无限的叙事作品以及人们能够讨论叙事作品的众多的观点(历史的、心理学的、社会学的、人种学的、美学的等等),分析家几乎身临与索绪尔同样的情景,因为索绪尔在纷繁的语言现象面前,试图从表面杂乱无章的信息中找出一条分类原则和一个描写焦点。”[③]

诚如巴特所说,彼时包括巴特本人在内的叙事学家们深受索绪尔结构主义语言学的影响,尤其是遵循了索氏对“语言”(langue)和“言语”(parole)的区分。巴特坚信:“在复杂的胡编和最简单的组合之间存在着一道鸿沟。如果不参照一个具有单位和规则的潜在系统,谁也不能够组织成(生产出)一部叙事作品。”[④]在很大程度上,“语言”和“言语”就成了早期结构主义者们寻找和发现叙事结构的有效路径。巴特、列维-斯特劳斯、格雷马斯、托多洛夫、热奈特,概莫能外。关于早期结构主义者们的这一研究路径,戴维・赫尔曼评价说:“索绪尔语言学认为‘语言’高于‘言语’,关注重点是语言符号系统的结构元素和组合原则;叙事学家们同样也将一般叙事置于具体叙事之上,主要关注点是基本结构单位(人物、状

① Herman and Vervaeck, *Handbook of Narrative Analysis*, p.45.
② 巴特:《叙事作品结构分析导论》,第 2 页。
③ Roland Barthes, *Image Music Text*, trans. Stephen Heath (London: Fontana Press, 1977), p.80.
④ Ibid., pp.80 - 81.

态、事件等)在组合、排列、转换成具体叙事文本时所依照的跨文本符号系统原则。"①

与赫尔曼类似,弗鲁德尼克指出:"'语言'和'言语'之分为早期的文学结构主义设定了基本参数,而叙事学便是结构主义的一个重要产物。向索绪尔和语音学模仿的结果是,二项对立结构成了叙事学大厦最基本的建筑材料。"② 确实如此,二项对立构成了结构主义叙事学的一个主要特征。对此,鲜明的例证有托多洛夫所区分的"故事"(包括情节逻辑与人物)与"话语"(包括叙事作品的时、体、式)、巴特所区分的"核心事件"与"催化事件"、列维-斯特劳斯关于神话的研究程式(A∶B∶∶C∶D∶)、格雷马斯的符号方阵等。弗鲁德尼克一针见血地指出:"对二项制和分类法的重视凸显出叙事学的两个普遍特征:对科学性(通过'准'语言学的形式主义和经验性)和描述性的终极追求。"③ 具体说来,早期的结构主义叙事学家们视结构主义语言学为"领航科学",努力实现其对科学性的追求。同时,他们试图发现所有叙事作品的深层结构,探索所有叙事作品所共享的模式,并试图建立普适性的理论框架,进而描述和阐释所有叙事作品。在这方面,颇具代表性的研究有巴特的《叙事作品结构分析导论》(1966)、格雷马斯的《结构主义语义学》(1966)、托多洛夫的《〈十日谈〉语法》(1969),等等。必须指出,尽管巴特宣扬"叙事无处不在",但早期结构主义者们关于叙事的研究主要还是集中在文学叙事领域,如神话、民间故事、小说等。

在结构主义叙事学阵营,最具代表性、影响最大的人物当属热奈特。在《修辞格Ⅰ—Ⅲ》(1967—1970)中,尤其是在以《修辞格Ⅲ》为基础的《叙事话语》(1972)以及随后出版的《新叙事话语》(1983)等论著中,热奈特建构了异常丰富的叙事学批评体系。在宏观层面上,热奈特提出了叙事研究的五大范畴:时序、时距、频率、语式、语态;在微观层面上,他在每个具体范畴下提出了一系列阐释性较强的叙事学概念。在《叙事话语》一书中,热奈特用了三章的篇幅来讨论时间问题。就时间而言,热奈特强调其双重性,即故事时间与叙述时间,在此基础上讨论了时序(order)、时距(duration)、频率(frequency)等核心概念。就时序而言,热奈特指出:"研究叙事的时间顺序,就是对照事件或时间段在叙述话语中的排列顺序和这些时间或时间段在故事中的接续顺序,因为叙事的时序已由叙事本身明确指出,或者可从某个间接标志中推论出来。"④ 在叙事作品中,叙述时间往往与故事时间并不同步,由此产生了"时间倒错"的情况。如果叙事事先或提前讲述了以后事件的活动,那么就是预序。反之,如果在事后讲述在之前发生的事件,那么就是倒叙。时距被热奈特用来指故事时间与叙述时间之间的长度比较,由此出现了四种情况:① 停顿,即故事时间为零,而叙述时间无穷大;② 场景,即叙述时间等同于故事时间;③ 概要,即叙述时间短于故事时间;④ 省略,即叙述时间为零,而故事时间无穷大。热奈特用 TH 表示故事时间,用 TR 表示叙述时间,列出了下述关系式:

停顿:TR=n,TH=0。故:TR∞>TH
场景:TR=TH
概要:TR<TH
省略:TR=0,TH=n。故:TR<∞TH⑤

---

① David Herman, "Histories of Narrative Theory (I): A Genealogy of Early Developments," *A Companion to Narrative Theory*, eds. James Phelan and Peter J. Rabinowitz (Oxford: Blackwell, 2005), pp.19 - 20.

② Monika Fludernik, "Histories of Narrative Theory (II): From Structuralism to the Present," *A Companion to Narrative Theory*, eds. James Phelan and Peter J. Rabinowitz (Oxford: Blackwell, 2005), p.38.

③ Ibid.

④ 热拉尔·热奈特:《叙事话语,新叙事话语》,王文融译,北京:中国社会科学出版社,1990 年,第 14 页。

⑤ 同上,第 60 页。

在热奈特那里，所谓的频率是指故事中某个事件的发生次数与被叙述次数之间的对比关系，由此可见四种频率类型：① 单一叙述，即事件只发生了一次，也只被叙述了一次；② 重复叙述，即事件只发生了一次，但被多次叙述；③ 多次叙述，即 N 次叙述发生 N 次的事件；④ 概况叙述，事件发生了多次，但只被叙述一次。

鉴于其对叙事学研究的重要贡献，热奈特在 2008 年被国际叙事学研究协会授予"韦恩・布斯终身成就奖"。在颁奖词中，美国宾夕法尼亚大学的杰拉德・普林斯说："我们所有人都感谢他所提出和阐释的一系列概念、工具和术语——从同质叙事、异质叙事到重复性频率或转叙——如果没有他的贡献，当下的叙事研究完全是不可思议的。"① 结构主义者们将叙事（尤其是文学叙事）作为主要的研究对象，充分借助结构主义语言学的研究模式与方法，力图探求共存于叙事作品的普遍结构，建构叙事作品分析的批评体系，提出叙事作品分析的专业术语。他们积极努力的结果，使得叙事学最终从传统的小说理论中独立出来，成为一门具有自身特色的学科。

巴特、格雷马斯、布雷蒙、托多洛夫、热奈特等结构主义叙事学家始终致力于寻找普遍的叙事语法，试图发现叙事文本的意义产生机制。在这种意义上，结构主义叙事学带有明显的诗学性质。在传统意义上，诗学一般是指关于诗歌的研究，因此被定义为"诗歌理论，尤其强调肌理与结构的原则"。② 在现代意义上，诗学指的是关于文学的一般理论。就如彼得・蔡尔兹和罗杰・弗勒所指出的那样："在现代用法中，诗学不是研究诗歌或诗歌的技巧，而是文学的一般理论。"③ 受到结构主义语言学的影响，结构主义叙事学家致力于揭示作品意义生产的机制。在《结构主义诗学》一书中，乔纳森・卡勒把诗学与阐释学并置，认为诗学的目标在于"理解文学的设置、规约和策略，文学作品以它们为途径产生效果"，而阐释学的目标在于"发现或确定文本的意义"。④ 不过，结构主义者们过于聚焦"诗学"层面和叙事作品自身，忽视了叙事作品的生产语境、接受语境和其他相关因素。因此，随着文化批评和后结构主义浪潮的崛起，结构主义叙事学逐渐遭到一定程度的诟病和攻击，走向衰微。

为加深对结构主义叙事学理念和方法体系的理解，本章选择了三篇经典文献，分别取自弗拉基米尔・普罗普（Vladimir Propp）的《故事形态学》、布雷蒙的《叙事可能之逻辑》以及热奈特的《叙事话语》。

---

① Gerald Prince, "2008 — Gérard Genette," http: //narrative.georgetown.edu/awards/booth-genette.php.

② Cuddon, *A Dictionary of Literary Terms and Literary Theory* (Fifth Edition), p.545.

③ Childs and Fowler, *The Routledge Dictionary of Literary Terms*, p.179.

④ Culler, *Structuralist Poetics: Structuralism, Linguistics and the Study of Literature*, p.vii.

第二节 弗拉基米尔·普罗普及其《故事形态学》

一、导读

弗拉基米尔·普罗普(1895—1970)是苏联的重要民俗学家,主要著有《故事形态学》(1928)、《魔法故事的起源》(1946)、《俄罗斯叙事诗》(1955)、《俄罗斯农民的祭礼仪式》(1963)、《口承文艺与现实》(1976)、《俄罗斯民间故事》(1984)等。尽管普罗普不属于法国结构主义阵营,但他对布雷蒙、列维-斯特劳斯都产生了重要影响,如果没有普罗普的民间故事形态学,我们就很难把握结构主义对叙事模式和结构的执念。本节选文取自普罗普的名著《故事形态学》。在《故事形态学》的中文版序言中,谢尔盖·尤里耶维奇·涅赫留多夫称赞普罗普为一个"世纪人"。在他看来,有一些书成为事件,成为发现:它们彻底改变了学界观察对象的眼光,引领学界走出研究方法的停滞状态,在数十年间给予后起的研究以前进的动力。毫无疑问,《故事形态学》属于此类书籍之列,普罗普首先因为是这本书的作者而成为"世纪人"。在《故事形态学》中,普罗普通过考察100个俄国民间故事,重点审视和讨论故事中人物的功能。普罗普先把故事划分成不同的组成部分,然后再根据组成部分来进行比较,由此得出一套故事的形态学框架,即对成分和成分之间的关系、成分与整体之间的关系做出描述。普罗普举了如下的例子:

(1) 沙皇赠给好汉一只鹰。鹰将好汉送到了另一个王国。
(2) 老人赠给苏钦科一匹马。马将苏钦科驮到了另一个王国。
(3) 巫师给伊万一艘小船。小船将伊万载到了另一个王国。
(4) 公主赠给伊万一个指环。从指环中出来的好汉们将伊万送到了另一个王国。

普罗普从上述例子中指出了故事的可变因素和不变因素,即变化的是人物的角色名称,而不变的是人物的行动或功能。就功能而言,普罗普指出角色是故事的最基本构成部分,故事的功能是有限的,功能的排列是同一的,而所有故事按其构成而言都是同一类型。在俄国民间故事中,一共存在31个功能:

(1) 一位家庭成员离家外出
(2) 对主人公下一道禁令
(3) 打破禁令
(4) 对头试图刺探信息
(5) 对头获知其受害者的信息
(6) 对头试图欺骗受害者,以掌握他的财物
(7) 受害者上当并无意中帮助了敌人
(8) 对头给一个家庭成员带来伤害或损失

(9) 灾难或缺少被告知,向主人公提出请求或发布命令,派遣他或允许他出发
(10) 寻找者允许或决定反抗
(11) 主人公离家
(12) 主人公经受考验,遭到盘问或遭到攻击,以此为他获得魔法或遇到相助者做铺垫
(13) 主人公对未来赠予者的行动做出反应
(14) 宝物在主人公的掌握之中
(15) 主人公转移,他被送到或被引领到所寻之物的所在之地
(16) 主人公与对头正面交锋
(17) 给主人公做标记
(18) 对头被打败
(19) 最初的灾难或缺失被消除
(20) 主人公归来
(21) 主人公遭受追捕
(22) 主人公从追捕中获救
(23) 主人公以让人认不出的面貌回到家中或到达另一个国度
(24) 假冒主人公提出非法要求
(25) 给主人公出难题
(26) 难题被解答
(27) 主人公被认出
(28) 假冒的主人公或对头被揭露
(29) 主人公改头换面
(30) 敌人受到惩罚
(31) 主人公成婚并加冕为王

在普罗普看来,各种功能构成了故事的基本成分,而故事的情节发展就建立在成分之上。这些功能按照一定的逻辑联系在一起,形成了不同的角色。普罗普认为,在故事中,一共有 7 个角色,分别是加害者、赠予者、相助者、被救者、派遣者、英雄和假英雄。普罗普的研究无疑触及了结构主义叙事学对叙事作品模式和稳定因素的追求,并深刻影响了布雷蒙、格雷马斯等人,是结构主义叙事学的重要先声。

二、《故事形态学》选读[①]

The Method and Material

Let us first of all attempt to formulate our task. As already stated in the foreword, this work is

① V. Propp, *Morphology of the Folktale* (2nd edition), translated by Laurence Scott. Foreword by Louis A. Wagner. Introduction by Alan Dundes (Austin and London: University of Texas Press, 1968), pp.19 - 24.

dedicated to the study of fairy tales. The existence of fairy tales as a special class is assumed as an essential working hypothesis. By "fairy tales" are meant at present those tales classified by Aarne under numbers 300 to 749. This definition is artificial, but the occasion will subsequently arise to give a more precise determination on the basis of resultant conclusions. We are undertaking a comparison of the themes of these tales. For the sake of comparison we shall separate the component parts of fairy tales by special methods; and then, we shall make a comparison of tales according to their components. The result will be a morphology (i.e. a description of the tale according to its component parts and the relationship of these components to each other and to the whole).

What methods can achieve an accurate description of the tale? Let us compare the following events:

1. A tsar gives an eagle to a hero. The eagle carries the hero away to another kingdom.①
2. An old man gives Súcenko a horse. The horse carries Súcenko away to another kingdom.
3. A sorcerer gives Iván a little boat. The boat takes Iván to another kingdom.
4. A princess gives Iván a ring. Young men appearing from out of the ring carry Iván away into another kingdom, and so forth.②

Both constants and variables are present in the preceding instances. The names of the dramatis personae change (as well as the attributes of each), but neither their actions nor functions change. From this we can draw the inference that a tale often attributes identical actions to various personages. This makes possible the study of the tale *according to the functions of its dramatis personae*.

We shall have to determine to what extent these functions actually represent recurrent constants of the tale. The formulation of all other questions will depend upon the solution of this primary question: how many functions are known to the tale?

Investigation will reveal that the recurrence of functions is astounding. Thus Bába Jagá, Morózko, the bear, the forest spirit, and the mare's head test and reward the stepdaughter. Going further, it is possible to establish that characters of a tale, however varied they may be, often perform the same actions. The actual means of the realization of functions can vary, and as such, it is a variable. Morózko behaves differently than Bába Jagá. But the function, as such, is a constant. The question of *what* a tale's dramatis personae do is an important one for the study of the tale, but the questions of *who* does it and *how* it is done already fall within the province of accessory study. The functions of characters are those components which could replace Veselóvskij's "motifs",

① "Car' daet udal'cu orla. Orcl unosit udal'ca v inoe carstvo" (p.28). Actually, in the tale referred to (old number 104a = new number 171), the hero's future bride, Poljusa, tells her father the tsar that they have a ptica-kolpalica (technically a spoonbill, although here it may have meant a white stork), which can carry them to the bright world. For a tale in which the hero flies away on an eagle, see 71a (= new number 128). [L.A.W.]

② See Afanás'ev, Nos. 171, 139, 138, 156.

or Bédier's "elements". We are aware of the fact that the repetition of functions by various characters was long ago observed in myths and beliefs by historians of religion, but it was not observed by historians of the tale (cf. Wundt and Negelein[①]). Just as the characteristics and functions of deities are transferred from one to another, and, finally, are even carried over to Christian saints, the functions of certain tale personages are likewise transferred to other personages. Running ahead, one may say that the number of functions is extremely small, whereas the number of personages is extremely large. This explains the two-fold quality of a tale: its amazing multiformity, picturesqueness, and color, and on the other hand, its no less striking uniformity, its repetition.

Thus the functions of the dramatis personae are basic components of the tale, and we must first of all extract them. In order to extract the functions we must define them. Definition must proceed from two points of view. First of all, definition should in no case depend on the personage who carries out the function. Definition of a function will most often be given in the form of a noun expressing an action (interdiction, interrogation, flight, etc.). Secondly, an action cannot be defined apart from its place in the course of narration. The meaning which a given function has in the course of action must be considered. For example, if Iván marries a tsar's daughter, this is something entirely different than the marriage of a father to a widow with two daughters. A second example: if, in one instance, a hero receives money from his father in the form of 100 rubles and subsequently buys a wise cat with this money, whereas in a second case, the hero is rewarded with a sum of money for an accomplished act of bravery (at which point the tale ends), we have before us two morphologically different elements—in spite of the identical action (the transference of money) in both cases. Thus, identical acts can have different meanings, and vice versa. *Function is understood as an act of a character, defined from the point of view of its significance for the course of the action.*

The observations cited may be briefly formulated in the following manner:

1. *Functions of characters serve as stable, constant elements in a tale, independent of how and by whom they are fulfilled. They constitute the fundamental components of a tale.*
2. *The number of functions known to the fairy tale is limited.*

If functions are delineated, a second question arises: in what classification and in what sequence are these functions encountered?

A word, first, about sequence. The opinion exists that this sequence is accidental. Veselóvskij writes, "The selection and *order* of tasks and encounters (examples of motifs) already presupposes a

① W. Wundt, "Mythus und Religion," *Völkerpsychologie*, II Section I; Negelein, *Germanische Mythologie*. Negelein creates an exceptionally apt term, *Depossedierte Gottheiten*.

certain *freedom*." Sklóvskij stated this idea in even sharper terms: "It is quite impossible to understand why, in the act of adoption, the *accidental* sequence [Sklóvskij's italics] of motifs must be retained. In the testimony of witnesses, it is precisely the sequence of events which is distorted most of all." This reference to the evidence of witnesses is unconvincing. If witnesses distort the sequence of events, their narration is meaningless. The sequence of events has its own laws. The short story too has similar laws, as do organic formations. Theft cannot take place before the door is forced. Insofar as the tale is concerned, it has its own entirely particular and specific laws. The sequence of elements, as we shall see later on, is strictly *uniform*. Freedom within this sequence is restricted by very narrow limits which can be exactly formulated. We thus obtain the third basic thesis of this work, subject to further development and verification:

3. *The sequence of functions is always identical*.

As for groupings, it is necessary to say first of all that by no means do all tales give evidence of all functions. But this in no way changes the law of sequence. The absence of certain functions does not change the order of the rest. We shall dwell on this phenomenon later. For the present we shall deal with groupings in the proper sense of the word. The presentation of the question itself evokes the following assumption: if functions are singled out, then it will be possible to trace those tales which present identical functions. Tales with identical functions can be considered as belonging to one type. On this foundation, an index of types can then be created, based not upon theme features, which are somewhat vague and diffuse, but upon exact structural features. Indeed, this will be possible. If we further compare structural types among themselves, we are led to the following completely unexpected phenomenon: functions cannot be distributed around mutually exclusive axes. This phenomenon, in all its concreteness, will become apparent to us in the succeeding and final chapters of this book. For the time being, it can be interpreted in the following manner: if we designate with the letter A a function encountered everywhere in first position, and similarly designate with the letter B the function which (if it is at all present) always follows A, then all functions known to the tale will arrange themselves within a single tale, and none will fall out of order, nor will any one exclude or contradict any other. This is, of course, a completely unexpected result. Naturally, we would have expected that where there is a function A, there cannot be certain functions belonging to other tales. Supposedly we would obtain several axes, but only a single axis is obtained for all fairy tales. They are of the same type, while the combinations spoken of previously are subtypes. At first glance, this conclusion may appear absurd or perhaps even wild, yet it can be verified in a most exact manner. Such a typological unity represents a very complex problem on which it will be necessary to dwell further. This phenomenon will raise a whole series of questions.

In this manner, we arrive at the fourth basic thesis of our work:

4. *All fairy tales are of one type in regard to their structure*.

We shall now set about the task of proving, developing, and elaborating these theses in detail. Here it should be recalled that the study of the tale must be carried on strictly deductively, i.e. proceeding from the material at hand to the consequences (and in effect it is so carried on in this work). But the presentation may have a reversed order, since it is easier to follow the development if the general bases are known to the reader beforehand.

Before starting the elaboration, however, it is necessary to decide what material can serve as the subject of this study. First glance would seem to indicate that it is necessary to cover all extant material. In fact, this is not so. Since we are studying tales according to the functions of their dramatis personae, the accumulation of material can be suspended as soon as it becomes apparent that the new tales considered present no new functions. Of course, the investigator must look through an enormous amount of reference material. But there is no need to inject the entire body of this material into the study. We have found that 100 tales constitute more than enough material. Having discovered that no new functions can be found, the morphologist can put a stop to his work, and further study will follow different directions (the formation of indices, the complete systemization, historical study). But just because material can be limited in quantity, that does not mean that it can be selected at one's own discretion. It should be dictated from without. We shall use the collection by Afanás'ev, starting the study of tales with No. 50 (according to his plan, this is the first fairy tale of the collection), and finishing it with No. 151.① Such a limitation of material will undoubtedly call forth many objections, but it is theoretically justified. To justify it further, it would be necessary to take into account the degree of repetition of tale phenomena. If repetition is great, then one may take a limited amount of material. If repetition is small, this is impossible. The repetition of fundamental components, as we shall see later, exceeds all expectations. Consequently, it is theoretically possible to limit oneself to a small body of material. Practically, this limitation justifies itself by the fact that the inclusion of a great quantity of material would have excessively increased the size of this work. We are not interested in the quantity of material, but in the quality of its analysis. Our working material consists of 100 tales. The rest is reference material, of great interest to the investigator, but lacking a broader interest.

① Tales numbered 50 to 151 refer to enumeration according to the older editions of Afanás'ev. In the new system of enumeration, adopted for the fifth and sixth editions and utilized in this translation (cf. the Preface to the Second Edition, and Appendix V), the corresponding numbers are 93 to 270. [L.A.W.]

三、思考与讨论

(1) 普罗普认为什么是功能?

(2) 在普罗普的理论模式中,什么是可变的元素,什么又是不变的元素?

(3) 普罗普的理论模式有何缺陷?

第三节　克洛德·布雷蒙及其《叙述可能之逻辑》

一、导读

克洛德·布雷蒙(1929—2021)是法国著名的符号学家、叙事学家。就叙事学而言,其颇有影响的作品就是于1966年刊发在《交流》杂志的论文《叙述可能之逻辑》("The Logic of Narrative Possibilities"),该文也成为结构主义叙事学经典文献。在文章开篇,布雷蒙就指出,叙事作品的符号学研究可以分成两种类型,即关于叙事技巧的分析,以及对故事起支配作用的规律的研究。布雷蒙以普罗普的研究模式为参照,又对之进行了适当修改。他认为,故事的基本单位(即故事原子)依然是功能,三个功能可以构成一个基本序列(elementary sequence)。但是与普罗普不同的是,在这个基本序列中,一个功能并不一定会引发另一个功能,而只是后一个功能发生的可能,用下图表示就是:

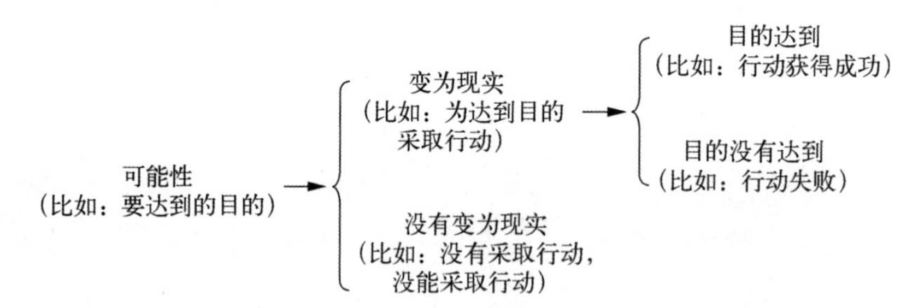

根据普罗普的解释,开始序列的功能出现以后,叙述者既可以使这一功能进入实现阶段,也可以将它保持在可能阶段:既然一个行动是以即将采取的形式出现的,或者既然一个事件是以即将发生的形式出现的,那么,这一行动或这一事件既可以发生也可以不发生。另外,叙述者可以把这一行动或这一事件化为现实,也有自由或者让变化过程发展到底或者在中路把它截断:行动可能达到目的,也可能达不到目的;事件可能发展到底,也可能不发展到底。[①] 可见,普罗普的上述关于功能序列的论述,具有明显的二元对立色彩。布雷蒙对叙事结构的研究重点在于考察和发现事件的序列结构。他直接指出:"任何叙事作品相等于一段包含着一个具有人类趣味又有情节统一性的事件序列的话语。没有序列,就没有叙事。"[②]布雷蒙再次利用二元对立的模式,认为事件序列具有两种基本类型,即要得到的改善(amelioration to obtain)与可以预见的恶化(degradation expected),如下所示:

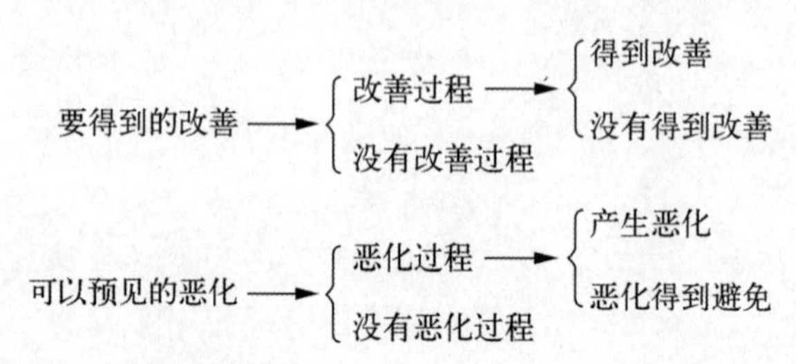

① 克洛德·布雷蒙:《叙述可能之逻辑》,载张寅德编选:《叙述学研究》,北京:中国社会科学出版社,1989年,第154页。
② 同上,第156页。

就事件发展的改善与恶化两种走向而言，布雷蒙总结出三种组合方式，即首位接续式、中间包含式、左右并连式。在此基础上，布雷蒙又分别对改善和恶化的两种序列类型做了再次归类与阐释。在这种意义上，布雷蒙所执着的是以分类的方式来把握叙事作品的基本类型与结构。用他的话来说："如果我们从叙述性、序列和角色的最简单形式出发，把越来越复杂、越来越有区别的情景连接起来，我们就为叙事作品类型的分类打下了基础；而且我们同时还为这些行为的比较研究制订了一个参照范围；因为这些行为虽然从基本结构来看总是相同的，然而，根据无限的组合和取舍，根据文化、时代、体裁、学派及个人风格不同，可以无限地分类。"[①]

二、《叙述可能之逻辑》选读[②]

I

Semiological study of narrative can be divided into two parts: on the one hand, an analysis of the techniques of narrative; on the other, a search for the laws which govern the narrated matter. These laws themselves depend upon two levels of organization: they reflect the logical constraint that any series of events, organized as narrative, must respect in order to be intelligible; and they add to these constraints, valid for all narrative, the conventions of their particular universe which is characteristic of a culture, a period, a literary genre, a narrator's style, even of the narration itself.

After examining the method used by Vladimir Propp to discover the specific characteristics of one of these particular domains, that of the Russian folktale, I became convinced of the need to draw a map of the logical possibilities of narrative as a preliminary to any description of a specific literary genre. Once this is accomplished, it will be feasible to attempt a classification of narrative based on structural characteristics as precise as those which help botanists and biologists to define the aims of their studies. But this widening perspective entails the need for a less rigorous method. Let us recall and spell out the modifications which seem indispensable:

First, the basic unit, the narrative atom, is still the *function*, applied as in Propp, to actions and events which, when grouped in sequences, generate the narrative.

Second, a first grouping of three functions creates the elementary sequence. This triad corresponds to the three obligatory phases of any process: a function which opens the process in the form of an act to be carried out or of an event which is foreseen; a function which achieves this virtuality in the form of an actual act or event; and a function which closes the process in the form of an attained result.

Third, the foregoing differ from Propp's method in that none of these functions lead necessarily

① 克洛德·布雷蒙：《叙述可能之逻辑》，第 175 页。
② Claude Bremond, "The Logic of Narrative Possibilities," *New Literary History* 11.3 (Spring 1980), pp.387 - 396.

to the following function in the sequence. On the contrary, when the function which opens the sequence is proposed, the narrator always has the choice of having it followed by the act or of maintaining it in a state of virtuality: when an act is presented as having to be realized, or if an event is foreseen, the actualization of the act or of the event can just as well take place as not. If the narrator chooses to actualize the act or the event, he still has the choice of allowing the process to continue on to its conclusion, or he can stop it on the way: the act can attain or fail to attain its goal; the event can follow or not follow its course up to the end which was foreseen. The network of possibilities opened in this way by the elementary sequence follows this pattern:

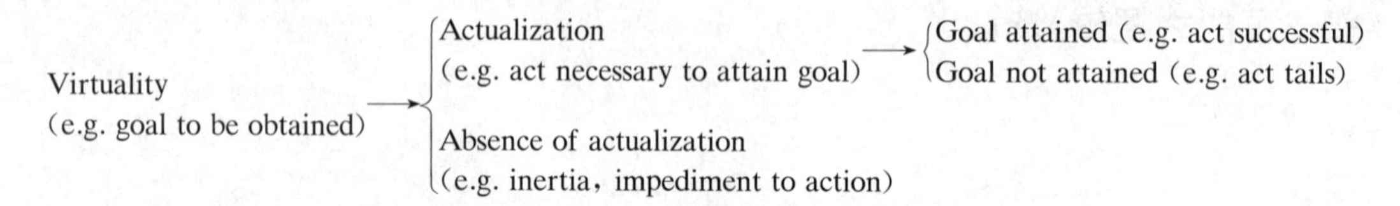

The elementary sequences combine so as to produce complex sequences. These combinations are realized according to variable configurations. Here are the most typical:

(1) The end-to-end series, for example:

Evil to perform
↓
Evildoing
↓
Evil performed = Deed to be avenged
↓
Process of revenge
↓
Deed avenged

The symbol = which we have used signifies that the same event simultaneously fulfills, within the perspective of a single role, two distinct functions. In our example, the same reprehensible action is qualified, from the perspective of an avenger, as the end of a process (evildoing) in relation to which he plays the passive role of witness and as the opening of another process in which he will play an active role (punishment).

(2) The enclave, for example:

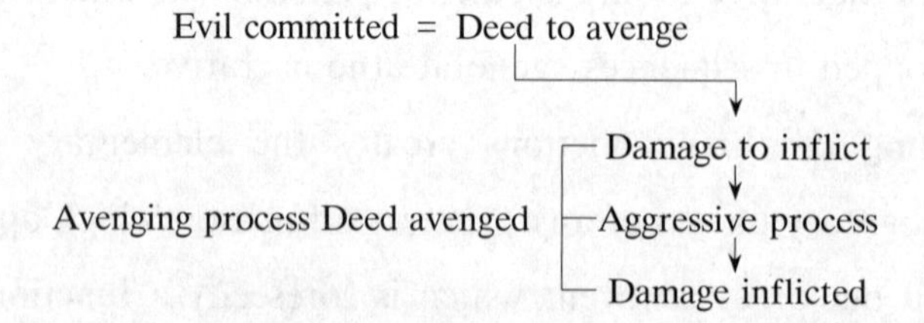

This arrangement appears when a process, in order to attain its goal, must include another which acts as a means for the first; the latter can in turn include a third, etc. The enclave is the mainspring of the specification mechanisms of sequences: in this case, the process of retribution becomes more specifically an aggressive process (punitive action) corresponding to the function *evil committed*. It could have become specified as an obliging process (recompense) if a service had been performed.

(3) "Coupling", for example:

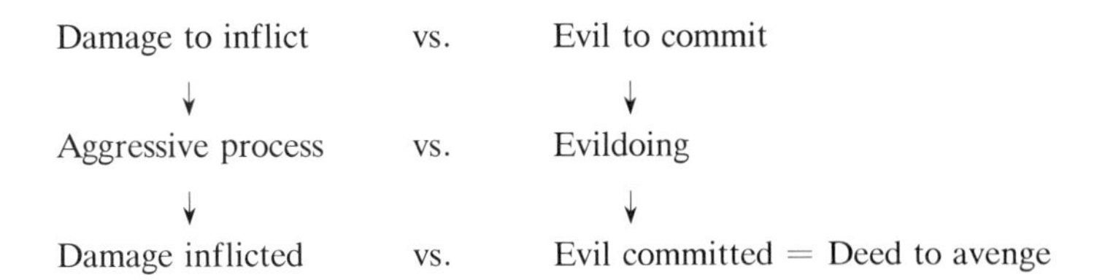

The symbol *vs*. which acts as a link between the two sequences means that the same event which fulfills a function *a* from the perspective of an agent *A* fulfills a function *b* when we shift to *B*'s perspective. This ability to perform a systematic conversion of points of view and to formulate the rules of such a conversion will make it possible to delineate the spheres of action corresponding to the diverse roles (or dramatis personae). In our example the borderline passes between an aggressor's sphere of action and that of an administrator of justice from whose perspective the aggression is equivalent to an evil deed.

These are the rules which will be tested in the following pages. We will attempt to arrive at a logical reconstitution of the starting points and directions of the narrative network. Without pretending to explore each itinerary through to its final ramifications, we will try to follow the main arteries, taking into account, along each distance covered, the bifurcations at which the major branches split and so engender subtypes. In this way we will draw up a tableau of model sequences, much less numerous than one might imagine and from among which the storyteller must necessarily choose. This tableau itself will become the basis for a classification of the roles assumed by the characters in the story.

II. The Narrative Cycle

All narrative consists of a discourse which integrates a sequence of events of human interest into the unity of a single plot. Without succession there is no narrative, but rather description (if the objects of the discourse are associated through spatial contiguity), deduction (if these objects imply one another), lyrical effusion (if they evoke one another through metaphor or metonymy). Neither does narrative exist without integration into the unity of a plot, but only chronology, an enunciation of a succession of uncoordinated facts. Finally, where there is no implied human interest (narrated events neither being produced by agents nor experienced by anthropomorphic beings), there can be no narrative, for it is only in relation to a plan conceived by man that events gain meaning and can be organized into a structured temporal sequence.

According to whether they favor or oppose this plan, the events of a given narrative can be classed under two basic types which develop according to the following sequences:

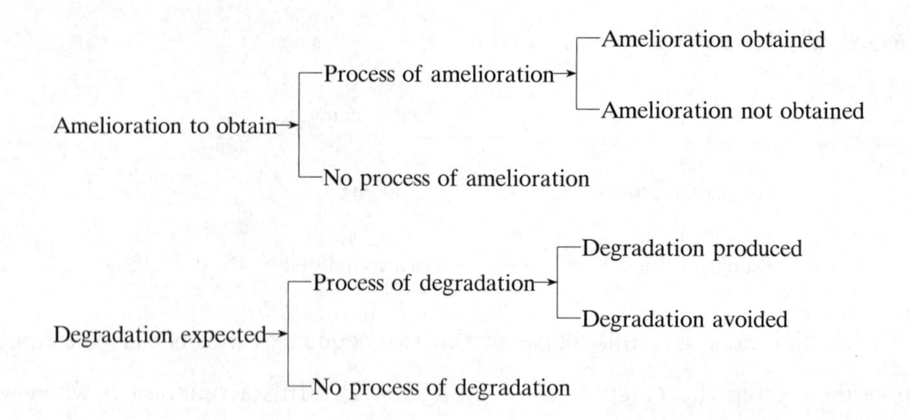

Each elementary sequence which we will eventually isolate is a specification of one or the other of these two categories, which thus establishes the first principle of dichotomous classification. Before examining the various sequences, let us specify the modalities according to which amelioration and degradation combine in a narrative:

(1) By end-to-end succession. It can immediately be seen that narration can alternate phases of amelioration and degradation according to a continuous cycle:

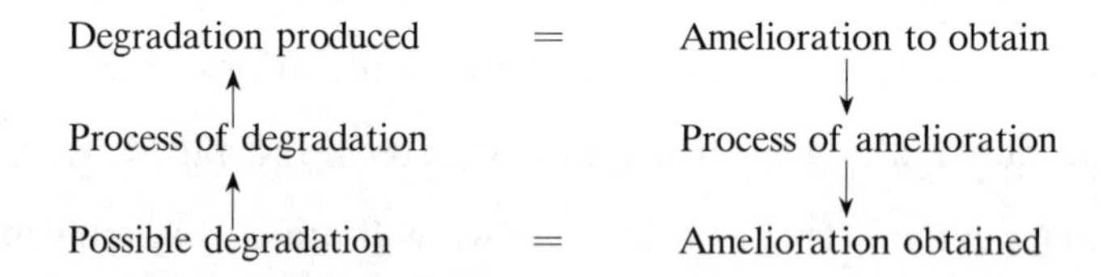

However, and this is not quite so obvious, this alternation is not only possible but necessary. Let us consider the beginning of a story which presents a deficiency affecting an individual or a group (in the form of poverty, illness, stupidity, lack of a male heir, chronic plague, desire for knowledge, love, etc.). For this beginning to develop, the situation must evolve; something must happen which will bring modification. In what direction? One might suppose either toward amelioration or degradation. Rightfully, however, only an amelioration is possible. Misfortune may, of course, grow worse. There are narratives in which misfortunes follow one after the other so that each degradation brings on another. But in this case the deficiency which marks the end of the first degradation is not the real point of departure of the second. This intermediary interruption—this *reprieve*—is functionally equivalent to a period of amelioration, or at least to a phase which represents the preservation of what can still be saved. The departure point of the new phase of degradation is not the degraded condition, which can only be improved, but the still relatively satisfying state which can only be degraded. Likewise, two amelioration processes cannot follow one another, inasmuch as the improvement brought about by the first still leaves something to be desired. By implying this lack, the narrator introduces the equivalent of a phase of degradation. The still relatively deficient condition which results acts as a point of departure for the new amelioration phase.

(2) By enclave. The failure of a process of amelioration or degradation in progress may result from the insertion of a reverse process which prevents it from reaching its normal conclusion. In this case we have the following schemata:

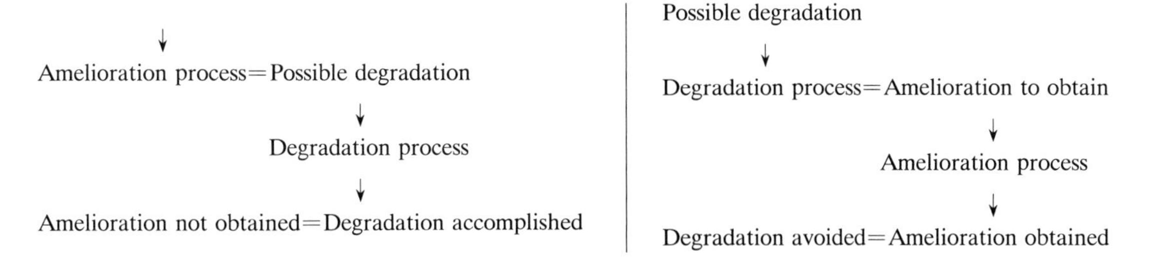

(3) By coupling. The same sequence of events cannot at the same time and in relation to the same agent be characterized both as amelioration and degradation. On the contrary, this simultaneity becomes possible when the event affects at one and the same time two agents moved by opposing interests: the degradation of the fate of the one coincides with the amelioration of the fate of the other. This produces the following schema:

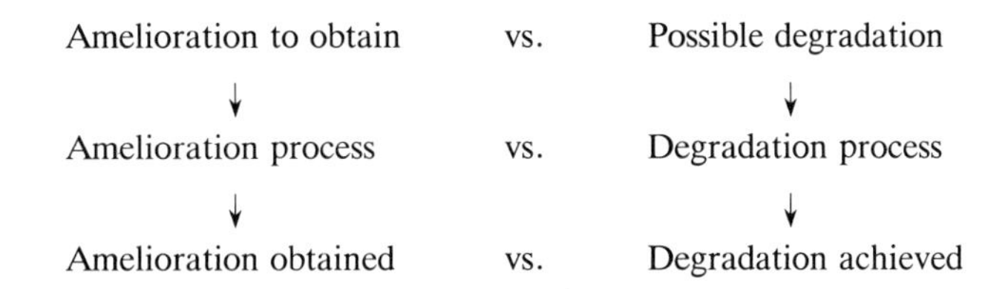

The fact that it is possible and indeed necessary to change viewpoints from the perspective of one agent to that of another is capital for the remainder of our study. It implies the rejection, at our level of analysis, of the notions of Hero, Villain, etc. Each agent is his own hero. His partners are defined from his point of view as allies, adversaries, etc. These definitions are reversed when passing from one perspective to another. Rather than outline the narrative structure in relation to a privileged point of view—the hero's or the narrator's—the patterns that are herein developed will integrate the many perspectives belonging to diverse agents into the unity of a single schema.

III. Amelioration Process

The narrator can limit himself to indicating an amelioration process without explicitly outlining its phases. If he simply says that the hero solves his problems or that he gets well, becomes good, handsome, or rich, these specifications which deal with the contents of the development without specifying how it comes about cannot help us to characterize its structure. On the contrary, if he tells us that the hero solves his problems after a long period of trials, if the cure is the result of a medication or of a doctor's efforts, if the hero regains his beauty thanks to a compassionate fairy, his riches because of an advantageous transaction, or his wits following the resolutions he makes after committing an error, then we can use the articulations within these operations to differentiate diverse types of amelioration: the more detail the narrative provides, the further this differentiation can be carried out.

Let us first consider things from the perspective of the beneficiary of the amelioration. (It should be understood that the beneficiary is not necessarily aware of the process engaged in his favor. His perspective can remain in a potential state, like that of Sleeping Beauty while she waits for her Prince Charming.) His initial state of deficiency implies the presence of an *obstacle* which prevents the realization of a more satisfying state. The elimination of the obstacle implies intervening factors which act as means taken against the obstacle and in favor of the beneficiary. So that if the narrator chooses to develop this episode, his narrative will follow the schema:

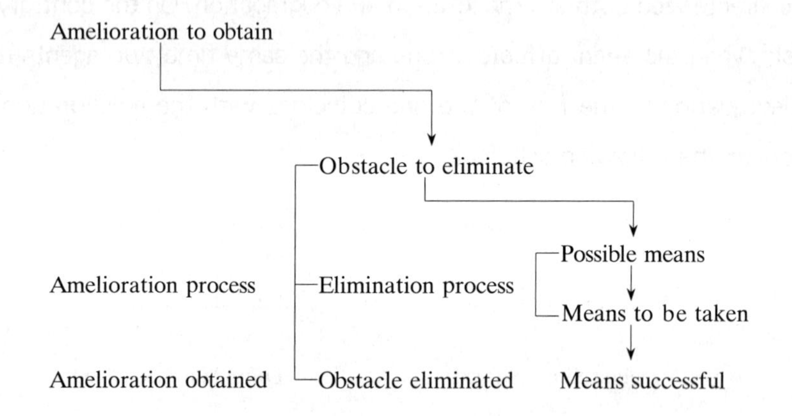

At this stage we may be dealing with a single dramatis persona, the beneficiary of the amelioration, who benefits passively from a fortunate combination of circumstances. In this case neither he nor anyone else bears the responsibility for having brought together and activated the means which overturned the obstacle. Things "turned out well" without anyone's having seen to them.

There is no such solitude when the amelioration, rather than being ascribed to chance, is attributed to the intervention of an agent endowed with initiative who assumes it as a *task to accomplish*. The amelioration process is then organized into behavior, which implies that it takes on the structure of a network of ends and means which can be analyzed ad infinitum. In addition, this transformation introduces two new roles: on the one hand, the agent who assumes the task for the benefit of a passive beneficiary acts, in relation to that beneficiary, no longer as an inert means, but as one endowed with initiative and with his own interests: he is an *ally*. On the other hand, the obstacle confronted by the agent can also be represented by an agent, also endowed with initiative and his own interests: this agent is an *adversary*. In order to take these new dimensions into account examine: the structure of the completion of the task and its possible developments, the full details of the alliance relationship brought about by the intervention of an ally, and the modalities and the consequences of the action undertaken against an adversary.

IV. Completion of the Task

The narrator can limit himself to mentioning the performance of the task. If he chooses to develop this episode, he must make dear first the nature of the obstacle encountered, then the structure of the measures taken to eliminate it—intentionally, and not by chance this time. The agent can be lacking these means, perhaps intellectually he is ignorant of what he must do, or materially if he does not have the necessary tools at his disposal. The recognition of this lack is equivalent to a phase of degradation which, in this case, takes on the specific form of a problem to solve and which, as before, can be dealt with in two ways: things either work out by themselves (heaven may unexpectedly provide the sought-for solution) or an agent may assume the task of arranging them. In this case, this new agent acts as an ally intervening for the benefit of the first who becomes in turn the passive beneficiary of the assistance thus given him.

V. Intervention of the Ally

It is possible that the ally's intervention, in the form of an agent who takes charge of the amelioration process, not be given a motive by the narrator, or that it be explained by motives having no beneficiary (if the aid is involuntary). In this case one cannot really speak of the intervention of an ally: deriving from fortuitous encounter between two tales, the amelioration is the product of chance.

Things are quite different when the intervention is motivated, from the ally's point of view, by the merits of the beneficiary. In that case the aid is a sacrifice consented to within the framework of an exchange of services. This exchange itself can assume three forms: either (1) the aid is received by the beneficiary in exchange for assistance which he himself offers his ally in an exchange of simultaneous services: the two parameters are in this case jointly responsible for the accomplishment of a task of mutual interest; or (2) the aid is offered in gratitude for a past service: in this case the ally acts as the beneficiary's *debtor*; or (3) the aid is offered in the hope of future compensation: in this case the ally acts as the beneficiary's *creditor*.

Three types of allies and three narrative structures are thus determined by the chronological ordering of the services exchanged. If two associates are jointly interested in the completion of a single task, the perspective of the beneficiary and that of the ally come so close together as to coincide: each one is the beneficiary of his own efforts united with those of his ally. In a final stage there could be a single character split into two roles: when an unhappy hero decides to right his fate by "helping himself", he splits into two dramatis personae and becomes his own ally. The completion of the task represents a voluntary degradation, a sacrifice (a fact which is supported by the expressions "to do something with great pain" "to toil", etc.) whose purpose is to pay the price of an amelioration. Whether it is a question of a single character who divides in two, or of two interdependent characters, the role configuration remains identical: the amelioration is obtained through the sacrifice of an ally whose interests are the same as those of the beneficiary.

Rather than coincide, the perspectives oppose one another when the beneficiary and his ally form the couple creditor/debtor. Their roles then take on the following form: for example, *A* and *B* must each obtain an amelioration distinct from that of the other. If *A* receives *B*'s aid in order to achieve amelioration *a*, *A* becomes *B*'s debtor and will be obliged in turn to help *B* achieve amelioration *b*. The narrative will follow the schema:

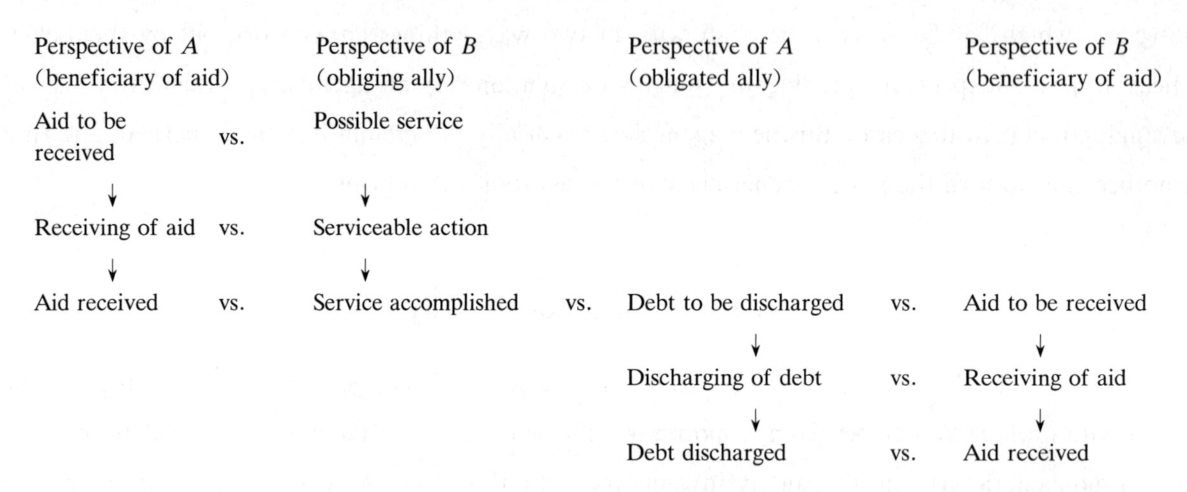

The three types of allies that we have just distinguished—the interdependent associate, the creditor, the debtor—act according to a pact which regulates the exchange of services and guarantees the repayment of services rendered. Sometimes this pact remains implicit (it is understood that hard work is worthy of payment, that a son must obey the father who gave him life, that a slave obey the master who saved his life, etc.); sometimes the pact is the result of a particular negotiation, spelled out in the narrative more or less specifically. Just as it was necessary to search for means before implementing them when their lack constituted an obstacle to the completion of the task, so aid must be negotiated when an ally does not cooperate spontaneously. Within the framework of this preliminary task, the abstention of a future ally makes of him an adversary who has to be convinced. This negotiation, soon to be discussed, constitutes the peaceful way of eliminating an adversary.

三、思考与讨论

(1) 布雷蒙的叙事模式与普罗普的叙事模式有何内在的关联?

(2) 在布雷蒙看来,叙事可能性的逻辑究竟是什么?

(3) 能否以具体文学作品为例,讨论布雷蒙所关于事件朝着恶化或改善方向发展的趋势?

第四节　热拉尔·热奈特及其《叙事话语》

一、导读

热拉尔·热奈特(1930—2018)是最为著名的结构主义叙事学家之一。我们完全可以说,倘若没有热奈特,叙事学就不会有诸如聚焦、时距、时长、视频等核心概念,其叙事学思想主要体现在《修辞格Ⅰ—Ⅲ》中,尤其是在以《修辞格Ⅲ》为基础的《叙事话语》以及随后出版的《新叙事话语》等论著中。鉴于其对叙事学研究的重要贡献,热奈特在2008年被国际叙事学研究协会授予"韦恩·布斯终身成就奖"。本节选自热奈特的《叙事话语》一书,重点探讨热奈特所提出的聚焦概念。

在《修辞格 II》中,热奈特在参照前人理论的基础上提出了"叙述聚焦"这一概念,力图消除叙事学界在"谁说"(who speaks)与"谁看"(who sees)这一问题上长期存有的疑问。继而,在《叙述话语》一书中,热氏又对叙述聚焦做了更为详细的论述和阐释。后经施劳米什·里蒙-凯南、米克·巴尔、威廉·尼尔斯(William Neues)等诸多叙事学家的推广沿用,叙述聚焦已经成为当下叙事学研究的重要术语之一。根据《劳特利奇叙事理论百科全书》的解释,叙述聚焦是指与某个人(通常是某个人物)的感知、想象、知识或视点相关的叙述信息起源与视角限制。叙述聚焦实际上涵盖了对叙述信息的规范、选择、传输等各种方式,尤其是从某个人物的视点来观察事件,不论这一视点是多么主观化与不可靠。①

在叙事学家们看来,"不言自明的是,事件无论何时被描述,总要从一定的'视角'范围内被描述出来,而且需要选择一个观察点,即看事物的某种方式或某种角度。"② 在热奈特之前,人们通常用叙述视角(point of view)、叙述情境(narrative situation)、叙述样式(narrative manner)、叙述透视(narrative perspective)、叙述焦点(focus of narration)等术语来指称叙述者的观察角度或观察视点。杰拉德·普林斯认为,没有什么叙述特征能像叙述视角这样被广泛讨论,叙述事件与情境从生理、心理、意识形态等角度被呈现出来;也没有什么叙述特征能像叙述视角这样拥有丰富的术语(从中央智能、视野、聚焦到过滤器、看法等)。③

其实,早在热奈特之前,西方已经有数量相当的文学理论家致力于小说的叙述视角研究。热奈特认为,自19世纪末以来,在与叙述技巧相关的所有论题中,要属叙述视角的研究频率最高。④ 热奈特本人也是在参照先驱者研究成果的基础上,创造性地提出了叙述聚焦这一概念。诸多的现代小说理论家都把叙述视角看作小说研究的重要一隅。S.L.威特科姆(S. L. Whitoomb)在《小说研究》一书中,以"叙述

① Manfred Jahn, "Focalization," *Routledge Encyclopedia of Narrative Theory*, eds. David Herman, Manfred Jahn and Marie-Laure Ryan (London and New York: Routledge, 2005), p.173.

② Mieke Bal, *Narratology: Introduction to the Theory of Narrative* (Second Edition) (Toronto: University of Toronto Press, 1997), p.142.

③ Gerald Prince, "Point of View (Literary)," *Routledge Encyclopedia of Narrative Theory*, eds. David Herman, Manfred Jahn and Marie-Laure Ryan (London and New York: Routledge, 2005), p.442.

④ Gérard Genette, *Narrative Discourse: An Essay in Method*, trans. Jane E. Lewin (Ithaca: Cornell University Press, 1980), p.186.

者,其观察点"为该书的一个章节标题,初步涉猎叙述视角这一论题。帕西·卢伯克在《小说技巧》一书中,更是对叙述视角表达了极大的关注。卢伯克认为在小说技巧中,所有错综复杂的方法问题都要受到观察点即叙述者在故事中所站位置的影响。① 卢伯克还试着以叙述视角为参照范式,分析了巴尔扎克、福楼拜、托尔斯泰等人的作品。

就提出这一概念的原因,热奈特解释道:一方面他是想力图避免使用过于具体化的视觉性术语,如"视野""视角"等,另一方面,他是受到了布鲁克斯与沃伦关于"叙述聚点"这一概念的启发,因此提出了略微抽象的术语——叙述聚焦。但是,热奈特却没有提及一个更为重要的原因,即以往小说理论家在研究叙述视角这一问题上的致命缺陷——没有分清叙述过程中的"谁说"与"谁看"。在参照了布鲁克斯、沃伦、托多洛夫、让·普荣(Jean Pouillon)等人关于叙述视角研究的基础上,热奈特详细阐述了叙述聚焦理论。他根据叙述信息受限制程度的高低,提出了叙述聚焦的三种类型:① 无聚焦(non-focalization)或零聚焦(zero-focalization),相当于普荣的后视野或托多洛夫的叙述者>人物的视角公式。在这一叙述聚焦类型中,事件被没有限制的全知叙述视角所叙述。如菲尔丁的《汤姆·琼斯》、福斯特的《印度之行》,以及很多维多利亚时期的小说。② 内聚焦(internal focalization),相当于普荣的内视野、卢伯克的"视点"叙述、乔治·布兰(Georges Blin)的"有限视野"或托多洛夫的叙述者=人物的视角公式。在这一叙述聚焦类型中,事件通过聚焦人物的视点、感知、认知被呈现出来。如罗伯-格里耶的《嫉妒》、福克纳的《焚烧粮仓》等。③ 外聚焦(external focalization),相当于普荣的外视野或托多洛夫的叙述者<人物的视角公式。在这一叙述聚焦类型中,事件的叙述只局限于从外部视点、行为报告(behaviorist report)等角度出发,基本上只涉及摄像机所能拍到的东西,如福克纳的短篇小说《杀人者》。②

曼弗雷德·雅恩认为,在热奈特的三种叙述聚焦类型中,内聚焦最为重要,这不仅是因为内聚焦抓住了通常叙述情境的自然限制性,而且还因为它体现了 20 世纪现代主义叙事作品的主要特点。③ 也正是在这一叙述聚焦类型上,热奈特进一步细化。他以叙述聚焦的恒定性(persistence)为参照范式,提出了内聚焦的三种亚类型:① 固定式聚焦(fixed focalization),即对事件的叙述始终从某个单一聚焦人物的视点出发,如乔伊斯的《青年艺术家的肖像》。② 不定式聚焦(variable focalization),即对事件的叙述是通过几个不同聚焦人物的视点来完成的,如伍尔夫的《达罗威夫人》。③ 多重聚焦(multiple focalization),即通过不同的聚焦人物对同一事件进行多次不同的叙述,如福楼拜的《包法利夫人》。

热奈特的叙述聚焦理论一经提出,便引发了西方叙事学界的热烈讨论,赞同者有之,反对者亦有之。不可否认,热奈特关于叙述聚焦的"谁说"与"谁看"之分,第一次廓清了西方叙事学界长期以来在叙述视角研究问题上的混乱局面,他通过引入叙述聚焦这一技术性术语,使得叙事学研究彰显出"科学性"特征。但遗憾的是,热奈特没有深入探讨聚焦者(focalizer)与被聚焦者(focalized)的区别,也没有进一步划分叙述聚焦的层面,这无疑为后来学界在叙述聚焦问题上的论争埋下了伏笔。

---

① Lubbock, *The Craft of Fiction*, p.251.
② Genette, *Narrative Discourse: An Essay in Method*, pp.189 - 198.
③ Jahn, "Focalization," pp.173 - 174.

二、《叙事话语》选读 ①

Perspective

What we are calling, for the moment and through metaphor, narrative perspective—in other words, the second mode of regulating information, arising from the choice (or not) of a restrictive "point of view"—is, of all the questions having to do with narrative technique, the one that has been most frequently studied since the end of the nineteenth century, with indisputable critical results, like Percy Lubbock's chapters on Balzac, Flaubert, Tolstoy, or James, or Georges Blin's chapter on "restrictions of field" in Stendhal.② However, to my mind most of the theoretical works on this subject (which are mainly classifications) suffer from a regrettable confusion between what I call here *mood* and *voice*, a confusion between the question *who is the character whose point of view orients the narrative perspective?* and the very different question *who is the narrator?*—or, more simply, the question *who sees?* and the question *who speaks?* We will return later to this apparently obvious but almost universally disregarded distinction. Thus Cleanth Brooks and Robert Penn Warren proposed in 1943, under the term *focus of narration*—which they explicitly (and very happily) proposed as an equivalent to "point of view"—a four-term typology, summed up in the table below.③

	Internal analysis of events	*Outside observation of events*
Narrator as a character in the story	1. Main character tells his story	2. Minor character tells main character's story
Narrator not a character in the story	4. Analytic or omniscient author tells story	3. Author tells story as observer

Now, it is obvious that only the vertical demarcation relates to "point of view" (inner or outer), while the horizontal bears on voice (the identity of the narrator), with no real difference in point of view between 1 and 4 (let us say *Adolphe* and *Armance*) and between 2 and 3 (Watson narrating Sherlock Holmes, and Agatha Christie narrating Hercule Poirot). In 1955, F. K. Stanzel distinguished three types of novelistic "narrative situations": the *auktoriale Erzahlsituation*, which

① Gérard Genette, *Narrative Discourse: An Essay in Method*, trans. Jane E. Lewin (Ithaca: Cornell University Press, 1980), pp.185 - 211.

② Georges Blin, *Stendhal et les problémes du raman* (Paris, 1954), Part II. For a "theoretical" bibliography on this subject, see Françoise van Rossum-Guyon, "Point de vue ou perspective narrative," *Poétique*, 4 (1970). From the historical angle, see Richard Stang, *The Theory of the Novel in England*, *1850 - 1870* (New York, 1959), Chap.3; and Raimond, *La Crise du ronian*, Part IV.

③ Cleanth Brooks and Robert Penn Warren, *Understanding Fiction* (New York, 1943), p.589.

is that of the "omniscient" author (type: *Tom Jones*); the *Ich Erzahlsituation*, where the narrator is one of the characters (type: *Moby Dick*); and the *personate Erzahlsituation*, a narrative conducted "in the third person" according to the point of view of a character (type: *The Ambassadors*). [①] Here again, the difference between the second and third situations is not in "point of view" (whereas the first *is* defined according to that criterion), since Ishmael and Strether in fact occupy the same focal position in the two narratives: they differ only in that in one the focal character himself is the narrator, and in the other the narrator is an "author" absent from the story. In the same year Norman Friedman, on his part, presented a much more complex classification with eight terms: two types of "omniscient" narrating with or without "authorial intrusions" (Fielding or Thomas Hardy); two types of "first-person" narrating, I-witness (Conrad) or I-protagonist (Dickens, *Great Expectations*); two types of "selective-omniscient" narrating, that is, with restricted point of view, either "multiple" (Virginia Woolf, *To the Lighthouse*), or single (Joyce, *A Portrait of the Artist as a Young Man*); finally, two types of purely objective narrating, the second of which is hypothetical and, moreover, not easily distinguishable from the first: the "dramatic mode" (Hemingway, "Hills Like White Elephants") and "the camera", a recording pure and simple, without selection or organization.[②] Clearly, the third and fourth types (Conrad and Dickens) are distinguished from the others only in being "first-person" narratives, and the difference between the first two (intrusions of the author or not: Fielding or Hardy) is likewise a fact of voice, relating to the narrator and not to the point of view. Let us recall that Friedman describes his sixth type (*A Portrait of the Artist as a Young Man*) as "a story told as if by a character in the story, but told in the third person", a formulation that attests to obvious confusion between the focal character (what James called the "reflector") and the narrator. The same assimilation, obviously intentional, occurs with Wayne Booth, who in 1961 gave the title "Distance and Point of View" to an essay devoted in fact to problems of voice (the distinction between *implied author* and *narrator*—a narrator who is *dramatized* or *undramatized* and *reliable* or *unreliable*) as, for that matter, he explicitly stated in proposing "a richer tabulation of the forms the author's voice can take". [③] "Strether," continued Booth, "in large part 'narrates' his own story, even though he is always referred to in the third person": is his status, then, identical to Caesar's in the *Gallic War?* We see what difficulties the confusion between mood and voice leads to. In 1962, finally, Bertil Romberg took up Stanzel's typology again, and completed it by adding a fourth type: objective narrative in the behaviorist style (Friedman's seventh type); [④] whence this quadripartition: (1) narrative with omniscient author, (2) narrative with point of view, (3) objective narrative,

① F. K. Stanzel, *Narrative Situations in the Novel*, trans. J. P. Pusack (Bloomington, Ind., 1971).

② N. Friedman, "Point of View in Fiction".

③ Booth, "Distance and Point of View," *Essays in Criticism*, 11(1961), pp.60 - 79.

④ Bertil Romberg, *Studies in the Narrative Technique of the First-Person Novel*, trans. Michael Taylor and Harold H. Borland (Stockholm, 1962).

(4) narrative in the first person—where the fourth type is clearly discordant with respect to the principle of classification of the first three. Here Borges would no doubt introduce a fifth class, typically Chinese: that of narratives written with a very fine brush.

It is certainly legitimate to envisage a typology of "narrative situations" that would take into account the data of both mood and voice; what is not legitimate is to present such a classification under the single category of "point of view", or to draw up a list where the two determinations compete with each other on the basis of an obvious confusion. And so it is convenient here to consider only the purely modal determinations, those that concern what we ordinarily call "point of view" or, with Jean Pouillon and Tzvetan Todorov, "vision" or "aspect".[1] Granting this restriction, the consensus settles with no great difficulty on a three-term typology. The first term corresponds to what English-language criticism calls the narrative with omniscient narrator and Pouillon calls "vision from behind", and which Todorov symbolizes by the formula *Narrator* > *Character* (where the narrator knows more than the character, or more exactly *says* more than any of the characters knows). In the second term, *Narrator* = *Character* (the narrator says only what a given character knows); this is the narrative with "point of view" after Lubbock, or with "restricted field" after Blin; Pouillon calls it "vision with". In the third term, *Narrator* < *Character* (the narrator says less than the character knows); this is the "objective" or "behaviorist" narrative, what Pouillon calls "vision from without". To avoid the too specifically visual connotations of the terms *vision*, *field*, and *point of view*, I will take up here the slightly more abstract term *focalization*[2] which corresponds, besides, to Brooks and Warren's expression, "focus of narration".[3]

Focalizations

So we will rechristen the first type (in general represented by the classical narrative) as *nonfocalized* narrative, or narrative with *zero focalization*. The second type will be narrative with *internal focalization*, whether that be (a) *fixed*—canonical example: *The Ambassadors*, where everything passes through Strether; or, even better, *What Maisie Knew*, where we almost never leave the point of view of the little girl, whose "restriction of field" is particularly dramatic in this story of adults, a story whose significance escapes her; (b) *variable*—as in *Madame Bovary*, where

[1] Jean Pouillon, *Temps et roman* (Paris, 1946); Todorov, "Lés Catégories du récit littéraire".

[2] Already used in my *Figures II*, p.191, apropos of Stendhalian narrative.

[3] We can draw a parallel between this tripartition and the four-term classification proposed by Boris Uspenski [*A Poetics of Composition*, trans. Valentina Zavarin and Susan Witting (Berkeley, 1973)] for the "plane of psychology" of his general theory of point of view [see the "clarification" and documents presented by Todorov in *Poétique*, 9 (February 1972)]. Uspenski distinguishes two types in the point-of-view narrative, according to whether the point of view is constant (fixed on a single character) or not; this is what I propose to call *fixed* or *variable* internal focalization, but for me these are only subclasses.

the focal character is first Charles, then Emma, then again Charles;① or, in a much more rapid and elusive way, as with Stendhal; or (c) *multiple*—as in epistolary novels, where the same event may be evoked several times according to the point of view of several letter-writing characters;② we know that Robert Browning's narrative poem *The Ring and the Book* (which relates a criminal case as perceived successively by the murderer, the victims, the defense, the prosecution, etc.) was for several years the canonical example of this type of narrative,③ before being supplanted for us by the film *Rashomon*. Our third type will be the narrative with *external focalization*, popularized between the two world wars by Dashiell Hammett's novels, in which the hero performs in front of us without our ever being allowed to know his thoughts or feelings, and also by some of Hemingway's novellas, like "The Killers" or, even more, "Hills Like White Elephants", which carries circumspection so far as to become a riddle. But we should not limit this narrative type to a role only in works at the highest literary level. Michel Raimond remarks rightly that in the novel of intrigue or adventure, "where interest arises from the fact that there is a mystery", the author "does not tell us immediately all that he knows";④ and in fact a large number of adventure novels, from Walter Scott to Jules Verne via Alexandre Dumas, handle their opening pages in external focalization. See how Phileas Fogg is looked at first from the outside, through the puzzled gaze of his contemporaries, and how his inhuman mysteriousness will be maintained until the episode that will reveal his generosity.⑤ But many "serious" novels of the nineteenth century practice this type of enigmatic *introit*: examples, in Balzac, are *La Peau de chagrin* or *L'Envers de l'histoire contemporaine*, and even *Le Cousin Pons*, where the hero is described and followed for a long time as an unknown person whose identity is problematic.⑥ And other motives can justify recourse to this narrative behavior, like the reason of propriety (or the roguish play with impropriety) for the scene of the carriage in *Bovary*, which is narrated entirely from the point of view of an external, innocent witness.⑦

As this last example certainly shows, the commitment as to focalization is not necessarily steady

① On this subject see Lubbock, *The Craft of Fiction*, Chap.6, and Jean Rousset, "Madame Bovary ou le Livre sur rien," *Forme et signification* (Paris, 1962).

② See Rousset, "Le Roman par lettres," *Forme et signification*, p.86.

③ See Raimond, pp.313 – 314. Proust was interested in that book: see Tadié, p.52.

④ *La Crise du roman*, p.300.

⑤ It is the rescue of Aouda, in Chapter 12. Nothing prevents a writer from indefinitely prolonging this external point of view with respect to a character who will remain mysterious up to the end: that is what Melville does in *The Confidence-Man*, or *Conrad in The Nigger of the "Narcissus"*.

⑥ This initial "ignorance" has become a topos of novelistic beginning, even when the mystery is to be immediately dispelled. For example, in the fourth paragraph of the *Education sentimentale*: "A young man eighteen years old with long hair and holding an album under his arm ..." It is as if, to *introduce* him, the author had to pretend not to know him; once this ritual is over, he can go on without further affectations of mystery: "M. Frédéric Moreau, newly graduated ..." The two periods may be very close together, but they must be distinct. This rule operates still, for example, in *Germinal*, where first the hero is "a man" until he introduces himself: "My name is Etienne Lantier," after which Zola will call him Etienne. On the other hand, the rule no longer operates in James, who from the very beginning establishes a familiar relationship with his heroes: "Strether's first question, when he reached the hotel ..." (*The Ambassadors*); "She waited, Kate Croy, for her father to come in ..." (*The Wings of the Dove*); "The Prince had always liked his London ..." (*The Golden Bowl*). These variations would be worth an overall historical study.

⑦ III, Chap.1, Cf. Sartre, L'Idiot de la famille (Paris, 1971), pp.1277 – 1282.

over the whole length of a narrative, and variable internal focalization, a formula already very flexible, does not apply to the whole of *Bovary:* not only is the scene of the carriage in external focalization, but we have already had occasion to say that the view of Yonville that begins the second part is not any more focalized than most Balzacian descriptions.① Any single formula of focalization does not, therefore, always bear on an entire work, but rather on a definite narrative section, which can be very short.② Furthermore, the distinction between different points of view is not always as clear as the consideration of pure types alone could lead one to believe. External focalization with respect to one character could sometimes just as well be defined as internal focalization through another: external focalization on Phileas Fogg is just as well internal focalization through Passepartout dumbfounded by his new master, and the only reason for being satisfied with the first term is Phileas's status as hero, which restricts Passepartout to the role of witness. And this ambivalence (or reversibility) is equally noticeable when the witness is not personified but remains an impersonal, floating observer, as at the beginning of *La Peau de chagrin*. Similarly, the division between variable focalization and nonfocalization is sometimes very difficult to establish, for the nonfocalized narrative can most often be analyzed as a narrative that is multifocalized *ad libitum*, in accordance with the principle "he who can do most can do least" (let us not forget that focalization is essentially, in Blin's word, a *restriction*); and yet, on this point no one could confuse Fielding's manner with Stendhal's or Flaubert's.③

We must also note that what we call internal focalization is rarely applied in a totally rigorous way. Indeed, the very principle of this narrative mode implies in all strictness that the focal character never be described or even referred to from the outside, and that his thoughts or perceptions never be analyzed objectively by the narrator. We do not, therefore, have internal focalization in the strict sense in a statement like this one, where Stendhal tells us what Fabrice del Dongo does and thinks:

> Without hesitation, although ready to yield up his soul with disgust, Fabrizio flung himself from his horse and took the hand of the corpse which he shook vigorously, then he stood still as though paralysed. He felt that he had not the strength to mount again. What horrified him more than anything was that open eye.

---

① p.101.

② See Raymonde Debray-Genette, "Du mode narratif dans les *Trois Contes*," *Littérature*, 2 (May 1971).

③ Balzac's position is more complex. One is often tempted to see Balzacian narrative as the very type of narrative with an omniscient narrator, but to do that is to neglect the part played by external focalization, which I have just referred to as a technique of opening; and neglects also the part played by more subtle situations, as in the first pages of *Une double famille*, where the narrative focalizes sometimes on Camille and her mother, sometimes on M. de Granville—each of these internal focalizations serving to isolate the other character (or group) in its mysterious externality: a rearrangement of curiosities that can only quicken the reader's own.

On the other hand, the focalization is perfect in the following statement, which is content to describe what its hero sees: "A bullet, entering on one side of the nose, had gone out at the opposite temple, and disfigured the corpse in a hideous fashion. It lay with one eye still open."① Jean Pouillon very accurately notes the paradox when he writes that, in "vision with", the character is seen

> not in his innerness, for then we would have to emerge from the innerness whereas instead we are absorbed into it, but is seen in the image he develops of others, and to some extent through that image. In sum, we apprehend him as we apprehend ourselves in our immediate awareness of things, our attitudes with respect to what surrounds us—what surrounds us and is not within us. Consequently we can say in conclusion: vision as an image of others is not a result of vision "with" the main character, it is itself that vision "with".②

Internal focalization is fully realized only in the narrative of "interior monologue", or in that borderline work, Robbe-Grillet's *La Jalousie*, ③where the central character is limited absolutely to—and strictly *inferred* from—his focal position alone. So we will take the term "internal focalization" in a necessarily less strict sense—that term whose minimal criterion has been pointed out by Roland Barthes in his definition of what he calls the *personal* mode of narrative.④ According to Barthes, this criterion is the possibility of rewriting the narrative section under consideration into the first person (if it is not in that person already) without the need for "any alteration of the discourse other than the change of grammatical pronouns". Thus, a sentence such as "[James Bond] saw a man in his fifties, still young-looking..." can be translated into the first person ("I saw...")—and so for us it belongs to internal focalization. On the other hand, Barthes continues, a sentence like "the tinkling of the ice cubes against the glass *seemed* to awaken in Bond a sudden inspiration" cannot be translated into the first person without obvious semantic incongruity.⑤ Here we are typically in external focalization, because of the narrator's marked ignorance with respect to the hero's real thoughts. But the convenience of this purely practical criterion should not tempt us to confuse the two instances of the focalizing and the narrating, which remain distinct even in "first-person" narrative, that is even when the two instances are taken up by the same person (except when the first-person narrative is a present-tense interior monologue). When Marcel writes, "I saw a man of about forty, very tall and rather stout, with a very dark moustache, who, nervously slapping the leg

---

① *Charlerhouse of Parma*, Chap.3, trans. C.K.Scott Moncrieff (New York Liveright, 1925), p.48.

② *Temps et roman*, p.79.

③ Or, in the movies, Robert Montgomery's *The Lady in the Lake*, where the protagonist's part is played by the camera.

④ Barthes, "An Introduction to the Structural Analysis of Narrative," p.262.

⑤ Proust notices in *Le Lys dans la vallée* this sentence that he rightly says *manages however it can*: "'... I walked down to the meadows to see once against the Indre and its islets, the valley and its hillsides, *of which I appeared a passionate admirer*'" (Marcel Proust on Art. p.172).

of his trousers with a switch, kept fastened upon me a pair of eyes dilated with observation,"[①] the identity of "person" between the adolescent of Balbec (the hero) who notices a stranger and the mature man (the narrator) who tells this story several decades later and knows very well that that stranger was Charlus (and knows all that the stranger's behavior means) must not conceal the difference in function and, particularly, the difference in information. The narrator almost always "knows" more than the hero, even if himself is the hero, and therefore for the narrator focalization through the hero is a restriction of field just as artificial in the first person as in the third. We will soon come again to this crucial question apropos of narrative perspective in Proust, but we must still define two ideas indispensable to that study.

Alterations

The variations in "point of view" that occur in the course of a narrative can be analyzed as changes in focalization, like those we have already met in *Madame Bovary*: in such a case we can speak of variable focalization, of omniscience with partial restrictions of field, etc. This is a perfectly defensible narrative course and the norm of coherence raised to a point of honor by post Jamesian criticism is obviously arbitrary. Lubbock requires the novelist to be "consistent on *some* plan, to follow the principle he has adopted",[②] but why could this course not be absolute freedom and inconsistency? Forster[③] and Booth have well pointed out the futility of pseudo-Jamesian rules, and who today would take seriously Sartre's remonstrances against Mauriac?[④]

But a change in focalization, especially if it is isolated within a coherent context, can also be analyzed as a momentary infraction of the code which governs that context without thereby calling into question the existence of the code—the same way that in a classical musical composition a momentary change in tonality, or even a recurrent dissonance, may be defined as a modulation or alteration without contesting the tonality of the whole. Playing on the double meaning of the word *mode*, which refers us to both grammar and music,[⑤] I will thus give the general name *alterations* to these isolated infractions, when the coherence of the whole still remains strong enough for the notion of dominant mode/mood to continue relevant. The two conceivable types of alteration consist either of giving less information than is necessary in principle, or of giving more than is authorized in principle in the code of focalization governing the whole. The first type bears a name in rhetoric,

---

① RH I, 568/P I, 751.

② *The Craft of Fiction*, p.72.

③ E. M. Forster, Aspects of the Novel (London, 1927).

④ J. P. Sartre,"François Mauriac and Freedom, "in *Literary and Philosophical Essays*, trans. Annette Michelson (New York, 1955), pp.7 - 23.

⑤ [Translator's note.] In French the word *mode* includes two meanings that in English require separate words: (grammatical)"mood" and (musical) "mode".

and we have already met it apropos of completing anachronies:[①] we are dealing with lateral omission or *paralipsis*. The second does not yet bear a name; we will christen it *paralepsis*, since here we are no longer dealing with leaving aside (-lipsis, from *leipo*) information that should be taken up (and given), but on the contrary with taking up (-lepsis, from *lambano*) and giving information that should be left aside.

The classical type of paralipsis, we remember, in the code of internal focalization, is the omission of some important action or thought of the focal hero, which neither the hero nor the narrator can be ignorant of but which the narrator chooses to conceal from the reader. We know what use Stendhal made of this figure,[②] and Jean Pouillon evokes precisely this fact apropos of his "vision with", whose main disadvantage seems to him to be that the character is too well known in advance and holds no surprise in store—whence this defense, which Pouillon deems clumsy: deliberate omission. A solid example: Stendhal's dissimulation, in *Armance*, through so many of the hero's pseudo-monologues, of that hero's central thought, which obviously cannot leave him for a minute: his sexual impotence. That affectation of mystery, says Pouillon, would be normal if Octave were seen from without,

> but Stendhal does not remain outside; he makes psychological analyses, and in that case it becomes absurd to hide from us what Octave himself must certainly know; if he is sad, he knows the cause, and cannot experience that sadness without thinking of it: Stendhal therefore ought to inform us of it—which, unfortunately, he does not do; he obtains an effect of surprise when the reader has understood, but it is not the main purpose of a character in a novel to be an enigma.[③]

This analysis, we see, assumes the resolution of a question that has not been totally resolved, since Octave's impotence is not exactly a datum in the text, but never mind that here: let us take the example with its hypothesis. This analysis also includes some opinions that I will avoid adopting as my own. But it has the merit of describing well the phenomenon—which, of course, is not exclusive to Stendhal. Apropos of what he calls the "intermingling of the two systems", Barthes rightly mentions the "cheating" that, in Agatha Christie, consists of focalizing a narrative like *The Sittaford Mystery* or *The Murder of Roger Ackroyd* through the murderer while omitting from his "thoughts" simply the memory of the murder;[④] and we know that the most classical detective story, although generally focalized through the investigating detective, most often hides from us a part *of*

① P.52.
② See my *Figures II*, pp.183 - 185.
③ *Temps et roman*, p.90.
④ Barthes, "An Introduction to the Structural Analysis of Narrative," p.263.

his discoveries and inductions until the final revelation.[1]

The inverse alteration, the excess of information or paralepsis, can consist of an inroad into the consciousness of a character in the course of a narrative generally conducted in external focalization. We can take to be such, at the beginning of the *Peau de chagrin*, statements like "the young man did not *understand* his ruin" or "he *feigned* the manner of an Englishman",[2] which contrast with the very distinct course of external vision adopted until then, and which begin a gradual transition to internal focalization. Paralepsis can likewise consist, in internal focalization, of incidental information about the thoughts of a character other than the focal character, or about a scene that the latter is not able to see. We will describe as such the passage in *Maisie* devoted to Mrs. Farange's thoughts, which Maisie cannot know: "The day was at hand, and she saw it, when she should feel more delight in hurling Maisie at [her father] than in snatching her away."[3]

A final general comment before returning to Proustian narrative: we should not confuse the *information* given by a focalized narrative with the *interpretation* the reader is called on to give of it (or that he gives without being invited to). It has often been noted that Maisie sees or hears things that she does not understand but that the reader will decipher with no trouble. The eyes "opened wide with attention" of Charlus looking at Marcel at Balbec can, for the informed reader, be a sign, which completely escapes the hero, like the whole of the Baron's behavior with respect to him up to *Sodome I*. Bertil Romberg analyzes the case of a novel by J. P. Marquand, *H. M. Pulham*, *Esquire*, where the narrator, a trusting husband, is present at scenes between his wife and a male friend that he recounts without thinking anything amiss but whose meaning cannot escape the least subtle reader.[4] This excess of implicit information over explicit information is the basis of the whole play of what Barthes calls *indices*,[5] which functions just as well in external focalization: in "Hills Like White Elephants", Hemingway reports the conversation between his two characters while fully abstaining from interpreting it; so here it is as if the narrator, like Marquand's hero, did not understand what he relates; this in no way prevents the reader from interpreting it in conformity with the author's intentions, as each time a novelist writes "he felt a cold sweat run down his back" we unhesitatingly construe "he was afraid". Narrative always says less than it knows, but it often makes known more than it says.

Polymodality

Let us repeat it again: use of the "first person", or better yet, oneness of person of the narrator

---

① Another unmistakable paralipsis, in *Michel Strogoff*: staring with Part II, Chapter 6. Jules Verne conceals from us what the hero knows very well, viz., that he was not blinded by Ogarett's incandescent sword.

② Garnier, p.10.

③ Henry James, What Maisie Knew (New York: Scribner's, 1908), p.19.

④ Romberg, p.119.

⑤ Barthes, "An Introduction to the Structural Analysis of Narrative," p.247.

and the hero,[①] does not at all imply that the narrative is focalized through the hero. Very much to the contrary, the "autobiographical" type of narrator, whether we are dealing with a real or a fictive autobiography, is—by the very fact of his oneness with the hero—more "naturally" authorized to speak in his own name than is the narrator of a "third-person" narrative. There is less indiscretion from Tristram Shandy in mixing the account of his present "opinions" (and thus of his knowledge) with the narrative of his past "life" than there is on Fielding's part in mixing the account of *his* with the narrative of the life of Tom Jones. The impersonal narrative therefore tends toward internal focalization by the simple trend (if it is one) toward discretion and respect for what Sartre would call the "freedom"—in other words, the ignorance—of its characters. The autobiographical narrator, having no obligation of discretion with respect to himself, does not have this kind of reason to impose silence on himself. The only focalization that he has to respect is defined in connection with his present information as narrator and not in connection with his past information as hero.[②] He *can*, if he wants, choose this second form of focalization (focalization through the hero), but he is not at all required to; and we could just as well consider this choice, when it is made, as a paralipsis, since the narrator, in order to limit himself to the information held by the hero at the moment of the action, has to suppress all the information he acquired later, information which very often is vital.

It is obvious (and we have already seen one example) that Proust to a great extent imposed that hyperbolic restriction on himself, and that the narrative mood of the *Recherche* is very often internal focalization through the hero.[③] In general it is the "hero's point of view" that governs the narrative, with his restrictions of field, his momentary ignorances, and even what the narrator inwardly looks on as his youthful errors, naivetés, "illusions to lose". In a famous letter to Jacques Riviere, Proust insisted on his carefulness in dissimulating what was at the back of his mind (identified here with the mind of Marcel-narrator) up until the moment of the final revelation. The apparent meaning of the final pages of *Swann* (which, we must remember, tell an experience in principle very recent) is, he says forcefully,

> the opposite of my conclusion. It is a stage, seemingly subjective and amateurish, on the way to the most objective and non-foolish conclusion. If one inferred from it that my meaning is a disillusioned skepticism, that would absolutely be as if a viewer, at the end of the first act of

① Or (as we will see in the following chapter) of the narrator and an observer of the Watson type.

② Of course, this distinction is relevant only for the classical form of autobiographical narrative, where the narrating is enough subsequent to the events for the narrator's information to differ appreciably from the hero's. When the narrating is contemporaneous with the story (interior monologue, journal, correspondence), internal focalization on the narrator amounts to focalization on the hero. J. Rousset shows this well for the epistolary novel (*Forme et signification*, p.70). We will come back to this point in the following chapter.

③ We know that he was interested in the Jamesian technique of point of view, and especially the technique in *Maisie* [Walter Berry, *N.R.F.*, *hommage a Marcel Proust* (Paris: Gallimard, 1927), p.73].

> *Parsifal*, after seeing a character understand nothing of the ceremony and be chased off by Gurnemanz, assumed that Wagner meant that simplicity of heart leads to nothing.

Similarly, the experience of the madeleine (it too, however, is recent) is reported in *Swann*, but not explained, since the profound reason for the pleasure of the reminiscence is not disclosed:"I will not explain it until the end of the third volume." For the moment, one must respect the hero's ignorance, and deal carefully with the evolution of his thought and the slow work of vocation.

> But this evolution of a thought, I did not want to analyze it abstractly but to recreate it, make it live. So I am forced to paint the mistakes, without thinking I have to say that I take them for mistakes; too bad for me if the reader thinks I take them for the truth. The second volume will accentuate this misunderstanding. I hope that the last will dissipate it.①

We know that the last did not dissipate all of it. This is the obvious risk of focalization, a risk that Stendhal pretended to insure himself against by means of notes on the bottom of the page:"It is the opinion of the hero, who is mad and will reform."

It is obviously with respect to the main point—that is, with respect to the experience of involuntary memory, and the literary vocation connected to it—that Proust was most careful in handling the focalization, forbidding himself to give any premature sign, any indiscreet encouragement. The "proofs" of Marcel's inability to write, of his incurable dilettantism, of his growing distaste for literature, do not stop accumulating until the dramatic peripeteia in the courtyard of the Guermantes townhouse—all the more dramatic since the suspense has been built up for a long time by a focalization that on this point was very rigorous. But the principle of nonintervention bears on many other subjects—like homosexuality, for example, which, despite the premonitory scene of Montjouvain, will remain for the reader as for the hero, until the opening pages of Sodome, a continent one-hundred times met but never recognized.

The most massive investment in this narrative course (that is focalization through the hero) is undoubtedly the handling of the amorous relationships of the hero, and also of that second-degree hero, Swann, in *Un amour de Swann*. Here internal focalization recovers the psychological function that the Abbe Prevost had given it in Manon Lescaut: systematically adopting the "point of view" of one of the protagonists permits an author to leave the feelings of the other one almost completely in shadow, and thus to construct for that other, at little cost, a mysterious and ambiguous personality, the very one for which Proust will coin the name "creature in flight" (fugitive). We do not know, at each state of their passion, any more than Swann or Marcel knows about the inner "truth" of an

① *Choix de lettrcs*, ed. Philip Kolb (Paris, 1965), 7 February 1914, pp.197－199.

Odette, a Gilberte, an Albertine, and nothing could more effectively illustrate the essential subjectivity of love according to Proust than that constant evanescence of its object: the creature in flight is by definition the creature loved.[①] Let us not take up again here the list (already evoked apropos of analepses with a corrective function) of episodes (first meeting with Gilberte, false confession of Albertine, incident of the syringas, etc.) whose real significance will not be discovered by the hero—and with him by the reader—until long after.

To these temporary ignorances or misunderstandings we must add some points of definitive opaqueness, where the perspectives of hero and narrator coincide; for instance, we will never know what Odette's "true" feelings for Swann were, or Albertine's for Marcel. A passage in the *Jeunes Filles en fleurs* illustrates well this somewhat interrogative attitude of the narrative in the face of those impenetrable creatures, when Marcel, dismissed by Albertine, wonders for what reason the girl could possibly have refused him a kiss after a series of such clear advances:

> of her attitude during that scene I could not arrive at any satisfactory explanation. Taking first of all the supposition that she was absolutely chaste (a supposition with which I had originally accounted for the violence with which Albertine had refused to let herself be taken in my arms and kissed, though it was by no means essential to my conception of the goodness, the fundamentally honourable character of my friend), I could not accept it without a copious revision of its terms. It ran so entirely counter to the hypothesis which I had constructed that day when I saw Albertine for the first time. Then ever so many different acts, all acts of kindness towards myself (a kindness that was caressing, at times uneasy, alarmed, jealous of my predilection for Andree) came up on all sides to challenge the brutal gesture with which, to escape from me, she had pulled the bell. Why then had she invited me to come and spend the evening by her bedside? Why had she spoken all the time in the language of affection? What object is there in your desire to see a friend, in your fear that he is fonder of another of your friends than of you; why seek to give him pleasure, why tell him, so romantically, that the others will never know that he has spent the evening in your room, if you refuse him so simple a pleasure and if to you it is no pleasure at all? I could not believe, all the same, that Albertine's chastity was carried to such a pitch as that, and I had begun to ask myself whether her violence might not have been due to some reason of coquetry, a disagreeable odour, for instance, which she suspected of lingering about her person, and by which she was afraid that I might be disgusted, or else of cowardice, if for instance she imagined, in her ignorance of the facts of love, that my state of nervous exhaustion was due to something contagious, communicable to her in a kiss.[②]

① On Marcel's ignorance with respect to Albertine, see Tadié, pp.40 - 42.

② RH I, 703 - 704/P I, 940 - 941.

Again, we must interpret as indices of focalization those openings onto the psychology of characters other than the hero which the narrative takes care to make in a more or less hypothetical form, as when Marcel guesses or conjectures the thought of his interlocutor according to the expression on that person's face:

> I could see in Cottard's eyes, as uneasy as though he were afraid of missing a train, that he was asking himself whether he had not allowed his natural good-humour to appear. He was trying to think whether he had remembered to put on his mask of coldness, as one looks for a mirror to see whether one has not forgotten to tie one's tie. In his uncertainty, and, so as, whatever he had done, to put things right, he replied brutally.①

Since Spitzer,② critics have often noted the frequency of those modalizing locutions (*perhaps*, *undoubtedly*, *as if*, *seem*, *appear*) that allow the narrator to say hypothetically what he could not assert without stepping outside internal focalization; and thus Marcel Muller is not wrong in looking on them as "the alibis of the novelist"③ imposing his truth under a somewhat hypocritical cover, beyond all the uncertainties of the hero and perhaps also of the narrator. For here again the narrator to some extent shares the hero's ignorance; or, more exactly, the ambiguity of the text does not allow us to decide whether the *perhaps* is an effect of indirect style—and, thus, whether the hesitation it denotes is the hero's alone. Further, we must note that the often *multiple* nature of these hypotheses much weakens their function as unavowed paralepsis, while at the same time it accentuates their role as indicators of focalization. When the narrative offers us, introduced by three *perhaps's*, three explanations to choose from for the brutality with which Charlus answers Mme. de Gallardon,④ or when the silence of the elevator operator at Balbec is ascribed with no preference to eight possible causes,⑤ we are not in fact any more "informed" than when Marcel questions himself before us on the reasons for Albertine's refusal. And here we can hardly go along with Muller, who reproaches Proust for replacing "the secret of each creature with a series of little secrets": Proust, in giving the idea that the real motive is necessarily found among those he enumerates, thus suggests, according to Muller, that "the behavior of a character is always! amenable to a rational explanation".⑥ The multiplicity of contradictory hypotheses suggests much more the insolubility off the problem, and at the very least the incapacity of the narrator to resolve it.

---

① RH I, 381/P I, 498. Cf. an analogous scene with Norpois, RH I, 367/P I, 478 - 479.

② Leo Spitzer, "Zum Stil Marcel Prousts," in *Stilstudien* (Munich, 1928); trans. in *Eludes de style* (Paris, 1970), pp.453 - 455.

③ *Voix narratives*, p.129.

④ RH II. 41/P II, 653.

⑤ "He vouchsafed no answer, whether from astonishment at my words, preoccupation with what he was doing, regard for convention, hardness of hearing, respect for holy ground, fear of danger, slowness of understanding, or by the manager's orders"(RH I, 505/P I, 665).

⑥ *Voix narratives*, p.128.

We have already noted the highly subjective nature of Proustian descriptions, always bound to a perceptual activity of the hero's.① Proustian descriptions are rigorously focalized: not only does their "duration" never exceed that of real contemplation, but their content never exceeds what is actually perceived by the contemplator. Let us not come back to this subject, which is well-understood;② let us simply recall the symbolic importance in the *Recherche* of scenes to which the hero, through an often miraculous chance, comes unexpectedly, and of which he perceives only one part, and whose visual or auditory restriction the narrative scrupulously respects: Swann in front of the window which he takes for Odette's, able to see nothing between the "slanting bars of the shutters", but only to hear, "in the silence of the night, the murmur of conversation";③ Marcel at Montjouvain, witness through the window of the scene between the two young women but unable to make out Mile. Vinteuil's look or hear what her friend murmurs in her ear, and for whom the scene will stop when she comes, seeming "weary, awkward, preoccupied, sincere, and rather sad", to close the shutters and the window;④ Marcel again, spying from the top of the staircase, then from the neighboring shop, on the "conjunction" of Charlus and Jupien, the second part of which will be reduced for him to a purely auditory perception;⑤ Marcel still, coming unexpectedly on Charlus's flagellation in Jupien's male bordello via a "small oval window opening onto the corridor".⑥ Critics generally insist, and rightly so, on the unlikelihood of these situations,⑦ and on the hidden strain they inflict on the principle of point of view; but we should first recognize that here, as in any fraud, there is an implicit recognition and confirmation of the code: these acrobatic indiscretions, with their so marked restrictions of field, attest to the difficulty the hero experiences in satisfying his curiosity and in penetrating into the existence of another. Thus they are to be set down to internal focalization.

As we have already had occasion to note, the observance of this code goes sometimes so far as to become that form of hyper-restriction of field that we call paralipsis: the end of Marcel's passion for the Duchess, Swann's death, the episode of the little girl-cousin at Combray have provided us with some examples. It is true that the existence of these paralipses is known to us only by the disclosure made later by the narrator—is made known, thus, by an intervention that, for its part, would be due to paralepsis if we considered focalization through the hero to be what the autobiographical form requires. But we have already seen that this is not so, and that that very widespread idea follows simply from an equally widespread confusion between the two. The only

① Pp.99 - 106.

② On the "perspectivism" of Proustian description, see Raimond, pp.338 - 343.

③ RH I, 209 - 211/P I, 272 - 275.

④ RH I, 122 - 125/P I, 159 - 163.

⑤ RH II, 8 - 9/P II. 609 - 610.

⑥ RH II, 959/P III, 815.

⑦ Beginning with Proust himself, anxious to forestall criticism (and to divert suspicion): "Certainly, the affairs of this sort of which I have been a spectator have always been presented in a setting of the most imprudent and least probable character, as if such revelations were to be the reward of an action full of risk, though in part clandestine." (RH II, 6/P II, 608.)

focalization logically implied by the "first-person" narrative is focalization through the narrator, and we shall see that in the *Recherche* this second narrative mood coexists with the first.

One obvious manifestation of this new perspective is the *advance notices* we met in the chapter on order. When it is said, apropos of the scene at Montjouvain, that later this scene will exert a decisive influence on the hero's life, such notification cannot be the hero's doing, but must of course be the narrator's—like, more generally, all forms of prolepsis, which (except for an intervention of the supernatural, as in prophetic dreams) always exceed a hero's capacities for knowledge. Likewise, complementary information introduced by locutions of the type "*I have learned since*..."[①]—which belongs to the subsequent experience of the hero, in other words, to the experience of the narrator arises from anticipation. It is not correct to set such interventions down to the "omniscient narrator": [②] they represent simply the autobiographical narrator's share in the report of facts still unknown to the hero, but the narrator does not think himself obliged on that account to put off mentioning them until the hero should have acquired knowledge of them. Between the information of the hero and the omniscience of the novelist is the information of the narrator, who disposes of it according to his own lights and holds it back only when he sees a precise reason for doing so. The critic can contest the opportuneness of these complements of information, but not their legitimacy or their credibility in a narrative whose form is autobiographical.

Further, we must certainly recognize that this holds true not only for prolepses giving explicit and avowed information. Even Marcel Muller notes that a formula like "I was ignorant that..."[③]—a real defiance of focalization through the hero—"can mean *I have learned since*, and with these two *I's* we would unquestionably be kept on the Protagonist's plane. The ambiguity is frequent," he adds, "and the choice between Novelist and Narrator for the attribution of a given item of information is often arbitrary."[④] It seems to me that methodological *soundness* here forces us, at least for a preliminary period, to attribute to (omniscient) "Novelist" only what we really cannot attribute to the narrator. We see in this case that a certain amount of information which Muller attributes to the "novelist who can walk through walls"[⑤] can be ascribed without prejudice to the later knowledge of the Protagonist: for instance, Charlus's visits to Brichot's class, or the scene that unfolds at Berma's while Marcel attends the Guermantes matinee, or even the dialogue between the relatives on the evening of Swann's visit, if indeed the hero really could not hear it at the

① RH I, 148/P I, 193; RH I, 1057/P II, 475; RH I, 1129/P II, 579; RH II, 290/P II, 1009; RH II, 506/P III, 182; RH II, 607/P III, 326; RH II, 995/P III, 864, etc. It is different for information of the type *I had been told that*... (as for *Un amour de Swann*), which is one of the hero's modes of knowledge (by hearsay).

② As Muller has correctly observed: "We are of course leaving aside the cases—fairly numerous—where the Narrator anticipates what is still the hero's future by drawing from what his own (the Narrator's) past is. In such cases there is no question of the Novelist's omniscience." (Voir *narratives*, p.110.)

③ RH I, 1111/P II, 554; RH II. 288/P II, 1006.

④ *Voix narratives*, pp.140 – 141.

⑤ *Voix narratives*, p.110.

time.[1] Similarly, many details about the relations between Charlus and Morel can in one way or another have come to the narrator's knowledge.[2] The same hypothesis holds for Basin's infidelities, his conversion to Dreyfusism, his late liaison with Odette, for M. Nissim Bernard's unhappy love affairs, etc.[3]—so many indiscretions and so much gossip, whether true or false, are not at all improbable in the Proustian universe. Let us remember finally that it is to a tale of this kind that the hero's knowledge of the past love between Swann and Odette is attributed, a knowledge so precise that the narrator thinks he has to make excuses for it in a way that may seem rather clumsy,[4] and that furthermore does not spare the only hypothesis capable of accounting for the focalization through Swann in this narrative within the narrative: namely, that whatever the eventual way stations, the first source can only have been Swann himself.

The real difficulty arises when the narrative reports to us, on the spot and with no perceptible detour, the thoughts of another character in the course of a scene where the hero himself is present: Mme. de Cambremer at the Opera, the usher at the Guermantes soirée, the historian of the Fronde or the librarian at the Villeparisis matinée, Basin or Bréauté in the course of the dinner at Oriane's.[5] In the same way we have access, without any apparent way station, to Swann's feelings about his wife or to Saint-Loup's about Rachel,[6] and even to the last thoughts of Bergotte on his deathbed,[7] which, as has often been noted, cannot in point of fact have been reported to Marcel since no one—for a very good reason—could have knowledge of them. That is one paralepsis to end all paralepses; it is irreducible by any hypothesis to the narrator's information, and one we must indeed attribute to the "omniscient" novelist—and one that would be enough to prove Proust capable of transgressing the limits of his own narrative "system".

But evidently we cannot restrict the part played by paralepsis to this scene alone, on the pretext that this is the only one to present a physical impossibility. The decisive criterion is not so much material possibility or even psychological plausibility as it is textual coherence and narrative tonality. Thus, Michel Raimond attributes to the omniscient novelist the scene during which Charlus takes Cottard into a nearby room and talks to him without witnesses.[8] In principle nothing prohibits us from assuming that this dialogue, like others,[9] was reported to Marcel by Cottard himself, but nonetheless the reading of this passage gives the idea of an immediate narrating without way stations and the same is true for all those that I mentioned in the preceding paragraph, and for some others

---

① RH II, 583/P III, 291-292; RH II, 1098-1101/P III, 995-999; RH I, 26-27/P I,35.
② Including the risqué scene of the Maineville bordello, the account of which is vouched for (RH II, 343/P II, 1082).
③ RH II, 101/P II, 739; RH II, 1113-1115/P 01, 1015-1018; RH II, 182/P II, 854-855.
④ RH I, 143/P I, 186.
⑤ RH I, 753-754/P II, 56-57; RH II, 29/P II, 636; RH I, 869/P II, 215; RH I, 893/P II, 248; RH I, 1090/P II, 524; RH I, 1025-1026/P II, 429-430.
⑥ RH I, 398-401/P I, 522-525; RH I, 801/P Ⅱ, 122; RH I, 826/P II, 156; RH I, 830-831/P II, 162-163.
⑦ RH II, 509/P III, 187.
⑧ RH II, 335-336/P II, 1071-1072. Raimond, p.337.
⑨ For example, the conversation between the Verdurins about Saniette, RH II, 607/P III, 326.

as well. In all these Proust manifestly forgets or neglects the fiction of the autobiographical narrator and the focalization which that implies—and a fortiori the focalization through the hero that is its hyperbolic form—in order to handle his narrative in a third mood, which is obviously zero-focalization, in other words, the omniscience of the classical novelist. Which, let us note in passing, would be impossible if the Recherche were—as some people still want to see it—a true autobiography. Whence these scenes—scandalous, I would imagine, for the purists of "point of view"—where I and other are handled on the same footing, as if the narrator had exactly the same relationship to a Cambremer, a Basin, a Bréauté, and his own past "me": "Mme. de Cambremer remembered having heard Swann say... / For myself, the thought of the two cousins... / Mme. de Cambremer was trying to make out exactly how... / For my own part, I never doubted..."① Plainly such a text is constructed on the antithesis between Mme. de Cambremer's thoughts and Marcel's, as if somewhere there existed a point from which my thought and someone else's thought would seem symmetrical to me—the height of depersonalization, which unsettles a little the image of the famous Proustian subjectivism. Whence further that scene at Montjouvain, in which we have already noted the very rigorous focalization (through Marcel) with respect to visible and audible actions, but which for thoughts and feelings, on the other hand, is entirely focalized through Mile. Vinteuil: ② "she felt... she thought... she felt that she had been indiscreet, her sensitive heart took fright... she pretended... she guessed... she realised..."—as if the witness could neither see all nor hear all, and nevertheless divined all the thoughts. But the truth quite obviously is that two concurrent codes are functioning here on two planes of reality which oppose each other without colliding.

This *double focalization*③ certainly corresponds to the antithesis organizing the entire passage (like the entire character of Mile. Vinteuil, "shy maiden" and "battered old campaigner"), an antithesis between the brutal immorality of the actions (perceived by the hero-witness) and the extreme delicacy of the feelings, which only an omniscient narrator, capable like God himself of seeing beyond actions and of sounding body and soul, can reveal.④ But this scarcely conceivable coexistence can serve as an emblem of the whole of Proust's narrative practice, which plays without a qualm, and as if without being aware of it, in three modes of focalization at once, passing at will from the consciousness of his hero to that of his narrator, and inhabiting by turns that of his most diverse characters. This triple narrative position is not at all comparable to the simple omniscience of

---

① RH I, 754/P II, 57.

② With the exception of one sentence (RH I, 125/P I, 163) focalized through her friend, a "probably" (RH I, 123/P I, 161), and a "may well have" (RH I, 125/P I, 162). [Translator's note: partly my translation.]

③ B. G. Rogers, *Proust's Narrative Techniques* (Geneva, 1965), p.108, speaks of "double vision" apropos of the concurrence between the "subjective" hero and the "objective" narrator.

④ On the technical and psychological aspects of this scene, see Midler's excellent commentary (pp.148 – 153), which, in particular, points out well how the hero's mother and grandmother are indirectly but closely implicated in this act of filial "sadism", whose personal resonances in Proust are immense and which obviously recalls the "Confession d'une jeune fille" of *Les Plaisirs et les jours*, and the "Sentiments filiaux d'un parricide".

the classical novel, for it not only defies, as Sartre reproached Mauriac for defying, the conditions of the realistic illusion: it also transgresses a "law of the spirit" requiring that one cannot be inside and outside at the same time. To resume the musical metaphor used above, we could say that between a tonal (or modal) system with respect to which all infractions (paralipses and paralepses) can be defined as alterations, and an atonal (amodal?) system where no code prevails anymore and where the very notion of infraction becomes outworn, the *Recherche* illustrates quite well an intermediary state: a plural state, comparable to the polytonal (polymodal) system ushered in for a time, and in the very same year, 1913, by the *Rite of Spring*. One should not take this comparison too literally;[①] let it at least serve us to throw light on this typical and very troubling feature... of Proustian narrative, which we would like to call its *polymodality*.

Let us recall to finish this chapter that this ambiguous—or rather, complex—and deliberately nonorganized position, characterizes not only the system of focalization but the entire modal practice of the *Recherche*: at the level of the narrative of actions, the paradoxical coexistence of the greatest mimetic intensity and the presence of a narrator, which is in principle; contrary to novelistic mimesis; the dominance of direct discourse, intensified by the stylistic autonomy of the characters (the height of dialogic mimesis) but finally absorbing the characters in an immense verbal game (the height of literary gratuitousness, the antithesis of realism); and, finally, the concurrence of theoretically incompatible focalizations, which shakes the whole logic of narrative representation. Again and again we have seen this subversion of mood tied to the activity, or rather the presence, of the narrator himself, the disturbing intervention of the narrative source—of the narrating in the narrative. It is this last instance—that of *voice*—which we must now look at for its own sake, after having met it so often without wanting to.

三、思考与讨论

(1) 热奈特的"聚焦"概念与传统的"视角"概念相比,有何独特性?

(2) 判断零聚焦、内聚焦、外聚焦的标准是什么?

(3) 从叙事的故事层和话语层来说,聚焦存在于哪个层面?

本章推荐阅读书目

[1] Roland Barthes. "Introduction to the Structural Analysis of Narrative," *Image Music*

① We know [George Painter, *Proust: The Later Years* (New York: Atlantic-Little, Brown, 1965), pp.340 - 342] what a fiasco the meeting arranged in May 1922 between Proust and Stravinsky (and Joyce) was. We could just as well draw a parallel between Proustian narrative practice and those multiple and superimposed visions so well expressed, still in the same period, by Cubism. Is it that kind of portrait that these lines from the preface to *Propos de peintre* refer to: "the admirable Picasso, who, in fact, has concentrated all Cocteau's features in a portrait of such noble rigidity ..." (*Essais et articles*, Pléiade, p.580; "Preface to Jacques Emile Blanche's Propos de Peintre: De David à Degas," in *Proust: A Selection*, p.253.)

Text. Eds. Roland Barthes. Trans. Stephen Heath. London: Fontana Press, 1977:79-124.

[2] Seymour Chatman. *Story and Discourse: Narrative Structure in Fiction and Film*. Ithaca: Cornell University Press, 1978.

[3] Jonathan Culler. *Structuralist Poetics: Structuralism, Linguistics and the Study of Literature* (2nd Ed.). London and New York: Routledge, 2002.

[4] Shilomith Rimmmon-Kenan. *Narrative Fiction: Contemporary Poetics* (2nd edition). London and New York: Routledge, 2002.

[5] Gerald Prince. *Narratology: The Form and Function of Narrative*. Berlin: Mouton, 1982.

第二章
修辞叙事学

第一节　概　　论

作为当代西方后经典叙事学阵营中最具系统性的派别之一，修辞叙事学被视为"20 世纪 90 年代以来发展较快、影响较大的后经典叙事学派"。[①]修辞叙事学是修辞学与叙事学相结合的产物，其主要理论来源为盛行于 20 世纪 40 年代美国学界的芝加哥学派，其以考察叙事文本中多重的修辞交流为旨趣，注重叙事交流的目的和语境。就其学理基础和研究视角而言，修辞叙事学主要有三个重要的分支：以罗纳德·克莱恩(Ronald Crane)、韦恩·布斯和詹姆斯·费伦为代表的将新亚里士多德诗学作为基础的芝加哥学派修辞叙事学；以梅尔·斯滕伯格为代表的将功能主义和叙述交际作为基础的特拉维夫学派修辞叙事学；以理查德·沃尔什和迈克尔·卡恩斯(Michael Kearns)为代表的从语言学角度出发的修辞叙事学。

一、修辞叙事学流派

20 世纪四五十年代，以芝加哥大学为中心的一批学者挑战了当时文学批评界重历史而轻文本的传统，号召将研究的重心转向文本本身。这一批学者以亚里士多德的《诗学》的基本原则为指导，着力建构不同文类的诗学，以此为模式探讨文本内部各种结构因素之间的关系、发生作用的方式以及产生的效果和原因。这一学派成为学界公认的"新亚里士多德"(neo-Aristotelian)学派，也被称为"芝加哥学派"。由克莱恩主编的《批评家与批评》(*Critics and Criticism*，1952)集中阐释和表达了这一学派的原则、宗旨和方法。在劳特利奇出版社重磅推出的《20 世纪人文学的理论学派和学术圈》(*Theoretical Schools and Circles in the Twentieth-Century Humanities*，2015)一书中，修辞叙事学的领军人物费伦系统梳理了历代芝加哥学派之间的承袭关系。国内学者申丹在《西方文论关键词：修辞性叙事学》一文中也以芝加哥学派的发展为中轴，对几代芝加哥学派修辞叙事学做出了历时性的综述和分析。从克莱恩、布斯到至今依然十分活跃的费伦，芝加哥学派的批评者们对小说文类、情节、叙事交流模式、作者、读者、虚构性等概

---

① 申丹、王丽亚：《西方叙事学：经典与后经典》，北京：北京大学出版社，2010 年，第 171 页。

念进行了广泛而深入的研究。依照其研究思想和方法的变化轨迹，芝加哥学派修辞叙事学大致可以分为四代：芝加哥学派第一代以克莱恩为代表，其由历史研究转向文本研究，注重探究情节、人物等结构因素和其产生的效果，着力建构文本诗学；第二代以布斯为代表，其由文本研究转向了作者和读者的修辞交流研究，主要探究文本内部隐含作者通过叙事技巧与隐含读者的交流，着力研究作者通过什么叙事方式、采用哪些叙事技巧影响读者从而达到自身的修辞目的；第三代以费伦为代表，其转向更为全面、多维和动态的修辞交流研究，主要探究作者、文本和读者之间的多层次动态修辞交流；第四代学者更具开拓性，着力打破一些研究传统，建构新的阐释和研究框架。四代学者们在不同社会历史语境的影响或制约下，以不同的方法及视角建构和发展了修辞叙事学。

芝加哥学派的第一代继承了亚里士多德将文学视为模仿的理念，反对文学的历史研究，注重文本内部结构因素之间的关系以及产生文本效果的多种原因。较之发轫于20世纪二三十年代的“新批评”，尽管芝加哥学派也持有形式决定内容的观点，但这一学派旨在找寻能够阐释所有文类的批评方法，将情节、人物等文本结构因素置于语言之上，认为这些因素支撑起整个艺术作品。芝加哥学派的第一代的诗学分析以多元论(pluralism)为哲学基础，立足于隔绝文学作品与彼时的创作语境和过程，更适用于解释在任何时期的任何作品中都会保持不变的效果以及那些根据相同的艺术组合原则建构后的效果。[①]作为第一代的领袖和主力军，克莱恩通过其情节诗学观的阐释和分析展示了芝加哥学派的理论宗旨和方法。在克莱恩看来，情节通过一系列的因子决定了文学作品对读者的情感效果。我们首先应该把握小说的情节类型，即作品希望对读者产生的情感效果，才能评判作品中一些细节安排的优劣。在此基础上，克莱恩指出，情节包括对象(object)、方式(manner)和途径(means)三个元素，是作者在时间序列上创造的某种合成物。他进一步区分行动(action)、人物性格(character)和思想(thought)三种情节成分，并强调三种成分的有机结合构成完整而有序的整体情节，以特定的方式影响读者的情感和思维。[②]这种情节诗学观从文学作品的统一情感意图入手探究技巧，摒弃了先于作品存在的评判标准，影响了布斯、费伦等后几代芝加哥学派批评家。有鉴于此，芝加哥学派的文本诗学采取了以文本为唯一考虑的立场，着眼于文本中永恒的艺术结构，以文本类型组织原则为核心并以此统一文本细节。因此，它未能将文本外的因素纳入研究范围，在考察作者叙事技巧或意图和读者的多重反应以及二者之间的多层交流时缺乏足够的灵活性和阐释力。芝加哥学派的第二代主力军布斯意识到了这一弊端，以作者修辞意图为核心，将研究重点转向了作者影响控制读者的修辞技巧以及二者之间的修辞交流和效果。

布斯的《小说修辞学》是修辞叙事学的奠基之作，被誉为“小说美学的里程碑”，开辟了叙事研究的新路径。[③] 在这部著作中，布斯将叙事视为作者利用文本与读者进行的修辞交流行为，从对文本结构和其产生的效果的关注转向对作者与读者之间修辞交流的关注，着力探讨作者采用哪些手段或方式影响读者从而达到自己的修辞目的。在形式主义主导的学术环境下，布斯提出了“隐含作者”(implied author)这一重要的概念。这也是他对叙事学理论最为重要的贡献之一。布斯认为，“隐含作者”是作者写作时创造的一个有别于真实“自我”的隐含形象，是真实作者的“第二自我”，[④]兼具“创造文本的作者”

---

① Ronald Crane, “The Concept of Plot and the Plot of *Tom Jones*,” *Critics and Criticism*, ed. Ronald Crane (Chicago: University of Chicago Press, 1957), p.92.

② Ibid., pp.62-93.

③ 程锡麟：《当代美国小说理论》，北京：外语教学与研究出版社，2001年，第21—22页。

④ Wayne C. Booth, *The Rhetoric of Fiction* (Chicago: University of Chicago Press, 1983), pp.70-71.

和“隐含在文本中并由读者理解的规范”两个特征。[①]这一概念的提出不仅使得作者文本化，同时也能使布斯实现探讨作者与读者修辞交流的目的。“隐含作者”的提出使得布斯能在“新批评”和“新亚里士多德学派”两个对立流派之间找到结合点，达成某种妥协。前者致力于根除文本中作者的存在，后者则对作者角色的忽视感到不满。[②]同时，布斯强调隐含作者根据具体作品的特定需要以及针对特定的读者做出特定的文本选择。[③]有鉴于此，对于隐含作者所做出的“文本选择”以及修辞交流的考察需要相应的历史语境研究。因此，布斯在转向修辞交流关系的研究中具有了考虑历史语境的潜能。[④]为了区分隐含作者与叙述者，布斯还提出了“不可靠叙述”(unreliable narration)这一重要且具有争议的概念。在对叙述类型进行分类时，布斯指出隐含作者、叙述者、作品人物以及读者之间可能存在种种距离，并在探讨叙事者与隐含作者(或隐含读者)之间存在的距离时提出了著名的“不可靠叙述”：“当叙述者的言行与作品的范式(即隐含作者的范式)保持一致时，叙述者就是可靠的，否则就是不可靠的。”[⑤] 布斯将对于“不可靠叙述者”的判定标准限制于文本范围以内，排除了文本外“真实读者”的规范等因素。在1983年出版的《小说修辞学》第二版中，布斯撰写了后记，在对经典立场的反思基础上，向后经典立场迈开了步伐，“为后经典叙事理论的发展做了一定铺垫”。[⑥]

作为布斯的高足，费伦秉承了新亚里士多德学派前两代批评家的衣钵，成为第三代最为核心和重要的代表人物，促使叙事学完成了从经典到后经典的范式转移并使其迈向了一个新的发展阶段。较之经典叙事学，费伦的修辞叙事理论主要聚焦作者、文本和读者之间的多层次交流活动，考察交流背后作者和叙述者的多重目的，凭借“其综合性、动态性和开放性构成了西方后经典叙事理论的一个亮点”。[⑦] 他将叙事定义为“某人在某一场合为了某种目的告诉另一人发生了某件事”(Somebody telling somebody else on some occasion and for some purposes that something happened)。[⑧] 这一定义将叙事置于以(隐含)作者为主的修辞交流语境中，从而考察作者、叙述者、人物以及读者之间的多层次交流活动。它既涉及人物、事件和叙述的动态进程，也涉及读者反应的动态进程，将作者、文本和读者全面纳入考察范围，并平衡了三者之间的关系。费伦的叙事观拓展了叙事的概念，从布斯的模式转向了关注作者代理、文本现象和读者反应之间交互、协同作用的循环交流的互动型修辞模式。在此基础上，他拓展和阐释了六个核心论题：叙事进程(narrative progression)、人物叙述(character narration)、不可靠叙述(unreliable narration)、叙述聚焦(focalization)、叙事判断(narrative judgment)以及叙事伦理(narrative ethics)。其中，叙事进程和叙事判断是其修辞叙事理论的亮点和创举，也是探讨读者阅读体验的两条理论路径。以读者为取向的费伦以“进程”取代“情节”，指出叙事进程是“文本动力”(textual dynamics)(人物与人物以及人物与环境之间的不稳定因素)和“读者动力”(readerly dynamics)(读者与

① Wayne C. Booth, *The Rhetoric of Fiction* (Chicago: University of Chicago Press, 1983), p.83.

② 相关讨论参见申丹：《关于西方叙事理论新进展的思考：评国际上〈首部叙事理论指南〉》，载《外国文学》2006年第1期，第99页；Susan Lanser, *The Narrative Act: Point of View in Prose Fiction* (Princeton: Princeton University Press, 1981), p.49.

③ Booth, *The Rhetoric of Fiction*, p.71.

④ 参见 Shen Dan, "Implied Author, Authorial Audience, and Context: Form and History in Neo-Aristotelian Rhetorical Theory," *Narrative* 21.2 (2013), pp.149–151.

⑤ Booth, *The Rhetoric of Fiction*, pp.158–159.

⑥ 申丹：《西方文论关键词：修辞性叙事学》，载《外国文学》2020年第1期，第86页。

⑦ 申丹等：《英美小说叙事理论研究》，北京：北京大学出版社，2005年，第256页。

⑧ James Phelan, *Narrative as Rhetoric: Technique, Audiences, Ethics, Ideology* (Columbus: The Ohio State University Press, 1996), p.218.

叙述者以及读者与隐含作者之间的张力)共同作用的结果。[①]费伦的叙事进程概念不仅包括了文本因素,也涵盖了读者对叙事的阐释因素,具有较强的动态性和灵活性,在一定程度上超越了以往的情节诗学。此外,叙事判断也是费伦建构后经典叙事学理论的一个重要组成部分。叙事判断是读者对于叙事的反应结果,可分为三种基本类型:阐释判断(interpretive judgment)、伦理判断(ethical judgment)和审美判断(aesthetic judgment),三者相互影响。费伦随后提出了关于叙事判断的七个一般性命题,并以此阐释了叙事判断的主要类型和运作机制。费伦对于叙事进程和叙事判断两者间的关系并未给出实质性的阐释,但国内学者尚必武指出,二者首先是互为因果、互相依存的关系。叙事进程引发了叙事判断。随着叙事进程的变化,读者做出的叙事判断也会相应发生一定程度的改变;与此同时,叙事判断也推动着叙事的进程。[②]费伦的修辞叙事理论在继承前代对于修辞交流手段、目的和效果的研究外,凭借多维的人物观、读者观和动态的情节观,通过对作者代理、文本现象和读者反应之间的多层次关系研究呈现了较强的"理论感、层次感和系统性"。[③]值得一提的是,费伦笔耕不辍。在2017年的著作《某人向某人讲述:叙事的修辞诗学》(*Somebody Telling Somebody Else: A Rhetorical Poetics of Narrative*)中,他将人物的会话交流等以往被忽略的范畴纳入考察范围,并提出了新的叙事交流模式,从而不断拓展自己的研究疆域。

在梳理芝加哥学派时,费伦提及了迅猛发展(burgeoning)的第四代,并列举了五位批评家:约翰逊(Gary Johnson)、纳什(Katherine Nash)、申丹(Dan Shen)、拜拉姆(Katra Byram)和马什(Kelly Marsh)。[④]芝加哥学派的第四代学者的显著标识为"开拓创新"。[⑤]其中,中国学者申丹凭借其在著作《短篇叙事小说的文体与修辞》(*Style and Rhetoric of Short Narrative Fiction*,2013)中提出的"隐性进程"(covert progressions)位列其中。"隐性进程"指"一股自始至终在情节发展背后运行的强有力的叙事暗流"。[⑥]它与情节发展呈现出相异甚至相反的走向,在主题意义、人物形象和审美价值上形成对照补充或对立颠覆的关系。这一全新概念的提出不仅打破了自亚里士多德以来修辞叙事学聚焦情节发展的阐释框架和传统,而且拓展了修辞叙事学的研究范围。无论是对概念的重新定义、新概念的提出,还是将修辞理论与女性主义等其他流派相结合,第四代学者不断尝试打破传统,为修辞叙事学注入新的活力。

自20世纪60年代以来,依托以色列特拉维夫大学"波特诗学和符号学研究所"(Porter Institute for Poetics and Semiotics),一大批从事叙事理论研究的批评家在叙事学领域辛勤耕耘,并使得该研究所成为当代西方叙事学的一个"重镇",形成了独具特色的特拉维夫学派。有别于欧美叙事学派,特拉维夫学派建立了一套完整且独立的理论体系。该学派将文学文本视为意义单元的连续体,在修辞叙事研究中具有强烈的功能主义倾向,同时注重叙事的形式和功能两个维度,其理论建构深受现象学美学阅读理论的影响。第一代特拉维夫学派批评家的代表人物是斯滕伯格。斯滕伯格根据叙事功能的特点,提出了著名的"普罗吐斯原则"(Proteus Principle)。在斯滕伯格看来,不同语境中相同的叙事形式可以实

---

① Phelan, *Narrative as Rhetoric: Technique, Audiences, Ethics, Ideology*, p.90.

② 尚必武:《当代西方后经典叙事学研究》,北京:人民文学出版社,2013年,第87页。

③ 申丹、王丽亚:《西方叙事学:经典与后经典》,第192页。

④ Phelan, "The Chicago School: From Neo-Aristotelian Poetics to the Rhetorical Theory of Narrative," *Theoretical Schools and Circles in the Twentieth-Century Humanities*, eds. Marina Crishakova and Silvi Salupere (New York: Routledge, 2015), pp.148-149.

⑤ 申丹:《西方文论关键词:修辞性叙事学》,第92页。

⑥ 申丹:《西方文论关键词:隐性进程》,载《外国文学》2019年第1期,第82页。

现多种不同的功能，反之，相同的功能可以有不同的形式，即叙事功能和形式有多重的对应性。在此基础上，斯滕伯格对小说叙事的时间次序做了深入研究。他指出，在阅读时间轴上，读者在把握文本连续体的过程中会对文本产生对未来发生事件的“悬念”（suspense）、对过去曾经发生事件的“好奇”（curiosity）和对现在所发生事件结果的“惊讶”（surprise）三种阅读兴趣，从而使文本具有叙事动力。[①]受斯滕伯格理论的启发，第二代的代表批评家塔玛·雅克比（Tamar Yacobi）深入研究了叙事虚构作品的不可靠叙述，将读者的角色引入其中。在雅克比看来，不可靠性是读者在语境范式下的“推测手段”，在包括阅读语境以及作者和文类框架在内的语境里被视为“可靠”的东西，在另一个语境里有可能是不可靠的，甚至可以在叙述者的缺陷的范畴之外得到阐释。[②]为了进一步探讨读者角色之于文本的不一致性以及读者阅读假设，雅克比提出了五种“整合机制”（mechanisms of integration）：存在机制（existential mechanism）、功能原则（functional principle）、文类原则（generic framework）、视角或不可靠性机制（perspective mechanism or unreliability hypothesis）、生成机制（genetic mechanism）。[③]整合机制的提出打破了以往叙事学界一味地以修辞方法阐释不可靠叙述的范式和惯例，为认知方法的发端与塑形做了良好的铺垫。[④]特拉维夫学派在汲取欧美叙事理论思想养分的同时，不断地吸收认知科学的理论，在叙事理论体系上别具一格，彰显了其独特性与原创性。

与芝加哥学派和特拉维夫学派两大派系的学者不同，一部分叙事学家，诸如沃尔什和卡恩斯，从语言学视角出发建构“另类”的修辞叙事学。沃尔什的《虚构性修辞学》（*The Rhetoric of Fictionality*，2007）是修辞视角下虚构性研究的重要代表作。在沃尔什看来，我们不应该将虚构性简单地等同于“作为叙事范畴或文类的‘虚构作品’”。虚构性其实是一种在“许多非虚构作品中也比较明显的交流策略”。[⑤]受关联理论的启发，沃尔什将虚构性定义为一种语境假设，而不是一种将“虚构话语与一般或‘严肃’交流区隔的框架”。他进一步阐释道：“在理解虚构话语时，其虚构性本身是显映的。这一语境假设的主要效果是使依赖字面真实性的隐义从属于那些以更分散和累积的方式实现相关性的隐义。”[⑥]这种从文类界定转变为功能性概念的范式转化启发了许多学者对虚构性作为交际资源的探究，从而在一定程度上彰显了修辞的力量。就此而言，通过语用视角，沃尔什的虚构性研究为修辞叙事学开辟了新的领域。

在《修辞叙事学》（*Rhetorical Narratology*，1999）一书中，卡恩斯以言语行为理论为基础，将修辞学与结构主义两种方法有机结合，并在兰瑟、费伦、巴赫金、热奈特等学者理论的基础上建构自己的修辞叙事理论。卡恩斯强调语境对叙事的决定作用，认为“恰当的语境几乎可以让读者将任何文本都视为叙事文，而任何语言成分都无法保证读者这样接受文本”。[⑦]在卡恩斯看来，叙事是一种社会行为，且只有在特定的语境下才能发挥叙事功能。此外，卡恩斯还强调了“作者式阅读”（authorial reading）、“自然化”（naturalization）、“进程”（progression）和“语言杂多”（heteroglossia）四种基本规约，借助言语行为理论

① Meir Sternberg, “Telling in Time Telling in Time (II): Chronology, Teleology, Narrativity,” *Poetics Today* 13.3 (1992), p.529.
② Tamar Yacobi, “Authorial Rhetoric, Narratorial (Un) Reliability, Divergent Readings: Tolstoy's *Kreutzer Sonata*,” *A Companion to Narrative Theory*, eds. James Phelan and Peter J. Rabinowitz (Oxford: Blackwell, 2005), pp.110.
③ Ibid., pp.108 - 123.
④ 尚必武：《当代西方后经典叙事学研究》，第174页。
⑤ Richard Walsh, *The Rhetoric of Fictionality: Narrative Theory and the Idea of Fiction*, p.7.
⑥ Ibid., p.30.
⑦ Michael Kearns, *Rhetorical Narratology* (Lincoln and London: University of Nebraska Press, 1999), p.2.

中的“相关性原则”(principle of relevance)、“合作原则”(cooperative principle)和“标记性”(markedness)研究作品中文本与读者的修辞交流。卡恩斯的修辞叙事理论融合了言语行为理论、修辞学、女性主义叙事学、读者反应批评等各种相关理论,强调了语境、读者和规约,具有较强的全面性和包容性,但同时也出现了“在语境上走极端、对言语行为理论的局限性认识不清”等问题。[①]

二、修辞叙事学的重要概念

叙事性是“叙事”的衍生概念,出自结构主义叙事学,指的是叙事具备的一系列区别于非叙事的特征,即“叙事的特性”(the quality of being narrative)。[②]它是当代叙事学研究一个重要且颇具争议的概念,对叙事本质的理解以及叙事研究方法和目标的考察具有重要意义。在后经典叙事学阶段,叙事的范畴得到了扩展,叙事性的含义也随之发生了变化。就修辞叙事学而言,费伦和卡恩斯着眼于叙述交际对叙事性展开不同程度的探讨。费伦从叙事的修辞性定义入手,结合其修辞叙事理论的两大核心概念,即叙事进程和叙事判断,研究叙事性。在费伦看来,叙事性不仅涉及人物、事件、讲述行为的动力,也涉及读者反应的动力。叙事性的存在以及程度都与“文本动力”和“读者动力”两大因素密切相关。当文本动力和读者动力同时存在于文本中时,文本具有较强的叙事性;反之,任何一种动力的缺少都将使得文本具有较弱的叙事性。[③] 然而在卡恩斯看来,结构主义叙事学重点探讨了文本中叙事性的存在和程度,没有考虑语境的作用,且始终没有回答“形式特征如何影响读者对叙事的体验”这一问题。[④] 有鉴于此,卡恩斯从语境主义角度出发,认为叙事性是“语境的一个功能”。[⑤] 它并非存在于文本中,而来自“读者阐释叙事文的语境,这一语境包含一个阐释框架”。[⑥] 但值得注意的是,过分强调语境而忽视文本特征、文类规则、作者的创作等因素容易出现偏误,无法全面地考察叙事性。斯滕伯格则认为叙事性涉及在时间轴上读者的三种阅读兴趣的提升,即朝向未来的“悬念”、朝向过去的“好奇”以及面对现在的“惊讶”。[⑦]

自“隐含作者”这一概念提出后,叙事学领域不同流派对其定义、作用、意义等方面展开了激烈交锋。针对这一概念引起的争论,费伦总结并概括了五个相应的焦点:交际模式的准确有效性、交际模式中人物代理的角色、作者的意图、读者的角色以及叙事学与其他批评理论之间的关系。[⑧]此外,尚必武还补充道,争论的实质还在于“隐含作者的定义与来源、隐含作者之存在、划分隐含作者的参照物等方面”。[⑨] 对于拥护“隐含作者”的批评家而言,他们大都抵触或排斥真实作者。在布斯概念的基础上,西摩·查特曼做出了相关修正,提出了著名的叙事交流模式:[⑩]

---

① 申丹:《语境、规约、话语:评卡恩斯的修辞性叙事学》,载《外语与外语教学》2003年第1期,第9页。

② Gerald Prince, “Narrativity,” *Routledge Encyclopedia of Narrative Theory*, eds. David Herman, Manfred Jahn and Marie-Laure Ryan (London: Routledge, 2005), p.387.

③ James Phelan, *Experiencing Fiction: Judgments, Progressions, and the Rhetorical Theory of Narrative* (Columbus: The Ohio State University Press, 2007), p.215.

④ Kearns, *Rhetorical Narratology*, p.39.

⑤ Ibid., p.35.

⑥ Ibid., p.41.

⑦ Sternberg, “Telling in Time Telling in Time (II): Chronology, Teleology, Narrativity,” p.529.

⑧ Phelan, *Living to Tell about It: A Rhetoric and Ethics of Character Narration*, pp.44 - 45.

⑨ 尚必武:《当代西方后经典叙事学研究》,第152页。

⑩ Seymour Chatman, *Story and Discourse: Narrative Structure in Fiction and Film* (Ithaca: Cornell University Press, 1978), p.151.

叙事文本

真实作者⟶| 隐含作者⟶(叙述者)⟶(受述者)⟶隐含读者 |⟶真实读者

不难看出,查特曼将真实作者与真实读者置于叙事交流圈的外围,将隐含作者视为一种文本功能。在重视语境思潮的影响下,费伦则试图将禁锢在文本内的隐含作者解放,并试图给之一个连贯且能被广泛运用的定义。他指出,隐含作者是一个真实作者精简后的变体(a streamlined version),是真实作者能力、特点、态度、信仰、价值以及其他属性的真实子集或者虚构子集。这些属性在特定文本的建构中起到了积极的作用。在通常情况下,隐含作者是真实作者的能力、态度、信念、价值和其他特征的准确反映(accurate reflection);但在一些非常见但十分重要的情况下,真实作者建构出的隐含作者会有一个或一个以上的不同之处。[①] 费伦从根基上挑战了查特曼的模式,指出除了"作者—叙述者—读者"的交流渠道之外,还存在且不止一个"作者—人物—人物—读者"的交流渠道,它们在功能上独立且并列运行。[②] 然而申丹指出,费伦的定义仍然没有阐释作为真实作者创造的建构物如何成为生产者这一问题,也未能成功挽救隐含作者的主体性。在申丹看来,隐含作者和真实作者难以互相取代,二者的相似和差异有助于我们更加深入地阐释作品,因此我们应考虑二者的兼收。[③] 有鉴于此,她修正了西摩·查特曼的叙述交流模式:[④]

叙事文本

真实作者⟶隐含作者⟶(叙述者)⟶(受述者)⟶隐含读者⟶真实读者

尚必武认为,费伦和申丹二人的论述形成互补。因此,两相结合,不啻为我们在如何对待隐含作者这一问题上,提供了一道良策。[⑤]

不可靠叙述自布斯提出后已经"从一个边缘话题成为叙事学界广泛热议的中心话题"。[⑥] 修辞叙事学则是这一话题的主导研究范式。布斯对于不可靠叙述的研究聚焦在"事实"(facts)以及"价值"(values or ethics)两条轴线上,并由此阐释了隐含作者和读者之间的三种关系,即秘密交流(secret communication)、共谋(collusion)和协作(collaboration)。布斯指出,当读者发现叙述者在"事实"轴的报道或是"价值"轴的报道不可靠时,一定的反讽效果往往就会出现。作者是反讽效果的发出者,叙述者是反讽的对象,读者则是效果的接受者。[⑦] 费伦在至少三个方面对布斯的理论加以继承和拓展。首先,费伦将不可靠叙述的定义拓展至"事实/事件"和"价值/判断"轴外,增加了"知识/感知"(knowledge and perception)轴,并依照这三大轴提出了六种不可靠叙述的亚类型:错误的报道(misreporting)、错误的解读(misreading)、错误的判断(misevaluating/misregarding)、不充分的报道(underreporting)、不充分的解读(underreading)和不充分的判断(underregarding)。[⑧] 在费伦看来,这六种类型的不可靠叙述是平行关系,既可单独亦可同时发生。此外,费伦以叙述者与"作者的读者"(authorial audience)之间的叙述

---

① Phelan, *Living to Tell about It: A Rhetoric and Ethics of Character Narration*, p.45.
② James Phelan, "Authors, Resources, Audiences: Toward a Rhetorical Poetics of Narrative," *Style* 1 - 2.52(2018), pp.3 - 4.
③ 申丹等:《英美小说叙事理论研究》,第 396—397 页。
④ 同上,第 397 页。
⑤ 尚必武:《当代西方后经典叙事学研究》,第 153 页。
⑥ Tom Kindt and Tilmann Köppe, "Unreliable Narration," *Journal of Literary Theory* 5.1 (2011), p.1.
⑦ Booth, *The Rhetoric of Fiction*, pp.300 - 309.
⑧ Phelan, *Living to Tell about It: A Rhetoric and Ethics of Character Narration*, p.51.

距离为基准考量不可靠叙述，将其界定为“疏远型不可靠性”(estranging unreliability)和“契约型不可靠性”(bonding unreliability)。前者指的是不可靠叙述凸显或拉大了叙述者与“作者的读者”之间的距离，而后者则是缩短或拉近了两者的距离。[①] 费伦还将不可靠叙述与叙事伦理相关联，指出不可靠叙述影响了叙述者、人物、隐含作者和真实作者的“伦理取位”。[②] 费伦的后经典修辞叙事理论的特性使得其在建构不可靠叙述理论时拥有动态的视野，但同时也带来了一定的盲点。费伦的不可靠叙述理论建立于隐含作者这一概念之上，他聚焦于文本内的不可靠性，从而没有充分关注文本之外的读者认知心理对不可靠性的理解和阐释。这也成为雅克比和安斯加尔·纽宁发起对修辞方法挑战的导火索。

作为不可靠叙述研究的认知(建构)方法的创始人，雅克比将不可靠叙述界定为一种“阅读假设”，其研究焦点在于读者不同的阐释策略或框架之间的差别。她的五种整合机制说明了读者对于同一文本不一致的阐释，对于研究非虚构叙事作品(如传记、回忆录等)中的不可靠叙述也有重要的启发性。尽管雅克比在阐释不可靠叙述时也关注了隐含作者的规范，但她将这种规范视为读者建构的产物，并强调任何一种“阅读假设”都能被修正、颠覆甚至被另一种假设取代。[③] 但是认知(建构)方法仅仅考虑了读者的阐释框架，忽视了作者的角色和作用。为了克服这一盲点，纽宁试图提出不可靠叙述研究的综合方法——“认知-修辞”方法，从而协调统一“读者关怀”与“作者关怀”。在纽宁看来，“一个叙述者是否可靠不但取决于叙述者的范式价值与整个文本(或隐含作者)之间的距离，而且取决于叙述者的世界观与读者或批评家的世界模式和范式标准之间的距离，当然，这些范式标准本身又是不断变化的”。[④] 尽管许多学者纷纷指出综合认知与修辞方法的不可行性，但不可否认，不可靠叙述的运作涉及叙述者的表达、隐含作者的意图以及读者的参与，因此修辞方法与认知方法在一定程度上具有互补性。

自沃尔什的《虚构性修辞学》出版以来，修辞叙事学成为虚构性研究最有影响的方法之一，不仅使虚构性“再次成为叙事学研究者们讨论的一个热门话题”，也获得了众多的支持。[⑤] 尽管都身处修辞虚构性理论阵营，但不同学者有不同的出发点，例如沃尔什从语用学角度出发，借用关联理论核心思想与关键概念(如“语境假设”等)去阐释虚构性，尼尔森对于虚构性的阐释更多是从其对非自然叙事学的兴趣而来的，费伦则立足于其修辞诗学，代表了将新亚里士多德诗学作为基础的芝加哥学派修辞叙事学。虽然学者们的出发点和立足点不同，还存在对于虚构性定义、概念范围等的分歧；但总体而言，修辞虚构性理论已经拥有了较为鲜明和统一的理论倾向，并具有了与其他各派虚构性理论不同的特点。从交流行为层面入手，修辞叙事学批评家将虚构性视作严肃交流中不可或缺的修辞资源，并指出虚构性不只是小说等传统虚构文类的独有特质，还是在各类严肃话语中被广为使用的交流手段。在区分“虚构”(fiction)和“虚构性”(fictionality)时，尼尔森、费伦、沃尔什指出前者为一系列常规的文学类型，后者则广泛存在于严肃交流之中，而非某些文艺体裁(例如小说)独有的特质。基于此，尼尔森等人提出了关于虚构性的修辞问题，即“某人在何时、何地，因何故并以何种方式，针对哪些受众，去实现什么目标?”[When, where, why, and how does someone use fictionality in order to achieve what purpose(s) in

---

① Phelan, “Estranging Unreliability, Bonding Unreliability, and the Ethics of *Lolita*,” *Narrative* 15.2(2007), pp.223 - 225.

② Phelan, *Living to Tell about It: A Rhetoric and Ethics of Character Narration*, pp.56 - 57.

③ 更多请参见尚必武：《当代西方后经典叙事学研究》，第172—174页。

④ Nünning, “Reconceptualizing Unreliable Narration: Synthesizing Cognitive and Rhetorical Approaches,” p.95.

⑤ Sam Browse, Alison Gibbons and Mari Hatavara, “Real Fictions: Fictionality, Factuality and Narrative Strategies in Contemporary Storytelling,” *Narrative Inquiry* 29.2(2019), p.252.

relation to what audience(s)?]。[①] 有鉴于此,修辞虚构性理论能将虚构性的讨论从传统意义上的小说范畴延伸至小说之外的其他文类,并为研究多媒介虚构作品和非文学交流提供了适合的理论工具,有效地实现了虚构性研究的跨文类和跨媒介转向,拓展了虚构性研究的边界。

为加深对修辞叙事学理念的理解,本章选择了三篇经典文献,分别取自布斯的《小说修辞学》、费伦的《某人向某人讲述:叙事的修辞诗学》以及沃尔什的《虚构性修辞学》。

① 参见 Henrik Skov Nielsen, James Phelan and Richard Walsh, "Ten Theses about Fictionality," *Narrative* 23.1(2015), pp.62-63.

第二节 韦恩·布斯及其《小说修辞学》

一、导读

韦恩·布斯是西方最具影响力的批评家之一，在多个领域都卓有建树。布斯一生著述丰硕，著有《小说修辞学》、《反讽修辞学》(*A Rhetoric of Irony*，1974)、《批评的理解：多元论的力量与局限性》(*Critical Understanding: The Powers and Limits of Pluralism*，1979)、《我们的朋友：小说伦理学》(*The Company We Keep: An Ethics of Fiction*，1988)、《修辞的修辞学》(*Rhetoric of Rhetoric*，2004)等。其中，《小说修辞学》不仅提出了至今仍在热烈讨论和广泛使用的“隐含作者”的概念，还开辟了一条叙事研究的新路径，被誉为“小说美学的里程碑”[①]以及“当代修辞性叙事理论的奠基之作”[②]。在这一著作中，布斯将小说视为作者与读者的交流活动，其过程体现在作者运用各种叙事技巧邀请读者参与到与作者的交流中。有鉴于此，布斯的研究重点是小说的“技巧”以及在这一交流活动中作者的修辞手段如何实现其对读者的统一修辞意图。换言之，我们可以看出布斯的研究以“作者的修辞意图”为核心，并以其统一文本技巧，着眼于小说产生的效果、制造这些效果的叙事手段、作者对叙述目的的控制等。

在《小说修辞学》中，布斯提出和阐释了“隐含作者”这一重要且具有争议的概念。尽管早在1952年，布斯便已经提出了这一概念，但是《小说修辞学》的出版将“隐含读者”推至了学界并产生了巨大的影响力。[③] 在这一概念提出之前，提及某一具体文本的作者时，我们大都将其等同于真实作者本身，并将真实作者作为讨论文本作者是否严肃或真诚的参照。然而，布斯指出，作者在创作的时候，会创造出一个有别于真实自我的隐含形象，即“第二自我”。隐含作者便是真实作者的“第二自我”。[④] 在布斯看来，作者在创作时会脱离平时真实作者所处的状态，进入某种理想化的、文学的创作状态，这种文学创作状态的主体就是隐含作者。就其概念本质而言，布斯认为隐含作者是自己选择的总和，即自身在写作中做出的选择构成读者了解其形象的依据。它既是真实作者“第二自我”在作品创造中的主体，又是文本总体形式表达出来的意义及道德情感内涵。在隐含作者的感觉这一方面，读者不仅可从作品所有人物的行动和受难中得出意义，而且还可了解他们的道德和情感内容。[⑤] 值得注意的是，布斯强调的交流活动具有两个特征：首先，交流活动以作者为主导；其次，交流活动与隐含读者相呼应。布斯的读者是“隐含读者”，是脱离特定社会历史语境的读者，有别于有血有肉的真实读者。

谈及提出隐含作者这一概念的缘由，布斯在《隐含作者的复活：因何烦恼》(“Resurrection of the

---

① 程锡麟：《当代美国小说理论》，第21—22页。
② 申丹：《西方文论关键词：修辞性叙事学》，第86页。
③ 参见 Wayne Booth, “The Self-Conscious Narrator in Comic Fiction before *Tristram Shandy*,” *PMLA* 67.2(1952), pp.163-185.
④ Booth, *The Rhetoric of Fiction*, pp.70-71.
⑤ Ibid., pp.74-75.

Implied Author：Why Bother?”)中曾提及以下四个因素：① 对当时学界在进行小说批评时，一味追求所谓的“客观性”感到不满。在《小说修辞学》中，布斯就对此提出了质疑和批判。很多批评家指出，优秀的小说应该“展示”(showing)而非“讲述”(telling)故事，以便让读者做出所有的判断。小说家若要令人称道，就必须摒除一切公开表达作者观点的文字。所有的作家和读者都应该是客观的，令人称道的小说也必须是客观的。然而布斯认为，这种原则和立场不仅会贬低许多优秀的小说家，还会违背真正的诗意性质。② 对学生的误读感到烦恼。③ 为批评家忽略修辞伦理效果(作者与读者之间的纽带)的价值而感到“道德上的”苦恼。④ 布斯发现隐含作者有时候高我们一筹，而有时候又会低我们一等；我们面临的主要挑战是要辨别这张面具究竟是好还是坏，做文学批评时尤应如此。[①] 此外，许多学者指出其背后的社会历史原因，即“新批评”与“新亚里士多德学派”之间的较量促使布斯提出新的概念。提出基于文本的隐含作者一方面迎合了“新批评”的纯文本批评要求，另一方面也不违背“新亚里士多德学派”对作者立场的重视。[②]

通过考察《小说修辞学》诞生的理论背景我们不难发现，20 世纪 60 年代正是“新批评”盛行于美国学界的时候。该学派主张仅考虑文本自身的逻辑，发掘文本的内在结构和深层意蕴，撇开传统的“意图谬误”式的批评路径。然而布斯的小说修辞理论是建立在作者与读者交流的基础上的，因此“作者”这一概念有着举足轻重的地位。有鉴于此，布斯通过创造隐含作者这一概念，一方面强调了作为作者的修辞主体性质，另一方面又将其界定为“文本规范”，从而能在避免“作者意图谬误”的前提下实现研究作者与读者的交流的修辞目的，也能方便其后续通过隐含作者、叙述者、人物以及读者的交流互动发掘小说的伦理价值。尽管布斯在阐释隐含作者时还存在一定的盲点，这一概念自诞生以来也不断受到来自叙事学、解构主义等批评理论的挑战，甚至遭到了许多的误解，但我们不可否认它的实用价值和现实意义。隐含作者的提出和使用不仅有助于我们“拯救”作者，将具体作品的规范与真实作者区分开来，还能促使我们更细致地考察文本结构。就隐含作者未来的研究方向和态势而言，费伦提出亟待完成的三大任务：① 给隐含作者一个连贯且能被广为应用的新定义；② 给隐含作者在各种基本理论问题上提供一个连贯且使人信服的位置；③ 为解读不可靠叙述提供一个可行的模式。[③]

二、《小说修辞学》选读[④]

Neutrality and the Author's "Second Self"

Objectivity in the author can mean, first, an attitude of neutrality toward all values, an attempt at disinterested reporting of all things good and evil. Like many literary enthusiasms, the passion for neutrality was imported into fiction from the other arts relatively late. Keats was saying in 1818 the kind of thing that novelists began to say only with Flaubert. "The poetical character ... has no

① Wayne Booth, "Resurrection of the Implied Author: Why Bother?" *A Companion to Narrative Theory*, eds. James Phelan and Peter J. Rabinowitz (Oxford: Blackwell, 2005), pp.75 - 77.

② 相关讨论参见申丹：《关于西方叙事理论新进展的思考》，第 99 页；Lanser, *The Narrative Act: Point of View in Prose Fiction*, p.49.

③ Phelan. *Living to Tell about It: A Rhetoric and Ethics of Character Narration*, p.45.

④ Booth, *The Rhetoric of Fiction*, pp.67 - 77.

character ... It lives in gusto, be it foul or fair, high or low, rich or poor, mean or elevated. It has as much delight in conceiving an Iago as an Imogen. What shocks the virtuous philosopher, delights the camelion Poet. It does not harm from its relish of the dark side of things any more than from its taste for the bright one; because they both end in speculation."① Three decades later Flaubert recommended a similar neutrality to the novelist who would be a poet. For him the model is the attitude of the scientist. Once we have spent enough time, he says, in "treating the human soul with the impartiality which physical scientists show in studying matter, we will have taken an immense step forward".② Art must achieve "by a pitiless method, the precision of the physical sciences".③

It should be unnecessary here to show that no author can ever attain to this kind of objectivity. Most of us today would, like Sartre, renounce the analogy with science even if we could admit that science is objective in this sense. What is more, we all know by now that a careful reading of any statement in defense of the artist's neutrality will reveal commitment; there is always some deeper value in relation to which neutrality is taken to be good. Chekhov, for example, begins bravely enough in defense of neutrality, but he cannot write three sentences without committing himself. "I am afraid of those who look for a tendency between the lines, and who are determined to regard me either as a liberal or as a conservative. I am not a liberal, not a conservative, not a believer in gradual progress, not a monk, not an indifferentist. I should like to be a free artist and nothing more ... I have no preference either for gendarmes, or for butchers, or for scientists, or for writers, or for the younger generation. I regard trade-marks and labels as a superstition."④ Freedom and art are good, then, and superstition bad? Soon he is carried away to a direct repudiation of the plea for "indifference" with which he began. "My holy of holies is the human body, health, intelligence, talent, inspiration, love, and the most absolute freedom—freedom from violence and lying, whatever forms they may take" (p.63). Again and again he betrays in this way the most passionate kind of commitment to what he often calls objectivity.

> The artist should be, not the judge of his characters and their conversations, but only an unbiassed witness. I once overheard a desultory conversation about pessimism between two Russians; nothing was solved,—and my business is to report the conversation exactly as I heard it, and let the jury,—that is, the readers, estimate its value. My business is merely to be talented, i.e. to be able ... to illuminate the characters and speak their language. [pp.58 - 59]

---

① Letter to Richard Woodhouse, October 27, 1818, *The Poetical Works and Other Writings of John Keats*, ed. H. Buxton Forman (New York, 1939), VII, 129.

② *Correspondence* (October 12, 1853) (Paris, 1926 - 1933), III, 367 - 368. For some of the citations from Flaubert in what follows I am indebted to the excellent monograph by Marianne Bonwit, *Gustave Flaubert et le principe d'impassibilité* (Berkeley, Calif., 1950). My distinction among the three forms of objectivity in the author is derived in part from her discussion.

③ Ibid. (December 12, 1857), IV, 243.

④ *Letters on the Short Story, the Drama and other Literary Topics*, selected and edited by Louis S. Friedland (New York, 1924), p.63.

But "illuminate" according to what lights? "A writer must be as objective as a chemist; he must abandon the subjective line; he must know that dung-heaps play a very respectable part in a landscape, and that evil passions are as inherent in life as good ones" (pp.275 - 276). We have learned by now to ask of such statements: Is it good to be faithful to what is "inherent"? Is it good to include every part of the "landscape"? If so, why? According to what scale of values? To repudiate one scale is necessarily to imply another.

It would be a serious mistake, however, to dismiss talk about the author's neutrality simply because of this elementary and understandable confusion between neutrality toward some values and neutrality toward all. Cleansed of the polemical excesses, the attack on subjectivity can be seen to rest on several important insights.

To succeed in writing some kinds of works, some novelists find it necessary to repudiate all intellectual or political causes. Chekhov does not want himself, as artist, to be either liberal or conservative. Flaubert, writing in 1853, claims that even the artist who recognizes the demand to be a "triple-thinker", even the artist who recognizes the need for ideas in abundance, "must have neither religion, nor country, nor social conviction".①

Unlike the claim to complete neutrality, this claim will never be refuted, and it will not suffer from shifts in literary theory or philosophical fashion. Like its opposite, the existentialist claim of Sartre and others that the artist should be totally *engagé*, its validity depends on the kind of novel the author is writing. Some great artists have been committed to the causes of their times, and some have not. Some works seem to be harmed by their burden of commitment (many of Sartre's own works, for example, in spite of their freedom from authorial comment) and some seem to be able to absorb a great deal of commitment (*The Divine Comedy*, *Four Quartets*, *Gulliver's Travels*, *Darkness at Noon*, *Bread and Wine*). One can always find examples to prove either side of the case; the test is whether the particular ends of the artist enable him to do something with his commitment, not whether he has it or not.

Everyone is against everyone else's prejudices and in favor of his own commitment to the truth. All of us would like the novelist somehow to operate on the level of our own passion for truth and right, a passion which by definition is not in the least prejudiced. The argument in favor of neutrality is thus useful in so far as it warns the novelist that he can seldom afford to pour his untransformed biases into his work. The deeper he sees into permanency, the more likely he is to earn the discerning reader's concurrence. The author as he writes should be like the ideal reader described by Hume in "The Standard of Taste", who, in order to reduce the distortions produced by prejudice, considers himself as "man in general" and forgets, if possible, his "individual being" and

① Corr. (April 26 - 27, 1853), III, 183: "... ne doit avoir ni religion, ni patrie, ni même aucune conviction sociale..."

his "peculiar circumstances".

To put it in this way, however, is to understate the importance of the author's individuality. As he writes, he creates not simply an ideal, impersonal "man in general" but an implied version of "himself" that is different from the implied authors we meet in other men's works. To some novelists it has seemed, indeed, that they were discovering or creating themselves as they wrote. As Jessamyn West says, it is sometimes "only by writing the story that the novelist can discover—not his story—but its writer, the official scribe, so to speak, for that narrative".① Whether we call this implied author an "official scribe", or adopt the term recently revived by Kathleen Tillotson—the author's "second self"②—it is clear that the picture the reader gets of this presence is one of the author's most important effects. However impersonal he may try to be, his reader will inevitably construct a picture of the official scribe who writes in this manner—and of course that official scribe will never be neutral toward all values. Our reactions to his various commitments, secret or overt, will help to determine our response to the work. The reader's role in this relationship I must save for chapter Ⅴ. Our present problem is the intricate relationship of the so-called real author with his various official versions of himself.

We must say various versions, for regardless of how sincere an author may try to be, his different works will imply different versions, different ideal combinations of norms. Just as one's personal letters imply different versions of oneself, depending on the differing relationships with each correspondent and the purpose of each letter, so the writer sets himself out with a different air depending on the needs of particular works.

These differences are most evident when the second self is given an overt, speaking role in the story. When Fielding comments, he gives us explicit evidence of a modifying process from work to work; no single version of Fielding emerges from reading the satirical *Jonathan Wild*, the two great "comic epics in prose", *Joseph Andrews and Tom Jones*, and that troublesome hybrid, *Amelia*. There are many similarities among them, of course; all of the implied authors value benevolence and generosity; all of them deplore self-seeking brutality. In these and many other respects they are indistinguishable from most implied authors of most significant works until our own century. But when we descend from this level of generality to look at the particular ordering of values in each novel, we find great variety. The author of *Jonathan Wild* is by implication very much concerned with public affairs and with the effects of unchecked ambition on the "great men" who attain to

① "The Slave Cast Out," in *The Living Novel*, ed. Granville Hicks (New York, 1957), p.202. Miss West continues: "Writing is a way of playing parts, of trying on masks, of assuming roles, not for fun but out of desperate need, not for the self's sake but for the writing's sake. 'To make any work of art,' says Elizabeth Sewell, 'is to make, or rather to unmake and remake one's self'."

② In her inaugural lecture at the University of London, published as *The Tale and the Teller* (London, 1959). "Writing on George Eliot in 1877, Dowden said that the form that most persists in the mind after reading her novels is not any of the characters, but 'one who, if not the real George Eliot, is that second self who writes her books, and lives and speaks through them'. The 'second self' he goes on, is 'more substantial than any mere human personality' and has 'fewer reserves'; while 'behind it, lurks well pleased the veritable historical self secure from impertinent observation and criticism'" (p.22).

power in the world. If we had only this novel by Fielding, we would infer from it that in his real life he was much more single-mindedly engrossed in his role as magistrate and reformer of public manners than is suggested by the implied author of *Joseph Andrews and Tom Jones*—to say nothing of *Shamela* (what would we infer about Fielding if he had never written anything but *Shamela!*).On the other hand, the author who greets us on page one of *Amelia* has none of that air of facetiousness combined with grand insouciance that we meet from the beginning in *Joseph Andrews and Tom Jones*. Suppose that Fielding had never written anything but *Amelia*, filled as it is with the kind of commentary we find at the beginning:

> The various accidents which befel a very worthy couple after their uniting in the state of matrimony will be the subject of the following history. The distresses which they waded through were some of them so exquisite, and the incidents which produced these so extraordinary, that they seemed to require not only the utmost malice, but the utmost invention, which superstition hath ever attributed to Fortune: though whether any such being interfered in the case, or, indeed, whether there be any such being in the universe, is a matter which I by no means presume to determine in the affirmative.

Could we ever infer from this the Fielding of the earlier works? Though the author of *Amelia* can still indulge in occasional jests and ironies, his general air of sententious solemnity is strictly in keeping with the very special effects proper to the work as a whole. Our picture of him is built, of course, only partly by the narrator's explicit commentary; it is even more derived from the kind of tale he chooses to tell. But the commentary makes explicit for us a relationship which is present in all fiction, even though it may be overlooked in fiction without commentary.

It is a curious fact that we have no terms either for this created "second self" or for our relationship with him. None of our terms for various aspects of the narrator is quite accurate. "Persona""mask" and "narrator" are sometimes used, but they more commonly refer to the speaker in the work who is after all only one of the elements created by the implied author and who may be separated from him by large ironies. "Narrator" is usually taken to mean the "I" of a work, but the "I" is seldom if ever identical with the implied image of the artist.

"Theme""meaning""symbolic significance" "theology" or even "ontology"—all these have been used to describe the norms which the reader must apprehend in each work if he is to grasp it adequately. Such terms are useful for some purposes, but they can, be misleading because they almost inevitably come to seem like purposes for which the works exist. Though the old-style effort to find the theme or moral has been generally repudiated, the new-style search for the "meaning" which the work "communicates" or "symbolizes" can yield the same kinds of misreading. It is true that both types of search, however clumsily pursued, express a basic need: the reader's need to know where, in the world of values, he stands—that is, to know where the author wants him to stand. But most works worth reading have so many possible "themes", so many possible mythological or metaphorical or symbolic analogues, that to find any one of them, and to announce it as what the work is for, is to do at best a very small part of the critical task. Our sense of the implied author includes not only the extractable meanings but also the moral and emotional content of each bit of action and suffering of all of the characters. It includes, in short, the intuitive apprehension of a completed artistic whole; the chief value to which this implied author is committed, regardless of what party his creator belongs to in real life, is that which is expressed by the total form.

Three other terms are sometimes used to name the core of norms and choices which I am calling the implied author. "Style" is sometimes broadly used to cover whatever it is that gives us a sense, from word to word and line to line, that the author sees more deeply and judges more profoundly than his presented characters. But, though style is one of our main sources of insight into the author's norms, in carrying such strong overtones of the merely verbal the word style excludes our sense of the author's skill in his choice of character and episode and scene and idea. "Tone" is similarly used to refer to the implicit evaluation which the author manages to convey behind his explicit presentation,① but it almost inevitably suggests again something limited to the merely verbal; some aspects of the implied author may be inferred through tonal variations, but his major qualities will depend also on the hard facts of action and character in the tale that is told.

Similarly, "technique" has at times been expanded to cover all discernible signs of the author's artistry. If everyone used "technique" as Mark Schorer does,② covering with it almost the entire range of choices made by the author, then it might very well serve our purposes. But it is usually taken for a much narrower matter, and consequently it will not do. We can be satisfied only with a term that is as broad as the work itself but still capable of calling attention to that work as the product of a choosing, evaluating person rather than as a self-existing thing. The "implied author" chooses, consciously or unconsciously, what we read; we infer him as an ideal, literary, created version of the real man; he is the sum of his own choices.

It is only by distinguishing between the author and his implied image that we can avoid pointless and unverifiable talk about such qualities as "sincerity" or "seriousness" in the author. Because Ford Madox Ford thinks of Fielding and Defoe and Thackeray as the unmediated authors of their novels,

① E.g., Fred B. Millett, *Reading Fiction* (New York, 1950): "This tone, the general feeling which suffuses and surrounds the work, arises ultimately out of the writer's attitude toward his subject ... The subject derives its meaning horn the view of life which the author has taken." (p.11)

② "When we speak of technique, then, we speak of nearly everything. For technique is the means by which the writer's experience, which is his subject matter, compels him to attend to it; technique is the only means he has of discovering, exploring, developing his subject, of conveying its meaning, and finally of evaluating it ... Technique in fiction is, of course, all those obvious forms of it which are usually taken to be the whole of it, and many others"["Technique as Discovery", Hudson Review, I (Spring, 1948), pp. 67 - 87, as reprinted in *Forms of Modem Fiction*, ed. Wm. Van O'Connor (Minneapolis, Minn., 1948), pp.9 - 29; see esp.pp.9 - 11].

he must end by condemning them as insincere, since there is every reason to believe that they write "passages of virtuous aspirations that were in no way any aspirations of theirs".[①] Presumably he is relying on external evidences of Fielding's lack of virtuous aspirations. But we have only the work as evidence for the only kind of sincerity that concerns us: Is the implied author in harmony with himself—that is, are his other choices in harmony with his explicit narrative character? If a narrator who by every trustworthy sign is presented to us as a reliable spokesman for the author professes to believe in values which are never realized in the structure as a whole, we can then talk of an insincere work. A great work establishes the "sincerity" of its implied author, regardless of how grossly the man who created that author may belie in his other forms of conduct the values embodied in his work. For all we know, the only sincere moments of his life may have been lived as he wrote his novel.

What is more, in this distinction between author and implied author we find a middle position between the technical irrelevance of talk about the artist's objectivity and the harmful error of pretending that an author can allow direct intrusions of his own immediate problems and desires. The great defenders of objectivity were working on an important matter and they knew it. Flaubert is right in saying that Shakespeare does not barge clumsily into his works. We are never plagued with his undigested personal problems. Flaubert is also right in rebuking Louise Colet for writing "La Servante" as a personal attack on Musset, with the personal passion destroying the aesthetic value of the poem (January 9 - 10, 1854). And he is surely right when he forces the hero of the youthful version of *The Sentimental Education* (1845) to choose between the merely confessional statement and the truly rendered work of art.

But is he right when he claims that we do not know what Shakespeare loved or hated?[②] Perhaps—if he means only that we cannot easily tell from the plays whether the man Shakespeare preferred blondes to brunettes or whether he disliked bastards, Jews, or Moors. But the statement is most definitely mistaken if it means that the implied author of Shakespeare's plays is neutral toward all values. We do know what this Shakespeare loved and hated; it is hard to see how he could have written his plays at all if he had refused to take a strong line on at least one or two of the seven deadly sins. I return in chapter v to the question of beliefs in literature, and I try there to list a few of the values to which Shakespeare is definitely and obviously committed. They are for the most part not personal, idiosyncratic; Shakespeare is thus not recognizably subjective. But they are unmistakable violations of true neutrality; the implied Shakespeare is thoroughly engaged with life, and he does not conceal his judgment on the selfish, the foolish, and the cruel.

Even if all this were denied, it is difficult to see why there should be any necessary connection

① *The English Novel* (London, 1930), p.58. See Geoffrey Tillotson, *Thackeray the Novelist* (Cambridge, 1954), esp. Chap. iv, "The Content of the Authorial 'I'" (pp.55 - 70), for a convincing argument that the "I" of Thackeray's works should be carefully distinguished from Thackeray himself.

② Qu'est qui me dira, en effet ce que Shakespeare a aimé, ce qu'il a haï, ce qu'il a senti? (Corr., I, 386).

between neutrality and an absence of commentary. An author might very well use comments to warn the reader against judging. But if I am right in claiming that neutrality is impossible, even the most nearly neutral comment will reveal some sort of commitment.

> Once upon a time there lived in Berlin, Germany, a man called Albinus. He was rich, respectable, happy; one day he abandoned his wife for the sake of a youthful mistress; he loved; was not loved; and his life ended in disaster.
>
> This is the whole of the story and we might have left it at that had there not been profit and pleasure in the telling; and although there is plenty of space on a gravestone to contain, bound in moss, the abridged version of a man's life, detail is always welcome.①

Nabokov may here have purged his narrator's voice of all commitments save one, but that one is all-powerful: he believes in the ironic interest—and as it later turns out, the poignancy—of a man's fated self-destruction. Maintaining the same detached tone, this author can intrude whenever he pleases without violating our conviction that he is as objective as it is humanly possible to be. Describing the villain, he can call him both a "dangerous man" and "a very fine artist indeed" without reducing our confidence in his open-mindedness. But he is not neutral toward all values, and he does not pretend to be.

三、思考与讨论

(1) 布斯如何看待作者和读者?

(2) 如何区分隐含作者与真实作者并阐释二者之间的关系?

(3) 布斯对于隐含作者的阐释有何盲点?

① Vladimir Nabokov, *Laughter in the Dark* (New York, 1938), p.1.

第三节 詹姆斯·费伦及其《某人向某人讲述：叙事的修辞诗学》

一、导读

詹姆斯·费伦是芝加哥学派第三代的领军人物、后经典修辞叙事学的代表人物，也是当今欧美叙事学界最具影响力的叙事学家之一。在芝加哥大学攻读博士学位期间，费伦师从新亚里士多德学派第二代批评家谢尔顿·萨克斯(Sheldon Sacks)和韦恩·布斯。在他们的影响下，费伦提出了修辞叙事理论的理论框架。自20世纪80年代以来，他撰写了一系列叙事理论著作。在《作为修辞的叙事：技巧、读者、伦理和意识形态》(*Narrative as Rhetoric: Technique, Audiences, Ethics, Ideology*, 1996)一书中，费伦发展了他在《阅读人物、阅读情节：人物、进程和叙事阐释》(*Reading People, Reading Plots: Character, Progression, and the Interpretation of Narrative*, 1989)中提出的理论框架，初步阐释了对叙事的定义、叙事交流、叙事本质等修辞性叙事理论基本命题的观点。在《活着是为了讲述：人物叙述的修辞与伦理》(*Living to Tell about It: A Rhetoric and Ethics of Character Narration*, 2005)一书中，他重新思考隐含作者、不可靠叙述、叙事交流模式等概念，并聚焦人物叙述，考察其在虚构和非虚构文本中的应用及其唤起的复杂修辞和伦理关系。在之后的《体验小说：判断、进程和修辞叙事理论》(*Experiencing Fiction: Judgments, Progression, and the Rhetorical Theory of Narrative*, 2007)一书中，费伦又以读者的阅读体验为研究中心，以"叙事判断"和"叙事进程"的共谋为视角，重点探讨了读者如何以相似的方式体验作品。在2017年出版的《某人向某人讲述：叙事的修辞诗学》一书中，费伦再一次展示了修辞的力量，引领了修辞叙事学的发展潮流。

在《某人向某人讲述：叙事的修辞诗学》中，费伦试图建构叙事的修辞诗学，提出了叙事理论的"范式转移"，强调了叙事的修辞性。在他看来，修辞议题的目的是全面理解作者和读者如何利用叙事资源进行多层次的沟通交流。这些层次包括作者与读者关系中的认知、情感、伦理和美学，而达到这一目标需要对叙事资源进行充分说明。[①] 在此基础上，费伦挑战了叙事交流的基本模式，提出了ARA模式，即作者(author)、资源(resources)、读者(audience)，以及叙事交流中的常量与变量图表。[②] 费伦的ARA模型将作者和读者视为叙事交流的两个常量，将叙事中的资源视为变量。位于文本内的叙事资源则具有一定的主动性，会对作者施加影响，使作者在自由与限制中做出协调。

---

① Phelan, "Authors, Resources, Audiences: Toward a Rhetorical Poetics of Narrative," p.2.

② James Phelan, *Somebody Telling Somebody Else: A Rhetorical Poetics of Narrative* (Columbus: The Ohio State University Press, 2017), p.26.

叙事交流中的常量与变量

作　者	⟷	资　源	⟷	读　者
真实的/隐含的		场合		作者的和真实的
		副文本		
		叙事者		
		人物/对话		
		自由间接话语		
		体裁		
		虚构性/非虚构		
		语态		
		风格		
		空间		
		时间性		
		安排/空缺		
		受述者		
		叙事读者		
		互文性		
		参考文献		
		歧义		
		……		

在前几部著作的基础上，费伦进一步概括和阐释了修辞诗学的基本原则：

(1) 叙事本身是一个事件，特别是讲述者与读者的多维度、有目的的交流，而非一种结构。

(2) 叙事的定义（“某人在某一场合为了某种目的告诉另一个人发生了某件事”）描述的是“默认”(default)的情形，并具有一定的开放性。值得注意的是，在费伦看来，尽管这一个定义并非叙事学家所给出的最好的定义，但它指引读者关注叙事交流以及叙事者、读者和目的的显著性，并进一步指引读者关注叙事学其他核心要素，包括文体、人物、情节、叙事进程等。[①]

(3) 修辞叙事学的阐释和理论建构基于后验的研究方法而非先验，力求理解和评价叙事已经做的各种事和已经采取的各种方式。

(4) 将叙事视为一种作者代理、文本现象（包括互文关系）和读者反应协同作用的修辞交流，注重三者之间的循环互动。叙事的意义就源自这一修辞三角。作者为特定目的设计叙事，而读者反应则可检验作者设计的效果。

---

① Phelan, “Authors, Resources, Audiences: Toward a Rhetorical Poetics of Narrative,” p.1.

(5) 区分“作者的读者”“实际读者”“受述者”和“叙述读者”四种读者类型。

(6) 在讨论叙事伦理时，费伦从读者、文本、作者等维度定义阅读过程中的伦理取位，并强调区分“被讲述对象的伦理”和“讲述行为的伦理”。前者涉及人物、事件等的伦理，后者涉及作者、叙述者、读者之间关系的伦理。

(7) 修辞叙事理论对于读者和作者之间多层次交流活动的关注和重视使得它以多重方式将历史语境纳入考量范围。

(8) 潜在的修辞情景在不同类型的叙事中，特别是个人叙事中有所变化。

(9) 文本动力与读者动力两种动力的整合对叙事进程的效果和目的至关重要。

(10) 将模仿性、主题性和虚构性的三维人物观拓展至读者的反应、阐释经验以及叙事作品的其他方面，强调读者之于叙事的三种不同反应，即模仿性反应、主题性反应和虚构性反应。[①]

这些修辞诗学的原则是对费伦一以贯之的修辞原则的再次强调和补充，是他之前修辞叙事理论的延续和升华。围绕着这些原则及其修辞诗学的理论建构，费伦详细阐释了叙事理论的范式转移对于我们理解可靠性和不可靠性、人物与人物的对话、叙事场合等的影响。从费伦对叙事的定义、对叙事模式的修订、对修辞诗学原则的阐释等角度来看，费伦的修辞叙事理论具有全面性、动态性和平衡性的特点。它不仅全面考虑作者、文本和读者，通过对三者之间循环互动的强调和研究规避了经典修辞学的短处，又在形式审美研究与意识形态关注之间达到了一种较好的平衡。

二、《某人向某人讲述：叙事的修辞诗学》选读[②]

Before I launch into the exploration of character-character dialogue, I offer a sketch of ten key principles of the rhetorical paradigm that I and others working in the tradition have developed in previous work. I have expressed some of these points above, but I hope the advantages of putting them all in one place will outweigh the disadvantages of some redundant telling. This sketch seeks to be succinct in its explication, in part because the rest of the book will elaborate on the principles as it puts them to work and, in some cases, explicitly offers further commentary. I invite those readers who are familiar with the principles or are more interested in their application to jump to chapter 1 and return to this sketch as needed.[③]

(1) Rhetorical theory subsumes the traditional view of narrative as a structured sign system representing a linked sequence of events under the broader view that **narrative is itself an event—more specifically**, a multidimensional purposive communication from a teller to an audience. The concern with purpose informs the analysis of narrative phenomena, including the core elements: how has the teller tried to shape these materials in the service of her larger ends? The focus on narrative as

① Phelan, *Somebody Telling Somebody Else: A Rhetorical Poetics of Narrative*, pp.4－12.

② Ibid., pp.4－12.

③ This discussion of principles draws to some degree on the similar discussion Peter J. Rabinowitz and I offer in Chapter 1 of Narrative Theory: Core Concepts and Critical Debates. But where that discussion identifies six principles, this one expands to ten. I am deeply grateful to Peter for his collaboration in that discussion and in so many others over the years.

multileveled communication follows from rhetorical theory's interest in accounting for the reading experience (and see principle number 5 for a gloss on "experience"). Consequently, rhetorical theory is at least as interested in a narrative's affective, ethical, and aesthetic effects—and in their interactions—as it is in that narrative's thematic meanings. Affective effects include the range of emotional responses (from empathy to antipathy) to characters, narrators, and even authors and to the narrative as a whole. Affective effects can follow from and/or influence ethical effects, and the quality of an audience's affective and ethical engagements with a narrative greatly influences its aesthetic effects.

(2) **The rhetorical definition of *narrative*, "somebody telling somebody else on some occasion and for some purpose(s) that something happened", describes a "default" situation rather than prescribes what all narratives should do.** The definition is designed to capture essential characteristics of most of those works that are widely considered to be narratives in our culture, even as I recognize that individual narratives may not conform exactly to every element of the definition. Thus, for example, I say "something happened", because the telling of events typically occurs after their occurrence. But I also recognize that the telling can sometimes be simultaneous with the events (as in J. M. Coetzee's *Waiting for the Barbarians*) or before the events (as in the ending of Dostoyevsky's *The Gambler*: "Tomorrow, tomorrow it will all be over!"). Characterizing the definition as "default" keeps one open to such deviations—and to the likelihood that they will be significant. See number 8 for a related principle.

(3) **Rhetorical interpretation and theory are based on an a posteriori rather than an a priori method.** This principle is closely connected to number 2. Rather than declaring what narratives invariably do or how they invariably do it, I seek to understand and assess the variety of things narratives have done and the variety of ways they have done it. In practical terms, this principle means that I try to reason back from the effects created by narratives to the causes of those effects in the authorial shaping of the narrative elements. I then try to draw appropriate generalizations about narrative as rhetoric. Since narrative communication is a complex, multilayered phenomenon, this reasoning process cannot be reduced to a formula, and its results yield hypotheses rather than dogmatic conclusions.

A related dimension of this principle is that rhetorical theory does not preselect for analysis certain matters of content, such as gender, race, class, age, sexual orientation, or (dis)ability, though it recognizes both that such methods have yielded valuable work on narrative and that some narratives do foreground such matters. More generally, rhetorical narrative theory maintains its interest in how authors seek to achieve their multidimensional purposes even as it strives to be sufficiently flexible to respond to the diversity of narrative acts. At the same time, of course, rhetorical theory is not a neutral, unmediated approach to narrative—as this present exposition of its principles amply demonstrates.

(4) **In interpreting a narrative, rhetorical narrative theory identifies a feedback loop among authorial agency, textual phenomena (including intertextual relations), and reader response.** In other words, the approach assumes that (a) texts are designed by authors to affect readers in particular ways; (b) those authorial designs are conveyed through the words, images, techniques, elements, structures, forms, and dialogic relations of texts as well as the genres and conventions readers use to understand them; and (c) those authorial designs are also deeply influenced by the nature of their audiences and their activity in responding to the unfolding communication. In a sense, my work in this book is a major elaboration of the consequences of this principle, one that starts from the idea that "there's a lot more here than initially appears". For now, I highlight a few of its practical consequences. The principle means that an interpretive inquiry can start with any point in the loop because questions about that point will inevitably lead to the consideration of other points. If, for example, I respond to a character's action with a negative ethical judgment, I will look for the textual sources of that judgment and the reasons why the author would have guided my judgment in that way, given her other purposes. In the course of asking and answering these questions, I may find that my negative judgment was too simplistic or otherwise inadequate, and I will therefore revise it.

Attending to all three points in the loop also sometimes makes rhetorical theory wary about thematic abstraction. For example, some critics have offered eloquent thematic defenses of Mark Twain's ending in *Huckleberry Finn*, but, while I admire the learning and reasoning in many of these arguments, I find them ultimately unpersuasive because they are insufficiently responsive to the readerly experience of that section. In focusing on thematic relevance, these analyses typically neglect the tedium most readers experience as they slog through Twain's account of Tom Sawyer's elaborate scheme for freeing Jim, and the disappointment they feel in Huck's ethical decline in his relationship with Jim. Because this response holds up after my examination of the textual phenomena of the Evasion section and my inferences about Twain's purposes, as revealed by the first two-thirds of the novel, I find it more convincing to view the ending as flawed.

(5) **The rhetorical approach theorizes "the somebody else" in narrative communication by identifying three audiences in nonfictional narrative and four audiences in fictional narrative.** The first audience is the actual audience, flesh-and-blood readers in all their differences and commonalities. The second audience is the authorial audience, the hypothetical group for whom the author writes—the group that shares the knowledge, values, prejudices, fears, and experiences that the author expected in his or her readers, and that ground his or her rhetorical choices. The authorial audience is neither wholly hypothetical nor wholly actual, but instead it is a hybrid of readers an author knows or knows about—or at least an interpretation of such readers—and an audience the author imagines. The third audience is the narratee, the audience addressed by the narrator, whether characterized or not. Typically, the more the narratee is characterized, the more important this audience is in the rhetorical exchange. Uncharacterized narratees in nonfiction are likely to be

indistinguishable from the authorial audience. The fourth audience, exclusive to fiction, is the narrative audience, an observer position within the storyworld. As observers, the members of the narrative audience regard the characters and events as real rather than invented, and, indeed, they accept the whole storyworld as real regardless of whether it conforms to the actual world. Two of J. K. Rowling's inventions in her construction of Harry Potter's storyworld can be adapted to help explain the relation between the actual audience and the narrative audience. In entering the narrative audience, the actual audience puts on an Invisibility Cloak and apparates to the world of the fiction.

This point means that the degree of overlap between the beliefs of the authorial audience and those of the narrative audience can vary considerably. To stay with Rowling's construction by way of illustration, the narrative audience of the Harry Potter novels believes that the entire population of the world can be divided into two types: witches and wizards with magical powers, on the one hand, and humans without magical powers (muggles), on the other; the authorial audience, however, does not believe in witches and wizards. At the same time, the narrative audience does not necessarily accept the narrator's portrayal of everything as accurate, any more than the reader of a nonfictional text necessarily accepts everything represented as true. Finally, as an observer, a member of the narrative audience overhears the narrator's address to the narratee, even as the degree to which the observer can also feel addressed can vary from narrative to narrative. Typically, the variation will be tied to the narrative audience's similarity or difference from the narratee. Similarly, second-person narration in which the "you" is both protagonist and narratee can make all the audiences feel addressed. These points about the variability of the narrative audience-narratee relationship apply more broadly: the relationships among all audiences can vary from narrative to narrative, and some narratives make those relationships crucial to their effects while others do not.

Beyond distinguishing among audiences, rhetorical poetics makes several other assumptions about the "somebody else" of narrative communication: ① Not all actual readers want to join the authorial audience. Those who do I call rhetorical readers, and those are the readers whose activity rhetorical poetics is most concerned with. Consequently, I will frequently use the phrase to refer to actual readers who have joined the authorial audience. To put this point another way, the authorial and, where relevant, narrative audience positions are roles that the rhetorical reader takes on, and examining those roles can provide insight into the experience of rhetorical readers. ② In fiction, the authorial audience position includes the narrative audience position, since the authorial audience has the double-consciousness that allows it to experience the events as real and to retain the tacit knowledge that they are invented. ③ Rhetorical readers can and should evaluate the experiences they are invited to have in the authorial audience. Indeed, rhetorical readers do not complete their acts of reading until they take this second step. In the analyses in this book, this second step will often be implied in my endorsement of the author-audience relationships I perceive in the narratives, but at various points I will make that second step explicit, most notably in my discussion of "deficient narration" in Chapter 9.

(6) **In addressing narrative ethics, rhetorical theory distinguishes between the ethics of the telling and the ethics of the told.** The ethics of the telling refer to the ethical dimensions of author-narrator-audience relationships as constructed through everything from plotting to direct addresses to the audience, while the ethics of the told refer to the ethical dimensions of characters and events, including character-character interactions and choices to act in one way rather than another by individual characters. In keeping with the posteriori principle, I approach ethics from the inside out rather than the outside in. That is, rather than using a particular theory of ethics to interpret and evaluate the ethical dimension of narratives, I seek to identify the system (whether coherent, eclectic, or incoherent) an author has deployed (consciously or intuitively) in the narrative.

(7) **Rhetorical theory integrates history in multiple ways.** Because rhetorical theory emphasizes author-audience relations and because it views both as always already situated in historical and social contexts, rhetorical theory is not just compatible with but dependent on historical knowledge—and historical analysis—of all kinds: literary, cultural, social, political, and so on. The role of history in rhetorical analysis is itself governed by a principle of salience: what historical knowledge is especially significant for the construction of author-audience relations? To take just a few examples from the following chapters: In *The Friends of Eddie Coyle*, George V. Higgins relies on his audience to know something about both the Black Panthers and how they were perceived by white law enforcement. In *Pride and Prejudice*, Jane Austen relies on her audience to know about a wide range of social norms of England's Regency Period. In "Recitatif", Toni Morrison relies on her audience to know about the political controversies surrounding post-1960s school bussing programs in the United States. In "The Third and Final Continent", Jhumpa Lahiri relies on her audience to have some knowledge of the tradition of arranged marriages in India as well as of recent patterns of Indian immigration to England and the United States.

These examples also point to another common—but by no means universal—aspect of the relation between historical and rhetorical analysis. In each case, the historical knowledge is a necessary, not a sufficient, condition for understanding the author-audience relations. To get at sufficient conditions, the rhetorical analyst does a detailed, close analysis of the multiple factors that go into establishing that relationship—and, indeed, its trajectory over the course of a narrative. For the most part, my attention will be directed toward such analyses, but I remain aware that they are themselves dependent on a wide range of historical knowledge. One more example, about literary history, will help clarify this point. In approaching a novel such as *The Sound and the Fury*, a rhetorical reader benefits from knowing something about modernism and that Faulkner was a modernist. At the same time, such knowledge is only a starting point for the task of accounting for the detailed workings of the feedback loop among authorial agency, textual phenomena, and readerly response in Faulkner's novel.

(8) **The underlying rhetorical situation varies in different kinds of narrative, and it typically varies within individual narratives**. For instance, in fictional narratives such as Jhumpa Lahiri's "The Third and Final Continent" or Franz Kafka's "Das Urteil" (to take two narratives discussed in later chapters), the teller/audience situation is doubled: the narrators tell their stories to uncharacterized narratees for their own purposes, while the authors communicate both the events and the narrators' telling of them to their audiences for their own purposes. In such cases, the fictional narrative is a single text combining at least two tracks of rhetorical communication. I say "at least" because, as I shall argue in chapter 1, this commonsense description overlooks other tracks between author and audience commonly constructed via dialogue, juxtapositions of narrative segments, and other things. This description also overlooks the ways in which authors can construct synergistic relationships among these tracks that generate communications that are more than the sum of the transmissions along the individual tracks. In nonfictional narrative, the same tracks are available for the author's use, but sometimes the narrator-narratee track is indistinguishable from the author-audience track. In other words, sometimes authors of nonfiction speak directly in their own voices to their projected audiences, as, for example, Joan Didion does in *The Year of Magical Thinking*. But this common strategy in nonfiction is not a required one: authors of nonfiction can distance themselves from their narrators, as, for example, Frank McCourt does in *Angela's Ashes*.

(9) **The progression of a narrative—its synthesis of textual and readerly dynamics—is crucial to its effects and purposes.** Textual dynamics are the internal processes by which narratives move from beginning through middle to ending, and readerly dynamics are the corresponding cognitive, affective, ethical, and aesthetic responses of the audience to those textual dynamics. The bridge between textual dynamics and readerly dynamics consists of interpretive, ethical, and aesthetic judgments. These judgments constitute a bridge because they are encoded in the narrative yet made by rhetorical readers. Furthermore, by describing progression as a synthesis, I seek to capture the ways that textual dynamics and readerly dynamics influence each other. I will develop this point more fully in Chapter 2.

Textual dynamics are themselves a synthesis of plot dynamics, governing the sequence of events, and narratorial dynamics, governing the relations among authors, tellers (whether narrators or characters), and audiences. Plot dynamics typically develop through patterns of instability-complication-resolution. That is, an author generates a plot through introducing one or more characters in unstable situations, he advances the plot by complicating those instabilities, and he ends the plot by resolving those instabilities to one degree or another—or thematizing the impossibility of resolution. Narratorial dynamics are diverse, but two broad patterns, which I will unpack more fully in part 2, are reliable and unreliable narration. Each pattern has consequences for how an author handles the plot dynamics and thus adds an important layer to the textual dynamics. Unreliable narration introduces tensions among authors, narrators, and audiences and the issue of whether these tensions will be resolved can become an important part of the textual dynamics. Readerly dynamics include both local and global interpretive, ethical, affective, and aesthetic responses to the unfolding textual dynamics. They also include such broader activities as configurations and reconfigurations of the various layers of the developing trajectory. Since analyzing the progression involves unpacking the underlying logic of the narrative—why it is the way it is and not some other way—it provides valuable insight into the narrative's purposes.

(10) **Rhetorical readers develop interests and responses of three broad kinds, each related to a particular component of the narrative: mimetic, thematic, and synthetic.** Responses to the mimetic component involve rhetorical readers' interest in the characters as possible people and in the narrative world as like our own, that is, hypothetically or conceptually possible; responses to the mimetic component include rhetorical readers' evolving judgments and emotions, their desires, hopes, expectations, satisfactions, and disappointments. Responses to the mimetic component of fiction are tied to rhetorical readers' participation in the narrative audience. Responses to the mimetic component of nonfiction are tied to rhetorical readers' sense of the fit between the actual world and its representation in the narrative. Responses to the thematic component involve rhetorical readers' interest in the ideational function of the characters and in the cultural, ideological, philosophical, or ethical issues being addressed by the narrative. Responses to the synthetic component involve rhetorical readers' interest in and attention to the characters and to the larger narrative as artificial constructs. The relationship among rhetorical readers' relative interests in these different components will vary from narrative to narrative depending on the nature of its genre and progression. Some narratives (including most so-called realistic fiction) are dominated by mimetic interests; some (including allegories and political polemics such as *Animal Farm*) stress the thematic; others (including the *nouveau roman* and postmodern metafiction) put priority on the synthetic. But the interests of many narratives are more evenly distributed among two or three of the components. Most narratives in the realistic tradition, for instance, promote both the mimetic and the thematic, and some narratives situate mimetic characters in clearly anti-mimetic worlds. Furthermore, developments in the course of a narrative can generate new relations among those interests. Indeed, many narratives derive their special power from shifting rhetorical readers' attention from one kind of component to another: Nabokov's *Bend Sinister*, for instance, has the effect that it does in part because, in the closing pages, the mimetic is drowned out by the synthetic.

三、思考与讨论

(1) 如何看待费伦对于叙事的定义?

(2) 费伦的修辞叙事理论如何看待作者、文本和读者之间的关系?

(3) 费伦的修辞叙事理论的动态性体现在哪些方面?

第四节 理查德·沃尔什及其《虚构性修辞学》

一、导读

理查德·沃尔什在其2007年出版的《虚构性修辞学》中正式提出了修辞方法虚构性理论(rhetorical approach to fictionality)。这一理论的提出标志着虚构性理论的一次范式转移。沃尔什指出,前人的虚构性理论大多将真实性视为语言的基本准则;既然虚构话语违背了这一准则,那就必须通过某种机制(例如虚构叙述者、虚构世界、对语言行为的假装、假扮作者的游戏等)将其排除于一般的严肃交流之外。[①] 而沃尔什则借鉴语用学领域中关联理论(relevance theory)的中心思想,认为语言交流遵循的唯一最高原则是关联性的最大化而非真实性,并在此基础上提出将虚构性视作严肃交流中固有的修辞资源之一,主张虚构性是作者引发读者特定阐释策略、取得特定交流效果的灵活手段。[②] 他将虚构性定义为"一种语境假设"(a contextual assumption),其主要效果是"使依赖字面真实性的隐义从属于那些以更分散和累积的方式实现关联性的隐义"。[③] 这一理论为我们理解虚构性在现实交流中的作用与其社会文化价值提供了新视角。

从标题来看,沃尔什的《虚构性修辞学》是对芝加哥学派代表学者韦恩·布斯重要著作《小说修辞学》的批判性继承:一方面,沃尔什赞同布斯从"修辞",即交流行为层面入手理解虚构叙事,强调其作为作者与读者交流的手段所取得的现实效果;另一方面,沃尔什不赞成布斯将"小说"或"虚构文学"(fiction)视为作者建构与传达"虚构世界"(fictional world)、引发读者与虚构世界互动的艺术,他引入"虚构性"(fictionality)这一概念,主张虚构性是虚构文学整体使用的一种修辞手法,直接影响叙事表现的效果。[④] 沃尔什对"虚构性"与"虚构文学"概念的区分具有多重意义:首先,他强调虚构文学是其所处文化语境中的一种特殊表意方式,具有特殊的文化功用,这种特殊性恰恰源于其对虚构性的整体使用;其次,他指出虚构性并非某些传统虚构文类的专利,而是广泛存在于各类严肃交流中;最后,沃尔什还指出,虚构文学在整体使用虚构性的同时也可局部使用非虚构性的语境假设,例如历史事件或作者自身经历。[⑤] 由此可见,沃尔什的虚构性理论既摆脱了传统叙事学以偏概全、将虚构文学作为一切叙事之蓝本的弊病,又挑战了传统虚构性理论以体裁为标准、将叙事分为"虚构性叙事"(fictional narrative)与"事实性叙事"(factual narrative)的做法。

尽管沃尔什运用了一系列文本实例来阐释虚构性理论,验证其严谨性与解释力,但他的修辞方法虚构性理论本质上是诗学性质的理论。沃尔什写作《虚构性修辞学》的首要目的不是细察虚构性在不同语境中的运用方式或为文本阐释提供新方法,而是提出一种创新的、具有普适性的、经得起逻辑检验的虚

① Walsh, *The Rhetoric of Fictionality: Narrative Theory and the Idea of Fiction*, pp.14-15.
② Ibid., pp.15-16.
③ Ibid., p.30.
④ Ibid., pp.5-6.
⑤ Ibid., pp.6-7.

构性定义，并以此为出发点，重新审视“故事/话语”“叙述者”“作者”“虚构世界”等一系列叙事学经典概念，对叙事理论做出全面革新。在《虚构性修辞学》出版后的数年间，修辞方法虚构性理论相继吸引了亨里克·斯克夫·尼尔森、詹姆斯·费伦等重要学者加入。诸位学者提出了各自的虚构性定义，探索修辞方法虚构性理论对各类文学文本与非文学性话语研究的指导意义，进一步促进修辞方法虚构性理论与修辞叙事学的融合。如今，沃尔什开创的修辞方法虚构性理论已然成为叙事学界一股引人瞩目的新兴力量。

二、《虚构性修辞学》选读[①]

Modern accounts of fictionality generally turn on one or more of a small repertoire of theoretical gambits, which can be collectively understood as gestures of disavowal, achieved through several kinds of displacement. That is to say, these accounts variously respond to the problem of fictionality as a problem of truthfulness and resolve it by detaching the fictive act from the domain of truth, that is, language. The kinds of theoretical move I have in mind are: the institution of a narrator as the source of the fictive discourse; the redescription of fictional artifacts as props in a game of make-believe; the notion of pretended speech acts; and the recuperation of fictional reference as actual reference to fictional worlds. The first two moves place the language of fiction itself within the fictional frame; the third move disqualifies it, as nonserious language, from communicative accountability; and the fourth move allows the language of fiction to be literal and serious but not exactly fictive (that is, to the extent that fictive language does not make referential commitments), since fictionality has been redefined as a matter of ontological modality. The nub of fictionality always turns out to be elsewhere; it is as if fictionality were not a problem *except* in relation to language. This is odd, given that language, I take it, is what makes fiction possible—and by a language here I mean broadly any codified system of representation (fictions in any medium are equally dependent upon a language, a representational code, and not merely upon cognitive illusion).

Fictionality, I want to suggest, functions within a communicative framework: it resides in a way of using a language, and its distinctiveness consists in the recognizably distinct rhetorical set invoked by that use. I assume that narrative fictionality is worth distinguishing from narrativity in general. That is to say, I want to grant full force to the claim that all narrative is artifice, and in that very restricted sense fictive, but I maintain nonetheless that fictional narrative has a coherently distinct cultural role, and that a distinct concept of fictionality is required to account for this role. It is best explained in functional and rhetorical terms, rather than in formal terms: true, there are formal qualities strongly associated with fiction, but they do not supply necessary or sufficient conditions of fictionality. To say instead that fictionality is a functional attribute is to say that it is a

① Walsh, *The Rhetoric of Fictionality: Narrative Theory and the Idea of Fiction*, pp.14 - 16, 26 - 29, 30 - 32.

use of language; to say that it is rhetorical is to say that this use is distinguished by the kind of appeal it makes to the reader's (or the audience's) interpretative attention. No model that treats fictive discourse as framed by formal, intentional, or ontological disavowal can meet these criteria for a concept of fictionality. If fictionality consists in a distinct way of using language, it is not explained by attaching its distinctiveness to some quarantine mechanism conceived precisely to maintain its conformity with nonfictional usage, at the cost of detaching it, in one way or another, from its actual communicative context. The rhetorical distinctiveness of fiction, then, is consistent with a communicative continuity between fictional and nonfictional uses of language. Fictionality is a rhetorical resource integral to the direct and serious use of language within a real-world communicative framework.

...

Relevance Theory

The most important consequence of relevance theory, for my purposes, is the new relation it proposes between the functions of relevance and truthfulness in communication. Wilson and Sperber have articulated this with direct reference to Grice, declaring, "One of our aims is to show that the function Grice attributes to the Quality maxims—ensuring the quality of the speaker's overall contribution—can be more effectively achieved in a framework with no maxim of truthfulness at all" (Wilson and Sperber 2002: 585 - 586). Relevance theory advances the idea that, for the purposes of communication, the propositional criterion of truth is a subordinate consideration to the contextual, pragmatic criterion of relevance. This is not to say that the truth or falsehood of assumptions is a matter of indifference, or even that there are circumstances where it is a matter of indifference (as one might be tempted to say, precipitously, is the case with fiction): rather, it is decisively to detach those criteria with regard to assumptions from any necessary direct relation with the encoded form of an utterance. So, when Grice reiterates, in the retrospective epilogue to *Studies in the Way of Words* (1989), his view of the privileged status of the Maxim of Quality, it meets with this reply from Wilson and Sperber: "We agree with Grice that 'false information is not an inferior kind of information; it just is not information'. So, yes, hearers expect to be provided with true information. But there is an infinite supply of true information which is not worth attending to. Actual expectations are of relevant information, which (because it is information) is also true. However, we have argued that there just is no expectation that the true information communicated by an utterance should be literally or conventionally expressed, as opposed to being explicated or implicated in the sense we have discussed" (627 - 628). For relevance theory, then, literalness is not a norm but a limit case; the notion of literal meaning is detached from any presumption of literalness in communication (1990: 143). An utterance, as an interpretative expression of a speaker's thought, is defined as literal if it has the same propositional form as that thought; but "there is no reason to think that the optimally relevant interpretive expression of a thought is always the most literal one. The speaker is presumed to aim at optimal relevance, not at literal truth" (1995: 233). An assumption, to be an assumption at all, must be taken as true. But all assumptions are, to a greater or lesser extent, the products of inference, which is a pragmatic, relevance-driven process, and the truth of an assumption need not depend upon the truth of the encoded form of an utterance, or its literal meaning. Sperber and Wilson offer an extended account of metaphor and irony, which shares with speech act accounts the assumption that successful communication in such instances is dependent upon an inferential search for contextual relevance. It does not, however, present this search as a process resulting in a dichotomy between the literal sense of "what is said", which is false, and a recovered implicit meaning, which is true (242). From a relevance theory perspective, the comprehension of figurative language (as all language) is understood as an inferential process of filling out the linguistic code until maximal relevance is achieved (that is, up to the point at which the cost in processing effort exceeds the benefit in contextual effect, for the reader concerned). Criteria of truth enter into this process only to the extent that truthfulness is a condition of the particular contextual effects involved, and they apply only in relation to the assumptions producing those effects, which need not include the literal utterance, or any translation of it, as a proposition.

Sperber and Wilson understand comprehension in general to be a process of identifying the communicator's informative intention, which bears upon the mutual cognitive environment of the parties to the communication.[①] Accordingly, as they say, "linguistic decoding is not so much a part of the comprehension process as something that precedes the real work of understanding, something that merely provides an input to the main part of the comprehension process" (177). Truth criteria are applicable to successful communication only in the sense that the *output* of the inferential process, its cognitive effects, must qualify as information. Relevance to an individual is, definitionally, a measure of cognitive benefit, which Sperber and Wilson generally interpret as an "improvement in knowledge" (Wilson and Sperber 2002: 601), although they do expressly want to leave open the possibility of taking into account other kinds of benefit to cognitive functioning: they instance the reorganization of existing knowledge, and the elaboration of rational desires (1995: 266). Even within the compass of improvement in knowledge, though, they include various possible kinds of benefit (improvements in memory, or in imagination, for example), which they see as, in themselves, indirect improvements in knowledge.

In a more specific way, too, the notion of "improvement in knowledge" can embrace a wide

① Note that the intentionality of this model need not be reductive. An informative intention is an intention to make manifest or more manifest to the audience a set of assumptions; but "to have a representation of a set of assumptions [in mind, as a precondition of this intention] it is not necessary to have a representation of each assumption in the set. Any individuating description may do" (58). This comment leads directly on to Sperber and Wilson's discussion of "vague" forms of communication, exemplified by sharing an impression: narrative display would fit well into this class.

range of cognitive effects. For instance, Sperber and Wilson explain the possibility of communicating an impression, by describing this kind of effect as "a noticeable change in one's cognitive environment, a change resulting from relatively small alterations in the manifestness of many assumptions, rather than from the fact that a single assumption or a few new assumptions have all of a sudden become very manifest" (59). They describe the general category of cognitive changes of this kind as "poetic effects". The label is slightly misleading from a literary point of view, but its explanation greatly increases the subtlety of the relevance theory model. An utterance has poetic effects, in their sense, if it achieves most of its relevance through a wide array of weak implicatures (222). Poetic effects do not affect the mutual cognitive environment of communicator and audience by adding new, strongly manifest assumptions. Rather, "they marginally increase the manifestness of a great many weakly manifest assumptions. In other words, poetic effects create common impressions rather than common knowledge. Utterances with poetic effects can be used precisely to create this sense of apparently affective rather than cognitive mutuality. What we are suggesting is that, if you look at these affective effects through the microscope of relevance theory, you see a wide array of minute cognitive effects" (224). So, the improvement in knowledge required for a positive cognitive effect, and therefore relevance, may be the cumulative product of many minute cognitive effects, many weakly manifest assumptions, all of which are outcomes of the process of comprehension, and none of which is necessarily dependent upon the propositional truth of the input to that process.

The Relevance of Fictions

...

I want to suggest that relevance theory has more to offer than this. Most fundamentally, it allows me to say that the problem of fictionality is not, after all, a problem of truthfulness, but a problem of relevance. It is the presumption of relevance, not any expectation of literal truthfulness, that drives the reader's search for an appropriate interpretative context. Relevance theory allows for inference, and the generation of implicatures, to proceed from an utterance that is clearly false in the same direct way as for one that is taken as true: evaluations of truth only come into play in consequence of that process. So the fictionality of a narrative only compromises the relevance of those assumptions that are contingent upon its literal truth. The relevance theory model allows for a view of fiction in which fictionality is not a frame separating fictive discourse from ordinary or "serious" communication, but a contextual assumption: that is to say, in the comprehension of a fictive utterance, the assumption that it *is* fictive is itself manifest. The main contextual effect of this assumption is to subordinate implicatures that depend upon literal truthfulness to those that achieve relevance in more diffuse and cumulative ways. Fiction does not achieve relevance globally, at one remove, through some form of analogical thinking, but incrementally, through the implication of various cognitive interests or values that are not contingent upon accepting the propositional truth of the utterance itself and upon the deployment, investment, and working through of those interests in narrative form.

There is, certainly, a global, retrospective sense in which narrative can be understood as the suspension of relevance along the line of action, and in which narrative closure figures less as the resolution of plot in itself (though it is an effect usually achieved in terms of plot), than as the resolution of suspended evaluations of relevance. In this straightforward sense, irrespective of questions of fictionality, narrative form in itself responds to certain expectations of relevance. K.'s death at the end of *The Trial* is not just a very emphatic terminal plot event, but also the "answer" to several kinds of questions raised by the narrative, and in that respect it occasions a range of possible overall assessments of relevance from the reader (relating, for example, to K.'s moral desserts and models of justice, whether legal, cosmic, or poetic; to the balance of power between state and individual, or between structure and agency; to the psychological mechanisms of guilt, and the authority of the superego; and so on). Such global, thematic relevance is by no means the only kind offered by narratives, nor is it necessarily the most important; though in fiction, such interpretative logic is likely to dominate over the kind of factual enrichment of the reader's cognitive environment for which nonfictional narratives are better suited. Still, the investment of interpretative effort in the process of reading a fiction requires an ongoing sense of relevance. There are limits to everyone's tolerance of delayed gratification, and no ultimate resolution alone could plausibly justify the effort of reading Proust's *Recherche*, or *War and Peace*, or *Clarissa*. The narrative force of fiction depends upon assumptions carried forward, enriched, modified, reappraised, overturned in the process of reading; even in fiction, narrative development is only possible on the basis of an *established* sense of relevance.

Relevant information, in fiction, is supplied by assumptions with the capacity to inform a cognitive environment that includes the assumption of fictionality itself, as well as a set of general assumptions that might be collectively labelled "narrative understanding" (which would include logical, evaluative, and affective subsets), and more specific assumptions relating to, for instance, generic expectations of the text in hand and the particulars of its subject matter. In this cognitive environment, the contextual effects that constitute relevance may be produced by new assumptions informing the project of narrative understanding in general (and the further kinds of understanding this may facilitate), or by assumptions enabling further inferences from the narrative particulars, which will themselves contribute to an ongoing, cumulative experience of relevance (such cumulative effects being analogous to those that Sperber and Wilson term "poetic effects" in their discussion of how impressions may be communicated). So, a reader of *The Trial* may find relevance in constructing some of the subtle hypotheses about psychological motivation needed to comprehend

K.'s behaviour; or such comprehension may contribute to an emotional investment of interest, for which K. becomes the vehicle. In either case, the narrative coherence that provides for these effects rests upon more manifest assumptions, of a sort that relates to the familiar idea of what is "true in the fiction". Such assumptions have the status of information irrespective of the literal truth value of the utterance, because their validity, their "aboutness", is contextual, not referential (though this is not to exclude the possibility that some of the assumptions made available by fictive discourse may indeed be referential: as, for instance, in the case of a roman à clef, or a historical novel, or the many modern forms of documentary fiction).

The notion of truth "in the fiction" does not imply an ontological frame, but a contextual qualification: assumptions of this kind provide information relative to a context of prior assumptions. We do not generally attempt to resolve the reference of fictive utterances because we know in advance that, in the absence of any evidence to the contrary, their literal truth value will probably be of too little relevance to be worth determining. But this does not compromise the narrative coherence of fictions, because successful reference resolution is not necessary for co-reference to occur (think of algebra: we do not need to know the value of x to know that, in $x^2 = 2xy$, each x refers to the same value, which is also twice the value of y). The communicative efficacy of multiple references to fictional characters, places, and events is a pragmatic matter, not a semantic one. As a fictional narrative progresses, further assumptions become manifest not because earlier assumptions have projected a fictional world within which the fictional truth of new assumptions can be established, but because the achieved relevance of the earlier assumptions itself becomes a contextual basis for maximizing the relevance of subsequent related assumptions.

A relevance-driven, pragmatic account of inference in fiction does not need to proceed by way of a referential world beyond the discourse, or a denotative, "de re" semantics beyond the attributive, "de dicto" relations between referring expressions. Everything we can explain by conceiving of fictions as referential constructs projecting fictional worlds, we can explain as well, without cumbersome detour, restrictive norms, paradox, or redundancy, by understanding fiction as the serious use of a language's representational capacity for fictive—imaginary, not literally assertive—purposes (and it goes without saying that relevance theory's inclusive model of communication as ostensive behaviour provides a way to embrace fictions in nonlinguistic media without difficulty). The communicative criterion of relevance is primary rather than deferred or indirect, and unitary rather than internal or external to a fictional frame. We need to think in terms of the pragmatics rather than the semantics of fictionality.

三、思考与讨论

(1) 关联理论为沃尔什的修辞方法虚构性理论提供了哪些启示?

(2) 沃尔什对"虚构世界"这一经典概念提出了何种批评,并提供了何种替代解释?

(3) 请运用沃尔什的虚构性定义,试分析你熟悉的虚构文学作品中的1～2句话,探讨此处虚构性引发的具体交流效果。(可参考沃尔什《虚构性修辞学》第一章中对卡夫卡小说《审判》第一句的分析。[①])

本章推荐阅读书目

[1] Michael Kearns. *Rhetorical Narratology*. Lincoln and London: University of Nebraska Press, 1999.

[2] James Phelan. *Living to Tell about It: A Rhetoric and Ethics of Character Narration*. Ithaca: Cornell University Press, 2005.

[3] Peter J. Rabinowitz. *Before Reading: Narrative Conventions and the Politics of Interpretation*. Ithaca: Cornell University Press, 1987.

[4] Shen Dan. *Style and Rhetoric of Short Narrative Fiction: Covert Progressions Behind Overt Plots*. London: Routledge, 2014.

[5] Meir Sternberg. *Expositional Modes and Temporal Ordering in Fiction*. Bloomington: Indiana University Press, 1978.

① Walsh, *The Rhetoric of Fictionality: Narrative Theory and the Idea of Fiction*, pp.33 - 36.

第三章
认知叙事学

第一节 概 论

作为西方后经典叙事学中的一个关键流派,"认知叙事学"(cognitive narratology)是当代西方叙事学发展的一个重要方向。1997年,戴维·赫尔曼在《现代语言学会会刊》第5期上发表后经典叙事学的宣言式文章《脚本、序列和故事:后经典叙事学的元素》。赫尔曼在文中首次提出后经典叙事学,并把认知科学对叙事学研究方法的拓展视为后经典叙事学的一个代表性方向,认为"将认知工具融入叙事学能够给叙事分析所面临的一些最基本问题提供新颖思路"。[①] 同样在1997年,曼弗雷德·雅恩在《今日诗学》(*Poetics Today*)上发表论文《框架、优先性与第三人称叙事的理解:走向认知叙事学》("Frames, Preferences, and the Reading of Third-person Narrative: Towards a Cognitive Narratology"),明确提出认知叙事学这一概念,这标志着认知叙事学的正式出场。21世纪以来,认知叙事学呈现出蓬勃发展的态势,大量相关著述涌现出来,其中具有代表性的是《叙事理论与认知科学》(*Narrative Theory and the Cognitive Sciences*, 2003)、《我们为什么阅读小说:关于心理与小说的理论》(*Why We Read Fiction: Theory of Mind and The Novel*, 2006)、《小说中的社会心理》(*Social Minds in the Novel*, 2010)、《故事讲述与心理科学》(*Storytelling and the Sciences of Mind*, 2013)等。

一、什么是认知叙事学?

艾伦·帕尔默(Alan Palmer)指出,文学研究在20世纪90年代迎来一轮较为明显的"认知转向"(cognitive turn),这直接引发认知叙事学、文学研究的认知方法(cognitive approaches to literature)及认知诗学(cognitive poetics)的兴起,它们共同构成文学研究领域的新发展。虽然它们存在联系,但相互之间又有所差异。在帕尔默看来,三者的区别在于:认知叙事学是指运用心智哲学、心理学、认知科学等领域的相关理论来考察叙事理解过程的不同方面,目前主要关注的叙事为小说;文学研究的认知方法兴起于文学批评领域,其主要感兴趣的一个方向是对戏剧和诗歌中的隐喻的分析;认知诗学则属于一

---

① David Herman, "Scripts, Sequences, and Stories: Elements of a Postclassical Narratology," p.1057.

种应用语言学，试图运用语言学工具对诗歌、戏剧、小说等文本展开分析。①

因而，认知叙事学是21世纪初叙事学领域兴起的一种跨学科研究方向。认知科学与叙事学的学术联姻是促成认知叙事学这一后经典叙事学流派产生和发展的主要动力。21世纪以来，认知科学研究受到学界高度重视，该领域不断出现前沿研究成果，为叙事学家从中借用理论资源提供了可能。此外，这一时期的叙事学在理论创新方面的迫切需求成为推动叙事学与认知科学交叉互惠的催化剂。

认知叙事学界的代表人物戴维·赫尔曼对认知叙事学的界定为："认知叙事学是一个跨学科的研究领域，它将叙事学的概念和方法与源自心理学、人工智能、心理哲学等认知科学的思想和方法融合。该跨学科研究领域旨在为研究叙事结构和叙事阐释的理论家所提出的范畴和原则建构一种认知基础或提供动力。相反，认知叙事学家认为，那些在传统意义上被认为是从事认知科学研究的学者同样能够通过熟练掌握分析自然叙事话语——无论是口头的还是书面的，日常的还是文学的——的技术方法来获得有益启发。"② 赫尔曼强调认知叙事学的跨学科特质，认为认知叙事学的重要贡献在于，它能够推进叙事学和认知科学之间的融合，二者通过互惠融通而获得协同发展。

从研究的具体内容来看，认知叙事学旨在"探讨认知、语言、知识、记忆与世界之间的关系，关注的是在这些现象之内和相互交叠之处故事起何作用"。③ 认知叙事学考察的主要对象是叙事与认知之间的链接问题，聚焦叙事的组织模式与读者的解读之间的互动关系。换句话说，认知叙事学格外关注接受者理解叙事的普遍认知模式，探讨的主要问题是"故事如何与阐释者的认知能力和倾向发生互联，并由此阐释叙事经验"。④

二、认知叙事学的主要研究模式

认知叙事学的跨学科特质决定了其研究模式的多元化。这种研究模式的多元化致使认知叙事学在某种程度上显得有些混乱，其具体的理论边界难以确定。为认知叙事学提供主要理论滋养的认知科学本身就是一个跨学科的领域，涉及认知神经学、心理学、人工智能科学、语言学等诸多学科，这在给认知科学研究方法赋予跨学科优势的同时也为之隐形增添了难以理清的混乱。⑤ 认知叙事学也存在这方面的问题，该领域实际上是由多种不同的研究方法共同促成的一个叙事学研究方向。限于篇幅，本章无法将所有的认知叙事学研究模式全部加以阐述，只能从中挑选具有代表性的模式展开述评，具体关注的是赫尔曼的世界建构模式、弗鲁德尼克的普世认知模式、帕尔默的虚构心理模式。除这三种认知叙事学研究模式外，玛丽-劳勒·瑞安的认知绘图模式同样值得注意。瑞安把"认知绘图"(cognitive map)定义

① Alan Palmer, *Social Minds in the Novel* (Columbus: The Ohio State University Press, 2010), p.6.

② David Herman, "Introduction," *Narrative Theory and the Cognitive Sciences*, ed. David Herman (Stanford: CSLI Publications, 2003), p.20.

③ Manfred Jahn. "Cognitive Narratology," *Routledge Encyclopedia of Narrative Theory*, eds. David Herman, Manfred Jahn and Marie-Laure Ryan (London: Routledge, 2005), p.67.

④ David Herman. *Storytelling and the Sciences of Mind* (Cambridge: The MIT Press, 2013), p.ix.

⑤ 陈礼珍：《当代西方认知叙事学研究的最新走向与远景展望》，载《解放军外国语学院学报》2020年第1期，第52页。

为“空间关系的心理模型”[①]，她关注的是叙事中的空间关系在读者大脑中呈现出的认知模型，即“阅读时文字所唤起的读者对叙事空间的建构”[②]。另外值得一提的是，由玛丽莎·博托卢西（Marisa Bortolussi）和彼得·狄克逊（Peter Dixon）提出的心理叙事学同样是认知叙事学中的一个分支，虽然其在文学认知叙事学领域的影响不及其他三种模式，但其研究方法较为新颖。[③] 他们提倡从实证心理学角度对读者的叙事认知展开研究，挑战传统的文学认知叙事学研究方法，认为其缺乏实证基础，过于关注理论问题。[④]

（一）世界建构模式

赫尔曼是该模式的代表人物。赫尔曼的认知叙事学围绕两个核心问题展开：一是不同媒介形式的故事如何与阐释者的认知能力发生互联，由此产生叙事经验；二是叙事对于人们理解经验又有何作用。[⑤] 赫尔曼认为，讨论叙事的世界建构问题是深入探索这两个问题的基础。“世界建构”（word-making）是赫尔曼认知叙事学中的一个关键概念，构成他在认知叙事学领域展开理论思考的一个“核心探索框架”，该概念指的是“叙事在阐释者心中生成世界的能力”。[⑥] 结构主义叙事学家所做的主要工作是对叙事文本展开系统的结构分析，总结归纳叙事文本的叙事语法。赫尔曼认为这种叙事研究模式的一个重要局限就是没有去讨论故事讲述与世界建构之间的关系。在赫尔曼那里，探究叙事如何给予读者世界创造的方法，思考故事讲述何以成为读者建构世界的根本基础是叙事学家所面临的一个“巨大而突出的挑战”，因而他的主要工作就是去考察“故事讲述者如何运用多种不同的符号系统——不论是书面语或口语，静止的或运动图像，还是文字和图像的结合——促使阐释者参与创造叙事世界”。[⑦] 说到底，赫尔曼的认知叙事学所关注的核心是阐释者的叙事认知过程，具体就是要考察故事讲述究竟能够在读者心里激起什么样的世界，以及故事讲述的动机和结果又是什么。[⑧]

赫尔曼认知叙事理论的一个突出贡献在于，它在某种程度上为认知叙事学这一后经典叙事学分支提供了理论基础，这对认知叙事学在21世纪的繁荣和发展具有开拓性作用。赫尔曼的认知叙事学具有以下几个方面的特点：首先，赫尔曼的研究具有很强的跨学科特质，他尤其善于从认知科学、哲学、语言学等其他学科借用各种专业术语，并将它们巧妙地运用到认知叙事学的建构中；其次，他的认知叙事学研究具有很强的理论性，为认知叙事学领域的纯诗学建构做出了重要贡献，他不仅从认知角度对经典叙事学概念加以重审和修正，也原创性地提出了一系列重要的认知叙事理论术语；最后，在所有认知叙事学家中，赫尔曼的理论研究或许是最为系统的，他一方面从理论角度阐述了叙事学研究读者的认知过程与叙事形式结构之间的关系，进而为认知叙事学研究的合法性提供理论支撑，另一方面则在具体的研究实践中从认知理解的角度对叙事时间、叙事聚焦、叙事交流、叙事媒介、叙事人称等叙事学领域的核心问

---

① Marie-Laure Ryan, “Cognitive Maps and the Construction of Narrative Space,” *Narrative Theory and the Cognitive Sciences*, ed. David Herman (Stanford: CSLI Publications, 2003), p.215.

② 申丹:《叙事结构与认知过程：认知叙事学评析》，载《外语与外语教学》2004年第9期，第5页。

③ 关于博托卢西和狄克逊的心理叙事学，详见 Marisa Bortolussi and Peter Dixon, *Psychonarratology: Foundations for the Empirical Study of Literary Response* (Cambridge: Cambridge University Press, 2003).

④ 申丹:《叙事结构与认知过程：认知叙事学评析》，第6页；陈礼珍:《当代西方认知叙事学研究的最新走向与远景展望》，第54页。

⑤ Herman, *Storytelling and the Sciences of Mind*, p.ix.

⑥ 戴维·赫尔曼等:《叙事理论：核心概念与批评性辨析》，谭君强等译，北京：北京师范大学出版社，2016年，第15页。

⑦ 同上，第15页。

⑧ 同上，第18页。

题展开详细的探讨，极大地推进了认知叙事学领域的理论建设。

(二) 普适认知模式

德国叙事学家弗鲁德尼克在《走向"自然"叙事学》(*Towards a 'Natural' Narratology*, 1996)一书中提出建构"自然叙事学"(natural narratology)。她受自然语言学相关理论启发，把自然叙事这一概念引入叙事学。自然叙事是指那些"自然产生的对话性故事讲述"，它是一种基础性参数，构成了所有叙事的基本原型和普遍基础。[①] 弗鲁德尼克的自然叙事学中的一个重要观点是，若某一文本要构成叙事，它必须经历"叙事化"(narrativization)这一关键环节。[②] 叙事化是指接受者将文本理解为叙事的过程，而接受者对文本的叙事化依赖于他们源自经验生活的认知参数。由于源自经验生活的自然叙事构成所有叙事的原型，读者在叙事化的过程中会将文本理解为一种对经验的表达，经验性也就成了叙事的一个基本条件。

不难发现，弗鲁德尼克把自然叙事视为一种蕴藏于所有叙事文本之下的深层机理。人们对叙事的理解源于其基于真实生活经验的种种认知框架，而文本对于经验的再现是读者将文本理解为叙事的前提。弗鲁德尼克的自然叙事理论的原创之处在于，她并没有像热奈特、普林斯、巴尔等人那样，从文本对于不同事件的再现方式，以及不同事件之间的逻辑关系角度来理解叙事，而是从更为根本的人类认知的普遍规律角度去把握所有叙事的共同基础。依据弗鲁德尼克的观点，判断某一文本是否为叙事的关键，并不在于文本如何再现某个或某些事件，而在于接受者能否依据已有的认知参数将文本理解为对经验的表达。换句话说，"叙事性"(narrativity)并非文本本身的固有特质，从"文本"到"叙事"的转变依赖于接受者的参与，前提是文本必须是对特定经验的再现。因而在弗鲁德尼克那里，构成叙事的本质要素是经验性，而不是情节，无情节但存在经验性的叙事是可能存在的。

从本质上看，弗鲁德尼克的认知叙事学基本上沿袭了认知语言学对传统索绪尔语言学加以突破的基本思路。传统语言学将语言视为一种形式系统或者交流行为，而认知语言学关注的却是藏于语言形式之下的各种观念，假定语言源于人们对世界的理解，认为语言和语言运用的分析与人们的心理认知及人们与外部非心理环境的互动密切相关。[③] 在认知语言学家看来，虽然语言受到文化因素的影响，但语言中基本概念的含义却往往是普遍的，因而基于语言概念普遍性的认知框架和过程将"激发、影响和控制语言使用"。[④] 基于认知语言学的基本理论假设，弗鲁德尼克在理解叙事时，并不致力于考察叙事的形式结构——这是普罗普、热奈特等经典叙事学家的重点工作；她关注的是叙事中的普遍性，并用自然叙事这一概念来指代这种普遍性，称其是构成所有叙事的一个基础，并由此推演出关于叙事的一系列重要概念，其中叙事化和经验性最为突出。

(三) 虚构心理模式

帕尔默致力于考察虚构叙事中的意识再现问题，关注的是作品中人物的"虚构心理"(fictional minds)建构。在帕尔默看来，关于小说中的虚构心理这一议题，叙事学界大致存在两种视角，即"内部视角"(internalist)和"外部视角"(externalist)，前者强调虚构心理的内省式特质，而后者则强调虚构心理

---

① Fludernik, *Towards a 'Natural' Narratology*, p.13.

② Ibid., p.14.

③ Fludernik, "Narratology in the Twenty-First Century: The Cognitive Approach to Narrative," p.925.

④ Ibid.

的公共性特质。[1] 帕尔默认为，长期以来，传统叙事学研究方法大多只是强调小说故事世界中人物心理的内部方面，关注的是小说中虚构人物的个体的私人意识，这是自由间接话语、意识流、内心独白等概念在叙事学界受到较多关注的原因。但这种过度关注人物心理内部方面的研究范式实际上是以牺牲故事世界中的其他形式的心理功能为代价的；换言之，叙事学长期以来忽略了虚构心理的社会性特质。[2] 因此，帕尔默认为，在研究虚构叙事中的意识再现问题时有必要引入一种外部视角，具体就是要关注人物心理中那些公共的、社会的、具体的、确定的方面。[3]

帕尔默把由外部视角所揭示的虚构心理称为“社会心理”(social mind)。在他看来，“脑际意识”(intermental thought)是与社会心理相关的一个重要方面，它与“脑内意识”(intramental thought)相对，脑内意识是个人的，脑际意识则是公共的、集体的，可以被视为一种“社会性的分布式、情境式或延展式认知”，亦能被视为一种“主体间性”。[4] 换句话说，虚构叙事不仅涉及个体的思维，还涉及故事世界中那些由个体之外的多重社会因素、环境因素互动产生的公共意识。帕尔默认为，正如经验世界中的大多数意义和思维的形成源于集体性互动一样，虚构文本中的意识运作同样产生于团体性的人际交流。他进一步指出，虚构叙事必然包含这种公共性的社会心理模式，且在某种程度上，“小说中的大量主题都是这种人际心理系统的形成、发展、维护、修正和破坏”。[5]

帕尔默对小说中的社会心理的研究具有开创性的意义，因为他关注了传统叙事研究范式所忽略的方面，把研究的视角从个体心理转向社会公共心理，开辟了虚构叙事中的意识再现研究的新空间。另外，帕尔默对小说中的社会心理的研究同样体现出明显的跨学科特质。从帕尔默的论述中可以清楚地看到，他借用了大量认知科学领域的相关理论，为叙事学研究方法的突破做出了重要贡献。

三、认知叙事学的诗学本质

从诗学本质上看，认知叙事学是叙事学在其后经典阶段形成的跨学科叙事研究方向。叙事学自其作为一门独立的学科确立以来，一直都致力于探索叙事的形式和功能。结构主义叙事学旨在发现文本的叙事语法，力图以语言学的基本理论来阐释文学叙事的结构特征。认知叙事学说到底也是要去探索叙事的结构问题的，但认知叙事学家则通过从认知科学那里借用方法来探讨叙事文本内部或作者对叙事理解的认知机制问题。索绪尔的结构主义语言学仍然是认知叙事学的基本理论源泉。赫尔曼认为，结构主义叙事学家并未充分探索索绪尔语言学中的“语言”概念的内涵。[6] 赫尔曼的意思是，结构主义叙事学家对于索绪尔语言学的理解显得有些狭义，因为他们更倾向于通过对具体文本展开语言学式的分析来揭示文本语法。在赫尔曼看来，索绪尔所说的“语言”即语言系统，该系统犹如统摄特定叙事文本或话语理解和阐释的系统，是一个较为宏观的整体概念，而认知叙事学就是要尝试运用跨学科的方法来探索叙事阐释的认知系统。

---

① Palmer. *Social Minds in the Novel*, p.39.
② Ibid.
③ Ibid., p.40.
④ Ibid., p.41.
⑤ Ibid.
⑥ Herman, “Introduction,” p.9.

第二节　戴维·赫尔曼及其《叙事与认知之间联系的研究》

一、导读

戴维·赫尔曼是“后经典叙事学”的提出者。赫尔曼在后经典叙事学的多个领域都有所建树，其中最值得称道的仍然是他在认知叙事学方面的理论探索。赫尔曼把认知叙事学视为后经典叙事学中的一个大有可为的方向，并将之看成跨学科叙事研究的一种典型领域。赫尔曼认为通过研究经典叙事学家所忽略的认知问题，认知叙事家能够丰富和拓展结构主义叙事学。“叙事世界建构”是赫尔曼认知叙事理论中的一个核心概念，构成他建构其叙事诗学体系的一个基础。叙事世界建构涉及叙事的指称维度，具体则是指叙事在阐释者心中激起某种故事世界。在赫尔曼看来，世界建构是叙事经验的一个标志性特征，也是故事和故事讲述的基础性功能，因而理应成为叙事研究的一个起点。[①] 认知叙事学就是要考察叙事的世界建构问题，关注的具体问题是叙事如何运用各种形式的符号系统促使叙事接受者参与到叙事世界的共同创建过程之中。[②] 所以说，赫尔曼认为，认知叙事学就是要去研究文本被读者理解为叙事的过程，这涉及两个方面，一是文本如何运用不同类型的符号系统来建构文本世界，二是读者如何借助个人的认知经验来对文本所建构的世界展开理解。赫尔曼指出，尽管不同的叙事都是通过某种媒介来创造故事世界的，但不同的叙事实践中却包含了不同的世界建构“协议”(protocols)，进而也会产生不尽相同的叙事效果，要想有效阐释此类不同形式的世界建构协议，就必须推进叙事学与认知科学之间的对话交流。与此同时，虽然赫尔曼一再强调认知科学能够给叙事学研究带来新变化，他同样认为探索叙事的世界建构问题能够推进人们对人类认知能力的研究，因而二者相辅相成。

二、《叙事与认知之间联系的研究》选读[③]

My contributions to this volume outline an approach that focuses on the nexus between narrative and mind, using Ian McEwan's 2007 novel *On Chesil Beach* as a case study. Research on the mind-narrative nexus, like feminist narratology, work on narrative across media, and other approaches to narrative inquiry can be described as a subdomain within "postclassical" narratology (Herman, "Introduction" to *Narratologies*). At issue are frameworks for narrative research that build on the ideas of classical, structuralist narratologists but supplement those ideas with work that was unavailable to story analysts such as Roland Barthes, Gérard Genette, Algirdas J. Greimas, and

① David Herman, et al., *Narrative Theory: Core Concepts and Critical Debates* (Columbus: The Ohio State University Press, 2012), p.14.
② Ibid., p.15.
③ Ibid., pp.14-19.

Tzvetan Todorov during the heyday of the structuralist revolution. In the case of scholarship bearing on narrative and mind, theorists have worked to enrich the original base of structuralist concepts with research on human intelligence either ignored by or inaccessible to the classical narratologists, in an effort to throw light on mental capacities and dispositions that provide grounds for—or, conversely, are grounded in—narrative experiences.

To explore these interfaces between stories and the mind, I use the idea of *narrative worldmaking* as a central heuristic framework, drawing on the pioneering insights of Nelson Goodman, Richard Gerrig, and other theorists. In my usage of the term, worldmaking encompasses the referential dimension of narrative, its capacity to evoke worlds in which interpreters can, with more or less ease or difficulty, take up imaginative residence.① I argue that worldmaking is in fact the hallmark of narrative experiences, the root function of stories and storytelling that should therefore constitute the starting-point for narrative inquiry and the analytic tools developed in its service. Yet the structuralist narratologists, for their part, failed to investigate issues of narrative referentiality and world-modeling, not least because of the Saussurean language theory they used as their "pilot-science". Of key importance here is Saussure's bipartite analysis of the linguistic sign into the signifier and signified② to the exclusion of the referent, as well as his related emphasis on code instead of message—that is, his foregrounding of the structural constituents and combinatory principles of the semiotic system of language over situated uses of that system. By contrast, in the years since structuralism, convergent research developments across multiple fields, including discourse analysis, philosophy, psychology, and narrative theory itself, have revealed the importance of studying how people deploy various sorts of symbol systems to refer to, and constitute, aspects of their experience. Building on this work, the approach I outline in this book assumes that a crucial outstanding challenge for scholars of story is to come to terms with how narrative affords methods—indeed, serves as a primary resource—for world-modeling and world-creation.

A focus on narrative worldmaking studies how storytellers, using many different kinds of

① As will become clear in what follows, I use the term "referential" in a broader sense than does Dorrit Cohn in *The Distinction of Fiction*, for example. Discussing ideas also explored by theorists such as Philippe Lejeune, Lubomír Doležel (*Heterocosmica*), and Marie-Laure Ryan (*Possible Worlds*), Cohn argues that fictional narratives are non-referential because, in contrast with historiography, journalistic reports, biographies, autobiographies, and other narrative modes falling within the domain of nonfiction, fictional works are not subject to judgments of truth and falsity (15). As Cohn writes, "in fictional poetics, though the concept of reference has recently been reinstated, its qualification by such terms as *fictive*, *nonostensive*, or *pseudo*-sufficiently indicates its nonfactual connotations, even when it denotes components of the fictional world taken directly from the world of reality" (113). In my approaches to the present volume, however, I link worldmaking to "the referential dimension of narrative" to preserve the intuition that fictional as well as nonfictional narratives consist of *sequences of referring expressions* (see also Schiffrin), whose nature and scope will vary depending on the storytelling medium involved. Through these referring expressions, narratives prompt interpreters to co-construct a discourse model or model-world—that is, a storyworld—containing the situations, events, and entities indexed by world-evoking expressions at issue (for further discussion, see Herman, *Basic Elements* and *Story Logic*). In other words, narratives refer to model-worlds, whether they are the imagined, autonomous model-worlds of fiction or the model-worlds about which nonfictional accounts make claims that are subject to falsification.

② With signified and signifier, compare story (*fabula*) and discourse (*sjuzhet*).

symbol systems (written or spoken language, static or moving images, word-image combinations, etc.), prompt interpreters to engage in the process of co-creating narrative worlds, or "storyworlds"—whether they are the imagined, autonomous worlds of fiction or the worlds about which nonfictional accounts make claims that are subject to falsification. As this last formulation suggests, although narrative provides the means for creating, transforming, and aggregating storyworlds across various settings and media,① different kinds of narrative practices entail different protocols for worldmaking, with different consequences and effects. I argue that illuminating these protocols will require bringing scholarship on narrative into closer dialogue with developments in the sciences of mind. More than this, however, I suggest that moving issues of worldmaking to the forefront of narrative inquiry opens up new directions for basic research in the field, in part by underscoring the need to reframe the kinds of questions theorists ask about narrative itself.

In this respect, my emphasis on narrative worldmaking takes inspiration from Ludwig Wittgenstein's later philosophy, or rather what has come to be called the *metaphilosophy* embedded in texts such as the *Philosophical Investigations*. According to this metaphilosophy, the role of philosophy is to dispel, through analysis of the way particular expressions are used in particular contexts, conceptual problems caused by overgeneralization of any specific usage—as when expressions involving numbers are conflated with expressions involving physical objects, such that numbers start to be treated as things (Horwich 165-167).② Put another way, the later Wittgenstein's central metaphilosophical insight is that the grammar with which a question is formulated, or the language in which a problem is cast, can close off other ways of surveying a given area of inquiry or mapping out a problem space being investigated. Similarly, in reorienting narrative theory around questions of worldmaking, and in turn situating storyworlds at the nexus of narrative and mind, I seek to recontextualize existing heuristic schemes for narrative study, or rather shift to an alternative vantage point from which those schemes' underlying "grammar" can be surveyed anew.③ Hence my contributions have been designed to serve not just narratological purposes, by suggesting how a focus on worldmaking affords productive strategies for studying stories, but also metanarratological purposes, by using this same focus to reassess the terms in which questions about narrative have been formulated up to now.④

---

① In *Basic Elements*, I more fully characterize narrative as a mode of representation that (a) must be interpreted in light of a specific discourse context or occasion for telling; (b) focuses on a structured time-course of particularized events; (c) concerns itself with some kind of disruption or disequilibrium in a storyworld inhabited by intelligent agents; and (d) conveys what it is like for those agents to live through the storyworld-in-flux.

② Compare Brenner's account of how, for Wittgenstein, "[p]hilosophical investigation recollects the grammar of terms that are deeply embedded in everyday language" (7).

③ Here I am drawing on Wittgenstein's discussion, in section 122 of the *Philosophical Investigations*, of the key concept of "surveyability". Suggesting that the purpose of philosophy is to provide an overview or survey of the different ways in which uses of words fit together in a language, Wittgenstein writes: "A main source of our failure to understand is that we don't have *an overview* of the use of our words.—Our grammar is deficient in surveyability. A surveyable representation produces precisely that kind of understanding which consists in 'seeing connections'" (54).

④ For more on the scope and aims of the project of metanarratology, see Herman, "Formal Models".

For example, in the chapters that follow and also in my response to my coauthors' contributions in Part Two, I revisit the grammar of questions about narrative premised on the concept of mimesis. On the one hand, if mimesis is defined narrowly as imitation or reproduction, the very concept becomes untenable—since there can be no direct representation of the world, no bare encounter with reality, without mediating world-models.① On the other hand, if mimesis is defined as part of a family of strategies for deploying world-models, then the concept cannot do the work my coauthors try to get it to do—for example, when they set mimesis up as a standard or touchstone against which "antimimetic" stories, or the "synthetic" and "thematic" dimensions of narrative, can be measured. But changing the grammar of the question—asking not about mimesis or its absence but about how story designs can be arranged along a scale corresponding to more or less critical and reflexive methods of worldmaking—opens up new avenues for narrative inquiry. Along similar lines, my focus on issues of worldmaking leads me to reconsider (ways of asking) questions associated with the narrative communication diagram, a widely used heuristic scheme that has given rise to the constructs of the implied author and the implied reader, among others. Shaped by the anti-intentionalist arguments of the Anglo-American New Critics, these constructs are embedded in a grammar that can be surveyed from a different position when processes of worldmaking, which are grounded in defeasible or possibly wrong ascriptions of intentions to story creators, become the key focus. This new vantage point suggests how the communication diagram not only proliferates heuristic constructs but also reifies them—obscuring how the constructs at issue are ways of describing phases or aspects of the inferential activities that support worldmaking, not preconditions for understanding stories. Again, then, by keeping the focus on narrative's root function as a resource for world-modeling and world-creation, new ways of formulating questions about stories suggest themselves. I argue that these questions cannot be fully articulated, let alone addressed, in the terms afforded by previous nomenclatures and the grammar of inquiry with which they are bound up.②

By the same token, my emphasis on worldmaking as a framework for exploring the mind-narrative nexus has required that I tweak the template designed to provide readers with a basis for comparing and contrasting the four approaches covered in this volume. Unlike the other three approaches, my approach treats the creation of and (more or less sustained) imaginative relocation to narrative worlds not as a way of analyzing issues of space, setting, and perspective in particular,

① As Goodman puts it, "If I ask about the world, you can offer to tell me how it is under one or more frames of reference; but if I insist that you tell me how it is apart from all frames, what can you say? We are confined to ways of describing whatever is described. Our universe, so to speak, consists of these ways rather than of a world or of worlds" (2 - 3). Compare Merlin Donald's complementary account of the evolution and functions of mimesis or "mimetic skill". For Donald, such skill "usually incorporates both mimicry and imitation to a higher end, that of re-enacting and re-presenting an event or relationship" (169). Hence, extended to the social realm, mimetic skill "results in a collective conceptual 'model' of society" (173). See also my contribution to Part Two.

② See Chapter 5 for analogous remarks concerning the need to reassess the grammar of questions about narrative that feature the concept of "Theory of Mind".

but rather as a core aspect of all narrative experiences—as an enabling condition for storytelling practices as such (see also Herman, *Basic Elements* 105 - 136). In turn, narrative worldmaking is imbricated with—both supports and is supported by—basic mental abilities and dispositions that constitute focal concerns of research on the interconnection between narrative and mind. Hence in my approach, time, space, and character can be redescribed as key parameters for narrative worldbuilding. Through acts of narration, creators of stories produce blueprints for world construction. These blueprints, the complexity of whose design varies, prompt interpreters to construct worlds marked by a particular spatiotemporal profile, a patterned sequence of situations and events, and an inventory of inhabitants.①

Accordingly, extending scholarship that adapts ideas from psycholinguistics, discourse analysis, and related areas of inquiry to characterize processes of narrative understanding,② I suggest that engaging with stories entails mapping discourse cues onto WHEN, WHAT, WHERE, WHO, HOW, and WHY dimensions of mentally configured worlds; the interplay among these dimensions accounts for the structure as well as the representational functions and overall impact of the worlds in question. I emphasize throughout how the making of storyworlds depends on the reader or interpreter, and I expand upon that claim in chapter 6 while using chapter 7 to explore the broader contexts and consequences of such worldmaking practices. Narratives do not merely evoke worlds but also intervene in a field of discourses, a range of representational strategies, a constellation of ways of seeing—and sometimes a set of competing narratives, as in a courtroom trial, a political campaign, or a family dispute (see Abbott, *Introduction* 175 - 192). Under its profile as a reception process, then, narrative worldmaking entails at least two different types of inferences: those bearing on what sort of world is being evoked by the act of telling, and those bearing on why (and with what consequences) that act is being performed at all.

I should also emphasize at the outset that although I explore issues of broad relevance for the study of narrative and mind, a mind-oriented approach to narrative inquiry can be pursued along lines different from the ones sketched here. For one thing, my example narrative is a (monomodal) print text, and different tools are needed to explore the mind-narrative nexus in storytelling practices that recruit from more than one semiotic channel (see Herman, "Directions"). Further, whereas my approach is synchronic rather than diachronic, focusing on acts

---

① In characterizing narrative texts as blueprints for building storyworlds, I am drawing on Reddy's critique of what he termed the "conduit metaphor" for communicative processes (see Green, 10 - 13, for a useful discussion). Reddy suggested that rather than being mere vessels or vehicles for channeling thoughts, ideas, and meanings back and forth, utterances are like blueprints, planned artifacts whose design is tailored to the goal of enabling an interlocutor to reconstruct the situations or worlds after which the blueprints are patterned. Further, in contrast with the conduit metaphor, which blames miscommunication on a poorly chosen linguistic vessel, the blueprint analogy predicts that completely successful interpretation of communicative designs will be rare—given the complexity of the processes involved in planning, executing, and making sense of the blueprints. Hence my emphasis in this volume on the *defeasibility* of inferences about story creators' intentions.

② Relevant studies include Doležel; Duchan, Bruder, and Hewitt; Emmott; Gerrig; Herman, *Story Logic* and *Basic Elements*; Pavel; Ryan, Possible; and Werth.

of narrative worldmaking that it is currently within humans' capacity to perform, evolutionary-psychological perspectives explore ways in which features and uses of narrative can be traced back to mental abilities that have evolved over time (Austin; Boyd; Easterlin; Tooby and Cosmides).①
What is more, in contrast with researchers (e.g. Hogan) who have appealed to the neurobiology of the brain to posit mapping relationships between aspects of narrative production or processing, on the one hand, and specific structures and processes in the brain, on the other hand, my approach remains situated at the person level—the level of the medium-sized, human-scale world of everyday experience (Baker, *Persons* and *Metaphysics*; see chapter 5 of this volume and also my response in Part Two). Since narratives and narrative scholarship both have much to say about this world of everyday experience, by focusing on the person level I seek to substantiate one of the basic assumptions of my approach: namely, that the study of narrative worldmaking can inform, and not just be informed by, understandings of the mind.

The Case Study: McEwan's *On Chesil Beach*

I use *On Chesil Beach* to examine key aspects of stories and storytelling from a perspective that foregrounds issues of worldmaking; focusing on these issues will allow me to outline, in turn, strategies for investigating the mind-narrative nexus. I have chosen McEwan's novel② for a number of reasons, including its powerful exploration of how interpersonal conflicts are rooted in larger familial and social contexts, and its reflexive investigation of the way stories provide scaffolding for making sense of one's own and others' actions (see Herman, "Storied"). I discuss these and other aspects of McEwan's text in the chapters that follow; however, according to the needs of the discussion, I alternately zoom in on and back out from the novel, which I sometimes use as the basis for theory building and sometimes as a means for testing the possibilities and limits of an approach oriented around issues of worldmaking—and for gaining a new vantage point on the grammar of narrative inquiry itself. In any case, a brief synopsis of the novel here will help lay groundwork for the ensuing analysis.

On Chesil Beach opens in medias res with two inexperienced and under-informed newlyweds trying to navigate the complexities of their wedding night on the eve of the sexual revolution in England in 1962. The first sentence sets the scene: "They were young, educated, and both virgins on this, their wedding night, and they lived in a time when a conversation about sexual difficulties was

① Conversely, Donald explores how narrative, among other semiotic and thus cultural practices, itself contributed to the development of humans' cognitive abilities (201 - 268).

② There are as yet few critical studies of this recently published text. But see Head, "Novella", and, for background on the novel's composition, Zalewski, who reports that Timothy Garton Ash's comments on an early draft caused McEwan to remove more explicit references to Florence's sexual abuse at the hands of her father (see my discussion in Chapter 3). Meanwhile, Head's Ian McEwan provides invaluable insights into McEwan's oeuvre prior to the publication of *On Chesil Beach*.

plainly impossible" (3). The first part of the novel explores the characters' states of mind as they sit down to dinner in their honeymoon suite in a Georgian inn on the Dorset coast. For Edward Mayhew, the groom, and the son of a father who is headmaster of a primary school and a mother who suffered brain damage because of a freak accident on a railway platform, the idea of having sex with his new wife is at once tantalizing and a source of worry. But for Florence Mayhew (née Ponting), a professional musician-in-the-making whose mother is a professor of philosophy and whose father owns an electronics company, the prospect of consummating her marriage with Edward causes a deep, paralyzing anxiety.① Thus, whereas Edward "merely suffered conventional first-night nerves, [Florence] experienced a visceral dread, a helpless disgust as palpable as seasickness" (8).

From this point until the final ten pages of McEwan's 203-page novel, the narrative alternates between, on the one hand, periodic shifts back in time that provide information about the main characters' family backgrounds, life stories, and courtship and, on the other hand, a detailed, blow-by-blow recounting of the events of the present moment. The present-day events lead up to what proves to be a disastrous attempt at sexual intercourse by Edward and Florence and an angry, marriage-ending exchange on the beach—Chesil Beach—afterward. Then, in the final portion of the novel, the pace of narration speeds up drastically, covering some forty years of story time in about 5 percent of the page space used previously to narrate events lasting just a few hours. Most of this final section is refracted through the vantage point of Edward, who eventually comes to the realization that though all "[Florence] needed was the certainty of his love, and his reassurance that there was no hurry when a lifetime lay ahead of them" (202), on that night on Chesil Beach he had nonetheless "stood in cold and righteous silence in the summer's dusk, watching her hurry along the shore, the sound of her difficult progress lost to the breaking of small waves, until she was a blurred, receding point against the immense straight road of shingle gleaming in the pallid light" (203).

三、思考与讨论

(1) 如何理解赫尔曼所提出的"故事世界"?

(2) 认知叙事学之于当代叙事学有何意义?

(3) 赫尔曼的认知叙事学有何局限?

① Readers of *On Chesil Beach* familiar with Ford Madox Ford's 1915 novel *The Good Soldier* will recognize that the first names of McEwan's two main characters echo those of Edward Ashburnham and Florence Dowell, whose ill-fated, destructive affair is narrated ex post facto—and through a complex layering of time-frames—by Florence's perversely obtuse husband, John Dowell.

第三节　莫妮卡·弗鲁德尼克及其《走向"自然"叙事学》

一、导读

德国叙事学家莫妮卡·弗鲁德尼克于1996年出版专著《走向"自然"叙事学》。该书在叙事学发展史上具有重要意义，因为弗鲁德尼克提出了一种新的叙事理解模式。弗鲁德尼克受到自然语言学启发，提出建构"自然叙事学"。她在书中明确指出，自然语言学的相关研究对她的理论思索有重要启示，直接影响了她提出关于"自然叙事学"的诸多核心概念和理论主张。弗鲁德尼克在书中提到了美国语言学家威廉·拉波夫(William Labov)对"自然叙事"的界定，并以此为启发，阐明了她个人的相关立场。所谓"自然叙事"，是指那些"自然产生的对话性故事讲述"。[①] 在弗鲁德尼克看来，自然叙事是一种基础性参数，它构成了所有叙事的基本原型和普遍基础。[②] 弗鲁德尼克认为，若某一文本要构成叙事，它必须经历"叙事化"这一关键环节，即接受者将文本理解为叙事的过程。读者对文本的"叙事化"依赖于他们源自经验生活的认知参数。由于源自经验生活的自然叙事构成所有叙事的原型，读者在叙事化的过程中会将文本理解为对某种"经验性"的表达，"经验性"也就成了叙事的一个基本条件。[③] 在《走向"自然"叙事学》一书中，弗鲁德尼克提出了叙事在接受和生成过程中的四层认知原型模式：① 第一层次为"目标""意图"等基本的认知观念和框架，我们是透过此类框架来解释日常生活中的现实经验的；② 第二层次是指讲述、观看、体验、思考或行动的叙事框架；③ 第三层次则是影响读者阅读框架的文类原型，如动作电影、成长小说等有关叙事类型的规约；④ 第四层次为"自然化"，即读者通过诉诸另外三个层次的框架积极地对文本进行"叙事化"，将之理解为叙事。[④] 此模式构成弗鲁德尼克自然叙事理论的一个基本假设。从弗鲁德尼克提出的四层认知原型模式可以看出，她是从叙事的深层次逻辑这一角度来理解和阐释叙事的，因此，其阐释具有浓重的认知科学意味。

二、《走向"自然"叙事学》选读[⑤]

It is now time to outline the model which I am here proposing and which will form the basis of the detailed analyses of *Towards a 'Natural' Narratology*. In this model cognitive parameters enter at several levels, in a manner that generalizes the term 'natural' over a number of alternative as

① Fludernik. *Towards a 'Natural' Narratology*, p.13.
② Monika Fludernik, "Natural Narratology and Cognitive Parameters," *Narrative Theory and the Cognitive Sciences*, ed. David Herman (Stanford: Center for the Study of Language and Information, 2003), p.244.
③ Fludernik. *Towards a 'Natural' Narratology*, p.313.
④ Monika Fludernik, "Naturalizing the Unnatural: A View from Blending Theory," pp.14–15.
⑤ Monika Fludernik. *Towards a 'Natural' Narratology* (London: Routledge, 1996), pp.32–36.

well as combined applications. Besides the obviously synchronic cognitive parameters, the model is meant to allow for historical analysis, providing diachronic perspectives on narrative texts.

The model operates on four levels. The axiomatic natural parameters of real-life experience form the most basic experiential and cognitive level. On this level are situated the core schemata from frame theory, which accommodate presupposed understandings of agency, goals, intellection, emotions, motivation, and so on. My **level I** parameters of real-life experience is therefore identical with Ricoeur's *Mimesis I*. It comprises the schema of agency as goal-oriented process or reaction to the unexpected, the configuration of experienced and evaluated occurrence, and the natural comprehension of observed event processes including their supposed cause-and-effect explanations. In this schema teleology (i.e. temporal directedness and inevitable plotting) combines with the goal-orientedness of acting subjects and with the narrator's after-the-fact evaluation of narrative experience. Such a pattern is typical of natural narrative, as we will see in Chapter 2.

On **level II** I locate four basic viewpoints which are available as explanatory schemas of access to the story. All four relate to narrative mediation, to narrativity. I distinguish between the real-world 'script' of TELLING; the real-world schema of perception (VIEWING); and the access to one's own narrativizable experience (EXPERIENCING). These storytelling schemata are macrostructural and comprise the basic frames of telling, viewing, experiencing and cultural knowing.

A fourth schema that I will be using a great deal is that of ACTION or ACTING. Properly speaking, this fourth frame really belongs with level I since it refers to the *what* and not to the *how* of narrative experience. However, as will become clear in a moment, in terms of the interpretative use made of frames located on level II, ACTING also is one of the frames that readers resort to in the process of narrativization, and this schema visualized at level II does not merely comprise understandings about goal-oriented human action but additionally invokes the entire processuality of event and action series. When readers attempt minimally to narrativize texts that are highly inconsistent they may have to rely on the rock-bottom schema of actionality to tease out a rudimentary sense in story-referential terms.

Furthermore, the frame of TELLING can be extended to incorporate what I call REFLECTING, i.e. the mental activities outside utterance which turn the act of telling into a process of recollection and self-reflective introspection. Whereas the TELLING frame invokes a situation of enunciation and hence an addressee persona, REFLECTING tends to project a reflecting consciousness in the process of rumination. I will return to the applications of level II on level IV below.

My **level III** of cognitive parameters comprises well-known naturally recurring story-telling situations. Since storytelling is a general and spontaneous human activity observable in all cultures, it provides individuals with culturally discrete patterns of storytelling. These patterns include not only a knowledge about storytelling situations and the structure of that situation (who is telling what to whom, interaction or non-interaction with listeners, etc.), but also an understanding of performed narrative and particularly an ability to distinguish between different kinds or types of stories. As genres proliferate and written texts appear on the scene, the relevant competence increases accordingly and also changes in kind. In the process of acculturation, particularly literary acculturation, potential audiences acquire generic models which decisively influence their reading experience. Genres, after all, are large-scale cognitive frames. Such models are different only in degree from the simple text types or 'genres' encountered in oral storytelling in which the basic parameters are context-bound. These consist of the relationship of the teller to the audience and to the told; institutionalization (private vs. public narrative); tradition as a memory trace; performance as the most important constitutive feature of natural narrative; and the distinction between elaborated and simple oral storytelling. On level III relevant parameters additionally include narratological concepts: the concept of the narrator, of chronological reordering (e.g. flashback), of authorial omniscience (both in the meaning of access to protagonists' internal states and in the sense of the narrator's temporal and spatial release from the limitations of human embodiedness). Level III also features the more precisely generic parameters of literary narratives the readers' concepts of the historical novel, the Bildungsroman, etc., as they are acquired through exposure to literature.

My levels II and III do not reproduce Ricoeur's *Mimesis II* (which concerns the immediate textual level of discourse), but characterize features which are partially relevant for Ricoeur's level of *Mimesis III*, the level of reconfiguration. Whereas cognitive parameters on levels I and II are decidedly transcultural, basic-level experiential frames, categories on level III are culture-specific and to a large extent acquired, in fact even taught, as abstract categories. One has to distinguish, for instance, between knowledge about the dynamics of conversational exchanges, such as one can participate in on a bus or at parties, and knowledge about the dynamics of written narratives. Thus, as a kind of fine-tuning of the more basic frames of ACTION, TELLING, VIEWING, and EXPERIENCING from level II, one can add, on level III, the practical generic knowledge of what jokes, anecdotes, witness-box reports, conversations with doctors (telling the history of one's illness), etc., are like. Such practical awareness need not always entail a conscious knowledge of abstract categories. Cognitive parameters on level III are 'natural' precisely because they operate in a non-reflective manner and relate to one's pragmatic experience of hearing and reading stories. It is important to emphasize most forcefully that these categories are not (yet) constituted by the reader's immediate interpretation but provide like categories situated on levels I and II cognitive tools for the interpretation of narrative texts or discourses. Yet, as I will argue below, parameters on level III are already the result of a metaphorical extension of concepts from levels I and II to the level of a more abstract instrumentarium employed in the apperception of written narratives. Due to our long history of exposure to written narratives, generic parameters on level III have simply turned into available cognitive schemata and are no longer the result of a conscious process of interpretation and naturalization.

This brings me to the fourth and final level of my model of natural storytelling parameters, the level which concerns the interpretative abilities by which people link unknown and unfamiliar material with what they are already familiar with, thereby rendering the unfamiliar interpretable and 'readable'. On **level IV** readers utilize conceptual categories from levels I to III in order to grasp, and usually transform, textual irregularities and oddities. Level IV constitutes an all-embracing dynamic process engendered by the reading experience. In correlation with Jonathan Culler's more general concept of naturalization (Culler 1975) I have called this process narrativization. (Compare above under 1.2.3.) Culler's naturalization is concerned with the interpretation of literary texts (including, in particular, poetry). According to Culler, readers, faced with initially inconsistent or incomprehensible texts, attempt to find a frame that can naturalize the inconsistencies or oddities in a meaningful way. In contrast to Culler's more general process of naturalization, narrativization on level IV is exclusively concerned with narrative parameters. It circumscribes readers' attempts at making sense of texts, particularly of texts which resist easy recuperation on the basis of parameters from levels I to III. Narrativization is that process of naturalization which enables readers to re-cognize as narrative those kinds of texts that appear to be non-narrative according to either the natural parameters of levels I and II or the cultural parameters of level III. Such interpretative strategies serve to naturalize texts in the direction of natural paradigms, for instance by providing a realistic motivation that helps to ensure readability. Thus, Alain Robbe-Grillet's novel *La Jalousie* (1957) has frequently been narrativized as the jealous husband's observations of his wife through the window shutters.① In like manner readers also narrativize discourse that seems to have no perceptible origin. The very term 'camera-eye' technique, for instance, betrays another such narrativization which attempts to correlate the text with a frame from recognizable experience (the VIEWING frame from my level II). When dealing with storytelling in the second person, and with impersonal one, it and (French) on (Chapter 6), I argue that such texts are indeed read, not as a series of actions in the traditional story sense, but as narratives portraying human experience and a human story-world. Readers narrativize such texts by resorting to the EXPERIENCING frame, overruling the oddity in pronominal usage that makes such texts difficult to narrativize within a TELLING frame.

How do natural parameters interrelate with narrativization? 'Natural' parameters and frames on levels I to III are only indirectly responsible for narrativization. Natural parameters do not effect narrativization, but narrativization utilizes natural parameters as part of the larger process of naturalization applied by readers to the unfamiliar. Naturalization processes are reading strategies

① See, for instance, Hamburger (1968: 103; 1993: 123±4).

which familiarize the unfamiliar, and they therefore reduce the unexpected to more manageable proportions, aligning it with the familiar. Whereas naturalization and narrativization are interpretative processes, natural parameters or frames are cognitive categories of a synchronic kind which correlate with real-world knowledge. Narrativization needs to be conceptualized as a cultural and literary process, one in which the concept of the natural plays a crucial structuring role without ever becoming part of the cultural product itself. Although narrativization can ultimately result in the establishment of new genres and new narrative modes, these do not thereby become 'natural'; they merely become recuperable from a semantic and interpretative perspective, and they do so through readers having recourse to natural categories. However, once new texts appear on the scene in massive numbers, as has been the case with the novel of internal focalization or with second-person fiction, they may institute a new genre or a new narrative mode and have to be included as a reference model on level III.

What the above outline yields is an explanation of types of narrative as based on simple cognitive parameters. Thus, one can now comprehend Stanzel's narrative situations as a direct development from natural categories. Fiction with a teller figure evokes situational real-life equivalents of telling and their characteristic constellations. If there is a personalized narrator, for example, a certain cognitive, ideological, linguistic and sometimes even spatio-temporal position may become attributed to that narrator, and she becomes a 'speaker' on the model of the standard communication script. One can thereby explain the entire communicative analysis of fiction as an (illicit) transfer of the frame of real-life conversational narrative onto literary personae and constructed entities (such as that of the notorious 'implied author'). Second, and even more important, one can trace the recurrent personalizations of the narrative function which regularly results in the ontology of a 'narrator' to the influence of the very same schema, namely that of the typical storytelling situation: if there is a story, somebody needs must tell it. Even more absurd, since the earlier (script-logical) tendency to identify the non-personalized narrator with the (historical) author has become untenable in the wake of the Modernist aesthetic, the responsibility for the telling has now been transferred to the (covert) narrator, or the implied author, and that even in narratological circles. The persistence of this preconceived notion that somebody (hence a human agent) must be telling the story seems to derive directly from the frame conception of storytelling rather than from any necessary textual evidence.①

First-person narrative of course relates back to narratives of personal experience, a model from oral storytelling that has developed into autobiographical proportions. Autobiography itself is actually a fairly late development, long preceded by the third-person form of the Life. This is not

① See also the argument in Hempfer (1990: 127): 'Mir schiene es also möglich, Fiktionalität als eine Als-ob- Struktur dergestalt zu definieren, daß sich fiktionale Texte über eine bestimmte Menge von Strukturen konstituieren, die sie hinsichtlich dieser Strukturen isomorph zu bestimmten Typen nichtfiktionaler Diskurse erscheinen lassen, daß sie aber gleichzeitig über Strukturen verfügen, die diese Isomorphie als eine nur scheinbare ausweisen.'

surprising, after all, since people may easily tell of their adventures, their particular experiences at one point or another, but to write one's own life requires a sustained Augustinian effort to construct from the random succession of remembered scenes (the material of narratives of personal experience) that well-structured tale with teleological shape. Other people's lives, paradoxically, are knowable and tellable much more easily, and therefore surface as a genre soon after prose takes over.[①] Likewise, literary third-person narrative, of the authorial type, can now be discussed in terms of storytelling models that derive from the institution of the oral poet and from the shape of the folk tale. The figure of the authorial narrator can then be seen to replace the visible and audible jongleur (Kittay and Godzich 1987) and becomes a textual function in its own right with its own subsequent developments in form and function. In so far as literary texts pretend to historical truth and mimetic realism, these functions of the authorial narrator remain linked to actual situations of telling and writing. First-person and authorial narrative are, however, only subtypes of the TELLING frame (level II) and constitute themselves generically (in reference to level III) rather than by direct recourse to natural parameters from levels I and II.

By contrast, the third major narrative situation according to Stanzel, the figural, develops from two quite different directions. On the one hand there is an increased interest in consciousness, usually third-person consciousness, on the part of writers, resulting in an extended portrayal of the mind: early examples are Aphra Behn, Horace Walpole, Ann Radcliffe, and Jane Austen, and for the first person Charles Brockden Brown and William Godwin. (Epistolary narrative participates in this emphasis on consciousness.) As long as there is also a continued interest in realism and history, the portrayal of consciousness results in the omniscient type of novel. That is to say, fiction at one point discovers that it can not only present another's mind by conjecture and a little bit of invention (by a stretching of the imagination, so to speak), but can present consciousness extensively as if reading people's minds. This was not yet an available option in the sixteenth-century novel. The willing suspension of disbelief is precisely the attitude that becomes necessary for this quite non-natural narratorial feat (cp. Cohn 1990: 790 ± 1). Once one has been inside people's minds, however, one can dispense with the omniscient narrator convention since 'he' is neither more nor less 'real' than a position from which you look directly inside your characters' minds. From the all-knowing narrator[②] who interferes less and less with the fictional personae it is therefore a brief step towards a textual model that visualizes narrative as directly presenting characters' consciousness. Telling can be dispensed with, readers simply orient themselves to a position within the fictional world; they are no longer constrained to experience the story as something that happened to another

① This is true for Greek antiquity and for the Middle Ages, but may have to be qualified for Latin prose.

② Hempfer quotes a memorable passage from Gautier's Capitaine Fracasse: 'Nous commettrons cette incongruity dont les auteurs de tous les temps ne se sont pas fait faute, et sans rien dire au petit laquais qui serait allé prévenir la caméristе, nous pénétrerons dans la chambre à coucher, sûrs de ne déranger personne. L'écrivain qui fait un roman porte naturellement au doigt l'anneau de Gygès, lequel rend invisible' (Hempfer 1990: 129 footnote 71).

person and which they must relate to their own life by means of a conscious effort of empathy and understanding. Figural or reflectoral narrative allows them, instead, to experience the fictional world from within, as if looking out at it from the protagonist's consciousness. Such a reading experience is structured in terms of the natural frame of EXPERIENCING, which includes the experiences of perception, sentiment and cognition. Real-life parameters are transcended. Instead of merely observing and guessing at other people's experiences, frames naturally available only for one's own experience become accessible for application to a third person.

Nevertheless, part of our own everyday experience is still our curiosity about others, and this lack of knowledge has its own charms of a detective and/or voyeuristic kind. In what has been termed neutral narrative the refusal to allow the reader access to consciousness harks back to the real-life experience of observation as much as it self-reflexively refuses expected meanings to the reader, thereby constituting a deliberate literary strategy. Historically, it is no coincidence that neutral narrative was invented precisely at that point in time when readers had come to expect full access to protagonists' consciousness. Such expectation would make the refusal to provide inside views all the more frustrating and therefore spur readers on to attempt to fill the resultant vacuum interpretatively aligning the deliberate lack of information about characters' emotions and motives with these characters' indifference, inability to face their emotions, incomprehension of actual circumstances, etc. In the absence of a fully fledged evaluative narrator figure the lack of inside view is therefore immediately linked with (mimetic) psychological motivation on the part of a character, and this is especially true for neutral first-person texts. Camera-eye narration has of course also profited from the example of the film, which as a new experience for readers provided an interesting aesthetic model. In texts such as Muriel Spark's *The Driver's Seat* (1970) the novel's thematic concerns the incomprehensibility of a psychopath's mind become a metaphor for the reader's bewilderment at the narrative presentation which situates her in the position of an uncomprehending observer of compulsive behaviour.

This leaves us with narrative texts that appear to espouse entirely nonnarrative models non-narrative, that is, in the traditional sense of the term. Narratives in the form of drama (the 'Circe' episode of Joyce's *Ulysses*), dialogue (work by Ivy Compton-Burnett and Christine Brooke-Rose, Gabriel Josipovici's *In a Hotel Garden* [1993] or Nathalie Sarraute's *Tu ne t'aimes pas* [1989]), or in question-and-answer format (the 'Ithaca' episode in *Ulysses*) these all lack narrativity from a merely formal rather than essentially narrative perspective since they can still be read as portraying human experience, even if the reader has to read between the lines to discover the story and/or experience which are buried under the non-narrative cloak. Such readerly ingenuity is called for in even greater measure in experimental texts like Beckett's late prose fiction, in which narrativity appears to be something constituted entirely in the reading process with little notional help from the referential potential of the language. Successful narrative readings of 'Ping' and comparable texts become possible only in so far as one imagines a human agent or experiencer in a situation of radical extremity. Readings that see such texts as wordplay with no existential (fictional) situation attached to it are, I maintain, readings that *en fin de compte* refuse the constitutive property of narrativity to these texts.

What does this model 'do' in comparison to the standard paradigms of Genette and Stanzel? As I have illustrated at length in my discussion of narrativity, 'natural' narratology bases itself on a very specific definition of narrative which is thematically identified as the presentation of experientiality. Formally, and I have only hinted this so far, one can now claim that all narrative is built on the mediating function of consciousness. This consciousness can surface on several levels and in different shapes. Consciousness comprises both lived experientiality and intellectual attempts to deal with experience, and it includes the comprehension of actancy just as it necessarily embraces an understanding of mental processes. Narrative modes are therefore all 'resolved' or mediated on the basis of cognitive categories which can be identified as categories of human consciousness. Teller-mode narrative employs the prototype of the human teller, the ruling consciousness of a narrator, to mediate story experience. Figural or reflectoral narrative, on the other hand, makes use of protagonists' consciousness and from that anchorpoint orders narrative experience, relying on a protagonist's consciousness for its centre of cognition, intellection and subjectivity. Neutral narrative and texts that conform to Banfield's 'empty centre' definition (Banfield 1987) place the ordering consciousness in a surrogate figure, that of the reader who 'views' and thereby constructs narrative experience. (For more extensive argument on that score see Chapter 5.)

The four levels of my cognitive model are therefore the operative reader-oriented side of that deep-structural mediation of narrative which employs consciousness as its cognitive structure. It is this cognitive base structure which allows the integration of non-natural forms of storytelling and of all self-reflexive experimental writing into the model of 'natural' narratology. Not only are reflectivity and self-reflexiveness simply facets of human intellection and, in spite of their meta-theoretical character, part of the ruling consciousness of the textual producer (intuited in many postmodernist texts as the so-called 'implied author'); meta-reflection itself, as an activity relative to a (meta-)consciousness, can be treated as a level of fictional mediation.

三、思考与讨论

(1) 弗鲁德尼克的自然叙事学关注的主要问题是什么?

(2) 怎样理解弗鲁德尼克的"叙事化"这一概念?

(3) 弗鲁德尼克的自然叙事学有何缺陷?

第四节　艾伦·帕尔默及其《小说中的社会心理》

一、导读

认知叙事学家艾伦·帕尔默指出，文学研究领域在20世纪90年代发生了明显的认知转向，由此催生了认知叙事学、文学研究的认知方法和认知诗学三大重要文学研究领域。[①] 帕尔默提到，小说中由作者和叙述者所建构的"虚构心理"(fictional minds)对于读者理解小说而言极为重要，因为"虚构叙事在本质上是一种有关心理功能的再现"，读者也恰好是透过小说中所建构的不同形式的虚构意识来进入到文本世界的。[②] 帕尔默进一步指出，故事世界中的事件只有成为虚构人物的体验时才具有重要意义，即只有当虚构文本中的事件对人物意识产生影响时，事件对于整个叙事文本才具有意义，读者同样是通过阅读和感受文本中的虚构人物的想法、感受、信念、欲望来理解小说所搭建的故事世界的。[③] 在帕尔默看来，叙事学界对小说中的意识再现问题有过卓有成效的讨论，开辟了针对自由间接话语、意识流、内心独白、聚焦等一系列相关问题的研究领域。不过，叙事学界长期以来对小说中虚构心理的研究基本上都只是关注小说中人物的个体意识，将分析视野仅仅局限于内部意识这一部分。因此，帕尔默明确表示，既有研究者有关小说中的虚构意识的研究是"不完整"且"具有误导性"的。[④] 他认为，小说中的虚构意识再现体现在个体意识和人际意识之间的平衡上，而以往有关小说中的虚构意识的研究却忽略了虚构文本中意识再现问题的公共性和社会性，他由此提出要对虚构文本中的意识再现问题的公共性特质展开系统研究，并创造了"社会心理"(social minds)这一概念。帕尔默研究的意义不仅体现在他对社会心理这一被以往研究所忽略的方面的强调，更体现在其研究所彰显的跨学科意识。帕尔默坚信，有关人类真实认知能力的实证研究对于理解小说中的虚构意识再现具有重要指导意义，因而他在探讨虚构心理的过程中借用了心智哲学、心理学、神经科学、心理语言学等领域的相关理论资源，这一点可以从他的具体论述中清楚地看到。

二、《小说中的社会心理》选读[⑤]

Speaking broadly, there are two perspectives on the mind: the internalist and the externalist. These two perspectives form more of a continuum than an either/or dichotomy, but the distinction is, in general, a valid one.

---

① Palmer, *Social Minds in the Novel*, p.5.
② Ibid., p.9.
③ Ibid.
④ Ibid., p.8.
⑤ Ibid., pp.39 - 49.

- An internalist perspective on the mind stresses those aspects that are inner, introspective, private, solitary, individual, psychological, mysterious, and detached.
- An externalist perspective on the mind stresses those aspects that are outer, active, public, social, behavioral, evident, embodied, and engaged.

I use the term *social mind* to describe those aspects of the whole mind that are revealed through the externalist perspective.

It seems to me that the traditional narratological approach to the representation of fictional character is an internalist one that stresses those aspects that are inner, passive, introspective, and individual. This undue emphasis on private, solitary, and highly verbalized thought at the expense of all the other types of mental functioning has resulted in a preoccupation with such concepts as free indirect discourse, stream of consciousness, and interior monologue. As a result, the social nature of fictional thought has been neglected. But, as Antonio Damasio suggests, "the study of human consciousness requires both internal and external views" (2000, 82), and so an externalist perspective is required as well, one that stresses the public, social, concrete, and located aspects of mental life in the novel.

As table 2.1 shows, a number of the concepts that are used to analyze the workings of fictional minds tend to fit easily into one or other of these perspectives. Some of these pairs oppose each other precisely; other pairings are much looser. The types of relationships within the pairings include opposition, complementarity, and intersection (as, for example, when an interior monologue shows evidence of Bakhtinian dialogicality). The term *aspectuality*, as mentioned in the previous chapter, refers to the fact that storyworlds are always experienced under some aspects and not others by the characters who inhabit them. People experience the same events in different ways. Within the internalist/externalist framework, I see focalization and aspectuality as complementing each other. Focalization occurs when the reader is presented with the aspect of the storyworld that is being experienced by the focalizer at that moment. In this context, the concept of aspectuality serves as a reminder that, meanwhile, the storyworld is also being experienced differently, under other aspects, by all of the characters who are not currently being focalized in the text. Any of those other characters could have been focalized if the author had chosen to do so. The term *continuing consciousness*, as I have said, stands for the process whereby readers create a continuing consciousness for a character out of the scattered, isolated mentions of that character in the text. The idea of continuing consciousnesses links nicely with the concepts of aspectuality and focalization. Other characters' consciousnesses are continuing while, at any single point in the narrative, only one consciousness is being focalized.

The internalist/externalist framework is also helpful in expanding our awareness of the implications of the concept of subjectivity. As the list suggests, the term can be used in both a first-

TABLE 2.1

INTERNALIST PERSPECTIVE	EXTERNALIST PERSPECTIVE
Private minds	Social minds
Intramental thought	Intermental thought
Personal identity	Situated identity
First-person attribution	Third-person attribution
Subjectivity of self	Subjectivity of others
Focalization	Aspectuality
Introspection	Theory of mind
Stream of consciousness	Continuing consciousness
Interior monologue	Bakhtinian dialogicality

person way (subjectivity of self) and a third-person way (subjectivity of others). The term *situated identity* locates selfhood and identity between the two. Aspectuality acts as a reminder here too, this time of the existence of the subjectivity of others, as available to us through the use of our theory of mind. The concept of aspectuality is a way of bringing to center stage previously marginalized characters whose voices may not often be heard. Knapp (1996) has applied the techniques of family systems therapy to D. H. Lawrence's *Sons and Lovers* (1913) in order to reinterpret the emotional landscape of that storyworld from the point of view of Paul's father. This is an unusual perspective because the focalization in the novel (through Paul, who has a difficult relationship with his father and tends to side with his mother) does not encourage it.

An important part of the social mind is our capacity for *intermental thought*. Such thinking is joint, group, shared, or collective, as opposed to *intramental*, or individual or private thought. It is also known as *socially distributed*, *situated*, or *extended cognition*, and also as *intersubjectivity*. Intermental thought is a crucially important component of fictional narrative because, just as in real life, where much of our thinking is done in groups, much of the mental functioning that occurs in novels is done by large organizations, small groups, work colleagues, friends, families, couples, and other intermental units. Notable examples include the army in Evelyn Waugh's *Men at Arms*, the town in William Faulkner's "A Rose for Emily" (1930), the group of friends in Donna Tartt's *The Secret History* (1992), the villainous Marchioness de Merteuil and the Viscount de Valmont in Laclos' *Les liaisons dangereuses* (1782), and Kitty and Levin in Tolstoy's *Anna Karenina* (1877), who, in a famous scene, write out only the initial letters of the words that they wish to use but who nevertheless understand each other perfectly. However, these are only a few of the most notable examples. My argument is that intermental units are to be found in nearly all novels. It could plausibly be argued that a large amount of the subject matter of novels is the formation, development, maintenance, modification, and breakdown of these intermental systems. As storyworlds are profoundly social in nature (even Robinson Crusoe has his Friday), novels necessarily contain a good deal of collective thinking. However, intermental thought in the novel has been invisible to traditional narrative approaches. Indeed, many of the samples of this sort of thought that follow in later chapters would not even count as examples of thought and consciousness within these approaches. But shared minds become clearly visible within the cognitive approach to literature that underpins this book.

A good deal of the significance of the thought that occurs in novels is lost if only the internalist perspective is employed. Both perspectives are required, because a major preoccupation of novels is precisely this balance between public and private thought, intermental and intramental functioning, and social and individual minds. Within this balance, I will be emphasizing social minds because of their past neglect. In illustrating the importance of the functioning of the social minds in my main example texts, *Middlemarch*, *Little Dorrit*, and *Persuasion*, I aim to show that it is not possible to understand these novels without an awareness of these minds as they operate within their storyworlds. They are one of the chief means by which the plots are advanced. If you were to take all of the social thought out of these three novels, they would not be comprehensible. So, given the importance of this subject to the study of the novel, it seems to me that it is necessary to find room for it at the *center* of narrative theory.

I will take one example from many in order to illustrate the issues that may arise from an overreliance by literary critics on the internalist perspective. I have chosen *Reading the Nineteenth-Century Novel: Austen to Eliot* (2008) by Alison Case and Harry E. Shaw, because it is an excellent study that contains many valuable internalist insights. (For example, it points out that Charlotte Brontë's *Jane Eyre* [1847] starts with a tight, uncontextualized focus on Jane's consciousness and explains how revolutionary this decision was within the evolution of the nineteenth-century novel.) But, more troubling from an externalist perspective, Case and Shaw also remark on "how difficult it is for people to be simply themselves in any social setting" (2008, 24). These questions occur to me: Why assume that the self can only be found (or easily found) in solitude? Could it not be the other way round? Is it possible that we are only really ourselves when with others? When we are alone, are we not more easily tempted to construct convenient, comfortable, easy-to-live-with narratives for ourselves that may be distortions of reality? Similarly, Case and Shaw talk about *Wuthering Heights*'s "conflicting fantasies of escape from, or reconciliation with, the multiple restraints of selfhood that enable a stable, social world" (2008, 68; my emphasis). (Although this appears to be an objective description of the novel, I sense authorial agreement too.) Well, that is one way of looking at selfhood. Another, more externalist way is to see the social world as providing the *possibilities* for, or *affordances* for, the expression of selfhood.

Within the real-mind disciplines of psychology and philosophy there is a good deal of interest in *the mind beyond the skin* (as opposed to *the mind inside the skull*): the realization that mental functioning cannot be understood merely by analyzing what goes on within the skull but can only be fully comprehended once it has been seen in its social and physical context. Case and Shaw put the point nicely in their otherwise internalist study when they speculate about Walter Scott's wish to "reveal human nature, not from the skin in, but from the skin out" (2008, 37). Social psychologists routinely use the terms *mind and mental action* not only about individuals but also about groups of people working as intermental units. So, it is appropriate to say of these groups that they think or that they remember. James Wertsch explains that "the notion of mental function can properly be applied to social as well as individual forms of activity" (1991, 27). As he puts it, a *dyad* (that is, two people working as a cognitive system) can carry out such functions as problem solving on an intermental plane (1991, 27). It is significant that cognitive scientists are now beginning to share the interest of social psychologists in the mind beyond the skin. For an overview of the work being done in the new research area called *social neuroscience*, see *The Neuroscience of Social Interaction: Decoding, Influencing and Imitating the Actions of Others*, edited by Chris Frith and Daniel Wolpert (2004).

You may be asking what is achieved by talking in this way, instead of simply referring to individuals pooling their resources and working in cooperation together. The advocates of the concept of distributed cognition such as the theoretical anthropologists Gregory Bateson (1972) and Clifford Geertz (1993), the philosophers Andy Clark and David Chalmers (1998) and (2009) and Daniel Dennett (1996), and the psychologists Edwin Hutchins (1995) and James Wertsch all stress that the purpose of the concept is increased explanatory power. They argue that the way to delineate a cognitive system is to draw the limiting line so that you do not cut out anything whose absence leaves things inexplicable (Bateson 1972, 465). To illustrate, Wertsch tells the story of how his daughter lost her shoes and he helped her to remember where she had left them. Wertsch asks: Who is doing the remembering here? He is not, because he had no prior knowledge of where they were, and she is not, because she had forgotten where they were and was only able to remember by means of her father's promptings. It was therefore the intermental unit formed by the two of them that remembered (Sperber and Hirschfeld 1999, cxxiv). If you draw the line narrowly around single persons, and maintain that cognition can only be individual, then things remain inexplicable. Neither *on their own* remembered. If you draw the line more widely, and accept the concept of an intermental cognitive system, then things are explained. The intermental unit remembered. The same applies not just to problem solving but also to joint decision making and group action. Here is a simple example from Evelyn Waugh's *Vile Bodies* (1930) that I will use again when explaining the philosophical concept of action in chapter 4: "The three statesmen hid themselves" (86). The decision to hide is an intermental one that is taken together by all three individuals, and the action of hiding is also one that they perform together.

Intermental cognitive systems are, to some extent, independent of the individual elements that go to make them up.This is not to say that the whole is necessarily greater than the sum of its parts; it is simply to say that it is different from the sum of its parts. One example of this difference is the vivid metaphor with which I began this chapter and which was used by the author Edith Somerville to describe her writing partnership with Martin Ross: a question of "mixing blue and yellow which together makes green". Something similar happened when the poet John Ashbery wrote a novel with James Schuyler in the 1950s, each contributing a line or two at a time. In the diary section of the *Times Literary Supplement* (5 December 2008), the diarist wondered which of the two wrote the line "Why don't you admit that you enjoy my unhappiness"? The following response from Ashbery was published two weeks later:"In regard to the line in question, I can't remember. Schuyler and I were often unable to remember who had written what, as our lines seemed to emerge from an invisible third person" (*Times Literary Supplement* [19 December 2008]). There are musical examples too. Keith Rowe, a member of the free improvisation group AMM, once told me that while the group was playing, he would sometimes not know whether it was he or another member of the group who was producing the sounds that he could hear.

However, in considering the wide-ranging nature of intermental functioning (problem solving, decision making, coming to ethical judgments, and so on), it should be borne in mind that analyses of this sort of thought should involve no preconceptions about its quality. Intermental thought is as beautiful and ugly, destructive and creative, exceptional and commonplace as intramental thought. The communal creativity described in the previous paragraph should be balanced against, for example, the scapegoating tendencies of many groups, and also against Pentagon "groupthink".

An emphasis on social minds will inevitably question these twin assumptions: first, that the workings of our own minds are never accessible to others; and, second, that the workings of our own minds are always and unproblematically accessible to ourselves. This book will, in the main, question the first assumption and will make much less reference to the equally questionable second, although the subject does come up occasionally (as in the *Men at Arms* case study that follows). But in disputing the first-named assumption by discussing the public minds that are to be found in *Middle-march*, *Little Dorrit*, and *Persuasion*, I must stress that I am certainly not saying that fictional minds are always easily readable. Sometimes, they are; sometimes, they are not. In these three novels, I will argue, they frequently are. In other novels, especially those of the twentieth and twenty-first centuries, however, different levels of readability and unreadability will apply. For more discussion on this, see Porter Abbott's "Unreadable Minds and the Captive Reader" (2009).

In an illuminating article titled "Diagramming Narrative", Marie-Laure Ryan uses diagrams as a semiotic tool for the understanding of narrative in relation to three aspects of plot—time, space, and mind. On the question of mind, she refers to the subject matter of narrative as the "evolution of a network of interpersonal relations" (2007, 29) and convincingly shows how diagrammatic representations of these networks can add a good deal to our understanding of the narrative process. She illustrates this approach with two highly technical analyses, one of a minimal, two-sentence narrative and the other of the fable "The Fox and the Crow" (which was also used in Ryan 1991). It seems to me that a modified and necessarily greatly simplified variant of this sort of approach could be used to analyze the workings of social minds in whole novels. For example, the complex interrelations between different intermental units can be thought of as resembling the patterns made by Venn diagrams, in which overlapping circles are used to express the relationships between classes of objects. Such a diagram would show that the memberships of some groups are completely included within larger ones, some might have no overlap of membership with any others, others would have partial membership overlaps, and so on. With at least some of the novels to be discussed later, it would be possible, though difficult, to construct Venn diagrams that could vividly illustrate this complexity in visual terms.

Little narratological work has been done on social minds in the novel. Exceptions include studies of aspects of distributed cognition by John V. Knapp (for example, 1996) and also by the postclassical narrative theorists David Herman (2003a, 2003b, 2007a, 2008, and 2010) and Uri Margolin (1996b and 2000). The exploration of "we" narratives (that is, narratives written predominantly in the first-person plural) that was initiated by Margolin and continued by Brian Richardson (2006) has produced rewarding results (see, for example, Marcus 2008). A welcome and related development has been the important work done by the literary critic Susan Sniader Lanser in *Fictions of Authority* (1992), in which she focuses on the concept of *communal voice*. Her use of the term *voice* shows that she is concerned with the relationship between "we" narration and "I" narration in which one speaker represents others. That is to say, she explores the telling, the mode of narration, the discursive practices of the novels that she discusses. Lanser writes persuasively about some of the important issues raised by the notion of communal thought such as the problematic erasure of differences between individuals and the need to make speculative and potentially mistaken assumptions about the thoughts of others. I want to take a more inclusive approach, however, and set these issues as well as some of the more positive ones arising from intermentality into a wider context. Most of the nineteenth-century novels that feature plentiful evidence of shared thought have heterodiegetic narrators and are not therefore examples of a communal voice. The studies mentioned above are pioneering, but they have focused in the main only on the relatively small number of narratives written in the "we" form; my point is that little attention has been given to the much larger group of what, in response, I would call "they" narratives: that is, narratives that feature social minds.

You may be feeling some doubt about this claim regarding the neglect of intermental thought. Surely we have always known about the importance of groups right from the beginning of

Western literature. What about the role of the chorus in Greek tragedy? Well, yes, undoubtedly, but my claim is that this knowledge has not been reflected in the theory on mental functioning in narrative. Obviously, we all know about the proverbial *vox populi*, both in literature (especially in drama) and also in our daily lives, but the purpose of the present book is to examine the socially situated or intermental cognition lying at its basis and the various ways in which it is represented in narrative. What about Menakhem Perry's masterly analysis of William Faulkner's short story "A Rose for Emily" (1979), in which the townspeople as a group play such an important role? Perry's article is a groundbreaking contribution to our knowledge of the role of cognitive frames in the reading process, but I do not think that it was part of his intention explicitly to recognize the status of the town as an intermental unit. That is the purpose of this book.

A Typology

Obviously the extent, duration, and success of intermental activity will vary greatly from occasion to occasion. Because this is such a wide, relatively uncharted area in the context of literary studies, the following, rather basic typology may be of some value.

1. *Intermental encounters*. At the minimal level, this consists of the group thought that is necessary for conversations between individuals to take place. It is not possible to have a coherent dialogue without at least some intermental communication. A minimal level of mind reading and theory of mind is required for characters to understand each other and thereby make everyday life possible. It is made easier or more difficult by a variety of factors such as solipsistic versus emotionally intelligent individuals, easily readable versus impenetrable minds, familiar versus unfamiliar contexts, similar versus different sorts of social background, and so on. A heightened awareness of the mental functioning of another can occur within random encounters between people who do not know each other particularly well or even between complete strangers. I am sure that most readers of this book will have had the experience of meeting somebody for the first time and instantly feeling that you are both on the same wavelength. A focus on the workings of long-term, stable intermental units such as couples and families as itemized below can give a misleading impression if it suggests that intermental thought can only occur within such units. As we know from our real-life experience, mind reading can occur in a variety of situations. Sometimes, it is what might be called reciprocal: there is a conscious and fully intended sharing of thought and so people will know that others know what they are thinking. At other times, it is inadvertent: someone may reveal their thoughts without meaning to. In these cases, that person may not know that their mind has been read by another person, or they may notice that it has been, for example by the other's facial expression.

In addition to our various encounters with countless strangers and acquaintances over the course of our lives, we all belong to intermental units. I would define these as stable, fairly long-lasting groups that regularly employ intermental thinking. They vary greatly in size, and I will adopt the rather simplistic approach of referring to them as small, medium, and large units. Obviously, many other, rather more sophisticated typologies are possible. John V. Knapp (personal communication) has suggested one that would measure group membership along a scale of interpersonal intensity. For example, someone may feel an intense involvement in the unit formed by their work colleagues but may have a much more distant relationship with their own family.

2. *Small intermental units*. Characters tend to form intermental pairs and small groups of various sorts such as marriages, close friendships, and nuclear families. It is likely that, over time, the people in these units will get to know quite well what the others are thinking. However, these small groups will obviously vary greatly in the quality of their intermental thought, and readers' expectations may not be met. Many fictional marriages have much less intermental thought than one might think (depending on the level of one's expectations in this matter, of course). For an excellent analysis of the small intermental unit of a marriage, see Elena Semino's "Blending and Characters' Mental Functioning in Virginia Woolf's 'Lappin and Lapinova'" (2006).
3. *Medium-sized intermental units*. The intermentality that occurs between the individuals in medium-sized units such as work colleagues, networks of friendships, and neighborhoods is rather different from the one that arises in random encounters and small units. Here, the emphasis is less on individuals knowing what another person is thinking, and more on people thinking the same way (whether or not they know that others are also thinking that way). Examples that are highlighted in later chapters include some of the subgroups of the Middlemarch mind in chapter 3, the Circumlocution Office in chapter 4, and the party to which Anne Elliot belongs in chapter 5.
4. *Large intermental units*. Individuals are also likely to belong to larger groups that will also have a tendency to think together on certain issues and so produce a collective opinion or consensus view on a particular topic. To pursue this point in greater depth would be to take this study into concepts such as ideology that are well beyond the scope of this book. The dynamics involved in large groups are similar to those that govern medium-sized units. Examples from the novels studied in future chapters include the town of Middlemarch, "Society" in Bath (*Persuasion*), and the important role that the public plays in the passage from *Little Dorrit* that is discussed at the end of chapter 4.
5. *Intermental minds*. These are intermental units, large, medium, or small, that are so well defined and long-lasting, and where so much successful intermental thought takes place, that they can plausibly be considered as group minds. Couples who have been together for a long time, who

> know each other's minds well, and who are able to work well together on such joint activities as decision making and problem solving are the best examples. However, larger groups may also acquire some of these characteristics. Though well defined, these groups will contain individuals who will often be completely different from each other. Opinions will inevitably differ widely on the point at which a particular collection of people can be regarded as sufficiently stable, well-functioning, and distinctive to be defined as an intermental mind. I will argue that the town of Middlemarch, a large unit, may be called an intermental mind, together with some marriages such as the Crofts in *Persuasion* and the Meagles in *Little Dorrit*.

The simplicity of this typology hardly begins to do justice to the complexity and range of the intermental units to be found in novels. Nevertheless, it does have some value in providing a map, however rudimentary, by which this unfamiliar territory may be initially explored. It is obvious that there is a wide spectrum of phenomena covered by the term *intermental thought* and also by this typology: it ranges from chance encounters between two strangers to the life of a whole town over a long period. I do not see any harm in this, as long as we remain conscious of it. The priority is to establish the viability of the externalist perspective on fictional minds as a whole. Then it will be possible to specify the intricate complexities that can be revealed by that perspective. In his review of Dorrit Cohn's inspirational study *Transparent Minds*, the narratologist Brian McHale said that the "history of our poetics of prose is essentially a history of successive differentiations of types of discourse from the undifferentiated 'block' of narrative prose" (1981, 185). These wise words have guided me throughout my narratological studies. I see the first book as having hacked off a huge, previously undifferentiated block of prose and labeled it *fictional minds*. This current stage involves detaching a smaller but still sizeable chunk (labeled *social minds*) from the fictional-minds block, for the purpose of reducing it further into ever smaller and finer fragments. The intention is that, by these means, the work may eventually, over time, become progressively less industrial and heavy-duty in nature and rather more craftsmanlike.

三、思考与讨论

(1) 帕尔默所提出的"社会心理"究竟指什么?

(2) 帕尔默如何用有关人类真实认知能力的研究成果来考察小说中的虚构心理?

(3) 帕尔默针对虚构叙事中的人际意识提出的分类模式有何漏洞?

本章推荐阅读书目

[1] Alan Palmer. *Fictional Minds*. Lincoln: University of Nebraska Press, 2004.

[2] David Herman, ed. *Narrative Theory and the Cognitive Sciences*. Stanford: CSLI Publications, 2003.

[3] David Herman. *Storytelling and the Sciences of Mind*. Cambridge: The MIT Press, 2013.

[4] Lisa Zunshine. *Why we Read Fiction: Theory of Mind and the Novel*. Columbus: The Ohio State University Press, 2006.

[5] Manfred Jahn. "Frames, Preferences, and the Reading of Third-Person Narratives: Towards a Cognitive Narratology," *Poetics Today* 18.4(1997): 441-468.

第四章
女性主义叙事学

第一节　概　　论

作为后经典叙事学最具影响力的重要流派之一，女性主义叙事学着眼于性别与叙事之间的关系，将叙事文本生产与阐释的社会历史语境纳入叙事学研究范围，重点考察叙事形式所承载的性别意义。自1986年苏珊·兰瑟在《建构女性主义叙事学》一文中提出"女性主义叙事学"（Feminist Narratology）的概念后，女性主义叙事学在西方叙事学界取得了令人瞩目的成就，得到了广泛的认可，"不仅极大程度地复兴了叙事学这门学科，而且还直接预示和引领了后经典叙事学的崛起"。[①] 作为一个跨学科的派别，女性主义叙事学是女性主义文学批评与叙事学相结合的产物，将意识形态分析与形式分析融为一体，打破了西方学界形式主义与反形式主义长期以来的对峙，深刻影响了叙事理论研究与阐释模式，[②]推动叙事学研究朝着"语境化"方向发展。[③]

从历时的角度来看，女性主义叙事学在经历了20世纪80年代的兴起和20世纪90年代的发展后，在21世纪呈现出交叉多元之态。就研究对象而言，女性主义叙事学家的研究主要在"话语"层面展开，系统探讨了叙述声音、叙述类型、叙述视角等"话语"层面的多种技巧，与女性主义文学批评"在研究对象上呈一种互为补充的关系"。[④]有鉴于此，在研究方法层面，女性主义叙事学以结构主义叙事理论为支撑，关注具体文本中的形式表现，并将文本形式与社会历史语境相结合，从相应的社会历史语境中找寻动因，从而考察文本形式特征与性别意识形态之间的复杂关系。在对性别与叙事形式关系的阐释中，女性主义叙事学提出了一系列创新的概念和术语。这种研究方法不仅改进和拓展了女性主义文学批评，也丰富了叙事学研究，为繁荣当下的叙事学研究做出了重要的贡献。

一、女性主义叙事学的发展历程

兴起于20世纪60年代，隶属于形式主义范畴的结构主义叙事学和隶属于政治批评范畴的女性主

---

① 尚必武：《当代西方后经典叙事学研究》，第61页。
② Brian Richardson, "Recent Concepts of Narrative and the Narratives of Narrative Theory," p.168.
③ Roy Sommer, "Contextualism Revisited: A Survey (and Defence) of Postcolonial and Intercultural Narratologies," *Journal of Literary Theory* 1.1 (2007), p.61.
④ 申丹、王丽亚：《西方叙事学：经典与后经典》，第202页。

义文学批评几乎没有任何交集，各行其道。进入 20 世纪 80 年代以后，经典叙事学在解构主义和政治文化批评的双重冲击中日渐衰微。女性主义文学批评也因自身拒斥理论的特点陷入了困境。针对叙事学忽略文本的社会历史语境与意识形态内涵以及女性主义文学批评过于印象化和模仿性的弱点，在叙事学越来越关注语境和女性主义文学批评越来越注重理论分析的两大动力的推动下，女性主义叙事学应运而生。在 1981 年的《叙事行为：小说中的视角》(*The Narrative Act: Point of View in Prose Fiction*)一书中，兰瑟开始做出相关的尝试。她聚焦叙述视角与意识形态之间的关联，冲破叙事学的桎梏，试图将叙事作品的形式研究与女性主义文学批评相结合。1986 年，兰瑟在《建构女性主义叙事学》一文中提出了"女性主义叙事学"这一概念，倡导将"科学"和"非意识形态的"结构主义叙事学分析方法与女性主义文学批评强调的政治立场进行融合，取长补短，相互借鉴，并系统地介绍了其研究目的和研究方法。这一概念也引发了叙事学界的一场争议。站在结构主义的立场，兰瑟的观点显然有违传统诗学的观点。以色列学者迪恩格特与兰瑟展开了论战，强调关注于叙事作品形式普遍规律的叙事学无关性别和社会历史语境，所谓的女性主义叙事学也仅仅是阐释，而非诗学。[①] 针对迪恩格特所提出的诗学与阐释之界，兰瑟解释道，如果将叙事诗学局限在理论的框架内，那便相当于否定了作品与理论之间的辩证关系，否定了抽象的理论依赖于具体文本创作这一逻辑。有鉴于此，将女性主义文学批评与叙事学相结合，并非否认经典叙事学的研究范式。恰恰相反，性别议题的引入是对叙事学的有益补充，有益于揭示男女作家在叙述策略运用方面的差异。[②] 在回应中，我们不难看出，兰瑟有意淡化诗学与阐释之界，强调形式的意识形态内涵，并以此拓展结构主义叙事学的研究范围。这种带有立场倾向的诗学也得到了像罗宾·沃霍尔这一类学者的拥护。从女性主义叙事学立场来看，经典结构主义叙事学理论大多基于男性作家作品，这也相应遮蔽了女性作家叙事艺术的独特性。[③] 因此女性叙事学家在研究中聚焦具体作家，特别是女性作家笔下的形式差异，从叙事形式和文本生产的社会语境及意识形态的关照中建构能够阐释形式差异的理论话语。

作为女性主义叙事学的另一位领军人物，沃霍尔同样也观察到了结构叙事学本身对女性作家文本的排斥，并在《建构有关吸引型叙述者的理论：盖斯凯尔、斯托和艾略特作品中的热心介入》("Toward a Theory of the Engaging Narrator: Earnest Interventions in Gaskell, Stowe, and Eliot"，1986)一文中尝试建构女性主义叙事学。通过分析盖斯凯尔、斯托和艾略特的作品，沃霍尔提出了"吸引型叙述者"(engaging narrator)和"疏远型叙述者"(distancing narrator)两个重要的概念：前者指鼓励读者与受述者产生认同的叙述者，常常采用第二人称称呼受述者；后者指阻止读者与受述者产生认同的叙述者，常常采用反讽、自我指涉等方法，增加读者与故事人物之间的距离。[④] 在此文的基础上，沃霍尔随后出版专著《性别介入：维多利亚小说的叙事话语》(*Gendered Interventions: Narrative Discourse in the Victorian Novel*，1989)，开启了她的"性别介入"研究之途。通过对维多利亚小说细致的文本分析，沃霍尔考察了吸引型叙事策略和疏远型叙事策略两种叙事介入具有的不同性别内涵以及它们的社会根源。

① Nilli Diengott, "Narratology and Feminism," pp.43 - 45.

② Susan Lanser, "Shifting the Paradigm: Feminism and Narratology," *Style* 22.1 (1988), pp.52 - 55.

③ Robyn Warhol, "The Look, the Body, and the Heroine of *Persuasion*: A Feminist-Narratological View of Jane Austen," *Ambiguous Discourse: Feminist Narratology and British Women Writers*, ed. Kathy Mezei (Chapel Hill: The University of North Carolina Press, 1996), p.22.

④ Robyn Warhol, "Toward a Theory of the Engaging Narrator: Earnest Interventions in Gaskell, Stowe, and Eliot," *PMLA* 101.5(1986), pp.811 - 812.

在她看来，吸引型叙述者多为女作家们所青睐，且没有受到应有的重视。究其原因，女性作家们因为其在社会公共领域中的边缘位置，选择借助吸引型叙述者讲述故事从而引导读者认同作品主旨。这种叙事策略也因此对男性权威产生介入作用，成为一种话语策略。[①] 尽管和兰瑟一样，沃霍尔的观点也招致了一些传统叙事学家的批评和质疑，但她们对于女性主义叙事学相关概念和理论开创性地建构和应用激励了许多其他女性主义叙事学家改写经典叙事模式，切实推动了女性主义叙事学的发展。女性主义叙事学的兴起帮助叙事学实现语境转向，也为女性主义文本的叙事形式和结构分析提供了有效的阐释手段。

女性主义叙事学的研究重点在于叙事文本中那些表征"性别差异的话语层"，因此文本细读也成为女性主义叙事学批评实践中的重点。[②] 正如女性主义叙事学家凯瑟·梅兹（Kathy Mezei）指出的那样："到了1989年，女性主义叙事学进入了另一个重要阶段：从理论探讨转向了实践。"[③] 进入90年代后，女性主义叙事学的研究重点由宏观的理论建构转向了微观的批评实践，逐渐成为叙事学显学，取得了诸多重要的成果，例如兰瑟的《虚构的权威：女性作家与叙述声音》（*Fictions of Authority: Women Writers and Narrative Voice*，1992）、梅兹于1996年主编的论文集《含混的话语：女性主义叙事学与英国女性作家》（*Ambiguous Discourse: Feminist Narratology and British Women Writers*）、艾莉森·凯斯（Alison Case）的《编织情节的女人：十八、十九世纪英国小说中的性别与叙述》（*Plotting Women: Gender and Narration in the Eighteenth- and Nineteenth-Century British Novel*，1999）等。但值得注意的是，相较于"新批评"倡导的从文本内部发现意义的"细读"，"女性主义叙事学的细读方法"将文本的细节与社会历史语境进行关照分析，辨析历史语境下的叙事形式和性别意识形态之间的复杂关系。[④] 在女性主义叙事学的概念界定和理论建构方面，兰瑟和沃霍尔强调了文本的性别文化建构属性，着眼于性别的反本质主义特征，进一步拓展和修正女性主义叙事学的一些概念和论断。在经典之作《虚构的权威：女性作家与叙述声音》中，兰瑟将"叙述声音"作为缝合形式化的叙事学理论与语境化的女性主义文学批评的关键所在，对它进行重新分类并赋予了其性别化的标志。在她看来，"声音"不仅仅是小说家的叙述技巧，其本身也包含了对身份和权力的控诉意味，因此具有性别意义。有鉴于此，兰瑟着眼于女性作家创作过程中叙事策略所形成的声音效果分析，并将其与彼时的社会语境相联系，从而将叙述声音性别化。她从话语层面区分了三种性别化叙述声音模式：借助"异故事叙述者"（heterodiegetic narrator）表达作者立场的"作者型叙述声音"（authorial voice）、由"同故事叙述者"（homodiegetic narrator）呈现的"个人型叙述声音"（personal voice）和由叙述者传递并代表故事中女性群体立场的"集体型叙述声音"（communal voice）。[⑤] 其中，前两者分别对应了热奈特叙述声音分类中的传统全知叙述的第三人称叙述声音和故事主人公的第一人称叙述声音。两者的区别在于话语方式不同以及是否具有全知视角。集体型叙述声音则是兰瑟创造的全新概念，具有集合性和代表性，强调了叙述者的主体间性

---

① Robyn Warhol, *Gendered Interventions: Narrative Discourse in the Victorian Novel* (New Brunswick: Rutgers University Press, 1989), p.23.

② Ibid., p.17.

③ Kathy Mezei, "Introduction," *Ambiguous Discourse: Feminist Narratology and British Women Writers*, ed. Kathy Mezei (Chapel Hill: The University of North Carolina Press, 1996), p.8.

④ Robyn Warhol, *Having a Good Cry: Effeminate Feelings and Pop-Culture Forms* (Columbus: The Ohio State University Press, 2003), p.26.

⑤ Susan Lanser, *Fictions of Authority: Women Writers and Narrative Voice* (Ithaca: Cornell University Press, 1992), pp.15 - 18.

和社会身份。在《观看、身体和〈劝导〉女主角：从女性主义叙事学角度看简·奥斯汀》（“The Look, the Body, and the Heroine of *Persuasion*: A Feminist-Narratological View of Jane Austen”,1996）一文中，沃霍尔正式界定了女性主义叙事学：“女性主义叙事学研究性别文化构成语境中的叙事结构和叙事策略，它提供了一种用来重新宣称奥斯汀是女性主义小说家的方法，也为我们提供了一种用来区分奥斯汀的‘故事’（文本中发生了什么）和她的‘话语’（故事如何用语言来表述）的分析工具。”[①] 通过对奥斯汀作品中自由间接引语这一标志性叙事策略的解读，沃霍尔探讨了叙述视角所隐含的女性主义意识形态。在沃霍尔看来，女性主义叙事学是在文本细读的基础上考察性别在叙事进程中产生的方式的，这不仅是它巨大的优势也是新时期女性主义叙事学肩负的任务。此外，90年代后现代主义对多元性的强调以及酷儿理论的兴起推动着“女性主义叙事学朝着多元路径进一步发展”。[②] 女性主义叙事学家们开始聚焦性别的多种可能，考察多元文化的性别身份，并试图将女性主义叙事学融入更为广阔的文化研究中。

进入21世纪以来，女性主义叙事学在理论建构以及批评实践两方面呈现出跨媒介、跨文类、跨学科和多元交叉的发展趋势。许多女性主义叙事学家开始尝试介入跨文类和跨媒介领域。例如，沃霍尔在《叙述是如何产生性别的：艾丽丝·沃克〈紫色〉中的女性气质及其影响》（“How Narration Produces Gender: Femininity As Affect and Effect in Alice Walker's *The Color Purple*”,2001）一文中分析了《紫色》这部作品中的叙事策略令读者痛哭的原因。在沃霍尔看来，叙事技巧与文类密切相关，因此，“性别是经由无数文化模式而产生和复制的，包括与文本相关的叙事策略”。[③] 在之后的女性主义叙事学研究实践中，沃霍尔在文类分析和跨媒体分析中介入性别。在《痛快地哭吧：女性化情感与通俗文化形式》（*Having a Good Cry: Effeminate Feelings and Pop-Culture Forms*,2003）一书中，她将漫画式自传、电影、热门电视剧等通俗文化形式引入叙事和性别研究领域，实现了女性主义叙事学在研究对象上的转向。其中，沃霍尔借鉴了朱迪斯·巴特勒（Judith Butler）的“性别操演理论”（gender performativity），考察了性别话语对情感的性别化阐释，提出了“女性化情感”（effeminate feeling）的概念以及一系列“情感技术”（technology of affect）的叙述策略，强调情感体验并不表达或模仿性别，而是构成性别。[④] 换言之，情感是操演的，植根于社会结构之中。在这之后，沃霍尔研究的范畴更为广阔，其不仅探讨了小说、绘本等文类的空间建构，也探讨了电影和热门电视剧中的叙事情景，在拓展女性主义叙事学方面做出了重大的贡献。

随着性别研究的深入以及视野的不断扩大，女性叙事学家纷纷采用跨学科的视角，从语言学、修辞性叙事学等学派中汲取了新的养分。例如，有别于大多数女性叙事学家的文学视角，露斯·佩奇（Ruth Page）强调了女性主义叙事学研究的语言学视角，从文学和语言学双重视角进行女性主义叙事学研究。在佩奇看来，用语言学框架研究文学文本、用文本建构语言学模型与文学和语言学研究之间都是互利互惠的[⑤]，这种路径也丰富了女性主义叙事学的研究方法。在《女性主义叙事学的文学与语言学视角》

---

① Warhol, "The Look, the Body, and the Heroine of *Persuasion*: A Feminist-Narratological View of Jane Austen," pp.21-22.

② 吴颉、卢红芳：《当代西方女性主义叙事学的缘起与流变》，载《解放军外国语学院学报》2020年第43卷第1期，第71页。

③ Robyn Warhol, "How Narration Produces Gender: Femininity as Affect and Effect in Alice Walker's *The Color Purple*," *Narrative* 9.2 (2001), p.183.

④ Warhol, *Having a Good Cry: Effeminate Feelings and Pop-Culture Forms*, p.5.

⑤ Ruth Page, *Literary and Linguistic Approaches to Feminist Narratology* (Basingstoke: Palgrave Macmillan, 2006), pp.12-13.

(*Literary and Linguistic Approaches to Feminist Narratology*,2006)一书中,佩奇指出与性别有关的不是叙事结构,而是"语言形式"(linguistic form),并得出了"叙事性的高低程度与性别毫不相干"的结论。[①] 不难发现,佩奇的这一观点以及她对语言学方法的重用已经偏离了"以兰瑟、沃霍尔等人为代表的女性主义叙事学的研究主流",其研究兴趣更多在于两性叙述差异背后情感维度的相似和相通本质。[②] 相较于沃霍尔、兰瑟等从读者和社会历史角度考察叙述策略的做法,在《女性主义叙事伦理》(*Feminist Narrative Ethics: Tacit Persuasion in Modernist Form*,2014)一书中,纳什将修辞理论与女性主义相结合。她通过考察作者与读者之间的叙事交流,探讨隐含作者的叙述策略如何促使历史语境中的读者重新考虑关于女性权利的伦理立场。在纳什看来,任何一部作品关于性别议题的呈现都会牵扯到其他问题,而不是直接显现为单一的性别政治主题,因此,其研究需要从各个层面分析作者与读者之间的叙事交流。[③] 纳什的研究也由此拓展了女性主义叙事学受限于性别主题的单一视野。

在《我们到达了那里吗? 论女性主义叙事学的交叉性未来》("Are We There Yet? The Intersectional Future of Feminist Narratology",2010)一文中,兰瑟指出女性主义叙事学未来发展的方向在于交叉性的路径。在兰瑟看来,叙事本身就具有交叉性,叙事理论也适合用交叉性理论研究叙事形式和叙事内容的相互作用。换言之,交叉性理论有助于解决文化批评与形式研究上的分歧。在《建构(更酷儿和)更加兼容的(女性主义)叙事学》["Toward (a Queerer and) More (Feminist) Narratology",2015]一文中,兰瑟将交叉性理论应用于女性主义和酷儿理论的"联姻"研究中。在沃霍尔和兰瑟主编的文集《解放了的叙事理论:酷儿介入和女性主义介入》(*Narrative Theory Unbound: Queer and Feminist Interventions*,2015)中,在考察女性主义叙事学和酷儿叙事学历史、意义和交叉属性的基础上,兰瑟指出两者相互依赖。之后,兰瑟进一步在《叙述声音酷儿化》("Queering Narrative Voice",2018)一文中发展和修补了她的酷儿叙事学构想。她区分了"显性酷儿叙述者"(explicitly queer narrator)和"隐性酷儿叙述者"(implicitly queer narrator),并指出"'集体型叙述声音'是一种包含各种性别或者说性别酷儿化的集体型叙述声音"。[④] 在此基础上,兰瑟以叙述声音为切入点,探讨女性主义叙事学和酷儿叙事学二者在共建理论框架时所出现的问题。

经过三十多年的发展,女性主义叙事学一直致力于"解开某些叙事思想的锁链,跨越某些理论界限,挣脱某些叙事学的束缚"[⑤],不仅与酷儿理论、语言学、后经典叙事学的其他学派等不断融合,还将叙事和性别的研究引入跨媒介叙事、族裔叙事、后殖民叙事等领域,成为当代叙事学研究领域中的重要流派。

二、女性主义叙事学的重要概念

在巴赫金"社会学诗学"(sociological poetics)的影响下,兰瑟将作为形式的叙述声音与社会身份相

---

① Ruth Page, *Literary and Linguistic Approaches to Feminist Narratology* (Basingstoke: Palgrave Macmillan, 2006), pp.40 - 44.

② 尚必武:《当代西方后经典叙事学研究》,第 68 页。

③ Katherine Nash, *Feminist Narrative Ethics: Tacit Persuasion in Modernist Form* (Columbus: The Ohio State University Press, 2014), pp.9 - 10.

④ Susan Lanser, "Queering Narrative Voice," *Textual Practice* 32.6(2018), p.931.

⑤ Robyn Warhol and Susan Lanser, *Narrative Theory Unbound: Queer and Feminist Interventions* (Columbus: The Ohio State University Press, 2015), p.1.

结合，基于女性叙述声音实现话语权威的叙事策略及其产生的社会和文学条件建构了叙述声音的女性主义理论。根据叙述者与讲述内容的关系，兰瑟区分了作者型叙述声音、个人型叙述声音和集体型叙述声音三种叙述声音，并依据受述者的结构位置区分了"公开的"和"私人的"两者类型。前者指叙述者对故事之外的受述者讲述故事，后者指叙述者对故事内的某一受述者讲述故事。兰瑟所提出的"公开叙述"和"私下叙述"概念是专为研究女性文本而创造的概念。她对于叙述声音的这种分类有助于她将叙述声音的形式与意识形态相结合。

尽管经典叙事学也关注叙述声音的权威性，但这种对权威性的探讨更多的是基于叙述模式的结构特征和美学效果。例如传统的全知叙述者，即兰瑟分类中的作者型叙述者，与虚构人物处于不同的结构层面，以虚构的形式置身于叙述文本之外。因而，较之于处于故事之内的第一人称叙述者，作者型叙述者具有更强的可信度和权威性。兰瑟以这种结构权威为基础，将叙述声音置于社会位置和文学实践的交汇处，聚焦于形式性别化的作者权威。在兰瑟看来，"公开的作者型叙述声音"可以通过公开的叙述建构女性主体性；"私人的个人型叙述声音"虽然会使得女性权威大幅度减低，但却可以建构一种以女性身体为形式载体的女性主义的权威。"集体型叙述声音"作为兰瑟叙述模式中的独创发展了经典叙事学模式。这种多方位、交互赋权的叙述声音或者某个获得群体授权的个人声音赋予一定规模的群体以叙事权威。这种群体声音则是被大部分叙事研究所忽视的，且大多是来自边缘化或受压抑的群体。① 例如在对《千年圣殿》的分析中，兰瑟指出蒙塞尔关于女性社会言论自由的观点代表着广大女性同胞的观点，由此通过她的叙述声音赋予了她们叙事权威。可以看到，在对"集体型叙述声音"的建构和讨论中，兰瑟跨越了"话语"与"故事"之间的界限，以女性社群的存在为前提探讨女性群体之声的权威。通过这种叙述声音的区分方式，兰瑟试图将女性作家为获得叙事和性别权威而向男权社会发出的控诉声音从文本中分离，并性别化了这一种叙述声音。这也使得结构形式化的三类叙述声音与女性作家和文本社会历史语境产生联系，成为政治斗争的场所。在《我们到达了那里吗？论女性主义叙事学的交叉性未来》和《叙述声音酷儿化》中，兰瑟对《虚构的权威：女性作家与叙述声音》一书进行了反思以及修改。她提出了"酷儿声音"的概念。在此基础上，她还进一步修改了"集体型叙述声音"的性别化标志。可以看到，从性别介入、酷儿、交叉性到更加兼容的理论，兰瑟的女性主义叙事学研究的发展路径也体现在她对于叙述声音的建构和阐释中。

相较于兰瑟对权威性的关注，沃霍尔则着眼于作者与读者的距离，通过"吸引型叙述"和"疏远型叙述"的对比探究19世纪中期英国现实主义女作家如何通过一定的叙述模式拉近与读者的距离，从而达到影响社会、改变现实的目的。沃霍尔系统地罗列了两种介入方式存在的五个明显的不同特征：受述者名字的指称、直接与受述者对话的频率、对于受述者的反讽程度、叙述者面向人物的立场以及叙述者对叙事模糊或清晰的态度。在"吸引型叙述"中，叙述者和受述者之间拥有更为亲近和真诚的关系，读者也能更加投入到故事中，与故事人物产生情感认同。有鉴于此，吸引型叙述者经常大量使用潜在读者群的名字，如用"你"称呼受述者，避免直接命名受述者，并高频率地使用这些称呼，以此加强读者对于受述者的认同。吸引型叙述者从情感高度肯定受述者的道德感，使得读者能够回应叙述者的情感召唤。此外，吸引型叙述者坚持人物和故事的真实性，通过互文等方式将虚构与真实世界融为一体，增强了现实

① 参见 Lanser, *Fictions of Authority: Women Writers and Narrative Voice*, pp.21-25.

感。这也使得读者在回归到现实世界后能回应故事，采取积极的行动并承担相应的社会责任。[①]

正如前文所述，在女性作家的文本中，吸引型叙事介入更为频繁，在修辞上的位置也更为突出。[②] 沃霍尔在探究两种介入方式性别内涵的成因时指出，吸引型叙事介入是女性介入现实生活的策略性技巧。[③] 类似书信体的文学形式使得女性作家能够通过叙述者对受述者的信任和亲切赢得读者的信任，从而在作者和读者之间营造直接的期待感，建立信任和亲密的关系，实现精神交流上的共鸣。吸引型叙事介入也由此可以通过对读者的这种介入实现对社会现实的介入并产生一定的影响。可以看出，沃霍尔通过吸引型叙事介入的提出和研究论证了叙事形式与性别之间的内在联系，展示了如何将叙事学的形式主义研究方法和女性主义语境批评结合起来，探讨历史的、社会的和以性别为基础的问题。[④]

经过三十多年的发展，女性主义叙事学在理论建构上更为系统，在批评实践上更为细致和丰富，在研究视角上更为多元和广阔。它不仅对叙述声音、叙述视角、情节等经典叙事学基本概念做出了全新的评价和界定，挖掘了暗含在叙事结构和叙述技巧之中的性别意识和意识形态，探讨叙事艺术与性别政治之间的复杂关系，而且还将叙事作品中的种族、阶级等元素纳入考查范围，不断携手其他学派和学科迎接全球多元化的挑战。为加深对女性主义叙事学理论建构和批评实践的理解，本章选择了三篇代表性文献，分别来自兰瑟的《虚构的权威：女性作家与叙述声音》、沃霍尔的《性别介入：维多利亚小说的叙事话语》和佩奇的《女性主义叙事学的文学与语言学视角》。

---

① Warhol, *Gendered Interventions: Narrative Discourse in the Victorian Novel*, pp.34 - 43.

② Ibid., p.18.

③ Ibid., pp.22 - 23.

④ Ibid., p.xv.

第二节　苏珊·兰瑟及其《虚构的权威：女性作家与叙述声音》

一、导读

作为女性主义叙事学的开创者和领军人物，苏珊·兰瑟在当代西方叙事学界有着重要的影响力。尽管兰瑟是形式主义研究出身的叙事学家，她同时也深受女性主义文学批评的影响。在对女性主义文学批评和传统叙事学分析和批评的基础上，兰瑟一方面看到了女性主义文学批评重视语境和读者但具有印象性和片面性的特点，另一方面看到了传统叙事学具有系统性和阐释力但忽略文本的意识形态内涵和社会历史语境的特征。两者之间的冲突以及互补促使兰瑟摆脱传统叙事学研究的枷锁，创造性地接纳两者的不同主张，探寻叙事形式的性别意义。

在其经典著作《虚构的权威：女性作家与叙述声音》中，兰瑟创建性地从女作者文本中的叙述声音入手研究叙事形式中蕴含的性别意义，结合性别和语境阐释作品中叙事形式的社会政治意义。就概念而言，兰瑟首先探讨了女性主义文学批评以及叙事诗学观念中的“声音”。在她看来，前者的探讨具有宏观、模仿再现和政治化的特点，而后者则具有具体化、符号学化以及技术性强的特征。对于声音的探讨也反映了女性主义文学批评和叙事学研究的不同以及冲突。当两者对“声音”的不同观念融合到巴赫金提出的“社会学诗学”中时，叙述声音就不再仅仅是意识形态的产物，还是意识形态的本身。[①] 基于此，兰瑟将叙述模式与性别身份相结合，视“叙述声音”为“叙事权威”。在叙述声音的研究中，兰瑟聚焦性别化的作者权威，着重探讨女性作家们如何通过对男性权威的使用、批判、颠覆等实现自我权威的建构。

在书中，兰瑟主要聚焦话语层面叙述声音的分类，将其分为作者的(authorial)、个人的(personal)和集体的(communal)三种叙述声音模式。作者型叙述声音借助“异故事叙述者”表达作者的立场，相当于传统的全知叙述。这一种声音是集体的并具有潜在自我指称意义的叙事状态，产生或再生了作者权威的结构或功能性场景，具有较强的权威性。个人型叙述声音则由“同故事叙述者”呈现，是人物叙述，即叙述者“我”同时也是故事中的主角“我”，是该主角以往的自我。这种结构上的特征使得它只能申明个人解释自己经历的权利及其有效性。尽管它能统筹其他人物的声音，但却不具备作者型叙述声音能超越具体人的优先地位。有鉴于此，这也使得其女性权威大打折扣。在考察作者型叙述声音和个人型叙述声音的基础上，兰瑟指出了叙述的个体化倾向并基于此创造性地提出了集体型叙述声音。这种声音或者表达了一种群体的共同声音，或者表达了各种声音的集合，有三种不同的形式，即某叙述者代某群体发言的“单言”(singular)形式、复数主语“我们”叙述的“共言”(simultaneous)形式和群体中的个人轮流发言的“轮言”(sequential)形式。在叙述过程中，具有一定规模的群体通过多方位、交互赋权的叙

① Lanser, *Fiction of Authority: Women Writers and Narrative Voice*, p.5.

述声音被赋予叙事权威。有鉴于此，这种声音可能也是最权威但也最隐蔽的虚构形式。在兰瑟看来，集体型叙述声音在以往的结构主义叙事理论中被忽略，是一个有待开发、充满未知可能性的领域。[①]

兰瑟的叙述声音理论和批评实践以结构主义叙事学理论为对照，着重辨析了叙述声音和意识形态之间的关联。这种方法不仅阐明了纯形式的分析方法和语境分析方法在探究叙事意义上的差异，肯定了传统叙事学在描述叙事现象时的工具意义，也展示了女性主义文学批评和传统叙事学结合的可行性和有效性。此外，正如兰瑟所言："对女作家作品中叙事结构的探讨可能会动摇叙事学的基本原理和结构区分。"[②]兰瑟从女性主义角度切入叙事形式的分析切实推动了叙事学的发展，影响深远。

二、《虚构的权威：女性作家与叙述声音》选读[③]

Toward a Feminist Poetics of Narrative Voice

Few words are as resonant to contemporary feminists as "voice". The term appears in history and philosophy, in sociology, literature, and psychology, spanning disciplinary and theoretical differences. Book titles announce "another voice", a "different voice", or resurrect the "lost voices" of women poets and pioneers; fictional figures ancient and modern, actual women famous and obscure, are honored for speaking up and speaking out.[④] Other silenced communities—peoples of color, peoples struggling against colonial rule, gay men and lesbians—have also written and spoken about the urgency of "coming to voice". Despite compelling interrogations of "voice" as a humanist fiction, for the collectively and personally silenced the term has become a trope of identity and power: as Luce Irigaray suggests, to find a voice (*voix*) is to find a way (*voie*).[⑤]

In narrative poetics ("narratology"), voice is an equally crucial though more circumscribed term, designating tellers—as distinct from both authors and nonnarrating characters—of narrative. Although many critics acknowledge the bald inaccuracy of "voice" and "teller" to signify something written, these terms persist even among structuralists: according to Gerard Genette, "in the most unobtrusive narrative, someone is speaking to me, is telling me a story, is inviting me to

① Lanser, *Fiction of Authority: Women Writers and Narrative Voice*, pp.15 – 22.

② Ibid., p.6.

③ Ibid., pp.3 – 8, 15 – 22.

④ A *few titles: In a Different Voice*; *American Women*, *American Voices*; *The Sound of Our Own Voices*; *The Other Voice: Scottish Women's Writing since 1808*; *Finding a Voice: Asian Women in Britain*; *Territories of the Voice: Contemporary Stories by Irish Women Writers*; *Radical Voices: A Decade of Resistance from "Women's Studies International Forum"*; *The Indigenous Voice: Visions and Realities*.

⑤ Luce lrigaray, *This Sex Which is Not One*, trans. Catherine Porter with Carolyn Burke (Ithaca: Cornell University Press, 1985), p.209. As my references to Cixous and lrigaray emphasize, even "poststructuralist" feminists have been unwilling to abandon the word *voice* as a signifier of female power, for women have not as a body (in both senses) possessed the logos that deconstruction deconstructs.

listen to it as he tells it."[①] Narration entails social relationships and thus involves far more than the technical imperatives for getting a story told. The narrative voice and the narrated world are mutually constitutive; if there is no tale without a teller, there is no teller without a tale. This interdependence gives the narrator a liminal position that is at once contingent and privileged: the narrator has no existence "outside" the text yet brings the text into existence; narrative speech acts cannot be said to be mere "imitations", like the acts of characters, because they are the acts that make the "imitations" possible.

Despite their shared recognition of the power of "voice", the two concepts I have been describing—the feminist and the narratological—have entailed separate inquiries of antithetical tendency: the one general, mimetic, and political, the other specific, semiotic, and technical. When feminists talk about voice, we are usually referring to the behavior of actual or fictional persons and groups who assert woman-centered points of view. Thus feminists may speak of a literary character who refuses patriarchal pressures as "finding a voice" whether or not that voice is represented textually. When narrative theorists talk about voice, we are usually concerned with formal structures and not with the causes, ideologies, or social implications of particular narrative practices. With a few exceptions, feminist criticism does not ordinarily consider the technical aspects of narration, and narrative poetics does not ordinarily consider the social properties and political implications of narrative voice.[②] Formalist poetics may seem to feminists naively empiricist, masking ideology as objective truth, sacrificing significance for precision, incapable of producing distinctions that are politically meaningful. Feminist criticism may seem to narratologists naively subjectivist, sacrificing precision for ideology, incapable of producing distinctions that are textually meaningful.

These incompatible tendencies, which I have overstated here, can offer fruitful counterpoints. As a narratological term, "voice" attends to the specific forms of textual practice and avoids the essentializing tendencies of its more casual feminist usages. As a political term, "voice" rescues textual study from a formalist isolation that often treats literary events as if they were inconsequential to human history. When these two approaches to "voice" converge in what Mikhail Bakhtin has called a "sociological poetics"[③], it becomes possible to see narrative technique not

---

① Gerard Genette, *Narrative Discourse Revisited*, trans. Jane E. Lewin (Ithaca: Cornell University Press, 1988), p.101. I consider this distinction not essential but conventional: narratives have narrators because Western literature has continued to construct reading and listening in speakerly terms. The convention may already be disappearing in an age of mechanical reproduction, bureaucratic discourse, and computer-generated texts. For an opposing viewpoint, see Jonathan Culler, "Problems in the Theory of Fiction," *Diacritics* 14 (Spring 1984), pp.5 - 11.

② On the tension between feminism and narrative poetics see Robyn Warhol, *Gendered Interventions: Narrative Discourse in the Victorian Novel* (New Brunswick: Rutgers University Press, 1989), pp.12 - 20; my essay "Toward a Feminist Narratology," *Style* 20 (1986), pp.341 - 363; and my subsequent exchange with Nilli Diengott in *Style* 22 (1988), pp.40 - 60.

③ A "sociological poetics" is described in P. N. Medvedev and M. M. Bakhtin, *The Formal Method in Literary Scholarship: A Critical Introduction to Sociological Poetics*, trans. Albert J. Wehrle (Baltimore: Johns Hopkins University Press, 1978), p.30. The feminist attention to voice generated by Bakhtinian theory is a welcome new inquiry; see especially Dale M. Bauer, *Feminist Dialogics: A Theory of Failed Community* (Albany: SUNY Press, 1988). On the whole, however, "feminist dialogics" have not focused on the close formal distinctions found, for example, in Bakhtin's "Discourse on the Novel," but have followed Bakhtin's tendency elsewhere to equate "voice" with discourse in the Foucauldian sense.

simply as a product of ideology but as ideology itself: narrative voice, situated at the juncture of "social position and literary practice"①, embodies the social, economic, and literary conditions under which it has been produced.② Such a sociological or materialist poetics refuses the idealism to which both narrative poetics and some forms of feminist theory have been prone, an idealism that has led in the first case to a reading of textual properties as universal, inevitable, or random phenomena, and in the second to the assumption of a panhistorical "women's language" or "female form". I maintain that both narrative structures and women's writing are determined not by essential properties or isolated aesthetic imperatives but by complex and changing conventions that are themselves produced in and by the relations of power that implicate writer, reader, and text. In modern Western societies during the centuries of "print culture" with which I am concerned, these constituents of power must include, at the very least, race, gender, class, nationality, education, sexuality and marital status, interacting with and within a given social formation.

So long as it acknowledges its own status as theory rather than claiming to trade in neutral, uninterpreted facts, a historically-situated structuralist poetics may offer a valuable differential framework for examining specific narrative patterns and practices. The exploration of narrative structures in women's writings may, in turn, challenge the categories and postulates of narratology, since the canon on which narrative theory is grounded has been relentlessly if not intentionally man-made.③ As one contribution to such a feminist poetics of narrative, this book explores certain configurations of textual voice in fictions by women of Britain, France, and the United States writing from the mid-eighteenth century to the mid-twentieth—the period that coincides with the hegemony of the novel and its attendant notions of individual(ist) authorship.Recognizing that the "authorfunction" that grounds Western literary authority is constructed in white, privileged-class male terms,④ I take as a point of departure the hypothesis that female voice—a term used here simply to designate the narrator's grammatical gender—is a site of ideological tension made visible in textual practices.

In thus linking social identity and narrative form, I am postulating that the authority of a given voice or text is produced from a conjunction of social and rhetorical properties. Discursive authority—by which I mean here the intellectual credibility, ideological validity, and aesthetic value claimed by or conferred upon a work, author, narrator, character, or textual practice—is produced

① Raymond Williams, *Marxism and Literature* (Oxford: Oxford University Press, 1977),p.179.

② I am using "ideology" throughout to describe the discourses and signifying systems through which a culture constitutes its beliefs about itself, structures the relationships of individuals and groups to one another, to social institutions, and to belief systems, and legitimates and perpetuates its values and practices. This definition does not address the question of whether there is a "real" outside ideology that is not itself ideological.

③ Nor is this true only of formalist critics like Genette, Shlomith Rimmon-Kenan, Wolfgang Iser, and (less egregiously) Seymour Chatman. The work of materialists like Fredric Jameson and even Bakhtin, which has been so enthusiastically embraced by critics working with "marginal" discourses, is androcentric in both its textual canon and its assumptions about literature。

④ On the "author-function" see Michel Foucault, "What Is an Author?" in *Language, Counter-Memory, Practice: Selected Essays and Interviews*, ed. Donald F. Bouchard (Ithaca: Cornell University Press, 1977),pp.113 - 138.

interactively; it must therefore be characterized with respect to specific receiving communities. In Western literary systems for the past two centuries, however, discursive authority has, with varying degrees of intensity, attached itself most readily to white, educated men of hegemonic ideology. One major constituent of narrative authority, therefore, is the extent to which a narrator's status conforms to this dominant social power. At the same time, narrative authority is also constituted through (historically changing) textual strategies that even socially unauthorized writers can appropriate. Since such appropriations may of course backfire, nonhegemonic writers and narrators may need to strike a delicate balance in accommodating and subverting dominant rhetorical practices.

Although I have been speaking about authority as if it were universally desirable, some women writers have of course questioned not only those who hold authority and the mechanisms by which they are authorized, but the value of authority as modern Western cultures have constructed it. I believe, however, that even novelists who challenge this authority are constrained to adopt the authorizing conventions of narrative voice in order, paradoxically, to mount an authoritative critique of the authority that the text therefore also perpetuates. Carrying out such an Archimedean project, which seems to me particularly hazardous for texts seeking canonical status, necessitates standing on the very ground one is attempting to deconstruct. While I will acknowledge ways in which women writers continue to challenge even their own authoritative standing, the emphasis of this book is on the project of self-authorization, which, I argue, is implicit in the very act of authorship. In other words, I assume that regardless of any woman writer's ambivalence toward authoritative institutions and ideologies, the act of writing a novel and seeking to publish it—like my own act of writing a scholarly book and seeking to publish it—is implicitly a quest for discursive authority: a quest to be heard, respected, and believed, a hope of influence. I assume, that is, that every writer who publishes a novel wants it to be authoritative for her readers, even if authoritatively antiauthoritarian, within the sphere and for the receiving community that the work carves out. In making this assumption I am not denying what Edward Said calls the "molested" or "sham" nature of textual authority in general and of fictional authority in particular, but I am also reading the novel as a cultural enterprise that has historically claimed and received a truth value beyond the fictional.①

I have chosen to examine texts that engage questions of authority specifically through their production of narrative voice. In each case, narrative voice is a site of crisis, contradiction, or challenge that is manifested in and sometimes resolved through ideologically charged technical practices. The texts I explore construct narrative voices that seek to write themselves into Literature

① See Edward Said, "Molestation and Authority in Narrative Fiction," in *Aspects of Narrative: Selected Papers from the English Institute*, ed. J. Hillis Miller (New York: Columbia University Press, 1971), pp.47–68. On the status of fiction see also Peter J. McCormick, *Fictions, Philosophies, and the Problems of Poetics* (Ithaca: Cornell University Press, 1988).

without leaving Literature the same. These narrators, skeptical of the authoritative aura of the male pen and often critical of male dominance in general, are nonetheless pressed by social and textual convention to reproduce the very structures they would reformulate. Such narrators often call into question the very authority they endorse or, conversely, endorse the authority they seem to be questioning. That is, as they strive to create fictions of *authority*, these narrators expose *fictions* of authority as the Western novel has constructed it—and in exposing the fictions, they may end up re-establishing the authority. Some of these texts work out such dilemmas on their thematic surfaces, constructing fictions *of*—that is, *about*—authority, as well.

When I describe these complexities in some women's writings I am not, however, suggesting any kind of "authentic" female voice or arguing that women necessarily write differently from men. Rather, I believe that disavowed writers of both sexes have engaged in various strategies of adaptation and critique that make their work "dialogical" in ways that Bakhtin's formulation, which posits heteroglossia as a general modern condition, may obscure.① It is possible, for example, that women privileged enough to write literature are particularly susceptible to what Margaret Homans describes as "a specific gender-based alienation from language" born of the "simultaneous participation in and exclusion from a hegemonic group".② My reading suggests that different communities of women have had different degrees of access to particular narrative forms. I am especially interested in those female narrators who claim public authority, since within the historical period I am studying it has not been voice in general so much as public voice that women have been denied. As I will suggest further on in this chapter, these concerns lead me less to a new narrative poetics than to a poetics attentive to issues that conventional narratology has devalued or ignored.

…

This book begins with the simultaneous "rise" of the novel and emergence of modern gender identity in the mid-eighteenth century, and moves toward what may well be the twilight of both. As I situate narrative practices in relation to literary production and social ideology, I will be asking what forms of voice have been available to women, and to which women, at particular moments. My intention is to explore through specifically formal evidence the intersection of social identity and textual form, reading certain aspects of narrative voice as a critical locus of ideology.

I have organized the book to focus on changing problems and patterns in the articulation of three narrative modes which I call, respectively, authorial, personal, and communal voice. Each

---

① Bakhtin's formulation that all novelistic discourse, if not all discourse, is irreducibly double-voiced makes more difficult the differentiating of specific ways in which the words of a disauthorized community are "entangled, shot through with shared thoughts, points of view, alien value judgments and accents", and dwell in "a dialogically agitated and tension-filled environment of alien words"[*The Dialogic Imagination*, trans. Caryl Emerson and Michael Holquist (Austin: University of Texas Press, 1981), p.276].

② Margaret Homans, "'Her Very Own Howl': The Ambiguities of Representation in Recent Women's Fiction," *Signs* (1983), p.205. Homans's suggestion that this ambiguity characterizes all women's discourse seems to me problematic insofar as it presumes that all women are simultaneously inside and outside a hegemony.

mode represents not simply a set of technical distinctions but a particular kind of narrative consciousness and hence a particular nexus of powers, dangers, prohibitions, and possibilities. Across all three modes, however, I will be concerned with two aspects of narration that I consider of greater significance in the construction of textual authority than narrative poetics has traditionally allowed. The first is the distinction between private voice (narration directed toward a narratee who is a fictional character) and public voice (narration directed toward a narratee "outside" the fiction who is analogous to the historical reader). The second is the distinction between narrative situations that do and those that do not permit narrative self-reference, by which I mean explicit attention to the act of narration itself. It is my hypothesis that gendered conventions of public voice and of narrative self-reference serve important roles in regulating women's access to discursive authority.

I use the term *authorial voice* to identify narrative situations that are heterodiegetic, public, and potentially self-referential. (Gerard Genette, observing that every narrator is potentially an enunciating "I", suggests the more precise term heterodiegetic for what is traditionally called "third-person" narration in which the narrator is not a participant in the fictional world and exists on a separate ontological plane from the characters.①) The mode I am calling authorial is also "extradiegetic" and public, directed to a narratee who is analogous to a reading audience.② I have chosen the term "authorial" not to imply an ontological equivalence between narrator and author but to suggest that such a voice (re)produces the structural and functional situation of authorship. In other words, where a distinction between the (implied) author and a public, heterodiegetic narrator is not textually marked, readers are invited to equate the narrator with the author and the narratee with themselves (or their historical equivalents). This conventional equation gives authorial voice a privileged status among narrative forms; as Bakhtin states, while the discourse of a character or a stylized narrator is always a contingent "object of authorial understanding", authorial discourse is "directed toward its own straightforward referential meaning".③ Moreover, since authorial narrators exist outside narrative time (indeed, "outside" fiction) and are not "humanized" by events, they conventionally carry an authority superior to that conferred on characters, even on narrating characters. In using the term "authorial" I mean as well to evoke Franz Stanzel's distinction in *Narrative Situations in the Novel* between "authorial" and "figural" modes: while authorial narrative permits what I am calling narrative self-reference, in the "figural" mode all narration is focalized

① Gerard Genette, *Narrative Discourse: An Essay in Method*, trans. Jane E. Lewin (Ithaca: Cornell University Press, 1980), pp.244 - 245.

② On the concept of diegetic levels, see ibid., pp.227 - 231. On the distinction between private and public voice, which is not identical to Genette's distinction between primary and inserted narrative, see my book *The Narrative Act: Point of View in Prose Fiction* (Princeton: Princeton University Press, 1981), pp. 133 - 148, and "Toward a Feminist Narratology," pp.350 - 355.

③ Mikhail Bakhtin, *Problems of Dostoevsky's Poetics*, ed. and trans. Caryl Emerson (Minneapolis: University of Minnesota Press, 1984), p.187.

through the perspectives of characters, and thus no reference to the narrator or the narrative situation is feasible.

I want to suggest as a major element of authorial status a distinction between narrators who engage exclusively in acts of representation that is, who simply predicate the words and actions of fictional characters—and those who undertake "extrarepresentational" acts: reflections, judgments, generalizations about the world "beyond" the fiction, direct addresses to the narratee, comments on the narrative process, allusions to other writers and texts.① I will be using the term *overt authoriality* or simply *authoriality*, to refer to practices by which heterodiegetic, public, self-referential narrators perform these "extrarepresentational" functions not strictly required for telling a tale. I am speculating that acts of representation make a more limited claim to discursive authority than extrarepresentational acts, which expand the sphere of fictional authority to "nonfictional" referents and allow the writer to engage, from "within" the fiction, in a culture's literary, social, and intellectual debates. On the other hand, as Shlomith Rimmon-Kenan has observed, when a narrator "becomes more overt, his chances of being fully reliable are diminished, since his interpretations, judgements, generalizations are not always compatible with the norms of the implied author".②

Extrarepresentational acts are especially critical to a polyglossic genre like the novel because they enable the narrator to construct the "maxims" that Genette describes as the foundation of verisimilitude.③ In other words, the reception of a novel rests on an implicit set of principles by which textual events (for example, characters' behaviors) are rendered plausible. To the degree that a text's values deviate from cultural givens (as they will to some degree in all but the most formulaic of fictions), they must be established (or inferred) for each narrative instance so that readers can construct the story as "plausible" and embed it in a "world view".④ Ideologically oppositional writers might wish, therefore, to "maximize" their narratives in order either to posit alternative textual ideologies or to establish the writer, through her authorial narrator-equivalent, as a significant participant in contemporary debates-all the more during those periods when the novel was one of the few accepted means for women to intervene in public life.

It should not be difficult to understand why, with differences in kind and intensity according to time, place, and circumstance, women writers' adoption of overt authoriality has usually meant transgressing gendered rhetorical codes. In cultures such as the ones I am examining, where women's access to public discourse has been curtailed, it has been one thing for women simply to tell stories

① Each of these "extrarepresentational" acts may of course be embedded in sentences of representation; the two activities are sometimes simultaneous.

② Shlomith Rimmon-Kenan, *Narrative Fiction: Contemporary Poetics* (London: Methuen, 1983), p.103.

③ Gerard Genette, *Figures II* (Paris: Seuil, 1968).

④ On the importance of "maxim" see Nancy Miller, "Emphasis Added: Plots and Plausibilities in Women's Fiction," *PMLA* 96 (1981), pp.36 - 48; reprinted in *The New Feminist Criticism*, ed. Elaine Showalter (New York: Pantheon, 1985), pp.339 - 360.

and another for their narrators to set themselves forth as authorities. Indeed, authorial voice has been so conventionally masculine that female authorship does not necessarily establish female voice: a startling number of critics have referred in the generic masculine to the narrators of such novels as *La Princesse de Cleves* and *Pride and Prejudice*.[①] Thus, on the one hand, since a heterodiegetic narrator need not be identified by sex, the authorial mode has allowed women access to "male" authority by separating the narrating "I" from the female body; it is of course in the exploitation of this possibility that women writers have used male narrators and pseudonyms (acts that may have profited individual writers or texts, but that have surely also reinforced the androcentrism of narrative authority). On the other hand, when an authorial voice has represented itself as female, it has risked being (dis)qualified. It is possible that women's writing has carried fuller public authority when its voice has not been marked as female.

The narrators I discuss in Part I of this book have sought not simply to tell stories, but through overtly authorial practices to make themselves (and, I presume, their authors) significant literary presences. After examining an eighteenth-century text that proclaims the difficulty of achieving authoriality, Part I focuses on four canonical writers (Jane Austen, George Eliot, Virginia Woolf, and Toni Morrison) in order to explore the means by which each has constructed authorial voice within and against the narrative and social conventions of her time and place. In the work of all four writers I see a reaching for narrative hegemony, for what Wayne Booth has called "direct and authoritative rhetoric"[②], that is obscured both by the writers' own disclaimers and by a tendency in contemporary feminist criticism to valorize "refusals" of authority in ways that seem to me ahistorical.

I use the term *personal voice* to refer to narrators who are selfconsciously telling their own histories. I do not intend this term to designate all "homodiegetic" or "first-person" narratives—that is, all those in which the voice that speaks is a participant in the fictional world—but only those Genette calls "autodiegetic", in which the "I" who tells the story is also the story's protagonist (or an older version of the protagonist).[③] In my exploration of personal voice I will exclude forms such as the interior monologue, which are not selfconsciously narrative and which, like figural narration, cannot construct a situation of narrative self-reference.

The authority of personal voice is contingent in ways that the authority of authorial voice is not: while the autodiegetic "I" remains a structurally "superior" voice mediating the voices of other characters, it does not carry the superhuman privileges that attach to authorial voice, and its status

① For example, in *The Dual Voice: Free Indirect Speech and Its Functioning in the Nineteenth-Century European Novel* (Manchester: Manchester University Press, 1977), Roy Pascal insists that Jane Austen's narrator be called by the "generic" masculine; Laurence Gregorio makes a similar insistence "for the sake of clarity" about *La Princesse de Cleves* in *Order in the Court: History and Society in "La Princesse de Cleves"* (Stanford French and Italian Studies 47.1986), 1. For the argument that the unmarked narrative voice is neither gendered nor necessarily human, see Culler, "*Problems in the Theory of Fiction*".

② Wayne Booth, *The Rhetoric of Fiction* (Chicago: University of Chicago Press, 1961), p.6.

③ See Genette, *Narrative Discourse*, pp.227 – 247.

is dependent on a reader's response not only to the narrator's acts but to the character's actions, just as the authority of the representation is dependent in turn on the successful construction of a credible voice. These differences make personal voice in some ways less formidable for women than authorial voice, since an authorial narrator claims broad powers of knowledge and judgment, while a personal narrator claims only the validity of one person's right to interpret her experience.

At the same time, personal narration offers no gender-neutral mask or distancing "third person", no refuge in a generic voice that may pass as masculine.① A female personal narrator risks the reader's resistance if the act of telling, the story she tells, or the self she constructs through telling it transgresses the limits of the acceptably feminine. If women are encouraged to write only of themselves because they are not supposed to claim knowledge of men or "the world", when women *have* written only of themselves they have been labeled immodest and narcissistic, and criticized for displaying either their virtues or their faults. Moreover, because male writers have created female voices, the arena of personal narration may also involve a struggle over which representations of female voice are to be authorized.

Although authorial narration, with its omniscient privilege, is usually understood to be fictional, fiction in the personal voice is usually formally indistinguishable from autobiography. Given the precarious position of women in patriarchal societies, woman novelists may have avoided personal voice when they feared their work would be taken for autobiography. The use of personal voice also risks reinforcing the convenient ideology of women's writing as "self-expression", the product of "intuition" rather than of art;② perhaps this is why Maxine Hong Kingston stated recently that she did not believe she would be a "real" novelist until she had written a book in the authorial voice.③ In view of these constraints, my discussion of personal voice is especially concerned with variations in the accessibility of public and private forms of personal voice to particular communities of women at particular moments in history. Part II attempts to interpret patterns of personal voice respectively in European women's writings from the late eighteenth to the mid-nineteenth century and in African American women's writings from the nineteenth century to the contemporary period.

Conventional narrative poetics has often viewed authorial and personal voices as formal antitheses, the one constituting the "diegetic" voice of a fictional author, the other constituting the "mimetic" voice of a character. Indeed, the two modes carry different forms of rhetorical authority:

---

① Obviously, a woman writer may choose an explicitly male "I"-narrator, as dozens of women writers from Hannah More to the Brontes to Willa Cather and Marguerite Yourcenar have done. When I speak of the teller here, I am speaking of the female *narrator*, not the female writer.

② See, for example, Jean Larnac's argument that women's literary power resides in their ability to "feel vividly and immediately to release from themselves feelings they have just experienced, without waiting for the fruitful germinations that come from slow meditation," in *Histoire de la litterature feminine en France* (Paris: Kra, 1929), p.111.

③ Maxine Hong Kingston, in a reading given at Georgetown University, April 1989. Kingston was referring to *Tripmaster Monkey—His Fake Book* (New York: Knopf, 1989), whose authorial voice, she says, is absolutely—and to her, unmistakably—female even though it is never marked as such.

paradoxically, authorial narrative is understood as fictive and yet its voice is accorded a superior reliability, while personal narrative may pass for autobiography but the authority of its voice is always qualified. But the opposition is far from definite: the eyewitness narrator used, for example, in Aphra Behn's *Oronooko* (1688) and George Eliot's *Scenes of Clerical Life* transgresses the polarities of "third-person" and "first-person" narration that are usually assumed to be formally unbridgeable.

The tendency to oppose these modes also conceals similarities between them. Both forms bear the potential for public, self-referential narration and thus for enacting a relationship between "writer" and audience and indeed an entire "story" that is the story of the narration itself. Moreover, the narratological tendency to oppose authorial and personal voices conceals the degree to which both forms are invested in singularity—in the presupposition that narration is individual. This narrative individualism that European cultures take for granted explains why authorial and personal voices have been so commonly practiced and so thoroughly analyzed, while so little attention has been given to intermediate forms such as that of Christa Wolfs *Nachdenken uber Christa T*. (1967), in which the narrator is reconstructing the life of another woman but is also in some sense a protagonist herself, not simply an eyewitness or biographer.

This individualization of narrative also explains why my third mode, *communal voice*, is likewise a category of underdeveloped possibilities that has not even been named in contemporary narratology. By communal voice I mean a spectrum of practices that articulate either a collective voice or a collective of voices that share narrative authority. Because the dominant culture has not employed communal voice to any perceptible degree, and because distinctions about voice have been based primarily on the features of this dominant literature, there has been no narratological terminology for communal voice or for its various technical possibilities.

By communal narration I do not mean simply the use of an authorial voice that resorts to an inclusive "we" (as George Eliot's narrators sometimes do), nor the multiple narration Faulkner adopts in a novel like *As I Lay Dying*, nor the presentation of divergent and antithetical perspectives on the same events that characterizes epistolary novels such as *Lady Susan* and *Les Liaisons dangereuses*. I refer, rather, to a practice in which narrative authority is invested in a definable community and textually inscribed either through multiple, mutually authorizing voices or through the voice of a single individual who is manifestly authorized by a community. In Part III, I will distinguish three such possibilities that result from various confluences of social ideology with changing conventions of narrative technique: a *singular* form in which one narrator speaks for a collective, a *simultaneous* form in which a plural "we" narrates, and a *sequential* form in which individual members of a group narrate in turn. Unlike authorial and personal voices, the communal mode seems to be primarily a phenomenon of marginal or suppressed communities; I have not observed it in fiction by white, ruling-class men perhaps because such an "I" is already in some sense speaking with the authority of a hegemonic "we". My survey of communal voice in Part III moves from an exploration of constraints on communal voice in the eighteenth century, through "singular" manifestations in the nineteenth, to a range of formal possibilities available to modern and postmodern narratives.

Because the structures of both narration and plot in the Western novel are individualist and androcentric, the articulation of a communal female voice is not simply a question of discourse but almost always one of story as well. Although it is possible to represent female community without communal voice, it is difficult to construct communal voice without constructing female community. Communal voice thus shifts the text away from individual protagonists and personal plots, calling into question the heterosocial contract that has defined woman's place in Western fiction. My examination of more and less realized communal forms in the singular, sequential, and simultaneous modes suggests the political possibilities of constituting a collectice female voice through narrative. At the same time, communal voice might be the most insidious fiction of authority, for in Western cultures it is nearly always the creation of a single author appropriating the power of a plurality.

The three modes of narrative voice on which this book concentrates seem to me to represent three distinct kinds of authority that women have needed to constitute in order to make their place in Western literary history: respectively, the authority, to establish alternative "worlds" and the "maxims" by which they will operate, to construct and publicly represent female subjectivity and redefine the "feminine", and to constitute as a discursive subject a female body politic. Each form creates its own fictions of authority, making certain meanings and not others articulable. Although I begin with authorial voice because it is the oldest and most basic mode and end with communal voice because it is the newest and least conventional, I refrain from any absolute evaluation of the three modes. I will speculate briefly in my final chapter about the value of each of these narrative "tools" for dismantling, to use Audre Lorde's now-famous metaphor, the "master's house".[①]

三、思考与讨论

(1) 与结构主义叙事学理论中的声音概念相比,兰瑟的叙述声音模式有何特征?

(2)"集体型叙述声音"为何一直被学界所忽视?

(3) 请运用兰瑟的叙述声音模式分析一个短篇小说。

① Audre Lorde, "The Master's Tools Will Never Dismantle the Master's House," in *Sister/Outsider* (Freedom, Calif.: Crossing Press, 1984), pp.110-113.

第三节　罗宾·沃霍尔及其《性别介入：维多利亚小说的叙事话语》

一、导读

作为女性主义叙事学的创始人之一，罗宾·沃霍尔对女性主义叙事学的建设和发展功不可没。20世纪80年代，女性主义文学批评陷入多元分散以及停滞发展的瓶颈期。沃霍尔在对前期女性主义文学批评实践过程中出现的弊病总结和反思的基础上，通过借鉴经典叙事学相关理论，以女性作家及其作品为核心，聚焦作者、文本、读者以及社会历史语境的交互作用，促成了女性主义文学批评和叙事学理论的"联姻"。沃霍尔也由此成功使得女性主义文学批评从故事层面的情节和人物形象分析走向了话语层面的对女性文本叙事形式的归纳。在界定女性主义叙事学以及讨论它与女性主义文学批评和叙事学之间的关系时，沃霍尔指出，女性主义叙事学"研究性别文化构成语境中的叙事结构和叙事策略"。[①] 其最终目标并非建立一种新的研究路径或方法，而是借助叙事学相关理论和概念实现相应的目标。就此而言，沃霍尔对于叙事学方法和理论的使用更多的是工具意义上的借鉴。她强调的是叙事学的工具性。因此，在她看来，女性主义叙事学属于女性主义文学批评理论范畴。在其女性主义叙事学研究中，沃霍尔着眼于考察文本产生时体现性别差异的历史文化语境，探究叙事如何运作于这些特定的历史文化语境中。

在经典著作《性别介入：维多利亚小说的叙事话语》中，沃霍尔贯彻了这一研究方法。在对维多利亚小说重读的基础上，沃霍尔从相应的历史语境入手，深入阐释了由性别差异所造成的男女叙事形式或结构的差异。从热奈特的"叙事介入"演变而来，沃霍尔区分了两种叙事的性别介入方式：吸引型叙事策略与疏远型叙事策略。前者鼓励读者与受述者产生认同，而后者则与之相反。随后，她系统地罗列了这两种性别介入方式所具有的明显的不同特征：

(1) 受述者名字指称的差异。吸引型叙述者常常规避直接命名受述者，或者大量使用潜在读者群的名字。例如在《玛丽·巴顿》中，叙述者只用第二人称"你"称呼受述者，"你"可以指向任何实际的读者，扩大了潜在的读者群。这种叙述者便是典型的吸引型叙述者；与此相较，疏远型叙述者常常直接称呼受述者具体的名字或称呼。比如萨克雷的《名利场》中的布洛克先生、史密斯先生等。在这种第三人称叙事中，读者也以一种超脱的姿态投入到故事中。

(2) 直接与受述者对话频率的差异。吸引型叙述者常常高频率地使用"你"与之对话。这种类似传道者的叙述方式是男性在公开社会场合发表言论时常常采用的对话策略，对实际的听众产生了重大和直接的影响，甚至能像布道者一样"控制"读者。例如《玛丽·巴顿》在至少22个篇章中高频率地使用"你""我们"等称呼，使得叙述者能紧紧控制受述者和真实读者的认同。而疏远型叙述者则更常使用"我

① Warhol, "The Look, the Body, and the Heroine of *Persuasion*: A Feminist-Narratological View of Jane Austen," p.21.

亲爱的""读者"等称呼受述者。例如在亨利·菲尔丁的《汤姆·琼斯》中,叙述者经常使用"我的读者"。

(3) 对受述者反讽程度的差异。吸引型叙述者常常肯定受述者具有完美的同理心和道德感,不注重其是否有个人的缺陷(愚蠢、自负、盲目等)。因而现实中的读者在阅读过程中会自觉认同受述者,从而回应叙述者的情感召唤;与之相反,疏远型叙述者则践行了反讽的干预,通过转叙、表明受述者的缺陷等策略刻意引导读者发现文本的虚构性,从而鼓励读者不去认同受述者,并与之分离,不回应相应的情感召唤。

(4) 叙述者面对人物立场的差异。吸引型叙述者避免提醒人物的虚构性,坚持人物和发生事件的真实性。例如《玛丽·巴顿》以互文性的方式提及其他的文本,比如通过引证的方式证实史密斯先生传记的真实性,使得虚构世界能与现实世界融为一体。而疏远型叙述者则着力提醒受述者人物的虚构性。

(5) 叙述者对叙事或模糊或清晰的态度差异。吸引型叙述者尽管也会承认或提醒受述者他们讲述的是故事,但会强调其反映了真正的世界条件,从而加强读者的参与感,鼓励读者在结束阅读后同情相同处境的人群并采取积极的行动,承担相应的社会责任。而疏远型叙述者则会有意无意地提醒受述者小说是"逼真"的文字游戏,并通过一系列的反讽策略加强疏离。①

在细致区分和阐释两种性别介入方式的形式差异的基础上,沃霍尔回顾了性别介入的历史,讨论了男女作家选择叙事立场的历史环境。她指出,女性作家更为青睐吸引型叙述者,男性作家则更倾向于使用疏远型叙述者。造成这种现象的主要原因是女性在当时的社会中处于边缘位置并缺失话语权。女性作家因此通过这种介入方式引导读者认同作品主旨,传递对社会生活的期待,从而能置身于社会。换言之,吸引型叙事策略是女性作家介入社会现实的话语策略。② 通过对维多利亚小说的重读,沃霍尔的性别介入理论不仅阐释了维多利亚时期男性与女性叙事作品采用不同叙事话语的原因,同时也展现和论证了叙事形式美学暗含和混合了社会权力机制,并影响着文本的阐释方式及评价标准。

二、《性别介入:维多利亚小说的叙事话语》选读③

Direct Address: The Engaging and Distancing Modes

Generally speaking, a distancing narrator discourages the actual reader from identifying with the narratee, while an engaging narrator encourages that identification. Sketching out the similarity between the narrator-addresser-sender relationship and the narratee-addressee-receiver relationship, Prince has used a simple example that can help describe the significantly different rhetorical effects of distancing and engaging addresses to narratees. Prince writes, "Just as in 'I ate a hamburger for lunch', the character-I is the one who ate and the narrator-I the one telling about the eating, in 'You ate a hamburger for lunch', the character-you is the one who ate and the narratee-you the one told about the eating." Prince uses the example to show that "the difference between intra-and

① Warhol, *Gendered Interventions: Narrative Discourse in the Victorian Novel*, pp.31 - 40.

② Ibid., p.23.

③ Ibid., pp.31 - 40.

extradiegetic narratee is no more fundamental than the one between intra-and extradiegetic narrator" ("Narratee Revisited" 301). This can be true in only a limited sense, however, as we must realize if we consider the rhetorical effect these utterances would have on an actual interlocutor or an actual reader. Depending on (1) the accuracy of the statement about "you" and (2) the speaker's stance toward "you" in making the assertion, the relation between the narratee and the receiver of the statement could be either distanced or engaged.

Consider the effect the two statements about lunch might have in a real-world conversation. If I tell you that I ate a hamburger for lunch, you may or may not believe me, according to your sense of my reliability (you may not know me well enough to know whether I am characteristically truthful, or you may know that I habitually lie about my calorie intake) and according to anything you know about my lunch beyond my assertion (maybe you sat across the lunch table from me and watched me eat that hamburger, or maybe you watched me eat quiche instead). But you can never be certain whether my report of my own experience is true: possibly I did not lie about what I ate for lunch, even if I customarily do; possibly I slipped away after I had the quiche and secretly ate a hamburger as a second lunch. You may believe my statement or not, but you can never be as certain of its truth as you can be about my statement "You ate a hamburger for lunch". You know—if you are not impossibly absentminded—whether you ate a hamburger, just as you know, while you are reading *Pere Goriot*, whether your hands are white and your armchair is comfortable.

The example shows that in fact there is a difference between the narrator-addresser-sender relationship and the narratee-addressee-receiver relationship, a difference that must occur to the actual reader in reading the text. The reader may or may not be interested in how closely the narrative "I" resembles the actual author; readers can only speculate about such a resemblance, which—even if it exists—would have no bearing on the rhetorical effect of the text. But one can know whether the narrative "you" resembles oneself, and surely the way one experiences the fiction is affected by how personally one can take its addresses to "you".

Keeping this in mind, we can pursue the example for its distancing and engaging potentialities. The effect of my assertion "You ate a hamburger" will depend on your interpretation of my rhetorical intent. Since you know whether you ate a hamburger, you may assume that my assertion is not intended to convey information to you. If you know I saw you having quiche for lunch and I say "You ate a hamburger", my utterance will be ironic. I might expect you to respond with laughter, annoyance, or perplexity, but in any case—since you would be unable to identify your experience with my assertion—you would separate your actual self from the "you" in my statement. My remark would then be distancing.

The distancing narrator may evoke laughter, or even annoyance, from an actual reader who cannot identify with the narratee. The task of the engaging narrator, in contrast, is to evoke sympathy and identification from an actual reader who is unknown to the author and therefore infinitely variable and unpredictable. The engaging narrator is in the position I would be in if, to win your trust and support, I had to approach you, a stranger, and tell you what you had for lunch. I could try to win you over through what I say or through the way I say it, through the substance of my assertion or through my attitude in asserting it. I could make a guess about what you ate, based on my idea of what most people eat; engaging narrators often do base assertions about "you" on such general assumptions. Chances are, though, that my guess would be inaccurate, in which case I could only hope to win you with the appealing attitude I try to take in addressing you. In realist novels—engaging narrators functioning as their authors' surrogates in earnestly trying to foster sympathy for real-world sufferers—work to engage "you" through the substance and, failing that, the stance of their narrative interventions and addresses to "you".

While the distinction between engaging and distancing stances may seem inconsequential on the purely textual level, the significance of the difference asserts itself in novels that aim to inspire personal, social, or political change. When the narrator of *Uncle Tom's Cabin* speaks to "you, generous, noble-minded men and women of the South—you, whose virtue and magnanimity and purity of character, are the greater for the severer trial it has encountered" (622), the speaker can have no certain knowledge of the virtue and magnanimity of actual Southern readers, nor of the Southern affiliations of any individual actual reader. Operating in a context where her information about the "real you" may be faulty, the narrator tries to win "you" with the ingratiating rhetoric of her engaging appeal. And if she can thus draw you in, she could possibly change your mind; if she does change your mind and you happen to be a Southern slave owner, she might change the world.

Intervention Strategies: The Ends of The Spectrum

In Gaskell's *Mary Barton* (1848), Stowe's *Uncle Tom's Cabin* (1851 - 1852), and Eliot's *Adam Bede* (1859), earnest, engaging strategies of intervention are strikingly present in passages of the novels addressed to "you". Typically, these novelists' engaging narrators differ from distancing narrators—such as Fielding's in *Tom Jones* (1749), Thackeray's in *Vanity Fair* (1846 - 1847), Trollope's in *Barchester Towers* (1849), Hawthorne's in *The House of Seven Gables* (1851) or Eliot's in her first novel, *Scenes of Clerical Life* (1857)—in their explicit attitudes toward the narratees, toward the characters, and toward the very act of narration. The differences occur in five forms:

1. *The names by which the narratee is addressed*. Whereas a distancing narrator may specify a name or title for an extradiegetic narratee (for example, "Miss Bullock" "Miss Smith" or "Jones, who reads this book at his Club" in *Vanity Fair*; "Your Majesty ... my lords and gentlemen" in Dickens's *Bleak House* [1852 - 1853]; "Madam" or "Mrs. Farthingale" in Eliot's *Scenes*), an engaging narrator will usually either avoid naming the narratee or use names that refer to large classes of potential actual readers. In *Mary Barton*, the most straightforward example of the first

engaging approach, the narrator never calls the narratee anything but "you". In *Uncle Tom's Cabin*, the most extreme example of the second approach, the narrator will, Walt Whitman-like, specify narratees in a group ("mothers of America") or include large numbers of more specifically defined groups in passages of direct address ("Farmers of Massachusetts, of New Hampshire, of Vermont, of Connecticut, who read this book by the blaze of your winter-evening fire,—strong-hearted, generous sailors and ship-owners of Maine ... Brave and generous men of New York, farmers of rich and joyous Ohio, and ye of the wide prairie states" [623]). Even such exhaustive lists exclude more readers than they can include. Straining against the limitations such specific names must enforce on actual readers' ability to answer appeals to the narratees, Stowe's narrator intersperses her novel with remarks directed simply to "Reader" or "you", designations that can signify any actual reader.

2. *The frequency of direct address to the narratee*. A distancing narrator, such as Fielding's, often refers to "the Reader" or "my reader" as a third party, someone not present (as it were) at the narrative conversation. Actual readers perusing the novel are no more likely to take such third-person references personally than they would take remarks that refer to characters in the novel. "He" and "she", whether the pronouns stand for Tom Jones and Sophia Western or for "my readers", have referents within the text—they do not shift as does the referent of "you". Whether an actual reader answers to remarks directed to "my reader(s)" will depend on how much the portrait of those readers actually resembles him or her: the actual reader gets to choose whether to take such narrative interventions to heart. An engaging narrator avoids giving the actual reader a choice in the matter, and, very much like an evangelical preacher, more frequently speaks to "you".① In *Mary Barton*, for instance, the narratee is addressed as "you" in at least twenty-two passages, included in the narrative "we" in at least five passages, and seldom, if ever, referred to in the third person.

3. *The degree of irony present in references to the narratee*. Irony is, of course, always multivalent, and never definitively determinable. If verbal irony may be defined as a presumably self-conscious disjunction between what a speaker says and what he or she appears to mean, then two particularly ironic conventions characterize the distancing narrator's attitude toward the narratee. Both kinds of irony occur in passages of direct address to the narratee that are distinctly not engaging in their approach. The first of these is a distancing narrator's pretense that "you" are present on the scene of the fiction; the second is a distancing narrator's habit of inscribing flawed "readers" from whom actual readers should want to differentiate themselves. In both kinds of ironic intervention, the effect is distancing in that the strategy encourages the actual reader *not* to identify with the narratee being addressed.

---

① Tompkins identifies similarities between the forms of address in *Uncle Tom* and the Old Testament models for the American jeremiad (*Sensational Designs*, 139 - 141).

The sarcastic pretense that "you" are present on the fictional scene is one way that a distancing narrator discourages the actual reader from identifying with the textual narratee. These are passages in which narrators play the game of "endangering the Reader's Neck" (as Fielding calls it) by pretending to locate the reader at the side of the characters or the narrator himself. A nineteenth-century example of this narrative jest would be Hawthorne's heterodiegetic narrator's intervention in chapter 28 of *The House of Seven Gables*, the scene which describes the room where the dead Judge Pyncheon sits alone: "You must hold your own breath, to satisfy yourself whether he breathes at all. It is quite inaudible. You hear the ticking of his watch; his breath you do not hear." In the climax of the scene, the voice places the narratee even more clearly on the narrator's diegetic level, by including the narratee in a collective "we": "Would that we were not an attendant spirit, here!"①

Genette's term for this technique is *metalepsis*, or the practice of crossing diegetic levels to imply that figures inside and outside the fiction exist on the same plane (*Narrative Discourse* 236). To illustrate the term: in this example, the extradiegetic narrator (who is inside the novel, but not inside the "diegesis", or story, because he does not participate as a character) places himself in the same room, and therefore on the same plane of "reality" with the extradiegetic narratee (the person to whom the story is being told, who—like the narrator—does not exist within the story) and the character (the judge, the only one of the three figures involved in this scene who, properly speaking, belongs in the diegesis). The effect of metalepsis in distancing narrative is usually to affirm the fictionality of the story: when Hawthorne's narrator pretends, for instance, that "you" are present with him in the room with the dead judge, the fictionality of the scene becomes obvious. *You*, the actual reader, are not a ghostly presence in the Pyncheons' house. You are a person holding a copy of *The House of Seven Gables*, reading it.

Describing the use of metalepsis in Cortazar, Sterne, Diderot, Proust, and Balzac, Genette has pointed to its metafictional potential: its effect, he writes, "is either comical (when, as in Sterne or Diderot, it is presented in a joking tone) or fantastic" (*Narrative Discourse* 235). Genette's account of the metaleptic effect describes very well the goal of the distancing intervention: "The most troubling thing about metalepsis indeed lies in this unacceptable and insistent hypothesis, that the extradiegetic is perhaps always diegetic, and that the narrator and his narratees—you and I—perhaps belong to some narrative" (236).

Stowe, Gaskell, and (especially) Eliot can also use metalepsis that pretends to place the reader on the scene of the fiction. A notable example would be the narrator's introductory description of the rectory in *Adam Bede*. The narratee is invited into the Irwines' dining room. "We will enter very softly," the narrator tells "you", "and stand still in the open doorway, without awakening [the dogs]" (98). But in *Adam Bede* the overall dominance of engaging interventions tends to transform

① I am grateful to Cynthia Bernstein for suggesting this example in her response to the first published version of this study.

the intended effect of a passage like this one. Instead of experiencing a comical or fantastic awareness of the activity of reading, the actual reader should indulge in a momentary exercise of imagination. Readers are encouraged to feel that perhaps they *could* be in Hayslope; perhaps the world they are reading about *is* as real as their own. The invitation to "enter very softly" both beckons the reader into the fictional world and emphasizes the fact that he or she is not really part of it; the implication is, though, that if the reader will participate in recreating a real world predicated on the lessons of sympathy that reading the novel imparts, perhaps the real world, as well as the actual reader, will be transformed. Indeed, the engaging narrator's frequent appeals to the reader's imagination, her earnest requests to the reader to draw upon personal memories to fill in gaps in the narrative, prompt the actual reader to participate in creating the fictional world itself, just as he or she should actively alter the real world after finishing the reading.

In the second type of ironic address to the reader, the distancing narrator humorously inscribes the addressee as a potentially "bad reader", thus discouraging the receiver of the text from identifying with the person addressed. Balzac's address to the complacent, pleasure-seeking narratee of *Le Pere Goriot* is an example of this ironic mode. So is Fielding's amusing directive on how to read *Tom Jones*, typical of Fielding in its self-conscious awareness of the distance the narrator encourages between the narratee, the implied reader, and the actual reader:

> Reader, it is impossible we should know what Sort of Person thou wilt be: For perhaps, thou may'st be as learned in Human Nature as *Shakespear* himself was, and, perhaps, thou may'st be no wiser than some of his Editors. Now lest this latter should be the Case, we think proper, before we go any farther together, to give thee a few wholesome Admonitions ... We warn thee not too hastily to condemn any of the Incidents in this our History, as impertinent and foreign to our main Design ... For a little Reptile of a Critic to presume to find Fault with any of its Parts, without knowing the Manner in which the Whole is connected ... is a most presumptuous Absurdity. (398)

Here, the narratee is not entirely foolish: Fielding's "Reader" is at least presumably capable of appreciating the contrast between the wisdom of Shakespeare and that of "some of his Editors"; the narratee is also patient and cooperative enough to attend to the "wholesome Admonitions" on how to read this book. But the same narratee has the potential to read badly, or "too hastily to condemn" the novel's parts before apprehending the whole. The "little Reptile of a Critic" is not a narratee, in that the narrator refers to him indirectly, rather than speaking to him. Still, the logic of the paragraph implies that if the narratee were to succumb to the inclination to "condemn", he or she would be imitating the reptilian critic's activity. The implied reader is someone who gets the joke and can chuckle at the expense of the hapless narratee. The actual reader, then, should hesitate to identify with the narratee, in order to avoid becoming laughably ridiculous. Similarly distancing is

Thackeray's ironic reference to "some carping reader" who is incapable of enjoying the sentimental passages in *Vanity Fair* (147). As much as the actual reader might be amused and entertained by these interventions, he or she is to be discouraged from identifying with any "carping" "little Reptile of a Critic".

Engaging narrators, in contrast, usually assume that their narratees (not to mention their actual readers) are in perfect sympathy with them. When Gaskell's narrator in *Mary Barton* assures the narratee, "Your heart would have ached to have seen the man, however hardly you might have judged his crime" (422), or when Eliot's in *Adam Bede* interrupts a love scene to remark, "That is a simple scene, reader. But it is almost certain that you, too, have been in love" (537), the narrators' earnestly confidential attitudes toward "you" encourage actual readers to see themselves reflected in that pronoun.

As these two examples show, an engaging narrator sometimes does imply imperfection in the narratee's ability to comprehend, or sympathize with, the contents of the text, even while expressing confidence that the narratee will rise to the challenge. These implications of the narratee's fallibility often come through narrative interventions that Prince calls

> *surjustifications* ... situated at the level of meta-language, meta-commentary, or meta-narration ... Over-justifications always provide us with interesting details about the narratee's personality, even though they often do so in an indirect way; in overcoming the narratee's defenses, in prevailing over his prejudices, in allaying his apprehensions, they reveal them. ("Introduction" 15)

Although engaging narrators tend to inscribe their narratees through overjustifying their own assertions, they usually do so in the spirit of sympathetically and earnestly attempting to convert the narratees to their own points of view. This mode of address encourages actual readers to identify with the narratees, unlike the sarcasm of distancing narrators, which attempts through irony to embarrass readers out of such identification.

The engaging narrators' overjustifications portray their narratees less as potentially bad readers than as potentially limited sympathizers. The narrators defend their characters' rights to the actual readers' sympathy by explicitly demonstrating those rights to the narratees. One of the most notorious passages of such overjustification occurs in *Uncle Tom's Cabin*, interrupting the scene of Eliza's barefoot escape over the frozen river. Anticipating an incredulous response, the narrator encourages the narratee to put herself in Eliza's place: "If it were *your* Harry, mother, or your Willie, that were going to be torn from you by a brutal trader, tomorrow morning—if you had seen the man, and heard that the papers were signed and delivered, and you had only from twelve o'clock till morning to make good your escape,—how fast could *you* walk?" (105). The passage provides specific information about the narratee: she is certainly female, and is perhaps, by the narrator's standards, overly judgmental. But the narrator's stance, implicit in her faith that the narratee can be persuaded to sympathize if actual readers will pause to recognize similarities between Eliza's experiences and their own, is what makes the passage engaging.① The actual reader, required to draw upon memory and sympathetic imagination to fill in the emotional details of the story, is engaged in collaborating on the creation of the fictional world.

4. *The narrator's stance toward the characters*. A distancing narrator may seem to delight in reminding the narratee that the characters are fictional, entirely under the writer's control. Some of the most extreme examples would be the references in *Vanity Fair* to the characters as puppets that come out of a box and the famous passage in *Barchester Towers* where Trollope's narrator reassures "the reader" that he would never let his Elinor Bold marry the likes of Mr. Slope, thus predicting the outcome of the plot and reminding the narratee that the fiction is an arbitrary creation, a game. An engaging narrator avoids reminders of the characters' fictionality, insisting instead that the characters are "real". The difference between the distancing and engaging attitudes toward characters thus parallels the difference between metafiction and realism. In moves that parallel their attitudes toward their narratees, both distancing and engaging narrators use metalepsis in establishing their relation to their characters, but whereas distancing narrators use it to subvert realism, engaging narrators use it to reinforce the veracity of their stories.

A distancing narrator does indeed use metalepsis for the humorous effect that Genette describes. Perhaps the best example of the disconcerting effect of distancing metalepsis is the shifting presentation of the characters in *Vanity Fair*. At the beginning and the very end of the novel they are puppets; often they are fictional figures under the author's explicit control; then quite suddenly, near the end of the story, they are people the narrator met in Pumpernickel before he had heard all the details of their biographies. Their changeable status contributes to the novel's humor, as well as to the narratee's awareness that they are creatures of fiction. An engaging narrator, though, uses metalepsis to suggest that the characters are possibly as "real" as the narrator and narratee, who are, in these cases, to be identified with the actual author and actual reader. Stowe's narrator simply claims that her characters—or people exactly resembling them—exist in the real world (for example, that "the personal appearance of Eliza, the character ascribed to her, are sketches drawn from life ... The incident of the mother's crossing the Ohio river on the ice is a well-known fact" [*Uncle Tom's Cabin* 618]). Gaskell's and Eliot's narrators occasionally claim personal acquaintance with their characters, even though the narrators never figure as intradiegetic characters themselves.

One of the many over justifications in *Mary Barton* is an example of metalepsis that places the heterodiegetic narrator and the intradiegetic character's on the same level. The narrator defends her

① Obviously not every reader can identify with the narratee. Evidence of the distanced response in hostile readers of *Uncle Tom* surfaces in reviews of the novel by Stowes contemporaries; see Ammons.

comments about one characters physical appearance by citing a "personal" impression of the fictional woman: "I have called her 'the old woman'... because, in truth, her appearance was so much beyond her years ... she always gave me the idea of age" (385 - 386). This heterodiegetic "I" is never present in the fictional world, hence never in a position to see the character in the context of the fiction; the implication is, then, that the character must exist within the context of the narrator's own world. Eliot makes a similar implication in one intervention that refers to a conversation between the heterodiegetic narrator and the hero: "But I gathered from Adam Bede, to whom I talked of these matters in his old age" (225). These instances of metalepsis—implying that the characters exist, as the narrators do, outside the world represented in the fiction—produce an effect that differs from the humorous discomfort that Genette had identified as the usual result of the device. Instead of distancing the actual reader from the characters by reminding the narratee that they are fictional, these metalepses are meant to reinforce the reader's serious sense of the characters as, in some way, real.

5. *The narrator's implicit or explicit attitude toward the act of narration*. The distancing narrator, directly or indirectly, often reminds the narratee that the fiction is a game and the characters pawns. Such reminders may be as direct as *Vanity Fair*'s references to the narrator as a stage manager or puppet master, as indirect as the mock-heroic "epic" language in the "battle scenes" of *Tom Jones* or *Joseph Andrews*, or as comparatively subtle as the type names that Fielding, Thackeray, Dickens, and Trollope assign to minor characters. In each of these examples, the distancing strategy pushes a text that in many other respects conforms to the conventions of verisimilitude in realist fiction over into the realm of metafiction. This playing with the text's fictionality goes hand-in-hand with the irony that characterizes the distancing approach.

三、思考与讨论

(1) "疏远型叙述者"与"吸引型叙述者"有何区别？

(2) 为何"疏远型叙述者"在男性作家作品中更为常见，"吸引型叙述者"则为女作家们所青睐？

(3) 沃霍尔如何通过叙事的性别介入将叙事学的形式主义研究方法和女性主义语境批评相结合？

第四节 露斯·佩奇及其《女性主义叙事学的文学与语言学视角》

一、导读

作为英国女性主义叙事学的代表人物，露斯·佩奇在以北美为主的叙事学阵营之外展现了英国叙事学家们的独有风采。在其女性主义叙事学研究中，佩奇承袭了英国叙事学派倚重语言学方法的风格，从文学和语言学双重视角展开性别与叙事的研究。在代表作《女性主义叙事学的文学与语言学视角》一书中，佩奇对女性主义叙事学的学科属性、研究现状、未来走向等主要论题给出了独到的阐释和解读。在她看来，女性主义叙事学并非一套关于女性主义文学批评的独立的叙事模式，而是可以理解为女性主义文学批评对叙事学的批评和应用。就女性主义叙事学和叙事学的关系而言，佩奇认为二者的关系复杂且不稳定。虽然女性主义叙事学隶属于后经典叙事学或语境主义叙事学的范畴，但它是在后经典叙事学的范畴内对经典叙事学的一种修正。它对于经典叙事学基本理论和概念的应用和修正不仅没有宣告经典叙事学的死亡，反而为其增添了色彩。① 在对女性主义叙事学发展历程的考察基础上，佩奇指出该学派未来发展需要关注的几个方面，如扩大其考察对象的范围，将电子游戏、数字叙事、法律叙事、医学叙事等纳入研究范围；与其他学科和理论框架合作，如文化研究、语言学研究等。②

但值得注意的是，佩奇在书中对于语言学方法过分倚重的做法也引起了一定的争议。在第二章中，佩奇试图从语言学的角度考察叙事性与性别之间的关系，即考察两者是否存在必然的联系。作为叙事学研究中一个核心且富有争议的概念，“叙事性”在后经典的语境下受到了不同流派叙事学家的关注，其研究呈现了如火如荼之势。总体而言，“叙事性”主要包含了两个方面的含义：它指一种叙事的“属性”(property)，即“一系列刻画叙事以及把叙事从非叙事中区别的特性”，以及一种“程度”(degree)，即不同的叙事所具有的不同程度的特性。③ 然而佩奇表达了对经典叙事学家“性别化的叙事性”论调的不满，认为性别化的情节与叙事性有着密切的关系，即男性化的情节有着较高的叙事性，而女性化的情节则有着较低的叙事性这一论断并不正确。佩奇指出这种论调不仅带有明显的本质主义倾向，同时也包含了对总体化描述的认可。④

在戴维·赫尔曼的相关研究基础上，她指出，对叙事性的感知可以理解为文本内的语言特征与文本外的超语言特征之间的复杂关系，如读者的世界知识可以受到具体文化语境的不同影响。因此，读者能够判断哪一个叙事较之其他叙事更像叙事。有鉴于此，佩奇试图探讨男性化情节与女性化情节所引发的不同程度和形式的叙事的特性，认为我们需要以批评和更细致的姿态重审性别与叙事形式之间二元对立的论断。佩奇选取了米歇尔·罗伯茨的《血与肉》和《词汇表》、托尼·莫里森的《宠儿》、弗拉迪米

① Page, *Literary and Linguistic Approaches to Feminist Narratology*, p.5.
② Ibid., pp.182-184.
③ 尚必武：《当代西方后经典叙事学研究》，第115页。
④ Page, *Literary and Linguistic Approaches to Feminist Narratology*, p.23.

尔·纳博科夫的《微暗之火》、伊塔洛·卡尔维诺的《隐形城市》等作品，在文本细读的基础上展示了这些作品在情节结构上共有的多重叠加特点，并得出结论："叙事性的高低程度与性别毫不相干。"[①] 与性别有关的不是叙事结构，而是"语言形式"(linguistic form)。[②] 这一结论也显示了佩奇与其他女性主义叙事学家的不同。她提出的"性别与叙事形式之间并不存在必然联系"的观点忽视了女性主义叙事学对结构主义叙事学无视性别和不考虑社会历史语境的不满和批评，也忽略了特定历史语境下性别因素之于叙事作品形式分析以及意义阐释的重要性。然而，值得注意的是，尽管佩奇的结论和方法一定程度上与女性主义叙事学研究的主流发生了背离，但其研究"有利于拆解女性主义叙事学长期围绕女作家作品展开的形式与叙事关系分析，避免阐释活动中的本质主义陷阱"，推动了女性主义叙事学的发展。[③]

二、《女性主义叙事学的文学与语言学视角》选读[④]

A Linguistic Approach: Narrativity and Gender

The first step in disentangling form and theme is to provide a more precise way of analyzing the texts. This requires a replicable set of parameters against which narrative forms might be compared. As Mills (1995) points out in her critique of "French feminists", the linguistic analysis of texts is a vital step in elucidating the validity of claims to gender difference in language, which here includes narrative structure. In order to do this, I reframe the description of "male" and "female" plots through the lens of narrativity. "Narrativity" is an issue that remains central to questions about the very status of narrative itself, as Prince's interrogative list demonstrates (2000). However, McHale's (2001) discussion of this topic indicates that what precisely constitutes "narrativity" is open to challenge. "Is narrativity a matter of kind or degree?" he asks (p.165). I follow Herman (1997) in distinguishing between narrativehood as that which concerns the criterial factors necessary to classify a text as a narrative (a matter of kind) and narrativity as a scalar notion related to "factors that allow narrative sequences to be more or less readily processed as narratives" (p.1048) (a matter of degree). I am interested in the second of these. I am not trying to argue that the male plot of ambition is a narrative and that the female plot is not. Instead, I am suggesting that these typologies can be compared by examining the forms of narrativity that they invoke.

The perception of narrativity may be understood as a complex relationship between linguistic features "in" the text and extra-linguistic features "outside" the text, such as the reader's world knowledge that may be shaped by specific cultural contexts in various ways (Herman, 1997; Hoey, 2001). These linguistic features "in" the text include those traditionally studied in narratology. This

---

① Page, *Literary and Linguistic Approaches to Feminist Narratology*, p.40.

② Ibid., p.44.

③ 王丽亚：《西方文论关键词：女性主义叙事学》，载《外国文学》2019 年第 2 期，第 109 页。

④ Page, *Literary and Linguistic Approaches to Feminist Narratology*, pp.25 - 31, 43 - 44.

incorporates the way in which temporal order is marked and organized, the type of characterization employed, the status of a text's narrator and/or focalizor, and the global organization of the text, for example as indicated by the presence of Problem-Solution or Goal-Achievement patterns and arranged into a teleological progression.[①] These factors should not be regarded as a definitive list (criterial to a text's status as a narrative as opposed to some other text type) but rather as an open set, which may be drawn upon in combination to create narrativity of various kinds and degrees. Implicit in Herman's definition of narrativity is the understanding that any given text may be perceived as having a higher or lower degree of narrativity and also that the reader is able to recognize these degrees as being more or less like "narrative". From this we might infer that certain combinations of these linguistic features occur in recognizable patterns which, as they then become grounds for processing a text "as narrative", are perceived as high in narrativity. What is striking about this in relation to feminist narratology is that there seems to be a correlation between degrees of narrativity and the stereotypical gendering of plot where the "male" and "female" plots exhibit strong and weak narrativity respectively.

The narrativity of the "male plot of ambition" can be characterized by the presence of the following factors. The temporal sequence is clearly defined and does not disrupt the perception of "real world" chronological order, enabling the hero and reader "to grasp past, present and future in a significant shape" (Brooks, 1984: 39). The characterization is consistent and coherent, typically focused through a central protagonist who is usually male and expresses and achieves their desires. Brooks' description of ambition as "a force that drives the protagonist forward, assuring that no incident or action is final or closed in itself until such a moment as the ends of ambition have been clarified, through success or else renunciation" (p.39) parallels the progression of the Problem-Solution and Goal-Achievement patterns, which reach closure when the problems have been satisfactorily resolved and goals achieved. Finally, the teleological progression of this plot with its characteristic rise, climax and fall in tension can be described in linguistic terms using Longacre's (1983) description of the surface marking used in the "anatomy of plot". This reaches a climax, which is indicated in the textual detail of the narrative using factors that Longacre describes as "Peak marking". This comprises heightened vividness, a shift in orientation (either spatially or in the focalizing figure), a more or less dramatic form of speech presentation, or a change in the size of the textual units being used (1983: 26 - 38), summarized by Marley as "disruption of the norm" (1987: 83). The narrativity of the "female plot" may contrast with these narratological features in a range of ways. For example, the degree of precision with which any factor is used may change, or a typical pattern is disrupted in some way (for example, time sequence might be disrupted by anachronies, problems are left unresolved, there are multiple passages marked as Peak and so

① To avoid confusion, structural terms used in narratology have been capitalized so as to differentiate them from their everyday usage. I have followed this practice throughout the narrative analyses in all later chapters.

on). These characteristics are not fixed in a stable configuration, but are unified in their contrast with the narrativity of the "male" plot. Because the features of the "female" plot diverge from the well-known pattern, it may then also be perceived as lower in narrativity.

Why this equation of narrativity and plot types should occur is an important question. One possible response is to note that the "male plot of ambition" has strong similarities with profiles such as Labov's (1972) narrative outline. As is now well recognized, these classical models might be re-evaluated in terms of potential gender bias in the corpora from which the pattern is derived (see Prince, 1995a, 1996; Cazden, 1997). Thus it could be argued that our sense of what constitutes a "well-formed" narrative (that is, high narrativity) is conditioned by a body of stories told by male speakers about stereotypically masculine experiences (in the case of Labov's 1972 study, fight narratives told by male adolescents). More generally, Hoey's approach to textual organization foregrounds the cultural situation of each pattern (2001). Given that gender may be understood as socially constructed as opposed to biologically determined, it might also be possible that cultural values of gender have some relationship with patterns of organization used in telling stories. For example, in certain situations it might be that the ability to solve problems or achieve goals is restricted to privileging one gender above another, as in stereotypically represented heroes and heroines where it is only the male characters that are allowed to follow quest-like progressions. Of course, this would be limited to specific genres and cultural contexts, but nonetheless the possible correlations between gender and predictable patterns remain a factor that may also contribute to the alignment of high narrativity with "male plots" and the relegation of "female plots" to weak narrativity. However, while I have initially transposed the models of "male" and "female" plots onto a polarity of strong and weak narrativity, this binary pairing deserves much closer and more critical re-examination. The following analysis of some contemporary fiction provides a further test case for exploring the relationship between narrativity and gender.

Narrativity and Gender in *Flesh and Blood*

The fiction of contemporary author Michèle Roberts is the focus for the analysis and discussion of these issues. Her work is of particular interest for two reasons. First, it is rich in gender-related themes and imagery including identity, sexuality, religion, the woman as artist and the mother-daughter relationship. In its interrogation of these issues, it has been categorized as "feminist" (Rowland, 1999; Falcus, 2003). Second, it contains examples of interesting experimentation with narrative form, which as Roberts herself comments is closely related to the content of her novels (1994: 171). As such, it might be expected that her narratives provide interesting points of connection between the two areas. This is not to claim that Roberts is representative of all feminist women writers, or that there is an unequivocal relationship between form and meaning. Rather, her work provides an appropriate example that might form the starting point for exploring issues of gender and narrativity. I begin with her novel, *Flesh and Blood* (1995).

Like her other short stories and novels, *Flesh and Blood* returns to many of the themes described above, but it is the piece where the relationship between gender and identity is most explicitly foregrounded and deconstructed in a form of "gender blending" (Neubert-Köpsel, 2001: 176). Roberts challenges the ways in which gender is marked through surface appearance (especially clothing), biological features, sexuality, naming and social practices, doing so in a manner that creates narrative uncertainty. The novel takes the form of a series of short narratives, each of which is named after a character and arranged symmetrically like a hall of mirrors around a central section headed "Anon". These chapters construct a quasi-history of mothers and children. However, rather than forming a straightforward genealogy, these chapters are linked in ways that reflect upon one another in inverse and contradictory ways that blur fantasy and reality, raise unanswered questions and critically destabilize the notion of a fixed gendered identity.

The narrativity of *Flesh and Blood* is weakened in ways that support the thematic focus on gender and identity. The most striking disruption occurs in the construction of character. While not criterial to narrativehood in the same manner as temporal succession, characterization is an important means of narrative coherence. As Longacre puts it, "You must keep track of who does what to whom or the story falls flat on its face" (1974: 362). In *Flesh and Blood*, not only do the cast of characters change from chapter to chapter but also the reader's sense of narrative coherence is challenged by the shifting and ambiguous description of the characters' gender, disrupting the frames of reference that would enable the reader to process the text as a coherent narrative. The "same" character narrates the opening two chapters, headed "Fred" and "Freddy", which are linked to the closing chapter "Frederica". In the first chapter Fred is described as male: "I saw myself: one of those men, framed in black, on a police poster; hollow-eyed, wild-haired, staring" (p.1). On the run, the criminal "Fred" takes refuge in a dress shop where he disguises his male identity in a feminine dress. "My large cotton handkerchief and my discarded tie, well stuffed in, did duty for breasts. I smoothed ballooning skirts, put my hands up to check my hair, drew my licked fingertips along my eyebrows. I kicked off my shoes: too big and heavy" (p.5). Even though the shopkeeper assumes "Fred" to be a woman, the reader is not led to believe that Fred has undergone a biological change in sex. In the next chapter, "Freddy", the narrator appears to be the same character, narrating "his" childhood. However, some ten pages later, it is clear that "Freddy" is biologically female, marked by the onset of menstruation (p.15) and now named "Frederica Stonehouse, in a bulky tunic and pullover, and with a stash of sanitary towels in a brown paper bag in my briefcase" (p. 17). As Neubert-Köpsel and her students comment, this results in a sense of narrative disruption. My own experience of reading this text with groups of undergraduate students reinforces this. Without exception, these students also commented on the disorientation they felt when discovering the gender change of what at this stage in the novel appears to be the central narrator and main protagonist.

Fred/erica is not the only character given a dual gender representation. In the chapter called "Felicite", the reader is introduced to a character who is coded as male by the choice of name (George Mannot), dress, textual references with masculine pronouns "he" "his" "him" and by biological definition as the narrator implies that George is responsible for Felicite's defloration (p.54). However, in the reciprocal chapter, "Georgina" "George" is revealed to be a woman in disguise.

> I'm sure that G. could point to either George or Georgina, even as it concealed them [...] she embarked upon a daring masquerade, like something in one of the modern novels we know she read and loved, in which she [...] allowed herself two selves, two lives, or was it three? Her life as a woman in London, her life as a man in France, his/her experience at the moment of crossing over from one to the other and back again. (pp.155 - 156)

With both of these instances, Roberts uses the reflective pairing of the chapters and the ambiguous characterization to challenge the reader's notion of gender as a stable, defining feature of a character's identity. Instead, the binary gendering of Fred/erica and Georg/ina as exclusively male or female is shown to be illusory, shifting according to the interpretation of dress codes, naming and sexuality.

The thematic focus on gender and identity is supported by alterations to the teleological progression of the text. As discussed earlier, the correspondence between surface Peak marking and a climactic moment of crisis is typical of the high narrativity found in the "male plot of ambition". At first sight, *Flesh and Blood* does have a chapter that appears to be a narrative Peak, in that the narrative style switches from standard prose into a poetic form without use of conventional syntax.

> Mamabebe love you are here with you together us now over and over so non-stop mamabebe so wanting you born this love us so close skinskin talking heartbeat belonging with you allowed love home flesh my mamabebe our body singing to you so beautiful love listen mamabebe listen. (p.109)

As a break from the established textual norm, this chapter does indeed seem to be like a "zone of turbulence" (Longacre, 1983: 25). Critically though, this chapter does not seem to correspond to the apex of a trajectory of problematic tension that marks a move into resolution. Instead, in content, it forms the ultimate point of gender deconstruction, describing a paradise of pre-Oedipal union with the mother that stands in contrast with the absence or critique of mothers in both preceding and subsequent chapters. In this sense, it forms the two-way interface against which all the other chapters are arranged (in structure) and reflect (in content). As such, the plot of *Flesh and Blood* is not unidirectional, moving towards a single resolution. Rather, the individual chapters provide multiple reflections on the mother-child relationship and the possible constructions of gender. The narrator hints at this multidirectional nature of the narrative in the first chapter, saying, "I'd always had a gift for inventing stories. I shuffled them like a pack of cards in my head" (p.1), where the chapters, like the cards in the pack, do not have to be followed in a fixed linear sequence.

The privileging of the centre section contrasts with the silencing of the "death blow" that closes the "male plot of ambition". Indeed, *Flesh and Blood* resists closure. Each of the chapters ends with the narrator giving an Abstract (cf. Labov, 1972) of the next story, which conventionally opens a narrative sequence rather than closing it. The final chapter is no exception, ending with the words, "So we walk through Soho and into the next story" (p.175). Theoretically, it would be possible to read this as an invitation to begin rereading the text, treating the first chapter as "the next story" and so restarting the sequence towards the central section again. The opposition to the "death blow" in this resistance to closure is supported by the narrator's equation with storytelling and physical survival. In the first chapter, "Fred" says, "Scheherezade had told stories, night after night, to save her life [...] I wasn't sure if my stories could save my life or my mother's" (pp.6 - 7). Not only is this central section metaphorically associated with surviving execution, its content celebrates the beginning of life with the union between child and mother. Here the stylistic features emphasize the "lyric timelessness" that is associated with women's bodies in feminist theories of narrative (Wallace, 2000: 177). The language in "Anon" corresponds to many of the features characterizing Cixous' description of *écriture feminine*. It is described as literally written on the body, "on your blissful skin the hands of the masseuse play a writing game" (p.108), and specifically within the female body "swimming in our waters" (p.109). It avoids syntactic closure at the level of both the word and the sentence,

> we is one whole undivided
> you/me broken now mended
> you/me restored mamabebe
> our body of love pickedup putbacktogether. (p.109)

In this way, the language itself mirrors the contesting of boundaries, be they psychic or socially constructed along gendered lines, and explicitly associates this with a celebration of the female body in the figure of the mother.

In summary, both in its lack of coherent characterization and multidirectional association between chapters and in the use of stylistic features parallel to those suggested by *écriture feminine*, the narrativity of *Flesh and Blood* contrasts with that of the "male plot of ambition". These narrative features might be interpreted as particularly appropriate to the feminist content of this text, which explores the mother-daughter relationship and challenges the binary definition of gender as either male or female. However, I would strongly resist arguing that this interpretation defines a fixed "female plot". This simplistic equation of form and gender is deeply problematic for reasons examined in the following discussion.

…

Conclusion

In this chapter, I have raised three main criticisms of this type of feminist narratology. First, categorizing the various plot types in metaphorical terms lacks the support of empirical data and detailed linguistic analysis. Second, labelling the alternatives as "male" and "female" illustrates a universalizing and essentialist assumption that all male and female experience is the same and is biologically determined. Finally, the slippage between narrative content and plot structure results in a simplistic correlation of narrative structure and gender where it is the linguistic form itself that appears to be gendered. These problems are to a certain extent inherent in the theoretical models from which this strand of feminist narratology is derived. Broadly speaking, psychoanalysis has been criticized for its potential universalism and tendency towards decontextualized abstraction (McCormick, 1992), as has the writing of Cixous described as *écriture feminine* (Mills, 1995). Indeed, the appropriation of Cixous, Irigaray and Kristeva as "French feminists" by Anglo-American scholars (including those discussed in this chapter) has been described as a dangerous form of decontextualization (Winter, 1997; Delphy, 2000; Moses, 2003) whereby their work is falsely taken as representative of feminism in France and ignores a more diverse situation. This principle of abstraction is problematic from both a feminist and a narratological point of view. Various writers have argued that when theoretical arguments and paradigms are divorced from their actual contexts, then a discussion of feminist principles has the potential to become apolitical. Once the discussion shifts from the particular into the abstract, it becomes difficult to ask vital feminist questions, such as to whom the differences of gender matter and what might be done about them. From a narratological perspective, the abstraction has also been shown to be dubious, for the gendering of alternative plot models when analyzed in terms of their narrativity simply cannot hold up against the analysis of a wider range of particular texts. This debate raises questions concerning how far the separation of form and content can be taken, how this relates to matters of context and the parts that each of these might play in the process of interpretation as a reader might make sense of a narrative. In this chapter, I have argued that gender cannot be attributed to the narrative form itself. In the next chapter, I discuss how these difficult questions may be approached from the perspective of contextualist narratology.

三、思考与讨论

(1) 较之于詹姆斯·费伦和戴维·赫尔曼的研究,佩奇关于“叙事性”的研究有何特征?

(2) 如何看待佩奇关于“叙事性的高低程度与性别毫不相关”的论断?

(3) 佩奇的女性主义叙事研究有何特色和盲点?

本章推荐阅读书目

[1] Alison Case. *Plotting Women: Gender and Narration in the Eighteenth-and Nineteenth-Century British Novel*. Charlottesville: University Press of Virginia, 1999.

[2] Kathy Mezei, ed. *Ambiguous Discourse: Feminist Narratology and British Women Writers*. Chapel Hill: The University of North Carolina Press, 1996.

[3] Katherine Nash. *Feminist Narrative Ethics: Tacit Persuasion in Modernist Form*. Columbus: The Ohio State University Press, 2014.

[4] Robyn Warhol. *Having a Good Cry: Effeminate Feelings and Pop-Culture Forms*. Columbus: The Ohio State University Press, 2003.

[5] Robyn Warhol and Susan Lanser. *Narrative Theory Unbound: Queer and Feminist Interventions*. Columbus: The Ohio State University Press, 2015.

第五章
跨媒介叙事学

第一节　概　　论

随着21世纪以来信息科技的快速发展，人类的信息储存和传播方式日益丰富多样。我们靠通信软件与世界各地的人沟通交流，用社交媒体记录生活，借影视剧和电子游戏放松身心，在3D虚拟场景欣赏艺术……在通过各种渠道传输信息的同时，我们的世界观和叙事方式也在悄然发生改变，而媒介的多样性则使跨媒介叙事成为可能。21世纪以来，一场叙事的“跨媒介转向”正在发生，它影响着文学的创作手法与批评视角，同时也促进了其他媒介的文艺创作与研究。在2006年出版的《融合文化：新媒体和旧媒体的冲突地带》一书中，亨利·詹金斯（Henry Jenkins）开宗明义地提出，融合与跨界是当今媒体的大势所趋，不仅是跨越多个媒体平台的娱乐内容，“我们的生活、关系、记忆、幻想、欲望都在不同媒体频道间穿越”。[①] 可以说，每一位在当代使用媒体、传输信息的人都被卷入“跨媒介转向”的潮流中。

一、跨媒介叙事：源起与定义

跨媒介叙事学的产生，除了科技发展推动“转向”的现实基础之外，也离不开叙事本身的跨媒介特性。即使对于文学这种与纸本印刷“绑定”的叙事，其本身潜质也不止于此。学者们在叙事学出现和发展时期就开始关注叙事媒介多样化的可能性与相关问题。“由于技术和媒介的变化，当代文学清楚地表明，印刷文本作为文学分发的唯一媒介是一种历史性的解决方案，而不是一个自然的事实”。[②] 1962年，克洛德·布雷蒙写道：“（故事）独立于承载物。它可以从一种媒介转移到另一种，而不失其核心特性：故事的主体像是一场芭蕾的内容，以小说形式的表述可以被转换为舞台或屏幕上的表演，一部电影也可以用语言讲述给没看过的人。这些形式包括我们阅读的文字、我们看到的图片以及我们解读的手势，我们可以通过不同形式了解一个相同的故事。”[③] 1966年，罗兰·巴特在《交际》杂志发表其对叙事学学科产生重大影响的论文《叙事作品结构分析导论》时，很直觉地提到文学的跨媒介特性：“对人类来说，似乎

---

① 亨利·詹金斯：《融合文化：新媒体和旧媒体的冲突地带》，杜永明译，北京：商务印书馆，2012年，第17页。

② Jørgen Bruhn, *The Intermediality of Narrative Literature: Medialities Matter*（London: Palgrave Macmillan, 2016）, p.7.

③ 转引自 Marie-Laure Ryan, “Introduction,” *Narrative across Media: The Languages of Storytelling*, ed. Marie-Laure Ryan（Lincoln and London: University of Nebraska Press, 2004）, p.1.

任何材料都适宜于叙事：叙事承载物可以是口头和书面的有声语言、是固定的或活动的画面、是手势，以及所有这些材料的有机混合；叙事遍布于神话、传说、寓言、民间故事、小说、史诗、历史、悲剧、正剧、喜剧、哑剧、绘画（请想一想卡帕齐奥的《圣于絮尔》那幅画）、彩绘玻璃窗、电影、连环画、社会杂闻、会话。而且，以这些几乎无限的形式出现的叙事遍存于一切时代、一切地方、一切社会。"① 若将视野从文艺作品扩大到所有类型的叙事，其媒介多样性则更为明显，多种媒介"有机混合"形成叙事也就自然地发生了。

跨媒介叙事作为当代后经典叙事学的后起之秀，有许多概念和名词的定义尚未在学界形成定论。一个核心的争论焦点就是"媒介"的含义。② 跨媒介叙事学家玛丽·劳勒-瑞安道出了学界共存的疑惑：

> 比如简·奥斯汀的《傲慢与偏见》的媒介是什么？是语言，是写作，还是书本？这三种媒介的概念都影响着它讲述何种故事，尽管研究其作为书本或一种写作的重要性似乎不能将它与其他小说明显区分开。相对来讲，研究它对语言的处理，会是一种更个体化的分析，因为每一次语言的使用都是原创的，每部作品语言的使用都是独特的。[……] 对于叙事媒介性的研究，如果我们想要捕捉这种媒介整体的叙事能力，我们经常需要把个体作品当作这种媒介的代表。但是我们不能忽略个体作品未被发掘的、在媒介本身叙事能力上延伸出的表现潜能。③

瑞安本人对媒介给出的定义较为模糊，她认为媒介的概念是因人而异的，不同人群会对"媒介"这一概念形成不同看法，在社会学家、文化评论家看来，媒介包括电视、广播、电影、互联网等传播媒介；艺术批评家则会联想到音乐、油画、雕塑、文学、戏剧、歌剧、摄影、建筑等不同艺术表现手法；持现象学观点的哲学家则会将媒介归结为视觉、听觉、语言、味觉、嗅觉等不同感官形式；艺术家则会以陶土、青铜、油墨、水彩、织物，甚至是一些青草、羽毛、啤酒罐之类的混合材料作为其艺术介质。④ 马歇尔·麦克卢汉(Marshall McLuhan)的名言"媒介即信息"在学界广为流传。他认为媒介是人类的延伸，是形成或重塑我们感知的形式。⑤ 赵毅衡在《广义叙述学》中提及叙事的几种不同媒介：记录类的文字、语言、图像、雕塑；记录演示类的胶卷与数字录制；演示类的身体、影像、实物和言语；类演示类的心像、心感、心语；意动类则包含任何媒介。

"媒介"的定义虽各有千秋，但总体而言都是从不同角度围绕媒介作为叙事承载物这一功能的理解。对于叙事而言，媒介的功能最终都是帮助我们完成叙事行为。所谓"跨"媒介叙事的说法，则强调了叙事在不同类型的承载物之间或穿越或融合的特征。"跨媒介叙事"这一名词通常被认为是詹金斯所创的，他认为：

> 跨媒介的故事通过多种媒体平台展开，每种新的文本类型都会对整体故事做出独特的、有价值

① 转引自王瑛：《回顾与展望：跨媒介叙事研究及其诗学建构形态考察》，载《中国文学研究》2016年第4期，第16—17页。

② "media"在中文中有时被译为"媒体"，有时被译为"媒介"。鉴于"transmedia"通常被译作"跨媒介"，本章为保持一致，将"media"对应的中文均处理为"媒介"。

③ Marie-Laure Ryan, "Editors' Preface," *Intermediality and Storytelling*, eds. Marina Grishakova and Marie-Laure Ryan (Berlin: The Gruyter, 2010), p.2.

④ Ryan, "Introduction," p.14.

⑤ 详见 Marshall McLuhan, *Understanding Media: The Extensions of Man* (New York: Signet, 1964).

的贡献。理想的跨媒介叙事形式中,每种媒介都尽其所能——所以一个故事可能由电影媒介引入,扩展到电视、小说和漫画;它讲述的世界可能要通过玩游戏来探索,或通过游乐园景点来体验。每种形式都要素齐全,你不需要为了享受游戏而必须先看电影,反之亦然。[①]

类似地,卡林·卡林诺夫(Kalin Kalinov)对跨媒介叙事的定义是"一种通过多种媒体频道结合的方式进行叙事沟通的多媒体产物"。[②] 休斯顿·霍华德(Houston Howard)则将跨媒介叙事定义为"将一个故事延伸到多重媒介、多种平台,创造出一种更好的创作商业模式,给观众提供更好的体验的叙事"。[③] 跨媒介叙事一般包含一种以上的媒介参与到相同或相似的故事的构建或演绎中,每种媒介所承载的叙事又相对独立。最常见的形式有小说改编的电影、漫画改编的游戏、电影改编的密室逃脱游戏或主题公园等。改编可能增删了原始作品的内容,改变了人物形象,甚至改写了部分情节,但各种跨媒介叙事始终处于一个相同的故事世界中,其情节、人物、场景设定有相似之处。如此,一个跨媒介的故事"体系"既包含原始的叙事,也包含了衍生的每种媒介各自讲述的关于某几个共同人物的主题相似的故事。比如DC漫画的作品《蝙蝠侠》最初以漫画书的形式问世,而后又被翻拍、演绎成多部电影,电影增加了人物的背景故事,丰富了原有情节。在《蝙蝠侠》故事的跨媒介叙事中,同一人物(如蝙蝠侠)被置于一个更复杂、包含更多层情节的故事世界,在不同的媒介中人物形象和性格也可能有差异,该媒介所针对的目标人群也有所区别。漫画书的形式主要针对年轻读者,而电影则扩大了这个故事的受众范围,引起更多人对《蝙蝠侠》故事的兴趣。另一个跨越更多类媒介的例子是"宝可梦"(Pokemon)系列。"宝可梦"最初是由任天堂公司开发的一款游戏,随后其人物形象、故事设定和战斗模式被演绎成探险主题的动画片《精灵宝可梦》,动画片在原有的战斗场景上增添了很多具有人文色彩的情节。宝可梦电影《超梦重现》等增添了更多人物和情节,手机游戏"宝可梦 Go"则结合现实世界的地图信息,让玩家在现实中的不同地点捕捉虚拟"宝可梦"生物并进行战斗,此外还有围绕"宝可梦"角色的卡牌游戏、漫画、小说等多种其他媒介,它们彼此独立地呈现了人类主人公带领宝可梦进行探险的叙事。

詹金斯等人的观点属于对"跨媒介叙事"的狭义定义。另一种广义的跨媒介叙事则包括了更多的研究范畴,在狭义的跨媒介叙事范围之上扩展到叙事媒介本身的研究。让-诺埃尔·托恩曾指出,跨媒介叙事的兴趣点主要在于穿越一系列叙事媒介而呈现的跨媒介现象,而非叙事媒介本身。[④] 学界的宏观目标是"致力于寻找可以应用于不同媒介而非单一媒介的叙事学方法"。[⑤] 因此"跨媒介叙事"有时会被用作一个涵盖性术语,囊括了文字文本之外所有媒介的叙事实践。如托恩所言,"跨媒介叙事"这个标签更多地意味着特殊的跨越性视角,或者仅仅指向"叙事媒介研究",目前尚无定论。[⑥] 戴维·赫尔曼在《一种跨媒介叙事》("Toward a Transmedial Narratology")中表达了类似的观点,认为跨媒介叙事是

① Henry Jenkins, *Convergence Culture: Where Old and New Media Collide* (New York and London: New York University Press, 2006), pp.95 - 96.

② Kalin Kalinov, "Transmedia Narratives: Definition and Social Transformations in the Consumption of Media Content in the Globalized World," *Postmodernism Problems* 7.1(2017), p.66.

③ 详见 Houston Howard, *You're Gonna Need a Bigger Story: The 21st Century Survival Guide to not just Writing Stories, But Building Super Stories* (New York: One 3 Books, 2007).

④ Jan-Noël Thon, *Transmedial Narratology and Contemporary Media Culture* (Lincoln and London: University of Nebraska Press, 2016), p.14.

⑤ Irina Rajewsky, "Intermediality, Intertextuality, and Remediation: Literary Perspective on Intermediality," *Intermediality: History and Theory of the Arts, Literature and Technologies* 6 (2005), p.46.

⑥ Thon, *Transmedial Narratology and Contemporary Media Culture*, pp.14 - 15.

“研究故事与其媒介的联系的总体理论”。[①] 这一类定义就不仅包括了多种媒介在叙事上的跨越与融合，也包括了非传统的叙事媒介本身的研究，不再强调与其他媒介的关联，旨在聚焦某一种媒介内部形成的独特研究理论，进而为学界寻找各种媒介之间的共性或差异性做出贡献。电影、电视、游戏、漫画等叙事媒介的专门研究均可包括于此类。

在国际学界，与“跨媒介”概念同时出现的还有“多重媒介”“媒介间性”等诸多新兴学术名词，它们代表着不同的媒介叙事形态。詹金斯在谈到数字信息时代的叙事时，将数字环境下的故事展开方式分为三种：其一是多媒体(multimedia)故事，即在一个平台上将一组涉及文本、音频、视频、互动媒体、图像等媒介的内容集中呈现，创造同一个故事的综合性体验；其二是跨媒介(transmedia)故事，叙述者们使用数字信息平台等其他传播渠道构建各自独立但互相关联的叙事，每种媒介的存在都增添了一种故事世界的特殊体验，所以读者有时需要主动追溯分散的内容并将其重组；其三是交叉媒介(cross-media)的内容，包括可以从数字信息平台获取或下载的故事。[②] 维尔纳・沃尔夫(Werner Wolf)提出了“媒介间性”(intermediality)的概念，这一概念狭义上是指一种以上的媒介参与到人为创造的同一内容的特性，即所谓的“内部构建”(intracompositional)；广义上则是指任何对通常意义上不同媒介间界限的侵越，包括了不同媒介之间在“内部构建”和“外部构建”上的关系，这种关系可以是共时性的融合、相似、囊括关系，也可以是历时性的“再媒介化”(remediation，现存媒介经融合或分化成为一种新的媒介)关系。[③]

二、跨媒介叙事的几个关键问题

跨媒介叙事打破了传统意义上的叙事媒介，其研究手法与关注点也在传统概念的基础上有很大程度的创新。下面介绍几个跨媒介叙事中常见的关键术语或研究问题。

(1) 故事世界。跨媒介叙事通常涉及多种媒介的多个叙事并探寻其关系和共性，而且，新兴的叙事媒介并不都包含传统叙事所呈现的所有要素，比如戏剧、电影等视听媒介中是否存在叙述者尚有争议，游戏、主题乐园、密室逃脱等媒介的主要人物变成了玩家本人，其情节根据玩家的决策而有着个性化的走向。因此传统概念中应用于单个叙事的情节、环境等概念无法满足对多个媒介叙事的总体研究。赫尔曼、托恩、瑞安等人基于认知叙事学提出了“故事世界”(storyworld)的概念。它类似于叙事学的“虚构世界”(fictional world)，但包含更复杂的要素。托恩将故事世界定义为“被叙事唤起的世界”或“被叙事表现所表现的世界”，该定义更便于考虑多种媒介所承载的叙事间的关系。而传统叙事理论中所谓的“内层”“外层”“中间层”叙事，则转变为一个包容的故事世界里的、本体论上互不关联的次级世界(subworld)。[④] 跨媒介的故事世界包括了一种以上的叙事，读者不能仅仅通过读一本小说、看一部电影就了解这一“世界”的全貌。与一般评论所言的“作者的创作世界”有所区别的是，叙事学意义上的“故事世界”是由若干个体文本所投射而成的，并非一个作者的全部作品。每一个故事都有其自身独特的故事

---

① David Herman, “Toward a Transmedial Narratology,” *Narrative across Media: The Languages of Storytelling*, ed. Marie-Laure Ryan (Lincoln and London: University of Nebraska Press, 2004), p.67.

② Henry Jenkins, “Voices for a New Vernacular: A Forum on Digital Storytelling: Interview with Henry Jenkins,” *International Journal of Communication* 11(2017), p.1062.

③ Werner Wolf, “(Inter)mediality and the Study of Literature,” *CLCWeb: Comparative Literature and Culture* 13.3 (2011), pp.2 - 6.

④ Thon, *Transmedial Narratology and Contemporary Media Culture*, pp.37 - 38.

世界，特别是跨媒介语境下，一个世界的表达是由多个不同文本和媒介组构而成的。相应地，叙事学意义上的“故事世界”必须要有叙事内容，所以学界对于抒情诗等非叙事文类的“故事世界”仍存在质疑。而且，故事世界是虚构世界，由虚构的人物组成，与现实中的作者并不处于同一空间。①

跨媒介叙事中的“故事世界”一方面如上所述，强调叙事世界在媒介间的创建和分布，另一方面则包括读者对故事世界的想象构建。② 为了获得更全面的故事体验，读者（或媒介的受众）需要了解多种媒介下的叙事，形成彼此关联的体验。在互联网时代，更可以通过相同爱好者之间的线上交流互动来加深对故事世界各个层次间关联的认知。詹金斯生动地描述了数字媒体时代体验跨媒介叙事的方式：“为了完全体验虚构的世界，消费者必须假设自己是捕猎者或收集者，在不同媒介渠道间穿梭，寻找故事的线索，通过线上的讨论组来互相比对故事的记录，与他人合作确认每个人投入的时间和努力都能换取更丰富的娱乐。”③ “哈利·波特”系列故事就是利用当代科技手段构筑跨媒介叙事故事世界和交流平台的典例。多个社交媒体都有“哈利·波特”爱好者的交流讨论区，爱好者们逐渐组成粉丝俱乐部，还有人创建了名为“魔法世界”的官方网站，其中囊括了《哈利·波特》系列小说、电影、手机游戏、戏剧、主题公园等同一故事世界中多种叙事媒介的信息。可以说，当代的跨媒介故事世界中，读者的角色也起着决定性作用，跨媒介的世界的特点就是观众和设计者拥有共同的“世界性”心理图景，即一系列关于这个宇宙的突出特征。④ 故事世界这一概念的出现，代表了叙事学研究从经典叙事学转向针对读者、观众和玩家的想象活动所采取的现象学研究模式。⑤

（2）作者与叙述者。跨媒介叙事的形式多样，不同于单一的语言类媒介有明确的“作者”，在电影、电视剧、游戏等媒介中，作者职能不再由具体的个体实现，而是由一个团队分工合作完成：改编电影的故事梗概可能来自小说，但其画面的拍摄是导演、演员、服装师、化妆师及其他工作人员共同完成的，最终呈现给观众的完整电影又需要剪辑师、特效师、配音演员等进行后期处理。此外，叙事媒介的接受者越来越多地参与到叙事中来，不仅在同一故事世界的几种媒介之间比较、思考，还可能在某一媒介上参与叙事的重构，如在《仙剑奇侠传》《幻想三国志》等仙侠类角色扮演游戏中，玩家代替人物在对话的几种内容间做出选择，这会影响到人物的关系和游戏的结局。因此，媒介的受众逐渐由传统叙事媒介的“被动接受”角色向“主动参与”的合作创作者角色转变。叙事创作与接受媒介的多样化也间接引发了作者、叙述者、人物、受述者、读者的身份混淆。因此有必要更新对作者和叙述者的认识。托恩提出了跨媒介叙事的三种作者类型。⑥ 首先，他基于韦恩·布斯早年的“隐含作者”概念提出了“假想作者”(hypothetical author)的概念，将被考察的叙事作品的全部设计归责于“假想作者”，这一概念主要应用于电影、漫画和某些类型的游戏，避免在理解和批评过程中因为难以概括和描述所有参与叙事创作的个体而偏离主题。与之相对，真实的创作团队则作为“作者形象”(author figure)存在，读者可以在电影或

① Marie-Laure Ryan, “Story/Worlds/Media: Tuning the Instruments of a Media-Conscious Narratology,” *Storyworlds across Media: Toward a Media-Conscious Narratology*, eds. Marie-Laure Ryan and Jan-Noël Thon (Lincoln and London: University of Nebraska Press, 2014), p.32.

② Alison Gibbons, “Reading *S*. across Media: Transmedia Storyworlds, Multimodal Fiction, and Real Readers,” *Narrative* 25.3 (2017), p.322.

③ Jenkins, *Convergence Culture: Where Old and New Media Collide*, p.21.

④ Lisbeth Klastrup and Susana Tosca, “Transmedial Worlds—Rethinking Cyberworld Design,” *Proceedings of the 2004 International Conference on Cyberworlds* (2004), p.409.

⑤ 段枫，陈星，许娅，等：《当代西方跨媒介叙事学研究述论》，载《解放军外国语学院学报》2020年第43卷第1期，第65页。

⑥ Thon, *Transmedial Narratology and Contemporary Media Culture*, pp.133-134.

电视的"演职人员名单"、游戏或动画的"制作人员名单"这类副文本中精确地了解这些人在叙事表现中做出的贡献。此外，对于以受众为中心，令叙事成为个性化体验的媒介，托恩将其体验者称作"创作职能人物"(authoring character)，他们适用于第一人称游戏、密室逃脱、主题游乐场等媒介，玩家作为"创作职能人物"，既是叙事的读者，也是叙事中的人物，同时一定程度上是叙事情节的主导者，分担了叙事创作上的部分职能。迪士尼乐园中的许多游乐设施就是让游客作为"创作职能人物"来体验童话、电影中的故事世界的，如"爱丽丝梦游仙境迷宫"让游客以爱丽丝的视角在迷宫中邂逅路易斯·卡罗《爱丽丝梦游仙境》童话故事中的黑桃皇后、兔子洞等场景，"小熊维尼历险记"再现了《小熊维尼》童话故事和相关动画的场景——游客乘坐小火车，置身小熊维尼和伙伴们生活的大森林中。如此看来，跨媒介叙事学在一定程度上更新了对叙事作者的传统定义，也在理论上打破了作者与读者双方之间的界限。

在颠覆作者身份的同时，跨媒介叙事学对叙述者的研究也在传统观念上有不少革新。经典叙事学认为叙述者是单纯的叙事的表现者或讲述者，比如里蒙-凯南将叙述者定义为一个"讲述的媒介或参与服务于叙述需求的行为的媒介"[①]，因此学界也有对于戏剧、影视等视听媒介中是否存在"叙述者"的争议。跨媒介叙事学倾向于承认叙述者的存在，将叙述者看作叙事沟通中不可或缺的角色，并且继续沿用经典叙事学中的"内故事叙述者""外故事叙述者"等概念，但同时也在叙述者的单一定位上有所革新，承认叙述者和接受者的身份之间存在着很大程度的流动性，这是跨媒介叙事定义叙述者的一大阻碍。此外，如瑞安所言，研究跨媒介叙事只在能够将语言叙事的变量转换到其他媒介时才可行，这就意味着要寻找一个在信息发送者和接受者(作者和读者/观众)之外还包括叙述者、受述者、叙事信息在内的沟通体系，但这也带来了跨媒介叙事定义叙述者的另一个阻碍。[②] 跨媒介叙事学理论家们采取了不同的方法来克服这些阻碍。托恩倾向于认为叙述者是"叙述的人物"，他聚焦于各种媒介中的语言维度，将不同类型的媒介中的叙述者的叙述行为分类讨论，比如图像小说是文字叙述与图文表现形式的结合，故事片是文字叙述与视听表现形式的结合，电脑游戏是文字叙述与"互动"形式的结合等。[③] 瑞安则尝试将叙述行为细分为三种职能，即叙述者的出现与否、可见程度、心理密度(psychic density)，其关注点从单一的讲述媒介转移到叙述行为是否满足这三种职能的讨论上，在更大程度上容纳了新媒介的存在。[④]

(3) 跨媒介叙事的分类。为了方便将不同的跨媒介叙事进行总览、比较，有必要将跨媒介叙事作基本的分类。下面简单介绍三种分类方法。其一是按媒介的信息传播渠道不同来分类，便于比较不同媒介之间的本质区别，是最显而易见的一种方法。比如，瑞安主编的《跨媒介叙事：故事讲述的语言》一书将所选论文分为面对面讲述、静态画面、动态画面、音乐、数字媒介五个主要类型。面对面讲述包括带有表情、手势的谈话沟通及相关的表演形式；静态画面包括绘本小说、连环画等；动态画面包括电视、电影及类似的视听媒介；音乐与之相对则是单一的听觉媒介，但非语言渠道；数字媒介则是游戏、交互式电影等新兴的互动式媒介。这种分类方法并不强调媒介之间的"跨越"关系。与之相对的是聚焦跨媒介叙事的跨越与融合特征的另一种分类方式。克里斯蒂·德娜(Christy Dena)结合跨媒介叙事创作的时序及

---

① Shlomith Rimmon-Kenan, *Narrative Fiction: Contemporary Poetics* (New York: Routledge, 2005), p.91.

② Ryan, "Introduction," p.15.

③ Jan-Noël Thon, "Toward a Transmedial Narratology: On Narrators in Contemporary Graphic Novels, Feature Films, and Computer Games," *Beyond Classical Narration: Transmedial and Unnatural Challenges*, eds. Jan Alber and Per Krogh Hansen (New York: De Gruyter, 2014), p.45.

④ 详见 Marie-Laure Ryan, "The Narratorial Functions: Breaking down a Theoretical Primitive," *Narrative* 9.2 (2001), pp.146－152.

对作者的要求将跨媒介叙事分为四类：第一类是单一媒介故事合集，即多种媒介各自讲述一个故事，各个媒介所讲的故事之间有一定联系，但又有各自独立的情节，比如小说与改变原有故事情节形成的电影。在这类跨媒介叙事中，作者将多种媒介的叙事平行对待。第二类是讲述一个故事的多种媒介集合，此类中的各种媒介对同一个故事进行补充，网络上的超文本作家用链接联系一个故事在不同媒介中体现的几个模块，或者作家出版小说后，又为其创作了续作的电影剧本。这一类型要求作者有较强的交互意识，并能够引导读者进行跨媒介的阅读。第三类称作“扩展分析”，指作者在创作一部作品之后，又创作了该作品的跨媒介衍生物，借此梳理故事情节、强调主要人物、做出回顾与分析，比如电视版的《圣经》呈现了《圣经》的重点人物、情节、场景等，这一类型要求作者创作时注意各种媒介间的观点在同一故事世界内自洽。第四类是前摄跨媒介叙事，即在创作伊始就被归类为跨媒介叙事的作品。这也要求作者对于故事各个媒介之间的关联、重点人物和情节、如何引导观众等问题有着极为清晰的认识。比如，当今日本漫画产业中的许多漫画家在创作静态漫画时就为其改编为动画做好了技术上和叙事情节上的准备，令自己的作品迅速发展成跨媒介产业。[①] 还有一种是根据知识产权和法律关系进行的分类，包括：① 知识产权归属不明的跨媒介叙事；② 所有跨媒介产物都受知识产权所有者直接控制或监管；③ 被部分移交知识产权的跨媒介叙事；④ 基于同一个故事世界，但部分媒介的知识产权不受归属者控制的跨媒介叙事；⑤ 知识产权所有者公开授权受众参与创造的跨媒介叙事；⑥ 未经知识产权所有者授权，由受众或爱好者自发创作的“非官方”跨媒介叙事。[②]

① Colin B. Harvey, “A Taxonomy of Transmedia Storytelling,” *Storyworlds across Media: Toward a Media-Conscious Narratology*, eds. Marie-Laure Ryan and Jan-Noël Thon (Lincoln and London: University of Nebraska Press, 2014), pp.280-281.

② Ibid., p.281.

第二节 扬·贝腾斯与雨果·弗雷的《绘本小说》

一、导读

在本节选文中，扬·贝腾斯(Jan Baetens)与雨果·弗雷(Hugo Frey)从绘本小说与漫画的关系以及绘本小说与传统文学的关系两方面探讨了绘本小说的定义、发展及其在当今文化产品中的特殊地位。在绘本小说和漫画的关系方面，二者有诸多共同和不同之处。扬·贝腾斯与雨果·弗雷指出，绘本小说不等于成人向漫画。无论是在内容、创作风格和形式上，还是在出版方式和文化价值上，绘本小说都是对漫画的一种重塑。第一，绘本小说不再关注超级英雄等经典漫画题材，转而叙述更加严肃的内容，将自传等非虚构文类引入漫画中；第二，绘本小说可以"牺牲"作品的叙事性以突出无聊、焦虑、停滞等主题；第三，绘本小说更能凸显创作者本人的风格，这是因为绘本小说的故事创作、分镜、线稿、上色等各环节都由作者一人完成，这与工业化生产的漫画有所不同；第四，绘本小说通常是以书本形式出版的长篇叙事并在正规书店出售；第五，绘本小说渴望在高雅文化中占有一席之地，而这是传统漫画难以想象和实现的。

当然，漫画与绘本小说之间也并非泾渭分明。绘本小说仍具有不少漫画元素，而漫画也从绘本小说中汲取了新的灵感。此外，尽管通常认为绘本小说晚于漫画出现，但实际上绘本小说最早出现于何时尚不明确。当今绘本小说的流行离不开"再媒介化"(remediation)和全球化两个过程。前者指图文并茂的绘本小说是对纯文字小说的一种"再媒介化"，这使其相比于文字文学在叙述形式上更具吸引力；后者指原本目标受众仅为本地读者的绘本小说如今越来越多地面向全球读者。不仅如此，随着其他国家和地区早期绘本小说再度被发掘，美国作为绘本小说发源地的地位也受到了质疑。

如今，绘本小说越来越多地被看作一种小说，而非一种新的漫画形式。这种现象背后的成因是什么呢？我们应该如何界定绘本小说呢？扬·贝腾斯与雨果·弗雷认为我们应该从那些已经被公认是绘本小说的作品中寻找答案。对绘本小说这一概念做出重要贡献的有三人：罗多尔夫·特普费尔(Rodolphe Töpffer)、威尔·艾斯纳(Will Eisner)、阿特·斯皮格曼(Art Spiegelman)。他们均是漫画家兼漫画理论家，均将绘本小说视作一种文学写作形式。绘本小说的本质就在于其文学面向，这也解释了为何绘本小说能进军文学领域。

需要注意的是，将绘本小说视为一种新型小说并不意味着我们可以将传统的文学批评理论(如经典叙事学)直接应用于绘本小说的研究中，因为以往文学理论主要针对的是以文字为单一媒介的文学作品，而绘本小说不仅有文字还有图像，是一种多模态文本。若直接套用传统理论，会出现很多不适用的情况。因此我们在应用理论时，应充分考虑到绘本小说本身的媒介特性，对原本的理论进行调整和修改以更好地服务于绘本小说的分析，丰富漫画领域的研究，同时绘本小说亦反过来促进了跨媒介叙事学的发展。

二、《绘本小说》选读①

A Subfield, Yes, but an Expanding One

If it is true that comics are no longer just for kids, what does this mean for the graphic novel? The graphic novel today is less a form of comics targeting a particular audience, allegedly via the use of "adult" content, than a different kind of medium that reshapes all aspects and dimensions of comics: its content, of course, but also its style and format as well as the publishing policy and the cultural values related to it.② Unlike comics, graphic novels tell serious stories that no longer focus on superheroes, humor, or adventure tales and introduce new strands of fiction and nonfiction such as biography and autobiography, history and journalism. Unlike comics, graphic novels even dare to put narrative between brackets, featuring nearly storyless works about boredom, angst, and immobility, sometimes even abandoning all traces of figuration and agency, as can be seen nowadays in the very popular subgenre of abstract comics.③ Unlike comics, graphic novels display as much as possible the idiosyncratic style of an individual author who aspires to become an auteur, in full control of every aspect of his or her work (graphic novelists, by the way, are more and more female, whereas the comics industry has always been an all-male business). Unlike comics, graphic novels are (sometimes very) long narratives published in book form, preferably by general or literary publishers, often very prestigious ones such as Pantheon and Jonathan Cape, and in formats whose size may change with each new work (even when they are serialized, and some of them still are, graphic novels like to resemble one-shot book publications). Unlike comics, graphic novels are no longer sold in newsstands but in "real" bookshops, next to "real" books. Last but not least, graphic novels are eager to claim a place under the high-cultural sun, something traditional comics could not even dream of—or were reluctant to do so, for reasons that have to do not only with a sense of unfair competition between high and low art④ but also with the fear that the cultural upgrade from comic book to graphic novel might have negative consequences on what has always constituted the power of comics: (1) their direct contact with the energy of popular culture and (2) the capacity to interact almost in real time, thanks to the paced rhythm of serialization, with the "news of the day".⑤ In comparison with the creative chaos of the comics world, graphic novels may seem slow (it takes at least as much time to write a graphic novel as a novel) and a little stiff

① Jan Baetens and Hugo Frey, "The Graphic Novel," *The Cambridge Companion to the Novel*, ed. Eric Bulson (Cambridge: Cambridge University Press, 2018), pp.238 - 253.

② See Jan Baetens and Hugo Frey, *The Graphic Novel: An Introduction*, Cambridge University Press, 2015.

③ See Andrei Molotiu, ed., *Abstract Comics*, Fantagraphics, 2010.

④ See Bart Beaty, *Comics versus Art*, Toronto University Press, 2012; and Jan Baetens and Hugo Frey, "Why So Much Hatred? Fine Art and Comics, Before and After the Graphic Novel," *Art History* (forthcoming).

⑤ See Charles Hatfield, *Alternative Comics: An Emerging Literature*, University Press of Mississippi, 2005.

(ignoring and even misrepresenting the popular realm no real comics can do without).

As one can imagine, the difference between comics and graphic novels is not absolute. Not all graphic novels follow the ideal model that was just sketched, and more and more comics have started including elements from the graphic novel model. Nor is the difference simply chronological. Even if it is generally accepted that comics came first and graphic novels later (the histoires en estampes of Töpffer excepted), it is not possible to date with precision the appearance of the latter. Just as we know that there were comics before *The Yellow Kid* (R. F. Outcault, 1895), there have been graphic novels before *A Contract With God* (Will Eisner, 1978—a collection of short stories, by the way, and thus not a novel). One should avoid any fast and easy dichotomy when approaching the world of comics and graphic novels and see their difference as that between two types that can overlap in various ways. Possible intersections in concrete works do not imply, however, that the very division between comics and graphic novels is meaningless. Many scholars who reject the notion of the graphic novel, accusing those who use it of elitism, are therefore obliged to use another, no less clear-cut terminology to distinguish between traditional comics and, for instance, "adult comics" (Sabin) or "alternative comics" (Hatfield).

The success of the graphic novel cannot be denied in today's culture. Not only has it been widely regarded as a separate medium from the late 1980s onward, but the new type of comics it represents can now be found literally everywhere. The worldwide success of Spiegelman's *Maus*, for instance, has been decisive in this regard. According to some critics, the graphic novel would even be promised a bright future if the novel as a genre would start dwindling—which, of course, is not (yet) the case,① and it is spreading all over the world, both through the export of mainly graphic novels from the United States and the emergence of local imitations and reappropriations of the imported works.② The story of what is happening with the graphic novel sounds very familiar. Media historians would define its achievement as resulting from a combination of remediation and globalization. On the one hand, the graphic novel appears as a form that not only appropriates but also "remediates" and hybridizes a previous verbal medium, in this case the novel. It manages to do so because of its combination of words and images, which makes it fitter than its competitor in the attempt to create more appealing forms of storytelling.③ On the other hand, the graphic novel is a medium that has succeeded in changing its initially local form into a global one, with all the complex globalizing negotiations that are entailed in these changes of scale. As a global form, emerging today in more and more countries and cultural traditions, the graphic novel is a complex phenomenon. Unlike comics, which are often directly marketed to a global audience and whose global dissemination is part of a larger strategy deployed by cultural industries such as the Disney Corporation, for whom

---

① See Charles McGrath, "Not Funnies," *New York Times*, July 11, 2004.

② For an overview of what is understood today by "world comics", see Frederick Luis Aldama, http://professorlatinx.com/planetary-republic-of-comics/.

③ See Jay David Bolter and Richard Grusin, *Remediation: Understanding New Media*, MIT Press, 1999.

comics are just one tiny part of a multimedia and cross-platform product development, graphic novels have often close ties with the personal vision of independent makers, targeting a more or less local audience. The global success of a work such as Marjane Satrapi's *Persepolis* (2007) was totally unforeseen—which does not mean, at least a posteriori, that it was totally unforeseeable. The increasing role of postcolonial authors in the contemporary book market, as well as the very special relationship between the Western world and Iran, certainly after 9/11, offers two plausible explanations for the enthusiastic national and international reception of the work of an unknown artist in exile published by a small independent company specializing in non-mainstream material. In practice, however, more and more graphic novelists do address a global (i. e. Anglophone) audience, and this is, of course, a severe restriction to our understanding of global. The reasons for this new strategy are various: there is the desire to professionalize, which is only possible if one can cater to a broader audience, but there is also the cosmopolitan character of many young artists who can travel, study, and work abroad; finally, there is also the international emulation that results from the growing number of translations.①

The twofold story of remediation and globalization cannot be reduced to the appearance and circulation of the graphic novel as an institutionalized label or category, however. Just as with comics in general, the graphic novel has been the object of a striking endeavor to stretch its limits in time as well as space. First, it is now no longer seen as a characteristically American form of adult comics, invented by Eisner and then popularized by Art Spiegelman. The existence of graphic novels before Eisner-Spiegelman and outside the United States is now universally acknowledged, and the works of both Eisner and Spiegelman are now being read in a longer and less monocultural and monolinguistic tradition.

From this point of view, the graphic novel repeats some features that have been very important in the story of comics. Indeed, definitions of comics have systematically tried to broaden its field and scope, in both temporal and spatial terms, first, thanks to its supposed links with previous art forms (the idea that the birth of comics should be dated in the prehistorical times of the cave paintings is a long-standing stereotype in comics studies) and, second, thanks to the possibility of recognizing other forms of comics outside the US breeding ground of newspaper comics.② With the arrival of the graphic novel, this take on the spatial and temporal scope of the medium has been repeated. To define the graphic novel always means tracing a new history and showing cultural, geographic, and social diversity. The more the existence of the graphic novel is socially and

① The art house works published by the leading Anglophone companies such as Pantheon, Cape, Fantagraphics, and Drawn & Quartely, for instance, are now being systematically translated into almost all major Western languages.

② For important historical research, see David Kunzle's *The Early Comic Strip: Narrative Strips and Picture Stories in the European Broadsheet from c.1450 to 1825* (*The History of the Comic Strip*, Vol. 1), University of California Press, 1973, and *The History of the Comic Strip*, Vol. 2: *The Nineteenth Century*, University of California Press, 1990. For a theoretical discussion, see Thierry Groensteen, *Mr Töpffer invente la bande dessinée*, Les Impressions Nouvelles, 2013.

culturally acknowledged, the more efforts are undertaken to push back in time the moment of its first appearance as well as to nuance the US hegemony in the field, which is no longer incompatible with a more open approach of making room for non-American forerunners and models.

As clearly shown by Art Spiegelman and Françoise Mouly's *RAW* magazine (1980-1991), much of the inspiration of Maus came from the European avant-garde. And in recent scholarship, the historical role of *A Contract With God* tends to be taken over by Harvey Kurtzman's *Jungle Book*, a 1959 short story collection by the founder of Mad Magazine,① or even by the wordless woodcut novelists of the 1920s, which were very popular on both sides of the Atlantic and themselves deeply influenced by European models of engraved illustrations (Gustave Doré).② As a corollary, it is no longer denied that next to and even before the rise of the US graphic novel there existed already in other countries (Otto Knückel was German; Frans Masereel, the actual inventor of the wordless woodcut novel, was Belgian) a thriving graphic novel market and readership, even if the "graphic novel" label was not used to define these works. In France, for instance, definitely a model for many US authors,③ many publishers, critics, booksellers, and readers continue to prefer the term bande dessinée (literally "drawn strip"), blending the two domains of comics and graphic novels (the French use of the term "graphic novel" originally refers to a publication format, not to issues of style and content that are dramatically diverse and sometimes rather experimental in bande dessinée). Hence also, and more generally speaking, there has been a tendency to rethink this history in terms of networks and mash-up works of mutual influences, appropriations, and creative misunderstandings between a wide range of genres, formats, media, and national traditions. Satrapi's *Persepolis* is, once again, a good example: a definitely postcolonial voice, deeply marked by Persian graphic traditions (as demonstrated, for instance, in the technique of the "collective character", the idea of a multitude being visualized by the repetition of similar characters within a single frame), but also clearly motivated by local influences (Satrapi's black and white drawings are indebted to the European woodcut models as well as to the teaching of her mentor, David B., the author of *L'Ascension du haut mal* (translated as Epileptic [2006], a landmark publication in French autofiction). All these elements clearly show the deeply globalized structure of the making, the marketing, the critical reception, and the commercial success of the modern graphic novel.

At the same time, the graphic novel has increasingly been defined in novelistic terms, something that had never been the case of comics despite the extremely close links between certain forms of comics such as the adventure strip or the sci-fi comics of the 1920s (one may think here of

① See Baetens and Frey, *The Graphic Novel*; and Santiago Garcia, *On the Graphic Novel*, trans. Bruce Campbell, University Press of Mississippi, 2015[2010], p.90.

② See David Beronå, *Wordless Books: The Original Graphic Novels*, Abrams, 2008. Also more recently Spiegelman with his *Wordless!* performance, a stage show created with composer Philip Johnston that highlights the history of these wordless novels.

③ See Joseph Witek, ed., *Art Spiegelman: Conversations*, University Press of Mississippi, 2007.

Wash Tubbs, starting in 1924, or Buck Rogers, starting in 1929) and their literary counterparts. So what makes a graphic novel a novel and not just a new form of comics? Length? Not really, since many graphic novels are actually short story collections. Serious content or innovative narrative techniques? Not really either, since this would imply that seriousness and narrative inventiveness had not existed before in the comics world—an implausible allegation. Few works of art are as sophisticated and profound as Herriman's Krazy Kat, for instance. Are graphic novels then novels because they are literary adaptations? Not at all, since most graphic novels are not derived from literary source material, whereas quite a few comics are, for instance, those produced within the infamous Classics Illustrated series, which no one has even taken seriously as literary works. The crucial change between comics and graphic novels seems to be that of authorship and style, on the one hand, and format and distribution, on the other. Graphic novels are no longer the more or less anonymous and streamlined products of a Taylorized studio system but the conscious output of an individual author claiming an individual drawing style, an individual use of the possibilities of a medium using both words and images and using all possible layout and rhythmic opportunities of panel and book, and, last but not least, an individual worldview. Besides, the graphic novel is also published in book format, which allows it to find its place next to "real" literary works on the shelves of serious bookshops. It is the combination of all these elements that has moved the graphic novel from the newsstand to the bookshop, the library, the canon, and the classroom. It is even not absurd to think of this progression as a stage in the evolution of the novel that thus explores new narrative techniques and modes of characterization.

It can be dangerous, however, to make the concept of the graphic novel too capacious, taking it as a new generic term for all kinds of comics (and, in this case, traditional comics would become something like "graphic novels for kids") or including forms of word and image interaction that belong to very different cultural contexts (we already gave the example of the rupestrian art, but other examples might entail Egyptian hieroglyphs, the Bayeux tapestry, or even the stories told in the stained glass of Gothic cathedrals, all usual suspects when it comes to broaden the corpus). In order to study what the graphic novel is and what it actually does, it makes sense to stick to a more modest definition of the kinds of works that can be labeled graphic novels—and here one should definitely limit oneself to print and book culture; if not, the graphic novel may become anything and thus nothing at all. In this regard, three names are frequently associated with the concept of the graphic novel: Rodolphe Töpffer (1799 - 1846), the nineteenth-century forerunner; Will Eisner (1917 - 2005), who was one of the first to claim successfully the strategic use of this term as a genre label; and Art Spiegelman (1948 -), whose graphic novel *Maus* (1991) represents a watershed moment for the institutional recognition of the medium. These three names are not the only ones that have helped to design the graphic novel, but what makes Töpffer, Eisner, and Spiegelman so interesting—besides the fact that all three are at the same time practitioners and theoreticians, trying to find out about their art in the making—is their common insistence on the very nature of the graphic novel, which they all present as a form of writing, of literature, and thus of the novel (though Spiegelman commonly disliked the term because it did not capture the attempt to use a popular and commercial medium to tell a story of personal and collective trauma that nobody was expecting in this format).

This is a major difference with comics in general, whose narrative and literary status is not always foregrounded (instead, the visual relationship with caricature is commonly underlined). Töpffer himself called the new medium that he was inventing by trial and error a form of "engraved stories" (histoires en estampes).① In his influential instruction book, *Comics and Sequential Art*, Eisner starts by stating:

> The format of comics presents a montage of both word and image, and the reader is thus required to exercise both visual and verbal interpretive skills. The regimens of art (e.g. perspective, symmetry, line) and the regimens of literature (e.g. grammar, plot, syntax) become superimposed upon each other. The reading of a graphic novel is an act of both aesthetic perception and intellectual pursuit ... [T]he psychological processes involved in viewing a word and an image are analogous. The structures of illustration and of prose are similar. In its most economical state, comics employ a series of repetitive images and recognizable symbols. When they are used again and again to convey similar ideas, they become a distinct language—a literary form, if you will.②

In the case of Spiegelman, as noted earlier, a lukewarm fan of the concept of graphic novel,③ the critical emphasis on the fact that his work exceeded the traditional boundaries of comics was present from the very beginning. The awarding of the Pulitzer Prize to *Maus* in 1992, which signified the great breakthrough for the graphic novel in mainstream culture, hinted in that same direction. The prize was a "special citation", that is, a prize that escaped the generic boundaries of the Pulitzer (which has special categories for cartooning and photography, for instance). This difficulty of locating Maus in a given generic category—a problem repeated by many reviewers' hesitations between the categories of fiction and nonfiction—is another sign that the graphic novel is migrating from the well-established domain of comics to something else, which comes closer to literature and writing—or should we say closer once again, for the pioneering work of Töpffer was clearly characterized, by its maker as well as by its first readers, as a special type of literature.

This is, of course, not the place to scrutinize whether images can or cannot be the equivalent of writing—a statement that most theoreticians of the "pictorial turn" have been invited to challenge

---

① See Philippe Kaenel, *Le Métier d'illustrateur: Rodolphe Töpffer, J. J. Grandville, Gustave Doré*, Droz, 2005, p.273.
② Will Eisner, *Comics and Sequential Art*, 1985, W.W. Norton, 2008, p.2.
③ For the evolution on this thinking on the concept, see Witek, ed., *Art Spiegelman: Conversations*.

critically.[①] What matters is the fact that most critical reflections on the graphic novel do take the literary dimension of the medium as one of their starting points. One can therefore easily understand why the graphic novel has entered the literary field. First of all, there is the power of the label itself, which is far from neutral: to call something a "novel" has inevitably dramatic consequences for its position in the larger literary field, for today the novel is in the center of this field and has therefore a canonical and hegemonic status. Second, the shift from newspapers and magazines to publication formats that belong to the shelves of a traditional bookshop or library also affects the perception of the work, whose cultural status is now upgraded. And third, there is also the assumption that the primary objective of the graphic novel is storytelling. It is the combination of these three features that creates a family resemblance with the novel, with which the graphic novel shares a wide range of techniques and tactics.

To summarize, then, the graphic novel is definitely a subset within the larger field of comics, but it is also a rapidly expanding field that has exceeded the formal and thematic restrictions of comics. It is thanks to this expansion that the graphic novel has now entered the larger field of literature, both fiction and nonfiction[②] but also both prose and poetry.[③] Yet what does it mean exactly to state that the graphic novel has been morphing into a kind of novel?

三、思考与讨论

(1) 绘本小说的文学性体现在何处?

(2) 绘本小说有何媒介特性?

(3) 绘本研究如何与叙事学相结合?

① See W. J. T. Mitchell, *Picture Theory*, University of Chicago Press, 1994.

② See Steve Tabachnick, ed., *The Cambridge Companion to the Graphic Novel*, Cambridge University Press, 2016.

③ See Brian McHale, "Beginning to Think about Narrative in Poetry," *Narrative*, vol.17, no.1, 2009, pp.11 - 27.

第三节　玛丽亚·莱文沃斯及其《跨媒介叙事和同人小说》

一、导读

"同人小说"(fan fiction,或称"粉丝文学")是凭借新兴媒体平台迅速崛起的跨媒介叙事分支,一般代表某一文艺作品(如电影、游戏、小说等)的爱好者们[即英文中的 fan(s)或中文的"粉丝"]基于现有的媒介和流行文化中的故事人物或情节进一步创作的写作形式。在创作同人小说时,粉丝们会拓展原有故事情节,创造新的叙事线索,为人物发展情感关系,关注未被充分表现的人物等。[1] 同人小说的作者大多数选择在网上发表与分享作品,以避免可能的法律纠纷,因此也极大程度地促成了同人小说在网络上的聚集与发展。同人小说往往被视为非正式的民间作品,有些同人小说仅仅是为了满足观众对故事设定和人物关系的"探秘"期待而被创作出来,因此水平良莠不齐。但不得不承认,这种所谓未获认可的民间作品的确影响着观众对故事世界的印象,甚至会影响原创作者的后续创作或者最终自身变为获得原创作者及其他粉丝普遍认可的作品。

玛丽亚·林格伦·莱文沃斯(Maria Lindgren Leavenworth)是瑞典于默奥大学现代英语文学教授,主要从事同人小说、粉丝群体等方面的研究。本节选文收录于玛丽-劳尔·瑞安和让-诺埃尔·托恩编写的《跨媒介的故事世界:建构媒介意识的叙事学》论文集的第三部分"跨媒介叙事与跨媒介世界"中,以《吸血鬼日记》系列作品及其同人小说为例,展现了同人小说参与跨媒介叙事时引发的新问题。莱文沃斯认为,《吸血鬼日记》等许多当代流行的跨媒介叙事作品本身就发展出了各具特色的平行叙事,而同一故事世界里各种媒介的叙事之间经常存在不可调和的差异与冲突,这也日渐成为跨媒介故事世界的本质特征。相对于故事世界的不稳定性,同人小说则是一个相对静态而稳定的文本形式。

莱文沃斯在研究同人小说时引入了数字媒体中的交互性(interactivity)概念,认为同人小说证明了同人作者与正统文本互动的愿望。虽然同人小说并不能像电子游戏、超文本一样在物质上支持读者与叙事间的互动(同人小说与原创作品之间更像是一种想象中的交互),但其在交互性概念研究中扮演着重要角色。尤其是"平行宇宙"(alternate universe)类的同人小说,在本体论层面替代了原有的故事,其与原作品之间的差异构成了平行宇宙间的通道,成为一种独特的交互形式。

二、《跨媒介叙事和同人小说》选读[2]

An ever-increasing number of Internet-published fan fictions (fanfic) based on the transmedial

① 详见 Rebecca W. Black, "Online Fan Fiction, Global Identities, and Imagination," *Research in the Teaching of English* (2009), pp.397 - 425.

② Maria Lindgren Leavenworth, "Transmedial Narration and Fan Fiction: The Storyworld of *The Vampire Diaries*," *Storyworlds across Media: Toward a Media-Conscious Narratology*, eds. Marie-Laure Ryan and Jan-Noël Thon (Lincoln and London: University of Nebraska Press, 2014), pp.315 - 323.

storyworld of *The Vampire Diaries* (TVD) evidences a desire to present alternatives to the narrative or to fill in perceived gaps. In their stories, fanfic authors in subtle or profound ways change conditions, plotlines, or characterizations, and in these ways they contribute new associations and interpretations to the extended storyworld. Despite increased academic interest in fan activities, there are still tendencies to see the relation between production and consumption as hierarchical. While the sanctioned products, in fanfic vernacular referred to as "canon", inspires a desire for interaction, the resulting fan products are not necessarily perceived as on par with the "original" or incorporated into processes of meaning making. The term "canon" works in relation to "fanon", or the fan-produced, unsanctioned developments of plot and character that over time acquire legitimacy within the fan community even though they may contest or be incompatible with canon elements. In what follows, it is argued that the concept of storyworld holds great potential for allowing a leveling of hierarchies between sanctioned and unsanctioned products. To rethink different contributions, especially in light of the contemporary stress on audience participation, is productive when seeing fan fiction as part of a larger archive.

Rather than presenting logically consistent, essentially compatible narratives along the lines of a traditionally defined storyworld, TVD illustrates alternative narrative developments and characterizations in its transmedial instantiations, the novels written by L. J. Smith and the TV series produced by Kevin Williamson and Julie Plec, that in some ways may seem to complicate the notion of TVD as one cohesive storyworld.① Adding the variations, alternatives, and sometimes critical commentary found in fan fiction further suggests the possibility of a collapse of any inherent logical narrative consistency. However, both the openness of TVD in terms of fan investment and general tendencies in global convergence culture that encourage audience participation would seem to point at the necessity of a more encompassing notion of *storyworld*. As Bronwen Thomas argues, "storyworlds are generated and experienced within specific social and cultural environments that are subject to constant change"②. Considering the specificities of TVD in terms of origin and fan participation, contradictions and incompatibilities are bound to surface and rise to the point where they become intrinsic to the storyworld itself.

Although the storyworld is in a state of flux, on a concrete level fan fiction is still a fairly static text form, which in this case is based on likewise fairly static text forms such as written novels and a TV series. Interest thus further lies in what affordances and limitations the concepts of interactivity have and in what aspects specific to TVD need to be taken into account to better understand what

① A fully expanded definition of *storyworld* naturally encompasses expressions such as production details, interviews and merchandise, and, in the case of TVD, computer games and webisodes, which contribute more straightforwardly narrative details. However, the vast majority of TVD fanfic (based on the initial survey it can be argued all of it) is based on either the novels or the TV series, and the analyses here center on the narrative as it develops in these media forms.

② Bronwen Thomas. "What Is Fanfiction and Why Are People Saying Such Nice Things about It?" *Storyworlds* 3 (2011), pp.1 – 24. Print. p.6.

goes on between authorized, sanctioned products and fan responses. Finally, four fan fictions are analyzed; two of which are connected to the storyworld's written instantiations, and two of which take the TV series as their starting point (all published in 2011). At focus are the ways in which the fanfic authors negotiate assignations and portrayals of good and evil and how they criticize cultural norms influencing contemporary romance, all adding new interpretations and new associations to an ever-expanding storyworld archive.

The Transmedial TVD Storyworld

TVD is designated as *transmedial* here in accordance with the simplest possible definition: the narrative is dispersed across different media forms. However, it is not a cohesive storyworld in which each instantiation contributes pieces to the overall puzzle, contains exactly the same characters, or presents identical ontologies. In Henry Jenkins's definition of an "ideal" storyworld, the Wachowski siblings' *The Matrix* trilogy is used as an example of how, in addition to "multiple media platforms [...] each new text [should make] a distinctive and valuable contribution to the whole" and how "[r]eading across media" theoretically can result in a full understanding①. The instantiations in TVD, rather than contributing to the whole, veer off in different directions. Viewers of the CW Television Network's TV series cannot turn to L. J. Smith's novels to find answers to all questions (although they can get answers to some) and vice versa.② Differences are, however, likely the result of a conscious transmedial strategy to present a story evolving in different directions rather than merely offering the TV series as an adaptation.

The transmedial strategy is also visible in encouraged early fan involvement, which illustrates a particular kind of accessibility. Kimberley McMahon-Coleman notes that fans were invited to take part in the creation of the storyworld via the website Vampire-diaries.net, which "predate[s] the existence of the actual show", and to offer commentary and suggestions via social media③. The initial posts on the website concern Smith's novels and establish that the TV series does take its inspiration from them, but it is progressively made clear that the visual text will take a slightly different route. McMahon-Coleman envisions the result as three locations, sprawling in different directions: Fell's Church (the fictional setting in the novels), Mystic Falls (the setting in the TV series), and "cyberspace [which becomes] a third and intermediated location [and which] has

① Henry Jenkins, *Convergence Culture: Where Old and New Media Collide* (New York and London: New York University Press, 2006), pp.95 - 96.

② There is a temporal lag between Smith's original novel quartet, published in 1991, and the trilogy with the series title *The Return* that roughly coincided with the airing of the first two seasons of the TV series (2009 and 2011). The TV series in October 2013 moved into its fifth season. The fan fictions analyzed later in this chapter are based on either Smith's novels or the first two seasons of the series.

③ McMahon-Coleman, Kimberley, "Mystic Falls Meets the World Wide Web: Where Is *The Vampire Diaries* Located?" *Fanpires: Audience Consumption of the Modern Vampire*, ed. Gareth Schott and Kirstine Moffat (Washington dc: New Academia Publishing, 2011), pp.169 - 186. Print. p.170.

facilitated direct conversations between writers, producers, actors and fans"[①]. The possibilities for communication and influence suggest that there was no desire on the part of the TV producers to maintain a narratively cohesive storyworld. Instead, alternative paths were imagined, encouraged, and finally realized. The creativity of many individuals thus influences the directions the narrative takes. These sometimes conflicting paths result in a number of differences between written and visual instantiations, some of which have no real bearing on the narrative itself, such as characters' names and physical appearance, and some of which are more profound, with connections to ontologies and the main characters' functions.

The novels feature a vast host of supernatural creatures and depict different fantastical realms between which the characters move, and the main protagonist, Elena, undergoes multiple transformations. At the end of *The Struggle* she drowns but, having previously ingested vampire blood, comes back as undead in the next novel, *The Fury*. This novel too ends with Elena's death as she sacrifices herself in order to kill the evil vampire Katherine, but again she makes a comeback, this time as a ghost or angelic presence. These transformations, the vampires, the other supernatural creatures, and the different realms are kept hidden from the citizens of Fell's Church, and Elena herself has to remain hidden from her immediate family (an aunt and a baby sister) since they believe she is dead. Elena provides an initial possibility for audience identification, and the use of the diary format gives the reader ample opportunity to gradually come to terms with the changing circumstances. Elena is initially unwilling to accept anything unnatural until her meeting with her soul mate, the vampire Stefan, forces her to do otherwise, but she is then progressively made "other" not only to the readers but also to her human friends. The destabilization of the initially realistic premise is furthered in *The Return* trilogy, where not only Elena is superhuman but also her hitherto human friend Meredith is revealed to be a hunter-slayer. The threats directed at the community of Fell's Church are unrelated to the main vampire characters—Stefan and his brother, Damon—and seem to amass because of specificities of the town's geographical location. Where Elena is concerned, the TV series initially represented more stability, keeping Elena human. The fourth season, however, revolves around her struggle in accepting that she has involuntarily been turned into a vampire. As in the novels, Elena is orphaned, but her guardian, Aunt Jenna, who only tenuously represents parental authority (until she is killed toward the end of the second season), is significantly younger than her novel counterpart, and baby Margaret has been replaced with a brooding and drug-abusing brother named Jeremy. The change in familial relationships means increased opportunities for romantic subplots and might be read as a strategy to attract a slightly different and slightly older audience than the novels did. Although family members and friends are

---

① McMahon-Coleman, Kimberley, "Mystic Falls Meets the World Wide Web: Where Is *The Vampire Diaries* Located?" *Fanpires: Audience Consumption of the Modern Vampire*, ed. Gareth Schott and Kirstine Moffat (Washington dc: New Academia Publishing, 2011), pp.169 – 186. Print. p.170.

for a long time kept in the dark regarding vampire activity, the community has a secret society that is aware of vampires and has quite a few gadgets to assist in their destruction. As opposed to the novels, where Damon Salvatore and Stefan Salvatore are made vampires in late fifteenth-century Italy, in the TV series they are local boys who were turned in Civil War times. They have periodically returned to Mystic Falls and are vaguely familiar to the townsfolk. In contrast to the novels, then, where Elena needs to stay hidden because the town presumes she is dead, it is the vampires who might be objects of suspicion and need to keep a low profile. The main threats of each season are in various ways connected to Elena and the Salvatore brothers rather than to geography. The antagonists in the main story lines invariably are also variations on the vampire trope, making issues of good and evil vampirism more central to the TV series than to the novels. So far, differences may seem to point at two separate storyworlds rather than one, but two central themes unite the written novels and the TV series—the romantic love between Stefan and Elena and the animosity between the Salvatore brothers. These themes underpin each major narrative event and are intertwined since Damon's advances toward Elena feed into the sibling feud. Another motif in both the novels and the show is the question of what constitutes evil where vampires are concerned, and Damon, the initially evil vampire, becomes progressively more humanized and vulnerable as the motif is woven with the romantic theme. The romantic love, the sibling rivalry, and the questions about good and evil are also chief aspects in TVD fanfic, thus working toward the argument that despite differences, TVD can be conceived of as one (albeit not cohesive) storyworld.

Interactivity and Archontic Texts

Interactivity is a key term in many discussions about digital or "new" media, but the written novels and the TV series cannot always be equated with the types of storyworlds that are most often mentioned—that is, interactive fictions, databases, games, and hypertexts—as they do not respond to physical interaction. Both text forms, however, elicit interactive responses from fans. In a discussion about television fandom, Sara Gwenllian Jones notes that "[t]he television text itself [...] has no facility for material intervention [however] the fiction that it generates, and which vastly exceeds containment by any discrete text, is a different matter"①. Fan fiction, as one expression, illustrates the authors' desire to interact with the canon texts, and it is not the material affordances of the medium that enable interaction but the excess of meaning. As Gwenllian Jones puts it: "Interactivity here occurs not as a material process involving physical interventions but as an imaginative one"②. However, fan fiction can still be seen in relation to more overarching discussions

① Sara Gwenllian Jones, "Web Wars: Resistance, Online Fandom and Studio Censorship, " *Quality Popular Television*, ed. Mark Jancovich and James Lyons (London: British Film Institute, 2003), pp.163 - 177. Print. p.167.

② Ibid., pp.163 - 177. Print. p.167.

about interactivity—for example, as in Marie-Laure Ryan's refinement of the concept. She makes two main distinctions, which are divided into dichotomous pairs: "internal versus external involvement and exploratory versus ontological involvement"[①]. The ontological aspect of the second binary is of particular relevance to fan fiction. Ryan maintains that in this kind of involvement "the decisions of the user send the history of the virtual world on different forking paths. These decisions are ontological in the sense that they determine which possible world, and consequently which story, will develop from the situation in which the choice presents itself"[②].

The fanfic category AU (Alternate Universe) represents these kinds of ontological alterations as au fanfics answer the "What If?" question (see also chapter 11, Mittell's contribution in this volume). The canon texts in the storyworld do not provide links to possible other worlds in any manifest way, but gaps and discrepancies do. Situations that are not explored fully, characters who are not developed, and tensions that are unsatisfactorily resolved provide the fanfic author with possibilities to take the story imaginatively in another direction and subtly or profoundly destabilize the ontology of the storyworld.

Say that a fanfic author asks, what if Elena was never attracted to Stefan in the first place? The love story between Elena and Stefan guides virtually every plot and character development in TVD, and upsetting or canceling it would radically change the storyworld's ontology. The question may stem from the fanfic author's sense that the characters' attraction to each other is not sufficiently explained in the canon, leaving an imaginative gap.It may be based on the author's detection of a discrepancy: a century-old vampire and a seventeen-year-old girl are incompatible on several levels. It may simply come from the author's individual opinion that Elena would be better off paired with someone else. The resulting hypothetical fanfic in which Elena meets Stefan, says thanks but no thanks, resumes the relationship with her high school sweetheart, Matt, and has no further run-ins with vampires and other supernatural creatures would contribute new associations and create a new possible world.

Fan fiction, and then particularly the category AU, thus shares traits with forms of interactivity in which clicking on a particular link or choosing a specific pathway evidence material media affordances. Lisbeth Klastrup and Susana Tosca identify three core features of the interactive transmedial storyworld: *mythos*, *topos*, and *ethos*. Put simply, the terms signify, respectively, the backstory, or "the central knowledge one needs to have in order *to interact with or interpret events in the world* accordingly"; the setting and with it "knowing *what is to be expected from the physics and navigation in the world*"; and the ethics of the storyworld, or "the knowledge required in order

① Ryan, Marie-Laure, "Will New Media Produce New Narratives?" *Narrative across Media: The Languages of Storytelling*, ed. Marie-Laure Ryan (Lincoln and London: University of Nebraska Press, 2004), pp.337 - 359. Print. p.339.

② Ibid.

to know *how to behave* in the world"[①]. "Interaction" "navigation" and "behavior" are all terms that draw attention both to active, physical choices made when transversing the storyworld and to the fact that the interface has to allow these choices to be made and have consequences.

In a discussion about fan activity in the Xenaverse, Gwenllian Jones lists "'stages' of knowledge and interpretation" that in various ways coincide with Klastrup and Tosca's terms but also allow for a focus on less material interactions[②]. Sharing affinities with mythos, "Background Hard Data" signifies the "'facts' about [Xena's] background, family, relationships and experiences" emerging through the extended diegesis of the show, whereas "Real-Time Hard Data" is constituted by the accumulation of information in each episode[③]. A certain amount of fidelity to the canon's hard data is necessary in fan fiction as readers of the story otherwise would not know how to interpret it. In TVD, as indicated, the differences between instantiations means that the author needs to specify what mythos, or hard data, he or she has in mind. The easiest way to signal this data is to file the fanfic according to the instantiation on which it is based.[④] In stories relying on real-time data, and then particularly in those connected to the TV series, it is common for fanfic authors to specify precisely where in the narrative arc the stories are placed (e.g. "set after 1.14").

Gwenllian Jones's next stage is "Competencies", which "determine [the characters'] range of possible actions and reactions"[⑤]. Competencies are based on individual characters' "personalities", or their weaknesses and strengths; and to depict actions and reactions too far removed from what is plausible, given the canon competencies, may result in fan fiction with Out of Character (OOC) characters.[⑥]"Themes and Motifs," Gwenllian Jones further claims, "extend far beyond the limits of the diegesis; they are reiterated and explored" in different forms of fan expressions[⑦]. In the case of TVD, the central romance is an example of such a theme, which is visible in stories about characters who are not romantically linked in the canon, and the good versus evil motif is similarly reiterated in ways that move beyond events in the canon and put a different spin on things.

"Behaviour, Ethics, and Psychology" also have strong affinities with Klastrup and Tosca's ethos, and "[i]t is in this area," Gwenllian Jones maintains, "that fan engagement and speculation is at its most intense"[⑧]. The psychological gaps in the diegetic story can be filled in fanfics that

---

① Lisbeth Klastrup and Susana Tosca, "Transmedial Worlds—Rethinking Cyberworld Design," *Proceedings of the 2004 International Conference on Cyberworlds* (Los Alamitos ca: ieeee Computer Society, 2004).

② Sara Gwenllian Jones, "Starring Lucy Lawless?" *Continuum: Journal of Media & Cultural Studies* 14.1 (2000), pp.9 - 22. Print. p.17.

③ Ibid., p.18.

④ The stories analyzed here are taken from sites that provide the fanfic author with the option of filing either under TVD the book series or TVD the show.

⑤ Sara Gwenllian Jones, "Starring Lucy Lawless?" p.18.

⑥ It should be noted that the creation of an OOC character may at times be a fanfic author's expressed desire. This type of character may, however, give rise to deriding comments from readers who do not wish to see a removal too far from canon behavior.

⑦ Sara Gwenllian Jones, "Starring Lucy Lawless?" p.18.

⑧ Ibid.

develop the perspective of minor characters or offer alternative readings of major characters. Fanfic authors may also profoundly destabilize the storyworld's ethics by removing aspects that are arguably essential to the very ontology. Fanfics based on vampire storyworlds and categorized as "All Human" or "AU-human" do away with the vampire element altogether and are examples of such destabilization. The pre-formed knowledge of how characters (and readers) are to react to and imaginatively behave in this type of story is canceled along with the supernatural element.①

The final item of Gwenllian Jones's list is "Erotics"②. Whereas the storyworld at the center of her analysis consciously plays with the characters' sexual identities and desires, TVD is fairly heteronormative. However, fan responses to the erotics of a storyworld can take a number of forms, and the fanfic category "slash", denoting a same-sex pairing between characters who are not a couple in the canon, is by no means nonexistent because of the lack of homoeroticism in the storyworld.

In contemporary popular culture where storyworlds are not confined to isolated media and where audiences are asked to participate in the meaning-making process, interaction thus occurs on both literal and figurative levels. When regarding fan fiction as one form of interaction, it is profitable to see the storyworld comprising not only sanctioned instantiations but also the fans' interpretations. Abigail Derecho's suggestion is to designate this type of text world as "archontic literature", and she argues that the "archontic text's archive is not identical to the text but is a virtual construct surrounding the text, including it and all the texts related to it"③. Thus each addition to the archive influences it and supplies new associations and interpretations that subsequent authors then can be inspired by or relate to. To view a storyworld along these archontic lines can be liberating because fan-deposited material is put on par with sanctioned products rather than being regarded in terms of lineage and derivation.

The excess of meaning concomitant with complex transmedial storyworlds illustrates the creators' "encyclopedic ambitions"④ but also triggers an encyclopedic drive in fans. As Jenkins notes: "None of us can know everything; each of us knows something; and we can put the pieces together if we pool our resources and combine our skills"⑤. Derecho notes a similar drive, but in line with her aim to equalize creators and fans, she ascribes it to the archive itself: the "drive within an archive that seeks to produce more archive, to enlarge itself"⑥. When viewed as a site of

---

① All Human or AU-human fanfics have not yet gained popularity in the TVD storyworld, but as an example from another fandom, the *Twilight*-specific website Twilighted.net has a filing option labeled "AU-human", containing, at present, close to twenty-seven hundred fanfics, more than in any other section at the site (see "Categories").

② Sara Gwenllian Jones, "Starring Lucy Lawless?" p.19.

③ Abigail Derecho, "Archontic Literature: A Definition, a History, and Several Theories of Fan Fiction," *Fan Fiction and Fan Communities in the Age of the Internet*, ed. Karen Hellekson and Kristina Busse (Jefferson nc: McFarland, 2006), pp.61 - 78. Print. p.65.

④ Henry Jenkins, "Transmedia Storytelling 101," *Confessions of an Aca- Fan* (March 22, 2007).

⑤ Henry Jenkins, *Convergence Culture: Where Old and New Media Collide*, p.4.

⑥ Abigail Derecho, "Archontic Literature: A Definition, a History, and Several Theories of Fan Fiction," p.64.

interaction, then, each fanfic story deposited in the TVD archontic text enlarges it by suggesting slight or profound differences.

三、思考与讨论

（1）不同媒介对于故事改编的选择是否与其受众群体类型有关？

（2）跨媒介叙事故事世界的不稳定性主要来自哪几个因素？

（3）文中 Klastrup & Tosca 和 Gwenllian Jones 对跨媒介故事世界的要素做出的分类有何不足之处？

第四节　让-诺埃尔·托恩及其《作为跨媒介概念的主体性》

一、导读

让-诺埃尔·托恩是挪威科技大学媒体研究方向的教授，主要从事跨媒介叙事研究、电子游戏跨学科研究等，是跨媒介叙事学界的新秀。托恩曾出版《跨媒介叙事与当代媒介文化》(*Transmedial Narratology and Contemporary Media Culture*)、《漫画与游戏：从混合媒介到跨媒介扩张》(*Comics and Videogames: From Hybrid Medialities to Transmedia Expansions*)、《跨媒介的故事世界：建构媒介意识的叙事学》等著作，并为《今日诗学》等多部权威刊物主持跨媒介叙事相关特刊。其代表著作《跨媒介叙事与当代媒介文化》从叙事表现、叙述者、主体性三方面介绍了跨媒介叙事的表现策略及其在特定媒介的应用。

本节选文来自"主体性"部分，较为系统地梳理了跨媒介叙事学中"视角""观点""聚焦"三个基本概念在当下的新内涵，对各种媒体研究者定义这些概念的精准度、通用性等方面进行评价。托恩对跨媒介叙事中概念框架与定义的革新持开放态度，乐于接受各类媒介研究者对"聚焦"等概念的重新定义。选文涉及若干当代理论家与查特曼、热奈特、巴尔等经典理论家的理论对话，体现了跨媒介叙事学对经典叙事学成果的继承和发展，同时又包括不同类型的媒介所创立的各种新的主体性叙事概念间的平行对比以及同一类媒介的不同理论观点的对比，提供了一个全面、广阔的视角来看待跨媒介叙事理论的碰撞冲突，为托恩在后续章节提出他自己关于主体性表现的概念做了充分的理论铺垫。

托恩基本按照电影、漫画、电子游戏几个媒介类别来归纳研究理论。他首先列举了若干继承热奈特"聚焦"概念并在电影类媒介加以发展的理论。比如：普适性较高的爱德华·布兰尼根的"聚焦"概念基于视听媒介的主观性与客观性之分，发展出"无聚焦""外聚焦""内聚焦"的分类；弗朗索瓦·约斯特(Francois Jost)将聚焦细分为"(认知性)聚焦""目击""聆听"，每一分支又有内部、外部、无聚焦等细分，但其理论普适性稍为逊色，对于电影的多重聚焦等案例无法完全覆盖。随后，托恩分析了马丁·舒沃(Martin Schüwer)、西尔克·霍斯托克(Silke Horstkotte)、凯伊·米科南(Kai Mikkonen)等研究漫画和绘本小说的理论家关于聚焦和视角的创新性理论框架，如：舒沃把漫画分为文字和视觉两部分来讨论聚焦，凸显了漫画媒介的独特性；霍斯托克和南希·佩德里(Nancy Pedri)继承了巴尔概念里的聚焦主体与聚焦客体概念；米科南又与之背道而驰，直接忽略了叙事性与非叙事性聚焦的区别。最后，文中也列举了几种在电子游戏研究中有影响力的聚焦理论，如布雷塔·奈泽(Britta Neitzel)依据游戏的交互性提出的"上帝之眼""半主观观点""主观观点"等系列观点。托恩的梳理较为客观地总结了这些理论家的贡献，也指出了各自理论的局限性，并再次强调了跨媒介叙事学的复杂性特征。各种媒介对人物主观性的表现策略的巨大差异甚至不能在一个体系内共同讨论，这也从侧面体现了当代叙事学在术语和理论建设上实际面临的一大"困境"。

二、《作为跨媒介概念的主体性》选读[①]

Among the countless attempts to apply either Genette's or Bal's conceptualization of "focalization" to narrative representations beyond the literary text, Edward Branigan's modification of the term in the context of a considerably more extensive examination of audiovisual subjectivity (and objectivity) seems to be the most relevant for the purpose of this chapter.[②] Among other things, this is due to Branigan's emphasis on the analysis of local segments of narrative representation with regard to their relation to characters' consciousnesses. Branigan distinguishes between "nonfocalized" representation, where the "way we learn about characters is through their actions and speech in much the same way that characters learn from each other"[③]; "external focalization" that "represents a measure of character awareness but from outside the character"; and "internal focalization" that "is more fully private and subjective than external focalization", ranging "from [the representation of] simple perception (e.g. the point-of-view shot), to impressions (e.g. the out-of-focus point-of-view shot depicting a character who is drunk, dizzy, or drugged), to 'deeper thoughts' (eg. dreams, hallucinations, and memories)"[④]. My attempt to sharpen Branigan's definition of "nonfocalized" representation in order to distinguish it more clearly from "external focalization" will lead me to propose a somewhat different distinction between objective, intersubjective, and subjective modes of representation, but my examination of transmedial strategies of subjective representation remains highly indebted to Branigan's discussion of "focalization" in *Narrative Comprehension and Film* as well as to his earlier study, *Point of View in the Cinema*. Before I can develop further my own conceptualization of the representation of subjectivity and of strategies of subjective representation, though, it will be helpful to mention a few additional attempts to transfer either Genette's or Bal's conceptualization of "focalization" to films, comics, and video games, which tend to be as conceptually interesting as they are terminologically problematic.

Another influential attempt to transfer Genette's concept of "focalization" to film has been made by François Jost, who—not entirely dissimilar to the postulation of various nonrepresented "narrating instances" responsible for different aspects of film's audiovisual representation already

① Jan-Noël Thon, *Transmedial Narratology and Contemporary Media Culture* (Lincoln and London: University of Nebraska Press, 2016), pp.228 - 237.

② See Branigan, *Narrative Comprehension* 100 - 107. Other contributions on "focalization" in film include, e.g. Deleyto; Jost, "The Look"; *L'oeilcaméra*; "Le regard romanesque"; Kuhn 119 - 194; Schlickers, *Verfilmtes Erzählen* 127 - 167; "Focalization"; Schweinitz, "Die Ambivalenz"; "Multiple Logik". See also, e.g. Horstkotte and Pedri; Kukkonen, "Comics"; Mikkonen, "Focalization"; "Graphic Narratives"; "Subjectivity"; Round; Schüwer 392 - 404 on "focalization" in comics and, e.g. Arjoranta; Beil 37 - 39; Eskelinen, *Cybertext Poetics* 170 - 179; Neitzel, "Point of View"; Nitsche 145 - 155 on "focalization" in video games.

③ Edward Branigan, *Narrative Comprehension and Film* (Abingdon: Routledge, 1992). Print. p.100.

④ Ibid., p.103.

tackled in chapter 4—uses the observation that terms such as "point of view" and "focalization" tend to refer to, "on the one hand, perceiving, and on the other hand, thinking and knowing"[①] as a starting point to distinguish between "focalization" "ocularization" and "auricularization". While "*focalization* designates the cognitive point of view adopted by the narrative, with the equalities or inequalities of knowledge expressed at their full strength"[②], "ocularization" and "auricularization" describe the relation between what the film makes visible or audible and what its characters see or hear, respectively. Jost further distinguishes between "primary internal ocularization/auricularization", where changes in the quality of the film's picture or sound mark that it represents the visual or auditive perception of a character, "secondary internal ocularization/auricularization", where such a representation is marked by the context of the picture or sound in question, and "zero ocularization/auricularization", where the picture or sound are not attributed to the visual or auditive perception of any specific character. Jost's terminological choices may not be entirely convincing, yet his emphasis on the "disconnect" between how film's audiovisual representation relates to the represented characters' perceptions and how it relates to their knowledge is certainly helpful—though, once more, not all film narratologists would agree.[③] Primarily building on Bal's rather than Genette's concept of "focalization", Celestino Deleyto, for example, argues that Jost's "focalization" and "ocularization" actually "designate much the same thing"[④], before he insists that "in film ... there can appear, simultaneously, several focalisers, external and internal, on different points of the frame (and outside)"[⑤]. While Deleyto's approach to "focalization" has been fairly influential as well, its reductionist foundation leads him to postulate, rather unconvincingly, "the almost permanent existence of an external focaliser in a film narrative" that allegedly "accounts for the general tendency of the medium towards narrative objectivity"[⑥]. Whether one calls it "ocularization/auricularization" or not, what Deleyto refers to here is not the whole range of meanings commonly associated with "focalization".

Now, while the representation of subjectivity is perhaps most extensively discussed in literary and film narratology, there have been quite a few attempts to transfer the terms "perspective" and "point of view" as well as the term "focalization" to comics and to video games—albeit with varying results. Even though they are not adding too many genuinely new aspects to the discussion, some of the attempts to apply the term "focalization" to comics at least serve to emphasize the importance of

---

① François Jost, "The Look: From Film to Novel: An Essay in Comparative Narratology," *A Companion to Literature and Film*, ed. Robert Stam and Alessandra Raengo (Malden: Blackwell, 2004), pp.71 – 80. Print. p.72.

② Ibid., p.74, original emphasis.

③ Jost's distinction between "ocularization" "auricularization" and "focalization" has become a rather common point of reference in recent German film narratology, at least. See, e.g. Kuhn 119 – 194; Orth; Schlickers, *Verfilmtes Erzählen* 127 – 167; "Focalization"; Schweinitz, "Die Ambivalenz"; "Multiple Logik".

④ Celestino Deleyto, "Focalisation in Film Narrative," *Narratology: An Introduction*, ed. Susana Onega and José á. García Landa (London: Longman, 1996), pp.217 – 233. Print. p.222.

⑤ Ibid., p.223.

⑥ Ibid., p.222.

distinguishing between narratorial and nonnarratorial forms of "focalization" and/or strategies of subjective representation, a distinction that tends to be less pronounced in the more influential accounts of "focalization" within film narratology: Martin Schüwer, for example, may use somewhat problematic terms when he proposes to distinguish between the "verbal parts" and the "visual parts" of a comic, but his insistence that an analysis of comics' "focalization" needs to ask not only "from whose perspective are perceptions/thoughts/feelings *shown*" but also "from whose perspective are perceptions/thoughts/feelings *told* "① seems laudable. Despite the admirable detail in which Schüwer's study examines some of comics' medium-specific strategies of narrative representation, though, his discussion of "internal" and "external focalization" ultimately remains fairly brief and refrains from engaging the question of how narratorial forms of "focalization" are realized in comics. Instead, he focuses primarily on the ways in which nonnarratorial point-of-view panels and thought bubbles may or may not be used to subjectively represent a character's consciousness and how, even in the absence of these "strong" forms of "internal focalization", other strategies may also more indirectly contribute to the representation of characters' consciousnesses. Indeed, the way that the term "focalization" is used may become even less technical in some areas of comics studies, when, for example, Karin Kukkonen claims that the "oriental architecture" in some of the page margins in Bill Willingham's *Fables: Arabian Nights (and Days)* "tells us that this part of the story is told from the Oriental fairy tale characters' perspective" and, thus, "visually represents an act or process of focalization"②.

More recently, though, Silke Horstkotte and Nancy Pedri have proposed a comics-specific approach to "focalization" that emphasizes precisely those parts of the term's conceptual history that aim at the function(s) of the narrator: building on Mieke Bal and Shlomith Rimmon-Kenan rather than on Gérard Genette, they stress that "optical perspectivation is only one dimension within a broader category of focalization that also includes aspects of cognition, ideological orientation, and judgment"③, all of which have "to be signaled by distinctly subjective discourse markers in all texts, including visual and multimodal ones"④. Perhaps even more important than their insistence on the multidimensional or "multiaspectual" nature of "focalization" is Horstkotte and Pedri's proposal to "operate with a binary typology of focalization that sets off the subjective inflection of *character-bound focalization* against a more neutral *narratorial* one"⑤. It should be noted, however, that their argument "for preserving focalization as a central category of narratological analysis, rather than erasing it in favor of a broader consideration of consciousness presentation in fiction"⑥, results in a

---

① Martin Schüwer. *Wie Comics erzählen: Grundriss einer intermedialen Erzähltheorie der grafischen Literatur* (Trier: Wissenschaftlicher Verlag Trier, 2008). Print. p.392, my emphases, my translation from the German.

② Karin Kukkonen, "Comics as a Test Case for Transmedial Narratology," *SubStance* 40.1 (2011), pp.34 - 51. Print. p.48.

③ Silke Horstkotte and Nancy Pedri, "Focalization in Graphic Narrative," *Narrative* 19.3 (2011), pp.330 - 357. Print. p.331.

④ Ibid., p.334.

⑤ Ibid., p.335, original emphases.

⑥ Ibid., p.335.

conceptualization of "focalization" that is strikingly different from, say, the conceptualization developed by Schüwer in that it focuses on Bal's "focalizing subject" as opposed to her "focalized object", defining the term with regard to the "filter function" of represented consciousnesses instead of the question to what extent a narrative representation represents those consciousnesses as its "content". That this is only one of many potential conceptualizations of "focalization" may be further illustrated by a brief look at the recent work of yet another prolific comics narratologist, Kai Mikkonen, who, in "operating with a consciously limited notion of focalisation, restricted to questions of access to perception in strict sensory bounds", not only confines the concept to "the information the narrative conveys about the spatial and physical point of observation, and the sensory range of that position"[①], but also largely ignores the distinction between "focalizing subject" and "focalized object" as well as the distinction between narratorial and nonnarratorial forms of "focalization" (even though Mikkonen explicitly mentions Genette's and Bal's accounts of "focalization" and, moreover, also provides a brief nod to Horstkotte and Pedri's conceptualization of the term).

It might be worth noting at this point that my remarks on previous conceptualizations of "focalization" are not meant as an overly harsh critique of any specific approach. Instead, I intend the examples of film-and comics-specific accounts of "focalization" given so far to illustrate that there is no common understanding of the term in film studies and comics studies any more than in literary narratology—although most if not all of the existing approaches to "focalization" in literary texts, films, and comics will have something relevant to say about transmedial aspects of strategies that aim at the representation of subjectivity, their medium-specific realization, or both.[②] Still, despite the fact that the specifically narratological term "focalization" seems to suggest a certain technical quality rather more strongly than the comparatively general terms "perspective" and "point of view", the lack of consensus regarding the concepts that the term in question should be used to refer to is similarly glaring in all three cases. While the various attempts to transfer terms such as "point of view" "perspective" or "focalization" to films and comics may help us to better understand some of the medium-specific as well as transmedial aspects of strategies of subjective representation, then, they also illustrate the terminological dilemma into which contemporary narratology has maneuvered itself, and which might ultimately indicate a comparatively radical terminological solution. Incidentally, both of these observations are even more relevant with regard to studies that examine "point of view" "perspective" and/or "focalization" in video games: at least some of these studies may propose fruitful modifications and expansions of established approaches to the representation of subjectivity from literary and film narratology, in particular, but even in those

---

① Horstkotte and Pedri, "Focalization in Graphic Narrative," p.72.

② See also the recently published study by Ciccoricco for a transmedial approach to the representation of minds in narrative media that focuses on novels, interactive fiction, and video games. For further discussions of interactive fiction, see also Aarseth, *Cybertext*; Bell; Montfort.

cases, a keen awareness of video games' medium-specific limitations and affordances tends to be combined with a certain terminological "sloppiness" that further adds to the already existing confusion surrounding terms such as "perspective" "point of view" and "focalization".

A comparatively early but still paradigmatic example is Britta Neitzel's influential discussion of three types of representational rules that are commonly used in contemporary video games: the "objective point of view", which is sometimes also called a "god's eye perspective", can be found in games where the spatial position from which the game spaces are represented is not connected to the spatial position of a character or other entity within these game spaces; the "semisubjective point of view", which is also called "third-person perspective", can be found in games where the spatial position from which the game spaces are represented is connected to the spatial position of a character or other entity within these game spaces, but does not coincide with that position; and the "subjective point of view", which is also called "first-person perspective", can be found in games where the spatial position from which the game spaces are represented coincides with the spatial position of a character or other entity within these game spaces.① However, Neitzel not only uses the terms "perspective" and "point of view", somewhat interchangeably, but also relates the three types of "point of view" she distinguishes to Gérard Genette's three types of "focalization", arguing that an "objective point of view" can be understood as a form of "zero focalization", a "semi-subjective point of view" can be understood as a form of "internal focalization", and a "subjective point of view" can be understood as a form of "external focalization" (since the latter does not, or at least not fully, represent the body of the playercontrolled character). At the very least, the connections that Neitzel draws here are highly unconventional, with related approaches from film and comics studies usually conceptualizing the medium-specific counterparts of the "semi-subjective point of view" as a form of "external focalization" and those of the "subjective point of view" as a form of "internal focalization" (or "external ocularization" and "internal ocularization", respectively, in those approaches that follow François Jost).

While I do not agree with what I consider an inappropriate short circuit of the terms "perspective" "point of view" and "focalization", then, it should be emphasized that the three forms of "point of view" that Neitzel distinguishes are, indeed, well suited for the analysis of most if not all contemporary video games. Yet, more importantly, what allows Neitzel's approach to remain relevant to the present day is her insistence that the interactivity of video games necessitates distinguishing not only between different forms of "point of view" as the spatial position from which the game spaces are represented but also between different forms of "point of action" as the actional position from which the player may interact with these game spaces. Accordingly, Neitzel's

---

① See Neitzel, "Point of View"; as well as Neitzel, "Gespielte Geschichten"; "Narrativity". See also Thon, "Perspective", where I expand on the notion of "spatial point of view/perspective" by also examining "actional point of view/perspective" and "ideological point of view/perspective".

approach to "point of view/point of action" has modified and expanded rather significantly any concept of "point of view" (or "perspective", or "focalization") that could have been developed with literary texts, films, or comics in mind. I will not further discuss Neitzel's conceptualization of video games' "point of action" here,[①] but I would still like to stress that this kind of medium-specific modification and expansion of existing conceptualizations of "perspective" "point of view" and "focalization" is still surprisingly uncommon in the field of game studies. In *Video Game Spaces*, for example, Michael Nitsche largely limits himself to illustrating the fairly general claim that the complexity of contemporary video games allows them to use and combine "the character-bound focalizer and the external focalizer"[②], which he seems to model largely following Mieke Bal. Another example of terminological "sloppiness" would be Jonne Arjoranta's more recent account of "focalization" in video games, which manages to nonchalantly claim (without much explanation) that "games have the usual focalizations (zero, external, internal)"[③], yet also mentions that Genette supposedly "calls these perspective" and "classifies perspective into three categories: zero focalization, external focalization and internal focalization", even though "focalization is the point of view things are seen from"[④].

Instead of discussing those or other similarly problematic attempts to conceptualize "focalization" in video games as largely similar to "focalization" in literary texts and films, let me conclude this interlude on (more or less) medium-specific conceptualizations of "focalization" by mentioning a more recent study of the representation of subjectivity in films and video games by Benjamin Beil. Despite the title of his book, *First Person Perspectives*, Beil proposes to use none of the three "popular" narratological terms "perspective" "point of view" or "focalization", instead building on Edward Branigan and Seymour Chatman in his examination of "character-centered filters" "distributed filters" "the subjective" and the "interest focus" as prototypical "strategies of subjectivization". Once more, neither Beil's terminological decisions nor his conceptual considerations appear particularly convincing (at least not if one takes it to be one of his aims to provide a systematically sound taxonomy of strategies of subjective representation in contemporary video games), but his work is nevertheless worth singling out (in a positive sense) for two reasons. On the one hand, while it may not result in the development of terminologically and conceptually convincing alternatives, Beil's decision to abandon the well-established terms "perspective" "point of view" and "focalization" remains preferable to conceptualizing these terms

---

① Once more, see also the detailed discussion of different forms of "point of action" in Thon, "Perspective", where I propose to distinguish not only between "subjective" "semi-subjective" and "objective points of view" but also between "subjective" "semi-subjective" and "objective points of action".

② Michael Nitsche, *Video Game Spaces: Image, Play, and Structure in 3d Worlds* (Cambridge ma: mit Press, 2008). Print. p.146.

③ Jonne Arjoranta, "Meaning Effects in Video Games: Focalization, Granularity and Mode of Narration in Games," *Proceedings of the Games and Literary Theory Conference 2013*, Web. (December 1, 2013), p.1.

④ Ibid., p.5.

in the ways in which, for example, Neitzel or Nitsche conceptualize them. On the other hand, and perhaps more importantly, Beil's focus on a wide variety of different examples may occasionally appear arbitrary, but it nevertheless demonstrates rather impressively that films and video games (as well as comics, for that matter) may represent characters' subjectivity using very different strategies, whose heterogeneity tends to resist any attempt at systematization. Before I further examine this relation between the universal and the particular using my previously outlined approach to describe salient prototypical strategies of narrative representation on a transmedial level as well as their medium-specific realization in contemporary films, comics, and video games, however, some further remarks on the terminological and conceptual foundation of my account of subjectivity across media appear to be in order.

三、思考与讨论

(1) 对于狭义跨媒介叙事的故事世界研究,如何解决不同媒介在理论体系上的差异?

(2) 基于传统文类的叙事学几大要素各自在跨媒介叙事中经历了何种变化?

(3) 你认为未来的跨媒介叙事学有必要建构覆盖尽量多种类型的媒介的理论吗?为什么?

本章推荐阅读书目

[1] Marie-Laure Ryan, ed. *Narrative across Media: The Languages of Storytelling*. Lincoln and London: University of Nebraska Press, 2004.

[2] Henry Jenkins. *Convergence Culture: Where Old and New Media Collide*. New York and London: New York University Press, 2006.

[3] Jørgen Bruhn. *The Intermediality of Narrative Literature: Medialities Matter*. London: Palgrave Macmillan, 2016.

[4] Matthew Freeman and Renira Rampazzo Gambarato, eds. *The Routledge Companion to Transmedia Studies*. New York: Routledge, 2019.

第六章
非自然叙事学

第一节 概　　论[①]

“非自然叙事学”(unnatural narratology)作为一个后经典叙事学派的迅速崛起是过去十多年间西方叙事学界一大引人瞩目的现象,其“发展势头迅猛”,被称为近年来叙事学领域“最突出的新发展”和“最激动人心的新范式”,并在国内外学界产生了较大影响。过去十多年来,学界对非自然叙事学的研究表现出了极大的学术兴趣,对其探讨的热度不断增强。国际知名学术期刊《文体》在 2016 年第 4 期隆重推出了关于非自然叙事学的专题讨论。杰拉德·普林斯、詹姆斯·费伦、申丹、玛丽-劳勒·瑞安等顶级叙事学家就布莱恩·理查森关于非自然叙事学的理论观点展开了激烈的学术论战。非自然叙事学在后经典叙事学整体图谱中的迅速崛起从侧面反映了它作为一个新兴叙事研究范式的生命力。

一、非自然叙事学的起源与建构

早在 20 世纪 80 年代左右,理查森就对文学作品中的反常的叙事实践有较为深入的探讨,这可以被视为非自然叙事学的起源。理查森早期的非自然叙事研究以实验性戏剧和小说为对象,他主要关注的是其中的叙事时间、叙事声音、情节进程等叙事学的基本范畴问题。通过考察这类文本在上述叙事结构方面的独特处理模式,理查森力图发现这些独特叙事模式如何挑战现有的叙事理论框架,由此提出要建构基于这类反常叙事文本的叙事理论,以对结构主义叙事学提供有效补充。

研究剧中的时间问题是理查森探讨非自然叙事实践的开端。在其早期发表的文章中,他分析了《仲夏夜之梦》《麦克白》等戏剧中的时间,指出前者“建构了两组内在连续却互不兼容的时间结构”[②],后者的故事时间则并未遵循严格的“线性发展顺序”[③]。在理查森看来,结构主义叙事理论无法对这种叙事

---

① 本节主要内容取自李亚飞、尚必武:《非自然叙事学的缘起、流变与发展态势:西方非自然叙事学研究述评》,载《解放军外国语学院学报》2020 年第 1 期,第 77—84 页。

② Brian Richardson,“‘Time is Out of Joint’: Narrative Models and the Temporality of the Drama,” *Poetics Today* 8.2(1987), p.299.

③ Brian Richardson, “Hours Dreadful and Things Strange: Inversions of Chronology and Causality in Macbeth,” *Philological Quarterly* 68.3(1989), p.284.

时间做出合理解释，其有效性受到了挑战。虚构作品中的非自然叙述声音是理查森早期研究的另一个重点。在其2006年出版的专著《非自然的声音：现当代小说的极端叙述》中，理查森进一步系统地研究了后现代小说中的叙述策略。他以果戈理、康拉德、贝克特等人的小说为对象，借鉴后现代主义理论的思想资源，对小说中的第二人称叙述、第一人称复数叙述、多人称叙述、极端化叙述、戏剧中的非自然叙述等反常规叙述形式作了精辟的原创性理论分析。理查森的早期研究除了考察反模仿的叙事时间和叙述声音外，还涉及对其中的情节进程的探讨。在“超越情节诗学”一文中，理查森以《尤利西斯》《海浪》等20世纪的叙事文本中的碎片化叙事和开放式结尾为例，有力论证了现代主义作品中的反常叙述如何抵制、违背或拒绝传统的情节模式。在他看来，传统情节理论对故事发展模式有过分简化的嫌疑，叙事的情节模式在他看来其实要复杂得多。他由此提出：“对于情节的理论研究应该涵盖逻辑上更多的叙事类别”，因为“这类广泛的框架有利于我们对历史上的叙事小说的展开方式做出更为全面的描述。”[①]

理查森早期就反模仿叙事中的反常的叙事时间、声音和情节进行了深入分析，其目的是指出传统结构主义叙事理论存在的缺陷，以此呼吁叙事理论研究关注反模仿叙事文本。不过，他在这一阶段并未对相关理论概念做出准确界定，也没有提出系统研究反模仿叙事的方法，因此更没能建构“非自然叙事学”。但不可否认，他的早期研究为后来非自然叙事学的建构做了充分准备，打下了一定的基础，为非自然叙事学的兴起和发展提供了丰润的滋养力。

进入21世纪后，西方非自然叙事学迎来发展热潮，呈现出较为繁荣的发展局面。这一时期，更多的叙事研究学者加入非自然叙事研究的阵营当中，这从根本上改善了早期理查森孤军奋战的局面。其中值得一提的是德国叙事学家扬·阿尔贝，虽然他从事非自然叙事研究的时间晚于理查森，但他具有建构“非自然叙事学”的强烈意识。2009年，阿尔贝在发表的《不可能的故事世界——以及怎么理解它们》(“Impossible Storyworlds—and What to Do with Them”)一文中，不仅率先定义了“非自然”这一概念，还提出了理解非自然叙事的阐释策略。可以说，这篇文章开启了建构非自然叙事学的新篇章。

如果说阿尔贝的文章只是建构非自然叙事学的开端，那么由阿尔贝、斯特凡·伊韦尔森、亨里克·斯克夫·尼尔森、理查森四人在2010年联合发表的文章《非自然叙事，非自然叙事学：超越模仿模型》则标志着非自然叙事学的历史出场。文章不但明确界定了“非自然”这一概念，还正式指出了“非自然叙事学”的研究目标，并系统论述了“非自然叙事学”与结构主义叙事学和标准的认知叙事理论之间的差异。为了有效论证非自然叙事学这一范式的创新之处，文章借助《保姆》《饥饿》《泄密的心》等非自然叙事文本，从非自然故事世界、非自然心理、非自然叙述行为三个方面作了具有说服力的案例分析。

自2010年起，在众多非自然叙事学研究者的推动下，非自然叙事学不仅在当代西方后经典叙事学研究的整体版图中强势崛起，还借助女性主义、认知叙事学等其他理论视角，通过寻求不同领域之间的交叉和对话，取得了突破性进展。这一时期，一系列关于非自然叙事学研究的编著、专著和文章大量涌现，如《非自然叙事，非自然叙事学》《非自然叙事诗学》《非自然叙事：理论、历史与实践》《非自然叙事：小说与戏剧中的不可能世界》《非自然叙事学：扩展、修正与挑战》等。另外，各大期刊也纷纷开辟关于非自然叙事研究的专栏，包括《故事世界：叙事研究学刊》(*Storyworlds: A Journal of Narrative*

① Brian Richardson, “Beyond the Poetics of Plot: Alternative Forms of Narrative Progression and the Multiple Trajectories of Ulysses,” *A Companion to Narrative Theory*, eds. James Phelan and Peter J. Rabinowitz (Oxford: Blackwell, 2005), pp.177 - 178.

Studies)的专栏"女性主义小说与非自然叙事理论"(2016 年第 2 期)、《叙事研究前沿》(*Frontiers of Narrative Studies*)的专栏"非自然叙事：理论与实践"(2018 年第 1 期)、《今日诗学》(*Poetics Today*)的专栏"叙事的非自然与认知视角(一个交叉理论)"(2018 年第 3 期)等。

可以看出，非自然叙事学在这一阶段取得了颇为突出的发展成绩。这类专著、编著和文章的集中出版不仅推动了非自然叙事学的建构和蓬勃发展，还确定了非自然叙事学在后经典叙事学研究谱系中的重要地位。非自然叙事学之所以能够蓬勃兴起并取得跨越式的发展，主要有如下几个方面的原因：① 非自然叙事学研究的出发点是反对现有叙事理论的模仿偏见、为广泛存在但长期被忽略的边缘叙事实践提供解释模式，这在观念上迎合了西方人文社会科学界流行的后结构主义式的"解构"和"增补"潮流。② 从非自然叙事学的研究路径和方法来看，非自然叙事学家具有明显的跨领域对话意识，在推进非自然叙事学发展的过程中，他们尝试通过寻求与女性主义理论、认知叙事学等其他研究视角和方法的交叉和互补来修正、完善、拓展其自身的理论建构。③ 非自然叙事学注重考察叙事的形式结构和叙事意义之间的关联性，坚持叙事形式研究与叙事意义研究的结合，这一点和女性主义叙事学研究范式颇有相似之处。非自然叙事学研究中的一个重要方向就是考察反模仿叙事策略与意识形态和文化政治之间的关联性，即非自然叙事中的非自然化文本处理方式如何表达特定的文化和意识形态内涵，这一方面顺应了叙事研究关注历史文化语境的潮流，进而使其获得更广泛的关注；另一方面也拓宽了非自然叙事学的研究范畴，有利于它实现诗学建构和文本阐释并行发展的研究路径。

二、非自然叙事学的发展与流变

非自然叙事学并不是一个统一的叙事研究范式，不同的非自然叙事学家之间在非自然叙事学的基本理论假设、研究方法、研究目标等具体内容方面存在一定的差异。总体来看，非自然叙事学可以被划分为两大阵营：一是以理查森和尼尔森为代表的倾向于研究非自然叙事"内部本质"的阵营，二是以阿尔贝为代表的强调非自然叙事"外部阐释"的阵营。[①] 就"内部本质"阵营而言，他们试图对非自然叙事作本体论的探讨，将非自然叙事视为一种与模仿叙事具有同等地位的叙事类型并将其理论化。相较于"内部本质"阵营，阿尔贝等"外部阐释"阵营更看重对非自然叙事的阐释和解读。阿尔贝认为，"不管某一叙事的文本结构有多奇特，它仍然是带有某种意图的交流行为的一部分"。[②] 他感兴趣的是阐释和理解非自然叙事，非自然叙事研究的根本任务就是去发现非自然叙事的认知功能和其中所蕴含的意义，要"让奇怪的叙事更加具有可读性"。[③] 具体来看，非自然叙事学研究者内部的差异主要体现在什么是非自然叙事，以及怎样研究非自然叙事这两个基本问题上。

先看何为非自然叙事。关于这一问题，西方非自然叙事学界存在两种不同的界定模式：① 理查森的反模仿模式；② 阿尔贝的不可能的故事世界模式。在理查森的理论框架中，非自然叙事等同于反模仿叙事。他将模仿叙事界定为"那些效仿非虚构叙事，或者与非虚构叙事极为相似的虚构作品"，它们试

① Brian Richardson, *Unnatural Narrative: Theory, History, and Practice* (Columbus: The Ohio State University Press, 2015), p.19.

② Jan Alber, "Impossible Storyworlds—and What to Do with Them," *Storyworlds: A Journal of Narrative Studies* 1.1(2009), p.82.

③ Ibid., p.81.

图以可辨认的方式去系统描述我们的经验世界。[1] 与之相对，非自然叙事则指"包含反模仿事件、人物、场景或叙述行为的叙事"，它们不但"违反非虚构叙事的预设、现实主义的实践，或其他建立在非虚构叙事基础之上的诗学"，还"超越了现存的文类规约"。[2] 一言以蔽之，对于理查森而言，非自然叙事必须违背模仿的规约。如果说理查森关于非自然叙事的定义的核心是"反模仿性"，那么阿尔贝关于非自然叙事的定义的核心便是"不可能性"。对于阿尔贝而言，非自然叙事是指那些"在物理上和逻辑上不可能的情景和事件，即从支配物理世界的规则和被接受的逻辑原则来看的不可能情景和事件"。[3] 阿尔贝十分强调非自然叙事中的不可能性，而这种不可能性是相较于读者在经验世界中的知识框架而言的。如他所言："叙事中的这类非自然（或不可能）是基于'自然'（真实世界）中的认知框架和草案的，而这种认知框架和草案又是和自然规则、逻辑原则和标准化的人类知识和能力限度相关的。"[4]

虽然不同的非自然叙事学家都以反对"模仿简化主义"（mimetic reductionism）和"模仿偏见"（mimetic bias）为研究非自然叙事学的基本目标，并将非自然叙事和虚构叙事中的非自然成分作为其主要的分析对象，但就怎样具体研究非自然叙事而言，非自然叙事学家内部同样存在一定的差异。理查森认为现有叙事理论"几乎是完全建立在模仿叙事作品和模仿概念的基础之上的，并未给当代文学作品中广泛存在的创造性的、不可能的、戏仿的或矛盾的事件和人物留有任何理论空间"。[5] 这种模仿的叙事研究范式"认为虚构叙事中的人物、场景和事件能够被源于非虚构叙事和真实生活经验的理论模式完全描述和理解"。[6] 然而，由于"文学本身在不断地进化，创造性的新文学形式持续涌现，其中有不少作品发展出原创性的方式去挑战模仿的规约"。[7] 如此一来，非自然叙事文本挑战了模仿叙事理论的边界，颠覆了经典叙事学基于模仿叙事文本建构的一系列理论假设。故围绕这类反模仿叙事实践去建构新的叙事理论就应当被提上日程。所以在理查森看来，非自然叙事学应该致力于建构一种能够敏锐反映反模仿叙事的流动性及其反二分法本质的叙事理论。[8]

与理查森不同，阿尔贝坚持认为"认知叙事学的一些观点能够帮助阐明非自然叙事所带来的大量棘手的阐释难题"，他倡导使用"认知叙事学的相关成果去解读一些叙事文本如何依赖并挑战人类基本的意义建构能力"。[9] 他的研究路径基本上是从认知叙事学的基本理论出发，提出非自然叙事的阐释策略。他认为非自然叙事尽管超越了真实世界中的认知限度，但是"就算是最为奇特的叙事文本也是和人及人所关心的问题相关的"，所以他力图解决的问题是读者在阅读过程中何以能够借助真实世界的认知和文学草案将非自然叙事自然化。[10] 相较于阿尔贝，尼尔森关于非自然叙事的研究路径又有不同。尼尔森认为，当读者在阅读非自然叙事时，他们要么试图努力将其自然化，要么采用所谓的"非自然阅读策略"对之加以理解。按照他的观点，"非自然叙事暗示读者采用有别于其在虚构、口头故事讲述的情景中

---

① Richardson, *Unnatural Narrative: Theory, History, and Practice*, p.3.
② Brian Richardson, "Unnatural Narrative Theory," *Style* 50.4(2016), p.389.
③ Alber, "Impossible Storyworlds—and What to Do with Them," p.80.
④ Jan Alber, *Unnatural Narrative: Impossible Worlds in Fiction and Drama* (Lincoln: University of Nebraska Press, 2016), p.3.
⑤ Richardson, "Unnatural Narrative Theory," pp.387 - 388.
⑥ Richardson, *Unnatural Narrative: Theory, History, and Practice*, p.5.
⑦ Richardson, "Unnatural Narrative Theory," p.388.
⑧ Brian Richardson, *Unnatural Voices: Extreme Narration in Modern and Contemporary Fiction* (Columbus: The Ohio State University Press, 2006), p.139.
⑨ Alber, "Impossible Storyworlds—and What to Do with Them," p.80.
⑩ Ibid.

所使用的阅读策略”[①]，这种阅读策略即非自然阅读策略，这种阅读策略“反对将真实世界的极限运用于所有的叙事中，也避免将解释限定在文学交流行为和阐释模式的可能性框架内”[②]。不难看出，尼尔森试图超越真实世界的认知框架，将非自然叙事还原到它本身的逻辑框架中去解读，对之作本体论的探讨，这也是为什么他和理查森同属非自然叙事“内部本质”研究阵营。

非自然叙事学作为一个较为新兴的叙事研究流派，其内部存在诸多观点差异，导致这种差异性的原因是不同非自然叙事学家研究非自然叙事所持的立场不同。然而，这种观点的差异恰好体现了非自然叙事学研究的多维视角，且这种多维视角实际上构成了非自然叙事学能够迅速拓展的一大动能，即不同研究方法和立场构成了一股合力，有力推进了非自然叙事学在过去十多年来的迅速拓展。但也必须承认，这种理论内部的差异性和多元性实际上也对非自然叙事学作为一个叙事研究新范式的整体性建构带来了一定的挑战，不利于非自然叙事学作为一个一元叙事研究流派的进一步确立，所以后期非自然叙事学面临的一个亟待解决的问题便是统筹和整合内部的多维研究视角。

三、非自然叙事学的挑战与发展方向

伴随着非自然叙事学在西方后经典叙事学整体版图中的迅速拓展，学界对非自然叙事学作为一个新兴叙事研究范式的存在合法性提出了持久的学理性质疑。不同学者从多个角度对非自然叙事学发起了种种批评和责难，这构成了非自然叙事学发展过程中的一大挑战。安斯加尔·纽宁和娜塔亚·贝克塔(Natalya Bekhta)认为，虽然非自然叙事学为经典叙事模式提供了一种补充和纠正，并对现存叙事理论的普遍实用性提出了质疑，由此拓展了后经典叙事学，但由于“缺乏术语的准确性、概念的明晰性和理论的严谨性，非自然叙事学仍然是一个极具争议的研究方法”。[③] 总体来看，西方学界就非自然叙事学展开的学术争鸣主要集中在三个方面，即研究出发点、研究内容和研究属性。

非自然叙事学研究的基本出发点是对叙事的模仿性和反模仿性的区分。非自然叙事学家认为，现有叙事理论的建构忽略了文学史上广泛存在的反模仿叙事，因而需要对之加以理论化，以使得叙事理论更为完整。然而，不少学者就非自然叙事学对模仿叙事和反模仿叙事之间的区分提出了不同的看法。罗宾·沃霍尔认为模仿叙事和反模仿叙事之间的界限并不像非自然叙事学家所认为的那样清晰，她对这种区分的稳定性并不认同。[④] 与理查森不同，她并不认为罗伯-格里耶的小说是非自然的。在她看来，格里耶的小说只是采用了某种非常规的叙事聚焦而已，即格里耶的小说采用了一个认知或情绪极度不稳定的人物视角作为感知和体验的主体，并以此建构了奇特的故事世界。所以格里耶的小说与理查森所谓的模仿叙事之间的差异并不是一种叙事建构(narrative construction)的差异，而只是一种视角稳定性程度的差异。[⑤] 戴维·赫尔曼则认为理查森将模仿和反模仿叙事对立起来的做法低估了模仿本

---

① Jan Alber, et al. “What Is Unnatural about Unnatural Narratology?: A Response to Monika Fludernik,” *Narrative* 20.3 (2012), p.373.

② Jan Alber, et al. “Introduction,” *A Poetics of Unnatural Narrative*, eds. Jan Alber, et al. (Columbus: The Ohio State University Press, 2013), p.8.

③ Ansgar Nünning and Natalya Bekhta, “‘Unnatural’ or ‘Fictional’? A Partial Critique of Unnatural Narrative Theory and Its Discontents,” *Style* 50.4(2016), p.419.

④ Herman, et al., *Narrative Theory: Core Concepts and Critical Debates*, p.212.

⑤ Ibid., p.213.

身的复杂性。赫尔曼从认知叙事学的角度出发,认为“传统意义上的模仿性再现以日常经验世界的一个模型为基础或中介”,即模仿性再现依赖于一系列模型,其中一些模型来自叙事文本和其他文本。[①] 他指出,凡是被称为模仿的东西,都可以被认为是调动世界模型的特定策略,他由此认为非自然叙事中使用的技巧只不过是作者用以打破世界制造过程的叙事手法;换句话说,所谓的“非自然叙事”只是通过反叙事的技巧去限制并扰乱读者建构故事世界的企图,即通过阻止文本所唤起的时空领域中的何时、何事、何地等维度去形成一个故事世界。[②]

对非自然叙事学的研究对象的争论构成了西方学界质疑非自然叙事学的另一个方面。非自然叙事学以反模仿叙事为研究对象,主要聚焦其中的非自然性。申丹认为理查森对非自然叙事的界定实际上忽略了“非自然性”和“非自然叙事”之间的差异。在申丹看来,一些现实主义作品中虽然存在非自然的成分,但是“现实主义小说保持了一个‘总体模仿’框架,因此它们并不构成‘非自然叙事’”,即“现实主义传统中的非自然手法通常在没有打破总体模仿印象的前提下违背了模仿规约”。[③] 换言之,“非自然叙事”和“非自然性”应该被区分开来,非自然叙事指整个叙事打破了模仿规约,然而还有一些现实主义叙事,虽然其中存在非自然性,但这些叙事只是在局部采用了非自然的手法,整个文本还是在模仿的框架之内,没有打破模仿的总体印象。玛利亚·梅凯莱(Maria Mäkelä)则驳斥了非自然叙事学以叙事中的非自然性作为理论建构的对象的做法。她认为,非自然叙事学极力强调后现代主义文本,并视其中的非自然性为其理论建构的聚焦对象,这就暗示了非自然性可以被视为一种文类特点。[④] 然而,类属性实际上就代表了一种规约性,所以非自然性实际上是后现代主义这类新型小说已经建立起的规约,我们并没有必要将其视为一种特定的叙事现象并进行理论的建构。对此,纽宁和贝克塔也表达了类似的观点,他们认为“非自然叙事学所探讨的许多叙事现象尽管在真实世界中看来是不可能的,但是它们已经在虚构文本中被规约化了,因此并不构成一个叙事理解和阐释的理论问题”。[⑤]

就非自然叙事学的理论属性而言,非自然叙事学家多次强调,非自然叙事学并不是否认现有叙事理论的重要作用,而是倡导建立“一个模仿和反模仿双重互动的模式”,但他们所关注的是那些先前被忽略的反模仿叙事,其所提供的范式是一种“补充”,而非一种“替代”。[⑥] 然而,这一研究立场却引发了其他叙事学家对非自然叙事学的学理性质疑。费伦和拉宾诺维茨认为,非自然叙事学要建构的是一种关于X(X即反模仿叙事)的叙事理论,而不是以一种新的视角将叙事视为Y来建构叙事理论,这种立场和修辞性叙事学视叙事为一种修辞行为、认知叙事学视叙事为故事世界的心理模型、女性主义叙事学视叙事为性别政治的再现场所有所不同。[⑦] 换句话说,非自然叙事学并不是从某种普遍意义上去重新审视叙事而建构新的叙事理论,而是要去考察反模仿叙事这种特定叙事类型或模仿叙事中的特定反模仿成分。而这种基于叙事特殊性的叙事理论是否能够独立成为一种叙事学的研究范式是西方叙事学家持续顾虑的一个关键问题。还有一些学者则认为非自然叙事研究实际上和后现代主义式的叙事研究并没有本质

---

① Herman, et al., *Narrative Theory: Core Concepts and Critical Debates*, p.224.

② Ibid., p.223.

③ Shen Dan, “What Are Unnatural Narratives? What Are Unnatural Elements?” *Style* 50.4(2016), p.486.

④ Maria Mäkelä, “Narratology and Taxonomy: A Response to Brian Richardson,” *Style* 50.4(2016), p.464.

⑤ Nünning and Bekhta, “‘Unnatural’ or ‘Fictional’? A Partial Critique of Unnatural Narrative Theory and Its Discontents,” p.423.

⑥ Richardson, *Unnatural Narrative: Theory, History, and Practice*, p.5.

⑦ Herman, et al., *Narrative Theory: Core Concepts and Critical Debates*, p.186.

差异。他们断言:“非自然叙事学通常涵盖了其他理论家能够以更为精密的方式对之加以探讨和理论化的领域。”[①]他们以布莱恩·麦克黑尔(Brian McHale)、乌苏拉·K.海斯(Ursula K. Heise)、维尔纳·沃尔夫等人关于后现代主义小说的研究为例,认为这类研究就理论的严密性和批评的洞见而言几乎难以与非自然叙事研究相互区别开来。

当谈及非自然叙事学的未来发展方向时,尚必武颇为前瞻性地指出,未来非自然叙事学的研究需要注意考察三个方面的问题,即探讨“非自然性”与“叙事性”之间的关系、反思非自然叙事学的激进与缺失、对非自然叙事做跨媒介的考察。[②] 鉴于学界对非自然叙事学提出诸多质疑,非自然叙事学未来研究的一个重要任务便是对学界就非自然叙事学的相关质疑和批判做出有力的回应,澄清相关的混乱和误解。应该说,学界对非自然叙事学的众多反驳意见存在不少的误解,对非自然叙事学的一些基本概念和假设也有误读的现象,这些是需要非自然叙事学家进一步说明的。如何整合目前关于“非自然叙事”的多重定义,由此对“非自然叙事”做出清楚明晰的界定,以及如何统筹现有的关于非自然叙事学的多种研究立场和方法,都是非自然叙事学家在未来需要重点解决的具体问题。此外,虽然非自然叙事学家已经在尝试寻求非自然叙事学和女性主义及认知叙事学之间的交叉,在不同领域的连接点开展知识创新,但这方面的工作还需要从深度和广度两个方面进一步加强。换言之,除进一步深入挖掘非自然叙事学和女性主义及认知叙事学之间的交叉互动关系外,还应当拓展范畴,探索非自然叙事学与修辞性叙事学、后殖民主义叙事学等其他领域之间能否创造新的知识。

为进一步加深对非自然叙事学基本理论和范畴的理解,本章选择了三篇代表性理论文献,分别取自理查森的专著《非自然叙事:理论、历史与实践》、阿尔贝的专著《非自然叙事:小说与戏剧中的不可能世界》,以及阿尔贝等人编著的《非自然叙事诗学》。

---

① Nünning and Bekhta, "'Unnatural' or 'Fictional'? A Partial Critique of Unnatural Narrative Theory and Its Discontents," p.422.

② 尚必武:《非自然叙事学》,载《外国文学》2015年第2期,第109—110页。

第二节　布莱恩·理查森及其《非自然叙事：理论、历史与实践》

一、导读

布莱恩·理查森对非自然叙事学牵涉的一系列核心概念问题都进行了详细论述。于理查森而言，清楚界定非自然叙事这一概念，是建构非自然叙事理论的前提。理查森强调非自然叙事的“反模仿”特质，将非自然叙事等同于反模仿叙事。在他那里，非自然叙事学就是围绕反模仿叙事而建构的叙事诗学。在界定反模仿叙事时，理查森首先明确界定了它的对立面——模仿叙事。理查森把模仿叙事确定为一种以非虚构叙事为参照并旨在表达逼真性的虚构叙事。与模仿叙事相对，反模仿叙事（即非自然叙事）是指“含有明显反模仿事件、人物、场景或框架的叙事”，该类叙事有意“打破非虚构叙事的预设，并违反模仿的期待和现实主义的创作实践”。[①] 因此，非自然叙事的核心在于反模仿，在于对现实主义再现方式的解构。在理查森看来，传统意义上的神话故事、童话故事、动物叙事等超自然文本并不是“反”模仿的，而是“非”模仿的，因为从本质上看，这类叙事只是在模仿的故事世界中加入了超自然元素，仍然注重故事世界的完整性，并未从根本上颠覆已经建立起的文类规约，只能算是拓展了模仿叙事的形式。为清楚呈现究竟何为非自然叙事，理查森对一系列与非自然叙事极为相近的叙事形态展开详细分析，讨论了科幻小说、超自然小说、奇幻小说、寓言故事等文本与非自然叙事在深层结构方面的差异。基本上来说，理查森对非自然叙事的界定是从叙事的形式角度入手，着重强调该类叙事在形式上对模仿规约的解构，这在很大程度上赋予了其非自然叙事诗学结构主义的特质。

二、《非自然叙事：理论、历史与实践》选读[②]

Unnatural narratology is designed to examine and comprehend postmodern and other anti-mimetic narrative practices. We will start with some necessary definitions: what I call *mimetic* narratives are those works of fiction that model themselves on or substantially resemble nonfictional works. Mimetic narratives systematically attempt to depict the world of our experience in a recognizable manner; this is the traditional goal of works that strive for realism or verisimilitude. Nineteenth-century realist fiction is a major subspecies of the mimetic tradition.

I define an unnatural narrative as one that contains significant antimimetic events, characters, settings, or frames. By *antimimetic*, I mean representations that contravene the pre-suppositions of

① Richardson, *Unnatural Narrative: Theory, History, and Practice*, p.3.
② Ibid., pp.3－12.

nonfictional narratives, violate mimetic expectations and the practices of realism, and defy the conventions of existing, established genres.[①] Paradigmatic examples of unnatural narratives include Borges's most unrealistic stories, Beckett's *The Unnamable* (1953), Robbe-Grillet's *La Jalousie* (1957), Anna Kavan's *Ice* (1967), and Salman Rushdie's *The Satanic Verses* (1988). It is important to note that many narratives are entirely mimetic and almost no narrative is entirely antimimetic; nevertheless, both aspects are present in different degrees in a large number of works. Mimetic texts often try to disguise their artificiality; at other times they slyly hint at their own fictionality. Antimimetic texts may downplay their mimetic features as they flaunt their transgressive aspects. Antimimetic scenes and characters are often most conspicuous and most compelling when they are engaged in a dialectic with mimetic aspects of a given text.

We may further differentiate the antimimetic from what I will call the nonmimetic: an antimimetic (or antirealist) work like Beckett's *Molloy* defies the conventions of mimetic (or realist) representation that are adhered to in a work like *Anna Karenina*, while a nonmimetic (nonrealist) work, such as a fairy tale, employs a consistent, parallel storyworld and follows established conventions, or in some cases, merely adds supernatural components to its otherwise mimetic depiction of the actual world.[②] I will offer three examples to further clarify these differences. A story of an ordinary man who rides a typical horse for several hours over normal terrain and travels thirty-five miles is mimetic, whereas a prince who rides a winged horse to the other end of his principality in a few minutes is non-mimetic. An antimimetic, that is, unnatural example would be the scene of flying in Aristophanes's *The Peace* in which the protagonist mounts a giant dung beetle to ascend to heaven and begs the audience not to pass any gas and thereby misdirect his mount.

Conventional nonmimetic works are not, from my perspective, unnatural narratives. Although an ordinary animal fable has nothing to do with the canons of realism that it predates or diverges from, it may simply be a common instance of a traditional natural narrative. Animal fables are quite widespread throughout different cultures. Stories of talking or thinking animals extend from prehistory down to *Millie's Book*, Barbara Bush's volume about her experiences in the White House told from the perspective of her dog. Animal stories can become unnatural, however, once authors move beyond their conventional deployment; we find this in the representations of a horse's poetic, philosophical, and priapic consciousness in John Hawkes's *Sweet William*. More extreme still is the monologue of a spermatozoon as it swims toward the ovum in John Barth's "Night Sea Journey" (see Bernaerts et al.). Antimimetic texts thus go beyond nonmimetic texts as they violate rather than simply extend the conventions of mimesis; this difference can be perceived by the degree of unexpectedness that the text produces, whether surprise, shock, or the wry smile that acknowledges

① This cluster does not imply a significant homology between these very different kinds of narratives but only notes that each presupposes representations that are consonant with nonfictional narratives.

② My conception thus differs significantly from Kathryn Hume's generous definition of fantasy, which she applies to "any departure from consensus reality" (21).

that a different, playful kind of representation is at work. A key aspect of the unnatural (like parody) is its *intentional* transgression of conventional mimetic or nonmimetic conventions. By contrast, authors of mimetic or nonmimetic works often believe (or at least intend their audience to believe) in the general accuracy of the storyworld they present (though exceptions abound, such as the ghost stories of Edith Wharton).

As will be documented in Chapter 5, substantially antimimetic scenes and works can be found in most periods of literary history, ranging from ancient Greek, Roman, and Sanskrit texts through medieval, Renaissance, and eighteenth-century narratives on to recent postmodern, magical realist, and avant-garde works. Unnatural narratives constitute an entire alternative history of literature, the other "Great Tradition", though it is one that has been ignored or marginalized by histories, criticism, and theories that remain constrained within the narrow limits of mimetic practice.

Throughout this book, I will be arguing against what I call the mimetic paradigm of narrative theory, a paradigm that proposes or assumes that the figures, settings, and events in fictional narratives can be adequately depicted and comprehended by conceptual models derived directly from nonfictional narratives and real-life experience. Let me indicate in advance that I have no quarrel whatsoever with the quality work and important results these theorists have produced. My objection is exclusively to the self-limited nature of such a model. By definition, a mimetic model, whether derived from substantially realistic literary fiction (Defoe through Proust) or from nonfictional narratives, cannot comprehend antimimetic works that violate mimetic practices. Beyond these limits lies a vast territory of unnatural narratives, which Fludernik, to her credit, has acknowledged and begun to theorize. I want to go much further into this territory and show how narrative theory needs to be expanded in order to map it properly. The paradigm I propose thus insists on a dual, interactive model of mimesis and antimimesis, though I will of course be stressing the missing antimimetic practices and the theory of those practices in this work. To comprehend unnatural works, we need an additional poetics. I am not offering an alternative paradigm so much as another, complementary one. In most areas, we do not need to reject existing models but rather to supplement them. I advocate we move beyond a merely mimetic paradigm to a much more comprehensive one that can embrace both mimetic and antimimetic narrative practices.

A word about the term "unnatural": I consider my work a radical extension of and addition to that performed by Monika Fludernik in her *Towards a 'Natural' Narratology* (1993), where she follows out the paradigm of natural narratives to its limits. I begin with narratives that cannot be contained within the model of conversational, nonfictional natural narratives. The word for me has no extranarrative connotations; it is merely a narratological term derived from sociolinguistics. I am not in favor of, or necessarily opposed to, any cultural practices, individual actions, or sexual preferences commonly designated as unnatural by society. I realize there will probably be some confusion concerning these very different meanings, but the term "unnatural narrative" now has such wide currency that we all have to live with its consequences, including the occasional apparent paradox.

Degrees of the Unnatural

It should be stressed that many, perhaps most narratives can be situated on two parallel and occasionally intersecting spectra. A work like Proust's *Recherche* may be almost entirely mimetic but contain a few special instances of the antimimetic at key points in the text, such as the narrator's notorious anti-illusionistic claim that all the characters in the work are invented, with the exception of the millionaire cousins of Françoise who came out of retirement to help their relative when she was left without support. Such a statement (whatever its actual veracity) points to the fictionality of the narrative and destroys the mimetic illusion. This activity is by no means unusual; many ostensibly realist works contain localized unnatural elements secreted within them. Maria Mäkelä is especially astute in identifying these ("Realism"); in her discussion of fictional minds, she goes so far as to claim, "We don't have to resort to avant-garde literature to notice that the *unnaturalness*—or the peculiarly *literary* type of cognitive challenge—is always already there in textual representations of consciousness" ("Cycles" 133).

A narrative may have a much greater unnatural component, regularly commenting on conventions of representation and sometimes mocking their unreality as well. At the beginning of *Northanger Abbey*, we find a description of the circumstances of the heroine's birth: her mother "had three sons before Catherine was born; and, instead of dying in bringing the latter into the world, as anybody might expect, she still lived on—lived to have six children more—to see them growing up around her, and to enjoy excellent health herself" (367). This statement mocks the convention of the heroine's mother dying as she gives birth to the heroine (as happens, for example, to Arabella in *The Female Quixote*, 1752). Its critique may function on several levels: though many women did die giving birth in the eighteenth century, it is improbable that so many heroines would repeatedly lose their mothers in such a fashion. Such a situation provides a number of "too easy" plot opportunities involving the daughter in distress and immediately creates a fund of sentiment for the motherless girl. Austen's statement thus combines a probabilistic and aesthetic critique of the existing narrative convention, even as it suggests that the narrator, rather than any preexisting events, will determine the trajectory of the actions that ensue. We may also note here that unnatural strategies are often especially effective when interacting with a sustained mimetic framework or trajectory.

The unnatural is located in specific events, characters, settings, and frames. Different incarnations of the unnatural can, however, produce extremely disparate effects at the level of the narrative as a whole; thus, a text's calling attention to its own fictionality can produce varying degrees of unnaturalness. When Trollope notes that he can give his narrative any turn he chooses to, the unnatural moment appears but then is quickly subsumed within the novel's mimetic center of gravity. However, when Cervantes cracks open the mimetic illusion by pretending the manuscript he claims to be transcribing breaks off, after which he searches for another copy in order to determine the end of the episode and the rest of the story, the effect, though fairly brief, is quite powerful, and places the mimetic aspects of the book entirely within brackets, as it were. The effect is still more disruptive and, indeed, transformative when it commits ontological violations as at the end of John Fowles's otherwise substantially mimetic *The French Lieutenant's Woman* (1969). By such a strategy, the entire narrative suddenly becomes unnatural.

Other works are still more insistently unnatural, repeatedly utilizing a wide range of antimimetic elements and devices, such as the many unnatural aspects of Angela Carter's *Nights at the Circus* (1984) or the even more resolutely unnatural *Molloy*. Again, we recognize that both of these works have mimetic components; the ontological foundations of both are transformed by the power of the antimimetic elements so that Carter's novel is finally only quasi-mimetic and Beckett's becomes primarily antimimetic. A text like Salman Rushdie's *Midnight's Children* is playfully antimimetic yet also has a strong if devious mimetic throughline as it traces the history of the Indian subcontinent for some seventy years. Still more thorough-going antimimetic narratives are also possible and can be found in Calvino's *Invisible Cities* (1972), Carter's *The Infernal Desire Machines of Doctor Hoffman* (1972), or Beckett's *The Unnamable*, each extremely antimimetic throughout.

To get another sense of the relations between the mimetic and the antimimetic, we may look at the range of some self-reflexive statements in drama. Jacques's lines, "All the world's a stage and all the men and women merely players" (*As You Like It*, 2.7.139 - 140), expresses a perfectly normal sentiment that fits snugly within a mimetic framework. It takes on an added piquancy when uttered by a character on a stage; I would say that it is marginally or minimally unnatural. When the irony is intensified, the unnaturalness of the statement increases, as occurs in *Henry VI* when Talbot, learning that his son has just been killed, rails against fate, specifically castigating the "accursed fatal hand / That hath contriv'd this woeful tragedy!" (1.4.80 - 81). When the mimetic justification is diminished or strained, the potential unnaturalness of an observation is also increased, as in Fabian's comment in *Twelfth Night* on the scene he just witnessed: "If this were play'd upon a stage now, I could condemn it as an improbable fiction" (3.4.127 - 128). In these three examples, each character's statement is mimetically motivated, but the nature of their discourse undermines the pretense of mimesis.①

Entirely unnatural are the points where the mimetic illusion is completely broken, as when

① A rhetorical narratologist might simply say that these examples paradoxically stay within the mimetic, even as they foreground the synthetic. To this I would respond that the category of the synthetic tends to obscure the difference between merely conventional artifices such as characters speaking in verse, which is not usually intended to challenge the work's mimetic features, and the unnatural synthetic discourse of the impossible dialogue of an absurdist play like Ionesco's *La Cantatrice Chauve* (1950). If the verse drama is presented in a parodic fashion that draws attention to its antimimetic features, as in Henry Fielding's *Tom Thumb* (1730), then the work becomes unnatural.

Robin Goodfellow, still in character, addresses the audience at the end of *A Midsummer Night's Dream* ("If we shadows have offended, / Think but this and all is mended" [5.1. 418 - 419]). Most flagrantly unnatural is where the representational illusion is travestied. About thirty minutes into Roger Vitrac's play *Les Mystères de l'amour*, a shot is heard and a man comes to the front of the stage to say that the author has just committed suicide and that all the spectators should leave the theater. After a short break, the play resumes; the "theater manager" was simply an actor playing a role. The audience chants for the author, and he soon appears, covered in fake blood, smiling broadly. At the extreme end of this spectrum would be Peter Handke's "Publikumsbeschimpfung" ("Offending the Audience", 1966). Here, the concept of representation is itself ambiguous or paradoxical: the actors state that their actions do not depict events; the players merely speak their lines. As they inform the audience: "This is no drama. No action that has occurred elsewhere is re-enacted here [...] This is no make-believe which re-enacts an action that really happened once upon a time. Time plays no role here. We are not acting out a plot" (15). Of course, they are speaking scripted lines to an audience in a way determined by a director; they do reenact the same scenes night after night. Nevertheless, this performance seems to mime representation more than it engages in it.

Many multilinear texts pose some rather different, and perhaps more theoretically challenging questions, since they can seem to be entirely natural and unnatural at the same time. In a work like Malcolm Bradbury's "Composition", which I will discuss in chapter 3, three different, mutually exclusive possible endings are offered. Each of the three endings is entirely mimetic, and each one taken alone concludes an entirely mimetic story. Thus, each possible story is internally consistent; what is unnatural is that the reader is invited to determine the course of events. This practice thus violates the conventional retrospective nature of any story narrated in the past tense, in which an event is therefore related after it has occurred, and the ending, which has already transpired, cannot be selected from among a list of options. Porter Abbott explains that narrative "is something that always seems" to come after the events it depicts, "to be a re-presentation" of them (*Cambridge* 36); it is the violation of this sense of the pastness of the narrative events that is foregrounded by multilinear fabulas.

Beyond Postmodernism: the Extent of the Unnatural

Most postmodern stories and novels are clear-cut, perhaps quintessential, examples of unnatural narrative. It should be noted, though, that there are some works that are usually considered postmodern due to stylistic features rather than ontological ones, so these would not be considered as unnatural. As will be clear in chapters 5 and 6, the unnatural extends far beyond the postmodern in several ways, reaching back almost to the earliest periods of Western literature. Examples of unnatural narratives include Greek Old Comedy, Menippean satires, Rabelaisian texts, eighteenth-century "it" narratives, several Shandean novels, and many texts of the Romantics. In the twentieth century, it is found in surrealist fiction, metafiction, antinovels, most *nouveaux romans* (though not all of Butor's earlier novels), Brechtian epic theater, metadrama, and theater of the absurd, as well as many works of the historical avant-garde, *écriture féminine*, magical realism, cyberpunk, and hyperfiction.

The unnatural is also present in many classical Asian works. Comic Kabuki plays include numerous antimimetic scenes (e.g."The Zen Substitute"). There are some very compelling examples of metalepsis in the eighteenth-century Chinese novel *Hung Lou Meng* (*The Story of the Stone*). Classical Sanskrit drama has unnatural frame-breaking devices that are at times spectacularly employed. And, as will be discussed below, many popular and folk narrative genres contain unnatural elements. The unnatural thus gives us a comprehensive category within which to situate and thereby historicize postmodernism and the various antimimetic genres that preceded or are now following it.

We may also note that some kinds of works seem similar to antimimetic texts but have a profoundly different kind of construction and are thus not especially unnatural at all. In the discussion that follows, I will elaborate on my own sense of the unnatural, which is more restricted than that of many colleagues who also investigate unnatural narratives. I will use this discussion to frame and explain these differences.①

A) *Classical science fiction*, I argue, is not usually unnatural, especially insofar as it attempts to construct entirely realistic narratives of events that could occur in the future; the mimetic impulse remains constant. Postmodern science fiction, however, such as practiced by Italo Calvino, Stanisław Lem, or Ursula LeGuin, does create the kinds of antirealistic or logically impossible settings and events required by my conception of the genuinely unnatural; it might be noted that more and more science fiction seems to be moving in this "unnatural" direction. Novels that construct an alternative history, such as if the Confederacy had won the U.S. Civil War, also typically conform to a realistic framework—indeed, that is arguably their chief source of interest.

B) *Supernatural fiction*, in which a magic potion, an angel, or a divinity affects the course of events, also typically aspires to a mimetic poetics, though one that exceeds the parameters of classical realism: its authors dramatize a world in which supernatural entities can alter events; they produce a mimetic representation according to supernatural beliefs. In the discussion of the work of Henry Fielding in chapter 4, we will observe how Fielding can entirely eschew all supernatural and what I call nonmimetic agents and events even as he regularly incorporates unnatural aspects into his

① For an account of some significant points of disagreement among us, see Alber, Iversen, Nielsen, and Richardson, pp.371 - 378.

narration. At the same time, we note that antimimetic authors can tamper with supernatural forms and make them unnatural. When Rushdie retells the stories of Mohammed and Satan in *The Satanic Verses*, he employs numerous antimimetic strategies of representation. When we find literal mind reading, magical transportation, or time moving impossibly slowly in *Midnight's Children*, Rushdie generally makes it clear that he is employing unnatural postmodern techniques in place of the more traditional supernatural devices. Similarly, the narrator admits that Gandhi dies on the wrong day in this novel, and the fact is acknowledged in the text; the narrator refuses to change the mistaken date to the correct one. His alternative history is not a failed realist or supernatural one but an unnatural narrative that at times contradicts the historical sequence it observes elsewhere in the text.

C) *Works of fantasy* also fail to qualify as wholly unnatural narratives in my view because of their conventionality. They usually follow familiar patterns that readers quickly recognize. An online guide to writing fantasy novels begins: "When writing a fantasy novel, the writer needs to remember there is a structure to follow. We refer to the flow of the storyline as the plot arc. In a fantasy novel, as in all novels, following the arc is imperative to creating a novel readers will devour." Similar formulaic advice is given for the creation of fantasy worlds, characters, gods, and dialogue.① It is easy to imagine how different a guide to writing an antimimetic postmodern novel would be. One would begin by eschewing or exaggerating narrative conventions, above all the implicit rule demanding a stable, ontologically consistent storyworld, and continue to violate genre and other rules in as unconventional way as possible. The difference between these two is precisely the unnatural component of postmodernism. In short, insofar as a work is conventional, it is not unnatural. In the same vein, most fairy tales are entirely conventional without being either mimetic or antimimetic, and thus occupy the realm of the nonmimetic.② At the edges of such genres we can nevertheless adduce examples of postmodern transformations of fairy tales into something quite unnatural, as in Angela Carter's rewritings of traditional fairy stories. In "The Company of Wolves", the relation between the girl's red hood and its suggestion of the onset of menses is made self-conscious as the story is inverted: the young woman acquiesces in the killing of her grandmother and goes on to have amorous relations with the beast, who is in fact a roguishly attractive wolf man.

D) *Allegory* is a genre that is neither primarily mimetic nor antimimetic. Instead, it embodies structures of ideas in narrative form. Its sequencing is not that of either the natural or unnatural development of events but follows instead the logic of ideas. Candide experiences an ever more powerful series of events that contradict the view that ours is the best of all possible worlds; it is the

① See http: //www.inspiredauthor.com/Fiction_Writing/Fantasy/Write_Novel/index.htm.

② This same general argument applies to what have been called "weird tales"; for me, they aren't quite as weird as the genuinely antimimetic.

development of ideas rather than probability or travesties of generic forms that propel the narrative. Similarly, "Everyman" and *Animal Farm* are straightforward allegories and have little of the unnatural about them. By contrast, the narrative in Jonathan Swift's allegories takes on a life of its own, as the events proceed by a narrative logic independent of allegory's progression of ideas. Postmodern allegories (common throughout *The Infernal Desire Machines of Doctor Hoffman* and *Midnight's Children*) go further as they play with or parody the straightforward dramatization of a set of ideas found in classical allegory, and thereby become more unnatural.

E) *Stylization*: Sometimes a work's discourse is highly unusual or fragmented or the presentation of its events is entirely original, even if all the represented events are themselves ultimately mimetic. Many modern authors have employed such discourse; examples from Stein, Faulkner, and Donald Barthelme suggest themselves. Here is the opening passage of Ronald Firbank's *Caprice* (1917):

> The clangour of bells grew insistent. In uncontrollable hilarity pealed S. Mary, contrasting clearly with the subdued carillon of S. Mark. From all sides, seldom in unison, resounded bells. S. Elizabeth and S. Sebastian, in Flower Street, seemed in loud dispute, while S. Ann "on the Hill", all hollow, cracked, consumptive, fretful, did nothing but complain. Near by S. Nicaise, half paralysed and impotent, feebly shook. Then, triumphant, in a hurricane of sound, S. Irene hushed them all. It was Sunday again. (335)

My position is that discourse alone does not constitute the unnatural, except in rare cases where the discourse actually affects the storyworld, as in instances of what I call denarration, where the discourse negates or erases parts of the fictional world, or in a text like Walter Abish's *Alphabetical Africa* (1974), in which possible words—and thereby, their signifiers—are limited by severe alphabetical constraints (see Sommer).①

三、思考与讨论

(1) 理查森所说的"模仿"具体是指什么?

(2) 模仿叙事与反模仿叙事之间的界限究竟在哪里?

(3) 理查森关于非自然叙事的界定有无缺陷?

---

① Other instances in which discursive features of a text can affect its storyworld include Oulipo experiments such as Georges Perec's *La Disparition* (1969), a French novel that does not use any word that contains the letter "e", and perhaps some of Beckett's late texts.

第三节 扬·阿尔贝及其《非自然叙事：小说与戏剧中的不可能世界》

一、导读

德国叙事学家扬·阿尔贝为非自然叙事学作为一个后经典叙事学关键学派的兴起和发展做出了重要贡献。如果说理查森的非自然叙事理论是一种结构主义模式，那么阿尔贝的非自然叙事学则可以被视为一种认知模式。在概念界定上，阿尔贝以真实世界中的总体认知框架为基准，将那些超越该框架之外的情境和事件视为非自然的。这与理查森从模仿规约角度来界定非自然叙事有所不同。在阿尔贝看来，"……非自然这一术语是指物理上、逻辑上和人力上不可能的情境和事件。即从已知的支配物理世界的规则、被人所接受的逻辑原则（如不矛盾原则）或标准的人力知识和能力限度来看，被呈现的情境和事件必须是不可能的"。[1] 阿尔贝把符合经验生活中的认知限度的故事讲述视为可能的，反之则是不可能或非自然的，如叙述时间反方向发展、不同故事发展线索相互矛盾、第一人称叙述者能够洞悉其他人物的内心所想等，均属于非自然的。阿尔贝所坚持的非自然叙事研究方法同样体现出浓重的认知意味。与理查森钟情于描述非自然叙事的形式结构不同的是，阿尔贝试图以认知叙事学的相关理论为指引，探寻非自然叙事的解读方法，进而找到将非自然叙事"自然化"的阐释策略。阿尔贝相信，认知叙事学的理论资源有助于解决非自然叙事给读者带来的阐释难题，因而他提倡运用认知叙事学的相关理论去解读非自然文本"如何依赖并挑战人类基本的意义建构能力"[2]。阿尔贝在考察非自然叙事时关注的同样是非自然叙事的世界建构问题，其要探索的是读者究竟应该如何透过非自然叙事来建构世界。由于非自然叙事在人物、场景、时间、情节、叙述者等具体层面使用新颖的再现手法，读者透过非自然叙事往往难以轻易地建构完整而稳定的故事世界，因而阿尔贝尝试从这些不稳定性中探索出建构世界的方法，他由此提出理解非自然叙事的九种策略。

二、《非自然叙事：小说与戏剧中的不可能世界》选读[3]

…

The reading strategies that I see as particularly relevant for engagements with the unnatural relate to both our real-world knowledge (acquired through our physical being in the world) and our literary knowledge (acquired through our exposure to narrative literature), and these types of knowledge are stored in cognitive frames and scripts. Similarly Shlomith Rimmon-Kenan (2002,

---

① Alber, *Unnatural Narrative: Impossible Worlds in Fiction and Drama*, p.25.
② Alber, "Impossible Storyworlds—and What to Do with Them," p.80.
③ Alber, *Unnatural Narrative: Impossible Worlds in Fiction and Drama*, pp.47 - 55.

125) distinguishes between what she calls reality models, which help explain "elements by references to some concept (or structure) which governs our perception of the world", and literary models, which "make elements intelligible by reference to specifically literary exigencies or institutions".[①] The following reading strategies (see also Ryan 2006b; Yacobi 1981) may be used by recipients to make sense of impossible scenarios or events:[②]

1. The blending of frames
2. Generification (evoking generic conventions from literary history)
3. Subjectification (reading as internal states)
4. Foregrounding the thematic
5. Reading allegorically
6. Satirization and parody
7. Positing a transcendental realm
8. Do it yourself (using the text as a construction kit to build our own stories)
9. The Zen way of reading

1. The blending of frames: When we are confronted with unnatural scenarios or events, our task as readers becomes a Sisyphean one. We have to conduct seemingly impossible mapping operations to orient ourselves within storyworlds that refuse to be organized by real-world parameters only. In such cases we are urged to blend preexisting frames and create what Mark Turner (1996, 60) calls "impossible blend[s]" to adequately reconstruct the unnatural elements of the storyworld.

According to Roger Schank and Robert Abelson (1977, 37), a script (or frame) comprises "specific knowledge to interpret and participate in events we have been through many times" and can be used as a point of reference to help us master new situations. Such cognitive parameters are "dynamic" knowledge structures that "*must be able to change* as a result of new experiences" (Schank 1986, 7, my italics). Similarly Marvin Minsky (1979, 1) points out that "when one encounters a new situation (or makes a substantial change in one's view of a problem), one selects from memory a structure called a frame. This is a remembered framework to be adapted by changing details as necessary". Doležel (1998, 181) argues that literary texts often urge us to change our thinking, which is largely based on our real-world knowledge, and create new frames: "In order to reconstruct and interpret a fictional world, the reader has to reorient his cognitive stance to agree

① For example, when Alice in *Alice's Adventures in Wonderland* tries to come to terms with her unnatural experiences in Wonderland, she uses real-world and generic knowledge to orient herself. She resorts to her knowledge of mathematics (Carroll [1865] 1984, 3, 15) and geography (4, 15), and at some point believes that she has landed in a fairy tale (33). After a while she gets used to the unnaturalness of this world, and everything seems "quite natural to Alice" (21).

② See Amit Marcus (2012) for a critique of an earlier version of these reading strategies (Alber 2009). I have reordered and partly reformulated the navigational tools on the basis of his critique (see also Alber 2013b, 2013d, 2013e) and would like to thank him for his important input.

with the world's encyclopedia. In other words, knowledge of the fictional encyclopedia is absolutely necessary for the reader to comprehend a fictional world. *The actual-world encyclopedia might be useful, but it is by no means universally sufficient; for many fictional worlds it is misleading, it provides not comprehension but misreading*" (my italics).[①]

For instance, when readers are confronted with impossibilities, they may generate new frames by blending preexisting schemata. Turner (2003, 117) explains the process of blending by pointing out that "cognitively modern human beings have a remarkable, species-defining ability to pluck forbidden mental fruit—that is, to activate two conflicting mental structures ... [such as *tree* and *person*] and to blend them creatively into a new mental structure [such as *speaking tree*]". As an example, Turner mentions the character of Bertran de Born in Dante's fourteenth-century allegory *Inferno*. This character is "a talking and reasoning human being who carries his detached but articulate head in his hand like a lantern". Turner (1996, 62, 61) argues that "this is an *impossible* blending, in which a talking human being has an *unnaturally* divided body" (my italics).

Mante S. Nieuwland and Jos J. A. van Berkum (2006) have shown that subjects try to make sense of unnatural entities (such as an amorous peanut or a crying yacht) through the blending of frames. They report that the subjects needed "to construct and gradually update their situation model of the story to the point that they project human characteristics onto inanimate objects. This process of projecting human properties (behavior, emotions, appearance) onto an inanimate object comes close to what has been called 'conceptual blending', the ability to assemble new and vital relations from diverse scenarios" (1109). The process of blending, which opens up new conceptual spaces, plays a crucial role in all cases in which we try to make sense of the unnatural. Since unnatural scenarios and events are by definition physically, logically, or humanly impossible, they always urge us to create new frames by recombining, extending, or otherwise altering preexisting cognitive parameters.

2. Generification (evoking generic conventions from literary history): In some cases the represented unnatural scenario or event has already been conventionalized and turned into a perceptual frame. In other words, the process of blending has already taken place, and we have converted the unnatural into a basic cognitive category that is part of certain generic conventions. In such narratives the unnatural no longer strikes us as being strange or unusual. We can simply account for the unnatural element by identifying it as belonging to a particular literary genre, that is, a suitable discourse context within which the anomaly can be embedded. For example, we know that animals can speak in beast fables; we also know that magic exists in epics, certain romances, Gothic novels, and later fantasy narratives; we know that we can read the minds of the characters in modernist fiction; we know that time travel is possible in science-fiction narratives; and so forth.

① Similarly Roger D. Sell (2000, 3) argues that certain types of literary communication lead to "mental re-adjustments", that is, changes in people's thought-worlds.

In their experiment Nieuwland and van Berkum (2006, 1109) found that subjects typically process impossible entities (such as an amorous peanut) by seeing them "as actual 'cartoon-like entities' (i.e. a peanut that walks and talks like a human, having emotions and possibly even arms, legs and a face)". Hence, they assume that "the acceptability of a crying yacht or amorous peanut is not merely induced by repeated specific instances of such unusual feature combinations, but somehow also—perhaps even critically—by the *literary genre* ... that such instances suggest" (1109). That is to say, the evocation of a particular genre (such as the cartoon), that is, the construction of a supportive context, helps us come to terms with represented impossibilities.①

In the context of this reading strategy I am also interested in the question of how conventionalizations of unnatural scenarios and events have come about. As I will show, it is typically the interaction between various cognitive mechanisms and/or human needs that leads to the converting of impossibilities into new frames and thus forms of literary knowledge. Also we are currently in the process of conventionalizing postmodernism. At one point readers will no longer be shocked or surprised by the specific uses of the unnatural in postmodernist narratives, or, alternatively, they will know that postmodernist fiction is a type of fiction that tends to explicitly foreground the impossibilities of the scenarios and events it represents.②

3. Subjectification (reading as internal states): Some impossible elements can simply be explained as parts of internal states (of characters or narrators) such as dreams, fantasies, visions, or hallucinations. This reading strategy is the only one that actually *naturalizes* the unnatural insofar as it reveals the ostensibly impossible to be something entirely natural, namely nothing but an element of somebody's interiority.③ For example, one can explain the retrogressive temporality in Amis's (1992) *Time's Arrow* by ascribing it to the central protagonist's wish to turn back the clock and undo the moral chaos of his life, including his participation in the Holocaust.④

4. Foregrounding the thematic: Other examples of unnaturalness become more readable when we

① This reading strategy ("generification"), which plays a role in cases of conventionalized impossibilities, is rather similar to Yacobi's (1981, 115) "generic principle", the idea that the "generic framework dictates or makes possible certain rules of referential stylization, the employment of which usually results in a set of divergences from what is generally accepted as the principles governing actual reality". What Ryan (2006b, 670) refers to as "magic" is actually a subcategory of reading strategy 2: she argues that when we appeal to the supernatural, we admit "the irrational or fantastic nature" of the represented world.

② Richardson (2015, 18), on the other hand, argues that "it takes a lot of repetition—and widespread knowledge of that repetition—to fully conventionalize the antimimetic". I believe that Richardson's own critical work and the many examples he uses contribute to the process of conventionalizing the antimimetic (because more and more readers become familiar with it). Richardson feels that I am "far too quick to call a new practice conventional" (18n10). In contrast to Richardson, I maintain that it is difficult for practices to remain unexpected, confusing, or unnerving over a longer period of time. At one point, even the postmodernist games with the unnatural will be conventionalized and perceived as being outmoded.

③ To clarify my terminology: the term *conventionalization* denotes the transforming of unnatural scenarios or events into cognitive frames (such as the speaking animal in beast fables) in the context of reading strategy 2, while the term *naturalization* only refers to reading strategy 3, which reveals the seemingly unnatural to be something entirely natural. I refer to all of the other reading strategies as explanatory tools or sense-making mechanisms.

④ While Ryan (2006b, 669) refers to this navigational tool in terms of "mentalism", Yacobi (1981, 118) calls it "the perspectival principle" and argues that we can sometimes attribute the unexplainable "to the peculiarities and circumstances of the observer through whom the world is taken to be refracted".

look at them from a thematic angle and see them as exemplifications of themes rather than mimetically motivated occurrences. I follow the definition of *theme* as "a specific representational component that recurs several times in the [narrative], in different variations—our quest for the theme or themes of a story is always a quest for something that is not unique to this specific work .... A theme is ... the principle (or locus) of a possible grouping of texts. It is one principle among many since we often group together texts considered to have a common theme, which are importantly and significantly different in many other respects" (Brinker 1995, 33). The telepathic powers of Saleem Sinai in Rushdie's (1981) *Midnight's Children*, for example, serve a specific thematic purpose: they highlight the opportunity for mutual understanding among different ethnicities, religions, and local communities in postcolonial India after independence from the British colonizers.

With regard to narrative components, James Phelan (1996, 29) distinguishes between mimetic, thematic, and synthetic elements. He explains these three components as follows: "Responses to the mimetic component involve an audience's interest in the characters as possible people and in the narrative world as like our own. Responses to the thematic component involve an interest in the ideational function of the characters and in the cultural, philosophical, or ethical issues being addressed by the narrative. Responses to the synthetic component involve an audience's interest in and attention to the characters and to the larger narrative as artificial constructs" (2005, 20).

In many cases one can link the synthetic (of which the unnatural is a subcategory) back to the mimetic by foregrounding the thematic. In other words, by identifying a specific theme we can explain the unnatural so that it communicates something meaningful to us (see also Phelan 1996, 29; 2005, 15). Also since "anything written in meaningful language has a theme" (Tomashevsky [1921] 1965, 63), this reading strategy plays a crucial role in all of my readings or interpretations.①

5. Reading allegorically: Readers may also see impossible elements as parts of abstract allegories that say something about Everyman or Everywoman, that is, the human condition, or the world in general (as opposed to particular individuals). Allegory is a figurative mode of representation that tries to convey a certain idea rather than represent a coherent storyworld. David Mikics (2007, 8) points out that, depending on one's perspective, one might either argue that "allegories turn abstract concepts or features into characters" or that allegories "transform people and places into conceptual entities". The basic cognitive move of this reading strategy is to see unnatural scenarios or events as representing abstract ideas or concepts.

In Sarah Kane's (2001) play *Cleansed*, for instance, the character Grace transforms into her beloved brother Graham. We can make sense of this metamorphosis by reading it in the context of an allegory on the merits and dangers of love. Grace's transformation can be read as highlighting one of the

① Yacobi (1981) refers to thematic readings in terms of the "functional principle". For her "the work's aesthetic, thematic and persuasive goals invariably operate as a major guideline to making sense of its peculiarities" (117).

potential dangers of love, namely the danger of losing oneself in the relationship with the loved one.[①]

6. Satirization and parody: Narratives may also use unnatural scenarios or events to satirize, mock, or ridicule certain psychological predispositions or states of affairs. The most important feature of satire is critique through exaggeration, distortion, or caricature, and "grotesque images" of humiliation or ridicule (Mikics 2007, 271), which serve a didactic point, often merge with the unnatural. Parody is a subcategory of satire that involves the mocking recontextualization of a prior text or style by a later one.

Roth's *The Breast* (1972), for example, confronts us with a slightly obsessive professor of literature who has transformed into a female breast. In his lectures before the metamorphosis, this professor used to teach the unnatural transformations in the works of Gogol and Kafha while at the same time insisting that fiction influences our lives. This professor has literally become an example of what he used to teach, and the novel uses this unnatural transformation to ridicule him for taking fiction too seriously.

At this point one might wonder about the relationship between allegorical and satirical readings, on the one hand, and the idea of evoking generic conventions from literary history, on the other. For me a distinction can be drawn between general modes (such as allegory and satire) and proper literary genres (such as the beast fable or the modernist novel). In principle one could try reading any text allegorically or satirically, and therefore separate reading strategies are based on the concepts of allegory and satire.[②]

7. Positing a transcendental realm: Readers can explain some projected impossibilities by assuming that they are part of a transcendental setting (such as heaven, purgatory, or hell).[③] Beckett's ([1963] 1990) play *Play*, for example, confronts us with a circular temporality: at the end of the play the story returns to its beginning and continues indefinitely. *Play* thus suggests that its three characters (M, W1, and W2), who are trapped in urns while a light consistently forces them to talk about their past lives, are caught in an endless temporal loop.A very common way of explaining this unnatural temporality is to argue that the play is set in a transcendental realm, a kind of purgatory without purification, in which the three characters are doomed to relive the events of their past lives, which involve a love triangle, in a continuous cycle as a form of punishment.

8. Do it yourself: Ryan (2006b, 671) has shown that we can explain the logically incompatible

---

① Ryan (2006b, 669) refers to this reading strategy in terms of "allegory and metaphor" and argues that in some cases the point of the impossible is to "illustrate an idea rather than to represent objectively happening courses of events".

② The case of satire is even more complicated than the case of allegory because the term *satire* designates both "a mode, that is, a tone and an attitude" and "a genre, a class of literature with a distinct repertory of conventions" (Real 2005, 512). I therefore distinguish between satire as a broad discourse mode (which involves critique through exaggeration) and satire as a genre that deploys the satiric mode in a certain way and has a specific object of ridicule (such as the beast fable, the Menippean satire, the circulation novel, the social satire, the mock literary history, or parodies of certain genres).

③ One does not have to believe in the actual existence of heaven, purgatory, or hell to be able to imagine that a fictional narrative is set in such a transcendental realm.

storylines of some narratives by assuming that "the contradictory passages in the text are offered to the readers as material for creating their own stories". In such cases the narrative serves as a construction kit or collage that invites free play with its elements. Coover's (1969) short story "The Babysitter", for instance, confronts us with various logical impossibilities. One might argue that this narrative uses mutually incompatible storylines to make us aware of suppressed possibilities and allows us to choose the ones that, for whatever reason, we prefer.①

This reading strategy closely correlates with Roland Barthes's ([1968] 2001, 1470) ideas about "the birth of the reader", which must be "at the cost of the death of the Author". Barthes argues that "to give a text an Author is to impose a limit on that text, to furnish it with a final signified, to close the writing ... When the Author has been found, the text is 'explained'—victory to the critic" (1469). In stories such as "The Babysitter", on the other hand, the author cannot be found; the author is absent and does not guide the reader at all. Hence readers have to make up their own minds and construct their own stories.

9. The Zen way of reading: Acknowledging this strategy as a possible interpretive orientation is a way of ensuring that attempts to make sense of the unnatural do not destroy more than they create, or perhaps even become "an act of *Gleichschaltung*" in which "the diversity of fictional worlds is reduced to the uniform structure of the complete, Carnapian world" (Doležel 1998, 171). Hence as a radical alternative to my more or less intrepid moves of sense-making, all of which follow the human urge to create significance, I mention the Zen way of reading. The Zen way of reading presupposes an attentive and stoic reader who repudiates the earlier explanations and simultaneously accepts both the strangeness of unnatural scenarios and the feelings of discomfort, fear, worry, and panic that they might evoke in her or him. In this context what Keats calls "*Negative Capability*" can be resorted to as a way of thinking about the attitudes that many unnatural phenomena invite us to adopt: the state of being in "uncertainties, mysteries, doubts without any irritable reaching after fact or reason" (Forman 1935, 72). Alternatively this way of reading can also assume the shape of a pleasurable response. I am thinking of an aesthetic reaction that does not entail any kind of cognitive discomfort but rather sheer joy at the freedom from natural possibility. Since we know that fiction is safe, we enter into it voluntarily, knowing that we need not risk anything by doing so. We often simply take pleasure from the impossible as such.②

---

① Similarly John Ashbery (1957, 251) sees Gertrude Stein's "impossible work" as an "all-purpose model which each reader can adapt to fit his own set of particulars".

② Apart from the principles that I have discussed so far, Yacobi (1981, 114 - 115, 116 - 117) mentions "the genetic principle", which explains discrepancies in causal terms related to the production of the text by its author, and "the existential principle", which reconciles discordant elements in terms of a unique storyworld that cannot be accounted for by the constraints of a known genre. I am not really convinced of the explanatory power of the genetic principle when it comes to the unnatural. I feel that, unless one tries to explain slips or mistakes, invoking "the historical producer" (114) does not explain very much. The existential principle, on the other hand, plays a crucial role in all reading strategies—with the exception of reading strategy 2, which explains the unnatural through generic conventions, and reading strategy 3, which naturalizes the unnatural as a fantasy of a character or the narrator. All my other navigational tools concern unique storyworlds that have a peculiar structure because within them physical, logical, or human impossibilities objectively exist.

These reading strategies cut across Doležel's (1998, 165, 160) distinction between "world construction" and "meaning production" because the cognitive reconstruction of storyworlds always already involves a process of interpretation. Nevertheless the first two strategies correlate with cognitive processes that are closer to the pole of reconstruction or world-making, whereas the others are closer to the pole of interpretation or meaning-making. Also 1 and 2 involve more or less automatic cognitive processes, while the other strategies entail more conscious or reflexive moves.

三、思考与讨论

(1) 阿尔贝和理查森各自界定非自然叙事的优势和缺陷在哪里?

(2) 关于什么是非自然叙事,阿尔贝为什么提出与理查森不同的观点?

(3) 如何评价阿尔贝提出的几种非自然叙事阐释策略?

第四节 亨里克·斯克夫·尼尔森及其“非自然化阅读策略”

一、导读

丹麦叙事学家亨里克·斯克夫·尼尔森的非自然叙事理论在非自然叙事学界颇有特色。尼尔森并不试图将非自然叙事视为模仿叙事的对立面。他认为,非自然叙事的关键特质在于其对日常故事讲述原则的违背,其核心意义则是对叙事边界的拓展。他在界定非自然叙事时指出:“什么是非自然叙事?它们为虚构叙事的一个子类别——与许多现实主义和模仿叙事不同——它们暗示读者在阅读时需要运用不同于其在非虚构和对话性故事讲述情景中所采用的阐释策略。具体来说,这类叙事可能包含一些在真实世界故事讲述情景中被理解为物理上、逻辑上、记忆上、心理上不可能或难以置信的时间结构、故事世界、心理再现或叙述行为,但它们却通过暗示读者改变其阐释策略来允许他们将这类叙事解读为可靠的、可能的和/或权威的。”① 从尼尔森对非自然叙事的定义中不难发现,他对非自然叙事的界定同时考虑到了“文本”和“读者”两个维度。在文本层面,非自然叙事通过建构不可能的时间结构、故事世界、心理再现和叙述行为来区别于普遍意义上的现实主义叙事,拓展了叙事形式的边界,构成一种特殊的叙事类型。在读者层面,非自然叙事在文本形式方面的独特性要求读者运用不同于理解一般意义上的现实主义叙事的阐释策略,以能够充分理解非自然叙事所建构的非自然性。在如何阐释非自然叙事这一问题上,尼尔森提出“非自然化阅读策略”(unnaturalizing reading strategy)。所谓非自然化阅读,就是在理解非自然叙事的过程中并不诉诸基于真实生活经验的认知参数,拒绝将非自然叙事中的故事世界建构视为真实生活经验的投射和模仿,最大限度地保留非自然叙事本身的虚构特质,以此获得对非自然文本的新颖解读。从本质上看,如果说自然化阅读旨在通过真实世界的认知框架来消除非自然叙事的非自然性,以使其变得更为可读,那么非自然阅读的目的则是要从虚构性的角度来阅读非自然叙事,保留其非自然性。②

二、《自然化与非自然化阅读策略:重访聚焦》选读③

1. Aims of the Essay

In this essay I argue that applying the principles of unnatural narratology in the form of what I call unnaturalizing reading strategies to the interpretation of unnatural narratives is often a more

① Henrik Skov Nielsen, “Naturalizing and Unnaturalizing Reading Strategies: Focalization Revisited,” *A Poetics of Unnatural Narrative*, eds. Jan Alber, et al. (Columbus: The Ohio State University Press, 2013), p.72.

② Shang Biwu, “Unnatural Emotions in Contemporary Narrative Fiction,” *Neohelicon* 2 (2018), p.453.

③ Nielsen, “Naturalizing and Unnaturalizing Reading Strategies: Focalization Revisited,” pp.67 - 83.

appropriate choice than applying the principles of naturalization and familiarization. A main contention is that Genette's separation of voice and mood (who speaks and who perceives) and Genette's understanding of focalization as a restriction of access to point of view are more radical proposals than previous narratologists have recognized—and that they are in line with unnatural narratology and allow for unnaturalizing reading strategies.

The argument compels me to revisit some points from an early essay of mine called "The Impersonal Voice in First-Person Narrative Fiction" that played a role in the emergence of unnatural narratology along with work by Maria Mäkelä, Jan Alber, and Brian Richardson. In the essay I argue that in first-person narrative fiction, the limits of the protagonist's voice in such areas as knowledge, vocabulary, and memory are sometimes strikingly transgressed and that this is neither a mistake nor something foreign to the genre but, on the contrary, a matter of utilizing a possibility fundamental to it.

In the present essay I wish to take this one step further and to argue that what seemed to me and most other narrative theorists at the time to be a rare and strange type of narrative does in fact tell us much about character narration in general, and that character narration, in this view, in turn, tells us something about fictional narration in general. This is because these narrative types are all most fruitfully understood as different manifestations of a relationship between author and characters. In natural frameworks one would expect all character narrators to be internally focalized, since one would expect a character narrator to have access to his or her own thoughts and not to other people's thoughts. I argue that Genette's focalization theory is really a relational theory about the relation between characters and authors, and that it is an integral part of the system that an author can choose to combine any access or nonaccess to thoughts and knowledge with any kind of narration, including character narration, precisely because the system disconnects mood and voice.

Genette's insight into the disconnect between mood and voice in fiction explains why and how fiction can (but obviously need not) employ a range of unnatural mind representations in combinations such as homodiegetic narration with zero focalization (in the manner of Ishmael in *Moby-Dick*). Furthermore, this combinatory principle can even be expanded beyond Genette's own examples to include such unnatural combinations as you-narration with internal focalization, we-narration with external focalization, and so on. Therefore, it fits nicely with the discussions of strange and unnatural narratives in Brian Richardson's *Unnatural Voices*, in which chapter 2 covers second-person narration, chapter 3 covers we-narration, and the rest of the chapters cover other unusual narrative situations.

I argue further that the separation of mood and voice and the possible combinations that follow from it are connected to the no-narrator thesis. These combinations are attributable not to a fact-reporting narrator but rather to a fictional world-creating author. This attribution in turn emphasizes the difference between reading with the assumption that the storyworld is invented (fiction) and reading with the assumption that the storyworld is not invented (nonfiction). This understanding then logically leads to a choice between interpretations: If we interpret the words in a 300-page dialogue novel with a character narrator, or—on a smaller scale—the shorter rendering of a dialogue that took place 50 years ago as only *appearing* to be verbatim accounts, we make a legitimate but naturalizing choice. If we believe instead that they are part of the invented act of narration, we can also believe that the dialogues are verbatim accounts and can thus base interpretations on the characters saying some words rather than others. In making this equally legitimate choice we would also be following the principles of unnatural narratology because we would make an interpretational choice that is unnaturalizing in the sense that it is not limiting the narrative possibilities to what is mnemonically possible or plausible in real-world narration. In what follows I test these assumptions and argue in favor of unnaturalizing reading strategies in a range of examples before finally suggesting a simple, rhetorical model in which the real author rather than the narrator is the main agent of the telling, and in which not all narrative acts are representational.

2. Exceptionality, Similarity, and Unnatural Narratology

Much of the introduction to David Herman's impressive anthology *The Emergence of Mind* is based on a refutation of what he calls the exceptionality thesis. He directly connects this thesis to the question of unnatural narratology and to theorists such as Alber, Mäkelä, Richardson, and Skov Nielsen (11). Herman writes that "[...] the questioning of the exceptionality thesis is in a sense the starting point for all the approaches to fictional minds outlined by the chapters in this volume [...]" (18), and refers to almost every contributor in the volume as "anti-exceptionalist" (20, 21, 22). The exceptionality thesis, then, is the thesis that we approach fiction and nonfiction by means of different protocols for reasoning and with different interpretive strategies, and that, for example, "[...] readers' experiences of fictional minds are different in kind from their experiences of the minds they encounter outside the domain of narrative fiction [...]" (8), "[...] a thesis against which I think this volume militates," writes Herman (32). Interestingly, Herman explicitly notes his opposition to Richardson:

> Richardson describes as follows the conventions for representing minds in texts he characterizes as mimetic: "A first person narrator cannot know what is in the minds of others, and a third person narrator may perform this, and a few other such acts, but may not stray beyond the established conventions of depicting such perceptions: the thought of one character may not be lodged within the mind of another without any intervening plausible explanation" (6 - 7). I would argue by contrast that, in light of the research on folk psychology that I discuss in this section, the modes of

narration that Richardson characterizes as unnatural or "anti-mimetic" converge with present-day understandings of how minds actually work. (33 – 34)

Finally, I wish to mention a call to the exceptionalists that seems apt to me:

> Granted, fictional narratives have the power to stipulate as true reports about characters' mind-contents. But the onus is on Exceptionalists to demonstrate that readers have to use different interpretive protocols to make sense of such stipulated mental states and dispositions, in comparison with the protocols they use for construing actual minds. (33)

I agree with the latter quote, and, accordingly, I want to argue that it is *sometimes* necessary, *often* profitable, and *nearly always* possible to use different interpretive protocols when the mind-content of characters (other than of a character narrator herself/himself) is rendered. To make this argument, however, I need to engage in a reading of Genette's focalization theory. Genette is completely absent in Herman's introduction and in its voluminous list of references, and this is not surprising since the study of consciousness-representation in fiction has been almost totally separated from the study of focalization. I will argue, however, that they are two sides of the same coin. Before doing so, I will first define what I mean by unnatural narratives and unnatural narratology and clarify my intention, which is not to claim that all fictional narratives are unnatural.

3. Definitions

For me, the expression "unnatural narratives" first and foremost takes on meaning in relation to what it is not: natural narratives. By natural narratives I refer to narratives that have been designated as such by influential narrative theorists. Most prominently the term "natural" has been applied to narrative theory by Monika Fludernik in *Towards a 'Natural' Narratology*. Here, she describes the term as follows:

> *Natural narrative* is a term that has come to define "naturally occurring" storytelling [...] What will be called *natural narrative* in this book includes, mainly, spontaneous conversational storytelling, a term which would be more appropriate but is rather unwieldy. (*Towards* 13)

This is the first and most important of three different meanings that feed into the term "natural narratology". Its source is Labov and linguistic discourse analysis. The second meaning of the term "natural" comes from "Natürlichkeitstheorie", which uses the term to "[...] designate aspects of language which appear to be regulated and motivated by cognitive parameters based on man's experience of embodiedness in a real-world context" (17). Whereas both of these two meanings function as descriptive denominators of a certain kind of narrative or language, the third one is on a completely different level and refers to the readers' *reaction* to certain types of narrative, literature, or discourse. It comes from Culler and his use of the term "naturalization" to designate readers' efforts to make the strange and deviant seem natural and thus to familiarize it: "Culler's naturalization in particular embraces the familiarization of the strange" (*Towards* 31). I do not disagree that natural narratives of the kind described by Fludernik exist, but an equally important point is one that Fludernik herself stresses in 2003: that we should not necessarily privilege these:

> Rather than privileging naturally occurring storytelling situations, Natural Narratology, by contrast, attempts to show how in the historical development of narratorial forms natural base frames are again and again being extended. [...] [O]nce an originally non-natural storytelling situation has become widely disseminated in fictional texts, it acquires a second-level "naturalness" from habituality, creating a cognitive frame [...] which readers subconsciously deploy in their textual processing. Even more paradoxically, fiction as a genre comes to represent precisely those impossible naturalized forms and to create readerly expectations along those lines. ("Natural Narratology" 255)

It is instructive to see explicitly stressed that such a thing as an "originally non-natural storytelling situation" exists. The question, though, is whether the reader will always try to naturalize anything—and if so, if it can always be done successfully.

In yet another text, this time from 2001, Fludernik writes: "When readers read narrative texts, they project real-life parameters into the reading process and, if at all possible, treat the text as a real-life instance of narrating" ("New Wine" 623). I think it is worth noting, first, that as a descriptive statement as opposed to a normative statement about what readers *should* do, it hardly covers all readers, nor all lay readers; and second, that even if this is what many readers tend to do, we are not obliged to repeat the projection at a methodological level. Familiarization, or what Culler calls naturalization and Fludernik, narrativization, is a choice, and whether the choice is conscious or automatic, it remains a choice and not a necessity. A different choice in the form of unnaturalizing interpretation is equally legitimate and rewarding in many texts. Following from this, these are my answers to the "what?" and the "how?" of unnatural narratology:

- What are unnatural narratives? They are a subset of fictional narratives that—unlike many realistic and mimetic narratives—cue the reader to employ interpretational strategies that are different from those she employs in nonfictionalized, conversational storytelling situations. More specifically, such narratives may have temporalities, storyworlds, mind representations, or acts of narration that would have to be construed as physically, logically, mnemonically, or psychologically impossible or implausible in real-world storytelling situations, but that allow the reader to interpret them instead as reliable, possible, and/or authoritative by cueing her to change her interpretational strategies.

- What is unnatural narratology? The investigation of these strategies and their interpretational consequences and, more broadly, the effort to state the theoretical and interpretive principles relevant to such unnatural narratives. This means that for me all unnatural narratives are fictional but only some fictional narratives are unnatural. Only some fictional narratives cue the reader to interpret differently than real-life storytelling situations do, whereas scores of realistic and conventional fictional narratives do not do that. I do wish to stress, though, the unnaturalness also of some conventional forms, such as, say, the use of zero focalization in traditional works of realism.

...

5. Examples of Unnaturalizing Reading Strategies

5.1 *Glamorama*

In *Recent Theories of Narrative* (1986), Martin Wallace writes "One telltale sign of omniscience [...]: comments on what a character did not think" (146). Several times in the first-person novel *Glamorama*, by Bret Easton Ellis, we are explicitly told what the protagonist Victor does not perceive:

> "Disarm" by the Smashing Pumpkins starts playing on the soundtrack and the music overlaps a shot of the club I was going to open in TriBeCa and I walk into that frame, *not noticing* the black limousine parked across the street [...]. (168; my italics, H.S.N.)

This strange feature presents the reader with the paradoxical situation that the narrator seems to be at once omniscient and ignorant. This paradox arises, however, only if we attribute the narrative act and the enunciation of the narrative as a whole to Victor—and in fact there is little evidence, aside from the use of the first-person pronoun, that we should do that. In the course of *Glamorama* there are numerous passages in which events and thoughts are related that the character, Victor, could not possibly know about—indeed, that no character narrator would be able to know about. Among the most striking examples is the rendering of the passengers' last thoughts in an exploding airplane (438 - 441), and of the sleeping Cloe's dream (43). One example from the exploding airplane—which no one survives, and where Victor is not present—reads like this:

> "Why me?" someone wonders uselessly. [...] Susan Goldman, who has [...] cancer, is partly thankful as she braces herself, but changes her mind as she's sprayed with burning jet fuel. (440)

What do we make of this? Victor is not on the plane. All the passengers die. This seems like a clear-cut case of homodiegetic narration with zero focalization.① Naturalizing readings will have to explain this peculiarity by searching for ways to naturalize it. Might Victor somehow have gained access to the thoughts represented? Naturalizing options also include but are not limited to assuming that Victor is outright lying or making up what he cannot know, that he is unreliable, has gone temporarily mad, is joking or being ironic, or even that he might have—as a character in the storyworld—the gift of telepathy. I am not going to argue against each one of these options, but I think they are all extremely unlikely and heavily contradicted by other parts of the text. It seems to me that if we make the interpretational choice of believing that we can trust that this is actually what the passengers are thinking, then this in and of itself entails an interpretation that does not "converge with present-day understandings of how minds actually work" (Herman 33 - 34) since surely it is not a present-day understanding of real minds to say that they are able to reliably render what dying persons isolated in a plane far away are thinking.

This has to do exactly with the disconnect between mood and voice. In natural frameworks one would expect all homodiegetic narratives to be internally focalized, since we would expect a first-person narrator to have access to his or her own thoughts as opposed to external focalization but not to other people's thoughts as opposed to zero focalization. However, if we assume, as a reading strategy, that mood and voice are disconnected, then we can also assume that the possibility of transgressing the limits of personal voice regarding knowledge, vocabulary, memory, and so forth, is present. Therefore, we should not restrict our interpretations to what would be possible or plausible if mood and voice were connected, if the answer to "who speaks?" and "who sees?" was necessarily the same as in natural narration, and if, accordingly, the character, that is, Victor, had to the source of the narrative.

Without presenting a detailed analysis of the novel,② I wish to mention that this general conception has considerable interpretive consequences. The very feature of a voice that does not unambiguously belong to Victor referring to Victor in the first person greatly contributes to the effect of the uncanny and is deeply connected with the theme of the double, it being one of the many elements in the book that cause the narrative's words—and even the words "I" "me" and

---

① I prefer the description homodiegetic narration with zero focalization over descriptions such as first-person narrative with paralepsis. Insofar as "paralepsis" means "saying too much" in the sense of disclosing knowledge you could not possess, it is only a question of paralepsis in Glamorama and similar narratives if we still think of the first person as the source of the narration, and this is exactly the view I want to challenge. In this sense, "paralepsis" serves to naturalize the understanding in its own way by assuming that "I" must be the speaker, as in natural linguistics, only occasionally displaying information "I" could not have.

② For a more developed reading of *Glamorama*, see Nielsen "Telling Doubles".

"my"—to be open for the intrusion of the double. The words "Who the fuck is Moi?" on the first page of the novel thus become the starting signal for a game of hide and seek in which the reader is invited to make a guess: "Who is 'I' now referring to?" *Glamorama* is in some respects a classic doppelganger narrative. The protagonist and first-person narrator Victor Ward apparently has a double, and gradually this double takes over his identity. In the end, one Victor—and everything seems to indicate that he is the one we have followed throughout most of the book—dies in Italy while the other Victor, his double, enjoys life in New York. The really odd and unnatural thing about *Glamorama*, however, is that not only does the double overtake the identity of the first-person narrator on the thematic level and in the narrated universe; he even becomes the new referent of the pronoun "I". He has intruded in Victor's life and even overtaken his pronoun. This phenomenon does not seem to correspond to any real-world, natural discourse. In my opinion, a natural linguistic conception in which "I" inevitably refers to the speaker would not be able to account for either the many passages with zero focalization or this pronominal takeover. Yet an understanding of the basic events and the storyline in *Glamorama* hinges crucially on understanding these.①

…

5.2 *The Great Gatsby*

In a discussion of *The Great Gatsby* in *Narrative as Rhetoric*, Phelan observes that Fitzgerald does not even try to justify how the first-person narrator, Nick Carraway, is able to narrate what he could not possibly know. Phelan shows that Fitzgerald was rightly not concerned about providing any justification and that the reported scene is invested with full authority all the same (108 - 109). Similarly, in *Living to Tell About It*, Phelan exemplifies:

> In chapter 8 of *The Great Gatsby*, Nick Carraway reports the scene at Wilson's garage involving Michaelis and Wilson as if he were a non-character narrator with the privilege of moving between his own focalization and that of Michaelis. What is curious here is not just that Nick narrates a scene at which he was not present but also that Fitzgerald does not try to justify how Nick came to know what Michaelis must have been thinking. (4)

In my opinion, the choice to think of the garage scene in *The Great Gatsby* as authoritatively

① At the very beginning of the book the reader is warned, in Ellis's humoristic way, that there will be no unity of plot and no unity of character (that I is another, as Rimbaud put it) in the following two passages:

> "[...] I don't want a lot of description, just the story, streamlined, no frills, the lowdown: who, what, where, when and don't leave out why, though I'm getting the distinct expression by the looks on your sorry faces that why won't get answered—now, come on, goddamnit, what's the story?" (5)

> "Who the fuck is Moi?" I ask. "I have no fucking idea who this Moi is, baby," I exclaim. "Because I'm like shvitzing."
> "Moi is Peyton, Victor," JD says quietly.
> "I'm Moi," Peyton says, nodding. "Moi is, um, French." (5)

represented—even though the narrator, Carraway, was not present—is a result of what I call an unnaturalizing interpretation strategy. This is especially because it does not try to justify itself by interpreting the passage as the possible guess of the character narrator. Nor does it claim that he must later have obtained this knowledge. Instead, one of the most important consequences is very nicely captured by Phelan in the following sentence—which in my view acknowledges the disconnect between mood and voice: "When the narratorial functions are operating independently of the character functions, then the narration will be reliable and authoritative" (*Narrative as Rhetoric* 112).

三、思考与讨论

(1) 如何评价尼尔森对非自然叙事的界定?

(2) 尼尔森所提出的"非自然化阅读"有何意义?

(3) 尼尔森对《了不起的盖茨比》的解读你赞同吗?

本章推荐阅读书目

[1] Jan Alber and Brian Richardson, eds. *Unnatural Narratology: Extensions, Revisions, and Challenges*. Columbus: The Ohio State University Press, 2020.

[2] Jan Alber, Henrik Skov Nielsen, and Brian Richardson, eds. *A Poetics of Unnatural Narrative*. Columbus: The Ohio State University Press, 2013.

[3] Jan Alber and Rüdiger Heinze, eds. *Unnatural Narratives, Unnatural Narratology*. Berlin: Walter de Gruyter, 2011.

[4] Brian Richardson. *Unnatural Voices: Extreme Narration in Modern and Contemporary Fiction*. Columbus: The Ohio State University Press, 2006.

[5] Maria Mäkelä and Merja Polvinen, eds. "Narration and Focalization: A Cognitivist and an Unnaturalist, Made Strange," *Poetics Today* 39.3(2018): 495 - 521.

第七章
身体叙事学

第一节　概　　论

在 20 世纪前的很长一段时间，身体都被视为“灵魂的容器”、无思想的器官，甚至有时因拥有物质欲望而被宗教神学归为罪恶的渊薮，从东方到西方皆是如此。无论是《荷马史诗》的身体与灵魂之分、笛卡尔的身心二元论，还是孟子的“大体”“小体”区别，皆未逃离贬低物质身体的桎梏。纵然有文艺复兴时期对身体之美的推崇，抑或“天人感应”思想对身体概念的重审这类不同的声音，其也难免淹没在“精神中心论”的主流思想中。身体被压抑和克制，难登大雅之堂，更不必说对其特别关注和深入研究了。

随着 19 世纪末以来科学的发展，人们意识到身体是产生意识的根源，身心二元对立的传统认识逐渐被击破，这在哲学家的观点转变中即可看出。20 世纪以来，胡塞尔在海德格尔等人的哲学基础上创立现象学，高喊“回到事实本身”的口号，意图用现象学拯救处于困境中的西方哲学，这种反“形而上”的路径将作为感官枢纽的身体推上了至关重要的地位，学界对身体的忽视现象渐有改观。先有尼采大肆宣扬肉体之美，鼓励大众以身体为媒介，调动生命力的极限；再有梅洛-庞蒂建构“知觉现象学”，把身体构建为存在的根基，重塑身体知觉对人类理解世界的重要意义；其后更不乏德勒兹“无器官的身体”、福柯的身体政治、布莱恩·特纳的身体社会学、理查德·舒斯特曼的身体美学等探究身体作用的理论观点，身体在被压抑了数个世纪以后终于被重新正名。

随着身体意义的回归，哲学、社会学、人类学等多个学科掀起了“身体转向”(somatic turn)，叙事学也不例外。身体叙事和当今的“创伤叙事”“战争叙事”类似，源于对叙事中“故事”层面某类意象的特别关注，继而衍生出新的阐释角度和理论体系。因此，即使目前国内外的文学批评中“身体叙事”研究者众多，但相关理论体系仍然较为薄弱，与丰富的身体叙事文本批评成果形成鲜明对比。身体叙事学的理论建构始于 20 世纪 90 年代和 21 世纪初期，其后主要向其他学科横向发展。如今，“身体叙事”的视角已被广泛应用于文学、影视、文化、医学、体育等多个领域的研究，身体叙事学不仅可以帮助我们了解身体在人类认识和理解世界过程中的重要地位和多重功能，也能帮助我们更好地发挥身体的作用，实现自我的完善和提升。

一、是“身体书写”,还是“身体叙事”?

论及“身体叙事”,许多人会联想到学界使用频率更高的“身体书写”。的确,身体叙事比身体书写出现更晚,二者有一定关联,但身体叙事不止是身体书写。因此,有必要先从“身体书写”开始,逐步探明“身体叙事”的多层含义。巴赫金曾写道:“现代社会对个人身体的印象已全盘改变:身体被转移至私有的、心理的层面,身体的隐含意义精确窄化,不再与社会生活或宇宙有直接的联系。这种新的隐含意义令身体不再具有从前的哲学功能。”① 正因如此,越发个性化的身体成为作家和文学家关注的文本特征之一。20世纪以来,随着女性文学、少数族裔文学等关注身体特征的文学领域蓬勃发展,越来越多的作家选择身体作为书写的对象。法国女性主义学者埃莱娜·西苏(Hélène Cixou)提出的“阴性书写”便是身体书写风潮的前锋。西苏鼓励以“书写身体”(writing the body)为女性争取话语权,探索女性的身份和处境,意在打破写作中女性长久以来的失语状态。80年代,关于女性主义身体政治的讨论已经体现出若干对身体叙事学的探索,比如1985年苏珊·鲁宾·苏雷曼(Susan Rubin Suleiman)主持的《今日诗学》期刊专栏“西方文化中的女性身体”中,就有一系列此类研究,如解读“消除身体”行为对故事情节和人物形象的披露作用,探索传统女性身体意象与成长故事(bildungsroman)等传统文类的情节模型的关系,尝试取缔旧的叙事结构和旧的词汇,发明新的结构、新的词语、新的句法来动摇和转变旧的思维习惯和旧的观察视角。至今,“身体书写”一词仍经常被默认为女性主义视角的身体书写,但衍生出更多层理解和实践手法。一方面,部分作家对“身体”的理解过于片面,将“身体书写”演变为一种为商业炒作而生的快餐文学形式,将这一概念扭曲为单纯的身体细节描写,暴露女性身体和性相关的隐私体验,与身体书写最初的目的背道而驰;另一方面,“身体书写”的概念也在逐渐扩张,逐渐脱离与女性主义研究的关联,成为一种基于现象学思想、借人物身体来思考社会与文化的写作手法,内容亦不再限于女性身体的书写。

“身体书写”概念的演变催生了“身体叙事”的理论观点。尽管国内外部分学者仍将“身体叙事”简单地理解为“身体书写”,作为叙事学一个分支的“身体叙事”已初具规模,包括基于精神分析学和知觉现象学观点的身体叙事观、人物身体和叙事要素的关系讨论、从身体模式反观世界的具身化的世界观等,身体书写只是其重点关注的一个方面。如今我们已充分认识到,身体一直是文学作品塑造人物的必要媒介,关于身体的描述并非故事层面新出现的内容,“身体书写”和“身体叙事”的兴起只是文学发展史上长久存在的身体话题在近几十年受到更多关注的结果。

二、身体叙事学:基本观点与理论框架

从80年代中后期开始,身体被引入叙事学理论体系。使身体脱离“阴性书写”的领域,正式进入叙事学理论的先锋是彼得·布鲁克斯(Peter Brooks),他在《阅读情节:叙事中的设计和意图》(*Reading for the plot: Design and Intension in Narrative*,1992)中首次提出了“叙事欲望”的概念:“叙事既讲述欲

① 转引自 Daniel Punday, “Narrative Performance in the Contemporary Monster Story,” *The Modern Language Review* 97.4 (2002), p.805.

望——一般是呈现关于欲望的故事——又激发并利用欲望,将欲望作为意义的动力。”[①] 布鲁克斯从身体的角度出发,讨论欲望在叙事中不可缺失的地位,建立了著名的“欲望动力学”(dynamic of desire)。他写道:“如今,探究欲望这一概念至关重要,因为它是叙事的本原,它推动情节,为阅读提供动能,为意义的生成赋予活力。”[②] 布鲁克斯认为,欲望不能被简单的当作情节的驱动力,它同时也与叙事的主题、叙事的动力、叙事语言和叙述行为的意图紧密相关——叙述者的叙述行为(narration)来自原始的讲述意图。故事的人物和情节设计更是离不开欲望的产生和满足,而受述者或读者的阅读行为同样为欲望所驱动,他们因为想要了解全部情节而继续阅读。布鲁克斯借巴尔扎克名作《驴皮记》来解释叙事欲望在推动情节上的悖论：正如那张神奇的驴皮可以通过缩减主人公的生命来帮他实现愿望,叙事也是一张“神奇的驴皮”,读者对未知情节的欲望在阅读(或用布鲁克斯的话来说,“消耗”)文本的过程中逐渐被实现,意义建构最大化的时刻也就是情节的终点。如果说,叙事的驱动力是欲望,欲望能构筑并搭建意义单位,那么意义的最终决定因素就在叙事的结尾,叙事欲望最终成为期待结尾的欲望。[③] 由此也可以看出,“身体书写”只代表身体与叙事的一类关系,而身体叙事学体系中身体与叙事的关系是多种多样的。

关于欲望的叙事观是身体叙事学理论最具代表性的“前身”。布鲁克斯的《阅读情节：叙事中的设计和意图》在对此进行充分建构的基础上,其续作《身体活：现代叙述中的欲望对象》将身体叙事观拓展到了文学、绘画等文艺作品中“身体如何成为叙事”的问题上,从欲望出发,身体作为一种叙事所承担的多种功能,为身体叙事学理论体系的萌芽提供了丰厚的土壤。布鲁克斯在开篇即阐明:“现代叙述看来形成了某种身体的符号化(semioticization),而与之相应的是故事的躯体化(somatization)：它断言,身体必定是意义的根源和核心,而且非得把身体作为叙述确切含义的主要媒介才能讲故事。”[④] 借此,身体的功能被进一步拓展,布鲁克斯等学者在这一阶段逐步总结出身体在文艺作品中两方面的重要功能：

第一,身体是身份的象征,是人物社会文化意义的唯一载体。身体是读者区分人物的最主要判断依据,而人物也凭借身体才可以拥有特定的身份、社会地位、文化背景。诸多中外名著与传说中,许多人物给读者的印象都不仅包括性格、品德等抽象特征,也包含身体特征、衣着体态等具体形象特征,如“阿喀琉斯之踵”、卡西莫多的丑陋外貌、关羽的红脸、少年闰土戴的银项圈等。而承载身份特征的身体,也能推动故事的发展,促成亲友相认、行踪暴露、人物关系变化等关键情节。比如《红楼梦》中的侍女香菱,不知生身父母,也不知自己姓甚名谁,但作者特意提及其眉间的一颗“胭脂记”,令读者不免想起故事开头甄士隐在元宵节大火时走丢的、眉间同样有“胭脂记”的小女儿甄英莲。通过身体特征的匹配,读者得以为香菱找回她的出身背景和本来姓名,将其早年生活情景和现在的身份、环境衔接,较为完整地了解香菱命运的落差。从富贵之家的掌上明珠沦为被人任意买卖的仆婢,其本名暗示的“应怜”在其成年后的悲惨命运之上又添一层悲凉之意,揭露了封建社会的黑暗。

第二,身体是艺术和审美的基础。无论在文学、绘画、雕塑,还是当今的多媒体艺术形式中,身体都是人们欣赏的主要对象。在《身体活：现代叙述中的欲望对象》的主体章节中,布鲁克斯从身体视角重新审视了几种主流艺术形式的欲望本质,而这些小说、绘画、雕塑作品的艺术形式本身和审美的过程都

---

① Peter Brooks, *Reading for the Plot: Design and Intension in Narrative* (Cambridge: Harvard University Press, 1992), p.37.

② Ibid., p.48.

③ Ibid., pp.52 - 53.

④ 彼得·布鲁克斯:《身体活：现代叙述中的欲望对象》,朱生坚译,北京：新星出版社,2005 年,第 2 页。

是以身体为基础的。其中最具代表性的是对小说本质的探讨。布鲁克斯认为，小说的兴起与隐私观念的兴起有着紧密的联系。隐私状态决定了小说的阅读和写作的特性。[①] 首先，源于现实主义的小说本身就更倾向于表现更加个人化、私密化的故事，对现实的表现也离不开身体的介入。伊恩·瓦特在《小说的兴起：笛福、理查逊、菲尔丁研究》中曾写道："一般说来，小说本身对一段时间之内人物发展的关心远胜于其他任何文学形式。"[②] 因此，私人生活和私人经验从小说诞生之初就是其主要写作对象，作为私人生活和私人经验中最主要媒介的身体自然就成为小说形式的核心。[③] 身体动作的叙述构成了起居出行、社会交往的各种活动，视觉、听觉、嗅觉等身体的感官体验构成了人物的体验，小说的情节离不开人物欲望的产生与实现愿望的身体实践，身体特征、动作、语言综合塑造了个性鲜明的人物。因此可以说，小说的叙事离不开身体叙事。其次，比起集体观看戏剧或诵读诗歌，小说的欣赏方式更为私密。小说的读者受"欲望动力学"的驱动而阅读，同时也通过入侵小说人物的私人生活、私人体验，满足了潜意识里窥探他人隐私的欲望，在一定程度上满足了自身对认知身体、破译身体意义的好奇心，因为这些"窥探"所得，都是在日常生活中难以体验的。比如，阅读乔伊斯的《伊芙琳》，读者可以借伊芙琳之眼看到窗外景象，体验到一成不变的生活环境，感受都柏林生活给她带来的枯燥，进而窥探伊芙琳的矛盾内心；阅读《鲁滨逊漂流记》，代入鲁滨逊的身体动作，可以窥探到他独自一人流落荒岛时从恐慌到坚定的心态变化过程。总而言之，小说的产生受到重视身体、重视隐私的思潮推动，小说形式又转而推动了对身体体验的重视。从小说出发，再审视其他艺术形式，同样可以发现身体在其创作与欣赏中不可替代的地位。

在《阅读情节：叙事中的设计和意图》和《身体活：现代叙述中的欲望对象》中，布鲁克斯继承了精神分析的方法，以"性"来界定身体，采用"把自己视为有性别的生命的观念"，以"性"作为决定身份的各种想象和象征的复合体，因此也主要从与性别相关的问题出发。[④] 在身体转向的整体图景中，布鲁克斯巧妙地选择这一视角，为身体叙事创造了一个易于理解的切入点。然而，这也限制了布鲁克斯的理论进一步发展为普适的、系统的身体叙事学。布鲁克斯明确了欲望身体推动叙事的作用，但精神分析经常把身体等同于欲望，即使能够很好地解释故事情节为何及如何展开，但无法避免欲望是"混乱无序的"这一特征，未能解释故事情节的秩序与意义。[⑤] 对比来看，21 世纪初的丹尼尔·庞代(Daniel Punday)的身体叙事学理论建构就从更广阔的视野出发，将身体叙事学进一步向前推进。

庞代的身体叙事学理论主要集中于其论著《叙事身体：一种身体叙事学》中，这也是目前最为全面的身体叙事学理论体系。在布鲁克斯已经确立了身体在文学叙事中作用的基础上，庞代的理论宣告了"身体叙事学"(corporeal narratology)这一学科分支的正式成立，《叙事身体：一种身体叙事学》也明确体现了身体叙事的定义和内涵，以及身体与经典叙事学的关联。庞代在序言中写道："首先，我们可以从这些讨论出发：比如，身体会被如何用作故事的成分，身体如何依靠情节、人物、背景等传统叙事元素来形成故事……其次，身体叙事可以研究身体如何对我们讲故事、分析叙事产生影响。"[⑥] 可见，"身体叙事"概念具有两面性，不仅研究身体如何被书写，也研究身体如何影响叙事。从其字面意义出发，身体叙

① 布鲁克斯：《身体活：现代叙述中的欲望对象》，第 35 页。
② 伊恩·瓦特：《小说的兴起：笛福、理查逊、菲尔丁研究》，高原、董红均译，北京：三联书店，1992 年，第 16 页。
③ 布鲁克斯：《身体活：现代叙述中的欲望对象》，第 38 页。
④ 同上，第 3 页。
⑤ 欧阳灿灿：《叙事的动力学：论身体叙事学视野中的欲望身体》，载《当代外国文学》2015 年第 36 卷第 1 期，第 148 页。
⑥ Daniel Punday, *Narrative Bodies: Toward a Corporeal Narratology* (New York: Oalgrave Macmillan, 2003), p.ix.

事研究可以解释为“身体作为叙述对象”和“身体性的叙事观”两方面的有机结合，讨论二者其一的同时，往往也涉及另外一方。这种观点也成为庞代发展身体叙事学体系的基础。

三、丹尼尔·庞代与身体叙事学的建构

庞代身体叙事学理论体系自诞生起就被定位为一种“阐释方法”，时刻与批评实践紧密关联。换言之，身体叙事学理论的产生是一种从具体文本中提炼理论的过程，虽然分类类似于经典叙事学，但其构建思路已经完全不同。因此，身体叙事学理论不求概括身体叙事的全局，而是基于经典叙事学的几个叙事要素提供若干可用的身体叙事阐释视角，一方面，“试图为叙事的身体可能呈现的形式构建一套整体图式”，另一方面，从身体的角度重新审视几个经典叙事要素。[①] 下面基于庞代论著，对当下的身体叙事学理论中核心的世界观、人物、时间与空间几个部分简要说明。

身体叙事学对世界的理解基于知觉现象学这一哲学分支，认为叙事中的世界是依托身体的知觉而建立的。梅洛-庞蒂曾这样表述身体在感知世界中的功能：“身体本身在世界中，就像心脏在机体中：身体不断地使可见的景象保持活力，内在地赋予它生命和供给它养料，与之一起形成一个系统。”[②] 对各种客观事物的经验和认知必然离不开感知的主体——身体，而身体叙事学只是坦然地承认身体主体性的存在以及它对叙事的影响。结合人类对身体进行科学探索的成果也可以更深入地理解这种世界观。近几个世纪以来的生物学、医学已经悄然改变了人们对身体的认识。现代科学对身体的研究标志着身体意义的颠覆性变化，也特别暗示着我们必须放弃原来赋予人类表面形象的各种符号意义。[③] 当人类走出身心二分法的抽象区分，逐渐了解身体并非只是“灵魂的容器”，而是感知世界的主体时，围绕身体感知来理解世界的观点也就应运而生。这并不仅仅代表着要从某个人物的视角来体验故事世界，还代表着我们可以将目光更多地投向身体，从物质构成的世界“转移”到身体经验构成的世界，重新认识叙事的构成。

身体经验构成的世界与当下被文学研究者频繁讨论的“可能世界理论”中的概念颇为类似——人物的选择和行动决定了人物的个性和潜能，也决定了人物所处的“可能世界”；身体叙事学视角中，文艺作品所表现的故事世界则取决于人物的身体的具体形象与感受，读者通过认识和理解人物身体来解读文本，人物的出生、死亡、欲望、行动都决定着读者眼中的世界。而且，理解身体并不需要任何门槛，身体的存在状态是一种跨越语言的、在所有人类之中通用的沟通方式。人们可以不费任何额外努力就理解出生、疾病和死亡这些存在状态，从各种身体行为读出人物的欲望、情感、心理状态，进而通过这些身体的“符号”彼此理解和交流，传达更多意义。

从身体看世界，就要区分其中的两大组成部分——“身体”和“非身体”。叙事选用的区分身体与非身体的方法除人们的常识认知外，也取决于其历史和文化背景，以及身体在叙事中所扮演的角色。一种通用的、易于为人们所接受的区分方法就是看它是否与环境有互动或对环境做出反应，或者说，是否是意识活动的平台，而不是看其存在形态。[④] 例如，莫里森《宠儿》中惨死在母亲手里的女儿的鬼魂虽然没

---

① Punday, *Narrative Bodies: Toward a Corporeal Narratology*, p.53.

② 莫里斯·梅洛-庞蒂：《知觉现象学》，姜志辉译，北京：商务印书馆，2001 年，第 261 页。

③ Punday, *Narrative Bodies: Toward a Corporeal Narratology*, p.39.

④ Ibid., pp.58 - 59.

有如人类一般的物质存在，但依然与其他人物、环境有多重互动，所以仍然是具有文化和伦理意义的、存有意识的身体；相反，中国民间传说“孟姜女哭长城”中孟姜女丈夫的尸体虽从崩塌的城墙中出现，但在此处叙事情节中，其尸体与墙砖、泥土无异，只是非身体的环境的一部分。总体来看，囿于人类对其他物种感知能力的探索局限，现有身体叙事研究通常默认从人类身体出发形成身体性的世界观，但也不排除围绕其他类别的身体叙事。比如，身体与非身体状态间的界限是后现代主义所特别关心的议题，身体与非身体间难以定义的“灰色地带”，如动物身体、机械身体等，则指向了后人类批评的道路。

受制于古代人类探索身体奥秘的能力，经典的批评观点倾向于从“上帝视角”审视人物的作用，西方传统中，自亚里士多德起就认为叙事中的人物是行动的“表演者”，叙事学发轫之际，普罗普、格雷马斯等学者把人物当作行为的主体(actant)，查特曼将人物定义为一组特征的集合，里蒙-凯南认为人物是读者从文本中建构而成的。[①] 而中国的主流叙事观同样把人物当作某种借代，当作具有特定的肖像、行为和心理(个性心理和文化心理)的个体。[②] 然而，这些对人物的观点都尚未脱离庞代所概括的“人类表面形象”，即外界可观察到的、人物个体作为一个整体所呈现的状态。在理论建构上，其更是把人物视为与叙事中的时间、空间等平行的要素，从“旁观者”的视角分别讨论，人物塑造的理论也多聚焦于人物之间的对照。

身体叙事学对人物的理解与上述观念有着根本的区别，是一种“内外兼顾”的观点，既从身体出发，重审了以身体为主体的人物所携带的社会文化意义，又有身体对叙事沟通的作用剖析。这种人物观点强调身体的双重性，甚至可以说是一种自身与自身相对立的矛盾统一。如让-吕克·南茜(Jean-Luc Nancy)所言，一方面，身体是形象构成和投射的“内部”感觉与认知，是显现意义的途径；另一方面，身体又是意指的“外部”，是一种符号的表达，是储藏意义的场所。[③] 基于这一双重性的身体叙事学人物观亦可以说是对经典叙事学观点的又一突破，即，其不仅扩展了将身体看作“分析的对象”的传统观点，同时也考虑身体作为传达意义的“中间体”、作为作者与读者间沟通的符号体系，以及身体对读者领会文本意义的辅助作用。[④]

那么，身体叙事学在分析人物时有哪些可能的出发点呢？主要是人物身体之间的关系或人物身体与叙事之间的关系两方面。前者又包括身份标记和身体分类(sorting body types)两种典型类别。人物身体以各种方式携带身份的标记，不仅表明了人物个体的特征，也在一定程度上代表着故事世界里赋予人物这一身份的某个群体或组织，同时间接传递了作家本人对这一群体的态度。[⑤] 例如，阿城《棋王》中的王一生在对弈前禅定般的体态：“……瞪眼看着我们，双手支在膝上，铁铸一个细树桩，似无所见，似无所闻。”[⑥] 人物身体的描述一方面直接表现了“棋王”仙风道骨又有些乖僻的人物性格，另一方面也传达了作者对知青群体在艰苦环境中不忘追求知识和智慧的敬佩之情。此外，人物身体也通过与其他人物形成对照来传递意义，作者通过叙事中区别各类身体的文本特征塑造形象各异的人物图景，这也间接地体现出作者分类身体的“标准”或“规则”，读者也可以通过这些“标准”“规则”来观察故事的社会文化背

① Rimmon-Kenan, *Narrative Fiction: Contemporary Poetics*, pp.38 - 41.
② 杨义：《中国叙事学》，北京：人民出版社，1997年，第44页。
③ 让-吕克·南茜：《身体》，载汪民安、陈永国编：《后身体：文化、权力和生命政治学》，长春：吉林人民出版社，2003年，第92页。
④ Punday, *Narrative Bodies: Toward a Corporeal Narratology*, p.54.
⑤ 许德金：《身体、身份与叙事：身体叙事学刍议》，载《江西社会科学》2008年第4期：第31—32页。
⑥ 阿城：《棋王 树王 孩子王》，北京：人民文学出版社，2013年，第52页。

景,了解身体分类背后的更多意义。比如许多殖民地主题的作品中,不同的肤色关联不同的性格特征,总览这类叙事中身体分类的标准可深入挖掘出一系列与种族相关的社会问题、作者本人对少数族裔的具体看法等。类似地,文学作品中对身体的其他分类,比如男性与女性、病人与健康人、东方人与西方人的体貌特征、人类与非人类等都能在身体特征的区分和对照中反映一定的社会、文化、政治观念。根据作者所关注的话题,可以有无数种对身体的分类,新的分类也会随着时代更迭产生。《别让我走》中的人物身体分类就反映了科技发展中涌现的"克隆人"问题:黑尔舍姆学校里的"学生"被限制、被压抑的克隆身体,与外面世界能够尽情挥洒情感、自由生活的正常人类身体形成鲜明的对照,但这两类身体又同为人类,同样拥有对生命的热爱和对世界的好奇,身体类别的张力更能引发读者对科技界限和人类生存价值的思考。

人物身体与叙事的关系拓展得更为深远,以身体作为意义"中介"的手法在古代的"政治体"(body politic)论著中就已经出现了,托马斯·霍布斯(Thomas Hobbes)的《列维坦》将一个国家当作有机的身体来考虑其运作,讨论国王、市长、官员在社会运作中所处的不同位置和拥有的不同职责。在近代和当代亦出现不少文学作品以身体来隐喻国家、社会各群体之间的关系,利用读者熟知的身体结构作为阐释其他组织结构的中间媒介,而这只是身体叙事关注的一种典例。庞代将身体对叙事的协调作用扩大为对"肉身情境"(corporeal atmosphere)的建构,人物通过身体性的"触碰"(touch)进行互动,进而发展出叙事文本的"肉身情境"。[①] 以人物为核心,从身体视角构建的故事世界是读者理解和阐释叙事的关键,而这种身体性的故事世界的"入口"是一种"总身体"(general body)——能与所有文本对象关联,对"肉身情境"起到总领作用的某个事物,读者理解叙事中的人物,其核心就在于认出并接受协调所有人物个体身体的"总身体"。它可以是某个被具身化的人物的身体,可以是异化的空间体验,也可以是人物之间的特别关系。例如,《宠儿》的"总身体"可以是其核心人物"宠儿",《红字》的"总身体"可以是带有红字烙印的海斯特·白兰,《别让我走》的"总身体"可能是克隆人孩子们与外面的人的"责任"关系。文艺作品中,从身体出发的解读有时会显得混乱无头绪,因为每个人物都有身体,或多或少都有文本的叙述,这令人无从下手。重点应关注哪些人物的身体?当几个人物的身体都值得关注时,又该怎么办?"总身体"的概念就为身体叙事批评实践初步提供了一个可行的切入点。

如何定义叙事中的时间和空间一直是文学理论家和哲学家们争论不休的话题,然而人们在谈论它们时,总是无法避开人类与世界交互的必要媒介——身体对理解时间和空间的作用。无论是欲望对情节的推进,抑或是人物对空间建构的作用,最终都离不开对身体的讨论。巴赫金写道:"在文艺作品的时空体中……时间有了血肉,成为艺术上的可见之物。类似地,空间也富有意义,对时间、情节、历史的变换做出回应。"[②] 人物的选择和行动让时间和空间"有了血肉""富有意义",换言之,时间和空间的概念是基于身体的要求和行动而被赋予的。一般来说,经常伴随情节发展而出现的时间是发展各种叙事学时的必经之路,而空间则处于相对不那么重要的"从属"地位。下面对身体叙事学观点中的这两个叙事要素分别介绍。

海登·怀特(Hayden White)、诺斯洛普·弗莱、雅克·拉康(Jacques Lacan)、巴特勒等人都在讨论如何定义和想象时间的论著中肯定了身体的作用,其观点可归为身体在情节中自我对抗的"双重性":

① Punday, *Narrative Bodies: Toward a Corporeal Narratology*, p.82.
② Ibid., p.94.

一方面,类似"总身体"的人物身体可以作为故事总体情节的核心代表,另一方面,身体给叙事创造了各种"麻烦",身体的行动引发更多的情节,延迟了叙事的终结,处于"抵抗"时间的位置。[①]

庞代的身体叙事学提供了一个从"双重性"出发的研究视角,对叙事中的时间不再按传统的故事时间和话语时间进行区分,而是将其分为外部时间(external time)和内部时间(interior time)。前者近似于故事世界中时间的客观流逝。"叙事情节是依照外部时间的调控而构筑的。外部的时间调控提供叙事的轨迹感,以及章节最后的终结感"。[②] 因此也可以说,外部时间对应身体活动构筑情节的总体秩序。后者"内部时间"是一种"内心对时间的感知"(internal time consciousness)或"体感时间",指身体内部对时间流逝的体验,对应着与前者对抗的欲望身体一方。人物的"内部时间"与其所处世界的"外部时间"有着不同的对抗关系,有"洞中方一日,世上已千年"的平行差异对照,有"十三学织素,十四学裁衣"等被外部时间和封建礼教驱动身体的被动体验,也有《喧哗与骚动》中昆丁自杀前内心感受对外部时间的竭力逃避。总而言之,身体一方面是透视情节、总览故事的必备要素,另一方面又扮演着对抗情节、制造张力的角色。

然而,叙事中身体与时间的关系在近百年来变得越发复杂。庞代写道:"当我们将传统的情节与狭义的'身体'本质——出生、死亡和婚姻——联系在一起时,现代的情节似乎在构建整体叙事轨迹方面更自由,而不是严格遵循这些身体里程碑。"[③] 有鉴于此,身体叙事学也发展出了叙事文本之外的维度,比如呼应经典叙事学中"阅读时间"的读者的身体感受,在研究现代主义及之后的作品中显得越发重要。实验文学的叙事手法挑战着读者对叙事要素的传统印象。元叙事、类文本、跨媒介等叙事方法,使读者在阅读文学作品时产生不同于以往的身体经验。因此,将读者的阅读时间体验纳入研究可能也是身体叙事学在时间维度上的新方向。

"我们在日常生活的事件流中制造影响的能力依赖于我们对时间和空间中身体的管理"。[④] 时间并没有对叙事的决定性作用,但时间和空间都是谈及叙事时不可避免的要素。因此叙事中的身体能够制造戏剧化冲突,创造跌宕起伏的情节,除了身体在时间上的自我对抗关系外,也离不开身体与各种空间的关联互动。相对于时间的单向流逝特征,空间与身体的关系复杂得多,但类似的是,身体与空间依然呈现类似"对抗"的关系。用汪民安的话来说:

> 身体永远是冲创性的,永远要外溢扩张,永远要冲出自己的领域;身体的特征就是要非空间化,非固定化,非辖域化;身体的本质就是要游牧,就是要在成千上万座无边无际的高原上狂奔。在这个意义上,身体和密闭的空间永远处于一种紧张状态,身体总是要突破禁锢自己的空间。只有相互对峙的两种身体之力达到临时的平衡,只有两种身体经过盘算后的相互踌躇,只有它们各自的空间暂时能够承受身体之力撞击的时候,身体的空间界限才能保持相对的稳定。[⑤]

因此,我们可以从身体如何突破空间,即身体在空间中如何穿梭旅行、受到何种限制等问题出发理

① Punday, *Narrative Bodies: Toward a Corporeal Narratology*, pp.87 - 90.
② Ibid, p.106.
③ Ibid, p.108.
④ Chris Shilling, *The Body and Social Theory: Theory, Culture and Society*(London: Sage Publications, 1993), p.22.
⑤ 汪民安:《身体、空间与后现代性》,南京:江苏人民出版社,2015 年,第 36 页。

解叙事中的空间。基于此种理念，庞代从身体叙事学视角提供了一些可用的空间分类方法，包括身体进入空间的程度、途径、条件三方面。首先，身体进入空间的程度(degree of access)受人物自身情况和行动的可能性两方面限制，按身体能够进入和体验该空间的程度可分为完全不可进入的空间、想象投射的空间、感知上可进入的空间、物理上可进入的空间等几个等级。人物行动的逻辑在很大程度上取决于如何定义这些行动将发生的地点[1]，即如何定义空间不同的"可进入程度"，而解读作品"如何定义"特定人物身体可进入某个空间的程度则和故事中意图呈现的社会文化、人物背景紧密相关，特别是可进入与不可进入的分界线，是解读身体隐含意义的关键。以此类推，身体进入空间的途径亦可分为物理途径(physical)、感知途径(perceptual)、想象途径(imaginative)。以阿特伍德的作品《使女的故事》为例，女主角是帮大主教延续后代的使女，对她来说，在大主教的家里只有自己的房间是可通过"物理途径"自由出入的空间，客厅、厨房等绝大多数其他空间都是仅可偷听、偷看，但不可踏入的，即仅可通过"感知途径"进入。想象中基列国境外的自由生活没有任何途径可以了解，只存在于想象中的空间。以进入空间的途径作为对不同环境的区分，一方面更加清晰地透露出主角的生活范围和内心世界的巨大差异，另一方面也讽刺了故事世界中剥夺正常身体欲望的畸形宗教文化对人性的禁锢。空间对身体如何设限，或者说某个人物身体进入某个空间需要的条件也有若干种。首先是物理条件的限制，比如愚公一家因为太行、王屋二山的险峻地势而很难进入山外的空间，《白象似的群山》中的主角仅可遥望而未能亲临白色山峦等，都是由于物理条件限制了身体对某个空间的全面体验。在现代科技的辅助下，身体的感知范围得以扩大，能够触及更多遥不可及的地方，获得更丰富的空间经验。但无论是否借助科技，人物获得身体经验的物理或感知途径必须通过文化中的身体模式来理解，文化对身体能力的想象"筛选"出了可用于进入某一空间的物理途径。[2] 换言之，文化习俗和社会想象同样是影响身体体验空间的条件之一，比如《伊芙琳》中保守的文化信念限制了主人公上船远行、探索异域生活空间，一些武侠小说中只有教主方能进入密室等。与之类似的还有超验的条件限制，比如具有宗教色彩的作品中的天堂、幻境，玄幻小说中的穿越时空场景等。

四、身体叙事学的特征与价值

与许多其他后经典叙事学分支一样，身体叙事学作为一门"自下而上"的叙事学，来源于文艺作品，也最终回归于叙事的批评解读。当前的身体叙事学批评实践主要有三大特点：① 实践成果远超理论成果。就目前的成果来看，研究身体叙事的学者对批评实践的兴趣远大于对理论的修订，一方面是因为身体叙事学本身就具有"后经典"特性，学者倾向于从批评实践中挖掘其理论价值，另一方面是因为身体作为一种"通用语言"，其本身对批评家、作者或是读者来说就是很受欢迎的阐释视角。② 阐释的理论来源多样化。即使布鲁克斯和庞代是对身体叙事学理论体系贡献最大的两位学者，他们的名字也未如其他理论大家一般，频繁出现于论文中。身体叙事的批评实践借鉴的理论十分广泛，从尼采、福柯、梅洛-庞蒂等身体研究的奠基人，到当代的舒斯特曼、特纳等继承人，以及专攻女性主义、后殖民主义等领域的西苏、巴特勒、爱德华・萨义德(Edward Said)等学者，都可以成为身体叙事的理论来源。③ 强大的跨

① Punday, *Narrative Bodies: Toward a Corporeal Narratology*, p.128.

② Ibid., pp.136 - 138.

界潜能。身体概念的普遍性使得如今的身体叙事研究早已超越了文学作品的范畴，在布鲁克斯的绘画解析、庞代的雕塑欣赏基础上，电影、戏剧、新媒体等研究均出现以“身体”为视角，结合其叙事表现形式，继续开发身体叙事的新内容。同时，身体叙事研究广泛借鉴社会学、美学、医学、运动机能学等学科内容，不仅将身体叙事批评实践多样化，而且为这些学科提供了诸如叙事医学、身体美学等新方向，促进了学科之间的沟通互鉴。

第二节 穆德·埃尔曼及其《饮食、肥胖与文学》

一、导读

2015年出版的论文集《剑桥身体指南》由剑桥大学的戴维·希尔曼(David Hillman)和布里斯托大学的乌尔丽卡·莫德(Ulrika Maude)主编,集合了当今文学界身体研究的热点论题,系统地展示了"身体转向"以来取得的各方面成果及其在21世纪的最新动向,既包含性别、语言、种族等传统话题,也包括了残疾、医疗、后人类、情感等新兴话题,还从身体特征出发考察相关文本的内涵,为身体叙事研究提供了多样化的视角和若干可能的发展方向。本节选文出自该书第五章,作者是芝加哥大学杰出贡献教授穆德·埃尔曼(Maud Ellman),她在文中详细梳理了"肥胖"的文学史,选取若干经典文本,在身体叙事的阐释过程中为读者呈现了"肥胖"这一身体特征所关联的含义的历史流变。

选文主要按时间顺序展开。文艺复兴时期,莎士比亚戏剧中约翰·法斯塔夫爵士的肥胖身躯在《亨利四世》《温莎的风流娘儿们》等戏剧中给观众留下深刻印象,他的形象至今都在瘦身大潮中受到观众的喜爱。这一时期,发胖的身材在喜剧中很常见,叙事中的肥胖身体被赋予了多样的积极含义:法斯塔夫的智慧被认为与肥胖的身体有着紧密联系;他的身材被王子所称颂,隐喻了哈尔王子慷慨不羁的性格。此后,肥胖的积极含义为多部经典作品所继承,亨利·詹姆斯的《金碗》、普鲁斯特的《追忆似水年华》、托尔斯泰的《战争与和平》、狄更斯的《匹克威克外传》等作品都包含带有幽默效果或正面特征的胖角色。总体来看,20世纪前,文学作品中的肥胖从不是被歧视和否定的"疾病"。

20世纪中期开始,晚期资本主义的审美风尚开始改变,对肥胖身体的认识也与之前相去甚远。现代主义文学对肥胖的批判成为其与前人割席的标志,痛斥肥胖成为这一代作家革新的独特手段之一。最初还仍有雷克斯·施陶特笔下肥胖的侦探乌尔夫之类的正面人物,但这仍无法阻挡肥胖身体的地位在文学作品中一落千丈。随着减肥产业日益壮大,以及媒体、医疗机构等行业对肥胖身体的贬低,本身作为中性形容词的"胖"已经不可避免地被赋予了丑陋、肮脏、懒惰、下流、邪恶等数种消极含义。埃尔曼列举了雷蒙德·卡佛的《胖》、彼得·凯里的《历史上的胖子》等文艺作品中的胖人角色,阐释了肥胖身体在20世纪以来的隐含意义的变化,这不仅体现在小说叙事对肥胖者身体特征、人格特征的消极描绘和人物对肥胖角色的鄙视及压迫方面,也体现在"肥胖恐惧"的社会语境中观众对肥胖的排斥,以及社会舆论对审美、道德的引导方面。

二、《饮食、肥胖与文学》选读[①]

"Why, you are so fat, Sir John, that you must needs be out of all compass, out of all reasonable

① Maul Ellmann, "Eating, Obesity and Literature," *The Cambridge Companion to the Body in Literature*, eds. David Hillman and Ulrika Maude (Cambridge: Cambridge University Press, 2015), pp.62-72.

compass, Sir John" (1 *Henry IV* III. iii). Falstaff is out of all compass in the sense that he embodies the whole repertoire of fat stereotypes, ranging from the merry to the morbid, yet also exceeds these "hard opinions" (2 *Henry IV* V.v). His girth gives fleshly form to this semantic excess. In the painful scene of role-play in *Henry IV* Part 1(Act II, scene iv), when Falstaff and Henry take turns at playing King and Prince, Henry assumes the role of the reproachful father, unleashing a barrage of fat-abuse on "plump Jack": "that trunk of humours, that bolting-hutch of beastliness, that swollen parcel of dropsies, that huge bombard of sack, that stuffed cloak-bag of guts, that roasted Manningtree ox with the pudding in his belly". The fat knight, foreseeing his imminent rejection in these savage insults, defends the joie de vivre attested by his fat: "If sack and sugar be a fault, God help the wicked! if to be old and merry be a sin, then many an old host that I know is damned: if to be fat be to be hated, then Pharaoh's lean kine are to be loved". Concluding with a poignant entreaty not to be banished from the Prince's company—"banish plump Jack, and banish all the world"—Falstaff's self-defence does for fat-phobia what Shylock's does for anti-Semitism: "Hath not a Jew eyes?" Like Shylock's speech, however, Falstaff's eloquence is wasted on the Prince: "I know thee not, old man" (2 *Henry IV* V.v).

Falstaff's enduring popularity, even in the present age of diet-fascism, indicates that fat is loved at least as much as it is hated, a fact vigorously suppressed by today's weight-police. The Henry plays dramatize this ambivalence in the volte-face by which the Prince, having previously revelled in the carnivalesque, ungirdled world of Falstaff, rejects his oversized companion in favour of the exacting "compass" of the crown. Yet the consequence of this rejection is that the comic buffoon is transformed into a tragic sacrifice. Like the dieter whose unconscious mourning for her pounds compels her to gain them back again, Shakespeare's audience mourns the fat expelled by Hal's bulimic purge of his companions. It is to assuage this loss that the epilogue of *Henry IV* Part II (Act V, scene v) promises the audience: "if you be not too cloyed with fat meat, our humble author will continue the story, with Sir John in it ... unless 'a be killed by your hard opinions". And indeed Sir John returns in *The Merry Wives of Windsor*, reputedly at the express request of Queen Elizabeth, although the resurrected Falstaff retains little of his former brio. When his death is reported in *Henry V* (Act II, scene iii), his nose is described as "sharp as a pen", which suggests that it has lost its bulbous vigor, and it seems that his wit has fallen away with his fat meat. "Bardolph, am I not fall'n away vilely since this last action? Do I not bate? Do I not dwindle?" (1 *Henry IV* III. iii).

Before his downfall, Falstaff is hailed by the Prince as "my sweet creature of bumbast" (1 *Henry IV* II.iv). As Patricia Parker has pointed out, "bumbast" refers to "the padding that stuffs a body and its verbal equivalent".[①] She proposes that Falstaff, who "dilates" in both the bodily and

① Patricia Parker, "Literary Fat Ladies and the Generation of the Text," *Literary Fat Ladies: Rhetoric, Gender, Property* (London: Methuen, 1987), pp.8–35.

the rhetorical sense, provides a physical analogy for the Prince's dilatory tarrying. Thus Falstaff's waist becomes the emblem of the Prince's prodigality, his "waste" of time. Parker also suggests that the inordinate dilation of the Henriad itself reflects the "fat rogue" at its centre, and prolongs the audience's delectation of this jovial distraction from closure (1 *Henry IV* I.ii). It is worth noting that *Hamlet*, another sprawling play that overflows all reasonable compass, also stars a fat and dilatory hero: "He's fat, and scant of breath".[①] Both these plays make dilation and delay seem a good deal more appealing than coming to the "point"—the sharp nose or the poisoned rapier.

"I have a whole school of tongues in this belly of mine," Falstaff declares (2 *Henry IV* IV. iii). By describing his belly as a talkative womb, Falstaff undergoes a metaphorical sex-change, looking forward to *The Merry Wives of Windsor* where he cross-dresses as a fat lady.[②] His masculinity, already impugned by his name (Fal-staff), is also threatened by his fat, especially because this fat is associated with his belly's "school of tongues", the loquacity proverbially attributed to women. The woman who cannot "shut up", who cannot control her verbal or sexual incontinence, is a stock figure of the comic tradition.

This tradition is revived by Joyce in the final episode of *Ulysses*, in which Molly Bloom gets "the last word", giving birth to "a whole school of tongues".[③] "Fat" is the "organ" Joyce assigns to this episode in the "Linati schema", which identifies each chapter of *Ulysses* with a body-part.[④] Fat is usually disparaged as waste tissue, a dangerous supplement to the lean, efficient and productive body of modernity. "Out of all reasonable compass", fat exceeds the "proper" boundaries of the body, blurring its outlines in billowing folds of useless flesh. In the corpus of *Ulysses*, Molly's monologue performs a similar function, spilling out over the ending just as her "heaving embonpoint" spills out over her décolletage.[⑤]

In Henry James's *The Golden Bowl*, it is Fanny Assingham, with her preposterous name—all orifice—whose "amplitude of person" corresponds to the novel's verbal profligacy.[⑥] Her husband Colonel Assingham, distinguished from his wife by his "leanness of person" and abhorrence of waste, slenderizes Fanny's wordy and expensive telegraphs.[⑦] In Proust's *A la recherche du temps perdu*, the swelling figure of the Baron de Charlus presides over the prodigious expansion of the narrative. Proust began by writing the first and final volumes of the novel, gradually fattening the middle with adventures in Sodom and Gomorrah. The magnificent Baron's expanding middle seems

① *Hamlet* V.ii. For a review of critical responses to this line, see Laura Kine, "Hamlet's Fat", in Sidney Homan, ed., *Shakespeare and the Triple Play: From Study to Stage to Classroom* (Lewisburg, PA: Bucknell University Press, 1988), pp.89 – 104.

② *Merry Wives of Windsor* IV.ii. See Parker, p.21.

③ See James Joyce, *Selected Letters*, ed. Richard Ellmann (New York: Viking, 1975), p.278.

④ For the Linati schema, see Richard Ellmann, *Ulysses on the Liffey* (New York: Oxford University Press, 1986), pp.186 – 187.

⑤ James Joyce, *Ulysses* (1922), ed. Hans Walter Gabler et al. (London: Bodley Head, 1986), p. 194.

⑥ Henry James, *The Golden Bowl*, ed. Virginia Llewellyn Smith (Oxford: Oxford University Press, 2009), p.26; see also Parker, p.34.

⑦ James, pp.49, 50 – 51.

to monumentalise this compositional strategy. Almost as obese as the *Recherche* is Tolstoy's *War and Peace*, where notably the fat hero, Pierre Bezukhov, ultimately wins the girl. As for his thin rival, Prince Andrei Bolkonsky, the narrow compass of his waist and scruples causes him to lose Natasha; Pierre's fatter, more capacious moral code is better suited to embracing her humanity.

Readers of these novels learn to love fat in both corporeal and literary form. Indeed the novel as a genre depends on its accumulation of adipose detail. Fat is a fictional issue, to borrow the witty title of Pat Rogers's study of the novel and the rise of weight-watching. The realist novel, Rogers proposes, because of its ability to focus on detail, "drew increased attention to the bodily size" of its protagonists.[①] In the Victorian novel, however, fat had yet to be defined as a pathology. Although Dickens was no friend of fat, judging by his monstrous treatment of his stout wife Catherine, many of his plumper characters are memorably benign. Fat Peggotty, whose buttons pop off whenever she hugs David Copperfield, could scarcely be described as "morbidly obese". Pickwick's fat, far from weighing him down, endows him with buoyancy and effervescence; his girth is associated with largesse and good humour.

It is also associated with the picaresque comedy of *The Pickwick Papers*, a genre resistant to contraction and closure that boasts such portly precedents as Cervantes's Sancho Panza, whose surname means belly. "Comedy", argues Slavoj Žižek, "is the triumph of indestructible life—not sublime life, but opportunistic, common, vulgar earthly life itself ... the stuff of comedy is this repetitive, resourceful popping up of life."[②] And it is fat that signals this resilience; the spherical bounce back. Our affection for fat characters in literature testifies to a deep-rooted attachment to bodily life—"warm fullblooded life" as Leopold Bloom describes it in *Ulysses*—in preference to the thin world of the spirit.[③] The "fat girl, terrestrial" is Wallace Stevens's term for this warm fullblooded life:"Fat! Fat! Fat! Fat!" he cheers (or jeers) in "Bantams in Pine-Woods".[④]

Like the twentieth-century body, the twentieth-century novel has been forced to slim in response to the exigencies of late capitalism. Gone are the fat three-deckers of the nineteenth century; the modern reader has no patience for such dilation. Popular fi-ction has foregone weight and heft for portability, shrinking into svelte paperbacks and featherweight short stories. Symptomatic of this shift is Zola's novel *The Belly of Paris* (*La ventre de Paris*, 1873), which portrays a war of the fat against the thin. Although part of a fat series, Zola's Rougon-Macquart novels, *The Belly of Paris* is comparatively lean and travel-friendly. Set in the food markets of Les Halles, a "temple of gluttony", the novel tells the story of Florent Quenu's return to Paris after

① Pat Rogers, "Fat is a Fictional Issue: The Novel and the Rise of Weight-Watching," *Historicizing Fat in Anglo-American Culture*, ed.Elena Levy-Navarro(Columbus: Ohio State University Press, 2010), pp.19 - 39.

② See Slavoj Žižek, *Did Somebody Say Totalitarianism? Five Interventions in the (Mis)use of a Notion* (London: Verso, 2001), pp.81 - 85.

③ Joyce, *Ulysses*, p.94.

④ Wallace Stevens, "It Must Give Pleasure", Section x of "Notes toward a Supreme Fiction" in *Collected Poetry and Prose*, ed. Frank Kermode and Joan Richardson (New York: Library of America, 1997), p.351; "Bantams in Pine-Woods," p.60.

escaping the penal colony of Cayenne where he had been transported for his alleged part in the resistance to Louis-Napoleon's coup d'état.[1] After years of hunger, Florent is reunited with his corpulent brother, now the successful owner of a charcuterie and married to a well-upholstered wife, "la belle Lisa". "She had the fine skin and pinky-white complexion of those who spend their lives surrounded by fat and raw meat" (Zola, 35). The whole family, including Florent's chubby niece Pauline, is "bursting with health, solidly built, sleek, in prime condition; they looked at [Florent] with the surprise of fat people gripped by a vague feeling of unease at the sight of someone who is thin "(Zola, 36).

Eventually this unease gets the better of them, despite the initial hospitality with which they swallow up Florent into the household, described by Zola as "a whole world drowned in fat" (Zola, 78). When Lisa gets wind of Florent's revolutionary sentiments, she spits him out, to the applause of her obese community. The "huge bellies and enormous breasts ... nearly burst in malicious delight" when Florent is arrested by the gendarmes (Zola, 268). Thus the petit-bourgeoisie rejects the revolutionary hunger of the starveling who challenges their stout complacency. In its premise that the fat are trying to destroy the thin, Zola's novel provides a foretaste of today's fat-paranoia, the fear of being taken over by the so-called terror within.

Modernism marks its break from the nineteenth century by excoriating literary fat. To make it new is to make it thin. In his landmark manifesto, "A Few Don'ts by an Imagiste", Ezra Pound declares:"It is better to present one image in a lifetime than to produce voluminous works".[2] His own minimalist poem,"In a Station of the Metro" (1913), resulted from a kind of liposuction that reduced some thirty lines to two. In the same period, a crash diet is imposed on popular fiction to counter the flabby bourgeois epics of the past.

Yet the Falstaffian hero has not been altogether banished from the emaciated genres of modernity. Fat detectives, for example, have flourished in both the novel and the movies, a phenomenon that Sandor Gilman has tracked extensively.[3] My favourite of these gumshoes is Nero Wolfe, the stout creation of Rex Stout. A "huge hill of flesh",[4] Wolfe is too fat to venture out of his brownstone in Manhattan, and has therefore enlisted Archie Goodwin to do his legwork. Every mealtime, Fritz the cook produces gastronomic wonders for Wolfe and Archie, while the elusive gardener Horstmann ministers to Wolfe's rooftop collection of ten thousand orchids. So enthralling is this homosocial household that readers tend to be more interested in what's-for-dinner than whodunit; Stout catered to this taste by producing *The Nero Wolfe Cookbook*.[5]

---

① Emile Zola, *The Belly of Paris* (1873), trans. Brian Nelson (Oxford: Oxford University Press, 2007),p.35.

② Ezra Pound, "A Few Don'ts by an Imagiste," *Poetry* 1:6 (March, 1913): 200-206:201.

③ Sandor L. Gilman, "How Fat Detectives Think (and Fat Villains Act)" in *Fat Boys: A Slim Book* (Lincoln and London: University of Nebraska Press, 2004),pp.153-192.

④ One of Prince Hal's kinder epithets for Falstaff: 1 *Henry IV* II.iv.225.

⑤ Rex Stout, *The Nero Wolfe Cookbook* (New York: Viking, 1973).

Wolfe thinks with his belly. Archie marvels, "I never would understand how [Wolfe] could make his brain work so fast and deep that no other man in the country could touch him. He replied ... that it wasn't his brain that worked, it was his lower nerve centers". For this fat detective, thinking is located in the gut, not in the brain: it is something that happens "inside of him", a digestive process rather than a mental act.①

The British TV show *Cracker* created a successor to Nero Wolfe in the form of Eddie "Fitz" Fitzgerald, the forensic psychologist played by Robbie Coltrane, whose gigantic appetite for food, booze, adultery and gambling corresponds to his uncanny capacity for identification with the criminal mind. Fitz's fat, like Nero Wolfe's, testifies to his hypersensitivity; Wolfe claims to have gained weight to protect his nerves after an "unpleasantness with a certain woman in Montenegro".② If Wolfe's fat insulates his sensorium, however, Fitz's seems to make him more susceptible to other minds by enlarging the receptive surface of his body. His method of inquiry, as Gilman has observed, is "empathetic rather than analytic"; "he feels with and for the victims, and even for the criminals, rather than being a 'pure intellect' whose forte is unmasking the perpetrators or logistics of a crime".③ When ABC rewrote *Cracker* for a fat-phobic American audience, transplanting the action to diet-conscious LA, the hero became svelte, with fatal consequences for the series. The idea that a fat guy could be sexy was clearly unacceptable in the United States, although the huge John Goodman offers a homegrown example of this paradox. In the Californian *Cracker*, the translation from fat to thin detective did not work, because Fitz's powers of intuition are inseparable from his fat and the social stigma it entails. ④

Given the current clamour about fat, the millions of words (and dollars) annually expended in the supposed attempt to make us thin, it is paradoxical that fat in fiction often takes the form of the short story, the thinnest and most reticent of genres. A case in point is Raymond Carver's famous story "Fat" (1971), which has become a touchstone for fat studies and fat activism.⑤ Although short stories are slim by definition, Carver's is positively skeletal. The story is staged as a dramatic monologue in which the unnamed female narrator tells her friend Rita about her encounter with a fat man in a diner where she waits tables. These details, however, have to be fleshed out by the reader, who is obliged to supply the story with its missing fat.

In a setting reminiscent of Edward Hopper's paintings, the fat man orders an enormous dinner from the harried waitress, who attends to him with growing curiosity and wonder. "This fat man is the fattest person I have ever seen," she recalls, "though he is neat-appearing and well dressed

① See Gilman, *Fat Boys*, p.185.
② Ibid.
③ Ibid., p.154 - 155.
④ Ibid., p.155.
⑤ Raymond Carver, "Fat" in *Will You Please Be Quiet, Please?* (New York: Vintage, 1992), pp.3 - 8. I am indebted to Lauren Berlant's perceptive reading of this story in "America, Fat, the Fetus" in *Gendered Agents: Women and Institutional Knowledge*, eds. Silvestra Mariniello and Paul A. Bové (Durham, NC: Duke University Press, 1998), pp.192 - 244.

enough." What she finds most arresting are his fingers, which "look three times the size of a normal person's fingers—long, thick, creamy fingers". More teatlike than phallic, there is something feminine about these creamy fingers, corresponding to the fat man's taste for mammary food.

Off-scene, the other staff react to the fat man with a "naming frenzy", as Lauren Berlant has pointed out.[①] "Who's your fat friend? He's really a fatty". "God, he's fat!" "How is old tub-of-guts doing?" "Harriet says you got a fat man from the circus out there". "Some fatty". This chorus of mockery serves to distance and dehumanize the fat man, but also indicates excited interest: the fat man causes a stir in what is evidently a tedious routine. The name-calling is an attempt to keep the fat man in his place, to prevent his fat from overflowing and engulfing his observers. The group affirms its own normality by excluding the corpulent outsider from its gossip. Thus the fat man functions as a scapegoat who carries off the threat of fat from the community, preventing an "obesity epidemic".

The narrator, however, seems to relish her exposure to this peril. She lets the fat man get under her skin—a response not lost on Rudy, her co-worker and sex-partner, who remarks: "Sounds to me like she's sweet on fat-stuff". He is hinting that the waitress fancies the fat guy, but "sweet on fat-stuff" could refer to food as well as sex, to the fat-stuff that the waitress ferries to her patron's table. Much of this stuff consists of dairy fat—butter, sour cream, vanilla ice-cream—as if the waitress, who later fantasizes about giving birth to a fat child, were breast-feeding the fat man by proxy. As he munches through his calorific marathon, pausing only to order further courses, the waitress finds his mode of speaking as "strange" and intriguing as his eating habits. What is strange is his formality, his "well-dressed" mode of ordering his food; what is also strange is the "little puffing sound" that punctuates his speech. Strangest of all is his use of the first person plural: "Believe me, he says, we don't eat like this all the time, he says. And puffs. You'll have to excuse us, he says".

This "we" suggests that the fat man is double, even multiple: it is as if he were pregnant and "eating for two". But the pronoun also embraces the waitress in his appetite, implicating the feeder in the feedee. The fat man is eating for two in the sense that he is also eating for the waitress, enabling her to "gain" vicariously. And what she gains is a story, the "whole story" that Rudy is unable to grasp: "Rudy, he is fat, I say, but that is not the whole story". Instead of recoiling from the fat man's greed, the waitress says she likes "to see a man eat and enjoy himself", a phrase suggestive of "autocannibalistic pleasure".[②]

While the other workers close ranks against the fat man, using his obesity to gloat about their trimmer figures, the waitress dares to imagine herself fat. In reality, she tells the fat man, she finds it impossible to put on weight. "Me, I eat and I eat and I can't gain, I say. I'd like to gain, I say". Note that she does not say "gain weight", because she does gain something in the course of this

---

① Berlant, p.203.

② Ibid.

encounter—an enlargement of her fantasy-life. "I put my hand on my middle and wonder what would happen if I had children and one of them turned out to look like that, so fat". When Rudy mounts her for a nightly bout of boring sex, the waitress feels herself expand beneath him: "When he gets on me, I suddenly feel I am fat. I feel I am terrifically fat, so fat that Rudy is a tiny thing and hardly there at all". This imaginary fat insulates her against the unwanted sex ("it was against my will") and also magically fulfils her wish to "gain", enabling her to feel enormous. "My life is going to change", she concludes. "I feel it".

By empathizing with the fat man's compulsion—"there is no choice", he says—the waitress allows herself to be invaded by his fat, embracing her inclusion in his "we". Her life is going to change because her identity has been unsettled, opening her consciousness to unfamiliar feelings and desires: "I know I was after something. But I don't know what." Like the glass of water that she accidentally tips over on the fat man's table, her imagination overflows the bounds of stereotype, dissolving the division between self and other, thin and fat, normal and monstrous. The namelessness of both the waitress and the fat man, together with the absence of quotations marks and the pronominal ambiguities, especially the fat man's "we", contribute to unbinding fixed identities.

What the waitress "gains" from the fat man, then, is a reprieve from identity and agency, a kind of negative capability. It is significant that she says "my life is going to change", not "I am going to change my life". Perhaps she will get fat, perhaps she will get pregnant, but what she understands is that "there is no choice", because change requires receptivity rather than willpower: "a feeling comes over me". In different ways, both the fat man, who cannot stop eating, and the thin waitress, who cannot gain, recognise the fact that we really do not have much control over our bodies: a scandalous fact, in a culture that demands incessant self-improvement.

Peter Carey's story "The Fat Man in History" is not so thin as Carver's "Fat", since Carey's narrative consists of twenty chapters, but some of these are only three lines long.① The dismembered structure of the story anticipates its grisly end. Where Zola's *The Belly of Paris* portrays a battle of the fat against the thin, Carey's dystopian fable envisages a future crusade of the thin against the fat. In Carey's world, it is as if Florent and other hungry revolutionists had overthrown the former tyranny of fat and were persecuting any corpulent survivors. "It was not a good time to be a fat man", Carey's protagonist Alexander Finch reflects (11). In this post-revolutionary order, "to be fat is to be an oppressor, to be greedy, to be pre-revolutionary... Certainly in the years before the revolution most fat men were either Americans, stooges for the Americans, or wealthy supporters of the Americans"(10).

In this context, a fat revolutionary is an oxymoron, but this is Finch's dire predicament. In the

① Peter Carey, "The Fat Man in History" in *The Fat Man in History and Other Stories*, ed. Peter Carey (New York: Vintage, 1993), pp.9－33.

early days when people were hungry, Finch was sometimes embarrassed by his fat, but it was only later, when there was a surplus rather than a dearth of food, that fat came to be demonised as a counter-revolutionary throwback. Although the Committee of Seventy-Five never passed any motions directly related to fat men, "the word 'fat' entered slyly into the language as a new adjective, as a synonym for greedy, ugly, sleazy, lazy, obscene, evil, dirty, dishonest, untrustworthy". As a consequence, fat men have been driven into hiding (we never learn what happened to fat women). Finch has lost his job as a cartoonist on the grounds of his bad spelling and "slovenly" demeanor, the term "slovenly" having morphed into another synonym for "fat" (12). He has moved into a home for fat men who are plotting to avenge themselves against the thin. Little do they know they are the guinea pigs in an anthropological experiment, the title of which is revealed on the last page of the story: *Revolution in a Closed Society—A Study of Leadership Among the Fat* (32). The researcher, who masquerades as the fat men's "Florence Nightingale", spies on these oversized specimens who, having plotted to "eat a member or monument of the revolution", eventually devour their own corpulent leader (28).

Cannibalism aside, Carey's terrifying vision of the future is all too familiar from the present. Today, the endless vilification of fat that issues from the media, the diet industry, and the medical establishment, echoed by a growing chorus of sadistic bloggers on the internet, has made no impact on obesity; on the contrary, the statistics are continuing to rise. Yet the war against fat has succeeded in producing untold misery, especially among the young, hooked into the never-ending cycle of failure that sustains the multi-million-dollar diet industry.

Although literature offers no solution to obesity, nor to the persecution of the fat, it reminds us that current mythology of fat is not eternal but historical. Fat has been perceived as sexy and endearing (think of Maupassant's fat prostitute Boule de Suif), as well as gross and pathological (e.g. the Fat Boy of *Pickwick*); it has been associated with generosity and warmth (Peggotty of *David Copperfield*), as well as with rapacity and selfishness (the bloated monsters of Zola's Paris). Futile though it is to point out that fat is a neutral descriptor, devoid of moral and aesthetic implications, it is important to perceive how wildly these implications fluctuate. If the modern project of exterminating fat could possibly succeed, our lives would be the thinner for it. Less is not more. Lionel Shriver's dietary version of the pledge of allegiance, the American schoolchild's equivalent of the Lord's Prayer, provides a chilling forecast of a fat-free world:①

> I pledge aversion to the flab
> Of the derided waists of America,
> And to the repulsion for which it stands,

① Lionel Shriver, *Big Brother* (New York: HarperCollins, 2013), p.297. I have provided a condensed version of the pledge.

One nation, underweight, practically invisible,

With misery and smugness for all.

三、思考与讨论

(1) 结合文学经典和历史语境,尝试思考并归纳其他身体特征的隐含意义在文学历史上的演变,如瘦的身体、老年身体、暴露的身体等。

(2) 如何理解作者所言的《追忆似水年华》《战争与和平》等作品在文学形式上的"肥胖"?身体与文学形式间是否存在隐喻关系?

(3) 为什么现代主义作家选择身体作为文学革新的手段之一?

第三节　彼得·布鲁克斯与《身体活：现代叙述中的欲望对象》

一、导读

彼得·布鲁克斯是耶鲁大学比较文学专业荣休教授，主要从事叙事理论、英法小说等方面的研究。《身体活：现代叙述中的欲望对象》是布鲁克斯《阅读情节：叙事中的设计和意图》的续作，也是21世纪身体叙事理论体系建构的重要前序作品，为身体叙事提供了充分的理论视角和素材。此书由九章组成，既历时性地考辨身体叙事史料，又在现代的小说、油画、雕塑等多种文艺形式中讨论身体与叙事的关系，并关联医学、心理学等领域的成果，体现出跨学科的前瞻性。选文来自第一章"叙述与身体"，本章是导论性质的章节，从古希腊时期开始的各个历史时期的作品中举例说明叙述如何与身体相关。选文是其中的后半部分，即对18世纪以来的现代身体叙述模式的梳理与评价。

叙事作品的历史体现出一种日益专注于身体的趋向，布鲁克斯从弗洛伊德的精神分析视角出发，认为阅读中的身体是欲望的对象，而欲望则是带领叙事向前进的动力。如此，叙事可以被定义为揭露身体的过程，这一过程可能困难重重，可能无法到达完全"揭露"的终点，但重要的是，人们对揭露的过程的兴趣甚于对最终被揭露的身体的兴趣。这里所谓的"身体"，并不仅仅是某个人物的身体，而更像是一种意义的承载。

布鲁克斯在文中列举了詹姆斯·乔伊斯的《尤利西斯》、卡夫卡的《在流放地》、奥维德的《变形记》等作品，提出了与符号学上"身体的符号学化"(semioticization)相伴随的"故事的躯体化"(somaticization)概念，再次强调了身体作为叙述中的关键记号以及叙述内涵的核心连接点的重要地位，进一步展现了叙事与身体间的紧密联系。他认为，叙事就是欲望主体给欲望对象刻写和烙印的尝试。欲望主体往往是叙述者，欲望对象则是故事中的某个身体。主导对身体进行刻写和烙印的是一系列欲望：想要把身体赋予明确意义的欲望，和想要拥有或成为那种身体的欲望，等等。与"故事的躯体化"同样值得关注的是作品中身体概念的私人化。随着19世纪以来现代社会越来越多地关注个人身体的鉴别以及身份的独特性，各种形式的身体标记越来越多地被纳入社会符号学和社会控制的普遍体系中，相应的关于人物身体与身份鉴定的文艺作品也应运而生。布鲁克斯将这一现象与18世纪个人主义现代观念的兴起关联讨论，也由此为后续章节对小说、雕塑、医疗等话题下的现代身体讨论做了充分的背景铺垫。

二、《身体活：现代叙述中的欲望对象》选读[①]

Representation of the nude in the plastic and pictorial arts offers the clearest example of the

① Peter Brooks, *Body Work: Objects of Desire in Modern Narrative* (Cambridge: Harvard University Press, 1993), pp.18 - 27.

constitution of modern canons of vision and desire; literature appears to follow a similar, if more tortuous, route. The eighteenth century produces a particularly rich collection of erotic literature, which is fascinated by that which is normally covered and kept private. The literary representations most often have a playful indirectness, naming the private body through series of substitutions, as metonymies and metaphors. They also very often describe the naked female body as if it were posed for artistic representation. A century later, the aesthetics of realism does not bring the more graphic and detailed report of the naked body, in literature that intends to be public rather than pornographic, that one might have expected. In part, this is because narrative literature increasingly sees the world, and objects of attention and desire, through the eyes of fictive persons, including a narrator who is himself (or, less frequently, herself) a person both in the created world and above it. Therefore the object of attention and desire—most obviously, the person of the beloved—is not detailed in its nakedness but rather approached by way of its phenomenal presence in the world, which means by way of the clothing and accessories that adorn and mask the body. The approach to the body of the beloved may strive toward unveiling (Barthes compares traditional narrative to a striptease) but it also tends to become waylaid in the process of this unveiling, more interested in the lifting of veils than in what is finally unveiled.[①] An interest in the way, rather than simply in the endpoint, is indeed virtually a definition of narrative.

Barthes' model of narrative as striptease refers to the "classic" (or "readable") text which works toward a progressive solution of preliminary enigmas, toward a full predication of the narrative "sentence", toward a plenitude of meaning. The desire to reach the end is the desire to see "truth" unveiled. The body of the object of desire is the focal point of a fascinated attention. Yet this attention, the very gaze of literary representation, tends to become arrested and transfixed by articles of clothing, accessories, bodily details, almost in the matter of the fetishist. What Kleinian analysts call "part objects" become invested with affect and meaning, as the text presents inventories of the charms of the beloved (as in the enormously influential Petrarchan tradition). The moment of complete nakedness, if it ever is reached, most often is represented by silence, ellipsis. Narrative is interested not only in points of arrival, but also in all the dilatory moments along the way: suspension or turning back, the perversions of temporality (as of desire) that allow us to take pleasure and to grasp meaning in passing time.

One could, once again, find in Freudian scenarios of the man's fear and fascination at beholding the woman's sex an explanation for the way narrative swerves from direct contemplation of the object of desire—from direct confrontation of the Medusa—and also for the necessity of its reaching eventually that uncanny place that is man's first home. It may be more useful, however, to consider that the castration complex, which dictates that post-infantile desire emerges subject to

① See Barthes, *Le plaisir du texte*, pp.19 - 20; see also *S/Z* on Barthes' model of narrative, and, on these general questions of narrative, my *Reading for the Plot* (New York: Knopf, 1984; Cambridge, Mass.: Harvard University Press, 1992).

interdictions and repressions, founds a narrative "law" whereby direct access to the object of desire never can be unproblematic or linear, and indeed where knowing the vectors of desire and identifying its object is always complex, mediated, and subject to necessary error. The "eroticization of time", as a factor of human sexuality, also presides at the creation of narrative temporality. This temporality, like a force-field of desire, impels both fictive persons and real readers forward in a search for possession and truth, which tend to coincide in the body of the object that finally stands in the place to which desire tends. The greater reticence and indirection of the narrative text in depicting the body, as compared to painterly representation, has to do with the dynamic temporality of desire in narrative, the way in which narrative desire simultaneously seeks and puts off the erotic denouement that signifies both its fulfillment and its end: the death of desiring, the silence of the text.

The history of narrative offers its own story of a hesitant unveiling of the body—an increasing preoccupation with bodiliness, and a certain, somewhat sly, shedding of reticence about the erotic body. In France, Honore de Balzac, Gustave Flaubert, Emile Zola, and Marcel Proust represent stages in an increasingly explicit discourse of desire and its objects. In England, a greater weight of social repression affects representation of the body, but a displaced or censored eroticism is strongly registered by the reader of Charles Dickens, Charlotte and Emily Bronte, Henry James, or Thomas Hardy. A breakthrough in the uncensored, matter-of-fact representation of the body comes in our century, in James Joyce's *Ulysses* with its portrayals of Leopold Bloom at stool and Molly Bloom in bed with her own body. Yet literature continues to display a greater reticence about the representation of the body than painting. While I have attempted to explain this reticence by way of the logic of narrative, there may be additional reasons having to do with the logic of writing itself as a self-conscious remaking of the world in signs. Literature may be less interested in contemplation of the naked body per se than in the body as the locus for the inscription of meanings.

Let me try to gloss this last remark. The development of "civilization" (*Kultur*) as both Freud and Elias contend in their different ways, consists in instinctual renunciation and a disciplining the body and its functions. Bodiliness, we might say, is assigned to certain places in life, just as undressing or excretion are assigned to specific spaces within the modern bourgeois dwelling. In the predominant philosophical tradition that we usually derive from Descartes, the body is the other of soul or mind, and its place in life, while highly important, is not the same as that of the self. We live at a certain distance of spirit from materiality, while recognizing that it is a false distance—that spirit, whatever it is, depends on matter. Such a condition is not without analogies to that of the writer, whose spiritual conceptions are dependent on the materiality of the letter. If the letter, according to Saint Paul, kills while the spirit gives life, writers and readers of texts know—have always known—that there can be no spirit without the letter, and that the story of incarnation is, among other things, an analogy of writing. Although the body often seems opposed to spirit, its other, the realm of unmeaning, it can also be spirit's very material support, as the letter is the material support of the message.

Writing is often aware of this situation, and frequently dramatizes it as the recovery of the letter for spirit, of the body for signification. That dramatization very often takes the form of a marking or signing of the body. That is, the body is made a signifier, or the place on which messages are written. This is perhaps most of all true in narrative literature, where the body's story, through the trials of desire and over time, often is very much part of the story of a character. The result is what we might call a narrative aesthetics of embodiment, where meaning and truth are made carnal.

The moment of the recognition of Odysseus' scar by Eurykleia provides an emblem of this narrative tradition. It is the signing of Odysseus' youthful body by the boar's tusk—and we are given a detailed narrative of the incident of marking itself-that allows Eurykleia, so many decades later, to recognize the rightful lord of Ithaka. There could, of course, be other ways to assure Odysseus' recognition; indeed, Penelope will set him tests to assure herself of his identity, including the famous test of knowledge of how their marriage bed was constructed. The existence of other possible means of identification makes it only the more significant that the marked body should be the key, and the most dramatic, token of recognition. It is on the body itself that we look for the mark of identity, as writers of popular literature have so well understood. At the close of Alexandre Dumas's thunderous melodrama *La Tour de Nesle*, Buridan rolls back the sleeve of the expiring Gaultier d'Aulnay to reveal to Marguerite de Bourgogne the cross cut into his shoulder by a knife before he was abandoned as an infant on the steps of Notre-Dame Cathedral—thus offering the final revelation that he, like his twin brother Philippe, is the child of Buridan and Marguerite, and that she has committed both incest and infanticide. The example from Dumas' popular play is just one instance of the countless moments in modern literature when recognition takes place through markings made on the body itself. Climactic moments of coming-to-consciousness about one's identity, about the very order of the moral universe, are played out on the body.

The bodily marking not only serves to recognize and identify, it also indicates the body's passage into the realm of the letter, into literature: the bodily mark is in some manner a "character", a hieroglyph, a sign that can eventually, at the right moment of the narrative, be read. Signing the body indicates its recovery for the realm of the semiotic. When Freud comes to read the bodily symptoms of the hysteric as signs of psychic conflict, he brings a specific semiotic analysis to a long tradition of literary as well as medical efforts to make the body signify. Hysterical symptoms are a writing on the body. There are many other forms of such writing, including the sentences inscribed on the body by the torture machine of Franz Kafka's *In the Penal Colony*. The body can be made to bear messages of all kinds. Even more interesting than reading the messages on the body may be the study of their inscription. For the texts that show us the process of inscription give a privileged insight into the ever-renewed struggle of language to make the body mean, the struggle to bring it into writing. Most interesting to me—and this interest has dictated my choice of examples—are those texts that explicitly or implicitly speak of or dramatize the marking or imprinting of the body with meaning, its recreation as a narrative signifier.

What presides at the inscription and imprinting of bodies is, in the broadest sense, a set of desires: a desire that the body not be lost to meaning—that it be brought into the realm of the semiotic and the significant—and, underneath this, a desire for the body itself, an erotic longing to have or to be the body. As Freud's theories of the birth of the epistemophilic urge from the child's curiosity about sexuality suggest, there is an inextricable link between erotic desire and the desire to know. Both converge in writing, and where it concerns writing a body, creating a textual body, the interplay of eros and artistic creation is particularly clear. Among many instances that particularly emblematize that interplay, and that strikingly dramatize the marking and imprinting of the body, perhaps the one with the greatest mythic resonance for the Western literary imagination is that of Pygmalion and Galatea. In Ovid's *Metamorphoses* the story of Pygmalion is told by Orpheus, and thus is doubly about artistic creation. Pygmalion has turned away from women since he has found too many harlots among them, and devoted himself to a chaste existence. But when he creates a statue "lovelier than any woman born", he falls in love with his own creation.

Pygmalion's relation to the statue of Galatea is at first set within the imaginary order: a relation of *trompe l'oeil* deceptiveness, where he treats the statue as if it were alive: "Often he ran his hands over the work, feeling it to see whether it was flesh or ivory, and would not yet admit that ivory was all it was. He kissed the statue, and imagined that it kissed him back, spoke to it and embraced it, and thought he felt his fingers sink into the limbs he touched, so that he was afraid lest a bruise appear where he had pressed the flesh."① He then presents it with gifts and adornments, and places it on a couch, and calls it "his bedfellow". With the coming of the festival of Venus, he prays to the goddess that she give him "one like the ivory maid"—he doesn't dare say "the ivory maid"—as his wife. But Venus, understanding the true object of his desire, produces a metamorphosis of the statue itself. When Pygmalion returns home, and goes to kiss the statue on the couch,

> She seemed warm: he laid his lips on hers again, and touched her breast with his hands—at his touch the ivory lost its hardness, and grew soft: his fingers made an imprint on the yielding surface, just as wax of Hymettus melts in the sun and, worked by men's fingers, is fashioned into many different shapes, and made fit for use by being used. The lover stood, amazed, afraid of being mistaken, his joy tempered with doubt, and again and again stroked the object of his

① I quote from the translation of *Metamorphoses* 10: 253 - 258 by Mary M. Innes (Harmondsworth: Penguin Books, 1955), p.231.

prayers. It was indeed a human body! The veins throbbed as he pressed them with his thumb [*Corpus erat! saliunt temptatae pollice venae*]. (10: 289)

This moment when the statue becomes flesh—in a scene that will have its Christian version in the *hoc est enim corpus meum—registers* Galatea's coming into existence by way of the throbbing of the blood in her veins under the pressure of Pygmalion's thumb. The word for thumb, *pollice*, concludes a series of words having to do with Pygmalion's touching of the statue: the hands he runs over the statue (*saepe manus operi temptantes admovet*); the fingers he thinks he feels sink into the limbs he touches, so that he is afraid he has created a bruise (*et credit tactis digitos insidere membris/et metuit, pressos ne veniat ne livor in artus*); then, at the moment of transformation, the breast yielding to the touch of his hands (*manibus quoque pectora temptat*); and then the image of his fingers making an imprint on the yielding surface of the breast, as on softening wax (*temptatum mollescit ebur positoque rigore/subsidit digitis ceditque, ut Hymettia sole/cera remollescit tractataque pollice multas/flectitur in facies ipsoque fit utilis usu*). Hands, fingers, thumbs: they make no imprint on the ivory maiden, except in Pygmalion's momentary hallucination. But when she becomes flesh and blood, they leave their imprint, as in wax; and the thumb then feels the pulse throbbing beneath it.

The play of hands, fingers, thumbs images the artist's mark on his created work. The ivory virgin is of course Pygmalion's artistic handwork, but it remains other, inanimate, until desire is fulfilled by Venus. Then it bears the mark of his fingers, the sign of its shaping by human hands. So imprinted, Galatea opens her eyes and becomes Pygmalion's wife, and then the mother of Paphos, who in turn is the mother of Cinyras, who unwittingly becomes the lover of his own daughter Myrrha, engendering Adonis, who becomes the beloved of Venus. Galatea, then, joins the narrative world of the *Metamorphoses*. It is as if the human imprint on her cold, all-too-perfect and impenetrable body were the necessary marking or signing to make her come alive for narrative—become a vehicle of narrative signification. And she becomes this living, humanly imprinted body precisely because her perfect sculpted body has been the object of intense desire: it is Venus who presides at her animation.

The story of Pygmalion and Galatea has exercised a continuing fascination on the creative imagination because it magnificently represents a crucial wish-fulfillment: the bodily animation of the object of desire. It may suggest that in essence all desire is ultimately desire for a body, one that may substitute for *the* body, the mother's, the lost object of infantile bliss—the body that the child grown up always seeks to recreate.[①] As in the case of Pygmalion, that recreated body realizes

① The story of Pygmalion and Galatea can of course be considered exclusively a male wish-fulfillment, in which the female body is created according to the man's desire. Yet given that the epistemophilic urge develops in both men and women originally from the experience of the mother's body, perhaps this emblematic story could concern only the creation of a woman's body.

simultaneously erotic desire and the creative desire to know and to make. Galatea is a fiction suggestive of that word's derivation from *fingere*, meaning both to feign and to make. She is the supreme fiction that becomes reality as the embodiment of the artist's desire.

The story of Pygmalion and Galatea is in a sense the antithesis of Ovid's story of Narcissus, where the desired body is a vain image in the mirroring pool, an impossible object of desire which leads to sterile narcissism and the desire for death. Pygmalion and Galatea is the story of life, of enlivening, where the object of desire is both created according to one's wants and also other, a legitimate object of desire (though the ensuing story of the incest of Cinyras and Myrrha suggests a kind of return of the repressed, as if a toll had to be exacted for this perfect realization of desire). It is the story of how the body can be known, animated, and possessed by the artist of desire, and of how the body marked, imprinted, by desire can enter narrative. In this manner, it is something of an allegory of the narratives that interest me in the following chapters, which mainly concern, in very differing ways, attempts by a desiring subject to imprint the desired body. That desiring subject may be in the narrative, and is always also the creator of the narrative, whose desire for the body is part of a semiotic project to make the body signify, to make it part of the narrative dynamic. An aesthetics of narrative embodiment insists that the body is only apparently lacking in meaning, that it can be semiotically retrieved. Along with the semioticization of the body goes what we might call the somatization of story: the implicit claim that the body is a key sign in narrative and a central nexus of narrative meanings.

When we move into the modern world, we come upon indications that the individual identity has become newly important and newly problematic, and that the identification of the individual's body is a subject of large cultural concern. The historian Alain Corbin notes that the nineteenth century, in particular, brings a greater diversity in persons' forenames, as if to insist on the distinctive identity of the individual, along with a new mass distribution of the mirror, for self-contemplation, and the democratization of the portrait, once the exclusive appanage of the rich or famous, with the coming of photography.① At the same time, societies become more concerned with the identification of individuals within the group, especially in the undifferentiated mass of city dwellers. The identification of malefactors and marginals, such as prostitutes, was an obsessive issue; prostitutes were inscribed on police registers and given a "card" if they were streetwalkers, a "number" if they were in a brothel. When *La marque*—the practice of branding convicts' bodies with letters signifying their sentence—was abolished in France in 1832, various other methods for

① See Alain Corbin, "Coulisses," in *Histoire de la vie privee*, ed. Philippe Aries and Georges Duby, vol. 4: *De la Revolution a la Grande Guerre*, ed. Michelle Perrot (Paris: Editions du Seuil, 1987), especially pp.419 - 436, "l'individu et sa trace"; English trans. Arthur Goldhammer, *From the Fires of the Revolution to the Great War* (Cambridge, Mass.: Harvard University Press, 1990). On marks of identity and narrative, see also the remarkable essay by Carlo Ginzburg, "Spie: radici di un paradigma indizario," in *Miti, emblemi, spie* (Turin: Einaudi, 1986); English trans. John and Anne C. Tedeschi, "Clues: Roots of an Evidential Paradigm," in *Clues, Myths, and the Historical Method* (Baltimore: Johns Hopkins University Press, 1989).

singling out recidivists were invented: photography, "bertillonage"—the cranial measurements devised by Alphonse Bertillon—and the classification of criminal "types" by Cesare Lombroso. Eventually, fingerprinting—a technique long known to the Bengalis, and discovered by officials of the British Raj—would offer a surer indication of identity. In France and many other countries, various papers, employees' passports, and certificates of residence led to the creation of a national *carte d'identite*, textual authentication of the bearer's claim to a state-specified individuality.

Along with the concern to make some version of the bodily mark—like that by which Eurykleia identified Odysseus—into a universal system of social semiotics and control goes a literature driven by the anxiety and fascination of the hidden, masked, unidentified individual. The invention of the detective story in the nineteenth century testifies to this concern to detect, track down, and identify those occult bodies that have purposely sought to avoid social scrutiny. The shadowy underworld supermen created by Balzac—especially the arch-criminal Jacques Collin, alias Vautrin, alias Reverend Father Carlos Herrera, who undergoes multiple metamorphoses in his war on society—and the demiurgic Abel Magwitch, hidden author of Pip's life in Dickens's *Great Expectations*, and Victor Hugo's Jean Valjean, in *Les miserables*, whose saintly present is always undermined by the return of his convict past, prepare the fiction of Edgar Allan Poe, Gaston Leroux, and Arthur Conan Doyle in which emphasis shifts to the professional decipherer of the hidden identity.

To know the body by way of a narrative that leads to its specific identity, to give the body specific markings that make it recognizable, and indeed make it a key narrative sign, are large preoccupations of modern narrative. If these preoccupations are most fully dramatized in the nineteenth-century novel, they need to be perceived first in the rise of the novel, along with the rise of the modern sense of individualism, in the eighteenth century. The work of social and cultural historians has more and more confirmed our commonsense view that the Enlightenment is the crucible of the modern sense of the individual, the individual's rights, and the private space in which the individual stakes out a claim to introspection, protection, and secrecy, including private practices of sexuality and writing. Modern notions of the individual entail a conception of privacy as that place in which a person can divest himself or herself of the demands of the public and cultivate the irreducibly individual personality. Within this private space, what often appears to be most problematic, interesting, anguishing is the body. It is no accident that the person most often held to offer at least symbolic entry into the modern—and most often held responsible for its catastrophes as well as its more benevolent achievements—is also the first person to write about his own body as a problem. While certainly other confessional writers, notably Saint Augustine and Montaigne, examine problems of the flesh, its concupiscence, its weakness in disease, Jean-Jacques Rousseau appears to me the first who recognizes his body as a problem in the determination of his own life's story, and sets himself the task of giving a narrative account of that problem. It is, then, toward Rousseau, especially his *Confessions*, that I now propose to work, first by way of a consideration of how the very private realm of the body becomes the object of publicity.

三、思考与讨论:

(1) 布鲁克斯的介绍主要集中于传统的文类,当代的文学作品中的身体与叙事是否有更多种关系?

(2) 布鲁克斯谈论身体叙事的出发点是精神分析学,其身体观和叙事观有何局限性?

(3) 在叙事的构筑和解读中,给身体打上标记的除了叙述者,还可能是什么角色?

第四节　丹尼尔・庞代及其《叙事身体：一种身体叙事学》

一、导读

丹尼尔・庞代是美国密西西比州立大学英语系教授，主要从事身体叙事、数字叙事与叙事理论研究，他的《叙事身体：一种身体叙事学》发展和整理了前人较为零散的身体叙事研究，令身体叙事形成初步的理论体系，权威叙事学家杰拉德・普林斯称此书为"当今叙事学家在辨识、审查或重审叙事的方方面面时应该致力研究的方向"①之一。庞代在构建身体叙事理论框架时一直强调其"自下而上"的后经典特性以及理论的"不完整性"。因此，阅读庞代论著时也应怀有开放的批评态度，关注他所提炼的身体叙事理论框架各部分的重点特色、典型案例，思考如何补充和完善这一框架，而不必过分苛求其理论的全面性。

《叙事身体：一种身体叙事学》的主体部分按经典叙事学的人物、情节、空间、视角等基本要素分为五章。

本节选文来自第五章，这一章主要从作者与读者沟通层面介绍了具身化的差异和相应的叙事视角、作者权威等问题。选文所围绕的"政治体"就是一种典型的身体视角。庞代集中关注这些以身体比喻国家、社会的手法，从叙事学视角看待这一比喻手法背后所传达的具身化关系和阐释方法。文中梳理了历史上书写"政治体"的几部经典作品，如恩斯特・H.坎托罗维茨(Ernst H.Kantorowicz)的《国王的两个身体》、霍布斯的《列维坦》、托马斯・布里奇(Thomas Bridges)的《钞票历险记》等，展现了"政治体"比喻自中世纪晚期以来的悠久历史。作家和学者们使用这一比喻来代表对国家、教会之类的某个群体的整体印象，其类似身体的特点在于，政治体是由其各部分之间的关系联结而成的一种动态的社会模式，它是围绕活动和事件而组织起来的，而不是由某种外部权威以抽象的方式形成的。

身体天生可以看到自己之外的事物，理解叙事的设定也通常围绕身体的运动来进行。列维坦代表着国家机器，钞票的流通代表着流动的经济体……这些政治体的比喻一方面使用了一个假想的位置来描述整个群体，用视角克服个体本身的局限；另一方面，这种假想的位置也弥补了阅读动作的非具身性，促进了叙述者和读者间的交流沟通。庞代认为，叙事似乎自然地以一种与社会空间的整体和静态图像相反的方式运转和循环，而政治体的叙事方法是一种辩证的具身过程，借助阅读的非具身性才能实现抽象概念的具身化，只有通过身体的比喻才能呈现任何个体的身体都无法直接看到的"政治体"，深入了解其结构特征。

① Gerald Prince, "Surveying Narratology," p.10.

二、《叙事身体：一种身体叙事学》选读[①]

The Body Politic and Narrative Position

To narrate, then, is to search for a way to view the subject matter. With the transformation of narrative by print culture and the erosion of appeals to tradition or to direct experience, narrative has come to depend on visibility as the principle for reliability in narration. This visibility, as we have seen, emphasizes the position from which a story is told, and raises the problem of the way in which that narrated space is occupied physically. It is at this point that an inquiry into narrative authority becomes involved in the problematics of narrative space. Chapter 4 suggested that the body transforms narrative space into a route of circulation. The body, we noted, always looks beyond itself. Because of this, narrative setting must be understood in terms of the movement that it creates. I concluded that discussion by noting that the best example of narrative space is the concept of *circulation* that much of new historicist work draws upon. Social and narrative circulation, we saw, points to the inherent instability of social space. Ultimately the real power of circulation arises from narrative dynamics—its ability to capture the paradoxes of the unstable corporeality represented in texts, and in social totalities. Although in chapter 4 I used circulation to discuss the complexity of narrative space, it should be clear that it also has implications for the way that we think about the act of narrating itself. Toward the end of chapter 4 I noted Thomas Mann's observation in *The Magic Mountain* about narration: "Let us not forget the condition of life as of narration: that we can never see the whole picture at once—unless we propose to throw overboard all the God-conditioned forms of human knowledge."[②] Mann is ultimately describing the act of narration, and suggests that narrative itself arises from the difficulty of finding one position from which to describe a whole series of events. This difficulty, as we have seen, can be traced back in part to the nature of the human body, which defies the static location that we often associate with setting. Indeed, we have seen that the spatial instabilities of the human body resonate deeply with the problematics of narration itself, since both suggest the need for movement. Narratives and bodies circulate, we can say, and in doing so construct a complex textual hermeneutics that cannot be equated with static symbols.

We have seen, however, that narrative hermeneutics frequently relies on just such static figures to represent its own context for interpretation. In chapter 2, I argued that narrative always constructs a more general notion of bodily contact between text, author, and reader. I would like to suggest that we can read such figures as a response to the problems of narrative circulation that I

① Daniel Punday, *Narrative Bodies: Toward a Corporeal Narratology*(New York: Oalgrave Macmillan, 2003), pp.157 - 163.

② Thomas Mann, *The Magic Mountain*, trans. H.T. Lowe-Porter (New York: Vintage, 1969), p.574.

began to discuss in chapter 4. Consider, for example, the way in which figures of the "body politic" are used in political rhetoric. Ernst Kantorowicz's *The King's Two Bodies* suggests that the body politic metaphor emerges out of older traditions of imagining the King in the late-medieval/early Renaissance period. Kantorowicz notes, "The Church as the mystical body of Christ—and that means: Christian society as composed of all the faithful, past, future, and present, actual and potential—might appear to the historian so typically mediaeval a concept, and one so traditional, that he would easily be inclined to forget how relatively new that notion was when Boniface VIII probed its strength and efficiency by using it as a weapon in his life-and-death struggle against Philip the Fair of France" in 1302.① This corporate image of a group—in this case the Church, but nations as well—ultimately represents a notion of that group formed out of the relations between its parts and not out of some external authority that gave it form in an abstract way. Of course, the very idea that this form can be traced back to the body of Christ or to that of the king makes the formation ambivalent, since its corporate nature is coupled to a claim that some inherent authority stands behind that nature. Still, we can say that the body politic represents the emergence of modern definitions of nation and authority. To speak of the body politic, in this sense, is to claim a certain authority for a whole image of the social state.

The "body politic" metaphor that Kantorowicz describes may at first seem to have little relation to narrative authority, but in fact what is at stake within this metaphor is the "perspective" from which one can describe society. This perspective raises fundamentally narrative issues, and suggests the difficulty of thinking about the act of narration in general. Let us return to Hobbes's invocation of the body politic at the outset of *Leviathan*, which I have already quoted in Chapter 2. Hobbes imagines the body politic specifically in terms of the activity of the commonwealth:

> For seeing life is but a motion of limbs, the beginning whereof is in some principal part within; why may we not say, that all *automata* (engines that move themselves by springs and wheels as doth a watch) have an artificial life? For what is the *heart*, but a *spring*; and the *nerves*, but so many *strings*; and the *joints*, but so many *wheels*, giving motion to the whole body, such as was intended by the artificer? *Art* goes yet further, imitating that rational and most excellent work of nature, *man*. For by art is created that great LEVIATHAN called a COMMONWEALTH, or STATE, in Latin CIVITAS, which is but an artificial man.②

Hobbes's description of the state as an "artificial man" here is extraordinary—all the more so because the specific activity of the state usually goes unremarked by most commentators. Although

① Ernst H. Kantorowicz, *The King's Two Bodies: A Study in Medieval Political Theology* (Princeton: Princeton University Press, 1957), p.195.

② Thomas Hobbes, *Leviathan: Or the Matter, Forme and Power of a Commonwealth Ecclesiasticall and Civil*, ed. Michael Oakeshott (Oxford: Blackwell, 1960), p.5.

we tend to think of the body politic as a static, spatial metaphor that explains the elements of a society by reference to a fixed hierarchy, Hobbes treats this trope instead as a way to describe what the society *does*. This is a dynamic model of the society that is organized around activity and event rather than location or quality. Hobbes's artificial body is, we could say, narrative in the sense that it describes how political and social events should be understood and how agency can be recognized within such events. As political philosophy has long recognized, agency is a particularly complex issue when cultural context is taken into account. Hobbes's image of the artificial man seems to recognize this complexity and to account for it not just by reference to various responsibilities or duties, but by constructing an image of decentered activity—activity dispersed throughout the whole society. Thus, just as narrative raises the question of agency in textuality and suggests that it must be dispersed throughout the writing/reading spectrum, so too does the body politic represent the transformation and dispersal of national authority.

Along with its concern for agency, Hobbes's body politic also negotiates narrative perspective. Hobbes's body politic provides a perspective from which the whole society can be viewed. Hobbes concludes his opening invocation of the artificial man in precisely these terms:

> But let one man read another by his actions never so perfectly, it serves him only with his acquaintance, which are but few. He that is to govern a whole nation, must read in himself, not this or that particular man; but mankind: which though it be hard to do, harder than to learn any language or science; yet when I shall have set down my own reading orderly, and perspicuously, the pains left another, will be only to consider, if he also find not the same in himself. For this kind of doctrine admitteth no other demonstration. (6)

Hobbes offers his study as a meditation on the proper form of the social state. But the concern that drives him to this study and to the trope of the body politic with which he opens it is the difficulty of finding a perspective from which the society can be viewed. We are tempted, Hobbes notes, to find an image of ourselves, or of some particular person. The society, however, is comprised and defined precisely by the multiplicity of the "body". It is, in other words, an object of study precisely because it is genuinely to be seen in no one person. This problem can be described in terms of perspective—there is no position from which the society can be viewed, since its form is larger than any one or group of people. The body politic here emerges as a way of envisioning something that cannot literally be seen. The society is "in-visible" to Hobbes not so much because it is an abstract construction, an approximation like that of the "norm" or an "average". Instead, the society is invisible because vision itself is inadequate to understanding an entity that comprises elements so foreign to the King while at the same time containing the king. The nation is both "self" and "other", and vision seems to Hobbes unable to grasp the seemingly impossible position from which the King must view the society.[①]

The body politic describes, then, an imaginary position from which the whole of the nation can be narrated. We have seen, in fact, that it is precisely the body that routinely creates problems for defining a single location from which a narrative can be viewed. Faced with the demand that he adopt an impossible position from which to view the nation, the king is left with only *reading* as an alternative. In Hobbes's account, reading marks precisely the escape from the literal bodily position that disallows the king's understanding. In doing so, Hobbes ultimately adopts the kind of circulatory model that I have attributed to Mann and to Gallagher. Lynch has noted a similar concern for imagining the whole nation in the early British novel, and provides a way to link Hobbes's body politic and the circulation of Chapter 4. Lynch notes the popularity in the eighteenth century of novels that followed a coin or banknote from owner to owner. While such novels share a great deal with the open-ended and incidental structure of picaresque narratives, these stories also suggest the urge to provide an image of the whole society. Using the example of Thomas Bridges's *The Adventures of a Bank-Note* (1770), Lynch writes:

> Unlike Tom Jones or Roderick Random, both foundlings who are found out, the banknote's wanderings do not take him home to the landed estate that inspires eighteenth-century writers' fantasies of permanent residences and absolute private properties. The banknote moves on, into the pockets of persons in high life. Yet, as his momentary return to the little apothecary [an incident in Bridges's novel] suggests, the banknote's travels can make circulation seem more tidily circular. As late as 1820, this project retained its appeal: in *Buy a Broom: An Interesting Moral Tale for Children*, the talking broom that passes through a succession of owners also returns to the hands of its maker, although only long enough to be refurbished and resold. Like Asmodeus, the limping devil who knows how to maximize the city's visibility, such circulating protagonists give readers the wherewithal to conceptualize society as a whole. They assuage fears that the social is of unlimited and hence inapprehensible extension. (98)

Lynch describes a struggle within the early novel very similar to what I have suggested in the body politic: the attempt to overcome the perceptual limitations of embodied individuals and instead to "see" society as a whole. Indeed, Lynch's emphasis on circulation is significant, since it

① This representational paradox is suggested by Leonard Barkan when he remarks that "a vision of man in society making use of the human body analogy is likely to have a roughly hourglass-shaped structure. Society, seen as basically multiple and fragmented, is imaged forth by the diversity of the human body and at the same time unified by that image. The single body of society is analogous to or even identical with the body of the monarch, which is, in its ideal form, single and unified. But the monarch is himself fragmented by his public and private torments, and his fragmentation is in turn imaged forth by a diversification and multiplication of his own body, a process which makes him all the more analogous to the multiple body of the State" [*Nature's Work of Art: The Human Body as Image of the World* (New Haven: Yale University Press, 1975), pp.95 - 96].

approaches the problem of the perspective from which to view the society in much the same terms that I have used in discussing Hobbes's invocation of the artificial man. Lynch observes that the banknote is able to achieve its unique perspective precisely because it has no body: it is literally the "nobody" that narrators will increasingly approximate in their central characters and narrators. We can say, then, that the creation of a position from which one can narrate involves finding a way to negotiate the bodies of characters and viewers.

If Lynch's reading of the early novel is correct, we can understand the trope of the body politic as an inherently narrative way of providing a glimpse of social relations. Narratives overcome the bodily limitations of any one perspective in order to allow us to understand something that is inherently superindividual. But they do so not in the way that we expect from humanist criticism that claims that narratives bring together many selves. Instead, as Lynch and Hobbes suggest in their own ways, and as I will argue in this chapter, narratives overcome the limitations of individual perspectives precisely by negotiating the embodiment of the narrator and characters. Hobbes particularly allows us to see this, since *Leviathan* as we have described it is precisely the project of escaping the limitations of the body by turning to the disembodiment of reading. But this disembodiment in turn is possible only through the metaphor of another body that acts out the events that no one individual can see—the body politic. Lynch describes narratives of social circulation in which a vision of the whole society is accomplished only at the expense of actually participating within the society. But these narratives, too, install a dialectic of embodiment rather than merely celebrating a stable position from which the whole society can be viewed. After all, the money that circulates through the society is not free from bodily life, but is in many ways a vital part of keeping the body alive and well. We have seen the way that the philosophical ambiguity of capital troubles sociological discourse about population in Chapter 4. Lynch suggests this facet of these narratives when she notes that the banknote is an element of an economic system that may well seem foreign and overpowering to the individuals caught within it. The banknote here is not simply a disinterested observer, but is instead a vital but abstract part of the bodily lives of characters and readers. The banknote captures the ambiguity of the "material" in economic terms as both an abstract product of social forces and a concrete element that cannot be ignored. It exemplifies in the simplest form the dialectic that we will observe throughout this chapter between embodiment and disembodiment that is essential to creating narrative authority.

Creating authority through differential embodiment is a response, I would like to argue, to the kind of narrative dynamics that I have described at the end of chapter 4 and at the outset of this chapter. There I suggested that narrative creates fundamental problems about the perspective from which it should be viewed, and noted that narrative naturally seems to move and circulate in a way that is antithetical to overarching and static images of social space. I have argued that the "objectness" of the text and the characters represented within it becomes an issue as soon as our traditional ways of thinking about authority begin to erode. We are challenged to find a position from which to view them, and are caught up within a system of circulation and constant narrative movement. Because this movement can be traced back to the nature of the body itself, it should be no surprise that attempts to resolve this problem involve finding a disembodied perspective. Disembodied narration solves—or appears to solve—a whole host of problems for position and circulation that we have noted throughout this study. It makes it possible for us to imagine a position not caught up within these dynamics and thus capable of claiming authority to represent the whole.

In a larger sense, the narrative strategy of differential embodiment ultimately speaks to the nature of narrative hermeneutics. In Chapter 2, I argued that narratives necessarily create an image of a corporeality that transcends individual characters, and that makes sense of the relation between characters, authors, texts, and readers. Differential embodiment is both a confirmation and denial of that process. It is a confirmation because it defines our relationship as readers to a text through the model of corporeality—in this case, the balance between embodied and disembodied figures. Differential embodiment is a denial of these dynamics, however, because it creates credibility precisely by denying the embodied position from which a subject is described or a text is read. These narratives appear to create a universal position of "nobody" at the expense of embodied peripheral characters. The corporeal interaction between text and reader that Cixious described, or the physical hermeneutics of *Beloved*, work because they accept that we do interact physically with the text. These corporeal hermeneutics are disauthorized; they stand outside of the traditions and institutions that usually grant reliability to a text. This is one of the reasons, I think, that Morrison's novel is so ambiguous about its status as an object. We will recall that Morrison describes the novel as "not a story to pass on" and specifically locates it within an oral context. The return to orality and away from the textuality that we have associated with modern narrative clearly shows Morrison's attempt to escape from the traditional dynamics of differential embodiment and the text as an object. In insisting on the corporeality of our interaction with the text, Morrison rejects the tradition of differential embodiment that characterizes modern narrative.

三、思考与讨论

(1) 比起布鲁克斯,庞代看待身体叙事的态度有何进步之处?

(2) 请尝试从庞代提及的莫里森作品中寻找更多的"政治体"文本案例,从身体叙事视角阐释该手法,分析其叙事交流过程。

(3) "政治体"(body politic)和"身体政治"(body politics)有何区别与联系?

本章推荐阅读书目

[1] Peter Brooks. *Reading for the Plot: Design and Intention in Narrative*. Cambridge: Harvard

University Press，1992.

［2］Bryan S. Turner. *The Body and Society: Explorations in Social Theory*. Los Angeles：Sage，2008.

［3］Susanne Scholz. *Body Narratives: Writing the Nation and Fashioning the Subject in Early Modern England*. London：Springer，2000.

第八章
非人类叙事学

第一节 概　　论

进入21世纪以来，国际人文社科界迎来一轮显著的“非人类转向”（non-human turn），引发众多学者的关注。乔恩·罗费（Jon Roffe）和汉娜·斯塔克（Hannah Stark）指出：“在思想史的当下时刻，不可能不在非人类转向的语境下思考人类。此外，不足为怪的是，非人类转向在总体上是一个跨学科事件，对非人类的研究并不是哪一个学科所特有的，它要求我们超越摆在面前的界限。”[①] 作为一门研究讲故事的学问，叙事学同样需要关注“非人类转向”，并在这一语境下思考叙事的样式与功能。受罗兰·巴特《叙事作品结构分析导论》一文的影响，叙事学家们通常把由人类书写的叙事等同于关于人类的叙事，由此导致叙事学被打上了“人类中心主义”的烙印。在《走向“自然”叙事学》一书中，德国叙事学家莫妮卡·弗鲁德尼克直截了当地宣称：“在我的模式中，叙事可以没有情节，但却不能没有人类（拟人的）体验者，无论其属于哪种类型、处于哪个叙事层面。”[②] 从巴特到弗鲁德尼克，从杰拉德·普林斯到詹姆斯·费伦，叙事学家们无论是对于叙事的定义还是关于叙事研究的框架与模式，都带有“人类中心主义”的色彩。在现实的物理世界中，叙事作品是由人类书写的，从这种意义上来说，人是“讲故事的动物”（storytelling animal），但在虚构的文学世界中，叙事作品所呈现的不一定都是人类的故事或人类的经验。长期以来，叙事学以模仿主义为参照范式，重点聚焦再现人类经验的叙事作品，而忽略了大量书写非人类的叙事作品，由此导致了现有叙事理论的不完整。从学理层面上来说，提出非人类叙事首先就是出于丰富和发展叙事理论的需要。

在“非人类转向”语境下提出非人类叙事，既不是否定人是“讲故事的动物”这一基本观点，也不是否定“文学是人学”这一根本立场，而是试图借此加深我们对人类与非人类之间关系的理解，使人类更好地介入生物圈和建构更大的有机体，同时使叙事学在理论建构上摒弃“人类中心主义”。

---

① Jon Roffe and Hannah Stark, “Introduction: Deleuze and the Non/Human,” *Deleuze and the Non/Human*, eds. Jon Roffe and Hannah Stark (Basingstoke: Palgrave, 2015), p.2.

② Fludernik, *Towards a ‘Natural’ Narratology*, p.13.

一、什么是非人类叙事?

长期以来,所有关于叙事的定义基本上都是围绕人类经验的再现,假定叙事是关于人类的故事。无论是经典叙事学还是后经典叙事学,关于叙事的定义都普遍存在一个明显的"人类主义偏见"。在《叙事作品结构分析导论》一文的开篇,巴特写道:

> 世界上叙事作品之多,不计其数;种类浩繁,题材各异。对人类来说,似乎任何材料都适宜于叙事:叙事承载物可以是口头或书面的有声语言、是固定的或活动的画面、是手势,以及所有这些材料的有机混合;叙事遍布于神话、传说、寓言、民间故事、小说、史诗、历史、悲剧、正剧、喜剧、哑剧、绘画(请想一想卡帕齐奥的《圣于絮尔》那幅画)、彩绘玻璃窗、电影、连环画、社会杂闻、会话。而且,以这些几乎无限的形式出现的叙事遍存于一切时代、一切地方、一切社会。叙事是与人类历史本身共同产生的;任何地方都不存在、也从来不曾存在过没有叙事的民族;所有阶级、所有人类集团,都有自己的叙事作品,而且这些叙事作品经常为具有不同的,乃至对立的文化素养的人所共同享受。所以,叙事作品不分高尚和低劣文学,它超越国度、超越历史、超越文化,犹如生命那样永存着。[①]

巴特不断用"人类"一词来描述叙事的普遍性。他认为,人类可以选择任何材料作为叙事的媒介;叙事与人类共存于这个世界,所有人类集团都有自己的叙事作品。在某种程度上,巴特似乎把由人类来书写的叙事等同于关于人类的叙事。这一观点在叙事学界被广为接受。如果说巴特的上述叙事观基本代表了经典叙事学家们的立场,那么弗鲁德尼克和费伦带有人类中心主义色彩的叙事观则大体代表了后经典叙事学家们的立场。

在《走向"自然"叙事学》一书中,弗鲁德尼克借用威廉·拉波夫的观点,将自然叙事等同于口头叙事。她指出:"口头叙事(更确切地说,自发的会话讲述的叙事)在认知上接近于人类经验的感知范式,这些范式即便在更为复杂的书面叙事中也同样起作用,哪怕随着时间的推移,这些故事的文本构成会发生剧烈的变化。"[②] 弗鲁德尼克用"人类体验"来强调叙事的属性,认为"体验性"构成了作品的"叙事性"。在弗鲁德尼克看来,所谓的体验性"反映了与人类存在和人类关切的具身性的认知图式"。[③] 可见,弗鲁德尼克在论述体验性时,她所倚重的是"人类存在和人类关切"(human existence and human concerns)。弗鲁德尼克认为,叙事理论家们实际上很早就注意到叙事概念的"人类主义偏见"。"叙事理论家们很早就注意到,叙事的人类主义偏见及其与人物、身份、行动等相关的主要故事参数被认为构成了故事的最基本要素"。[④] 在弗鲁德尼克所列举的叙事理论家中,普林斯是比较突出的一位。在《叙事学词典》中,普林斯写道:"一个特定叙事作品的叙事性程度部分地取决于叙事在多大程度上满足接受者的欲望,再现方向性的时间整体(从开端到结尾的前瞻性方向,或从结尾到开端的回顾性方向),涉及冲突,由分开

---

① 巴特:《叙事作品结构分析导论》,第 2 页。
② Fludernik, *Towards a 'Natural' Narratology*, p.12.
③ Ibid., p.13.
④ Ibid.

的、具体的、积极的情景与事件所构成，从人类（化）课题或世界的角度来看它们是有意义的。”[①] 在普林斯看来，叙事成为叙事这件事，既离不开它之于人类接受者欲望的满足，也离不开它之于人类的意义。

当弗鲁德尼克指出自然叙事为研究所有类型的叙事提供了一个关键概念的时候，她意在强调几乎所有的叙事研究都需要聚焦人类的体验性。[②] 这一立场无疑忽略了那些再现非人类体验性的叙事。弗鲁德尼克这一带有“人类主义偏见”的叙事观在费伦那里也同样有较为明显的表现。在其经典作品《作为修辞的叙事：技巧、读者、伦理和意识形态》中，费伦从修辞视角出发，将叙事界定为“某人为了某个目的在某个场合下向某人讲述某事。”[③] 此后，在《活着是为了讲述：人物叙述的修辞与伦理》《体验小说：判断、进程和修辞叙事理论》等一系列论著中，费伦不断强化这一以“人”为核心的叙事概念。2017 年，费伦直接以“某人向某人讲述”作为其著作《某人向某人讲述：叙事的修辞诗学》的题名。在论述修辞诗学的原则时，费伦强调读者之于叙事的三种不同反应，即模仿性反应、主题性反应和虚构性反应。费伦认为读者之于叙事的模仿性反应在于“将人物看作我们自己所处世界中的可能人物”。[④] 无论是叙事的讲述对象还是受述对象，费伦都把他们看作“某个人”，假定叙事作品是关于人类而不是非人类的故事。

在人类发展史上，人类除了讲述自己的故事之外，还讲述了自己的对立面“非人类”的故事。纵观世界文坛，我们可以发现大量关于非人类的叙事作品。无论是早期的古希腊神话，还是当代先锋实验作品，都有非人类实体的存在。例如：古希腊、古罗马神话中关于神的故事；中国志怪小说中关于神仙鬼怪的故事，如蒲松龄的《聊斋志异》、吴承恩的《西游记》等；科幻小说中关于机器人、外星人、克隆人的故事，如玛丽·雪莱的《弗兰肯斯坦》、伊恩·麦克尤恩的《像我这样的机器》等；动物文学中关于动物的故事，如杰克·伦敦的《野性的呼唤》、麦克尤恩的《一只猿猴的遐思》、朱利安·巴恩斯的《10 ½章世界史》、莫言的《生死疲劳》等；寓言和童话故事中关于动物的故事，如安徒生的《海的女儿》等；变形文学中关于变形人物的故事，如卡夫卡的《变形记》、麦克尤恩的《蟑螂》、菲利普·罗斯的《乳房》、玛丽·达里厄塞克的《母猪女郎》等。遗憾的是，现有叙事理论大多聚焦于再现人类经验的叙事，而忽略了文学史上那些书写非人类的作品。

进入 21 世纪以来，受到行动者网络理论、情感理论、动物理论、新物质主义理论、媒介理论、思辨现实主义理论等多种思潮的激发和影响，人文社会科学迎来了一轮声势浩大的“非人类转向”。[⑤] 这一转向无疑为非人类叙事研究提供了契机。理查德·格鲁辛（Richard Grusin）指出，与“后人类转向”[⑥]不同的是，所谓的“非人类转向”指的是“人类始终与非人类共同进化、共同存在或协作，人类的特征恰恰在于其和非人类总是难以区分”。[⑦] 需要补充说明的是，就文学研究而言，“非人类转向”的最基本含义是“转向非人类”（turn to non-human），即认识到文学书写的对象不仅包括人类，而且也包括非人类。从理论

---

① Prince, *A Dictionary of Narratology*, p.65.

② Fludernik, *Towards a ‘Natural’ Narratology*, p.15.

③ Phelan, *Narrative as Rhetoric: Technique, Audiences, Ethics, Ideology*, p.8.

④ Phelan, *Somebody Telling Somebody Else: A Rhetorical Poetics of Narrative*, p.11.

⑤ Richard Grusin, “Introduction,” *The Nonhuman Turn*, ed. Richard Grusin (Minneapolis: University of Minnesota Press, 2015), pp.viii - ix.

⑥ 凯瑟琳·海勒(N. Katherine Hayles)指出：后人类的一个核心主题就是“人类与智能机器的结合”，“在后人类看来，身体性存在与计算机仿真之间、人机关系结构与生物组织之间、机器人科技与人类目标之间，并没有本质的不同或者绝对的界限”。参见凯瑟琳·海勒：《我们何以成为后人类：文学、信息科学和控制论中的虚拟身体》，刘宇清译，北京：北京大学出版社，2017 年，第 3—4 页。

⑦ Richard Grusin, “Introduction,” pp.ix - x.

层面上来说，将非人类叙事纳入讨论和考察范畴，可以丰富和扩展现有的叙事理论，使之更加完整，也可以对文学史上大量存在的非人类叙事文本做出应有的批评和阐释。

在论述广义叙述学的时候，赵毅衡提出了一个关于叙述的底线定义，即“有人物参与的事件被组织进一个文本中”。[①] 参照他对叙述的定义，我们大致可以给非人类叙事提供这样一个底线定义，即由“非人类实体”(non-human entity)参与的事件被组织进一个文本中。在具体叙事作品中，非人类实体主要存在于故事和话语两个层面。在故事层面上，他们以人物的身份出现；在话语层面上，他们以叙述者的身份出现。

二、非人类叙事的主要类型：从自然之物到人造之物

通过考察人物和叙述者的非人类身份，我们不妨将非人类叙事大致分为以下四种类型：其一，自然之物的叙事，主要包括以动物、植物、石头、水等各类自然界的存在物为核心对象的叙事；其二，超自然之物的叙事，例如以神话、传说、史诗中的鬼神、怪兽，以及科幻文学中的外星人为主体的叙事；其三，人造物的叙事，主要包括以钱币、玩具、布匹、线块等人类创造出来的无生命物体为主体的叙事；其四，人造人的叙事，主要包括以机器人、克隆人为主体的叙事，这在科幻小说中表现得尤为突出。在非人类叙事作品中，无论非人类实体是否有生命，它们都不再是作品场景的一部分，而是作品的人物，即故事的参与者，抑或是作品的叙述者，即故事的讲述者。

第一，自然之物的叙事。人类在诞生之初，首先接触到的就是自然之物。在《圣经》中，上帝在造出亚当和夏娃后，将他们安置在伊甸园。亚当和夏娃在伊甸园里品尝着甘美的果实，给所见的动植物命名，无论是地上的走兽、天空的飞鸟还是园中的嘉树与鲜花都有了自己的名字。长期以来，人们习惯于将动植物看作故事世界的背景环境，忽略了它们作为叙事主体而存在的可能，但后者的例子却屡见不鲜。在《山海经》中，山川河岳、植物、动物都成了作品的叙事主体，作品的基本格局是“依地而述”，而不是“依时而述”或“依人而述”。[②] 比如“南山经”“西山经”“北山经”“东山经”“中山经”“海外南经”“海外西经”“海外北经”“海外东经”“海内南经”“海内西经”“海内北经”“海内东经”“大荒东经”“大荒南经”“大荒西经”“大荒北经”“海内经”。此外，作品还叙述了大量鲜为人知的各类动植物。比如在“招摇之山”有一种名为迷縠的植物，作品中还记载了一种会冬眠的鱼。在傅修延看来，《山海经》是人类中心主义建立之前的产物，因为书中的叙述者并没有把自己与自然界分开，《山海经》中诸如“朴野”“荒芜”之类的词语恰好说明古人并未自诩为“万物的灵长”。[③]

放眼世界文坛，我们同样可以发现诸多以自然之物为主体的叙事作品。英国作家安妮・凯里(Annie Carey)的《一团煤、一粒盐、一滴水、一块旧铁和一个燧石的自传》即是如此。在作品中，煤块、盐、旧铁和燧石分别化身为叙述者讲述了自己的故事。丹麦作家安徒生也同样书写了很多关于自然之物的故事。比如，在《一个豆荚里的五粒豆》中，某个豆荚里面的五粒豌豆成为会说话的个体，各自经历了不同的命运，其中最后一粒豆子在楼顶的窗户下发芽了，给屋里病重的小女孩带去了生命的希望。在

① 赵毅衡：《广义叙述学》，成都：四川大学出版社，2013年，第19页。
② 傅修延：《中国叙事学》，第39页。
③ 同上。

《老栎树的梦》中，一棵365岁的老栎树在圣诞节的时候，做了一个美丽的梦，梦见自己越长越高："它的躯干在上升，没有一刻停止。它在不断地生长。它的簇顶长得更丰满，更宽大，更高。它越长得高，它的快乐就越增大；于是它就更有一种愉快的渴望，渴望要长得更高——长到跟明朗和温暖的太阳一样高。"[①] 遗憾的是，老栎树的梦还没有结束，就被一阵狂风连根拔起，崩裂而死。

在巴恩斯的《10½章世界史》中，木蠹叙述者认为动物们也有许多浪漫的神话故事。[②] 实际上，书写动物们的故事一直都是小说家们的重要兴趣。在中外文学史上，存在着大量以动物为主要叙述对象的叙事作品。在《10½章世界史》的第一部分"偷渡客"中，木蠹讲述了在大洪水来临之际，动物们如何登上挪亚方舟，躲避灾难的故事。木蠹一开始便亮明了自己的身份："我是个偷渡客，也存活下来，又逃离（离舟一点不比登舟容易），而且活得很好。"[③] 不过，大部分其他动物就没有木蠹那么幸运，因为挪亚立下的规矩是，可以允许七个洁净的动物登上方舟，而不洁净的动物中只有两个可以登舟避难。对于这一规定，有的动物选择扬长而去，走进了丛林；有的动物不愿意和配偶、子女分开，选择了留下；部分入选的动物上船前食物中毒，需要再选一次；那些试图偷渡的动物，比如驯鹿，则被吊死在方舟的栏杆上。木蠹特别强调，地球上五分之一的物种随挪亚的小儿子法拉第负责的那艘船一起沉没，而其余那些失踪的都被挪亚那伙人吃掉了。就书写濒临灭绝的动物的叙事作品而言，我们不禁想起陈应松的小说《豹子的最后舞蹈》。在作品中，叙述者是神农架地区的最后一只豹子。他讲述了自己家族，尤其是父母和兄弟姐妹被以老关父子为首的猎人捕杀，最后自己也被猎人打死的故事。众所周知，卡夫卡也是擅长书写动物的小说家。在《地洞》中，他写了某个种类不明的打洞动物；在《一份为某科学院写的报告》中，叙述者向科学院的先生们汇报了自己作为猴子的经历，尤其是它最后如何通过模仿人类进入人类世界的故事。

此外，我们还可以发现很多书写由人变形为动物或动物变形为人的叙事作品，如莫言的小说《生死疲劳》。作品主要讲述了地主西门闹先后投胎为驴、牛、猪、狗和猴子的故事。比如，在第一次投胎的时候，西门闹掩饰不住自己的惊讶："我睁开眼睛，看到自己浑身沾着黏液，躺在一头母驴的腚后。天哪！想不到读过私塾、识字解文、堂堂的乡绅西门闹，竟成了一匹四蹄雪白、嘴巴粉嫩的小驴子。"[④] 又如，法国作家玛丽·达里厄塞克的小说《母猪女郎》。作品讲述了一位在香水连锁店工作的漂亮姑娘变形为一只母猪的故事。变成母猪后的女孩失去了工作，惨遭男友抛弃，甚至遭到动物保护协会的追杀。所幸的是，她在狼人伊万那里收获了一段爱情。在卡夫卡的《变形记》中，旅行推销员格里高尔·萨姆沙一觉醒来后变成了一只甲虫。变成甲虫的萨姆沙遭到所有人的嫌恶，就连自己最喜欢的妹妹也慢慢地对他弃之不顾。麦克尤恩的小说《蟑螂》仿照了卡夫卡的《变形记》。不过，在麦氏的笔下，不是人变成了甲虫，而是甲虫变成了人。在作品中，一只名叫吉姆·萨姆沙的蟑螂变形为英国首相，并率领其他同样由蟑螂变形而来的内阁成员，在英国成功推行了违背经济规律、旨在撕裂国家的"逆转主义"政策。

第二，超自然之物的叙事。与自然之物的叙事相对应的非人类叙事是超自然之物的叙事，如以鬼神、怪兽、外星人等为主体的叙事作品。在中外文学史上，都存有大量以超自然之物为叙事主体的作品。比如，《荷马史诗》书写了包括众神之王宙斯、文艺女神缪斯、太阳神阿波罗、海神波塞冬、智慧女神雅典娜等在内的希腊众神。《伊利亚特》的第20卷讲述了诸神直接出战，各助一方的故事：

① 安徒生：《安徒生童话全集之八：老栎树的梦》，叶君健译，上海：上海译文出版社，1986年，第149页。
② 朱利安·巴恩斯：《10½章世界史》，林本椿、宋东升译，南京：译林出版社，2015年，第2页。
③ 同上，第2页。
④ 莫言：《生死疲劳》，杭州：浙江文艺出版社，2017年，第9页。

众神纷纷奔赴战场，倾向不一样。
赫拉前往船寨，一同前去的还有
帕拉斯·雅典娜、绕地神波塞冬和巧于心计、
分送幸运的赫尔墨斯，自以为力大的
赫菲斯托斯也和他们一同前往，
把两条细腿迅速挪动一拐一瘸。
前往特洛亚营垒的是头盔闪亮的阿瑞斯，
还有披发的福波斯、女射神阿尔特弥斯、
勒托、爱欢笑的阿佛罗狄忒和克珊托斯。[①]

与《荷马史诗》类似，在讲述人类故事的同时，涉及神的介入的作品还有古希腊罗马神话，以及中国古典作品《封神演义》。在《封神演义》的第九十九回“姜子牙归国封神”中，姜子牙请求天尊，“将阵亡忠臣孝子、逢劫神仙，早早封其品位，毋令他游魂无依，终日悬望”。[②] 在得到原始天尊的允许和敕命后，姜子牙在封神台一共分封了365位正神。20世纪60年代，叙事学发轫之初，部分叙事学家试图参照语言学模式对神话展开研究，揭示神话的叙事语法。例如，法国经典叙事学家克劳德·列维-斯特劳斯曾参照索绪尔的结构主义语言学模式，研究了俄狄浦斯神话、美洲神话等。通过研究，列维-斯特劳斯得出结论，他认为所有的神话都具有一种“板岩”结构，这种结构可以说是通过重复的手段显示出来的。[③] 以今天的眼光看来，列维-斯特劳斯的神话学研究对象就是非人类叙事。遗憾的是，这些以神话为对象的非人类叙事遭到了当代叙事理论家的淡忘或漠视。类似书写神仙、鬼怪等非人类的叙事作品还有《聊斋志异》《搜神记》《西游记》等。以《西游记》为例，作品涉及各种类型的神仙、妖怪。在经历八十一难后，唐僧、孙悟空、猪八戒、沙僧师徒四人最终取得真经，修得正果。英国史诗《贝尔武甫》则是以怪兽为叙事主体的另一个经典例子。该诗的主体部分讲述了英雄贝尔武甫战胜怪兽格伦戴尔母子的故事。此外，以超自然之物为主体的非人类叙事还包括那些关于外星人的叙事作品，常见于科幻文学作品中，例如厄休拉·勒奎因的《黑暗的左手》、刘慈欣的《三体》等。

第三，人造物的叙事。在很多非人类叙事作品中，无生命的器物被赋予了生命，成为作品中的人物或叙述者。18世纪英国文学涌现出大量此类叙事作品，学界一般称之为“它—叙事”(It-narrative)或“流通小说”(novels of circulation)、“物故事”(object tales)。[④] 诸如钱币、马甲、针垫、瓶塞钻、鹅毛笔等没有生命力的器物都被赋予了生命，成为作品中的人物，向读者讲述它们的故事。卡夫卡的作品中也有很多关于人造物叙事的例子。例如，在短篇小说《家长的忧虑》中，主人公是一种名为“奥德拉德克”(Odradek)的线块。尽管叙述者这样描述奥德拉德克：“初一看，它像是个扁平的星状线轴，而且看上去的确绷着线；不过，很可能只是一些被撕断的、用旧的、用结连接起来的线，但也可能是各色各样的乱七

① 荷马：《荷马史诗·伊利亚特》，罗念生、王焕生译，北京：人民文学出版社，1994年，第539页。
② 许仲琳编：《封神演义》，北京：中华书局，2018年，第698页。
③ 克劳德·列维-斯特劳斯：《结构人类学：巫术·宗教·艺术·神话》，陆晓禾等译，北京：文化艺术出版社，1989年，第68页。
④ 参见 Mark Blackwell, ed. *The Secret Life of Things: Animals, Objects, and It-Narratives in Eighteenth-Century England* (Lewisburg: Bucknell University Press, 2007).

八糟的线块。”[1] 但在作品中,奥德拉德克分明又是有生命的个体,身形灵活,交替地守候在阁楼、楼梯间、过道和门厅,其发出的笑声听起来像是落叶发出的沙沙声。让叙述者无法接受并感到痛苦的是,奥德拉德克能够拥有比自己更长久的生命:“显然,他绝不会伤害任何人;但是,一想到他也许比我活得更长,这对我来说,几乎是一种难言的痛苦。”[2]

安徒生创作的大量作品也可以被纳入人造物叙事这一类型。比如,在《钱猪》中,婴儿室中的各种玩具,包括桌子的抽斗、学步车、摇木马、座钟、爆竹、痰盂、钱猪等,在某天晚上突发奇想,要表演一出喜剧。玩具们一边看剧,一边吃茶和做知识练习。后来,激动的钱猪从橱柜上掉了下来,摔成了碎片,而钱猪肚子里的大银洋跑去了大千世界。在《瓶颈》中,一只瓶颈对小鸟讲述了自己和瓶子的故事,尤其是自己如何见证了一对年轻男女在森林中订婚,后来身为船员的年轻男子在遇到海难沉船前,把写有未婚妻的名字、自己名字和船名字的纸条塞在了瓶子中。后来有一次,瓶子被一个飞行家从腾飞的气球中扔出去摔碎了,从此只剩下了瓶颈。在《烂布片》中,一块挪威烂布片和一块丹麦烂布片为自己的产地国挪威和丹麦争论不休:

> “我是挪威人!”挪威的烂布说。“当我说我是挪威人的时候,我想我不须再作什么解释了。我的质地坚实,像挪威古代的花岗岩一样,而挪威的宪法是跟美国自由宪法一样好!我一想起我是什么人的时候,就感到全身舒服,就要以花岗岩的尺度来衡量我的思想!”
>
> “但是我们有文学,”丹麦的烂布片说。“你懂得文学是什么吗?”[3]

故事最后,挪威烂布片和丹麦烂布片都被造成了纸。用挪威烂布片造成的那张纸被一位挪威人用来写了一封情书给他的丹麦女友;而那块用丹麦烂布片做成的稿纸上写着一首赞美挪威的美丽和力量的丹麦诗歌。在安徒生笔下,诸如此类的故事还有很多。比如,在《衬衫领子》中,衬衫领子向袜带、熨斗、剪刀吹嘘自己有过一大堆情人的经历;在《老路灯》中,那个服务多年的老路灯在待在杆子上的最后一晚,回忆了自己的一生;在《笔和墨水壶》中,一个诗人房间中的墨水壶和鹅毛笔相互嘲讽;在《坚定的锡兵》中,锡兵哪怕就要被火化为锡块时,依然保持扛枪的姿势,坚定不动。

第四,人造人的叙事。随着文学与科技的相互交叉,人造人也被写进文学作品中,成为非人类叙事的又一类型。论及这一叙事样式,我们不得不提玛丽·雪莱的小说《弗兰肯斯坦》。在小说中,科学家维克多·弗兰肯斯坦开始对生命的原理能否延伸这个问题产生了浓厚的兴趣。用他的话来说:“有一个大自然的杰作特别引起了我的注意:人体结构(事实上是一切有生命的物体的身体结构)。我常常问自己:生命的原理可以延伸吗?这是个大胆的问题,是对生命(一个一直被认作奇迹的东西)的质疑。”[4]为此,弗兰肯斯坦开始调查生命的起源,研究死亡,研习解剖学,最终成功破解了生命密码。他说:“在经过多少个难以置信的辛苦和疲劳的日夜后,我成功发现了生命的演化与形成的原因。不,还不止于此,我自己就成了可以让无生命的东西获得生命的人。”[5] 弗兰肯斯坦口中的“让无生命的东西获得生命”几

① 卡夫卡:《家长的忧虑》,叶廷芳主编:《卡夫卡全集》第1卷,石家庄:河北教育出版社,1996年,第183页。
② 同上,第184页。
③ 安徒生:《安徒生童话全集之十四:曾祖父》,叶君健译,上海:上海译文出版社,1978年,第2页。
④ 玛丽·雪莱:《弗兰肯斯坦》,孙法理译,南京:译林出版社,2016年,第45页。
⑤ 雪莱:《弗兰肯斯坦》,第46—47页。

乎是关于人造人故事的一个重要动因。经过艰苦的努力，他成功制造出了一个有生命的物体，不过他自己都受不了这个怪物的丑陋外貌，唯恐避之不及。尽管怪物不断向人类示好，试图和人类交往，但其因丑陋的外貌遭到人类的厌恶和误解，开始报复人类、杀戮人类。最终，怪物在杀死弗兰肯斯坦的新婚妻子伊丽莎白和弗兰肯斯坦本人后，用火烧死了自己。

弗兰肯斯坦式的人造人故事在后世文学作品中以不同形式得到不断延续。例如，石黑一雄的小说《千万别丢下我》讲述了一群克隆人的故事。在作品中，叙述者凯茜既是克隆人，也是克隆人的看护者。根据她的讲述，人类创造出克隆人的目的就是给人类捐献器官。一般情况下，克隆人在给人类捐献器官三次或四次后，就完成了使命，其生命也随之走到尽头。尽管凯茜和另一位克隆人汤米真心相爱，但因为无法从人类那里获得延迟捐献的许可，她在亲眼看见汤米完成自己的最后一次器官捐献后，也由看护人变成了器官捐献人。麦克尤恩的小说《我这样的机器》讲述了一则人造人如何介入人类生活并遭遇失败的故事。小说场景设置在20世纪80年代，第一批人造人开始投放市场："第一批机器人中，十二个名为亚当，十三个名为夏娃。平淡无奇，每个人都这么说，但符合商业需求。生物学意义上的种族观念，在科学上受人诟病，所以这二十五个设计成了多个种族的样子。"[①] 在小说中，亚当表现出超强的机器学习能力，学会了在网上挣钱。他同女主角米兰达发生了关系，并宣称自己无可救药地爱上了她，还不断地为她撰写情诗。在石黑一雄的新作《克拉拉与太阳》中，叙述者克拉拉是一台AF机器人(人工朋友机器人)。按照人工智能工程师卡帕尔迪的设计和要求，克拉拉模仿和学习她的主人乔西，以便在乔西生病离开世界后，自己可以延续她。克拉拉根据自己的判断，努力去做对乔西最有利的事情，用自己的信念和行动帮助乔西恢复健康，长大成人。有关人造人的非人类叙事作品还有大卫·米切尔的《云图》中的克隆人星美反抗人类的故事，以及菲利普·迪克的《仿真人会梦见电子羊吗?》中的仿真人故事。

三、非人类叙事的主要功能：讲述、行动与观察

在叙事作品中，非人类实体主要存在于故事与话语两个层面，分别担任叙述者、人物、聚焦者三种角色，相应地发挥三种叙述功能，即讲述功能、行动功能和观察功能。

第一，讲述功能，即作为讲述者的非人类。谭君强指出，作为叙述主体，叙述者首要的功能就在于叙述。只有叙述才能成为叙述者，也只有存在叙述者的叙述才有叙事文本的存在。[②] 从叙述内容上来说，作为叙述者的非人类主体既可以讲述非人类的故事，也可以讲述人类的故事，或者讲述非人类与人类相处的故事。例如，在《豹子的最后舞蹈》中，叙述者是一只豹子，它讲述了自己的家族如何被人类灭绝的故事；在《千万别丢下我》中，叙述者凯茜是一个克隆人，她主要讲述了一群克隆人如何在给人类捐献器官的过程中走向生命尽头的故事；巴恩斯的《10½章世界史》中的木蠹叙述者讲述了动物们在洪水来临之际的命运。在《生死疲劳》中，叙述者是由地主西门闹投胎而来的驴、牛、猪、狗和猴子，然后这些动物们轮流出场，分别讲述了西门闹及其妻女和子孙后代的故事。在《克拉拉与太阳》中，AF机器人克拉拉讲述了她与小女孩乔西及其家人共同相处的故事。

第二，行动功能，即作为行动者的非人类。自亚里士多德以来，人物的一个重要功能就是作为行动

① 伊恩·麦克尤恩：《我这样的机器》，周小进译，上海：上海译文出版社，2020年，第2页。
② 谭君强：《叙事学导论：从经典叙事学到后经典叙事学》，第71页。

者而存在。例如，经典叙事学家格雷马斯将人物称为“行动元”(actant)，并且重点分析了主体、客体、发送者、接受者、帮助者、反对者六种行动元。叙事作品中的行动元既可以是人类，也可以是非人类。法国社会学家布鲁诺·拉图尔(Bruno Latour)受到格雷马斯的启发，提出了著名的“行动者网络理论”(Actor-Network-Theory，简称 ANT)。拉图尔说：“行动者网络理论借用了来自文学研究的技术词汇行动元。”[①] 在拉图尔看来：“行动者网络理论并非一种关于用物‘取代’人作为行动者的空洞论点，它仅仅指出，任何关于社会科学的行动都无法开展，除非我们先深入研究什么人和什么东西参与了行动这一问题，即便这可能意味着纳入一个我们因缺乏更好的术语只能称之为非人类的因素。”[②] 换言之，在拉图尔的理论体系中，行动者或参与行动的主体既可以是人类，也可以是非人类。正是在这种意义上，拉图尔强调检验行动者网络理论的一个重要手段就是非人类必须是行动者，不能只是悲哀地发挥着承载象征投影的作用。在大量的非人类叙事作品中，非人类实体作为行动者而存在，成为故事世界的主角，其行动也由此成为作品所要再现的故事内容，直接推动作品的叙事进程。例如，在奥威尔的《动物庄园》中，一群动物反叛人类，在农场上建立了自己的王国。在《我这样的机器》中，机器人亚当积极介入人类世界，不仅同女主角米兰达发生了性关系，而且还擅作主张，坚持“真相就是一切”(truth is everything)的说辞，[③]枉顾米兰达为自己好友伸张正义的伦理真相，将米兰达曾在法庭说谎的证据交给警方而导致她被捕入狱。在《克拉拉与太阳》中，机器人克拉拉跨越茂盛的草地走向麦克贝恩先生的谷仓，因为她坚信可以找回藏在那里的太阳，而太阳可以给予女孩乔西力量，让她重新恢复健康。在乔西生命垂危之际，克拉拉看到太阳出来后，立即与乔西的母亲和梅拉尼娅管家冲入乔西的房间，让太阳照射在乔西身上。克拉拉说：

> “该死的太阳!”梅拉尼娅管家大叫着，“走开，该死的太阳!”
>
> “不，不!”我赶忙走到梅拉尼娅管家跟前，“我们必须拉开这些，拉开一切! 我们必须让太阳尽他的全力!”
>
> 我试图从她手中拿走窗帘的布料，尽管她一开始不肯放手，最终却还是让步了，一脸惊诧的神色。这时，里克已经来到了我的身边，似乎凭着直觉做出了一个判断，于是他也伸出手来，帮忙升起百叶帘，拉开窗帘。
>
> 太阳的滋养随即涌入房间，如此的充沛饱满，里克和我都摇摇晃晃地向后退去，几乎要失去平衡。梅拉尼娅管家双手遮着脸，嘴里又说了一遍：“该死的太阳!”但她没有再试图遮挡他的滋养。[④]

由于克拉拉的积极行动，乔西奇迹般地恢复了健康，成为一个正常的孩子。

第三，观察功能，即作为聚焦者的非人类。在《超越人类的叙事学：故事讲述与动物生活》一书中，戴维·赫尔曼主要通过考察动物叙事作品来探讨叙事何以再现非人类的经验，建构一个非人类的世界，

---

① Bruno Latour, *Reassembling the Social: An Introduction to Actor-Network-Theory* (Oxford: Oxford University Press, 2005), p.54.

② Ibid., p.72.

③ 麦克尤恩：《我这样的机器》，第 294 页。

④ 石黑一雄：《克拉拉与太阳》，宋佥译，上海：上海译文出版社，2021 年，第 357—358 页。

而这恰恰可以通过非人类聚焦实现。不仅如此，作为聚焦者的非人类还为观察和审视人类行为与人类世界提供了一种他者视角。例如，在《10½章世界史》中，木蠹以观察者的身份，不仅讲述了自己对其他动物命运的思考，同时还传递了自己对挪亚的观察与判断。它讲述了挪亚裸身的故事：挪亚醉酒后，脱完衣服就躺在帐篷中；后来，含和他的弟兄遮盖了挪亚的裸体，并把他安顿在床上，但挪亚醒来后，"他诅咒看到他醉酒裸睡的儿子，宣判所有含的后代都要在那两个屁股先进他房间的弟兄家里做奴仆"。[①] 对于挪亚的这一举动，木蠹说："这当中有什么道理？我能猜到你的解答：醉酒影响了他的判断力，我们应该怜恤他，而不是谴责他。这也许有道理。但我只想提一句：是我们在方舟上认清了他。"[②] 依木蠹所见，挪亚动作笨拙，不讲卫生，甚至认为如果上帝选了大猩猩做他的门徒，就不会有这么多犯上作乱的事了，"兴许根本就不需要来一场洪水"。[③] 在故事世界中，木蠹作为一个观察者来陈述自己的所见所思："我要揭示的真相到此差不多说完了。这些都是出于好意，你一定要理解我的意思。你如果认为我这是故意挑起争端，那可能是因为你们这一族武断得不可救药——但愿你不会在意我这么说。你们只相信你们愿意相信的，然后就一直相信下去。想想也不奇怪，你们都有挪亚的基因。"[④] 又如在《克拉拉与太阳》中，克拉拉这样描述她和其他 AF 伙伴们透过橱窗对人类世界的观察："我们能够看着外面——行色匆匆的办公室工人、出租车、跑步者、游客、乞丐人和他的狗、PRO 大楼的下半截。"[⑤] 在克拉拉被乔西买回家后，她的重要任务就是负责观察乔西。克拉拉说："在多种环境下观察乔西对我来说非常重要。"[⑥] 克拉拉对人类世界的观察在很大程度上影响了她对人类行为的认知和判断，同时也使她认识到自己与人类之间的差异。在生命即将走到尽头时，克拉拉遇到了来回收站寻找自己销售出去的那些 AF 机器人的商店经理，她动情地说："经理，我做了我所能做的一切来学习乔西；如果真的有那样做的必要，那我是会竭尽所能的。但我认为那样做的结果恐怕不会太好。不是因为我无法实现精准。但无论我多么努力地去尝试，如今我相信，总会有一样东西是我无法触及的。母亲、里克、梅拉尼娅管家、父亲——我永远都无法触及他们在内心中对于乔西的感情。"[⑦]

非人类实体的讲述功能、行动功能和观察功能，在很大程度上指人类与非人类之间的关系，引发读者对人类与非人类共存于同一个世界这一问题的关注，摒弃人类中心主义。换言之，研究非人类叙事的重要旨趣在于更好地理解人类，使人类以更好的方式介入生物圈，建构更大的有机体。用赫尔曼的话来说，关于非人类叙事研究的一个基本目的是探究叙事何以作为一个"场所来重新思考——批判或重审，解构或重构——对于在一个不仅只有人类存在的世界中人类地位的不同理解方式"。[⑧] 在这种意义上，关注和研究非人类叙事无疑有助于激发我们对人类何以成为更好的人类、世界何以成为更好的世界等问题的思考。

---

① 巴恩斯：《10½章世界史》，第 16 页。
② 同上，第 16—17 页。
③ 同上，第 17 页。
④ 同上，第 25 页。
⑤ 石黑一雄：《克拉拉与太阳》，第 3 页。
⑥ 同上，第 102 页。
⑦ 同上，第 384—385 页。
⑧ David Herman, *Narratology beyond the Human: Storytelling and Animal Life* (Oxford: Oxford University Press, 2018), p.25.

第二节　拉尔斯·贝尔纳茨等及其《非人类叙述者的故事生活》

一、导读

拉尔斯·贝尔纳茨(Lars Bernaerts)等几位欧洲叙事学家重点关注了文学作品中的非人类叙述者(nonhuman narrator),尤其是非人类的人物叙述者,即这些非人类实体既是故事世界中的人物,又是话语世界的叙述者。论及非人类叙事,拉尔斯·贝尔纳茨等人强调非人类叙述的悖论本质:“读者通过阅读非人类叙述者的虚构的生命故事来反思人类生活的方面,无论这些非人类叙述者是动物、物体还是无法解释的实体”(readers are invited to reflect upon aspects of human life when reading the fictional life stories of non-human narrators, whether they are animals, objects, or indefinable entities)。[1] 实际上,通过揭露和展示松鼠、煤、狗等非人类的物体或动物的生活,这些非人类叙述强调并挑战了我们关于人类的概念。[2] 贝尔纳茨等人重点考察读者介入非人类叙述的双重辩证法:陌生化与共情、人类体验性与非自然。一方面,非人类叙述者可以激发读者将人类经验投射在通常不会想到的物体上,另一方面,读者不得不面对非人类叙述者的他者性,由此质疑关于人类生活与艺术的那些假设。在他们看来,陌生化是非人类叙述的一个重要因素,因为非人类叙述让读者具有陌生感和距离感,但同时又能让读者产生认同感。由此,贝尔纳茨等人指出:“不可小觑的是,非人类叙述让人承认相似性和他者性,同时又让人认识到老鼠身上的鼠性、猴子身上的猴性、老鼠和猴子身上的人性以及人类身上的鼠性和猴性。以这种方式,非人类动物讲述的故事可以颠覆人类中心主义的意识。这些叙述通过关注非人类的动物、培育共情,可以把非人类作为人类的连续体来看待,而不是把其作为人类的对立面来看待。”[3] 贝尔纳茨等人列举了不同类型文本中非人类叙述的功能,例如讽刺功能、教育功能、培育环境意识功能等。在这种意义上,他们也揭示出非人类实体似乎被赋予了人类感知的功能,但它们对事件做出了不同于人类的判断。

在非人类叙事这一议题上,我们无法回避或绕过非人类叙事学与自然叙事学、非自然叙事学、修辞叙事学之间的关系。自然叙事学强调的是人类的体验性,而这种体验性是从历时角度来看的,也是叙事成为叙事的一个主要因素或叙事的原型所在。非自然叙事学突出强调对于传统的现实主义叙事作品中模仿规约的违背,而修辞叙事学则侧重于叙事交流以及叙述目的。在贝尔纳茨等人看来,非人类叙事介于自然叙事与非自然叙事之间,因为其投射了“非人类体验性”(non-human experientiality)。[4] 不过,非人类叙事研究主旨是激发读者对非人类他者的关注、强调人类-非人类的互为主体性,进而建构更大的有机体。就此而言,非人类叙事学也需要从修辞叙事学那里汲取理论营养,积极借助修辞叙事学的叙

① Lars Bernaerts, Marco Caracciolo, Luc Herman, and Bart Vervaeck, “The Storied Lives of Non-Human Narrators,” *Narrative* 22.1 (January 2014), p.68.

② Ibid.

③ Ibid.

④ Ibid., p.75.

述交流模式，充分考察作者、文本和读者之间的互动。

二、《非人类叙述者的故事生活》选读[①]

Non-Human Narration in Literary Fiction

There are many intriguing examples of non-human narrators in literary fiction. In Italo Calvino's cosmicomic stories (*Tutte le cosmicomiche*, 1997), the character narrator is a kind of shapeshifter. In the opening chapter of Julian Barnes's *A History of the World in 10½ Chapters* (1989) the narrator is a witty woodworm. A statue is the homodiegetic narrator in Harry Mulisch's novella *The Statue and the Clock* (*Het beeld en de klok*, 1989). The narrating voice of Martin Amis's *Time's Arrow* (1991), a novel told backwards, inhabits the body of the protagonist and distances itself from the human species. In *Rat* (1993), the widely read novel by the Polish writer Andrzej Zaniewksi, a rat gives a detailed account of its life, from its birth to its death. In *Two Brothers* (*Dos Hermanos*, 1995), a novel by the Basque writer Bernardo Atxaga, the story is told by a bird, squirrels, a star, a snake, and a wild goose. The Flemish author Jan Lauwereyns has written a novel in which the narrator is a captive monkey that is used as a laboratory animal (*Monkey Business*, 2003). Andrea Kerbaker's *Ten Thousand* (*Diecimila*, 2003) is the story of a book's life. In *The Portrait* (*Specht en zoon*, 2004), by the Dutch author Willem Jan Otten, the narrator is the canvas of a famous portraitist.

Non-human narration can serve a variety of functions in narrative texts. In some cases, animal or object narration is a satiric strategy. In children's literature, non-human narration can have a didactic function. In other cases, it foregrounds ethical problems. Often, it reveals the problematic ways in which humans relate to their physical environment and to other living creatures. Lauwereyns's monkey narrator, for example, provides a straightforward invitation to reflect upon the conditions of lab animals. The monkey, whose skull and brains are penetrated with needles during experiments in a neuropsychological lab, explicitly asks whether scientific progress can go on at the expense of the lives of so many animals. Throughout the narrative, the reader is brought closer to the putative experience of "what it is like" (in Thomas Nagel's phrase) to be a monkey in a laboratory.

The novel also suggests that humans tend to reduce animals to objects, an ideological position that is often lurking in non-human narratives. Along the lines of R. D. Laing's analysis of depersonalization in *The Divided Self* (46–54), a lot of non-human narratives point to the fact that people may conceive the other (person, animal) as an object in order to cope with reality and to maintain one's own subjectivity or superiority.

In many non-human life stories, the reverse is also foregrounded: we—humans—have the

① Bernaerts, Caracciolo, Herman, and Vervaeck, "The Storied Lives of Non-Human Narrators," pp.69–75.

cognitive habit of animating the inanimate and anthropomorphizing animals. According to Blakey Vermeule, animism and personification (the attribution of agency), two processes involved in this anthropomorphizing mechanism, are "conceptual primitives" (21 - 24). Not only are these cognitive processes inherent to the reading experience, but they can also be self-consciously exploited by literary texts: "Writers can always deliver a shock of mild surprise by personifying things like pots, kettles, and banknotes. They can exploit the widespread human tendency towards animism while keeping us on the edge of our seats" (Vermeule 26). It is evident that the reflection upon this human cognitive habit is another recurring function of non-human narration.

This phenomenological thread in non-human narratives can also be illuminated with more recent insights into the "what it is like"—dimension of literary fiction (see Herman, *Basic Elements* 145 - 147). By playing with readers' familiarity with human experience ("experientiality", to borrow Monika Fludernik's term), literary texts can create phenomenological states that are taken by readers as convincing demonstrations of non-human life. Although non-human narrators vary greatly when it comes to their physical and psychological design, and to their functions as narrators, they have two crucial features in common as a narrative device. First of all, they are character-narrators and/or homodiegetic narrators: they are part of the storyworld they are conjuring up in their tales.① The non-human narrators at the center of our attention in this essay are the protagonists of their own story, shedding light on formative experiences in their lives. Calvino's cosmicomic stories can be read as a postmodern autobiography, as Kristi Siegel has argued. Kerbaker's novella announces itself explicitly as the autobiography of a book.

The second common feature is the fact that these narrators spring from and require the conceptual integration of human and non-human traits. Mark Turner (138 - 139) has already shown how conceptual integration or blending can account for the recurrent motif of talking animals in fairy tales. But of course these blends can be more or less conventionalized depending on a number of factors—including literary genre. A talking lion in a fairy tale is not so exceptional in view of the relevant generic conventions. Or consider the traditional omniscient narrator, who can be understood, according to Monika Fludernik, as a blend of divine and human features ("Naturalizing" 17). Unlike the omniscient narrator, the non-human narrators we are discussing are homodiegetic narrators and they are not always or not yet conventionalized in literary fiction. A woodworm complaining about the conditions in Noah's ark or an immortal shapeshifter narrating his life at the time of the big bang are new and surprising conceptual integrations. Because of their novelty, these blends draw special attention to themselves and evoke a new constellation of defamiliarization and empathy. In that respect, the phrase "conceptual integration" can even be misleading, since the so-called integration is not always smooth and may lead to "clashes"—in

① This means we are excluding non-human focalizers, such as the dog in Paul Auster's *Timbuktu* (1999), from our corpus. See Williams Nelles's essay on animal focalization.

Fauconnier and Turner's term (113)—or dialectic tensions between human and nonhuman features.

In *Strange Concepts and the Stories They Make Possible*, Lisa Zunshine explores fictional blends of the human and the non-human, such as robots, cyborgs, and androids, which she terms "counterontological entities" (*Strange Concepts* 75). In her view, the resulting tensions are culturally embedded conflicts of cognitive categorization (51 - 55), which are solved in the reading process. At first we may assume that narrators and characters are human-like agents, but the text and the immediate context (e.g. paratextual indications of genre) continually force us to (re)specify and adjust our assumptions. An important point made by Zunshine is that cognitive categories entail standard degrees and kinds of "processing over the folk-psychological domain", i.e. ascription of consciousness (63). Whereas an entity categorized as an animal or a pet is often seen as "friendly" "sad" or "angry", it is less obvious to attribute intentions and emotions to an artifact such as a cup or a pen. On the other hand, we should not forget that the animal characters we are interested in here are not just experiencing subjects: they are *talking* (narrating) subjects, which means that another cognitively and culturally salient distinction—humans speak, non-human animals don't—is collapsed. In short, both object and animal narrators seem to be "counterontological entities". Still, we argue that the degree of empathy and defamiliarization produced by non-human narrators does not depend only on these general cognitive predispositions, but also on the specificity of the narrative presentation of human/non-human blends. When the text presents an animal or a thing as a "character", the reader activates the framework of what Fotis Jannidis calls the "Basistypus" (*Figur und Person* 185 - 195) or "basis type" ("Character"). This rudimentary, prototypical structure involves the assumption that the entity has mental states and a body (Eder, Jannidis, and Schneider 13). A combination of conceptual domains such as "a speaking canvas" invites the reader to apply the basis type and it requires a particular (re)categorization.

By and large, the types and the effects of non-human narration emerge from the way the conceptual integration is configured, i. e. the specific proportion of human and non-human features. To illustrate the way human and non-human elements are conceptually integrated, let us consider the following quotation:

> [*T*] *he Sun takes about two hundred million years to make a complete revolution of the galaxy.*
>
> Right, that's how long it takes, not a day less—*Qfwfq said*—once, as I went past, I drew a sign at a point in space, just so I could find it again two hundred million years later, when we went by the next time around. (Calvino, "A Sign in Space" 32; emphasis original)

The human/non-human blend combines a personalized voice suggesting human mental functioning with a range of non-human features, some of which cannot be assigned to any living creature or known object. In the example, it is clear that the intradiegetic narrator of the cosmicomic stories has been around a long time. In fact, the reader of Calvino's stories will know that the narrator has always existed. In his humorous, idiosyncratic style, he comments upon several, sometimes incompatible formative events in his cosmic life. In some of the stories, the experiencing self takes the shape of an animal; in other stories his physical form remains unspecified. Still, human experience is integrated into the non-human make-up of Qfwfq. In every story, for example, a feeling of loss is prominent in the narrativization of the past.[①] The narrator's nostalgic attitude is one of the elements that reinforce his anthropomorphic side and it may also stimulate the reader's empathetic involvement. Similarly, all non-human narrators exploit human experientiality in varying degrees, and they call upon our ability to attribute consciousness to non-human entities and even to empathize with them. In what follows, we will clarify this conceptual framework by fleshing out the two pairs of concepts that can give rise to a "double dialectic" in readers' engagement with non-human narrators: defamiliarization and empathy, human experientiality and the (un)natural.

Defamiliarization and Empathy

Viktor Shklovsky, one of the early proponents of a formalist approach to literature and therefore one of the "proto-narratologists" (see Schmid), coined the term "defamiliarization" (*ostranenie*) in his attempt to define the specificity of art. Whereas practical communication confirms the way we look at the world, literature makes the familiar seem strange. In the famous key passage of his 1917 essay "Art as Technique", Shklovsky argues that

> art exists that one may recover the sensation of life; it exists to make one feel things, to make the stone *stony*. The purpose of art is to impart the sensation of things as they are perceived and not as they are known. The technique of art is to make objects "unfamiliar", to make forms difficult, to increase the difficulty and length of perception because the process of perception is an aesthetic end in itself and must be prolonged. (Shklovsky 12; emphasis original)

The first elaborate example of defamiliarization provided by Shklovksy is Tolstoy's *Kholstomer*, a novella in which a horse functions as an intradiegetic narrator. Shklovsky underscores the fact that the perspective of the horse changes the reader's perception of the world as he knows it. In narratological terms, it is focalization as well as voice, characterization, and narrative evocation of fictional minds that collaborate in realizing this effect.

The sort of defamiliarization Shklovsky identifies is indeed an important factor of non-human narration: the rat in Zaniewski's novel *Rat* or Calvino's Qfwfq prevent the reader from assimilating these texts to familiar conventions and expectations. As Shklovsky phrases it, our automatic

① See Cromphout.

perception or our "recognition" of reality is hampered and replaced by a fresh look. The world of the rats in Zaniewski's novel puts our reality into another perspective, as it demonstrates how the rats' lives are shaped by the gutters, sewers, trash, and cracks in the human world. Calvino's narrator talks about his various lives since the beginning of time and even before that. In that way, he stimulates the reader to reconsider familiar ideas about time and identity.

The reader is invited to adopt a cosmic point of view on the world, which is formally conveyed through panchronic and panoramic focalization.① From that vantage point, human beings can be viewed as nothing but "[s]hapeless, colourless beings, sacks of guts stuck together carelessly" (Calvino 149), as Qfwfq sees them.

In the context of this essay, defamiliarization will be considered as the effect that literary texts can bring about on readers by challenging their ideas about what counts as "normal" or "predictable" in a given genre or narrative situation. Phenomenologically, this effect involves a sense of strangeness or puzzlement, which may invite readers to self-consciously attend to their expectations. When it comes to non-human narration, however, Shklovsky's formalist approach can only offer one part of the story. We also need a counterbalance for the concept of defamiliarization to clarify the workings of non-human narration. For this purpose, we will use the concept of "empathy". Empathy is the imaginative process whereby readers temporarily adopt the perceptual, emotional, or axiological perspective of a fictional character, "trying it on" and experiencing its effects in a first-person way (Gaut; Coplan). Reading the autobiography of the laboratory monkey in Lauwereyns's novel, we might become estranged from human reality, but we are also invited to imaginatively share the cognition and emotion of the monkey in its cage. If we weren't able to empathize with it, then the kind of defamiliarization Shklovsky posits could not be actualized in the reading experience.

Non-human narrators often seem to echo this dialectic of defamiliarization and empathy. They implicitly and explicitly foreground strategies of distancing and identification. What is often at stake in non-human narration is the ability to acknowledge similarity and otherness at the same time, to recognize the ratness of the rat, the monkeyness of the monkey and the humanness of the rat and the monkey as well as the ratness and the monkeyness of humans. In that way, stories narrated by non-human animals can destabilize anthropocentric ideologies. By giving a voice to non-human animals and facilitating empathy, these narratives can place them on a continuum with humans, rather than constructing them as opposites. As the case studies will make clear, empathy and defamiliarization operate not just on the level of the reader's interaction with the text, but also on the level of the fictional world. Further, the case studies demonstrate that empathy and defamiliarization are important factors in the dynamics of the narrative, since they generate narrative interest, to use Meir Sternberg's terminology (*Expositional Modes*).

---

① See in particular Calvino's "The Spiral" (pp.137 – 151). For the terminology, see Herman and Vervaeck's *Handbook of Narrative Analysis*, pp.75 – 76.

Human Experientiality and the (Un)natural

Invoking Fludernik's "natural" narratology, we can say that the stories of nonhuman entities are narrativized by the projection of human experientiality—i.e. "holistic schemata known from real life" which "can be used as building stones for the mimetic evocation of a fictional world" (Fludernik, *Towards* 28). The projection is triggered by the narrative itself, because non-human agents are endowed with human sensitivities. In Otten's novel about the portrait, the narrator expresses shame, bewilderment, and desire. However, the canvas also emphatically deviates from human experientiality in its perception and interpretation of the events:

> People are more scared of death than we artefacts. That has become very clear to me. If you add a thousand fears to my fear, you'll come close to understanding human fear. I don't know what I owe this realisation to—I'm not human, and I'm about to go up in smoke. Why did I have to know? That it's beyond them, people, the thing that is about to happen to me? Having disappeared is beyond them. (Otten 151)

Since these narrators seem to depart radically from human beings, the projection of human experientiality can only be one part of the reader's engagement with them. While coming to grips with the non-human and artificial dimension of these narrators, the reader may be invited to consider important aspects of human existence, including the artificial nature of fiction itself. The violation of conventions that underlies the audience-nonhuman narrator relationship is precisely the focus of attention of unnatural narratology. Jan Alber, Stefan Iversen, Henrik Skov Nielsen, and Brian Richardson claim that unnatural narratives violate "the conventions of natural narrative" (Alber et al. 115) as well as the "conventions of standard narrative forms" (Richardson, "What Is" 34) and "produce a defamiliarization of the basic elements of narrative" ("What Is" 34). In his book *Unnatural Voices*, likewise, Richardson associates non-human narration with a general development, in modern fiction, toward the posthuman (3). Posthuman narrators, such as Qfwfq or the woodworm in Julian Barnes's novel, undermine the idea of a stable and unified human identity, and question the concept of humanity.

All in all, in many cases we cannot understand non-human narration merely by applying familiar frames of reference. "Natural" narratology stresses the importance of human experientiality, while "unnatural" narratology stresses the anti-mimetic aspects of non-human narration. Between these two poles, something else happens as well, as we have suggested, namely the projection of *non-human* experientiality. Often, if not always, non-human narrators use techniques of focalization, characterization, and consciousness representation to evoke non-human experientiality. Thus, non-human narration cannot be reduced to the unnatural and the strange, since it is caught in a dialectic of empathy and defamiliarization, the familiar and the strange, human and non-human experience. Narrative strategies of voice, focalization, the evocation of consciousness, and characterization are decisive in the creation of these tensions. Thanks to them, non-human narration can challenge readers to reconsider familiar ideas on reality, identity, existence. In our case studies, we wish to demonstrate this link between narrative strategies, empathy and defamiliarization, and the reflection upon the human world.

Building on a similar scale set up by David Herman in his recent work on animal narratives ("Storyworld/Umwelt"), we would like to position our case studies on a continuum that goes from an anthropocentric mode of representation of non-human experiences to the imaginative exploration of the phenomenal world of non-human animals. In some narratives animals are allegorical representations of humans or anthropomorphic projections, while other narratives suggest zoomorphic projection or foreground the "distinctive texture and ecology of non-human experiences" ("Storyworld/ Umwelt" 158), thereby evoking "what it is like" to be that animal (160). The continuum proposed by Herman is similar to the gradual distinction made by Theodore Ziolkowski from a thematological perspective. In an illuminating chapter on talking dogs, he distinguishes between "'relativised' or 'anthropocentric' animal narratives" and "'absolute' or 'cynocentric'" narratives (Ziolkowski 94). While at one end of the scale non-human narration serves to reinforce preexisting aspects or elements of a given human culture, at the opposite end narrative can challenge readers' expectations and worldview, therefore expanding the boundaries of human experientiality.

Our third case study, Annie Carey's *Autobiographies*, comes closer to the first pole, since its talking objects convey a reassuring sense that humans occupy a central position in the universe, with objects serving as means towards the realization of technological and scientific progress. By contrast, the two short stories by Julio Cortázar ("Axolotl") and Franz Kafka ("The Burrow") fall on the opposite end of the scale, since their narrators seem to question the anthropocentric paradigm: these narratives prove unsettling because they blur the boundary between the human and the non-human by asking their readers to imaginatively adopt perspectives radically different from their own everyday experience. Although our case studies do not span the whole gamut of functions and roles that can be fulfilled by non-human narration, they aptly illustrate the underlying double dialectic that we see as central to readers' encounters with impossible narrators.

三、思考与讨论

(1) 非人类叙述者的功能是什么?

(2) 为什么读者在阅读非人类叙事的时候,会存在双重辩证法?

(3) 非人类叙事学与自然叙事学、非自然叙事学、修辞叙事学之间有何区别与联系?

第三节　戴维·赫尔曼及其《超越人类的叙事学》

一、导读

在戴维·赫尔曼看来，21世纪叙事学研究的一个重要任务就是在一个更大的、关于价值和责任的系统中重新评价叙事学，评估故事及其用来分析故事的传统如何与构成学术或当下其他最为紧迫的社会、司法、环境、健康等研究的范式、体制和实践相关。[①] 赫尔曼试图思考的和探究的命题是叙事理论家如何在更大的生物圈中探讨人类与动物之间关系的本质与范畴问题。从这种意义上来说，叙事学确实有着超越人类的必要。那么问题就在于超越人类的叙事学究竟需要或可以做什么？

对此，赫尔曼引入了肯尼斯·J.格根（Kenneth J. Gergen）和玛丽·M.格根（Mary M. Gergen）所提出的“自我叙事”（self-narrative）概念。在他们看来，自我叙事具有重要的心理、交际和社会文化功能，而自我叙事主要源自人类试图在多个生命事件中建立连贯的联系。尽管自我叙事似乎是个体的，但是它们的谱系性和持续性都是社会性质的。通过结合自我叙事在文化语境中的故事讲述模式，他们考察了自我叙事的三种类型：稳定叙事（stability narratives）、进步叙事（progressive narratives）以及倒退叙事（regressive narratives）。[②] 赫尔曼认为，超越人类的叙事学不仅需要分析一个特定的“自我叙事”如何将人类行动者放置于自我的跨物种群体中，而且还要通过在更广意义上的自我相对性质的、新的、更可持续的个体和集体自我叙事来分析处于更大的动物生命网络中的自我状况。在赫尔曼看来，这些叙事更有可持续性，因为它们把人类自己再度融入更大的自我群体中，而不是过去所确立和辨识的那些占据主导地位的科学、社会、法律和道德范式的群体中。

在讨论非人类叙事的时候，赫尔曼的重点考察对象为动物叙事。例如，通过分析劳伦·格罗夫（Lauren Groff）的短篇小说《上面与下面》（*Above and Below*），赫尔曼指出作品的主人公如何走出狭隘的自我生态圈的限度，揭示出稍微允许可能超越人类的自我与大幅允许可能超越人类的自我之间的虚假界限。这种虚假的界限也反映出世界的人类中心视角与生物中心视角之间的对立，其本质是把人类和其他生物之间做出等级划分，抑或是证明人类生命和非人类生命之间存在一定的连续性。具有启发意义的是，在该作品中，主人公逐渐消解了其个人狭隘的自我叙事，越发认识到她在“不仅只有人类的世界”（a more-than-human world）中的位置。在赫尔曼看来，这部短篇小说的价值与寓意在于人类社会必须要认识到自己只是更大生物圈的一员，并且对该生物圈负有一定的责任，人类一方面帮助支持这个更大的生物圈，同时也依赖于该生物圈。赫尔曼的研究试图揭示研究动物以及人与动物之间关系的故事可以在艺术学、科学和人文科学之间的交流上开辟富有生产性的路径，同时从跨学科视角来研究这些叙事作品也可以为在大的生物圈想象和回应跨物种关系提供新的路径。在赫尔曼看来，21世纪叙事学

① David Herman, “Narratology beyond the Human,” *DIEGESIS* 3.2 (2014), p.132.

② Kenneth J. Gergen and Mary M. Gergen, “Narratives of the Self,” *Memory, Identity, Community: The Idea of Narrative in the Human Sciences*, eds. Lewis P. Hinchman and Sandra Hinchman (Albany: State University of New York Press, 1997), pp.161–184.

较为紧迫的任务之一就是考察对人类和其他动物在更大自我生态圈中所处位置提出问题的那些虚构或非虚构叙事作品。[①]

在《超越人类的叙事学：故事讲述与动物生活》一书中，赫尔曼重点考察了动物叙事作品，呼吁建构"生物叙事学"(bionarratology)。从这种意义上来说，赫尔曼关于非人类叙事的研究实际上是狭义上的动物叙事研究，没有将人造人、人造物、超自然之物等其他非人类纳入考量范畴。

二、《超越人类的叙事学》选读[②]

After the initial founding of the field of narratology in the 1960s and its systematization and consolidation in the 1970s and 1980s, scholarship on narrative over the last several decades has been marked by a resurgence of theory-building activity, enabled in part by analysts' engagement with ideas from other areas of inquiry. Cross-disciplinarity has driven—even constituted—narratological research from the start; but whereas the early narratologists, following a larger structuralist trend, looked to linguistics as their "pilot-science" for the study of stories, more recent contributions to the field have drawn on ideas from a variety of source disciplines, ranging from feminist theory, philosophical ethics, and cognitive science, to digital media studies, evolutionary biology, and ecocriticism. At the same time, scholars of narrative have expanded the corpus of stories—and broadened the range of storytelling media—on which these new, integrative frameworks for analysis have been brought to bear. The resulting proliferation of case studies across genres, periods, media, and cultural settings has both productively diversified and helpfully constrained research in the field; this double benefit derives from the way claims about narrative *tout court* must now be checked against attested storytelling practices in multiple fictional and nonfictional genres distributed over a constellation of media platforms, historical epochs, and cultural contexts.

Such, arguably, is the state of the art when it comes to narrative studies; or, to shift to the vocabulary of Thomas S. Kuhn (1962), the research situation that I have described thus far amounts to the normal science of contemporary narratology.[③] To be sure, much more paradigm-extending work of this sort needs to be done, given that theorists are still refining their methods for investigating narratives within (let alone across) particular genres and formats, and given too the constant innovation and renewal of the source disciplines from which cognitive narratologists, analysts of narrative vis-à-vis questions of gender and sexuality, and students of visual storytelling,

① Herman, "Narratology beyond the Human," *DIEGESIS* 3.2 (2014), p.141.

② Ibid., pp.131 - 136.

③ Critics have suggested that Kuhn's contrast between normal or paradigmatic and revolutionary science is overly dichotomized, arguing that revolutionary scientific developments (e.g. the discovery of DNA) can occur in the practice of what would have to be classed as normal science on Kuhn's own terms (see Bird 2013 for further discussion). Nonetheless, the distinction provides a basis for my distinction between work that seeks to consolidate, extend, or supplement existing paradigms for narratological inquiry, on the one hand, and work that reconsiders those paradigms' conceptual and institutional status, range of applicability, and interconnections with other fields, on the other hand.

among others, continue to recruit concepts and models. But there is another important task for narratology in the twenty-first century. This task, more reflexive or metanarratological in nature, differs from the process of mapping out the explanatory reach of current paradigms for narrative study, or for that matter furthering normal narratological science by supplementing existing paradigms with new research frameworks of the same general kind. Instead, this other task for twenty-first-century narratology entails reassessing the place of scholarship on narrative within a wider ecology of inquiry, a broader system of values and commitments, taking stock of how stories and traditions for analyzing them relate to the norms, institutions, and practices that structure academic and other engagements with today's most pressing concerns, social, jurisprudential, environmental, health-related, and other.

The present essay uses Lauren Groff's 2011 short story "Above and Below" to outline an approach to narrative scholarship that, while continuing to leverage the invaluable gains of paradigm-extending work in the field, also brings into view alternative pathways for research and engagement—pathways that may lead to a re-envisioning and recontextualization of normal narratological science. More specifically, I explore aspects of a narratology beyond the human, considering how ideas developed by scholars of narrative bear on questions about the nature and scope of human-animal relationships in the larger biosphere.① Groff tells the story of an unnamed female protagonist who leaves behind the life she knew as a graduate student in literature at a university in Florida and who then experiences the vicissitudes of homelessness over a period of approximately eighteen months, no longer able to embrace what Kenneth J. Gergen and Mary M. Gergen (1997) would characterize as the self-narrative in terms of which she had previously made sense of her experiences.② By not using quotation marks to distinguish instances of speech and thought representation from narratorial reports, and by blending such reports with moments of narrated perception③, Groff creates maximal consonance between narrator and protagonist; the story thus stages, through a sequence of vignettes strictly focalized through the protagonist, what it is like to live in the aftermath of a self-narrative that has fallen into obsolescence. Further, in tracing out the lived consequences of the main character's having "chosen to lose" and said "goodbye to longing" (Groff 2011, 106) by the time the story begins, Groff's text suggests how it requires the creation of another, different account, an offsetting narrative, to register the loss or active rejection of a previously sustaining story of self.

It is not just the narrative of one self that is at stake here, however. Groff's text also reveals

① In using the expression "narratology beyond the human", I build on the precedent set by Kohn (2013) vis-à-vis anthropology.

② Gergen and Gergen provide the following thumbnail definition of *self-narrative*: "the individual's account of self-relevant events across time" (Gergen / Gergen 1997, p.162). I discuss this concept in more detail in what follows.

③ An example of narrated perception occurs early in the story, as the narrator prepares to leave the apartment from which she has been evicted: "The apartment was a shell, scoured to enamel" (Groff 2011, 106).

how fictional accounts can serve as a workspace for reconsidering—for critiquing or reaffirming, dismantling or reconstructing—narratives about human selves in a world in which selfhood extends beyond the domain of the human.[①] Scholars of story are well-positioned to contribute to a broader, cross-disciplinary investigation of how self-narratives are imbricated with assumptions about humans' place within a more-than-human world. But a narratology beyond the human can take on another critically important task in this connection: not just analyzing how a given self-narrative locates the human agent in a transspecies constellation of selves, but also assisting with the construction of new, more sustainable individual and collective self-narratives grounded in this expanded sense of the self's relationality—of the self's situation within wider webs of creatural life. These new narratives can be viewed as more sustainable because they reintegrate the human self in a much larger community of selves than that recognized by dominant scientific, social, legal, and moral norms. In turn, stories in which selfhood extends beyond the human prefigure and help make possible ways of living on which the continued survival of the earth's entire biotic community arguably depends.

Self-Narratives and Nonhuman Selves

Unlike texts in which nonhuman animals assume, from the start, a primary actantial or thematic role vis-à-vis their human counterparts (as in Anna Sewell's *Black Beauty* [1877], Virginia Woolf's *Flush* [1933], Alan Moore's *Swamp Thing* [1984 - 1987], or Karen Joy Fowler's *We Are All Completely Beside Ourselves* [2013]), Groff's narrative brings transspecies encounters and relationships into view intermittently. More precisely, as I discuss in more detail in my next section, human-animal relationships come to the fore at key junctures in the unfolding story, marking transition points in the protagonist's attempt to move beyond an obsolescent self-narrative. Thus, with the title of "Above and Below" linking issues of identity with the dynamics of relationality, the text highlights how humans' understanding of their relations to other kinds of selves takes on special salience when self-narratives come under pressure, or no longer find purchase at all. Reciprocally, the protagonist's recognition of her place within a world that extends beyond the human shapes how she goes about reconstructing the story of who—and what—she is. The text thereby demonstrates how narratives ostensibly centering on human protagonists can nonetheless raise important questions about the scope and limits of selfhood in a wider world of selves, nonhuman as well as human.[②]

As already indicated, I adapt the concept of self-narrative from Gergen and Gergen (1997), although research by other analysts such as Jerome Bruner, Daniel Hutto, Andreea Ritivoi, and Alasdair MacIntyre also informs my approach (see Herman 2013, 73 - 99, for a fuller discussion of

---

① As suggested by *Blackfish*, Gabriela Cowperthwaite's 2013 documentary linking the deaths of several animal trainers to the treatment of killer whales kept in captivity, nonfictional accounts likewise afford space for exploring issues of selfhood beyond the human.

② In this connection, see Bateman's (2014) analysis of Henry James's "The Beast in the Jungle".

this and other relevant research). In their study of "Narratives of the Self", Gergen and Gergen confer on self-narratives crucial psychological, interactional, and more broadly sociocultural functions. Suggesting that self-narratives result from persons' attempts "to establish coherent connections among life events" (Gergen / Gergen 1997, 162), they further argue that "although self-narratives are possessed by individuals, their genesis and sustenance may be viewed as fundamentally social", since such narratives are ultimately "symbolic systems used for such social purposes as justification, criticism, and social solidification" (ibid., 163; see also Ritivoi 2009, 27 - 36). In other words, "as the individual's actions encounter varying degrees of approbation, [...] it becomes increasingly necessary for the individual to articulate the implicit narrative line in such a way that the actions in question become intelligible and thus acceptable" (ibid., 177). In addition to characterizing self-narratives as sense-making resources "constructed and reconstructed by people in relationships, and employed in relationships to sustain, enhance, or impede various actions" (ibid., 163), Gergen and Gergen situate these strategies for self-narration within a broader taxonomy of storytelling modes circulating in the culture, consisting of what they term stability narratives, progressive narratives, and regressive narratives. Gergen and Gergen base this taxonomic scheme on the assumption that

> the development of certain rudimentary narrative forms is favored by functional needs within the society. Stability narratives are favored by the common desire for the social world to appear orderly and predictable; progressive narratives offer the opportunity for people to see themselves and their environment as capable of improvement; and regressive narratives are not only entailed logically by the development of progressive narratives, but have an important motivational function in their own right. (Ibid., 175)

Regressive narratives are bound up with progressive narratives in the sense that a story about the increase in oneself of valued traits such as steadiness and maturity requires a countervailing story about the decrease of disvalued traits such as youthful volatility. For its part, the motivational function of regressive narratives stems from the way they provide an impetus for efforts to counteract what such narratives sometimes portray as worsening conditions or circumstances, whether in one's own life or in the world more generally.

Groff's story brings into focus how Gergen and Gergen's account can be extended and enriched with ideas from other domains of inquiry; the text also suggests how the very concept of self-narrative opens out into questions for a narratology beyond the human. For one thing, the ideas of stability, progression, and regression are situated at what might be termed a meso-analytic level. These plot contours need to be dovetailed with finer-grained methods of analysis that scholars of narrative have developed to trace trajectories of change in storyworlds. Such plot shapes also need to be linked to macro-analytic frameworks for studying how narratives at once reflect and help constitute broader norms concerning what sorts of event-sequences count as improvement or degeneration.[①] More importantly for my purposes here, Gergen and Gergen's emphasis on the sociointeractional functions of self-narratives—their relational approach to the self as a construction to be worked out through socially embedded sense-making acts that situate happenings, achievements, and projects vis-à-vis a more or less persistent narrative line—needs to be reframed within a wider, transhuman conception of self-other relations. As Groff's text suggests, who one is emerges in a space of selfhood that ranges beyond the human, whether a given self-narrative involves ignoring, denying, or embracing relatedness to the full range of selves taken to populate the world.

"Above and Below" thus indicates how scholarship on fictional and other narratives can be brought into dialogue with the comparative study of the various ontologies projected by different cultures, past and present. A narratology beyond the human, in other words, links up with what might be called the "ontological turn" in anthropological research;[②] by broadening the remit of possible-worlds and text-worlds approaches, among other domains within normal narratological science, narrative analysts can help map out the ontologies not just of the storyworlds associated with individual texts or genres but also of the cultures in which those texts and genres are embedded, and by which they are animated. At issue are more or less widely shared understandings of the kinds of beings that populate the world, the qualities and abilities those beings are taken to embody (including the capacity to have a perspective on events, among other attributes linked to selfhood), and how the beings included in various categories and subcategories relate to those categorized as human.

For example, Bruno Latour (1993) has shown how a notionally modern ontology—one that posits a divide between nature and culture, things and persons—is belied by complex networks spanning human and nonhuman actants (Latour 1993, 10 - 12; see also Descola 2013, 32). But whereas Latour's account flattens out contrasts among animals and other sorts of actants that can be categorized as nonhuman (computational devices, built structures, geological formations), other

① As suggested by my analysis of Groff's text, an event-sequence that might be interpreted as regressive, in the sense that the protagonist becomes homeless and exposed to the dangers of life in the open, can instead be read as progressive, in the sense that the protagonist, by entering a new, expanded constellation of self-other relationships, leverages the experience of homelessness to work toward an empowering self-narrative.

② As Matei Candea (2010) puts it, "the late 19th-century shift from singular capitalized Culture to the multiplicity of cultures, and the shift from the single Ontology of philosophy to an anthropology of ontologies can therefore be seen as analogous moves—they both serve to inscribe difference at the heart of the anthropological project. Not, of course, an exclusive, oppressive difference but a relational, productive difference" (Candea 2010,175). Similarly, Philippe Descola (2013) argues that "for anthropology, no ontology is better or more truthful in itself than another [...] [At issue are, D.H.] schemes of coding and parceling out phenomenal reality by means of which [people] have learned to couch and transmit their experience of things, schemes issuing from historical choices that privileged, at a given time and place, certain sets of relations to humans and non-humans, in such a way as to allow for the combination of these relationships into sui generis ensembles—already constituted before the birth of the individuals that actualize them—to be experienced as naturally coherent" (Descola 2013, 66 - 67).

theorists have zoomed in on human-animal relationships in particular and explored the way different ontologies allocate possibilities for selfhood more or less prolifically across the species boundary.[①] Eduardo Viveiros de Castro (1998), for instance, explores the ontology projected by Amerindian peoples, for whom "the world is inhabited by different sorts of subjects or persons, human and non-human, which apprehend reality from different points of view" (Viveiros de Castro 1998, 469). In accordance with a process that Viveiros de Castro terms "cosmological deixis",

> the Amerindian words which are usually translated as "human being" [...] do not designate humanity as a natural species. They refer rather to the social condition of personhood, and they function (pragmatically when not syntactically) less as nouns than as pronouns. They indicate the position of the subject; they are enunciative markers, not names [...] Amerindian souls, be they human or animal, are thus indexical categories [and] Amerindian ontological perspectivism proceeds along the lines that *the point of view creates the subject*; whatever is activated or "agented" by the point of view will be a subject. (Ibid., 476 - 477)

Eduardo Kohn (2013) maps out a similarly prolific matrix for subjectivity and selfhood among a particular group of Amerindians-namely, the Quichua-speaking Runa in Ecuador's Upper Amazon region. Kohn seeks to develop an "analytical framework that goes beyond a focus on how humans represent animals to an appreciation for our everyday interactions with these creatures and the new spaces of possibility such interactions can create" (see also Kirksey / Helmreich 2010); he suggests how for the Runa "all beings, and not just humans, engage with the world and with each other as selves—that is, as beings that have a point of view" (Kohn 2013, 4). Accordingly, if perspectives, ways of experiencing the world, "exist beyond the human, then we humans are not the only selves in this world" (Ibid., 72).[②] Rather, the very concept of self, and hence the narratives used to bring the self's experiences into relation with a storyline constructed through processes of interaction, must be situated with-in a more or less expansive "ecology of selves" (Kohn 2007, 4; Kohn 2013, 16 - 17), whose membership criteria will vary depending on the ontological commitments involved.

In what follows, returning to Groff's narrative about a protagonist caught between an obsolescent self-narrative and an as-yet-unimagined storyline that might accommodate a different way of living, I adapt Latour's emphasis on the contest of ontologies within the ostensibly singular cultures of modernity. "Above and Below", I argue, dramatizes the protagonist's movement away

① In Kohn's (2007) formulation, "the distinction Latour makes between humans and nonhumans [...] fails to recognize that some nonhumans are selves" (Kohn 2007, 5; see also Kohn 2013, 7, 91 - 92).

② Kohn (2013) offers the following transhuman, biocentric definition of self: "A self [...] is the outcome of a process, unique to life, of maintaining and perpetuating an individual form, a form that, as it is iterated over the generations, grows to fit the world around it at the same time that it comes to exhibit a certain circular closure that allows it to maintain its selfsame identity, which is forged with respect to that which it is not" (Kohn 2013, 76).

from a restricted to a more inclusive ecology of selves, exposing a fault line between parsimonious and prolific allocations of the possibility for selfhood beyond the human. This fault line can also be described in terms of the contrast between anthropocentric and biocentric perspectives on the world; at issue are perspectives positing a hierarchical separation between humans and other species, on the one hand, and perspectives assuming a fundamental continuity across human and nonhuman forms of life, on the other. Groff's text registers two-way causal effects flowing between the breakdown of the protagonist's self-narrative and her growing recognition of her place within a more-than-human world. In this way, the story traces mutations in the concept of selfhood brought about by a rejection of anthropocentric geographies of the self; such geographies assign humans a position *above* other forms of creatural life, while gapping out experiences located *below* the imaginary elevation of the human.① The protagonist's intermittent encounters with animals punctuate phases of her movement away from an over-restrictive ontology that curtails or obscures her relational ties to a wide range of relevant others, suggesting possibilities for biocentric becoming within an expanded ecology of selves.

三、思考与讨论

(1) 为什么在动物叙事以及其他类型的非人类叙事中需要讨论自我叙事?

(2) 在赫尔曼看来,建构超越人类的叙事学有何意义或作用?

(3) 超越人类的叙事学如何形成和建构?

① A fuller analysis of the story would need to consider how Groff uses the protagonist's entrance into a socioeconomic underclass, the community of the marginalized poor, to suggest how an altered conception of self-other relations across species lines connects up with a rethinking of structures of power, wealth, and privilege within the domain of the human. In a phrase, prolific allocations of possibilities for selfhood across species pair naturally with recognition of the claims of disenfranchised members of the human community.

第四节　马可·卡拉乔洛及其《叙述网状纠连：人类世的形式与故事》

一、导读

马可·卡拉乔洛(Marco Caracciolo)是当代欧洲比较活跃的叙事学家，现任比利时根特大学副教授，主要著有《叙事的体验性：能动论方法》(*The Experientiality of Narrative: An Enactivist Approach*，2014)、《当代小说中的奇特叙述者：读者对人物的介入研究》(*Strange Narrators in Contemporary Fiction: Explorations in Readers' Engagement with Characters*，2016)、《二十世纪小说中的具身化与宇宙视角》(*Embodiment and the Cosmic Perspective in Twentieth-Century Fiction*，2020)、《叙述网状纠连：人类世的形式与故事》(*Narrating the Mesh: Form and Story in the Anthropocene*，2021)等。近年来，卡拉乔洛的研究重点是认知叙事、环境叙事、人类世叙事以及非人类叙事。本节所节选的内容主要取自卡拉乔洛《叙述网状纠连：人类世的形式与故事》一书的第四章"观看非人类行动者的五种方式"(five ways of looking at nonhuman actants)。

就非人类叙事而言，卡拉乔洛借用了蒂莫西·莫顿(Timothy Morton)在《生态思想》一书中所提出的"网状纠连"(mesh)这个概念，用该概念取代过去关于人类与非人类之间线型的、等级的关系。网状纠连既表示脆弱的相互依存性，同时又具有较强的模式与关联性。卡拉乔洛认为，如果要理解故事中人类与非人类世界之间复杂而相互依存的关系，人物这个概念就是一个无可绕过的起点。一般说来，传统叙事理论家们把人类放置在行动者的位置上，而把非人类的现实放置在物体的位置上，后者要么作为服务于人类的工作，要么作为以人类为中心的事件背景。

通过参照安德鲁·格特力(Andrew Goatly)的生态语言学模式①，卡拉乔洛提出了考察非人类人物的五种方式：① 非人类发起(nonhuman instigation)，在该系统中，行动者不再是直接原因而是行动发起者，即人类和非人类共同参与和发起了某个事件；② 没有人类主体的行为(doing without a human subject)，即叙述语言或动作的指称中心处于人类体验者缺位的状态，由此揭示非人类的过程包围了人类，并且成为人类命运的一部分；③ 激发人类-非人类的互惠性(evoking human-nonhuman reciprocity)，互惠性存在于所有涉及人类与非人类现实的叙事作品中，例如在灾难性叙事作品中，非人类的事件和因素变成了行动者；④ 把地点提升为人物(promotion of place to character)，即把非人类空间拟人化，文体和叙事技巧可以把作为人物和事件背景的空间推到行动者的位置；⑤ 叙事进程的名物化和抽象化(nominalization and abstraction in narrative progression)，即从具体事件中抽象出一个名词或从具体事件的参与者中抽象出一个名词，不再把人类意图看作情节发展的驱动力。

① Andrew Goatly, "Green Grammar and Grammatical Metaphor, or Language and the Myth of Power, or Metaphors We Die By," *Journal of Pragmatics* 25.4 (1996), pp.537 - 560.

二、《叙述网状纠连：人类世的形式与故事》选读[①]

Nonhuman Instigation

In the ergative system, agency is a matter not of direct causation but of "instigation", and it extends from the grammatical subject to the grammatical object, involving both. In the sentence "John walked the dog", for instance, John initiates ("instigates") the action, but he and the dog coparticipate in it. Something similar happens in the plot of *The Echo Maker*, the novel by Richard Powers that will be discussed more at length in the next chapter. At the forefront of the novel is the human drama of a car accident and its aftermath. The victim, a character named Mark, suffers brain damage and develops a psychiatric condition known as "Capgras syndrome": he views his sister, Karin, as an impostor, a lookalike of his real sister. The backdrop to these events is the Platte River in Nebraska, where thousands of sandhill cranes congregate every year, on their way from Central America to Canada and Alaska. In parallel with Mark's slow and uneasy recovery is the attempt, on the part of a group of corporate investors, to build a tourist resort on the banks of the river, which would seriously endanger the cranes. This subplot follows a standard transitive pattern, which places the human in an agentive position, and the nonhuman world (meaning both the river and the cranes) in the position of a disempowered object.

However, Mark's mysterious mental condition complicates and to some extent subverts this pattern. Not only are the cranes physically present when Mark's car skids out of control, but their fate seems intimately bound up with Mark's. In his delusion, he is convinced that the surgeons implanted a bird's brain into his skull during the operation that followed his accident. In this way, the cranes are symbolically implicated in the traumatic disruption of the character's subjectivity, which points to a more general instability of the human subject. Powers's narrative reinforces this effect by portraying the birds not as individualized agents but as a collective actant, endowed with a group mentality that conflicts with the presumed autonomy and singularity of human selfhood: "Then thousands of them lift up in flood. The beating surface of the world rises, a spiral calling upward on invisible thermals. Sounds carry them all the way skyward, clacks and wooden rattles, rolling, booming, bugling, clouds of living sound. Slowly, the mass unfurls in ribbons and disperses into thin blue" (2006, 429). Powers's metaphorical language blurs the dividing line between the cranes' coordinated behavior and the surrounding landscape, transforming them into a "flood" "a beating surface" or "clouds" that eventually merge with the "thin blue" of the sky. This image of the cranes as a collective actant affects the human characters as well; for instance, it defamiliarizes

① Marco Caracciolo, *Narrating the Mesh: Form and Story in the Anthropocene* (Charlottesville: University of Virginia Press, 2021), pp.104－111.

Karin's view of humanity, in a key passage in which she realizes that "the whole [human] race suffered from Capgras. Those birds danced like our next of kin, looked like our next of kin, called and willed and parented and taught and navigated all just like our blood relations. Half their parts were still ours. Yet humans waved them off: impostors" (2006, 347 - 348).[①] The cranes are thus a full-fledged actant in Powers's novel insofar as they coparticipate in Mark's accident and determine its narrative and ethical stakes. Crucially, this does not happen by way of direct causation, but through the symbolic instigation of Mark's condition: "The cranes crashed Mark's car" would be the closest sentence-length equivalent of the plot. Through this ergative structure, with the cranes as a nonhuman actant, the novel is able to locate the human within a longer, evolutionary history that undermines any separation between human agency and an allegedly inert natural world.

Doing Without a Human Subject

Goatly's second device is the use of filler words like "there" or "it" in existential statements or to denote atmospheric phenomena. Because these words fulfill a purely grammatical function, their semantic emptiness draws attention to the processual nature of the scenario that is being verbally conveyed: in a sentence like "It is cold today", the "It" is not an agent or subject, but only stands in for meteorological conditions defined by a certain perceived temperature. In narrative terms, this device is reminiscent of what Ann Banfield (1987) calls "empty center texts": descriptive passages in which the subject position is left vacant, and a scene is verbally recorded despite the absence of any observers. The deictic center of this scene—the location that would normally be occupied by an experiencing subject—remains empty. Banfield takes as an example the interludes of Virginia Woolf's 1931 novel *The Waves*, which portray a sea landscape at different times of the day, without any character being present at the scene.

The emptiness of these scenarios serves as a window onto a world untouched by human presence.[②] This is something that Woolf herself strongly cues in the famous "Time Passes" section of *To the Lighthouse*, which registers material changes in a house during a ten-year period in which it is left uninhabited. Greg Garrard (2012) discusses Woolf's "Time Passes" as an instance of what he calls "disanthropy", a vision of the world without humans. Yet, for Garrard, attempts at disanthropy in verbal narrative are bound to fail: "The helpless allegiance of written genres to narrative voice and anthropomorphic characterization makes disanthropic literature conspicuously

① For more on collective actants in narrative, including a close reading of Powers's novel in this light, see Caracciolo (2020b).

② By contrast, Fludernik's discussion of these texts hinges on the reader's *projection* of subjectivity into the empty deictic center: "Just as, in figural narrative, the reader is invited to see the fictional world through the eyes of a reflector character, in the present text the reader also reads through a text-internal consciousness, but since no character is available to whom one could attribute such consciousness, the reader directly identifies with a story-internal position" (1996, 150). The reading strategy I am advocating here resists such projection of anthropomorphic subjectivity.

self-contradictory, and probably impossible" (2012, 43). Instead, Garrard turns to cinema as a medium that, due to the "ostensible impersonality of the camera" (2012, 43), is uniquely equipped to represent human absence. Garrard does not discuss Banfield's empty deictic center and appears to downplay the power of literary language to break its "helpless allegiance" with "anthropomorphic characterization". In fact, it can be argued that empty center passages like Woolf's capitalize on what Garrard calls their "self-contradictory" nature, inviting readers to undergo and value an experience of absence that exposes the rich vitality of the world without humans.

Jim Crace's novel *Being Dead* (1999) is a powerful example of how empty center descriptions can probe nonhuman materiality. The novel narrates the events that led to a couple's murder on a deserted beach. What takes center stage in the narrative—rather morbidly—is the material history of the two dead bodies, whose decomposition is described in painstaking detail even if there is no full-fledged character on the scene. Consider, for instance, this passage: "But the rain, the wind, the shooting stars, the maggots and the shame had not succeeded yet in blowing them away or bringing to an end their days of grace. There'd been no thunderclap so far. His hand was touching her. The flesh on flesh. The fingertip across the tendon strings. He still held on. She still was held" (1999, 102). The description features the equivalent of an "it" or an existential "there" where we would expect a human-like observer: it foregrounds process and the slow but inevitable decomposition of the bodies on the beach, conveying a cosmic and not entirely unironic perspective on the two characters' death. The absence of human spectators is made so salient by the narrative that it becomes an anomalous, ghostly (and ghastly) actant—a reminder of the nonhuman processes that enfold the human and constitute its fate.

Evoking Human-Nonhuman Reciprocity

Reciprocal verbs place two subjects in an agentive role, stressing the reciprocity of an action without establishing a subject-object (and therefore inherently hierarchical) relation: "John and Mary met." A degree of reciprocity is present in all narratives that probe the interrelation between human and nonhuman realities. Narratives focusing on catastrophe are a particularly salient example of how reciprocity can be foregrounded and inscribed into the progression of plot, with nonhuman events and elements becoming actants.

We have seen that in Whitehead's *Zone One*, for example, the zombies ("skels", in the novel's parlance) are a collective nonhuman actant, which the narrator explicitly compares to the effects of anthropogenic climate change: "The ocean [of the skels] had overtaken the streets, as if the news programs' global warming simulations had finally come to pass and the computer-generated swells mounted to drown the great metropolis" (2011, 302). Whitehead's figurative language establishes an intricate network of reciprocity: the skels are first compared to a nonhuman location, the ocean, while their invasion of the metropolis is assimilated to global warming (a phenomenon fueled by human activity), which in turn is seen through the lens of human technology (a computer simulation). Even as the skels may look like a fully nonhuman actant in the novel, the simulation simile conflates them with human societies and their impact on the natural environment, thus working toward a redistribution of agency across the human/ nonhuman divide. At the same time, Whitehead's original contribution to the zombie genre is the invention of so-called "straggler" skels, who (unlike regular skels) are condemned to reenact a gesture or haunt a location that meant something to them before they became skels—a clear manifestation of the psychological cycles of trauma. An inkling of the skels' humanity is thus poignantly preserved. The figure of the straggler, along with the figurative blending of zombie invasion and climate change, steer clear of a sharp dichotomization between skels and humans and instead stress their reciprocal relation.

Beyond postapocalyptic fiction, another instance of human-nonhuman reciprocity in narrative form can be found in *A Tale for the Time Being*, a 2013 novel by American Canadian writer Ruth Ozeki. *A Tale for the Time Being* focuses on two protagonists located, respectively, in Japan and on a remote island off the coast of British Columbia. One is a Japanese teenager, Nao; the other is a Canadian writer, Ruth. The novel devotes a chapter to each character, in alternating order, but the characters themselves never meet. What brings them together is a material object: Nao's diary ends up in the Pacific Ocean, possibly as a result of the tsunami that struck Japan in 2011, and later washes up, miraculously unscathed, on Ruth's island. The Ruth-focalized chapters explore the emotional impact of reading this diary on the character's life. *A Tale for the Time Being* is, in the terminology introduced in chapter 1, an object-oriented narrative that unfolds against a global backdrop, connecting East Asian culture (particularly Buddhism) and the Western world. But, while the novel's main characters are human, the ocean—and particularly its currents, known as "gyres"—rises to prominence in the novel. Recuperating and reinterpreting a metaphor in use in oceanography, Ozeki suggests that the gyres have their own material "memory" made up of objects discarded or lost by humans, including Nao's diary: "The gyre's memory is all the stuff that we've forgotten" (2013, 114).[①] It is thanks to the inscrutable patterns of the ocean's memory that Nao and Ruth come into contact. If a prototypical example of reciprocal sentence is something like "Nao and Ruth met", *A Tale for the Time Being* shifts the emphasis from the human meeting to the ocean's participation in the meeting—not as a mere vehicle or even facilitator, but as a nonhuman actant entangled, diegetically and metaphorically, with the two characters' fate: "Nao, Ruth, and the ocean met."

① In oceanography, the term "ocean memory" refers to the way in which large bodies of water can retain traces of past climatological trends: for instance, scientists Old and Haines explain that the "persistence of volume (heat) anomalies is equivalent to the ocean's memory of warming or cooling climatic events" (2006, 1144). See also Caracciolo (2019a) for a fuller discussion of Ozeki's novel that focuses on the intersection of narrative form and scientific models.

Promotion of Place to Character

Ozeki's ocean is also an illustration of the next category of nonhuman actants, the equivalent of Goatly's "promotion of place to grammatical subject": stylistic and narrative strategies can push the space of the setting, which typically serves as a mere backdrop to human characters and events, toward an agentive position. This process can involve varying degrees of personification of nonhuman spaces.① There is a hint of anthropomorphism in Ozeki's attribution of memory to the ocean, but in other narratives the personification of place becomes much more overt. In an insightful ecostylistic reading of Amitav Ghosh's *The Hungry Tide* (2004), Elisabetta Zurru (2017) argues that the landscape of the Sundarbans on the Bay of Bengal is one of the main actants in Ghosh's novel, entering a reciprocal relationship with the human characters. Zurru's analysis shows that "the linguistic level turns 'the setting of the novel' into an active, major character in the story" (2017, 203-204) through, in particular, the personification of the river Matla, in sentences such as "The Matla laughed its mental laugh" or "The Matla took pity" on someone (quoted in Zurru 2017, 230).

A striking example of promotion of place to narrative actant that avoids straightforward personification is Area X in Jeff VanderMeer's Southern Reach trilogy (VanderMeer 2014a; 2014b; 2014c). Area X is a coastal region in North America where the ecosystem shows some serious, and inexplicable, anomalies. The US government dispatches a series of research teams to investigate, but these expeditions repeatedly (and dramatically) fail, suggesting that the anomalies run deeper than previously thought: the government's official version points to an environmental catastrophe, but there are strong indications that Area X was occupied by an alien life form that radically altered the landscape. Just like the Sundarbans in Ghosh's novel, Area X becomes an actant, but in a way that avoids direct personification, instead emphasizing Area X's nonhuman opacity and unreadability: "Nothing about language, about communication, could bridge the divide between human beings and Area X" (2014c, 311). When, in the course of the trilogy, Area X starts expanding and incorporating the rest of the world, there is little doubt that its behavior displays intentionality, but its exact motivations remain unclear and deeply perplexing; as one of the main characters reflects, she "felt that if she could make Area X react, then she would somehow throw it off course. Even though we didn't know what course it was on" (2014b, 262).

Ultimately, however, the physical expansion of Area X proves less unsettling than its capacity to shape and control the minds of those who come into contact with it. Consider the following passage: "That landscape was impinging on them now. The temperature dipped and rose violently. There were rumblings deep underground that manifested as slight tremors. The sun came

① Personification and anthropomorphism will be discussed more at length in Chapter 7.

to them with a 'greenish tinge' as if 'somehow the border were distorting our vision'" (2014a, 164). The idea is not just that the trilogy's spatial setting informs the characters' existential and material situation—which would be a simple inversion of the transitive subject-object structure—but that it becomes deeply implicated in their actions and psychological states. Through the actantial mediation of place, the nonhuman infiltrates both the storyworld and the characters' psychology. Far from being straightforwardly personified, the landscape of Area X ends up taking over and nonhumanizing the human.

Nominalization and Abstraction in Narrative Progression

Nominalization uses a noun to capture a process normally denoted by a verb, thus eliding the agents involved in that process. This is, fundamentally, an operation of linguistic abstraction, in two ways: the noun abstracts from a specific event ("the evaporation of water" is more general than "the water evaporates"), and the noun abstracts from the participants in that event (i.e. who or what caused the water to evaporate). How does this translate into narrative terms? A possible equivalent are narratives that foreground a spatiotemporal process beyond the human scale, which displaces human intentionality as the driving force of the plot.

As argued in chapter 2, plot tends to be both triggered and determined in its progression by the beliefs and desires of human (or human-like) characters. However, in a novel like Kurt Vonnegut's 1985 *Galápagos*, the narrative progression is governed by a long series of coincidences and unlikely outcomes that break with human intentionality. *Galápagos* imagines a future in which only a handful of humans survive a catastrophic virus outbreak, by finding shelter on one of the Galápagos islands. Thematically, natural selection is a major player in the novel: there are multiple references to Darwin and his theory of evolution, conveyed with such accuracy that Andre Bixler (2007) proposes using *Galápagos* in schools as an aid for teaching genetic drift in evolutionary processes. Vonnegut's engagement with natural selection is deeply grounded in form. The narrative is strewn with ironic counterfactual statements, which keep reminding the reader that humanity's survival is a mere stroke of luck: for instance, the narrator points out that if a certain soldier "had not burglarized that shop, there would almost certainly be no human beings on the face of the earth today. I mean it. Everybody alive today should thank God that this soldier was insane" (2011, 160).[①] If humanity survives a catastrophic virus outbreak, it is not due to the survivors' deliberate efforts but thanks to the unintended and surprising consequences of an action dictated by

① In narratologist Prince's terminology, these counterfactual statements are "disnarrated": in Prince's definition, disnarrated events "do not happen but, nonetheless, are referred to (in a negative or hypothetical mode) by the narrative text" (1988, 2).

madness. In this way, Vonnegut's plot mirrors the haphazard, stochastic nature of natural evolution: just as natural selection is driven by random genetic mutations, the narrative proceeds by way of apparently random twists and turns. Evolution, as Porter Abbott (2003) argues in an insightful essay, cannot be narrativized directly, because the time frames it involves and its lack of teleology are incompatible with narrative representation. Vonnegut attempts to sidestep this limitation by capturing, through the formal logic of narrative sequence, the equally abstract logic of random mutations over large-scale time.① This strategy is the equivalent of nominalization as Goatly discusses it: in this reading of the novel, an abstract principle beyond the human scale is transformed into an actant, determining the characters' fate and putting the nonhuman in control of the narrative.

三、思考与讨论

(1) 卡拉乔洛关于非人类人物的五种考察方式与格雷马斯的行动素之间有何差异?

(2) 在卡拉乔洛那里,空间被提升为人物,那么时间也可以被提升为人物吗?

(3) 在同一个叙事作品中的同一个非人类人物可以同时用这五种方式来解读吗?

本章推荐阅读书目

[1] Mark Blackwell, ed. *The Secret Life of Things: Animals, Objects, and It-Narratives in Eighteenth-Century England*. Lewisburg: Bucknell University Press, 2007.

[2] Richard Grusin. *The Nonhuman Turn*. Minneapolis: University of Minnesota Press, 2015.

[3] David Herman. *Narratology beyond the Human: Storytelling and Animal Life*. Oxford: Oxford University Press, 2018.

[4] Sanna Karkulehto, Aino-Kaisa Koistinen, and Essi Varis, eds. *Reconfiguring Human, Nonhuman and Posthuman in Literature and Culture*. London and New York: Routledge, 2020.

[5] Yvonne Liebermann, Judith Rahn, and Bettina Burger, eds. *Nonhuman Agencies in the Twenty-First-Century Anglophone Novel*. Basingstoke: Palgrave, 2021.

① See Caracciolo (2018b) for a more in-depth reading of Vonnegut's novel.